Zero 7

Wintworth Henry

For more information contact:
Independent Authors Publications
PO Box 7062,
Roselle, NJ 07203
www.independentauthorspublications.com

Cover Design – Webprint Lab
Edited – Catherine Felegi

Print ISBN: 978-1-950974-10-8
Digital ISBN: 978-1-950974-11-5
Library of Congress Control Number: 2022917499

"I would love to dedicate this book to my loving father and grandmother who passed away. This great accomplishment is for you. Everyday I wished that you were alive to see how much you contributed to my success in life. But I know you're with the angels looking down on me."

BIOGRAPHY:

Wintworth Henry who is the last of 3 children born and raised in the tiny island nation of Vieux-Fort, St. Lucia, on the 26TH of May, 1975, majored in topics such as English Literature, Social Studies, History, and a number of topics too numerous to mention.

He has always had a great love for traveling, and learning about the history of the armed forces, and after visiting a number of countries finally decided to emigrate to the United States to pursue his greatest passion in writing despite his many other talents.

Contents

PROLOGUE:

2005: IVORY COAST, WEST AFRICA:

A country plagued by years of civil war and genocide, causing over 100,000 deaths. It came to be known as The Ivory Coast Massacre.

Many more were lost to the Chimera Virus, one of the deadliest diseases known to man, killing more people than the war.

To contain the deadly threat, the infected were burnt alive. That event would forever be known as The Hellfire Campaign.

Out of the chaos came hope of finding a cure. His name was Dr. Alexander Weaver.

After receiving the message that a future was possible, many fled to the outpost near the tiny fishing village in search of a new beginning after discovering a way to combat the deadly disease.

Before a cure could be found, more than 350,000 more people would perish from the lethal strain.

The tiny fishing village near the coast that became an outpost to combat the Chimera virus became known as The First Genesis.

2010: PORT-AU-PRINCE, HAITI:

The capital city of Haiti was ravaged by an earthquake, wiping out almost one-third of the entire population, leaving thousands more to perish from the Cholera outbreak.

With foreign aid being intercepted by militia groups, left with no other alternatives, the United States intervened.

2025: UNIFIED KOREA:

Decades after the civil unrest between the North and South divided the entire country into two separate governments, North Korea once again dreamed of uniting the entire peninsula under their oppressive regime.

Despite protests from their ally, China, the North declared an all-out war on the South, waging a full-scale strategic assault, rendering their allies less than half strength.

China, left with no other alternative, allied with their once bitter rival, the United States, to help thwart North Korea's ruthless ambitions.

After North Korea's defeat by the new alliance, the Korean Peninsula was finally reunited under the South, where the people once again prospered.

After the bloody conflict ended, many became displaced, and fled to Genesis under the guidance of Dr. Weaver.

More people perished than at the Ivory Coast Massacre. The event that plunged both countries into chaos would forever come to be known as The Shattered Alliance.

2025: GENESIS HAVEN, QUEEN MAUDSLAND, ANTARCTICA:

Two decades passed since the incident at the Ivory Coast, leaving many displaced, and fleeing to Genesis: The Haven of Mankind, in search of a better life under the guidance of Dr. Weaver.

Once again, the dark cloud of war loomed an evil shadow over the haven, extinguishing many lives in its wake.

Mankind's haven became a battleground. Countless more perished, like the Ivory Coast and the Unified Korea campaigns.

Those who witnessed the genocide called it The Genesis Uprising. Many others called it The Genesis Massacre. But it would forever come to be known as The Great Fall.

2025: NAZCA LINES, PERU, SOUTH AMERICA:

After The Great Fall of Genesis, a number of atrocities were committed, executing an entire regiment of the Peoples' Liberation Army.

However, two survived to tell the tale of the gruesome events, and as a result of their testimony, the entire Latin American nation of Peru went into civil unrest. That chapter would come to be known as The Survivor's Testimony.

Like the Ivory Coast and Genesis, many perished.

2025: WASHINGTON D.C. - THE NATION'S CAPITAL:

Shortly after the events of The Great Fall of Genesis and The Survivor's Testimony, millions gathered in the streets of Washington, D.C. to protest against the atrocities committed by the armed forces, dwarfing that of the Vietnam and Gulf War combined. Like the Ivory Coast, Genesis, and Peru, many perished.

That event was much larger than the Million Man March that stemmed from the Civil Rights Era, spearheaded by the great Dr. Martin Luther King, and would forever be known as The Great March.

2025: AROUND THE WORLD:

Following the events of The Great Fall and The Survivor's Testimony, the entire world went into a state of unrest, losing all forms of law and order, removing the faith from the once faithful and optimistic citizens.

With The Great Fall of Genesis, the only chance to achieve world peace was forever shattered. The world-shattering event would forever be known as Anarchy.

2035: UNITED STATES:

Three decades had passed since The Ivory Coast Massacre, and ten years had passed since The Great Fall, The Shattered Alliance, The Survivor's Testimony, the atrocities of the People Liberation Front, and The Great

March that flooded the streets of the United State's capital.

A nation under the grip of a ruthless general who was eager to unite the entire continent under his rule remained divided from a civil war that consumed much of the country's population.

The rebel forces under the command of Acting President Dr. Alexander Weaver, though scattered, disorganized, outnumbered, out-manned, and leaderless, still continued to fight for freedom. Many of them continued to fight and die to liberate the embattled nation from the iron grip of tyranny that was the ruthless general and his forces.

In the heat of war, a warrior was forged, and ascended from the ashes like a phoenix during the endless conflict, and came to be known by many names.

To some, he was known as The Drone. Others called him The Rogue. He would later be known as The Ronin.

But those who bore witness to the legend in real life knew this great warrior as the infamous 0-7.

CHAPTER 1: SANCTUARY

Fifty years passed since the atrocities of the Civil War that killed 100,000 people, and the deadly Chimera outbreak that swept across the Ivory Coast, killing 350,000.

Thirty years passed since the Great Fall of Genesis, the uprising in Peru, the unification of the Korean Peninsula, and the Anarchy that consumed the world.

Twenty years passed since the entire union went into a state of unrest that led to a civil war, consuming many of its once faithful and optimistic citizens.

2055. 42ND STREET, PORT AUTHORITY, NEW YORK, NEW YORK:

The dirt spiraled off the streets as the stale winds blew, carrying the overwhelming stench of death from the many lives extinguished.

The streets remained desolate with the corpses that lay strewn about in the decrepit husks of police cruisers - people who were tasked to defend the city - and army-issued transports - men and women who dreamt of imposing martial law and tyranny on the entire country. The landscape told the horrific tale of the clash that ensued, forcing both sides to meet their untimely demise from tragic engagements from many years past. Crows perched on corpses, feasting upon what remained of their dried flesh, and immediately took flight after having their fill.

The giant television screens that once proudly broadcasted the late night news on the walls of the skyscrapers bore the image of a female freedom fighter who remained marooned on Genesis since the inception of the uprising.

2055: PRESENT DAY.

07:37 HOURS. THE SANCTUARY. SOMEWHERE IN NEW YORK, NEW YORK:

Elaina's appearance was deceiving to the untrained eye, but she was much stronger than she looked. She was a street-smart, tech-savvy young woman, with smooth, caramel-brown skin, born and raised in the dreaded favelas of Brazil's disproportionately black population of African descent, with waist-length curly black hair that she often wore in a ponytail. She once served as an enforcer against rival gangs during her early years as a teenager, up until she lost her entire family and many of her friends, becoming an orphan and the only living lineage at the tender age of 17.

After the Marines landed in her home country, she ran through the slums in pursuit of the war criminal responsible for the genocide of countless innocent civilians during the Great Civil War that divided the countries of the former Soviet Union.

He traveled in the guise of a businessman, paying the local militia huge bribes for protection against outside forces, using fortunes he unlawfully obtained from the people and places his regime plundered, only to meet Angelina's estranged father in a chance encounter during a raid.

After the raid ended, and narrowly escaping being a prisoner of war by the American forces, Elaina searched for a new path of purpose and enlightenment, fleeing to Genesis under the guidance of Dr. Weaver, where she met Kassandra, becoming lifelong friends.

Even after giving birth to Angelina, after reuniting with her daughter's estranged father, her alluring Amazon-like features still remained intact, and like some of her peers, she aged gracefully, with her black hair showing little signs of gray, as she was slowly approaching 47.

Elaina sat on the bed next to her daughter, like she always did, reminiscing of the day that fate united her and her daughter's estranged father. She noticed how much Angelina had blossomed as the years went by, and thought to herself how to tell Angelina how she once crossed paths with Angelina's father.

While Angelina slept, Elaina gently untangled her daughter's long, curly black hair, and took a deep breath, still reminiscing of the last night she spent with the man that she loved, and often thought about it, even in her later years.

Angelina bore the exact same caramel-colored complexion and alluring features as her mother, though her shy gaze and facial features undoubtedly bore a resemblance to her father. Angelina spent her entire life inside the sanctuary, and grew up not knowing who her father was.

Angelina slowly opened her eyes, and saw her mother sitting next to her as she laid her head on her pillow. She slowly sat upright, looked at her mother and asked, "What? Why are you smiling?"

"I was just looking at you, like when you were just a baby, growing up to be the young and beautiful woman that you have become. I have waited so long to tell you about your father. And I think that it's time that you should know who he was. I was just thinking of a way to tell you. If he were here today to see you, his greatest creation, he would've been so proud of you."

"I do think it's time to know, now that you mentioned it. Who was he really? How did you meet?" Angelina asked.

"Your father was a soldier. It's hard to believe that the first time we met was when he was on one of his missions when they came running through the slums chasing some war criminal, 30 years ago. It's hard to believe that it's been this long since we crossed paths. We were on opposite sides that day. He was about 27, and I was only 17 at the time.

"I know that it was an age difference by an entire decade, but when I saw him, I just knew that he was the man I would fall in love with someday. It's almost like I wanted him to capture me.

"And capture me, he did. He didn't know that I was a woman until he'd taken off my hood. I stabbed his arm while trying to escape, but he wouldn't let me. And I'm glad he didn't," Elaina said softly. "He was shocked to see my face, seeing that he had captured a young girl in the militia. Then we came under enemy fire. And he saved me. He put his life on the line for someone that he just met, and that was admirable to me.

"He even vouched for me when they tried to take me as a prisoner of war.

He saved me more times than I remember.

"Then this war came. We fought for 10 years. 10 long years to be free. As a matter of fact, it's still happening, which is why we are here in this sanctuary, living in hiding, hoping that we won't be discovered by enemy forces.

"Then fate reunited us again. I waited an entire decade, and it was worth it. He gave me the greatest gift of all."

"Waited 10 years for what? What did he give you?" Angelina asked.

"You. He gave me you. You're my entire world. And his entire world. But he doesn't know it yet, because he doesn't know he has a daughter," Elaina answered softly, gently passing her finger on her daughter's cheek, and added, "You look more and more like him, every single day." Angelina simply bowed her gaze with a straight face trying to process everything all at once after learning about her father for the very first time.

"You have that shy gaze, just like him," Elaina said. "That was the same look he gave me when we met.

"I remember looking into his eyes for the first time like it was yesterday. Some images remain fresh in my mind, even after all this time.

"One would think that soldiers are cold and heartless, who hide behind their guns. But your father, he was just different.

"But, every time I looked into his eyes, I sensed a troubled soul. They were very sad and weary, like a restless spirit always searching for something that they couldn't have, but they were sincere, soft, warm, and compassionate. A certain gentleness when I looked into his eyes that I had never seen before.

"There was a certain calmness in them. But I also sensed there was conflict in them, no matter how he tried to hide it.

"No one had ever looked at me the way he did. Not even others in the militia. They wouldn't even look twice at me. All they saw was just someone who was a part of the gang. But your father had something else that I never saw from any other man that I met. And it was from that moment, I can tell that he was different from the others, and that he was genuine. But he stayed away because of our age difference.

"But still, it was from that very moment I fell in love with him. Even through all the war around us. I was able to find love in him. It felt like he was the one thing that was missing in my life. But he couldn't love me back the way that I wanted him to, because I was too young at the time. He would never let me get too close to him because of it.

And I had to respect that. That's what made him so noble. He went by a code, and was not willing to sacrifice them for anyone or anything.

"But despite losing so many good friends, and all of my family, all I could ever feel was that unconditional love for him. I just couldn't help but have those emotions towards him.

"No one can deny that you are his daughter. You have his eyes. And they don't lie. They never do. They are the very windows to our souls.

"He lives inside you. You look more and more like him every single day. You are all that I have to remember him by. You're all that's left of the both of us.

"Tomorrow, you'll be the one to carry on our name, our bloodline, our legacy. And the key to preserving it at all costs is you."

"Do you think he still loves you?," she asked softly, with a straight face.

"Your father was a very conflicted man. I saw it from the moment we met. Despite his tough exterior he had to use during all his missions.

"But there was a certain calm to him. He never told me in so many words. But I know that he did, just like I know that if he's still alive, he still does.

"He was torn between his love for me, and duty to his country. He sacrificed so much to save me, even at the expense of losing all that he had worked so hard to achieve, or even losing his life.

"And that spoke volumes to me. More than a thousand words. It was a war between love and duty. It appeared that his love for me conquered his duty to his country. That was a testament that love, indeed conquers all.

"In a way, it was his love for me that caused all this to happen. He lived by what was right, even if it would cost him his life."

"What do you mean?"

"The last time your father saved me, I remember like it happened yesterday. Everything. Every single detail.

"He was given an order to kill me, but ended up protecting me instead. And that triggered an international incident, the likes of which no one had ever seen.

"And the world as we knew it was never the same after that."

"What did you do to cause that?" Angelina asked.

"Being the sole survivor of enemy soldiers didn't sit too well with the General. That was already one strike against me."

"What was the other one?"

"Your father was on his way to see me when it happened."

"When what happened?"

"The Genesis Uprising. Putting it mildly. Others called it, "The Great Fall." I suppose everyone had a different name for what happened that day."

"What's that?"

"The event that brought the entire world into chaos, and caused the entire country to fall into a civil war. All this.

"All of what you see going on, around you. That was the real cause of this civil war. The long and bloody war that never made any sense to begin with.

"It all started when someone thought I was his own personal sex toy. It was someone whom your father had really trusted, and served with.

"It appears that he had other ideas for me," Elaina, said recalling the tragic events, and continued, "I had only defended myself and for that, I was accused of espionage, and of instigating an attack on his troops.

"After fighting off my attacker, I was beaten so badly that I had barely escaped with my life. And your father was given an order to kill me.

"In the General's eyes, it was a crime to defend myself. And from the way it seemed, I had to die because of it.

"Your father defied the General's orders just to save me, and that was the beginning of the end, of all civilization as we know it. It's a long story. Some would call it the catalyst to the end of the world."

"What do you call it?"

"The ultimate act of love. That was all I needed to see. That said more to me than if he told me that he loved me. I just wish it wasn't under those circumstances.

"All my life, I was searching to belong to something greater than myself, or someone for that matter.

"And there he was. Your father. He was the real measure of a man. No matter what the situation was, he always found it in himself to do what was right.

"And at this very moment, it all comes down to you; my greatest creation. Our greatest creation."

"For all that happened in the past, is that really why he left?"

"Yes. He never said so, but I know it was. To protect me. To protect all of us. To protect you. And that was the greatest price that I've had to pay in so long. Not being in the arms of the man that I love.

"And the greatest price that he had to pay was not being in the arms of the woman he had come to love so much, that he was willing to lose everything that he worked so long and hard for.

"But to keep you safe, it was a small price to pay, I suppose. It's the one thing that I have to do. You are his legacy and you must be kept safe at all costs.

"So, I think that it's safe to say that we both have suffered all those years."

"Does he even know about me?"

Elaina shook her head, and answered, "Sadly, no, he doesn't. He doesn't know you're his world because he doesn't know that you exist."

"Then how could you be so sure?"

"Because your father never knew that I was pregnant with you. None of us did. I found out that I was pregnant with you after he had left. And there was no way that any of us in the sanctuary could reach him and tell him. It's like he just vanished off the face of the earth.

"He left to protect me and the rest of us, and at the same time, ended up protecting you without even knowing it. In a sense, it's better that way, that no one outside this sanctuary knows about you, even your father. At least, for now. He was a hunted man at the time. If he is still alive, he still is.

"But I do know that if he were here, he would love you like I have every single day."

"Where do you think he could be at this moment?"

"Probably somewhere still wreaking havoc on enemy forces. Or what's left of them. If he's still alive.

"I really don't know to tell you the truth."

"What were the best memories that you remembered of him?"

Elaina exhaled, while she reminisced on their final tender moments together, and answered, "My fondest memory of your father was the last time we were together, before he left. That single moment of warmth and soft embrace, touching every inch, every fiber of his brown skin against my entire being, feeling the light stubble on his face. Feeling him so close to me caressing his handsome physique, with his hands all over me, while he was inside of me.

"His hands were calloused. You can tell they belonged to a real man, but there was a certain gentleness to his touch.

"I still feel his touch, like it just happened. And I still long for it, even after all this time. There never has been any better moment in my entire life that could amount to that single moment alone with him, and all the joy it brought me afterwards.

"And I would give anything just to be back in his arms and relive that one moment. Forever. That was the best moment of my entire life. Nothing can amount to that one moment.

"That's why I can never bring myself to feel another man's touch. The last time I saw him, all he did was smile before he left.

"The same gaze he gave me when he came into my life was the same he gave when he went away.

"And at the end of it all, all I could do is watch him leave, hoping that once again, fate will reunite us. That was the most helpless moment of my entire life."

"Do you have any pictures of what he looks like?" Angelina asked, with a sudden hint of interest.

"Seeing your father's image was too painful to bear, so I rid myself of all memories of him. Or at least, I tried to.

"I preferred that such a man only exists in memory. No image of him can do him justice. All I can tell you is he was the most noble person that I've ever met. He always stood for what was right," Elaina said, smiling.

She reached into her pocket and took out a piece of cloth that enveloped a gleaming dark hue of a purple heart still in perfect condition after many years that she kept as a memento to the promise they made to one another if they were ever reunited, and said, "He gave me this a long time ago. He made me promise to give it back to him the next time we met.

"But I never had a chance to. This is just one of the many awards I have to remember him by."

"What happened to the others? The other awards I mean," Angelina asked.

"Who knows? I'm sure they're here somewhere waiting to be discovered by some turn of events.

"Only Adam knows the answer to that, I'm afraid."

"It's beautiful," Angelina said, the image of the purple heart filling up her vision.

"This is an award given to soldiers who died or were wounded in the tour of duty, fighting for their country. Very few people who are alive have received this award. And your father was one of those people.

"Maybe you can help me keep that promise. Maybe one day, we can give it to him together, if we ever see him," Elaina said, opening Angelina's hand, and gently placing the purple heart in her palm, closing it.

Angelina opened her mouth in great awe, the gleaming hue of the purple heart, encrusted with pure gold at its side, filling her eyes. She slowly opened her palm and said, "Mom, you shouldn't have."

"I'm sure he would've wanted you to have it. You are all that's left of him. All that's left of us. This is his legacy. And I'm passing it down to you, my child."

"Mom, I can't take this," Angelina answered softly.

"I'm sure he would've wanted you to have it. Your father was the youngest and most decorated in his unit. Your father was a real war hero, Angelina," Elaina said smiling.

Susan was of Japanese heritage, though American by birth, and was one of 2 survivors from an attack on the sanctuary where she once lived as a child at the tender age of seven in Virginia, during the late stages of the civil war.

She was average height, with a slim build and long, straight black hair that fell to her mid-back. For her height and size, she had grown to be deceptively strong, agile and very skillful with a blade after many years of training her mind and body in the skills of an assassin.

Ever since the fateful day when she and Angelina's estranged father crossed paths, she bore an intolerable hatred towards him for the ordeal that she'd suffered even after all these years, leading up to her adult life. Each day she'd hope that the next time they crossed paths, she would have her revenge for the tragic loss of her family.

Susan sat upright on her bed next to Angelina's, with her long, black hair falling over her knees, resting her head on her knees, and was ruminating about her narrow brush with death at the hands of Angelina's estranged father. She sat listening to the entire conversation between Elaina and Angelina and rudely interrupted, "I'd hate to break it to you, Angel, but your father was a murderer."

"What?" Angelina asked in surprise.

"You heard what I said. Your father was a murderer. He might've been a hero in his time, but it ended no differently for those who he once fought and killed, or the very ones who may still be hunting us as we speak," she said, brushing her long, jet-black hair to the back of her neck, exposing her face.

Kassandra was a dark-haired woman in her late 40s, like Elaina, with a height a little past average. She was the daughter of the brilliant and renowned scientist Dr. Alexander Weaver, who invented the world's first universal antidote vaccine against the Chimera outbreak that claimed the lives of more than 300,000. She followed in her father's footsteps to continue his work and became the world's youngest recipient of the Nobel Peace Prize for her work in genetic engineering in Stockholm, Sweden. She then moved to Genesis at the young age of 17, only to lose her mother during the Civil War Uprising, and fled back to the mainland. There, she was captured by the enemy forces just before the country went into a total state of civil war, and spent a lot of time in captivity. She escaped with the help of Angelina's estranged father, who once served under the General's leadership.

Like her father, she aged gracefully. Kassandra wore glasses throughout her entire childhood, bearing an uncanny resemblance to her father, and continued to use his research in hopes that it may someday save the world. She planned to pass on the research to her son, Scott, to continue their brilliant legacy.

Despite her sheltered upbringing, Kassandra had shown great courage and mental fortitude, rivaling that of almost any soldier on the field, even after witnessing many atrocities during her escape from Genesis, the mass executions in Peru, and the number of atrocities committed when the country went into civil war.

Over the years, after she escaped the General's grasp, she lost contact with her father, not knowing if he was still alive. She hoped that someday, they would once again be reunited.

She stopped in the room where everyone slept with a look of shock on her face after hearing Susan's comments about Angelina's estranged father and said, "That's enough, Susan."

"He saved you. He is the reason why you're still alive. He is the reason why all of us are alive. He is the reason why this sanctuary has thrived over the years. He saved all of us.

"None of this was his fault. He was not himself. He isn't the monster that you're making him out to be. He has been made into what he became.

"You were there when Adam told him everything. You know that if he was in his right mind, he would never have done what he did.

"I remember it all like it was yesterday. Every word that Adam spoke, just like Elaina remembers her warm embrace with the man who murdered my entire family.

"But it does not change the fact that he stole my family from me. So long have I dreamt to look into the eyes of the man who took away all that was most precious to me," Susan replied.

"And what do you plan to do if you ever cross paths?" Kassandra asked, glancing at Elaina and her daughter, while Susan stared with a distant gaze.

Susan continued, "All these years, I've waited to kill the man who took everything away from me. To look into his eyes before I rob him of his life, the same way he did to my family. Only he never looked into their eyes when he did it."

"Vengeance will not bring your family back. It won't bring you peace, Susan."

"No one said anything about peace, Kassandra. Every night for the past

20 years, I still dream of the day my family was taken from me.

"There isn't one moment that I don't see the face of the man who stole everything from me."

"Mom, what is she talking about?" Angelina asked with a look of shock on her face. "Is that true? Did he really do what Susan said he did?"

Elaina nodded her head and answered softly, "Yes."

"They know. They all do. None of you can deny what he did," Susan said.

"Don't do this, Susan. Please. None of this was his fault," Kassandra pleaded.

"That's easy for you to say considering that the rest of you grew up with the ones you loved.

"I was the only one who never had my own family. I was the one who was robbed of all of it."

"I know how you feel, Susan, but all these years have been difficult for us, too. You are not the only one who has lost your family. I lost mine too in all this conflict.

"I lost my mother during the Genesis uprising, and haven't seen my father since the Civil War began.

"We've all lost people we love. That's why we're here, so we can pick up the pieces. Together.

"He is the reason why this sanctuary is thriving. He made the greatest sacrifice of all. He left to save the only woman that he has ever loved, along with the daughter that he never knew he had.

"To save the rest of us. To save you. And even after all this time, you don't see that."

"Please forgive me if I do not share the same ideals as you do, Kassandra," Susan said sharply, and added, "My actions may not bring back the ones I love, but such a deed should never be overlooked, nor should it go unpunished.

"My soul will never be at rest until I face the man who took everything away from me. For years, I trained my body and mind, hoping and praying for the day that our paths would once again cross, so I can settle the score between him and myself.

"I was only 7 when all that I ever loved was taken away from me, right before my very eyes. All I've ever known was being chased from place to place, and being forced to live like a scavenger, scurrying underground like a rodent, feasting on whatever scraps we could find, living in this old broken-down, decrepit, abandoned building that that was once a school that we now call a sanctuary. And because of it, I will never know what it is like to have a family of my own, or live like a decent human being.

"I've heard all the stories of how he hunted and murdered all those who served under his command," Susan said, and continued, "I heard the bullets from his machine gun tearing through the door and walls all around the sanctuary, wreaking havoc, claiming the lives of all those who stood in their way.

"I still hear the screams of all the people who were murdered right in front of me, just before they fell right on top of me.

"I still see their faces, and remember how their eyes stared back at me, every time I close my eyes at night.

"I still remember lying still for a brief moment, and the quietness, with only the empty shells falling, breaking what little silence there was left, while I lay beneath the lifeless bodies of my parents, after I struggled to free myself from all the other bodies that lay over me, all covered in their blood.

"I looked down and saw my family, and countless other innocent people lying dead all around me.

"Though I was too young to understand what had happened, I knew that I would never see my family again.

"I didn't know what emotions were at the time, but I knew that deep down inside, what I was feeling towards him was an intolerable hatred that I knew I'd never feel towards anyone else.

"He took my family away from me. I found myself looking down the barrel of his gun, with the smell of fresh blood from all the corpses, and smoke from his machine gun filling the confines of the sanctuary the day we both crossed paths.

"I remained standing, frozen with fright, quietly listening to his shallow breaths behind the mask that concealed his face. He slowly took it off, forcing me to look into his eyes, with the chamber of his gun still pointed at my face, waiting for fate to deal its final blow.

"But all he did was remain perfectly still, staring back at me with a straight face, as if to say that all the lives he'd taken had meant nothing to him, much like a mindless machine bent solely on my destruction.

"But what I remembered most was when I looked into his eyes. They were cold and empty, without a soul. Void of all life, all humanity.

"Until that point, I had felt like I was staring in the eyes of the devil himself. A doorway to pure evil. And anyone who saw those eyes could never forget.

"But, for some reason, he decided to spare my life. And even now, I still don't know what caused him to do it to this very day. Even now, the reason for this deed remains shrouded in mystery.

"But as I looked into his eyes, I could tell that he had no sense of his own identity, after seeing all the atrocities he had committed. I can tell that all of what he really stood for had been taken away from him.

"Imagine the government's deadliest and most prolific assassin, who was just a walking, breathing shadow of himself.

"Then I remember someone came, putting herself in harm's way, carrying me away to safety, with no regard for her own life, running from our pursuers, becoming a fugitive like the rest of you.

"After all the conflict, we had a brief respite from all the war and carnage. But even that was not enough. I suppose it never will be.

"Then after you had brought him back to life, I finally learnt the secret of the man who had taken my entire family from me. And for that, I want to make his death slow and painful, until he begs me to end his life.

"From that point on, my eyes remained fixated on him like a hawk, pursuing its prey. I never said a word.

"I was consumed with hate and vengeance towards him, though I was too young to comprehend what that really was. I remained close to all who knew him and listened to every word of his past.

"After learning of the horrible things he had done in the past, I remember seeing the look on his face, though knowing that deep down in his heart, he knew that he'd done everything that Adam said he did.

"And after he had finally come to his senses, he had learnt that he was once a man of great honor, disgraced by the one man who he'd pledged his allegiance to, and had trusted most.

"He turned back one last time saying his final goodbye, with a timid, half-hearted smile, and all I could do was watch him leave through the night as the rest of you slept.

"But when he looked into my eyes, I finally saw the remorse that I sought for for so long. Even that was not enough solace for all that I had endured at his hands.

"Even after he left, I remained empty, seeing everyone happy with families of their own, though I was robbed of mine.

"Then his seed came into the world. Born into this cesspool of total anarchy, misery, and suffering, just like the rest of us.

"An era of uncertainty, leaving us to carry the burden from all the mistakes of those who came before us.

"When you came into this world, Angelina, I watched as the whole world revolved around you, while slowly, but certainly, I came to be forgotten.

"Again, the same man had somehow taken all that I had longed to have for so long. And since then, I have been living in that shadow. Your shadow, Angelina.

"You're his daughter, and in a sense, that makes you my enemy. So, if you get in my way, I will be forced to kill you.

"This is between your father and me. Plain and simple. So, for your sake, it would be prudent to not cross my path."

An eerie silence filled the sanctuary. Everyone remained speechless, as Susan gave her accounts of the fateful day.

"That is the real story of all the events that changed the world, and with it, my life changed forever," said Susan.

"Everything happened after the uprising on Genesis, which history remembers as 'The Great Fall.'

"The event that forever altered the course of an entire country. And the entire world, as we knew it, was never the same. And human existence as we know it would no longer coexist.

"I often wondered how my life would've been if all the conflict, and all the bloodshed, hadn't taken root in history.

"This is the truth about the so-called man of honor that you've been thinking about for so long, Elaina. And all he really was, was just a hired gun like all the others he killed, while pursuing us…."

CHAPTER 2: OPERATION TALON

The president of the free world has gone missing.

A nation, once united, is now divided, with civil war looming on the horizon.

Its entire fate lies in a bitter power struggle between the battle-hardened and seasoned marines of a ruthless general, and the young and inexperienced liberation forces of the acting president, Dr. Alexander Weaver.

12:57 HOURS. SOMEWHERE IN THE MOJAVE DESERT. 208 MILES FROM LOS ANGELES, CALIFORNIA:

The year is 2026. A year has passed since "The Great Fall of Genesis."

The sun burned brightly in the afternoon skies, scorching the desert sand, with the entire horizon enveloped by the giant screen of a mirage.

The hot and humid winds blew across the barren and unforgiving tundra, tossing about the tumbleweeds, spiraling the dust off the scorched earth.

A sidewinder viper crawled through the scorching desert sands in search of prey, leaving behind the imprints of its scaly body, quickly vanishing with each passing moment over the burning sands.

The fast moving wings of a hummingbird flapped through the winds, whistling with the passing winds of the unforgiving tundra, feeding on the nectar of desert cacti, quickly taking leave to safety.

A red-tailed hawk quickly pounced on the unsuspecting rattlesnake, constricting its entire life from its body with its talons, until it became completely motionless, and quickly flew away squawking, with its prey tightly gripped.

A big horned sheep suddenly stopped grazing on the shrubs of the barren wasteland, suddenly alarmed at the ground shaking under its feet, and fled to safety.

Turkey vultures circled the sky, squawking at the carcass of a mule-deer, and made their rapid descent, joining the others who continued to have their fill.

A group of lizards, sensing danger, quickly scampered to safety after feeling the trembling earth under their bellies.

The rumbling of the desert sand grew louder, quickly overwhelming the howling desert breeze that continued sweeping across the unforgiving tundra.

The massive bodies of reinforced steel from countless heavy battle tanks stormed through the tundra, leaving deep impressions in the endless ocean of the infinite and sweltering desert sands.

A loud explosion echoed, exploding into another advancing armored enemy unit, triggering an exchange from the opposing side.

"Direct hit! We have more incoming!" Adam called out.

He was one of the few African-Americans to be promoted to the rank of general when the entire country went into a state of civil war after the Fall of Genesis. After switching his allegiances to Dr. Weaver against the General and his forces, after having spent many years under his command. Now, he was Dr. Weaver's most trusted general, and was the first to join Unit-13 after serving a tour in the Ukraine, where he hunted the ones responsible for shooting down an airliner carrying 288 people. The attack was the deadliest since the bombing over Lockerbie, Scotland in 1988.

The deafening roars from the tanks and artillery turrets echoed in unison, engaging one another in armored warfare for complete control to decide the fate of the nation.

Adam manned the turret in his armored unit, and deployed an artillery round into one of the enemy units, and cried out, "Direct hit! Reload. All units advance!"

As Adam led the charge against the General's forces, he was greeted by a relentless barrage of shells.

As the shells pounded the position of his armored battalion, the hull of his unit shuddered uncontrollably, temporarily throwing him and his crew off balance.

He rose from the floor, grabbing one of the subordinates sprawled on the floor, shoving him back into position.

The heavy shells continued to rain destruction around them while they fought back gallantly in their courageous counter offensive, holding out against the vast enemy forces.

"We gotta press the attack!" Adam yelled. "If the enemy forces take this position, we might not have another chance! We need to hold!"

Radio chatter from another platoon trying to keep the General's stubborn offensive at bay bounced around the hull, then turned to static as they were decimated.

A look of nervousness shrouded over one of the troops, as he opened his eyes wide at the thought of enemy forces breaking through, and cried out, "My God! They're all dead! It's up to us until reinforcements come!"

"What are we going to do?" asked one of the soldiers.

"What's your name, soldier?" Adam asked.

"Owens! Chris Owens!"

"Do you have any kids?"

"Yes. A daughter!" Chris answered.

"What's her name!?"

"Christine."

"How much does she mean to you, Chris?"

"Everything. I would do anything to protect her. I'd give my life for her."

"Well, here's your chance, soldier! We're all that stands in the way of total tyranny and freedom, even at the cost of making the ultimate sacrifice!

"I know you're afraid. We all are. But if we don't fight, our children and their children will be enslaved, dictated by people like the General, and your daughter will be one of them.

"Either she fights for people like the General, being controlled like a puppet, or dies for the greater good.

"And there is no in-between. It's either we're slaves, or we live and die like free men and women, like we're doing right now.

"We have to fight, and we have to hold. This is where we have to show our resilience. You hear me?

"Now, man your battle stations. Reload!" Adam said, patting Chris on his helmet.

"Yes, sir!" Chris answered, regaining his confidence. "Enemy, 12 o'clock!"

"Fire!" Adam yelled, and deployed the tank's massive shell into an oncoming enemy unit, temporarily stopping its advance.

A giant column of black smoke rose to the skies, as the enemy unit remained immobilized from the attack. The unit's turret slowly turned towards Adam's tank, ready for its counter-attack.

"We've only delayed it! It's getting ready! We need to fire now!" Adam yelled.

"Ready to fire!" Chris yelled, after reloading the next round.

Chris was a young man in his mid-20s, blessed with a boyish visage, short blonde hair, piercing blue eyes, and a well-built physique. He had recently become a father, right before joining the armed forces in strong support of Dr. Weaver during the countries' separation to fight the General.

Adam deployed the next round into the paralyzed enemy unit, this time completely destroying it, triggering another massive explosion and showering the landscape in a giant wall of red flame.

"Direct hit! Reload and advance. We need to score more hits and punch a hole in the enemies' offensive!"

"Ready to fire, sir!"

"Enemy at 11!"

"Weapons hot!"

"And loose!" Adam said as he fired at the next enemy unit, scoring a direct hit. "We have more incoming, at one o'clock!"

"Weapons hot! Weapons hot!" Chris yelled, while under constant pressure to reload.

Though outnumbered, Adam and the remaining armored units continued to advance.

Adam deployed the tank's shell through the enemy unit.

"Enemy down! Reload!" Adam yelled.

While Adam and his crew continued to engage, their tank shuddered uncontrollably, coming to a complete stop after an explosion knocked them off their position, causing their armored unit to be engulfed in thick, black smoke.

The alarms in the tank's battle station began to blare. They had taken a critical hit from enemy artillery.

"What the fuck was that?" he asked with a frantic look on his face.

"What do you think it is? We've been hit! Man the controls!"

"We can't move! The controls are jammed!" Chris shouted.

"We can't move, but we're still combat capable! We need to hold on! Reload and fire!" Adam yelled.

They turned their tank's turret, and continued to fire at the advancing enemy positions, destroying as many as they could.

They tried to maintain balance in their disabled unit, while their defensive lines continued to be pummeled from enemy fire.

The rain of artillery barrage whistled through the skies, triggering giant explosions around them, scoring critical hits on their tank.

A chain of explosions riddled through the liberator's defensive lines, destroying countless armored units, still trying desperately to break the General's offensive lines, causing them to suffer more heavy casualties.

Within moments, the barren wasteland became consumed with death, littered with the burning vessels of armor and corpses of soldiers from both sides.

"Enemy forces are still closing in! We're losing more units and sustaining more heavy casualties! We need to hold the line!" Adam yelled. "Taylor, lead the charge with your units, and flank their positions! We can't charge head on! But we still need to hold this line! Rollout and engage!"

Adam's armored unit was consumed with black smoke, which was quickly filling their lungs, after sustaining another critical blow, while they remained in the embattled unit.

"Holding the line! All units, fire!" Robert yelled.

Robert was a tall and well-built soldier, with brown weary eyes and auburn hair, who was drafted into Unit-13 after serving a tour in France. He was promoted to one of Dr. Weaver's most trusted lieutenants in the Civil War after switching his allegiance from the General.

On Adam's command, the tanks' hulking mass of metal, led by Robert's unit, continued to charge through the desert, flanking enemy positions, still trying to break through the General's defensive lines. The muzzles of their turrets blazed blinding flashes of fire, leaving only destruction in their wake, remaining defiant to all enemy shells that rained down upon them, causing the ground to tremble from their awesome forces from impact.

The tide of battle had continued to turn slowly towards the iron will of the liberation forces, as the General's army began to suffer significant casualties from Adam's counter offensive. Though still outnumbered, Adam's unit stubbornly continued resisting the General's onslaught, wearing down the number of enemy armored units.

Even after scoring a few decisive victories against the General's forces, Adam's defensive lines still remained vastly outnumbered. It seemed that the scales of this epic battle for control would never tip in his favor, despite significant victories.

As they continued pressing their attacks, the valiant stand from the freedom fighters' courageous unit, still outnumbered, had finally paid off, causing a sizable gap in the General's defensive lines.

Through the liberator's unrelenting courage, the General's forces had begun to suffer heavier losses, causing the tide of the battle to turn completely in favor of the freedom fighters.

Adam, Chris, and the other troops climbed out of the burning tank, coughing from the thick, black smoke.

The lethal volley of ordinance from both factions whistled in the skies from the relentless exchange, causing the vast, unforgiving tundra where they stood their ground to tremble, causing massive tremors about to devour everything that roamed through it.

Adam used the tank for cover from the onslaught of artillery and peered into the distance, seeing more clouds of dust rising in the horizon.

He looked through his binoculars and saw light armored vehicles racing towards their positions. "Oh shit," he whispered, with a look of panic on his face.

"What is it, sir?" asked his navigator.

"We have armored units advancing to our position and they're coming in fast! And we need support!"

"What do you want me to do, sir?" Chris asked.

"What's your name, soldier?"

"Luke, Luke Mason!"

"Okay, Mason! We have more enemy troops heading to our position and I need you to man the machine guns and give me some cover fire, before air support arrives! Can you do that?"

"Yes, sir!"

"Wait for my order!"

"What about me, sir?" Chris yelled.

"Help me provide fire on the ground!"

Luke climbed on top of the burning tank, waiting nervously for the order to fire.

Adam took hold of his radio and yelled, "All available units, ground units, we have light armored units with infantry heading to their position and they're closing in fast! We need air support now!"

"Fong, take point on the infantry! We need more time before our gunship support arrives! Wait for my order to fire!"

"Read you loud and clear! Moving into the blockade position!" Eric answered.

Eric was a fourth-generation Chinese who came from a traditional Chinese background. He turned his back on all traditions when he transitioned into adulthood in search of his own path to keep his family's honor by joining the armed forces straight from high school.

After serving a tour in Brazil in search of a war criminal from the Great War that divided the former Soviet Union into different countries, he was drafted into Unit-13, after being seriously wounded from enemy fire.

Eric and his platoon moved into blockade positions, patiently waiting for Adam's order to open fire while the enemy troops drew closer into range.

They waited through constant bombardment from enemy artillery for the charging squad of enemy light-armored units, escorted by more enemy armored units, to help maintain their broken defensive lines against the freedom fighters.

"Taylor, man the 50-Cal!" Adam yelled through the deafening hail of gunfire, while they continued to advance.

Robert jumped on top of one of the heavy tanks, manning the machine guns, pounding into the General's armored units, punching a wider hole through his defensive lines.

"Fire!" Adam yelled, the light-armored units within range.

Gunfire erupted through the desert, while the freedom fighters held their ground, inflicting heavy casualties on the General's ground forces at the cost of losing their own.

In the midst of the lethal exchange from both factions, with total disregard for their own lives, they ignored the dangers of bullets from all the machine guns racing past them, slicing through the wind at supersonic speed.

Within a brief moment, gunfire from both sides erupted. The bullets from the exchange tore through the hull of the light-armored units, while the gunners that manned the oncoming enemy units returned fire, ricocheting off the armored units and causing significant casualties.

Even through the deafening barrage of artillery bombardments, the crackling sounds of gunfire from the heavy machine guns could be heard throughout the entire desert.

After hours of a long and brutal battle, the desert had become a mass grave of dead husks of metal, filled with corpses riddled with bullets, lacerated and dismembered from each other's onslaught, neither side in retreat from the other.

Like the iron will of the liberation and the resolve of the enemy, the battle for control did not go untested. Though the light-armored enemy units suffered significant losses, they continued to advance on the position of the liberation.

"Alvarez, we have the enemy troops still converging on our position. We need cover fire! Man those gatling guns! Where the fuck are you?" Adam demanded.

13:04 HOURS. EDWARDS FREEDOM FIGHTER AIR FORCE BASE - LOS ANGELES, CALIFORNIA:

The crew on the base scurried all about with the tedious process of arming and fueling the planes and gunships.

Shortly after receiving Adam's call for support, a group of Huey helicopters, armed with mini guns on both sides, lifted off the base to buy their planes and gunships time, while the planes were armed and fueled up. Paul's helicopter led the way towards Adam's position at full speed.

"Heading to your position, sir!" Paul answered over the radio.

Paul had a short and stocky build, with light brown complexion who was of a proud Mexican heritage. He was the first of 6 children from teenage parents, born in the United States, along with the remainder of his siblings. And searched for his sense of belonging, joining the armed forces and serving a number of tours under the General's command.

After serving one of his tours in his home country of Mexico on the hunt for some of the world's most vicious cartels, he was drafted in Unit-13, and switched his allegiance from the General to Dr. Weaver during the uprising on Genesis, becoming one of Dr. Weaver's most trusted lieutenants.

13:07 HOURS. FORT IRWIN ENEMY AIR FORCE BASE. 92 MILES AWAY FROM EDWARDS FREEDOM FIGHTER AIR FORCE BASE - LOS ANGELES, CALIFORNIA:

A group of nimble enemy Cayuse attack helicopters and Apache longbow gunships lifted off the base, en-route to the battlefield to provide support for their ground troops, while more of the crew continued to scramble.

13:08 HOURS. SOMEWHERE IN THE MOJAVE DESERT. 208 MILES FROM LOS ANGELES, CALIFORNIA:

Adam and the others continued to stave off the enemy assault as long as they could, while more light enemy armored units continued to converge on their position. The burst of heavy shells from their tanks' enormous turrets continued their exchange on the unforgiving tundra, exploding in the earth, leaving hallmark giant craters, rank with the heavy scent of smoke and gunpowder, as a tell-tale sign of their dominating presence on the field.

"Vaughan, Evans, Collins - we have more heavy-armored units heading to our position. We need to hold this position until air support arrives! Provide whatever support you can!"

"In position, awaiting your orders, sir!" Ahmad answered, his sweaty palms gripped on the tank's heavy machine guns, awaiting orders to fire.

"All weapons hot and waiting for your orders, sir," Henry answered while he manned the tank's machine guns, looking through his binoculars to see the countless columns of desert sands blanketing the horizon.

Henry was a mild-mannered, carefree soldier, with dirty blonde hair and chestnut brown eyes, accompanied with a good build and average height, moving in his late 30s. He was drafted into Unit-13 after serving a tour in Tunisia, on the hunt for insurgents.

Like a number of the soldiers in the armed forces, he once served under the General's command and turned his allegiances to Dr. Weaver after the Genesis Uprising, and was promoted to lieutenant when the country went into a state of civil war.

"These shells are landing a bit too close! But we're still engaging!" Christopher answered over the radio.

Christopher had a light-skinned and freckled face, still blessed with the fragile gift of youth. He finally became a member of Unit-13 after his tour in El Salvador hunting for the country's dictator, who was responsible for the assassination of many of their operatives. Though, after countless missions with Adam, his visage that once brimmed with youth began showing visible signs of stress.

"Fire at will! We need to buy more time before support arrives! They're not letting up!" Adam yelled.

The enemy artillery continued to pound Adam's position, confusing them and obstructing their vision with the thick clouds of desert sands and smoke.

The dust suddenly began to scatter from the ground from the blades of a squad of Huey helicopters, with Paul leading the charge.

Paul looked down at Adam as he flew over his position, heading towards the oncoming enemy units, while Adam and the others continued the fight, still sustaining casualties from the onslaught of the heavy enemy artillery barrage, with the towering poles of thick, dark smoke filling the desert, rising to the skies, obstructing their view from seeing the vast remainder of oncoming enemy forces.

The squad of helicopters cleared their way through the thick, black smoke and began barraging the enemy.

The helicopters' chain guns decimated the entire convoy of the oncoming light-armored units, leaving a wave of shock at the lethal volley of firepower that emitted large plumes of fire from their quick rotating chambers.

Adam exhaled a sigh of relief as Paul and the squad of helicopters hovered, and yelled, "We're repelling the light-armored units! Continue pummeling the positions with as much artillery as you can!"

The barrage remained constant through the wasteland, with both factions still fighting to gain control.

For a brief moment, Adam and his band of freedom fighters had finally begun to gain the upper hand after scoring a number of decisive victories against the General's forces, when their position suddenly came under fire from a squad of agile enemy helicopters, successfully strafing their armored units, causing the sudden shift in the tide of battle.

Bullets and heavy ordinance from the enemy helicopters tore through the desert sands, decimating ground troops, while they quickly continued to strafe Adam's position, causing them to suffer more casualties.

A sudden explosion from an enemy shell exploded into Adam's crippled tank, knocking him to the ground, face first, while the bullets from the enemy gunships continued burrowing through the sand.

Adam's ears rang loudly while he hyperventilated from the shock of the force of the explosion. He felt the grip of someone grabbing his clothes, turning the person over, standing on top of him, after dragging him to safety, hearing the soldier yelling while he tried to regain his senses.

His vision blurred, seeing multiple silhouettes of the shadowy figure standing on top of him, until Chris's visage came into focus, staring down at him.

"You alright? Thought I lost you there for a second," Chris said.

"Yeah," Adam answered, trying to regain his senses.

"We took a pretty good hit. Our tank's completely out of commission."

"Thanks for pulling me out," Adam said. "I have a lot to fight for and I need to know I'll make it back home to my wife and daughter."

"You will, I promise."

The enemy helicopters attacked, causing Chris and Adam to scramble for cover.

"We have a squad of flying eggs and Apaches incoming, and we need gunship support! We won't be able to hold out much longer without support! O'Hara, what's your position? Mason, man those guns!" ordered Adam.

When Luke hadn't responded to Adam's order to fire, he looked at the machine gun position and saw Luke slumping over his gun position lifeless, blood oozing down the hull of the battered tank.

"Mason?" Adam moved towards Luke and called out, gently nudging him. "Mason! Oh, shit! Mason's down!"

Adam's worst fear was realized, knowing that Luke had become another casualty of war. He climbed on top of the tank and pulled Luke's lifeless body from the machine gun position, grunting at his weight, pulling him to the ground to take his place as the tank's gunner.

Chris climbed to the top of the tank to assist Adam in pulling Luke's lifeless body out of his gunnery position, and was greeted by a barrage of machine gun fire from enemy helicopters, causing them all to fall to the searing desert sands.

Adam ran over to assist Chris, seeing his hand covered in blood, turning the scorching sands red. Adam turned Chris over on his back, and saw him choking on blood from the gaping wound that penetrated his throat.

Adam tried to contain the bleeding, while the soldier's senses slowly slipped away from his grasp.

Chris's eyes opened frantically looking back at Adam, while he took his last breath. He reached into his pocket and grabbed a photograph of himself, posing with his wife and daughter, and handed it to Adam, his hands trembling.

"Just hold on! You'll be fine! You'll see your wife and daughter again! Soon! I promise!" Adam said.

Adam wiped the blood off his face, while he applied pressure to Chris's wound. "Soldier down! Medic! I need a medic! Someone help!"

Chris grabbed Adam's uniform, a look of agony on his face, while his life slowly and painfully slipped away. Finally, his hand lost its grip, slapping the unforgiving tundra.

Adam stared at Chris's lifeless gaze, gently passing his hand over his face, closing his eyes. Now, Adam was the only one to defend the position.

He looked around him, shocked, seeing all the soldiers in his regiment lying dead.

He grabbed the bloody photograph of Chris and his family, looking at it for a brief moment, and came to his senses. He slipped it into his pocket, gently laid Chris's body on the sands, and manned the tank's machine guns to fire at the enemy gunships.

Paul raced to Adam's position, the glass from the cockpit of the helicopter shattered from a bullet, killing the pilot, and causing the aircraft to spin out of control.

The alarms of the helicopter blared while the craft careened towards the ground. Paul gripped his seatbelt tightly, delirious and confused, until he crashed with a deafening thud, banging his head on the machinegun's burning steel.

The other helicopters suffered the same fate, crashing and burning.

Adam heard the distress call from Paul and yelled over the radio, "Alvarez is hit by enemy fire, and we lost all our choppers! We need gunship support now!"

13:10 HOURS. EDWARDS FREEDOM FIGHTER AIR FORCE BASE - LOS ANGELES, CALIFORNIA:

The long and tedious task of the gunships being armed and fueled was complete, and the group of Apache longbow gunships, spearheaded by Patrick, quickly lifted off the base, en route to Adam's position, to provide support to their beleaguered ground forces.

Patrick was a proud man, like many others from an Irish heritage, and was one of the oldest living members in the armed forces still in the field, even before most of the soldiers joined. He celebrated after every tour with a stiff drink of whiskey. His dark hair, once as dark as night, showed the obvious signs of gray, completely receding on the top of his head. Lines streaked across his forehead as a tell-tale sign of his seniority, showing that he served a long life under the constant stresses of being a helicopter pilot. He was renowned as the best helicopter pilot in the armed forces, after serving many tours under the General, and was recognized after his tour of duty in Colombia, during the largest manhunt since Pablo Escobar in 1993, earning him a place in the Unit-13.

Like Adam and some of the other senior soldiers, Patrick changed his allegiance from the General to Dr. Weaver after the Genesis Uprising, and was promoted to captain to lead younger pilots into battle.

He listened to the constant radio chatter from Adam, and answered, "We've just armed and fueled all our gunships. Support is already en route to your position. Just hold on a little longer."

13:12 HOURS. SOMEWHERE IN THE MOJAVE DESERT. 208 MILES FROM LOS ANGELES, CALIFORNIA:

The small and nimble enemy Cayuse helicopters continued to strafe the freedom fighters' positions while Adam and the remainder of his squad members fought back from their tanks' gunnery positions.

Adam looked up and saw an enemy gunship charging towards him. He turned the machine gun and opened fire.

As the helicopter charged towards the wall of fire, the impact from the bullets tore through the egg-shaped hull, riddling the enemy pilot's body with holes, causing the helicopter to glide out of control, flying over his position, crashing and burning, causing Adam to breathe a huge sigh of relief.

In the brief moment of respite, after destroying one of the enemy units, Adam saw another enemy helicopter racing towards him.

He froze, unable to react in time to counter the enemy advance, knowing the inevitable was about to befall him.

He felt the thumping of his heart in his chest, knowing what was to be the outcome. Suddenly, the enemy helicopter erupted into a ball of flames, debris and shrapnel pounding his crippled armored unit from a group of friendly gunships swarming with a blitzkrieg attack.

"All remaining ground units, hold this line! We have gunship support!"

The fight between both factions was long and brutal as the day wore on, leaving both sides with heavy casualties.

13:14 HOURS. FORT IRWIN ENEMY AIR FORCE BASE. 92 MILES AWAY FROM EDWARDS FREEDOM FIGHTER AIR FORCE BASE - LOS ANGELES, CALIFORNIA:

After another long and tedious process of arming and fueling their planes, the large number of enemy attack fighter planes quickly lifted off the base on to their attack run to provide support against the freedom fighters who remained heavily outnumbered against the enemy forces, inflicting as many casualties as they sustained, while they continued to hold out courageously.

13:15 HOURS. SOMEWHERE IN THE MOJAVE DESERT. 208 MILES FROM LOS ANGELES, CALIFORNIA:

The combined clamors of heavy artillery from tanks and howitzer guns continued to echo in the distance, while they continued their relentless assault on each other's positions, causing tolls of great proportions, while the all-out war between the gunships from both factions quickly consumed the skies, shifting the course of the war into a stalemate, as they continued to fall from the skies, crashing and burning on the battlefield.

13:28 HOURS. SOMEWHERE OVER THE MOJAVE DESERT. 208 MILES FROM LOS ANGELES, CALIFORNIA:

Patrick and his band of Apache gunships were greeted by a hail of enemy fire, while they engaged more enemy gunships, pounding their heavy guns with long-range attacks, significantly reducing the enemies' rate of firepower on their artillery positions.

A volley of rounds from another enemy gunship tore through the canopy of Patrick's gunship, grazing his arm.

He felt the blood oozing through his clothes and yelled, "Enemy gunship on my tail. I need ground support!"

"Reading you loud and clear!" Ahmad yelled.

"Heading your way!" Patrick answered, heading to Ahmad's position, with the enemy helicopter in hot pursuit. "E.T.A., 4 seconds, 3, 2…."

Within moments, the enemy gunship was greeted by a hail of ordinance from the tank's heavy machine gun, causing it to spiral out in a ball of flames, becoming another casualty on the field.

13:29 HOURS. SOMEWHERE IN THE MOJAVE DESERT. 208 MILES FROM LOS ANGELES, CALIFORNIA:

Ahmad watched as the enemy Apache gunship swiveled out of control, trailing a long line of heavy black smoke and crashing on the sands. Seconds after the impact, the desert trembled as the helicopter scattered shrapnel in every direction.

"1," Ahmad said, completing the countdown.

Ahmad had a stocky build, was a little past average height, and was dark brown in complexion. As a youth, he led a troubled life, coming from a broken family in the drug-infested projects of Baltimore, Maryland. Eager to leave his troubled past behind, he joined the armed forces straight out of high school.

While serving a tour in China, he was seriously wounded in battle, but still completed his mission. Shortly after, he was inducted into Unit-13.

Like Adam, he changed his allegiance to Dr. Weaver after serving under the General's command after the uprising that consumed Genesis, becoming one of Dr. Weaver's most trusted lieutenants.

"What would you do without me, huh?" Ahmad remarked sarcastically.

13:33 HOURS. SOMEWHERE OVER THE MOJAVE DESERT. 208 MILES FROM LOS ANGELES, CALIFORNIA:

"Well, considering that I just saved your ass, we're even," Patrick answered.

13:33 HOURS. SOMEWHERE IN THE MOJAVE DESERT. 208 MILES FROM LOS ANGELES, CALIFORNIA:

"You got jokes, don't you?" Adam said.

13:33 HOURS. SOMEWHERE OVER THE MOJAVE DESERT. 208 MILES FROM LOS ANGELES, CALIFORNIA:

"Who said I was joking?" Patrick asked.

13:34 HOURS. SOMEWHERE IN THE MOJAVE DESERT. 208 MILES FROM LOS ANGELES, CALIFORNIA:

While Adam and the rest of his lieutenants returned fire from their tanks' machine gun emplacements, trying to hold back the swarm of enemy gunships at bay, the battlefield suddenly became quiet. The heavy shells from the artillery guns and tanks had suddenly stopped raining from the skies.

13:17 HOURS. EDWARDS FREEDOM FIGHTER AIR FORCE BASE - LOS ANGELES, CALIFORNIA:

Dillon lifted off the ground in a newly fueled fighter plane to join in the assault against the General's forces, a squad of fighter planes following off the runway.

He was of Korean lineage, born from a long line of pilots dating as far back as the Korean War when the Communist regime invaded the South. Before defecting to the allies for political asylum in the United States, Dillon's great-great-great-great grandfather flew for the Communist regime during the Great War of the Chosin Reservoir in 1950. Dillon joined the armed forces because of his love of flying, to follow in his ancestors footsteps, and was drafted into Unit-13 after providing support to ground troops during a tour of duty in Egypt, fighting against insurgents hired by the Egyptian government during the revolution.

Like Adam and some of the soldiers in his unit, he had served under the General's command for many years, and switched his allegiance to Dr. Weaver during the Genesis Uprising. Now, he was one of Dr. Weaver's most trusted pilots, and was promoted to captain of his squadron by Dr. Weaver himself, leading younger pilots into battle against the enemy forces.

13:16 HOURS. SOMEWHERE IN THE MOJAVE DESERT. 208 MILES FROM LOS ANGELES, CALIFORNIA:

After hours of a full-scale war in the heart of the barren and unforgiving tundra, the searing sands had become consumed with death and destruction, like a great plague had swept through the plain, consuming all in its wake.

The dark columns of smoke from all the destroyed units from both fronts rose to the skies, blocking out the sun.

The desert had grown quiet and peaceful, with only the sounds of the winds sweeping through the barren tundra, breaking its silence, along with the crackling flames that consumed the dead husks of armor and corpses that littered the battlefield.

Adam and the rest of his unit looked around, and saw how so many were consumed in the war.

They were saddened at knowing that these were the same soldiers they once served with proudly, calling them brothers. Now, they became bitter enemies, locked in a long, grueling power struggle.

Moments after the long battle, the soldiers had a brief respite to catch their breath, but still remained puzzled as to why the enemy positions had ceased their attacks, and the enemy gunships suddenly withdrew.

"Something isn't right," Eric said, looking all around the barren tundra.

"I agree," Henry answered, while he continued to man his machine gun position.

"Keep your eyes opened," Robert said, while he continued to look all around him.

"It may be another ambush. The General is full of surprises," Adam replied.

As the scorching sun continued to rise high in the noon sky, burning through the desert sands, the quietness was suddenly shattered by the distant screaming of an engine from a jet fighter.

Ahmad looked in the skies and fixated on the jet fighters rapidly approaching their position and shouted, "We have incoming! Hornets, and they are coming in fast! They're heading straight for us! Enemy planes! Assume defensive positions!"

"All gunships break formation and retreat!" Patrick yelled, breaking formation, trying to retreat to safer grounds.

"We have enemy planes incoming, on a bombing run, heading to strafe our positions. We need fighter support!"

13:20 HOURS. SOMEWHERE OVER THE MOJAVE DESERT. 208 MILES FROM LOS ANGELES, CALIFORNIA. ONE MINUTE AWAY FROM FREEDOM FIGHTER'S' DEFENSIVE LINES:

"Heading to your location. E.T.A., 60 seconds," Dillon answered.

13:23 HOURS. SOMEWHERE IN THE MOJAVE DESERT. 208 MILES FROM LOS ANGELES, CALIFORNIA:

"We don't have 60 seconds, damn it!" Adam cried out.

"Concentrate all fire on incoming enemy planes!" Robert yelled.

"I knew it," Eric said to himself. "This was too good to be true."

Ahmad opened fire at the squad of incoming enemy planes, causing the others to quickly follow in greeting the enemy planes from their defensive lines.

The temporary moment of peace that had come into the desert after the long and costly war was now shattered at the screaming of jet engines that raced through their volley of anti-aircraft fire.

As the enemy planes quickly flew over their position, the ground trembled, and a giant wall of flames from deployed enemy ordinances rushed towards the freedom fighters' positions, consuming many in its wake.

Patrick and his squad of gunships had tried to retreat from their position, but became overwhelmed by the enemy planes' awesome power from their strafing round that caused them to spin out of control. Patrick became completely disoriented, the enemy planes causing a great fluctuation of power from the vacuum as they flew over Patrick and the gunships. The rebels' guidance systems began to malfunction, their cockpits shuddering violently from the vibration caused by enemy jet engines, causing their canopies to shatter, slicing through their faces. They crashed into the desert sands.

Within a brief moment, Patrick and his entire squad of gunships were wiped out by a single attack, leaving the remainder of the ground troops unprotected.

After neutralizing the squad of gunships, the enemy fighter planes made another strafing run, deploying a number of their ordinance.

The ground shook from a giant plume of flame rushing towards them, while they watched with stunned looks on their faces.

"Get cover!" Adam yelled, and ran for safety, hiding inside his crippled tank.

The giant wall of flame caused the tank to flip over multiple times before coming to a complete stop.

After hours of intense fighting between both factions, the stalemate was now broken, shifting the balance in favor of the war General's forces.

Adam's position was almost wiped out from the attack, causing morale to plummet as quickly as it had risen.

He crawled out of his tank, the thick armor totally consumed in flames. His face was badly bruised and bleeding, his ears ringing from the deafening roar of the explosion, leaving only a few armored units left from the deadly onslaught from the enemy planes.

Adam stood, dazed and confused from the attack, blood trickling down his face.

He walked through the battlefield, seeing so many of his soldiers charred, impaled, and dismembered from the flame from the enemy planes and burning shrapnel.

He looked into the face of the survivors, and saw defeat in their faces, looking for cover in the remainder of the surviving ground units.

Patrick staggered over to Adam, his face lacerated from tiny shards of metal and broken glass from his gunship's canopy.

"What happened to the rest of your squad?" Adam asked.

"They didn't make it. They were all wiped out from the attack," Patrick said.

"I don't know. Looks like we're the only ones left," Adam said, in a worried tone.

"It looks like the General has already won. Our campaign hasn't even begun, but already has ended."

"We must hold, Patrick. This can't be over now. We're all that stands between the General's forces and our freedom. We must hold," Adam said, all the strength almost drained from his body from the punishment he endured.

"How do we do that? The rest of our squad has been wiped out. It's just us, and our air support hasn't arrived and probably never will. Maybe they were intercepted by the enemy planes. Not that it matters now, anyway."

Robert, Eric, and the other lieutenants crawled out of the surviving units, along with a few other soldiers, badly shaken from the onslaught of enemy strafing runs.

Adam smiled weakly and said, "Am I happy to see you."

"My God," Henry said softly. "How did it come to this?"

"It's over, isn't it?" Eric said, all hope faded from his voice.

"No, it's not. Remember when we served before? Remember North Korea? We've been outnumbered before and we somehow thought of a way to win," Adam answered.

"We're completely decimated, Adam. Our air support never came. And probably will never come to back us up. We're just a handful of men. What good can we do against this onslaught? We're hanging by a string right now," Patrick said looking around him in a complete state of hopelessness.

Adam looked back and saw the look of defeat on the faces of the remainder of his troop, and saw their courage hanging by a thread. He looked around the desert, watching all the soldiers that paid the ultimate price for freedom, lying amidst the burning wreckage.

The desert once again was silent after the exchanges that had echoed in it, with only the crackling of flames that consumed the dilapidated units breaking through.

Adam was in deep thought, thinking of a way to inspire morale, to resist the onslaught of the vast enemy forces, and heard the familiar screaming from jet engines from enemy planes. His concentration broke. "Shhh."

"What is it?" Ahmad asked.

"I hear something. Enemy planes making another strafing run!" Adam said, listening closely to the distant buzzing of jet engines drawing closer every passing moment.

He looked in the distance and saw enemy forces, and added softly with a look of complete shock, "My God, they're closing in."

"This is suicide! We can't hold this position! We need to fall back and regroup!" Eric yelled.

"We can't fall back now. We came too far to turn back now. We need to hold the line somehow, no matter the cost. This is the only chance we got against the enemy. If we turn back now, they win," Adam said. "Eventually, we'll be found and slaughtered like cattle. We're all that's left between freedom and oppression. We must hold at all costs, or all those soldiers would've died for nothing!"

The distant screams of jet engines roared in the skies, growing louder.

"Man your positions!" Adam yelled.

Though the war had shifted in favor of the enemy, the remainder of the freedom fighters who were vastly outnumbered stood their ground against the oncoming enemy planes that were quickly closing on their positions on another strafing run.

Although they were heavily outnumbered, the enemy planes were still greeted by stiff resistance, with whatever available units and fire power remained to make their stand.

After moments of constant skirmishing, the sun moved higher in the sky, and the clamor from the rounds from the machine gun positions could be heard from miles outside the battle zone.

Adam and his unit held their ground until another enemy plane burst into flames, crashing near their position.

The ground shook from the explosion, the giant wall of crimson flame turning into thick, black smoke rising to the skies in the infamous dark, giant mushroom shape.

A group of planes soared over the freedom fighters' position and headed straight to the skies in pursuit.

Adam watched the planes flying over their position with great jubilation and asked, "Where have you been, pilot?"

13:25 HOURS. SOMEWHERE OVER THE MOJAVE DESERT. 208 MILES FROM LOS ANGELES, CALIFORNIA:

"It took longer than I thought to get to your position. Sorry I couldn't be here sooner. What's your status?" Dillon asked, looking down at the beleaguered forces that suffered a number of casualties from the enemy forces.

13:27 HOURS. SOMEWHERE IN THE MOJAVE DESERT. 208 MILES FROM LOS ANGELES, CALIFORNIA:

"We're in bad shape, and Alvarez is down. We don't have a fix on his location, and we don't know if he is still alive. We lost most of our infantry during the last strafing run. We're just a handful remaining against an entire battalion. Before that, we lost most of our ground units and sustained heavy casualties.

We barely have enough men to repel another wave. We're hanging by a thread, and all morale is down, and continues to rapidly decline among what's left of our troops as we speak. Patrick's entire gunship squad is down from the attack. He and just a few others made it out alive, but they're in bad shape. They're hurt pretty badly. We won't be able to hold for long. And we have more enemy forces converging on our position. We need air support and more reinforcements. If we lose this position, then all is lost. We need to hold, before more arrive. We need to keep on punching a hole in the enemies' defensive lines, and the remainder of our artillery alone won't cause enough damage. We need you and your squad to take out their artillery positions, and I mean fast, before the shelling begins again. But, if it makes you feel any better, I couldn't be happier to see you. You came in the nick of time."

13:30 HOURS. SOMEWHERE OVER THE MOJAVE DESERT. 208 MILES FROM LOS ANGELES, CALIFORNIA:

"Read you loud and clear. Providing support," Dillon answered, still peering down at the battlefield, seeing total decimation among the thick clouds of dark smoke coming from all over the battered and destroyed units, rising to the skies from all the destruction the war had wrought upon the desert.

He turned his plane around and headed to engage the enemy ground forces as he quickly descended.

The alarms in his cockpit blared loudly while he primed his weapons for his assault, as the enemy ground troops held their defensive lines.

"All ground units - open fire! Combine all our artillery with the air support! Hit their positions with all you have!" Adam commanded, as they moved closer to the enemy positions.

The enemy ground forces were once again greeted by the massive guns from the remainder of Adam's battalion.

An enormous volley of enemy fire suddenly greeted Dillon from the ground as he flew towards their position, deploying a cluster bomb. In a brief moment, it consumed the bulk of the enemy ground units with a giant burst of flame. Dillon arrowed straight into the afternoon skies, performing a barrel roll with the screaming of his jet engines slowly drowning in the distance.

With a single blow, the war had once again shifted back in the favor of the freedom fighters, as they continued wearing down the enemy forces with fire from the remainder of their artillery positions, while air support made another attempt for a strafing run to quell the enemy firepower.

Dillon and his squadron of F-16s began another rapid descent towards the enemy position, when a sudden blinding light from an explosion flashed through his cockpit. He was greeted by a sudden barrage of enemy fire from another enemy plane, now in pursuit.

Dillon watched as one of his pilots headed to the ground, with his wounded plane trailing black smoke, shuddering and breaking into pieces, and yelled, "Milton, come in! Bail! Bail!"

The alarms in the cockpit of Milton's burning plane blared loudly, warning him to eject. The pilot was badly burnt, drenched in blood.

Though barely conscious from the impact, Milton pulled his ejection lever as strongly as he could, but to no avail. The canopy was jammed from the heavy damage his plane had sustained, trapping him inside.

He continued pulling the ejection lever as hard as he could and yelled, "I can't eject! It's jammed! I'm going down, and I can't bail! I can't eject! Someone help me!"

The pilot still continued pulling on the ejection lever during his rapid descent to the ground, and finally lost all hope, knowing that he was about to die. He resigned himself to the inevitable, embracing his fate.

Dillon, the other pilots, and all the other freedom fighters heard the chatter from the pilot trapped inside the burning cockpit that plummeted towards the scorching desert sands, and watched helplessly as the plane crashed, triggering a massive explosion of red flame.

The enemy plane began its pursuit of Dillon. Dillon headed straight to the skies, and skillfully maneuvered his plane, flying deadlocked on the tail of the enemy plane. He quickly deployed his missile, destroying the enemy aircraft, and said, "That's for Milton," watching it disintegrate.

Dillon flew towards Adam's position with another enemy fighter in hot pursuit, the alarms in his cockpit blaring loudly.

13:31 HOURS. SOMEWHERE IN THE MOJAVE DESERT. 208 MILES FROM LOS ANGELES, CALIFORNIA:

Eric saw the planes heading toward their position and yelled, "Enemy plane, incoming!"

13:32 HOURS. SOMEWHERE OVER THE MOJAVE DESERT. 208 MILES FROM LOS ANGELES, CALIFORNIA:

"Another on my tail! I need ground support!"

13:32 HOURS. SOMEWHERE IN THE MOJAVE DESERT. 208 MILES FROM LOS ANGELES, CALIFORNIA:

"Provide cover fire!" Adam yelled. "We need air support to finish off the enemy ground units!"

The enemy flew over their position and was greeted by a volley of flak and heavy artillery. It exploded, causing the plane to spin out of control, crashing near the freedom fighters' position.

"Got him!" Ahmad yelled.

"We're not out of the woods yet, Evans!" Adam replied through the deafening roar of gunfire. "We still have more incoming!"

13:35 HOURS. SOMEWHERE OVER THE MOJAVE DESERT. 208 MILES FROM LOS ANGELES, CALIFORNIA:

The fight for air superiority had only begun a few moments ago, but was fought with great intensity as both factions battled for supremacy over the skies.

13:37 HOURS. SOMEWHERE IN THE MOJAVE DESERT. 208 MILES FROM LOS ANGELES, CALIFORNIA:

The ground troops from both factions kept their gaze firmly to the skies to witness the engagement, even under a series of bombardments.

13:39 HOURS. SOMEWHERE OVER THE MOJAVE DESERT. 208 MILES FROM LOS ANGELES, CALIFORNIA:

"Another enemy plane on my tail, and I can't shake him!" Dillon yelled over the radio, while the bright flashes of bullets from the enemy plane's guns raced past his cockpit, a few rounds tearing through his aircraft.

Dillon performed a barrel roll, causing some of the rounds to narrowly miss his plane.

The enemy pilot burst into flames from one of Dillon's wingman's assists.

The blinding flash of light from the enemy plane's explosion lit the cockpit of his plane, causing him to look back. He saw the enemy plane engulfed in flames, making the evening skies look as bright as day, helping to keep the tide of battle narrowly in their favor by breaking the brief stalemate.

"I owe you one, pilot," Dillon said.

"No thanks required," the pilot answered.

"But you saved my ass. And I owe you one."

"My pleasure," his wingman, Bradley, answered. The call was cut short from the enemy rounds that tore through the wingman's plane, piercing through the wingman's chest, shattering through the canopy and cockpit, letting in the deafening roar of the artillery guns below.

The wounded pilot looked at himself, covered in his own blood, and at the cockpit in a state of disbelief, smeared in heavy spatters of red.

He took off his oxygen mask, gasping for air, and called out over the radio, "Captain."

"Yes, pilot! What's your status?"

"I'm hit. Don't think I'm going to make it."

"Yes, you will, pilot. We're going to get through this!" Dillon said.

"I'm hit by enemy fire. And I'm losing a lot of blood, Captain."

"It's Kim! Dillon Kim! Call me Kim!"

"I don't think I'll make it back," the wounded pilot replied softly.

"You need to hold on! You're going to make it!" Dillon yelled through the radio, a look of horror on his face, knowing that the wounded pilot would soon be meeting his demise.

"I can't hold it. I'm going down," the pilot answered calmly.

"You got family, pilot?" Dillon asked.

"Yes," the pilot answered weakly.

"We'll get you back to them safe and sound! I promise you!"

"It's no use. I'm losing too much blood. I'm losing my senses. I can't hold on anymore," the pilot said weakly, while he slowly began to slip into unconsciousness.

"What's her name, pilot?"

"Her name is Chelsea. Chelsea Bradley. She's my daughter. Tell her that I couldn't make it back."

"Just hang on, pilot! "You'll be fine. We'll get you home to your wife and family!" Dillon said.

"It's been a real honor, Captain. A true honor," the pilot said, taking his last breath. After losing total consciousness, his plane plummeted from the skies.

A complete wave of silence filled the other end of Dillon's frequency.

"Bradley! Come in! Bradley!" Dillon yelled.

Dillon closed his eyes in a brief moment of silence, listening to the radio static of another fallen comrade who paid the ultimate price, to be survived by his wife and daughter.

The long and arduous power struggle that continued to plague the desert had shifted back into a bitter stalemate.

As Dillon continued to fly through the skies in pursuit of more enemy planes, his cockpit shuddered violently from an enemy plane that soared over his canopy in pursuit of his other wingman.

He turned his plane around in pursuit, closing the distance, and greeted the enemy plane with a barrage of fire.

The enemy plane disintegrated from the lethal volley, exploding into a blinding ball of flame, and descended towards the surface, screaming against the warm desert winds.

After the skirmish for air supremacy, losing a number of their planes to the enemy forces, the skies were now clear of enemy planes. And despite the stubborn resistance from the enemy forces, Dillon and the remainder of his squadron flew over the enemy ground units, deploying a series of ordinance, destroying more of the enemy's vast firepower, though they remained unwilling to relent to the freedom fighters.

Though a vast number of the enemy forces were destroyed by their strafing run, they were greeted with stiff resistance from the remainder of the enemy ground forces.

Dillon looked outside of the cockpit of his plane and saw the blinding flashes from all the flak and tracers from the heavy machine guns racing past him.

14:01 HOURS. SOMEWHERE IN THE MOJAVE DESERT. 208 MILES FROM LOS ANGELES, CALIFORNIA:

Paul woke from his brief state of unconsciousness in the wreckage of the helicopter.

He struggled to free himself from the straps that secured him to his position, and climbed out of the wreckage. His face and neck were lined with cuts from shards of broken glass and shrapnel, his uniform ripped from the fall. Paul walked around looking through the shattered cockpit of the helicopter and saw the pilot and the other machine gunner lying motionless, blood trickling from their wounds.

He heard the clamor of heavy artillery guns still firing and saw the entire region blanketed with towering columns of thick, black smoke, and the bright muzzle flashes of heavy guns continuing their exchange, shooting to the skies. He remained stranded within striking distance of the enemy lines, and sat on the desert floor to regain his strength from the heavy shock he suffered from the fall.

He watched the group of planes heading towards the enemy ground units on their final run to the enemy's positions, destroying the last of their long-range guns.

The skies and ground were now clear of enemy forces, giving the ground troops a brief respite to catch their breaths.

Adam grabbed the radio and asked, "How's your ammo and fuel count, flight leader?"

14:03 HOURS. SOMEWHERE OVER THE MOJAVE DESERT. 208 MILES FROM LOS ANGELES, CALIFORNIA:

"A few missiles left. Mostly guns. But collectively, we have a great deal of ordinance left. What are your orders, sir?"

14:05 HOURS. SOMEWHERE IN THE MOJAVE DESERT. 208 MILES FROM LOS ANGELES, CALIFORNIA:

"As I said before, we've lost most of our men and ground units, and it's my duty to ensure the survival of what troops I have left. There are a few enemy positions a few miles away from our current position, and they may be mobilizing more planes and ground units. I need you to lead a strike force and make a strafing run on their positions and cripple whatever abilities they have left to make war. Or do you need to reload and refuel?"

14:08 HOURS. SOMEWHERE OVER THE MOJAVE DESERT. 208 MILES FROM LOS ANGELES, CALIFORNIA:

Dillon watched his fuel gauge and simply flew out of the battle area to head back to base.

14:10 HOURS. EDWARDS FREEDOM FIGHTER AIR FORCE BASE - LOS ANGELES, CALIFORNIA:

The ground crew immediately scurried across the base to once again begin the time-consuming task of reloading and refueling the planes as they landed on the tarmac. Moments after, they were reloaded and refitted with more ordinance, they lifted off the runway en-route to the enemy positions.

14:31 HOURS. SOMEWHERE IN THE MOJAVE DESERT. 208 MILES FROM LOS ANGELES, CALIFORNIA:

The ground troops continued to gather whatever surviving troops they had left to make their last stand against the remainder of enemy forces, when they heard the roar of the jet engines flying over their position, and looked to the skies, seeing the large number of planes.

14:35 HOURS. SOMEWHERE OVER THE MOJAVE DESERT. 60 MILES AWAY FROM NAVAL AIR WEAPONS CHINA LAKE ENEMY AIR FORCE BASE - RIDGECREST, CALIFORNIA:

Dillon looked down at Adam's position from his cockpit, seeing the remainder of the forces still maintaining their formation of the crumbling defensive lines. He broke radio silence and said, "We'll be within enemy air space within a few minutes. Reduce altitude, all weapons hot, maintain radio silence, and engage on my command."

14:49 HOURS. NAVAL AIR WEAPONS CHINA LAKE, ENEMY AIR FORCE BASE. 72 MILES NORTH EAST FROM EDWARDS FREEDOM FIGHTER AIR FORCE BASE - RIDGECREST, CALIFORNIA:

The group of planes spearheaded by Dillon continued flying at low altitude to avoid detection with their weapons armed and ready to engage.

Seeing the enemy tower in the distance, Dillon lined it in his crosshairs and fired a long-range missile. He watched it explode, placing the entire enemy base on high alert, and said, "All communications from the enemy tower have been severed. Engage at will. I repeat, engage at will."

The planes broke formation, engaging all targets in their direct line of sight. A number of enemy planes began to line the runway on their final ascent to take off, and came under attack from the freedom fighters' firing line.

One of the enemy planes quickly made it off the runway when it came under fire, falling back to the surface, crashing and burning, after being engaged by Dillon.

The hangars that housed many of the planes and ammunition erupted in a giant ball of flame from the awesome power of a bunker buster that tore through its foundation, destroying all the enemy's supplies that would further fuel their war efforts.

Within a brief moment of their assault, the enemy base was instantly reduced to complete rubble.

After the enemy position had been demolished, the group of planes made their departure as quickly as they had appeared, leaving death and destruction in their wake, moving on to their next objective.

15:16 HOURS. FORT IRWIN ENEMY AIR FORCE BASE. 92 MILES EAST OF EDWARDS FREEDOM FIGHTER AIR FORCE BASE - LOS ANGELES, CALIFORNIA:

While the squad of planes silently made their way towards the enemy position, the enemy communications tower suddenly burst into flames, placing the enemy base on high alert, and the group of planes continued their relentless blitzkrieg attack on their next objective, overwhelming the enemy positions.

The planes burst into flames, just as one infrastructure after the next continued to crumble and fall from their awesome firepower, as the rebels continued to cripple the enemy's ability to mobilize more planes, and be combat capable against them, leaving more destruction as they had done previously. After their blitzkrieg attack, the rebels vanished into the sky as quickly as they came, leaving behind more carnage and destruction as they headed to their next objective.

15:42 HOURS. MARCH AIR RESERVE ENEMY AIR FORCE BASE. 99 MILES SOUTHEAST OF EDWARDS FREEDOM FIGHTER AIR FORCE BASE - ARNOLD HEIGHTS, CALIFORNIA:

The enemy communications tower suddenly burst into flames, as the planes swooped from the skies. The explosions were soon followed by a blast to the hangars that stored the planes and ammunition, as well as the other planes that were neatly arranged throughout the blast radius of all their ordinance.

The rebels continued to attack the enemy positions with relentless precision, stopping them from mounting any kind of defensive capabilities against the freedom fighters.

After the onslaught, the group of planes flew into the skies as quickly as they began their assault, leaving behind their usual trail of carnage and destruction on the enemy's positions.

15:56 HOURS. CAMP PENDLETON ENEMY AIR FORCE BASE. 148.6 MILES SOUTH OF EDWARDS AIR FORCE BASE - CARLSBAD, CALIFORNIA:

Dillon led the final assault on the last remaining enemy stronghold, deploying his long-range missile, and watched it cause pandemonium.

Within moments, the enemy compound was swarmed, the hangars that housed all their ammunition and planes destroyed.

A series of explosions from their armored units and fuel depots burst into flames from the onslaught, as they continued to neutralize the enemies' capabilities to mobilize against them.

Within moments, their attacks were over, and the planes withdrew from the enemies' position, completely neutralizing the enemy's fighting capabilities to wage war against them.

16:42 HOURS. SOMEWHERE IN THE MOJAVE DESERT. 208 MILES FROM LOS ANGELES, CALIFORNIA:

After a few moments of recuperating near the wreckage of the helicopter, Paul gathered all his strength, looking all around him, trying to find his way back to Adam and the remainder of the troops.

Still suffering from the shock of the crash, he stared into the gaping hole that tore into the cockpit, seeing the pilot's lifeless body, and grabbed the radio to call for help.

For a brief moment, an eerie silence swept through the desert, with only the howling winds blowing. He looked around, trying to get his sense of direction to make his way back to Adam's position, when his gaze fixed on a familiar brown-skinned, handsome visage, now with a blank expression that seemed alien, dressed in an enemy uniform. "Lieutenant? Is that you?" Paul asked, but only received total silence.

Paul looked into the soldier's eyes, seeing the emptiness in them. The man who had once saved his life, who was once an honorable man, was now completely void of his humanity. He had become a walking shadow of himself after being transformed into the ultimate killing machine, and was now under complete allegiance to the General.

Paul heard the roar of the plane's engines drawing nearer to his position, and the rumbling echo from a chain of massive explosions once again resumed.

The deafening exchanges of artillery suddenly stopped. The stalemate between both sides had finally been broken for the moment, shifting the war narrowly in favor of Dr. Weaver's forces.

Adam and his band of troops cheered loudly as Dillon and the rest of his squadron flew over their position.

As Paul shifted his attention back to the familiar face that stood before him, the enemy soldier slowly drew his sidearm from his holster, pointing it at Paul with no sign of reasoning or remorse.

Paul put his hands up and said, with his finger keyed on the button of his radio, "Lieutenant, it's me. It's Alvarez. We served in Mexico back in the day, remember?"

Adam heard Paul's voice over the radio, and called out in surprise, "Alvarez? It's Alvarez. He's alive!"

"What's his position?" Ahmad asked.

"Alvarez, what's your position?" Adam asked.

"It's him. Oh my God. I can't believe it's him," Paul answered over the radio, and continued. "It's me, Lieutenant. It's Alvarez. You saved me back in Mexico. You pulled me out of the burning wreckage, remember? Come on, Lieutenant! Fight it!" Paul continued loudly, looking at the gun pointed at him.

"Don't do it, Lieutenant," Jason said softly, begging the soldier to save Paul's life. "We can use him. He's worth more to us alive than dead."

Jason was a young and impressionable soldier in his early 20s with straight jet-black hair and piercing blue eyes. He joined the armed forces straight from high school in search of fame after the Korean War had ended, uniting the entire Peninsula under Southern rule, wanting to be a part of the infamous Unit-13.

After the country entered civil war, he reluctantly joined the General's forces, and was ordered to accompany the assassin on all his missions.

Adam's eyes opened wide, listening to Paul over the radio being confronted by the assassin, and said, "Oh my God, it's him. It's really him. He's alive. What's your status? Alvarez! Respond!"

The rest of Adam's unit listened helplessly to the radio chatter, with Paul's nervous voice on the other end of the transmission. Jason continued pleading for Paul's life, reluctantly anticipating the outcome.

After a long battle, the desert was once again soundless, with only the crackling sounds from the radio chatter breaking the short-lived calmness that had once again befallen the desert.

Paul continued, staring helplessly at the man who had once saved his life, and was now about to end it. "Don't you remember?" A shot rang out through the desert, echoing through the vast plain, startling Adam and the others.

Paul looked at the bullet hole that tore into his chest and touched it, his blood oozing from the wound, staining the desert sands.

Paul knelt on the scorching desert sands in front of the man who he once trusted with his life, and now had become his executioner.

"Alvarez! Respond!" Robert called out.

Paul continued looking into the Lieutenant's eyes and smiled, suddenly resigned to his fate. Two more shots echoed through the vast expanse of wasteland, robbing the young lieutenant of his life.

As Dillon flew towards the base, listening to Paul's last words before he was executed by his own former squad member, he closed his eyes in sorrow.

After the long and epic battle that ravaged the desert, the stalemate was completely broken. For the moment, the epic battle to decide the entire fate of the country ceased.

Although the freedom fighters had narrowly won the first round of many battles to come, their celebration was short-lived after losing one of their high-ranking officers. The cost of their narrow victory came at a very heavy price.

"Oh my God, he killed him," Christopher said softly.

"What do we do now?" Henry asked Adam, and said, "If more enemy reinforcements come, we won't have the manpower to hold this position. None of us will make it back alive, for sure."

Adam looked at Henry with a distant look on his face, and looked at the bloody photograph of Chris and his family, and answered softly, "Now we regroup. And prepare for the next battle coming our way. This is far from over. This has barely even begun, I'm afraid."

They looked all around the desert, and saw the carnage that consumed all the brave men and women, novice and seasoned, who had sacrificed their lives in the name of freedom and tyranny alike.

"Where do we go?" Patrick asked.

"We head back to base and strengthen our numbers for the next round of battle. Naturally, we must be prepared to fight at all costs. Too much weighing on our shoulders to stop now. There's no turning back. It's official. We're now a nation at war."

"How long do you think until the next attack?"

Adam looked at the bloody photograph and answered, "I don't know. But what I do know is that we have to be prepared. The General won't take this defeat lightly. After all, there's a thin line between freedom and tyranny. And we're the only ones that stand between it, and make no mistake - more of us will pay the ultimate price.

"His retribution will be swift against us, and we must be prepared to counter his forces at all costs. We can only do so if we have enough manpower and resources, which I'm sure will come. I just hope it won't be too late, since we barely won this round. We may not be so fortunate next time.

"That was a great job that you did, General West. No one could've done what you did today. No one could've inspired the morale that you did on the battlefield, especially under those circumstances. We were outnumbered in all respects and still won. It was a narrow defeat, but we still won. What happens tomorrow is yet to be determined.

"But that's another day. Let's just live in this moment of victory, and take a moment of silence for our all fallen comrades, for Paul and all the others who made the ultimate sacrifice."

"We couldn't have won this round without you," Christopher said, placing his hand on Adam's shoulder, and continued, "At least for today."

Adam smiled timidly, nodding his head and said softly, "But we lost Alvarez. And nothing can change that."

"Wasn't your fault. There was nothing that you could do. There was nothing any of us could've done," Ahmad added.

"You did your best, General West. All we can do for now is live in this moment, and share a moment of silence for Alvarez and all our other fallen comrades," Eric said, placing his hand on Adam's shoulder.

They looked at the skies, hearing the screaming engines of the jet fighters soaring over their position and decided to depart the war-torn desert.

Within moments of winning the long, grueling battle, Adam's reinforcements finally arrived.

Another soldier from one of the other neighboring bases walked out of one of the transports and said, "Sorry we're late, sir."

"With good reason," Adam responded.

"It won't happen again, sir."

"Don't worry. You'll have your chance to prove yourselves. This is far from over. As a matter of fact, it has barely even started."

They looked all around the desert, appalled at the atrocities that filled the unforgiving plain, littered with countless corpses.

Though they had narrowly won the first of many confrontations to come, their morale and spirits remained low, as they contemplated the high cost of losing many of their close friends. They began their long and difficult journey across the tundra with all the strength drained from their bodies, with only the rumbling of their transports filling the void.

A great number under their command were dead from the skirmish, and the few survivors were badly wounded, unable to fight. The rest grimaced from the extent of the grave injuries they had suffered from the skirmish on the battlefield, their clothes torn and soaked in blood, serving as a painful reminder of what happened.

On the other side of the battlefield, enemy soldiers laid burning and mangled from the giant wall of flame, leaving the wasteland rank with the smell of burning flesh and metal.

A stark reminder even to their vast numbers that the freedom fighters were prepared to fight to the last man against the forces that dreamt of tyranny.

They continued their long and arduous march back to their position many miles away, until the night sky had finally cast its shadow over their faces, only to await their next trials in the baptism of blood and fire.

The war continues…

CHAPTER 3: OPERATION HAVOC

The year was 2027. Two years have passed since "The Great Fall of Genesis."

The cool morning breeze howled through the desert, spiraling the endless sands, tossing tumbleweeds with the slightest effort across the endless, barren tundra that stretched as far as the eyes can see.

A diamondback rattlesnake slithered slowly through the desert sands, rattling its tail, serving a warning to any predator that dared cross its path.

A bobcat quickly scurried about the vast and barren wastelands in search of prey, and suddenly paused after hearing the engines of a convoy racing on the long stretch of the interstate.

The rapid drumming-like sounds of a ladder-backed woodpecker, pecking relentlessly on the thick wood of a tree trunk to build its nest, in search of a new beginning, echoed through the wasteland.

A giant golden eagle soared through the skies, squawking, while its razor-sharp vision scouted for prey roaming across the desert floor.

A mule deer fed on the defiant desert shrubs until it had its fill, and once again began its nomadic exodus through the unforgiving tundra.

A cactus wren constantly pecked on the desert floor, feeding on the tiny insects, and quickly took to flight after having its fill.

A kangaroo rat scurried across the barren plain in search of food, and hopped into its burrow for sanctuary after its long search.

On the lonely stretch of interstate, the endless sands swept across, spiraling from the cool winds that swept through the tundra, as it continued to toss them in all directions.

Dead shells of numerous decaying vehicles stretched as far as the eye could see, littering the roadside like the skeletons of many other species that perished in the merciless tundra, becoming a sanctuary for many other smaller species of animals.

The makeshift marvels of the world's wonders - the Eiffel Tower and Statue of Liberty - from once prosperous casinos that brimmed with life, surrounded by the once gleaming and towering skyscrapers, became decrepit from the unchecked passage of time. The constant neglect from the conflict that was waged between factions of the country's once faithful and optimistic citizens, and those once charged to defend it, could be seen for miles, and served as a painful memory of all the battles past, and the ones yet to be ensued in the coming years.

A convoy with a number of light- and heavy-armored units, transporting countless troops, moved on the interstate, heading to their base out of the state capital.

The heavy rumbling of countless engines of the traveling convoy continued to fill the vast expanse of the interstate as they moved quickly towards their position, hoping to not be detected by the enemy forces, as the morning sun slowly rose beyond the horizon, giving birth to the new day.

Amanda looked into the skies and saw the blinking lights of a fighter aircraft heading towards their position, closing in very quickly.

She was a young woman in her early 20s, with a very light brown complexion and jet black hair, and joined the armed forces straight from college.

The screaming of the plane's engines grew louder, while it rapidly descended towards their position.

She continued fixing her gaze on the descending plane and yelled, "We have enemy planes! We have incoming!"

The soldiers quickly assumed their defensive positions, and greeted the enemy planes with a sky full of anti-aircraft fire, causing one of them to descend from the skies to crash and burn in the desert, leaving more enemy planes to descend upon their positions strafing them mercilessly, while they remained exposed throughout the entire interstate.

A volley of enemy bullets from the plane's heavy machine guns ricocheted through their positions, claiming the lives of those who stood in their wake, causing one of the light-armored transports caught in the crossfire to burst into flames, echoing through the vastness of the desert.

The attacks from the firepower between the ground forces and enemy planes had soon become ferocious, and within a brief moment, a number of light- and heavy-armored transports were quickly consumed in the crossfire, as the ground troops desperately tried to hold their ground against the enemies' onslaught.

"They're combining their firepower! They're trying to wipe us out! Get on the radio and call for air support! They are picking us off like flies at a picnic!" Adam called out.

"It's a good thing we diverted all air support to another location!" Ahmad shouted through the deafening roar of anti-aircraft gunfire.

"Let's hope they're not too late to give us cover!" Adam replied.

05:17 HOURS. FREEDOM FIGHTER SECRET OUTPOST. SOMEWHERE IN THE VALLEY OF FIRE, 46.2 MILES FROM NELLIS AIR FREEDOM FIGHTER AIR FORCE BASE, NEVADA:

As the distress call for air support came, a number of the personnel quickly scrambled across the base, arming all the gunships and planes to go intercept the enemy forces, as the fighter plane and gunship pilots waited for the ground personnel to finish arming and refueling, to be deployed to the warzone.

Immediately after loading and fueling, Dillon took off, even without confirmation from the ground personnel, as the others quickly followed suit, en-route to Adam's position, flying in formation, as a few more fighter planes followed closely behind, while the rest were being loaded and fueled by the ground crew, along with Patrick and his entire squad of gunships, to engage the enemy ground units and gunships.

The entire squad of fighter planes en-route to Adam's position continued listening to the radio chatter of their frantic distress call, with the clamor of explosions from artillery fire filling the other side of their call, almost drowning out the frantic transmissions of the ground troops.

05:19 HOURS. SOMEWHERE ON THE MOJAVE DESERT INTERSTATE 15 APEX. MORE THAN 40 MILES AWAY THE SECRET FREEDOM FIGHTER OUTPOST IN THE VALLEY OF FIRE, NEVADA:

The skies of dawn lit as brightly as day from all the anti-aircraft fire that continued to greet the enemy planes.

A missile from one of the enemy planes exploded into a ground armored unit, killing a number of soldiers who stood within range, with only a few surviving quickly evacuating their burning unit.

Ahmad grabbed one of the soldiers by her clothes, quickly pulling her to safety, and saw the frightened look on her face, grabbing it after tapping her lightly to help her get to her senses, and yelled, "Keep it together, soldier! You got a name?"

The soldier paused for a minute and answered, "Spencer! Amanda Spencer!" with a frightened look on her face.

"I know that you're scared! We all are, but I need you to keep it together! Being afraid won't help! We have no choice but to fight right now. You've gotten this far. Can't turn back now! Do you understand what I'm saying to you, Spencer?" Adam said through the hail of artillery fire.

Eric climbed atop one of the burning tanks and pulled one of the dead soldiers from the tank's gunnery position, manned it, and returned fire at the enemy planes that continued to strafe their position, while they continued to remain exposed in the open.

Another volley of rounds from the enemy planes scattered through the desert sands, claiming more lives, with Robert and his squad members quickly scrambling for cover from the lethal barrage of bullets and quickly returning fire, when the coast became clear.

He looked into the frightened soldier's face and asked, "Are you the one who made the call?"

"No, it was Amanda!" Tiara, the frightened soldier, answered, shaking her head.

"Good call, anyway! She probably saved more lives in that one second that she spotted that enemy plane. That was good thinking on her feet," Robert answered.

"Thank you, sir! But it doesn't look like any lives are being saved right about now," she answered.

"You got a name, soldier?"

"It's Tiara Edwards," she replied.

She was a woman heading towards her mid 20s, of mixed Irish and Scottish background, with flaming red hair.

Despite her smaller stature, she was deceptively effective in having great marksmanship skills, in shooting down air and ground enemy forces with either the armored unit's heavy guns or turrets.

"You're doing great, Edwards! But I need you to concentrate! Can you do that?" Robert asked.

"I'll do my best, sir," she said, when a shell from enemy artillery suddenly exploded near their position, throwing them to the ground, covering them in a thick blanket of desert sand.

Robert quickly pulled himself from the ground, grabbing Tiara by her sleeve, and said, "Our position is under heavy attack from ground forces. Can you man the tank's heavy guns?"

"Yes, sir! I'm a good shot! I can do either one! It's what I did during the last battle engaging the enemy forces in the Mojave Desert," she answered.

"You'll be of more use inside the tank! I'll man the machine guns!"

They climbed on top of one of the tanks and provided fire from their vulnerable position, when Tiara zeroed in on one of the armored units and fired the tank's heavy shell, scoring a direct hit on one of the enemy armored units.

"Keep on doing whatever it is that you're doing, Edwards! More enemy tanks moving on our position!"

Adam continued to return fire from his position and yelled, "They caught us with our pants down and are moving in to pincer our position! We need air support - now!"

05:33 HOURS. SOMEWHERE OVER THE MOJAVE DESERT INTERSTATE 15 APEX. MORE THAN 40 MILES AWAY FROM THE SECRET FREEDOM FIGHTER OUTPOST IN THE VALLEY OF FIRE, NEVADA:

Dillon heard the desperate radio chatter from Adam's position, constantly harassed from enemy attacks and answered, "E.T.A. about 60 seconds!"

05:33 HOURS. SOMEWHERE IN THE MOJAVE DESERT INTERSTATE 15 APEX. MORE THAN 40 MILES AWAY THE SECRET FREEDOM FIGHTER OUTPOST IN THE VALLEY OF FIRE, NEVADA:

Adam had continued to sustain a number of heavy casualties from the relentless assaults and was almost on the brink of defeat, with the remainder of his armored units holding their position, until their support arrived, as Christopher quickly manned one of the tank's heavy guns, exchanging fire against the enemy forces.

05:35 HOURS. CREECH ENEMY AIR FORCE BASE. 48 MILES FROM NELLIS FREEDOM FIGHTER BASE, NEVADA:

The alarms in the base blared, causing a squadron of enemy soldiers to scramble, running to their gunships, to reinforce their position against enemy forces, while more enemy tanks and gunships moved towards the freedom fighters' position, priming their weapons for assault.

05:36 HOURS. SOMEWHERE ON INTERSTATE 15 APEX. MORE THAN 40 MILES AWAY FROM THE SECRET FREEDOM FIGHTER OUTPOST IN THE VALLEY OF FIRE, NEVADA:

Meanwhile, on the interstate, the liberation forces valiantly continued to resist the onslaught of enemy forces that continued to harass them, inflicting more casualties in their defensive lines.

While Henry continued to man his tank's turret, in courageous retaliation against the horde of enemy forces, he scored a few significant victories, wearing down the number of armored units that continued to outnumber them, while his heavy unit shuddered violently from the constant barrage that continued to pommel their positions.

Another explosion from enemy fire caused the ground to tremble violently near Adam's position, temporarily knocking him to the ground, while he bravely continued to exchange fire against the vast number of enemy forces.

He quickly came to his senses, resuming the exchange of fire unflinchingly against enemy forces, while his machine gunner manned his position, doing as much as he could to stave off the enemy planes until reinforcements arrived, when another enemy plane crashed and burned far from their position after he scored a direct hit from the heavy volley of bullets from anti-aircraft fire.

"We have more armored units converging on our position, and we need air support! Where is our air support? We are hanging on by a string, and our position is almost overrun by enemy forces!" Adam cried out as another barrage of heavy enemy bullets and artillery rained down on their position. Christopher, with total disregard for his safety, ran through the barrage and pushed the soldier out the way.

He grabbed a soldier from the ground and handed him a weapon, while he breathed heavily trying to catch his breath from his close call.

The soldier grabbed the weapon, nodded his head, and said softly, and nervously, "Thanks."

"Don't mention it," Christopher answered, still catching his breath from the close brush with death.

"That was a gutsy move, Lieutenant Vaughan!"

"So is staying out here dodging fire from enemy planes and artillery shells! What's your name, soldier?" Christopher yelled as the enemy artillery landed closest to their position.

"It's Yamaguchi! Steven Yamaguchi!," Steven yelled back.

He was of Japanese heritage, with a very slender physique in his late teens, and the second of two children that stemmed from a Japanese background. His physical prowess was not as strong as other Marines, but his keen sense of observation to call down artillery strikes on the enemy positions more than made up for his lack of attributes, and was the determining factor in getting him drafted into the armed forces.

They took cover from the thick chunks of desert soil smacking their faces from the explosion of artillery fire.

"Okay, Yamaguchi, we've lost a lot of good soldiers today, and will lose more if our defenses don't hold until our support arrives! We need to hold this position! What's your expertise?"

"I can spot! I've got a good eye for range! I helped to drive the enemy back during the last skirmish in the Mojave Desert on our last campaign, sir!"

"Great! I need you to spot for our tanks! I'll man the tank's machine guns until our support arrives! Can you do that?"

Steven nodded his head nervously, and answered, "Yes! Yes, I can!"

"Okay, but we need to move quickly! I need you to help me make space on the gunnery position!"

They climbed atop the tank, pulling the dead soldier from his gunnery position, and manned the tank's gunnery positions, using its heavy guns to continue firing at the oncoming enemy units.

An enemy barrage suddenly slammed into Robert's armored unit, knocking them from their positions, setting its confines ablaze, causing Robert to fall into the tank's interior, forcing them to evacuate the burning unit after regaining their faculties.

Robert quickly scuttled the burning tank, pulling Tiara by her clothes through the hail of enemy fire and artillery, while she remained dazed from the critical blow their unit sustained, and jumped off the burning unit, moving as quickly as they could away from it. It suddenly erupted into flames, scattering chunks of shrapnel all over the battlefield as they shielded for cover.

The armored enemy units continued drawing nearer, ready to pincer them into total defeat, when the ground began to shudder from a giant wall of flame that engulfed a number of the ground units from the enemy position. The squad of planes deployed their ordinance and took their flight back into the dark morning skies to engage the enemy forces.

05:29 HOURS. SOMEWHERE OVER INTERSTATE 15 APEX. MORE THAN 40 MILES AWAY FROM THE SECRET FREEDOM FIGHTER OUTPOST, NEVADA:

"All units break free and engage all enemy air units. I repeat - all weapons free, and engage," Dillon ordered, while he spearheaded the air attack on the enemy air forces.

05:30 HOURS. SOMEWHERE ON INTERSTATE 15 APEX. MORE THAN 40 MILES AWAY FROM THE SECRET FREEDOM FIGHTER OUTPOST IN THE VALLEY OF FIRE, NEVADA:

"If you are being engaged by the enemy, bring them into the firing range of our guns! And we have more enemy gunships en-route to our ground forces. While some of us keep the enemy planes entangled, the rest of you concentrate your fire on all the ground units to give the ground troops some much needed breathing space," Adam called out.

05:31 HOURS. SOMEWHERE OVER INTERSTATE 15 APEX. MORE THAN 40 MILES AWAY FROM THE SECRET FREEDOM FIGHTER OUTPOST IN THE VALLEY OF FIRE, NEVADA:

"Reading you loud and clear, General West! What's your status?" Dillon asked, looking at the ground forces engaging each other from the cockpit of his plane soaring above the battle zone, with the thick black smoke from the burning units rising to the skies.

05:33 HOURS. SOMEWHERE ON INTERSTATE 15 APEX. MORE THAN 40 MILES AWAY FROM THE SECRET FREEDOM FIGHTER OUTPOST IN THE VALLEY OF FIRE, NEVADA:

"We got caught with our pants down and lost a lot of men and armor from enemy artillery and strafing runs. On our way to the outpost! We're hanging by a thread and our defensive lines are on the brink of collapse! We're heavily outnumbered and still sustaining more casualties from enemy attacks from the ground and skies! Most of my soldiers are green and terrified out of their minds, and I don't blame them! But they're dropping like flies! And given the circumstances, I don't have to stress on how much we need all the air support we can get until we evacuate to say the least, if we can't hold them back!"

05:34 HOURS. SOMEWHERE OVER INTERSTATE 15 APEX. MORE THAN 40 MILES AWAY FROM THE SECRET FREEDOM FIGHTER OUTPOST IN THE VALLEY OF FIRE, NEVADA:

"Read you loud and clear, General West! Heading to engage," Dillon answered, when an enemy plane flew past him pursuing one of his wingmen, causing the cockpit of his plane to shudder. He quickly turned his plane around, and headed to engage the enemy plane, when he was suddenly engaged from behind.

He quickly pulled the nose of his plane as high as he could fly into the morning skies, feeling the agonizing force pressing down on his body, almost bringing him to the brink of unconsciousness every passing moment, but still able to skillfully maneuver his plane, bringing it within close range behind the enemy pilot, pummeling him with a barrage of his plane's heavy machine gun fire, till he burst into flames, and watched it head to the surface, crashing and burning, when the alarms of his plane suddenly blared in the confines of his cockpit, warning him of an inbound enemy missile quickly closing in towards him.

As the missile quickly closed into the rear of his plane, he made a sharp turn and watched the missile narrowly miss him, and deployed the plane's countermeasures, causing the missile to fly into them, exploding in midair.

While the enemy plane continued its relentless pursuit after Dillon, he saw the bright flashes from the enemy rounds racing across the canopy of his cockpit.

He performed a daring maneuver by quickly jamming the brake of his plane and tilting it slightly, causing the enemy to over-commit in speed, over-shooting him, and quickly deploying a missile, destroying it.

One of his squad members flew over the enemy ground unit, deploying ordinances, destroying countless more of the armored units, but was in return greeted by stiff resistance, damaging his plane severely, causing him to spin out of control, crashing and burning near the enemy position, with the shrapnel from the blast rising through the flames as high and as far as the eyes can see.

05:41 HOURS. SOMEWHERE ON INTERSTATE 15 APEX. MORE THAN 40 MILES AWAY FROM THE SECRET FREEDOM FIGHTER OUTPOST IN THE VALLEY OF FIRE, NEVADA:

"You just neutralized a number of enemy ground units, but they're not letting up! They still outnumber us and still come in strong! They're throwing everything they have at us! They're doing everything they can to wipe out our resistance! We just lost another one of our tanks from enemy fire, and still need support," Adam called out.

05:41 HOURS. SOMEWHERE OVER INTERSTATE 15 APEX. MORE THAN 40 MILES AWAY FROM THE SECRET FREEDOM FIGHTER OUTPOST IN THE VALLEY OF FIRE, NEVADA:

Dillon and his squad of planes remained entangled by other enemy planes, and unable to provide support to the remainder of outnumbered ground units. He heard the distress call for support from one of his wingmen, and quickly headed to assist.

One of his fellow pilots, unable to evade her pursuer, suffered a barrage of enemy fire tearing through her cockpit into the control system, causing it to burst into flames, as she quickly lost control of her plane.

A blinding flash from an explosion filled the pilot's cockpit from the enemy plane exploding, scattering shrapnel through the skies, tearing through her plane's fuselage and canopy slicing through her face, causing her to bleed profusely, the blood from her wound obstructing her vision.

She looked down at her chest and saw a gaping hole oozing blood, and remarked, "You came in the nick of time, Captain," coughing, choking on her own blood, as the pain from the severity of her wounds began to take its toll.

"Are you okay, Vulture?" Dillon asked with concern.

"As okay as I'll ever be," she answered, as she stared helplessly, as her plane drew closer to the desert floor, trailing a long line of smoke.

"Come in, Vulture! What's your status? McCarthy, come in!" Dillon called back.

"I'm losing control of my plane, along with my senses. I can't hold on any longer. All my plane's controls are fried," she answered softly.

Samantha was a young woman in her early 20s, with blonde hair and soft blue eyes, who had once began her flying career flying sorties against the North Korean regime, during their unprovoked occupation of the south, just before the Fall of Genesis, and switched her allegiances to Dr. Weaver during the beginning stages of the civil war that tore the country apart.

"What about your ejection lever? Can you bail?"

Samantha tried as best as she could, but grimaced from the sharp pain from her bullet wounds, and answered softly, "It's no use. I can't move. The pain is just too much," and continued, while she resigned to her fate, as she flew towards the surface, "Tell my sister I couldn't make it back home," and plummeted to the surface, crashing and burning.

Dillon watched her plane plummet to the desert floor, with the crimson red flame engulfing the wreckage of her plane, and closed his eyes softly in a brief moment of silence after hearing the static from her lost transmission.

05:44 HOURS. SOMEWHERE ON INTERSTATE 15 APEX. MORE THAN 40 MILES AWAY FROM THE SECRET FREEDOM FIGHTER OUTPOST IN THE VALLEY OF FIRE, NEVADA:

Ahmad and many of the other soldiers did not fare any better, while they continued to do as much as they could to maintain the strength of their crumbling defensive lines against the remainder of the oncoming enemy forces, when a shell from an enemy tank exploded into their already dilapidated armored unit, causing it to be engulfed into flames, forcing Ahmad to evacuate the burning tank, and use it for cover from the enemy shells that continued raining from above, pummeling their positions.

The fighter planes that continued to soar through the vast expanse of skies kept each other entangled, while the vast reserves of enemy forces continued closing on their positions.

Henry and his team continued to try and repel the enemy ground forces, when they were suddenly rocked by an enemy shell, flinging them from their positions, with the interior of the armored unit engulfed in a thick cloud of black smoke, causing them to choke on its fumes as their tank to erupt into flames.

The alarms of the tank blared loudly while the tank deployed its countermeasures to extinguish the fire that engulfed it.

After the fire that consumed the confined space of their armored unit was extinguished from the unit's countermeasures, they got back into their positions and continued to fight against the enemy forces while the ground continued to rumble violently from the constant impact from the enemy artillery that fell all around them.

The teamwork with Christopher and Steven had begun to pay some dividends, scoring significant victories against the General's forces, while spotting the enemy positions, calling strikes for their guns.

Suddenly, a squad of enemy gunships strafed their positions in a blitzkrieg fashion, assaulting the remainder of their ground units, when another hellfire missile exploded into Henry's tank, completely destroying it, causing the entire crew to evacuate their quarters.

Just seconds after Henry and his crew evacuated the flaming tank, it erupted into another giant ball of flame, scattering shrapnel all around them, impaling one of the soldiers.

Henry ran over to her and dragged her near the dilapidated unit for cover, and tore open the thigh of her pants, exposing the wound with the chunk of burning shrapnel protruding deeply into her flesh. He took out his hunting knife and began the long and painful process of digging the shard out of her leg wound, while the soldier grimaced loudly from the pain.

After digging out the chunk of shrapnel, she cut a piece of cloth from her uniform and wrapped it tightly around her leg to help stop the bleeding.

He watched the young soldier succumbing to the sharp pain in her leg and asked, "What's your name, soldier?"

"It's Perez. Lena Perez!," she answered, wincing in pain.

She was of Latin descent with a light brown complexion in her late teens, just a tad below average height, with a number of piercings in her nose and ears, and often wore her hair extremely short, and well groomed, reaching as closely to her scalp, and often wore the top part of her uniform around her waistline to display the tattoos that covered her well-built tomboy-like physique.

Though young and inexperienced, she showed great courage on the field.

"Not what you imagined, after all the small steps that the good doctor and our acting president made towards world peace, is it?"

"No, it's not," Lena answered, shaking her head, while she continued to wince in pain.

Henry wrapped her arm around his shoulder and carried her to safety, when a barrage of heavy bullets from an enemy gunship's mounted machine gun riddled through their positions.

He quickly threw Lena to safety and fell to the ground. After the volley had passed, he realized that he was hit from the round from the enemy gunship.

The others dragged him to safety, while he lay helpless on the desert floor, and rested his back against the body of a dilapidated armored unit, while he bled profusely from his wound.

Lena watched as the rest of the soldiers tore his clothes open and saw the gaping hole from the enemy gunship's attack that tore through his abdomen, while he clutched it lightly, losing his strength from the heavy bleeding.

"Looks like this is it for me! My time has come," Henry remarked softly, looking into Lena's eyes.

"Don't say that, Lieutenant! Collins, You'll be fine! Someone get some help!" Lena yelled frantically.

Henry nodded his head and answered, "It's no use! I've been hit in the gut, and it's all the way in! I can feel it! I'll die in the next hour or so, maybe less, if the enemy doesn't get to me first!"

Adam heard the radio chatter of Lena's cry for help, that Henry was severely wounded from an enemy gunship attack, and yelled, "Collins is down! I repeat, Henry is down! All available units provide support! We have enemy gunships in the vicinity! We need air support!"

Christopher was the closest to his position and answered through the high volley of artillery fire, "Read you loud and clear! Heading to his position!"

Christopher and Steven headed to Henry's position through the enemy gunships' strafing run on their positions, and saw Henry sitting with his back against the hull of a burning tank, with his hand completely doused in his blood and said, "You'll be fine," with a look of concern of his face.

"He saved my life! He pushed me out of the way from the enemy gunship," Lena said, with the vision clouded with tears.

"You're wounded," Christopher answered.

"Our tank was hit by an enemy shell, so we evacuated! Then it exploded just seconds after we were out, and that's when I was impaled by burning shrapnel. And out of nowhere, the bullets from enemy gunship came, strafing our position. And after that, he was lying on the ground. It all happened so fast," she said.

An enemy shell suddenly whistled through the skies, and exploded near the position, tossing them away with the smallest of effort, banging them against the tank's broken and burning armor, raising a giant cloud of sand, smacking them in their faces, filling their eyes with dust.

Christopher looked at the other soldiers with masks on their faces, and shouted through the raining clamor of artillery barrage, "We can't stay here! We have to get him to safety!"

"We're pinned by enemy fire! What's your plan?" Steven cried out.

"Go on to the next armored unit with the next position! Steven and I will help provide cover fire!"

"These gunships are too fast for our guns! There's no way we can get past them without being cut to pieces!" Lena yelled amidst the deafening exchange of artillery.

"And if we stay here, we're sitting ducks! We can't stay here!" Christopher answered.

"What are your names?" Christopher asked.

"Yee. James Yee!" the soldier answered nervously.

His father was Chinese and his mother was American. James was the first of three children, in his mid 20s, like many of the young recruits who had joined the war after the Fall of Genesis, and was past average in height, with a normal build. He was highly adaptable, and quickly became seasoned as a soldier, able to cope with all the demands and stresses that came from the rigors of conflict.

"Perrini. Catherine Perrini! What's the plan?" she answered.

She was of a long line of Italian heritage with long dark hair and chestnut brown eyes, indicative of Italian women, whose ancestry dated as far back as to those who fought for the resistance against the Nazi regime and Italian fascism during the second world war, before migrating to the United States in search of a new life, continuing the long legacy of her ancestors like her other siblings who joined the armed forces.

To keep the tradition of upholding her ancestors' honor, she took up arms against the General's forces to secure her place in history among them.

"I take it that it's your first time in combat," Christopher asked, looking into their faces filled with anxiety and fear.

They simply nodded their heads, with their bodies almost paralyzed from fear, knowing that they must run through the barrage of enemy fire, exposing themselves, to save a wounded soldier.

"How is your leg holding up, soldier?"

"I think I can make it," Lena answered, with a nervous glance on her face.

"Just tell us what you plan to do! We'll be ready," James answered.

The whistling from another shell of enemy artillery suddenly fell from the skies, rocking their position and throwing them to the ground while they attempted their escape.

After the deafening roar from the explosion, they looked at Christopher, waiting nervously for instructions to make their move, as the adrenaline from their fear grew every passing moment.

"We can't stay here, as you can see. We're getting our asses torn up! When we make a run to the next position, I'll draw their fire and keep the focus on me, and give you a fighting chance," Christopher said.

"I'll stay back with you to give you some help," Steven added nervously.

"Now, go!" Christopher yelled.

The young soldiers ran through the battlefield, exposing themselves to danger, dragging Henry's wounded body behind them, with Lena taking the lead to their next position. Christopher and Steven returned fire at the strafing enemy gunships from whatever gunnery positions they could find, trying to draw their fire as a distraction to give the others a chance to get to a safer position, and began trailing behind, when the ground suddenly trembled violently from another enemy shell exploding near their positions, knocking them off their feet.

Christopher and Steven quickly rose to their feet and continued trailing them and grabbed one of the soldiers from the sands to drag her to safety. They rested her back against the tank, and stared at her charred face and body, with a gaping wound in her stomach from the shrapnel blast.

"My God," Lena said, looking at Catherine's charred face and body in horror, while her life quickly slipped away from her. She applied pressure on her stomach wound with her hands, covered in Catherine's blood spurting in their faces.

"What are we going to do?" James asked nervously, looking at Catherine's battered body, bleeding profusely from her face and stomach wound.

"Help contain the bleeding!" Christopher answered, applying as much pressure on her wound as hard as he could. Enemy fire continued to rain on their positions, leaving behind the massive craters from the explosions that caused the ground to shudder beneath their feet.

Catherine reached into her pocket and pulled out a crumpled photograph and handed it to Christopher with a trembling hand, while the enemy shells continued to rain on their positions relentlessly.

She gathered her last breath and said, handing the photograph to Christopher, "Give this to my sister."

"You're going to be fine! You'll give it to her yourself when you see her!" Christopher said, when he saw Catherine's hand slammed on the desert sands, after she had finally taken her last breath, after handing over the photograph of herself and sister, immortalized with their smiling faces.

After Catherine had passed, Christopher gently rested her charred and bloodstained corpse on the sands of the unforgiving tundra, closing her eyes.

The battle between both sides had proven to be fierce, and the freedom fighters continued losing more of their armored units, sustaining heavy casualties from the enemy shells and gunships.

Christopher looked in the air and saw an enemy gunship coming closer to him and looked helplessly, sensing imminent danger, with his eyes wide opened, along with the rest of the less seasoned soldiers. The enemy aircraft suddenly burst into flames, followed by a number of other enemy gunships.

The group of gunships, spearheaded by Patrick, quickly moved in to intercept the enemy gunships, giving them a much needed chance to get to a safer position, while their air support remained distracted by the greater number of enemy planes high above the clouds.

The roar from an explosion of another fighter plane suddenly filled the vast and uncharted skies of the morning skies from the intense air battle in their desperate, yet constant struggle for air superiority, suddenly attracting the attention of the troops of the surviving ground units.

They continued looking to the skies and saw the metal frame of another fighter plane burst into flames, plummeting towards the surface, as it disintegrated into fragments from a ball of flame, trailing a long line of thick, black smoke, and slammed into the desert, exploding on impact.

05:45 HOURS. SOMEWHERE OVER INTERSTATE 15 APEX. MORE THAN 40 MILES AWAY FROM THE SECRET FREEDOM FIGHTER OUTPOST IN THE VALLEY OF FIRE, NEVADA:

Patrick and his group of gunships continued engaging the enemy gunships, inflicting a number of casualties from their surprise attack. "What's your status!?"

05:46 HOURS. SOMEWHERE ON INTERSTATE 15 APEX. MORE THAN 40 MILES AWAY FROM THE SECRET FREEDOM FIGHTER OUTPOST IN THE VALLEY OF FIRE, NEVADA:

"Henry is badly hurt, and we're still sustaining heavy casualties! We've lost most of our heavy guns and tanks, and our position is almost wiped out from enemy armor and they're still moving close to our position! Dillon and the rest of his squad are entangled fighting the enemy planes, and unable to provide cover, to completely neutralize the enemy positions! They really got us this time, but you can help change that right now, and start by silencing those guns and enemy armor to give us some breathing space! We won't be able to hold out much longer if those guns are still trained on us," Adam called out.

05:48 HOURS. SOMEWHERE OVER INTERSTATE 15 APEX. MORE THAN 40 MILES AWAY FROM THE SECRET FREEDOM FIGHTER OUTPOST IN THE VALLEY OF FIRE, NEVADA:

"Read you loud and clear, General," Patrick answered, and ordered some of his gunships to attack as many ground units as they could to minimize enemy assault, while he and his squad of gunships intercepted the enemy helicopters.

The engagements of the gunships were quick, just as they were fierce, as the enemy units had rapidly begun to sustain a series of casualties.

The sun had begun to rise beyond the horizon, exposing the clear blue skies and the battlefield, warming the cool morning breeze that swept across the vast unforgiving tundra.

The sounds of helicopter blades that circled amidst the young and inexperienced freedom fighters quickly received their attention, as they watched and listened helplessly as the gunships continued to engage one another on the battlefield, reminding them all too well of their close and constant brush with certain death.

Though their makeshift defensive lines were almost on the brink of collapse, they bravely continued to hold their position against the vast horde of enemy forces, though they were gradually worn down by the relentless firepower of Patrick and his group of gunships.

Though the enemy ground units were being worn down by the formidable group of gunships, they suffered sporadic attacks, while focusing much of their attention on the enemy gunships that wreaked havoc on their positions, allowing Adam and the remainder of his demoralized ground forces temporary reprieve to combine their firepower along with their gunships and planes that provided much needed support.

Another enemy shell rained down on Eric's position, exploding near another one of their armored units, rupturing a fuel line, causing a giant cloud of thick black smoke that engulfed its entire confines.

He quickly jumped onto the burning tank, and reached for the gunner, and the other soldier that manned its heavy guns, pulling him from his gunnery position, and quickly dove into its confines filled with smoke, pulling the other soldier out.

Just moments after the soldiers were rescued from the burning tank, they waited nervously for Eric to evacuate, hoping that he hadn't met his demise.

After moments of waiting, they saw that Eric had finally climbed out of the burning tank, coughing heavily from the massive smoke inhalation he suffered, while trying to rescue the young and inexperienced soldiers, and was about jump from its flaming hull when it burst into flames, tossing Eric off his feet onto the scorching desert sands, instantly dazing him.

He struggled to regain control of his senses while the other soldiers surrounded him, trying to revive him from the fall.

His blurred vision slowly normalized, seeing the silhouettes from all the faces that stood around him, and slowly stood to his feet.

"We've lost almost all of our armored units, and we need support! All available units respond!" Adam yelled over the radio while he fought against the enemy forces that continued their onslaught despite suffering a number of losses from their gunship support.

Adam and the remaining group of soldiers continued to hold out courageously against the number of enemy forces closing in on their positions, and was suddenly rocked by the blast from an enemy shell, tearing through the armor of his tank, engulfing its interior.

He ran over to one of the soldiers and grabbed him, quickly pausing in his tracks, seeing him bathed in his blood from a gaping wound in his abdomen, with his innards falling out, and badly burnt from the artillery blast, blood gushing from his mouth.

Adam stood in front of the soldier, who was impaled with countless fragments of burning shrapnel in total shock, barely able to react, a frantic look on his face, knowing that his demise was imminent. The soldier's life was quickly slipping away. He slowly took his last breath, his eyes wide opened. Adam yelled, "Everybody out!"

They climbed out of the burning tank and ran to the nearest position for cover, exposing themselves amidst all the chaos that continued to befall the desert, until Adam and his smaller band of fighters came across an immobilized armored unit, with the body of a lifeless soldier manning its gunnery position. The soldiers pulled him out, gently resting his body on the ground. Adam peeped through his binoculars and saw the enemy units continuing to close in despite the heavy losses they sustained from their gunships.

A genuine look of concern became visible on his face, seeing he was about to be completely overwhelmed by the enemy armor moving in, and radioed to their base, "We can't hold out any longer! We still have enemy units converging onto our positions! Henry is down! And we are almost completely overrun, and still sustaining heavy casualties! We need to evacuate immediately!"

After a long moment of engaging the enemy gunships, the air was cleared, and they quickly moved on to engage the advancing enemy ground units.

The looks on all the faces of the young and inexperienced soldiers were etched with fear, waiting for their orders to fight while enemy artillery continued to rain on their positions, and the remnants of their broken defensive lines continuing to hold as valiantly as they could, but to no avail.

Adam looked up and heard the screams of the jet fighter engines roaring in the skies, while the planes continued to engage one another, high above the clouds, with no regard for ignoring the clamor from the barrage. Enemy shells rained on their positions. Adam looked on in hopelessness and disbelief, as if all the courage had drained from his face, and strength had left his body.

He looked around and saw the number of casualties laying on the desert sands, charred and dismembered from the enemies' constant onslaught.

Ahmad ran toward Adam yelling, though he remained completely oblivious to Ahmad's attempts to help him come to his senses, while being tapped constantly on his face, causing him to quickly regain consciousness, and yelled, "What do we do? We can't hold this position any longer! We don't have enough guns to repel the enemy forces!"

"We need to evacuate," Adam answered softly, and continued, "If we stay here, all of us will die for sure. So radio the outpost and tell them to send as many extraction teams as they could find."

05:50 HOURS. SECRET FREEDOM FIGHTER OUTPOST. SOMEWHERE IN THE VALLEY OF FIRE, NEVADA:

After hearing Adam's distress call, a number of Blackhawk helicopters lifted off the base en-route to their position to rescue what was left of the stranded platoon.

05:52 HOURS. SOMEWHERE ON INTERSTATE 15 APEX. MORE THAN 40 MILES AWAY FROM THE SECRET FREEDOM FIGHTER OUTPOST IN THE VALLEY OF FIRE, NEVADA:

Ahmad stood back for a brief moment and watched the look of defeat on Adam's face from losing his position to the enemy forces, as if he were rambling mindlessly to himself, and grabbed him by his uniform, nudging him to his senses.

Adam said to himself, "What the hell just happened?"

"I thought I had lost you there for a second, General! You need to help us get out of this! We're getting our asses kicked! And right now, you need to snap out of it," Ahmad answered, when another shell rained on their positions, shattering the brief moment of silence, knocking them to the ground.

"We need to retreat! We can't hold this position! Most of our guns are destroyed, and we still have enemy forces converging on our position!"

"What about our E-vac?" Adam asked.

"They're on their way," Ahmad answered.

"How long before we have an airlift?" Adam asked.

"About 20 minutes."

"We won't be able to hold!"

"We need to hold! At least long enough until E-vac arrives!"

"Our air support is entangled against the enemy fighters, and so are our gunships!"

The screams of the jet engines roared through the skies, while they continued to engage one another.

Adam looked at Ahmad with a renewed look of hope on his face and contemplated for a brief moment.

"If you have something to say, General West, now is the best time to do it! We're hanging by a thread and we're still losing ground troops and units!"

"I have an idea and I think it might work!"

"Right now, I'm open to suggestions! We all are! Anything to get out of this shithole!"

"Kim, what's your status!?"

05:50 HOURS. SOMEWHERE OVER INTERSTATE 15 APEX. MORE THAN 40 MILES AWAY FROM THE SECRET FREEDOM FIGHTER OUTPOST, NEVADA:

"We've inflicted a number of casualties on the enemy forces at the expense of losing a number of our own! We're still engaging the enemy forces! What are your orders?"

05:51 HOURS. SOMEWHERE ON INTERSTATE 15 APEX. MORE THAN 40 MILES AWAY FROM THE SECRET FREEDOM FIGHTER OUTPOST, NEVADA:

"I got an idea! It's risky, but it just might work! I need you to sweep over the enemy ground forces and provide a smokescreen!"

05:52 HOURS. SOMEWHERE OVER INTERSTATE 15 APEX. MORE THAN 40 MILES AWAY FROM THE SECRET FREEDOM FIGHTER OUTPOST, NEVADA:

"I'm open to just about anything right now! I have an enemy plane on my tail, and I'm trying to shake him," Dillon yelled through the radio.

05:54 HOURS. SOMEWHERE ON INTERSTATE 15 APEX. MORE THAN 40 MILES AWAY FROM THE SECRET FREEDOM FIGHTER OUTPOST, NEVADA:

"I know! Fly over the enemy positions and deploy your ordinance! But, whatever you do, just don't let the enemy pilot get a lock on you," Adam answered.

"I hope you know what you're doing," Ahmad said softly to himself, while he watched Dillon dodge the enemy attacks as he plummeted from the skies, quickly descending into the heart of the enemy gunnery positions.

05:56 HOURS. SOMEWHERE OVER INTERSTATE 15 APEX. MORE THAN 40 MILES AWAY FROM THE SECRET FREEDOM FIGHTER OUTPOST, NEVADA:

The wall of anti-aircraft fire grew fiercer as Dillon made his rapid descent into the heart of the enemy gunnery positions, causing the inside of his plane to shudder violently, trying as much as he could to maintain control with the alarms of the cockpit blaring, still warning of the enemy plane on his tail in relentless pursuit.

He was startled as the bullets from the enemy plane raced past him while they tore through the wing of his plane. He performed evasive maneuvers, hoping to stay alive long enough to get to enemy ground forces to deploy his ordinance and help change the fortunes of their battle.

06:00 HOURS. SOMEWHERE ON INTERSTATE 15 APEX. MORE THAN 40 MILES AWAY FROM THE SECRET FREEDOM FIGHTER OUTPOST, NEVADA:

The wall of anti-aircraft enemy fire grew thicker from flying closer to the heavily fortified position, severely damaging Dillon's plane. He deployed a cluster bomb and took to the skies after a wall of crimson flames shrouded the entire enemy position, scattering heavy chunks of burning shrapnel and debris throughout the entire enemy position.

As the giant wall of flames consumed the enemy position, the enemy pilot tried to make his ascent, only to be bombarded and consumed by the wall of flame. Countless shards of burning shrapnel tore into the hull of his plane, shattering the canopy of his cockpit, causing him to crash into the flames that already wiped out the enemy ground units.

The remainder of Adam's unit watched as Dillon flew back into the skies to rejoin his squadron, with looks of total awe on their faces, after witnessing Dillon's close brush with death, surviving his close bout against the lethal barrage of anti-aircraft fire.

After Dillon's bombing run, most of the guns from the enemy position were wiped out, leaving a sudden quietness and calm throughout the barren desert, with the crackling of flames over the burning shells of armor and lifeless enemy soldiers, and the screaming of jet engines, leaving the constant trails of their contrails high in the stratosphere.

"That was a close one. That'll buy us more time until our E-vac gets here," Adam said, expressing a big sigh of relief.

"You crazy bastard," Eric said with a hint of excitement.

"How long till our E-vac gets here?"

"About 12 minutes," Robert answered.

"We may have silenced most of the enemies' guns, but we still have contacts closing in, General. We don't know how long our defenses can hold," James said nervously.

"How many guns do we have?" Adam asked.

"Just a handful. Don't know if it will buy us enough time. All our planes and gunships are engaging the enemy. Don't know if they can provide assistance," Ahmad replied.

"Okay. Make another call for air support. We'll take whatever help we can find. In the meantime, let's do all we can to silence the rest of our guns with whatever forces we have left. Fire when ready. All we can do is buy enough time until our help arrives," Adam said.

"They're not stopping, even after suffering all those losses. And they won't either. They're throwing everything at us," Christopher said softly.

"And we won't stop either. That airstrike tipped the balance in our favor for the time being. So let's do all we can to ensure our survival," Adam said softly.

The brief moment of tranquility in the desert was once again shattered when the combined forces of the tanks and Howitzer guns fired upon the remainder of the enemy units, after the airstrike had destroyed the bulk of their forces, with the combined forces of the gunships with whatever remaining ammunition and fuel they had left, after their long bout against the other enemy forces.

Patrick soared over Adam's position and said over the radio, "We're running low on fuel and ordinance. We'll need to go back to base to refuel and rearm soon. But until then, we'll hold out for as long as we can before support arrives."

06:12 HOURS. SOMEWHERE OVER INTERSTATE 15 APEX. MORE THAN 40 MILES AWAY FROM THE SECRET FREEDOM FIGHTER OUTPOST IN THE VALLEY OF FIRE, NEVADA:

The planes continued to soar high through the heavens, in a deadly game of pursuit for total air supremacy.

Though Dillon and his squadron were heavily outnumbered, they still managed to tip the balance against the enemy forces, when the loud chatter from the radio suddenly came from Adam, requesting air support.

The alarms in his cockpit began to blare loudly, warning him that he was almost out of ordinance and running low on fuel.

He flew over the enemy forces, though most of them were destroyed from his first bombing run. He deployed another barrage of firepower, delaying the enemies' progress even longer and flew over Adam's position, and answered, "We're extremely low on ordinance and fuel! Our defenses won't hold for long! We have to head back to reload and refuel soon!"

06:17 HOURS. SOMEWHERE ON INTERSTATE 15 APEX. MORE THAN 40 MILES AWAY FROM THE SECRET FREEDOM FIGHTER OUTPOST IN THE VALLEY OF FIRE, NEVADA:

Christopher heard the sounds of their helicopters coming from afar and said, "It doesn't matter now! Look!" He pointed at all the Blackhawks that headed their direction to evacuate them from the beleaguered sector, landing just outside of their position.

"All gunships and planes, our E-vac is en-route. Provide assistance until all remaining personnel have been evacuated," Adam said in a renewed sense of vigor, as he watched the helicopters coming to rescue them.

As the helicopters landed on the sands, Adam said, "Our first priority is to get Collins onboard, along with all the other wounded."

As Henry was being lifted onto the Blackhawk helicopter, he screamed loudly from the pain of the wound in his stomach, startling everyone around him, and nodded his head, saying, "It's no use. I can't go on. I've lost too much blood. I can't make it. Moving me will only make it worse."

"We can't leave you here, Collins. They're gonna kill you. He's gonna kill you, and you know it," Eric said.

"Look at me. I'm already bleeding to death. I'm gonna die soon enough anyway. The way I see it, he'll be granting me mercy. And right now, it sounds like a good idea," Henry answered.

"This is where I made my stand, so this is where I'm going to die, and I've already accepted that," Henry answered, clutching his side, while his blood continued pouring through his fingers onto the desert sand.

"Our code is to leave no soldier behind. We won't leave you, sir," Tiara answered.

"Our base is a few miles by chopper. We can get you a good doctor," Lena said, with her eyes clouded with tears.

"Some things a doctor can't fix. Some people, he can't save. But, I can use it right now. My time is done. Probably by the time the enemy forces reach my position, I'll already be dead. There is no time. Go on save yourselves. Go on now."

"I can't do what you're asking me to, Collins," Adam answered, and continued, "Most of these soldiers are green and I need all the help that I can get to lead them through battle. We need you."

"Let's face it, General West. My time here is done. There is no hope for me. You must save yourself, and all the others, for now, and live to fight another day. It's been a great honor serving with you, sir. Now go before you and all the others end up like me.

God be with you. God be with you all."

"And you, Collins," Adam answered, shaking hands with Henry.

"It was an honor. Goodbye, old friend. See you in the next life."

Adam gave the signal for the remainder of the soldiers to board the Blackhawks for immediate extraction, and slowly and sadly released Henry's hand and boarded the helicopter, still maintaining his gaze on the wounded soldier, who laid helpless on the desert near one of their dilapidated armored units, feeling a complete sense of helplessness, knowing he would eventually meet his demise at the hands of the enemy.

As the helicopters made their way to their secret outpost, far from the state capital, carrying the survivors, many of them wounded from the enemies' attacks, Adam continued to maintain his gaze on Henry, until his position vanished in the distance.

After the long battle between both factions, the remainder of enemy soldiers arrived to reinforce their positions, only to be greeted by a barren wasteland filled with the broken and burning shells of armor, and rank with the stench of burning flesh, from the corpses that laid lifeless on the field, broken, mangled, and dismembered from the awesome powers of destruction that they unleashed upon each other.

The remainder of enemy reinforcements looked in the skies and saw the Blackhawk helicopters retreating to their outpost and walked through the war-torn wasteland amidst all the corpses, stumbling onto Henry's wounded body, barely clinging to life, with his back against one of the dilapidated transports, a radio in one hand, trying to muster up the strength to say his last words to Adam.

"Over here, sir! Found one! He's still alive! But barely conscious!," Jason called out.

Jason looked at Henry closely, recognizing him as one of the lieutenants from the elite Unit-13, just before the uprising, and said, "You're one of the president's lieutenants, aren't you? I remember you when I was new to the armed forces, on Genesis. Just before the uprising."

Henry opened his eyes, and saw Jason kneeling over him, checking his vitals and offered a timid smile, while he continued to clutch the wound in his stomach, bleeding profusely from it, causing his vital signs to slow every passing moment.

Henry simply smiled at Jason, while he tried to maintain his strength from his gushing wound, slipping in and out of consciousness, his face becoming pale and strength completely waned.

"We need to get you to a medic, sir," Jason said to Henry, tending to his wound.

The other enemy soldiers came across to the young Jason's position, seeing the trapped and wounded soldier, slowly and painfully slipping into his last moments, blocking the sun that struck his pale face and cold skin from his rapid loss of blood.

Henry opened his eyes, and looked up at the group of soldiers that surrounded him and saw the familiar face of the assassin. He smiled and said softly, "Been a long time, Lieutenant. How have you been?"

06:22 HOURS. SOMEWHERE OVER INTERSTATE 15. THREE MILES FROM GARNET, 43 MILES AWAY FROM THE SECRET FREEDOM FIGHTER OUTPOST IN THE VALLEY OF FIRE, NEVADA:

A look of total awe quickly took over Adam's face as he watched the assassin standing before Henry from the view of his binoculars, as they continued their destination aboard their helicopter. Christopher, Eric, Robert, and the other lieutenants were in a complete state of shock, looking at each other.

"What is it?" Steven asked softly, looking at Ahmad.

"Oh my God. It's him. It's really him," Patrick said softly, with a sudden look of shock on his face, listening to the radio chatter, as he continued flying, escorting the Blackhawk helicopters towards the outpost, with all their ammunition and most of his fuel depleted.

Dillon slowly took off his oxygen mask, with a complete look of shock on his face, listening to Henry's voice, knowing who he had encountered, while he continued to fly back to base.

06:24 HOURS. SOMEWHERE ON INTERSTATE 15 APEX. 46 MILES AWAY FROM THE SECRET FREEDOM FIGHTER OUTPOST IN THE VALLEY OF FIRE, NEVADA:

"It's strange how you once saved my life. Now, you're the one who is coming to take it," Henry remarked, smiling at the man whom he once knew, and trusted as his predecessor before him, who had perished a year before, from the last campaign.

Jason watched helplessly as the one of the General's most trusted lieutenants stood over the wounded soldier, his face rigid from his lack of empathy, and his usual cold, calculating gaze, knowing the assassin was about to end Henry's life, and said, "You don't have to do this. We can still save him if we get him to a hospital," trying to sway the assassin from executing Henry who laid helpless before his feet, and continued, "He is no good to us dead."

06:27 HOURS. SOMEWHERE OVER INTERSTATE 15. 40 MILES AWAY FROM THE SECRET FREEDOM FIGHTER OUTPOST IN THE VALLEY OF FIRE, NEVADA:

Adam and the others listened to the radio chatter, hearing Jason's familiar voice, while he continued to beg for Henry's life, hoping that the assassin would spare him.

06:29 HOURS. SOMEWHERE ON INTERSTATE 15 APEX. 46 MILES AWAY FROM THE SECRET FREEDOM FIGHTER OUTPOST IN THE VALLEY OF FIRE, NEVADA:

Jason watched helplessly as Henry was about to be executed and continued his appeal, saying, "You don't have to do this. Please."

06:30 HOURS. SOMEWHERE OVER INTERSTATE 15. 38 MILES FROM THE SECRET FREEDOM FIGHTER OUTPOST IN THE VALLEY OF FIRE, NEVADA:

Lena saw the look of shock on Adam's face and asked, "What is it, General?"

06:31 HOURS. SOMEWHERE ON INTERSTATE 15 APEX. 46 MILES AWAY FROM THE SECRET FREEDOM FIGHTER OUTPOST IN THE VALLEY OF FIRE, NEVADA:

Henry watched as the enemy soldier walked closer to him, his gun pointed to his face and concluded, "These were good times when we once served together. I wish it didn't have to be this way. But, I suppose that you have a job to do. I already said my goodbyes to Adam and the others, and now you're the only one left. I guess this is how we say our final goodbyes. Now, don't just stand there. Get on with it, and grant me mercy. Put me out of my misery. Give me a soldier's death. This pain is killing me enough as it is already."

The assassin remained calm and calculating, with a straight face, after listening to Henry's last words, with a gun still pointed to his face, when a shot suddenly rang loudly through the desert, followed by a few more, ending Henry's life.

Jason closed his eyes and bowed his head in remorse, after witnessing the brutal execution of one of Dr. Weaver's top lieutenants, silently consumed with anger, knowing there was nothing he could do to save Henry's life.

06:32 HOURS. SOMEWHERE OVER INTERSTATE 15. 36 MILES FROM THE SECRET FREEDOM FIGHTER OUTPOST IN THE VALLEY OF FIRE, NEVADA:

"My God," Eric said with a look of fright on his face.

"What is it? What just happened?" Tiara asked.

"He killed him," Adam said softly with a distant gaze on his face.

"They got Collins. He got Collins," Christopher said softly.

Patrick closed his eyes tightly after knowing that Henry had met his demise at the hand of his nemesis, while he continued to escort the Blackhawks back to their outpost.

"Who killed him?" Lena asked, with her tears running down her cheek.

"Who is he?" Tiara asked.

"Someone who we once knew. Who we once served with. Who is now one with the other side," Adam answered, looking back at the battlefield filled with the towering masses of black smoke rising to the skies where they had left one of their wounded soldiers behind.

"He was the best and most decorated soldier in his unit, in the entire corp, and was the General's most trusted subordinate. And now he serves as his right-hand to carry out his bidding. He once served with General West, and the rest of us, up until the uprising on Genesis," Christopher answered. "After that, he was captured and was never heard from again, up until the last campaign in the Mojave Desert. And now he's hunting us. All of us. And he won't stop until we're all dead," Adam continued.

"My God," Tiara answered softly, with a look of worry on her face.

"He died because of me. He died saving me," Lena remarked softly, with her tears rolling down her cheeks.

"No. He died a soldier's death. He died fighting for what was right. For what he believed in. He did his job, till the end," Eric answered.

"We'll make them pay. All of them. Their deaths will not go in vain," Robert remarked.

Robert looked back at the towering columns of black smoke, from the view of the Blackhawk helicopters, and said softly, "Losing our defensive lines is one thing. But losing another one of us is something else entirely."

After the execution of another of their own, they contemplated in silence, realizing how close they were to being wiped out from the grueling campaign, the test of blood and fire that took its' toll on all those who lived through the horror of seeing loved ones and comrades fallen in the name of duty of the ones they served, with either side knowing that more lives were yet to be lost, in all the battles yet to be ensued, for control to decide the fate of an entire nation.

07:02 HOURS. SECRET FREEDOM FIGHTER OUTPOST. SOMEWHERE IN THE VALLEY OF FIRE, NEVADA:

The helicopters safely landed, disembarking all the survivors and wounded alike, after their close call with death.

Brian walked towards Adam and saw the look of awe on his face and asked, "Are you okay, General? You look like you just saw a ghost."

He was short, with stringy dark hair and chestnut brown eyes, in his mid 20s, and studied medicine for a few years, and shifted his allegiance to Dr. Weaver, hoping to follow in his footsteps from all his great accomplishments of being a great doctor someday.

"He got him. He got Collins," Adam answered, with a distant gaze.

The medic just looked in awe, sharing Adam's grief in losing another one of his closest friends.

The war continues…

CHAPTER 4: OPERATION BLITZKRIEG

04:23 HOURS. SOMEWHERE NEAR THE GREAT SALT LAKE DESERT, UTAH:

The year was 2028. Three years had passed since "The Great Fall of Genesis."

The moon was full and lit brightly in the night skies, as the cool winds swept slowly across the almost plain infinite desert sands.

A coyote silently prowled across the barren desert, coming to a halt, with its eyes gleaming in the darkness.

A copperhead slowly slithered its way through the cool sands of the unforgiving tundra, under the blanket of the night skies.

A jack rabbit quickly hopped through the barren wasteland, and abruptly stopped, looking to the skies, and quickly scampered away.

A desert fox dug through a burrow, trapping a rat in its jaw, prying it from its burrow, quickly consuming it, and looking in the skies, with its large satellite-like ears locking onto sounds from miles away and quickly scampered off.

A pack of wolves howled in unison, and stopped abruptly, looking in the skies, and ran away, after picking up the sounds from a distance, growing louder.

04:27 HOURS. WENDOVER ENEMY AIR FORCE BASE. 159 MILES FROM THE GREAT SALT LAKE DESERT, UTAH:

A raven flew into an enemy guard post, alerting the guard that patrolled within its confines, cawing loudly, and quickly flew away, vanishing into the darkness that shrouded the desert of the Great Salt Lake.

The enemy soldier watched as the raven flew into the dark skies, until it vanished from sight, thinking nothing of the strange occurrence that took place, and lunged his head slightly out of the guard post and saw the blinking lights of a plane drawing nearer, focusing his gaze when his guard post suddenly burst into flames. The remaining guard posts also burst into flames in quick succession, causing the alarm of the base to blare throughout the entire compound, causing widespread panic among the enemy personnel.

Within seconds, Dillon and his squad of hornet fighter jets stormed over the enemy base, destroying the hangars that housed their planes and ordinance, along with all their fuel reserves, completely neutralizing whatever air capabilities they had left, with the base erupting in a giant explosion.

"Looks like we caught them with their pants down! All units charge! We have the element of surprise! Don't let them get back in the fight," Adam called out.

The front gate was quickly overwhelmed by the fearsome power of the armored units that stormed through the front gates with countless to their rear, using their armor for cover against enemy fire, quickly charging through the enemy stronghold, keeping them suppressed from getting back into the fight.

04:34 HOURS. SOMEWHERE OVER WENDOVER ENEMY AIR FORCE BASE. 159 MILES AWAY FROM THE GREAT SALT LAKE, UTAH:

Moments after Dillon made his strafing run over the enemy stronghold, he flew over the burning wreckage of all the fuel reserves and hangers that housed their fighter planes, watching all the destruction he had unleashed upon the enemy from the view of his cockpit, flying over his ground forces.

04:35 HOURS. WENDOVER ENEMY AIR FORCE BASE. 159 MILES AWAY FROM THE GREAT SALT LAKE, UTAH:

The once young and once inexperienced soldiers, after their last skirmishes, had now become battle-hardened after being forged through the fires of combat, as they continued their blitzkrieg attack through the enemy stronghold, with the enemy soldiers unable to defend.

The roar of heavy machine gun fire suddenly rang out through the base from enemy gun encampments pinning the oncoming soldiers' advance.

"Some of our boys are pinned by enemy heavy machine guns! All units, man those 50s, and give our boys some cover fire!"

Their tanks moved forward to deflect the incoming enemy fire, and the loud clamor of machine gun fire from their tanks' mounted 50-Caliber machine guns returning fire rang out throughout the base, providing cover for their advancing soldiers to continue their blitzkrieg offensive.

The burning wreckage from a number of transports scattered as a number of enemy tanks broke through in their advance towards them.

"I have a few enemy contacts moving in, 12 o'clock!" Christopher yelled.

"Hold the position!" Adam yelled.

The ground of the Salt Lake Desert trembled violently from the enemy tanks pounding their positions with heavy shells, tossing a group of the advancing soldiers in the air, stopping the freedom fighters' advance on their positions.

Adam and his armored unit moved into blockade positions, providing cover fire for their advancing infantry, greeting the enemy armor with a barrage of heavy fire.

As the shells and bullets from both sides whistled in the skies, pounding onto the desert sands, causing the grounds of the great salt lake to tremble, the ground troops continued to advance throughout the enemy stronghold in their efforts to seize it.

Tiara looked into the tank's scope and zeroed in on an enemy unit and called out, "Enemy in my sights!"

"Take the shot!" Robert yelled back.

Tiara fired at the enemy tank, and saw an enormous plume of flame erupting through the scope, and yelled, "Direct hit! I made a direct hit."

"Move on to the next target," Ahmad said loudly.

The freedom fighters continued to advance through the enemy base, the enemy resistance intensified, with an enemy shell exploding into one of their armored units, completely immobilizing it.

James climbed the gunnery position of the immobilized unit, pulling the lifeless soldier from his position, and manned the tank's mounted guns amidst heavy machine gun fire. Enemy shells continued to rain on his position as he returned fire at the enemy forces, with little regard for his own life.

Steven lined up the sight at the enemy unit and deployed his shell, and watched it explode into it, completely halting its advance. He continued moving further into uncharted enemy territory, quickly inching their way in attempts to seize the enemy stronghold.

Lena courageously led a small squad of soldiers in a charge under heavy enemy resistance.

She grabbed a rocket-propelled grenade and fired the missile after an oncoming enemy armored unit, only slowing down its advance from impact, and shouted, "Reload!"

She fired another round and watched while it burst into flames, and hopped onto another enemy unit, quickly chucking a grenade inside it, and waited till it exploded. She jumped inside the tank's cockpit, with others following suit in seizing the enemy armored units, using them against the enemy, giving them a better chance of success in seizing the enemy stronghold.

Amanda sat securely in the tank's cockpit, lining up shots at the enemy units, scoring a number of hits, significantly wearing down the enemy number, while they continued to push deeper into the enemy positions.

She loaded another shell into the turret and fired at the enemy unit, and watched another violent explosion. She clamored through the base, completely dismantling the turret, and said, "Scored another hit!"

"We need more!" Eric cried out while he manned the tank's machineguns.

04:49 HOURS. SOMEWHERE IN THE GREAT SALT LAKE DESERT. 167 MILES AWAY FROM THE GREAT SALT LAKE, UTAH:

A pack of wolves traversed the unforgiving plain, stopped in their tracks after hearing the thunderous roar from all the explosions of the artillery exchange echoing in the distance, seeing the bright flashes that looked like the forecast of a storm warning, fixing their collective gazes on the great battle that continued to ensue in the distance, for miles howling in unison, knowing that so much death had taken its course on the battlefield.

Though the freedom fighters seemed outnumbered, they had caught the enemy soldiers by surprise with their blitzkrieg attack, with the enemies' position being just moments away from being overwhelmed.

05:07 HOURS. WENDOVER ENEMY AIR FORCE BASE. 159 MILES AWAY FROM THE GREAT SALT LAKE, UTAH:

Within moments after the enemy base was invaded, it was finally overwhelmed, and cleansed from all enemy forces.

The air was rank with the stench of death and smoke, and a sudden calm swept through the base, allowing all the soldiers the opportunity to gain a brief moment of respite.

Adam climbed from the tank's gunnery position and looked all around him, seeing all the destruction and corpses of dead soldiers, and turned to James and asked, "How many casualties?"

"About 20 so far. Just a few injured, sir."

Adam looked all around him and said softly, "Something doesn't feel right."

"What do you mean, sir?" James asked with a puzzled look on his face.

"That was too easy," Adam answered.

"But we've secured the enemy base, sir," Steven remarked.

"He's right. Something isn't right," Eric answered.

"For a place this size, there was supposed to be more enemy personnel," Ahmad added.

"The objective was to draw us in and trap us. Damn. They're good, I'll give them that," Eric said, nodding his head.

"We're too deep in the enemy positions. If we make it out, they'll cut us to pieces for sure. We can't afford to be too far from our air support. Our air support should be right on top of us if we make a run for it," Ahmad said.

"Well, I won't stay here for us to be sitting ducks, either," Adam replied.

"It was a trap and we walked right into it. Damn," Robert added.

"Okay everyone, be on your guard," Christopher said softly, with his eyes probing all about searching for any enemy activity.

"We have a few wounded, and their best chance of survival is to load them into whatever surviving units we can salvage," Robert added.

"You heard the man, people! Let's move! And let's evacuate! Before more enemy forces box us in this shit hole," Adam ordered.

Lena climbed out of the enemy tank's cockpit, sat in the tank's gunnery position, looked into the dark morning skies, and saw the blinking lights of a fighter planet quickly closing in on their positions while they began to evacuate the enemy base, and called out softly, "General West."

"What's on your mind, soldier?" Adam answered, and said, "Make it quick. I'm on a time limit."

Lena pointed to the skies and said softly, "Look. Bogeys closing in and it's coming in fast. Don't think it's one of ours, sir."

"I knew it. This was too good to be true. This was too easy," Adam replied. He grabbed the radio and said, "We have an undisclosed number of enemy bogeys closing in, and have a number of wounded from the assault! Everyone assumes defensive positions! Rollout!"

"We need to call for air support!" Steven answered.

"Yamaguchi, get on the radio and radio for air support!" Adam yelled.

"I'm seeing more enemy planes, and they're closing in fast!" Lena yelled.

The oncoming enemy planes were suddenly greeted by a sky full of anti-aircraft fire, while they quickly closed in on Adam's position.

05:17 HOURS. SOMEWHERE IN THE GREAT SALT LAKE DESERT. 167 MILES FROM THE GREAT SALT LAKE, UTAH:

The pack of wolves that wandered the great plain of the desert remained fixated at the strange yet awesome spectacle as they continued to watch the bright streaks of anti-aircraft fire lighting through the skies, as they greeted the vast number of enemy planes, hearing the loud clamor of machine gun fire, even from the great distance that separated them from the battlefield.

05:19 HOURS. WENDOVER ENEMY AIR FORCE BASE. 159 MILES FROM THE GREAT SALT LAKE, UTAH:

"If we stay here, we'll be like sardines in a can! We have to evacuate now!" Adam called out.

05:22 HOURS. SOMEWHERE OVER WENDOVER ENEMY AIR FORCE BASE. 159 MILES FROM THE GREAT SALT LAKE, UTAH:

Dillon heard the distress call and moved in to provide support, along with a number of his fellow wingmen, their ground troops quickly evacuated the enemy stronghold with their wounded.

The squad of enemy planes rapidly descended upon them and deployed a bomb, causing a giant wall of flame, destroying a number of the smaller armored units, killing a number of their troops.

After their brief victory of capturing the base, Dillon and his planes quickly turned around and headed back to engage the enemy planes, when his canopy suddenly shuddered from the roaring engines of an enemy plane quickly flying past, causing him to quickly glance to his rear, and quickly turned around in pursuit and said over the radio, "All units break off and engage! I repeat, all units, weapons free!"

The planes soared above the skies ferociously, engaging one another while the enemy artillery guns pounded the freedom fighter's position, as they continued to evacuate the enemy base.

Dillon engaged the enemy closing in on his tail and switched to his guns, unleashing a lethal volley of bullets from its chain guns, watching it burst into flames.

Adam and the rest of the ground forces continued to exchange artillery fire, and sensed they were slowly being overwhelmed by the constant barrage. He yelled over the radio, "We're being pummeled by enemy guns, and we need to silence that position! We need air support now!"

05:25 HOURS. SOMEWHERE OVER WENDOVER ENEMY AIR FORCE BASE. 159 MILES AWAY FROM THE GREAT SALT LAKE, UTAH:

"We're swamped by enemy planes! We'll be there as soon as we can!" Dillon answered over the radio.

05:32 HOURS. WENDOVER ENEMY AIR FORCE BASE. 159 MILES AWAY FROM THE GREAT SALT LAKE, UTAH:

The enemy planes and the enemy artillery positions combined their firepower and continued to pound their positions with shells and air to ground ordinance, while they continued to move in closer range to the freedom fighters' positions to provide a counter attack. The freedom fighters returned fire from the tanks' heavy gunnery emplacements as they tried to evacuate from the base with all their wounded before they were sealed in the enemy position by the advancing enemy ground troops.

"There are too many enemy planes. We need to provide cover fire from our position!" Christopher yelled.

"Bring the enemy planes to our position! We'll provide ground support," Eric said to Dillon over the radio.

05:36 HOURS. SOMEWHERE OVER WENDOVER ENEMY AIR FORCE BASE. 159 MILES AWAY FROM THE GREAT LAKE, UTAH:

"Bringing them to your position!" Dillon answered, and ordered all his wingmen to lead their pursuers over Adam's position for added support.

05:42 HOURS. WENDOVER ENEMY AIR FORCE BASE. 159 MILES AWAY FROM THE GREAT SALT LAKE, UTAH:

The dawn skies lit brighter, as the fire from the ground intensified to help repel the enemy air assault, while they continued making their survival run out of the enemy position.

05:45 HOURS. SOMEWHERE OVER WENDOVER ENEMY AIR FORCE BASE. 159 MILES AWAY FROM THE GREAT SALT LAKE, UTAH:

The flashes from enemy bullets continued racing past Dillon's canopy, while he flew over Adam's position. He quickly pointed his plane to the skies, leaving the pursuing enemy plane to the mass volley of anti-aircraft fire, tearing through its fabric, causing it to shoot out of the skies, crashing and burning in the Salt Lake Desert.

05:48 HOURS. WENDOVER ENEMY AIR FORCE BASE. 159 MILES AWAY FROM THE GREAT SALT LAKE, UTAH:

"Keep them coming!" Ahmad yelled.

"Enemy guns are still knocking the wind out of us!" Robert yelled through the constant, thunderous rumbling.

"The sooner we knock those planes out the skies, the sooner we knock the fuck out those enemy guns!" Ahmad said.

They were very close to reaching out in their desperate run out of the enemy base, when their paths were suddenly blocked by the enemy armored units.

"We're boxed in by enemy armor. We need to punch a hole in their lines at all costs, or be sitting ducks! All tanks move into blockade positions, and return fire!" Adam said.

"I can't tell enemy planes from friendlies! It's still too dark!" Christopher said loudly from the deafening roar of artillery and gunfire.

"All units switch to night vision!" Adam ordered.

Adam and his heroic band of freedom fighters remained undaunted and moved closer in range of enemy artillery for a counterattack, with the turrets of their tanks blazing through the dark void of the desert.

Dillon and his squad of fighters kept the enemy planes entangled, bringing them over to Adam's position to increase their firepower, to aid in clearing the skies of the enemy planes.

The clamoring in the skies continued from the explosions of enemy planes, from the combination of air and ground fire that brought them closer to clearing the skies every passing moment.

"The skies are almost cleared of enemy planes! But we still have a number of enemy armor wreaking havoc on our positions! Move in and attack the enemy positions!" Adam cried out.

The enemy artillery continued raining down on their positions while they advanced with the massive turrets of their tanks blazing.

"We have more enemy units moving in to reinforce their positions!" Steven shouted, as he peered through his binoculars watching the horizon.

"It took them a while, but they took the bait! We're finally drawing them in! Our guns are finally moving into the flank, General West!" Lena yelled.

"Couldn't come at a better time! Yamaguchi, get on the radio and relay coordinates of the enemy position for our artillery to punch a hole in their defenses! It was a good thing we kept some of our guns on reserve during the assault, or we would've been wiped out!"

"All guns in position! Waiting on your order to fire, General!" Robert yelled.

"We need to flank the enemy artillery positions so we can limit their firepower, and help us tear through their defenses! We need to hold on long enough so our planes can rain hell on the enemy positions!" Adam cried out.

06:09 HOURS. SOMEWHERE OVER WENDOVER ENEMY AIR FORCE BASE. 159 MILES NEAR THE GREAT SALT LAKE, UTAH:

"We're still swamped by enemy planes, and we must keep them busy long enough, with our combined efforts from air and ground support!" Dillon answered over the radio, while he flew over Adam's position, seeing the flashes from artillery exploding all around him, while he and his group of planes cleverly continued engaging the enemy planes, luring them over Adam's position into the trap of a thick wall of anti-aircraft fire.

06:16 HOURS. WENDOVER ENEMY AIR FORCE BASE. 159 MILES AWAY FROM THE GREAT SALT LAKE, UTAH:

"We need a Plan B! Where are our gunships? We need them to attack enemy artillery positions!" Adam called out.

06:18 HOURS. SOMEWHERE OVER THE GREAT SALT LAKE DESERT. 15 MILES AWAY FROM WENDOVER ENEMY AIR FORCE BASE - TOOELE COUNTY, UTAH:

Patrick and his squad of gunships remained at a safe distance to intercept the enemy artillery positions and armored units with Dillon and his squad of planes and added, "All units, visibility is still low! Maintain night vision!"

"Our guns are beginning the assault! But the enemy forces are moving to counterattack our guns!" Eric added.

"It's like we flank and they outflank! It's like a game of cat and mouse, sir!" Steven said.

"But we're still outnumbered, and we still need to bring down their numbers!" Robert shouted.

Adam turned to Ahmad and said, "Tell our gunships to protect those guns at all costs!"

Their guns flanked the enemy positions and began their assault, wearing down the enemies' firepower.

Ahmad looked in the distance in his night vision goggles, saw the flashes of artillery fire exploding in the enemy position, and yelled, "It's working! Our guns are now active!

And our gunships are providing cover fire for our guns! They got the message!"

The enemy firepower is beginning to dwindle!" Robert said loudly.

"They'll keep them busy until our gunships come!" Adam yelled through the deafening roar of artillery fire.

The dust from the desert sand swirled constantly from the awesome fire power from their tanks' massive guns that spewed their shells from their turrets, while they drew closer within firing range of the enemies' blockade position.

06:19 HOURS. SOMEWHERE OVER WENDOVER ENEMY AIR FORCE BASE. 159 MILES AWAY FROM THE GREAT SALT LAKE, UTAH:

As Dillon engaged an enemy plane, the sensors in his cockpit blared loudly, while he locked on in his sights, deployed a missile, and watched it explode into the enemy plane's engines, causing a giant fireball.

06:23 HOURS. WENDOVER ENEMY AIR FORCE BASE. 159 MILES AWAY FROM THE GREAT SALT LAKE, UTAH:

The ground troops were suddenly alarmed, seeing the blinding flash of fire, and hearing the thunderous explosion that came moments after, watching the burning plane plummeting to the desert sands.

All the soldiers paused for a moment watching the burning plane heading to the surface in flames trailing black smoke, fascinated by the lethal form of air combat that circled high in the dark skies above their position, looking at each other with a look of awe on their faces, from its intensity.

"No matter how many times I see it, it never gets old," Christopher said softly, while he and the others watched the enemy plane crash and burn in the desert, close to their position.

"I'll share those sentiments as long as it's not one of us," Eric answered.

"Wow," Lena said softly to herself, while she continued to man the tank's heavy guns.

06: 27 HOURS. SOMEWHERE OVER WENDOVER ENEMY AIR FORCE BASE. 159 MILES NEAR THE GREAT SALT LAKE, UTAH:

"One more bites the dust," Dillon said over the radio.

The blinding flash from another explosion lit brightly into the confines of Dillon's cockpit, almost blinding him, followed by a sudden volley of enemy bullets, flying past him.

He glanced briefly over his shoulder, and saw the fighter plane heading straight to the surface in a giant ball of flame and said," Shit, I just lost one of my own!" while the volley of enemy rounds continued racing past his plane.

He pressed the thrusters of his engines and headed straight into the clouds, while the enemy plane trailed him relentlessly, and made a sharp turn, finding himself behind the enemy plane, locking onto it and quickly fired a missile, destroying his enemy, and watching it freefall to the ground, like many others had done before.

06:33 HOURS. WENDOVER ENEMY AIR FORCE BASE. 159 MILES NEAR THE GREAT SALT LAKE, UTAH:

The battle intensified between the ground forces. Many of the younger ground troops remained mesmerized at the awesome yet deadly spectacle of aerial combat that ensued, watching the planes rain from the skies like giant fireballs from the heavens.

"Snap out of it, all of you! Where you're going in this line of work, you'll be seeing plenty of it where we're going!" Ahmad said loudly.

"My God," Amanda said softly, with a look of total shock on her face, watching the towering wall of crimson flame consuming the enemy position from the barrage they sustained from their guns.

"It comes with the job. Now, move your asses closer within firing range of the enemy positions!" Adam yelled.

06:37 HOURS. SOMEWHERE OVER WENDOVER ENEMY AIR FORCE BASE. 159 MILES AWAY FROM THE GREAT SALT LAKE, UTAH:

"I lost a number of my planes from enemy fire. Don't know how long our air defenses can hold," Dillon yelled over his radio.

06:38 HOURS. WENDOVER ENEMY AIR FORCE BASE. 159 MILES AWAY FROM THE GREAT SALT LAKE, UTAH:

"Lure them to our position so we can provide support! We need to take out those guns and seize the advantage!"

06:40 HOURS. SOMEWHERE OVER WENDOVER ENEMY AIR FORCE BASE. 159 MILES AWAY FROM THE GREAT SALT LAKE, UTAH:

"Roger that!" Dillon flew past an enemy plane, causing it to pursue him over Adam's position.

The enemy plane pursued Dillon relentlessly, while he headed towards the large concentration of ground troops that continued making their way, from deep within the enemy fortress.

The alarms in his cockpit began to blare loudly from a missile deployed from the enemy plane that pursued him deep into the heart of his defenses. He skillfully maneuvered his plane while the enemy missile drew nearer, quickly deploying his counter-measures of sunburst, drawing the enemy missile away, exploding into them.

06:41 HOURS. WENDOVER ENEMY AIR FORCE BASE. 159 MILES AWAY FROM THE GREAT SALT LAKE, UTAH:

The ground forces watched the bright bursts of light deployed from Dillon's plane, luring the enemy missile away, exploding on impact, setting off a blinding flash of flame. There was a deafening roar from the blast, lighting the void of darkness that shrouded the Salt Lake Desert, as they eagerly anticipated the lure of more enemy planes into their clever ambush.

"We have incoming! All weapons hot!," Robert yelled.

Lena nervously anticipated the incoming enemy plane, with the sweat from her palms dripping down the tank's heavy machine guns, eagerly anticipating the enemy plane to fly into their trap, while the others waited patiently, nervously, with their hearts thumping heavily in their chests. They waited with bated breaths to repel the enemy air defenses and clear the way to assault the enemy ground positions, while the enemy artillery continued to explode around them in their retreat to open ground.

06:43 HOURS. SOMEWHERE OVER WENDOVER ENEMY AIR FORCE BASE. 159 MILES FROM THE GREAT SALT LAKE, UTAH:

Dillon saw more flashes of light, hearing the bullets racing past his plane at supersonic speed, while he was just mere seconds away from his position, hoping that he would not be shot down before he lured the enemy into his trap, and quickly took vertically to the skies, exposing the enemy plane to a giant volley of anti-aircraft fire from all their tanks' heavy machine guns.

As the heavy wall of bullets sped into the skies, they tore through the enemy plane's hull, through the enemy pilot's body, and through his canopy, causing his body to convulse violently, staining the confines of the entire cockpit with enormous blood spatters, rendering the controls of his plane completely immobile from the lethal barrage and quickly spun out of control, entirely consumed in flames.

The enemy plane continued to fall from the skies from the lethal barrage of gunfire, and the enemy pilot stared helplessly as he continued falling from the skies, knowing there was nothing he could do as the life from his body quickly slipped away. He became resigned to his fate, witnessing his final moments in combat, crashing and burning, becoming another casualty of what will be a long and brutal campaign.

06:52 HOURS. WENDOVER ENEMY AIR FORCE BASE. 159 MILES AWAY FROM THE GREAT SALT LAKE - TOOELE COUNTY, UTAH:

The barrage from enemy ground troops continued to rain all around their positions, while they fought back gallantly, and simultaneously provided ground fire in assisting their air support who were vastly outnumbered by the enemy forces.

After a long period of fighting between the both forces, the dawn of a new day had once again arrived, with the morning sun slowly rising beyond the horizon, causing the darkness that shrouded the endless desert to quickly fade as the cool morning breeze gently blew across the desert sands, tossing about the tumbleweeds, carrying the heavy stench of more death and smoke that festered in it.

The gallant freedom fighters had finally made it out of the enemies' stronghold to open road, en-route to their base.

06:57 HOURS. SOMEWHERE OVER THE GREAT SALT LAKE DESERT. 15 MILES AWAY FROM WENDOVER ENEMY AIR FORCE BASE - TOOELE COUNTY, UTAH:

Patrick and his squad of gunships remained within striking range of the enemy artillery guns, still engaging them, clearing the path for Adam and the other soldiers to make it to open ground. They scanned the area for heat signals for any signs of enemy gunships on the infrared scanners, while they continued hovering silently from a safe distance to stay out of the enemies' range, and saw more enemy armored units still converging on Adam's position and deployed their long range missiles. Patrick watched them track their target, exploding into them, and said, "We have more enemy tanks moving into your position. We'll continue to hold them off as much as we can for you to continue clearing a path before more support arrives! All units - maintain current positions and engage all enemy ground units moving converging to General West's position!"

07:00 HOURS. SOMEWHERE IN THE GREAT SALT LAKE DESERT. 3 MILES AWAY FROM WENDOVER ENEMY AIR FORCE BASE - TOOELE COUNTY, UTAH:

Amidst all the towering explosions from the heavy ordinance exchanging from both fronts, a series of explosions could be seen coming from behind the enemy lines.

Robert looked into his infrared scope and saw a number of enemy armored units being engaged and handed it over to James. "Look, our gunships have taken out more enemy tanks!"

"General West, our gunships are still in position engaging the enemy tanks" James yelled in excitement.

"What about the flank from our guns?" Adam asked while he continued providing fire from his gunnery position.

James looked into the binoculars and saw their tank and artillery gun formation still intact and answered, "They're still holding!"

"O'Hara, we're out on the open road heading towards your position! We need you to silence the rest of those guns!"

07:02 HOURS. SOMEWHERE OVER THE GREAT SALT LAKE. 15 MILES AWAY FROM WENDOVER ENEMY AIR FORCE BASE - TOOELE COUNTY, UTAH:

"Read you loud and clear, General! All units, attack all enemy guns until air support arrives," Patrick replied.

The gunships quickly attacked the enemy artillery positions with a massive volley of hellfire missiles and hydra missiles, decimating the enemy troops and destroying the guns, as they continued to hover out of enemy range, until the enemy artillery were reduced to into burning heaps of metal, with countless corpses laying among their wreckage.

07:04 HOURS. SECRET ENEMY OUTPOST. SOMEWHERE NEAR THE GOLDEN SPIKE NATIONAL HISTORIC SITE. 204 MILES FROM WENDOVER ENEMY AIR FORCE BASE - TOOELE COUNTY, UTAH:

The alarms of the enemy base blared loudly. The heavy footsteps of countless enemy personnel raced towards their planes and gunships to begin yet again another tedious process of arming another group of their planes to engage the smaller group of freedom fighters that continued to wreak havoc on their planes with meticulous precision.

After the long process, the sounds of helicopter propellers whirring filled the enemy base, as they lifted off to engage the freedom fighters, leaving behind a swirling cloud of dust. A number of the enemy planes quickly ascended to the skies from the long and dusty make-shift runway that stretched through the desert for miles.

07:16 HOURS. SOMEWHERE IN THE GREAT SALT LAKE DESERT. 5 MILES AWAY FROM WENDOVER ENEMY AIR FORCE BASE - TOOELE COUNTY, UTAH:

Steven intercepted a message of the enemy forces calling for reinforcements, and said to Adam, "General West, I just intercepted a radio transmission from the enemy base, calling on for more reinforcements! Along with more enemy armors already en-route. They should be within range soon. The enemy is hitting us with everything they have, sir! But the good news is, more of their planes are still being armed! We may still be able to get to them if he acts soon!"

"Good job, Yamaguchi!" Adam yelled through the hail of heavy artillery fire wreaking havoc on their positions, and continued, "Calling all available planes, we have multiple bogeys, and more enemy armored units converging to reinforce their positions! We have more being armed and fueled as we speak, but we need to take them out before they can get off the ground!"

07:30 HOURS. SOMEWHERE OVER THE GREAT SALT LAKE. 9 MILES AWAY FROM WENDOVER ENEMY AIR FORCE BASE - TOOELE COUNTY, UTAH:

The battle for air superiority continued, with enemy planes suffering heavy losses from the smaller number of freedom fighter planes, while they combined their efforts with the ground units.

While Dillon continued to engage the enemy planes, he heard the frantic distress call from one of his pilots over his radio, while he tried to evade the enemy pilot, as countless enemy bullets continued slicing through the air, speeding past the canopy of his plane. With a sudden look of frantic creasing on his face, he discovered he was locked on the enemy scope. He was surprised by a sudden blinding flash of light, causing the blaring of his alarms to suddenly cease, and inhaled, taking a deep sigh, glancing back through the transparent canopy of his plane. The enemy plane was heading down to the surface trailing heavy smoke, tallying the last of the enemy planes that they had to contend with.

The pilot rested his head back in his seat, breathing a giant sigh of relief that he had survived, and said to Dillon, "This is call sign, Razor. Thanks for saving my ass, Captain. I owe you one."

"You don't owe me anything. You would've done the same thing for me. We're on the same team."

He was a young pilot in his mid 20s, with blonde hair and green eyes, who was eagerly looking to prove himself, with Dillon being his role model during his early exploits serving with Adam on many of his missions before the Fall of Genesis that led to the civil war. He continued trying to catch his breath from his close brush with death, and said, "Thanks to you, I can fight for one more day. The name is James Tompkins, by the way. But you can call me by my moniker, although I was the one who was almost cut to pieces. Good to finally meet you, Captain Kim. And it's a real honor to be flying by your side, sir. You're my hero. You've been a great inspiration to me, ever since your early days of flying in your past missions before the war. You're the reason why I fought for Dr. Weaver instead of the General."

"Likewise Tompkins. Thank you for the compliment. That really means a lot to me. But we're not out of the woods yet. We have an unconfirmed number of enemy planes and gunships arming as we speak from an airstrip more than 200 miles away from our current location. Our job is to keep them from falling from the skies, so General West and the rest of the ground crew can make it home safely. We've shot down most of the enemy planes, but they're still combat capable. So we have to employ the same tactic to maximize our firepower. If our numbers are strong enough and we have enough fuel left, we will attack that base and level it to the ground. How is your fuel and ordinance holding up?" Dillon asked.

"I still have enough fuel and ordinance to engage. Ready whenever you are. Just give the signal."

"To all fighters, the good news is the skies are now clear from enemy fighters. But the bad news is, we have an unconfirmed number of enemy planes, gunships, and tanks heading this way to reinforce their position, taking off from an outpost more than 200 miles from here. The number of enemy contacts outnumber us, so we must use all available resources to keep them getting to the skies.

We have a number of our troops wounded from action and are to provide cover for them at all costs. We are running low on ordinance and fuel, so we need to make every shot count. We've received intel that they're still rearming. The best chance that all of us have to ensure the survival of all our troops is to launch a preemptive strike. Our orders are to head towards the enemy vector and engage. Our gunships will take care of the rest of the enemy ground troops. All weapons hot, and engage at will," Dillon concluded, as he flew towards the enemy outpost to launch their preemptive strike, after the skies had been cleared from the first wave of enemy planes, from the combined efforts of air and ground support.

07:45 HOURS. SOMEWHERE IN THE GREAT SALT LAKE DESERT. 10 MILES AWAY FROM WENDOVER ENEMY AIR FORCE BASE - TOOELE COUNTY, UTAH:

The ground troops paused for a brief moment to catch their breaths, watching the destruction that greeted them from all the wreckage of the enemy artillery positions, consumed in flames, with the bodies of countless enemy soldiers sprawled on the sands of the Great Lake Desert from their gunships.

They heard the buzzing engines from the remainder of the planes flying over their positions, heading towards the coordinates of the enemy base deploying fresh air and ground units, until they vanished beyond the horizon.

07:49 HOURS. SOMEWHERE OVER THE GREAT SALT LAKE DESERT, UTAH:

Patrick and his group of gunships watched from the view of their cockpits, as the remainder of their planes flew towards the enemy position on their preemptive strike, hovering in the desert to defend the column of light and armored vehicles making their way back to base.

08:17 HOURS. SECRET ENEMY OUTPOST. SOMEWHERE NEAR THE GOLDEN SPIKE NATIONAL HISTORIC SITE, 204 MILES AWAY FROM THE WENDOVER ENEMY AIR FORCE BASE - TOOELE COUNTY, UTAH:

After the long and tedious process of loading and fueling the enemy planes, they lined up on the runway ready to taxi the freedom fighters' positions.

The exhaust of all the enemy planes blew with full force, the deafening roar of their engines filling the vicinity of the outpost, gaining speed as they began to taxi off the dusty runway just moments from lifting off, when the tower that maintained all traffic erupted into a giant ball of flame, raining down wreckage on top of enemy soldiers, causing them to scurry about frantically.

As the leading enemy planes continued to lift off, they exploded from combined barrage of bullets and long-range missiles, causing them to fall back on the runway with deafening clamor in a heap of flaming wreckage, followed by a chain reaction of explosions of more enemy planes, that waited to lift off, remaining completely helpless to the freedom fighters' attack while they remained on the long and dusty stretch of runway.

Just seconds after the chain of explosions, the squadron of planes continued storming the enemy base, causing the enemy soldiers to flee for cover, while the others bravely confronted the swarming planes, only to meet their demise from the planes' awesome firepower.

A ball of flame, slowly transforming into a dreaded mushroom cloud, quickly consumed the hangar that housed the rest of the planes and ammunition, completely depleting their ammunition stores, with their fuel reserves following in quick succession.

A barrage of heavy bullets tore through the compound, causing another series of explosions, claiming a number of enemy lives indiscriminately in their wake. The hollow and painful screams of those burning and dying slowly from the onslaught of the freedom fighters echoed through the entire outpost, as the freedom fighters continued neutralizing all opposition against them.

08:29 HOURS. SOMEWHERE OVER THE SECRET ENEMY OUTPOST. 204 MILES AWAY FROM WENDOVER ENEMY AIR FORCE BASE - TOOELE COUNTY, UTAH:

Moments after the attack, the enemy outpost was completely neutralized, and the decimation that was left in the wake of their attack could be seen from high above, while they circled for their final moments, looking down from the view of their cockpits, seeing giant clouds of thick, blinding smoke from the sea of flames that shrouded the entire position.

08:32 HOURS. SECRET ENEMY OUTPOST SOMEWHERE NEAR THE GOLDEN SPIKE NATIONAL HISTORIC SITE. 204 MILES AWAY FROM WENDOVER ENEMY AIR FORCE BASE - TOOELE COUNTY, UTAH:

The surviving enemy soldiers searched for more survivors, carrying their dead and wounded throughout the outpost. They paused for a moment, and watched helplessly at the planes that had completely decimated their base flew away, vanishing into the clouds.

08:34 HOURS. SOMEWHERE OVER THE ENEMY SECRET OUTPOST NEAR THE GOLDEN SPIKE NATIONAL HISTORIC SITE. 204 MILES AWAY FROM WENDOVER ENEMY AIR FORCE BASE - TOOELE COUNTY, UTAH:

"Enemy base destroyed. All enemy units neutralized. I repeat, enemy base destroyed, all enemy planes and ground units neutralized. Heading back to the designated area to provide support," Dillon said, watching from the safety of his cockpit.

08:36 HOURS. SOMEWHERE IN THE GREAT SALT LAKE DESERT. 20 MILES AWAY FROM WENDOVER ENEMY AIR FORCE BASE - TOOELE COUNTY, UTAH:

Adam heard the news on the radio and yelled with a hint of excitement, "News well received, flight leader. Great job. Now get your asses over here and provide more support. I get the feeling we may be getting another surprise. And I hate surprises. Especially under those circumstances."

08:43 HOURS. SOMEWHERE OVER THE GREAT SALT LAKE DESERT, UTAH 20 MILES AWAY FROM WENDOVER ENEMY AIR FORCE BASE - TOOELE COUNTY, UTAH:

Meanwhile, over the desert, Patrick and his squad of gunships hovered safely out of range, searching for more enemy activity, as their planes were away. A sudden blinding flash lit through Patrick's cockpit from one of his gunships being hit from enemy fire. He suddenly heard radio chatter from one of his pilots, warning him that an enemy attack was imminent, and went silent.

08:45 HOURS. SOMEWHERE IN THE GREAT SALT LAKE DESERT, 21 MILES AWAY FROM WENDOVER ENEMY AIR FORCE BASE - TOOELE COUNTY, UTAH:

Although the enemy base was attacked by the freedom fighters' planes, a number of enemy gunships escaped unscathed and were able to intercept the freedom fighters while they continued to make their run towards their position to treat their wounded.

"We're under attack by enemy gunships! Looks like some made it out from their outpost undetected!" Patrick shouted.

"That's not possible! Weren't they supposed to have been intercepted on our strafing run?" Robert asked in surprise.

"It appears they made it out before our birds hit their base! And I just picked up two more gunships moving in towards your positions to engage! Unless they have another secret outpost in these parts," Patrick called out.

The look on Adam's face turned into a look of awe while he listened to the radio chatter, hearing the enemy planes had escaped their strafing run, and continued to listen in while they made their way back to their position, and said, "Let's just hope that we got all their planes!" Like the battle for control of the skies between both forces of fighter planes, another battle for control with gunships from both sides had begun to wage.

The enemy gunships quickly honed in on Patrick and his squad, and began their assault, trying to flush them out of their positions, causing them to be exposed to enemy ground fire. Meanwhile, the other enemy gunships moved in to engage their artillery positions not too far from their position.

"General West, I've just intercepted a message from our gunnery positions flanking the enemy artillery positions," Steven said.

"What's the message?" Adam asked.

"They're being overrun by enemy gunships, sir! Our enemy gunships are completely surrounded by enemy forces, and suffering significant losses!" Steven said, pausing for a moment, listening to the frantic radio from their artillery position, and concluded, "Our artillery flank has been completely overrun! They're gone! All of them! Our flank has been completely decimated, from enemy fire. They're attacking from both fronts! And now, they're closing in, along with a number of enemy armored units!"

"Same trick with enemy planes, O'Hara! Get your gunships out of the enemy position, and lead them within firing range of our guns until our planes get back! We have more enemy armor closing in! Move in to blockade position," Adam said loudly, when another blinding flash lit through Patrick's cockpit. Seeing another one of his gunships going down from enemy fire from the battle between both factions continued to intensify, Patrick's squad of gunships was left with mounting losses, as they were being surrounded by the enemy, while trying to punch a hole in their defenses.

09:07 HOURS. SOMEWHERE IN THE GREAT LAKE DESERT, 25 MILES AWAY FROM WENDOVER ENEMY AIR FORCE BASE - TOOELE COUNTY, UTAH:

Patrick felt enemy rounds bouncing off his gunship and glanced to his rear, seeing an enemy gunship in relentless pursuit, and said over the radio to Adam, "Hold on! The enemy just downed another one of my gunships, and they're coming in after me! I'm bringing him over to your position!"

09:10 HOURS. SOMEWHERE IN THE GREAT SALT LAKE DESERT, 26 MILES AWAY FROM WENDOVER ENEMY AIR FORCE BASE - TOOELE COUNTY, UTAH:

The enemy gunship remained distracted as it continued to pursue Patrick, while he continued to draw it into the ambush. It was greeted by a volley of anti-aircraft fire from Adam's position, causing it to fall into the desert sands, bursting into flames.

The ground troops were greeted by a volley of fire from a gauntlet of armored units and long range artillery guns.

Ahmad peered through his binoculars and saw the sea of enemy armored units. "We're closing in on their positions!" he yelled.

"We need to hold on long enough until our planes come!" Robert answered when an enemy shell exploded into the desert, severely immobilizing the transport that carried a number of their wounded back to their base.

"Our transports carrying our wounded are down! And we have no other means of transport!" Robert called out.

"We need to get them back to base, but our position is too hot! We'll have to hold for now!" Adam replied.

"Right now, our gunships are taking out as many of the ground units as possible!"

"I hope they do it soon, because we are sitting ducks down here!" Eric replied.

"Me too!" Adam replied.

09:12 HOURS. SOMEWHERE OVER THE GREAT SALT DESERT, 27 MILES AWAY FROM WENDOVER ENEMY AIR FORCE BASE - TOOELE COUNTY, UTAH:

"We need to create a diversion! I'll play the bait so I can draw their fire while the rest of you stay back and pick off as many units as you can!" Patrick said, flying towards the enemy ground units with a few of the other gunships to draw the enemies' fire towards them. They distracted the enemy from the other gunships that continued to wreak havoc on their positions.

Patrick continued flying into the heart of the enemy positions with another enemy gunship in relentless pursuit, greeting him with a lethal barrage of heavy bullets from the mounted cannon, while the rest of his squad continued to destroy a number of enemy ground units with a volley of ordinance, triggering a series of explosions. This created an instant smokescreen, blinding the pursuing gunship as they flew straight into the wall of heavy, black smoke, and quickly turned his gunship around, greeting the enemy pilot with a barrage of bullets, scoring a series of critical hits on the enemy gunship. It flew out of control, crashing and burning. Patrick said to Adam over the radio, "It seems that the old man still has a few tricks up his sleeves."

09:20 HOURS. SOMEWHERE IN THE GREAT SALT LAKE DESERT, 27 MILES AWAY FROM WENDOVER ENEMY AIR FORCE BASE - TOOELE COUNTY, UTAH:

"You need to get your wrinkled ass out of the enemy position! You are flanked on all sides by enemy units! It's too dangerous!" Christopher yelled.

09:20 HOURS. SOMEWHERE OVER THE GREAT SALT LAKE DESERT, 27 MILES AWAY FROM WENDOVER ENEMY AIR FORCE BASE -TOOELE COUNTY, UTAH:

"I have more of my units under fire! I need to provide some support until they can clear the enemy gun placements, at least!" Patrick answered.

09:21 HOURS. SOMEWHERE IN THE GREAT SALT LAKE DESERT, 27 MILES AWAY FROM WENDOVER ENEMY AIR FORCE BASE - TOOELE COUNTY, UTAH:

"Watch your old crazy ass, O'Hara! We still have enemy units wreaking havoc on our position and need support!" Adam answered.

09:21 HOURS. SOMEWHERE OVER THE GREAT SALT LAKE DESERT, 27 MILES AWAY FROM WENDOVER ENEMY AIR FORCE - TOOELE COUNTY, UTAH:

Patrick continued flying into the enemy artillery positions, engaging them and causing great losses in their ranks, decreasing their firepower, though they remained strong in numbers.

He heard the frantic distress call from one of his pilots and answered, "What is your position? Heading over to offer support! Hang on just a little longer!"

Patrick continued charging into the enemy position with little regard for his own life while enemy tracers flew past him. He continued engaging the enemy air and ground units in a desperate rush to save the life of one of his pilots before he became another casualty, and found himself pursuing the enemy gunship that trailed one of his pilots. He greeted it with extreme prejudice until it burst into flames, falling out of the skies in smoke and flame, crashing and burning near the enemy positions.

The pilot exhaled a sigh of relief, and said, "That was close. Thanks for saving my ass."

"Don't thank me yet. We still have a lot of enemy units and are still outnumbered. We need to clear the skies of enemy gunships, and the rest of those ground units blocking our path, so we can provide support for our ground units. You got a name or moniker that you go by, pilot?"

"It's Gary Stevens, sir. And I just wanted to tell you that I've heard a lot about you, and it's an honor to be flying by your side. Your flying skills are truly legendary."

He had brown hair and sharp green eyes, nearing his mid-20s. Despite his young age and inexperience, he showed great promise in being a helicopter pilot, often looking to prove his worth in the field of air combat.

Patrick smiled and replied, "Thanks for the compliment. The name is Patrick O'Hara. I know you're afraid. We all are. But don't worry. You're doing great. We'll get through this."

"I know who you are, sir. You need no introduction. I know we'll get through this," Gary replied, and continued nervously, "What are your orders?"

"We're completely outnumbered by enemy forces and we need to bring them away from our fighters' positions while they remain distracted pursuing us. We bring them closer to our ground so we can ambush them, and feel free to engage if necessary. We need to eliminate as many of these units as possible and wear down the number of their units to punch a hole through their defenses until our planes get here. Now, I'm going to play the bait, and I need you and the others to come up from behind and provide cover fire. I need you to strike hard and fast. Now is your chance to save my ass. Now is your chance to save all our asses. Are you all ready?" Patrick asked, and quickly attacked the enemy position before they could have a chance to respond.

"Okay, here it goes," Patrick added, and thrusted himself further into the enemy position, destroying as many of the enemy units to lure the enemy gunships towards him. He played the decoy, drawing the enemy gunships away from their positions while the others waited to ambush them in their line of fire.

"I'll be your wingman, sir. You can't hold out against all of them alone," Karen added.

"State your name, pilot," Patrick responded.

"Santiago. Karen Santiago."

She was of Latin descent, with light skin and long black hair reaching down her waistline that she often tied up in a ball to the back of her head, of average height and slim build, and trying to conform to life as a gunship pilot in her first mission to hone her flying skills.

At her young age, she hoped to prove her prowess under extreme pressure to live up to being a great gunship pilot, someday in the ranks of Patrick's level.

"Okay, Santiago. You go left, I'll go right. Here we go."

The enemy fire erupted as Patrick flew his gunship over the enemy position, while the others waited close to their positions to spring their trap in ambushing the enemy gunships.

After destroying more of the enemy armored units and artillery guns, the enemy gunships pursued Patrick and Karen through the sea of enemy artillery positions in hot pursuit unleashing a volley of enemy ordinance.

Patrick heard the rounds from the enemy gunships tearing through the hull of his gunship, and shouted, "Taking enemy fire! How's it on your end, Santiago?"

Patrick heard the alarms in the cockpit blare loudly from a missile from an enemy gunship closing in, and deployed as his countermeasures, causing the enemy missile to fly into it and explode.

"Taking heavy fire, sir! Don't know how much I can hold on before I get back to our position!"

Karen continued to fly back to her position under heavy enemy fire, and heard the heavy bullets from the enemy gunship's cannons tearing through the hull of her gunship, causing a major fire in the cockpit.

"Just hold on a little longer! You're almost there!"

"I'm trying as much as I can, sir!" she answered, while she continued to lead the enemy gunships back to their positions, still under heavy fire, when it suddenly burst into flames, spinning out of control, crashing heavily in the desert.

"Santiago, are you reading me! Santiago, come in!" Patrick called out, only to receive no response.

Within moments after Karen crashed near Adam's position, the enemy gunships were quickly greeted with a sky filled with fire from the gunships and ground units, drastically decreasing their numbers, immediately turning the deadly clash of gunships in the enemies' favor.

09:32 HOURS. SOMEWHERE IN THE GREAT SALT LAKE DESERT, 27 MILES AWAY FROM WENDOVER ENEMY AIR FORCE BASE - TOOELE COUNTY, UTAH:

Although the enemy defenses has suffered a number of casualties from their combined firepower, they still continued attacking the freedom fighters' positions with the remainder of their long range guns and tanks, with the shrapnel from the debris scattering from the blast radius, landing near Robert's position, ripping through his helmet and lodging deeply into his skull. Robert was immediately rendered unconscious as he bled profusely from his head wound, the battered helmet falling from his head as he slumped over the tank's gunnery position.

Christopher ran towards Robert's position and pulled him from the tank's gunnery position. "Taylor's down!" he yelled. "Sustained massive trauma to the head and we need to contain the bleeding!" He applied pressure on Robert's head wound.

"How's he doing?" Adam asked frantically.

"He's losing a lot of blood, and completely unresponsive," Christopher replied.

Adam grabbed one of the soldiers by her shirt and asked, "What's your name?"

"Amanda Spencer!" she answered, looking at the massive trauma of Robert's head wound, with a look of total franticness on her face.

"I need you to take Taylor's place! I need you to man those guns!"

"Yes, sir!" she replied.

"I see more enemy gunships closing in on our positions!" James yelled, while he peeped through his binoculars.

"Man all guns and prepare for assault! And get Taylor to a safe position!" Eric called out.

The enemy gunships were within range of their position, and were quickly ambushed by Patrick's smaller group and the ground forces. They immediately began inflicting heavy losses.

Moments passed as Karen lay unconscious for a moment in the confines of her burning gunship, and suddenly regained consciousness, dazed and confused from the fall, looking all around her. She remained strapped in the cockpit in the haze of the thick, black smoke. She tried to radio her status to Patrick, only to receive no response.

She watched her palms covered in blood from a piece of metal that impaled her deeply in the leg.

She looked at the radio and saw that it had been badly damaged from the attack. Karen began punching the shattered canopy, trying to fight her way out of her dilapidated gunship.

She slowly crawled out, and looked around the desert, trying to get the sense of where she was. She saw the towering columns of smoke rising from both sides, when the sudden deafening roar of artillery fire exploding into one side of the defensive lines got her attention, followed by an exchange from the other front, causing her the mental debate - which side was her ally, and which side was foe?

She looked in her binoculars and seeing the dilapidated transports that carried the wounded, suddenly realized which side she was on. She turned back for a brief moment, glancing at the enemy defensive lines, seeing the destruction that they had inflicted on the enemy forces. The cost of their success was dear. She saw clouds of dust rising from a formation of enemy tanks that continued closing in, and said softly, "Oh no."

As Karen stood in the middle of the opposing side, she began to make a run to her allies as quickly as she could, while ordinance from both sides flew over her position.

Steven looked through the lens of his binoculars and saw someone running to their positions and shouted, "General West, we have incoming! Someone is heading to our position!"

"Who is it?" he asked.

"I don't know," he answered, shrugging his shoulders, and continued, "I think it's the gunship pilot who crashed, sir! And it looks like she's limping! I think she may be wounded from the crash! And we still have enemy tanks closing in on our positions behind her! If she doesn't get here fast, she will be captured - or worse!"

"O'Hara, how's your squad holding up?" Adam said loudly.

09:53 HOURS. SOMEWHERE OVER THE GREAT SALT LAKE DESERT, 27 MILES AWAY FROM WENDOVER ENEMY AIR FORCE BASE - TOOELE COUNTY, UTAH:

"Trying to clean up whatever enemy units left! But there's so many! They're still not letting up!" Patrick answered, with an enemy gunship locked into his sights. He unleashed a lethal barrage of heavy rounds from his gunship's mounted cannons until it burst into flames, impacting the desert sands with great force.

09:55 HOURS. SOMEWHERE IN THE GREAT SALT LAKE DESERT, 27 MILES AWAY FROM WENDOVER ENEMY AIR FORCE BASE - TOOELE COUNTY, UTAH:

"We still have ground units heading our way and I don't know how long we can hold!" Eric said loudly.

09:59 HOURS. SOMEWHERE OVER THE GREAT SALT LAKE DESERT, 27 MILES AWAY FROM WENDOVER ENEMY AIR FORCE BASE - TOOELE COUNTY, UTAH:

"Heading to your position and moving to engage all enemy air and ground units! All gunships - clear the area! Moving in to engage!" Dillon said over the radio.

"Read you loud and clear!" Patrick answered, as he and the others retreated to a safer distance, waiting for their planes to unleash total destruction on the enemy defensive lines.

As Dillon flew over the enemy gunships' position, with his plane, causing a giant vacuum, he caused them to swivel out of control, falling on the desert's barren tundra, and flew straight into the clouds, as the enemy forces greeted them with a thick volley of anti-aircraft fire. He skillfully maneuvered in the skies, avoiding fire.

10:04 HOURS. SOMEWHERE IN THE GREAT SALT LAKE DESERT, 27 MILES AWAY FROM WENDOVER ENEMY AIR FORCE BASE - TOOELE COUNTY, UTAH:

As Karen continued to limp towards the freedom fighters' position, she paused for a brief moment, hearing the roaring engines of a lone fighter plane making its strafing run towards the enemy position from the skies, and saw the pilots while they were trapped in their cockpits. They continued to swivel out of control, crashing and burning in the desert all at once, while Patrick and the rest of his squad continued to watch from a safe distance.

"I'd hate to be one of those enemy pilots right about now!" Ahmad said to himself, after seeing the group of enemy gunships slamming to the desert floor.

"Still not the time to celebrate yet! We still have incoming! And pray our planes have enough ordinance left!" Adam called out.

Within a brief moment, a giant wall of red flame blanketed the bulk of the enemy ground armored units, completely ceasing their attacks, causing the entire ground to tremble uncontrollably, while the lone fighter jet flew into the skies, the sounds of roaring engines fading as it vanished in the distance into the clouds.

The remainder of the planes followed over the enemy ground position, deploying their ordinance, causing another giant wall of flame, blanketing the entire enemy position for good measure. They made certain that the entire enemy position was completely silenced, allowing them safe passage to their base.

Though the bulk of the enemy forces were wiped out after the bombing, the remainder of the enemy artillery guns from a determined enemy continued pounding their positions, intending to carry out their mission to the very end.

Karen witnessed the entire scene in awe, while she continued to Adam's position with the shard still in her leg, and laid on the parched sands of the desert, after being hampered by the pain, and struggled to get back up. She continued towards Adam's position until she arrived safely, only to be greeted with a number of rifles pointing to her face.

"State your name and rank, soldier! Who are you?" Adam said firmly.

"Karen Santiago! One of Captain O'Hara's pilots, sir! Was shot down bringing the enemy gunships to our position!" she answered frantically, with her hands up.

They lowered their guns and wrapped her leg wound with fresh gauze, and searched through the wreckage that carried all their wounded.

"All enemy armored units destroyed! But those guns are still active! We can't advance unless we take out the rest of those guns!" Eric shouted.

"What's Taylor's status?" Adam yelled.

"He's still bleeding badly and we can't contain it. He's still totally unresponsive from the shock of the impact, sir," Steven answered.

"We can't leave him outside! Get him inside one of our armored units! Perez, you provide the assist!" Adam called out.

"Yes, sir!" she yelled, climbing from her tank's gunnery position.

The artillery continued to assault their positions. While they paused for a brief moment, they loaded Robert's body in the steel facade of the tank. He remained unconscious from the massive trauma his head sustained from the shrapnel that tore through his helmet.

An enemy shell exploded into Karen's crashed gunship, causing its stockpile of ordinance that still remained intact from the fall to explode, maximizing the explosion, violently scattering shrapnel and debris in all directions with violent force, ricocheting through the remaining armored units in Adam's position, causing them to scramble for cover.

Adam got up and shouted, "Is anyone hurt?"

"Spencer's down, sir! She's impaled by shrapnel from the blast, sir," Christopher said, frantically pulling her from the tank's gunnery position.

Amanda laid on the desert sands, gasping for breath from the large piece of shrapnel that sliced deeply into her chest.

"We have soldiers down, and we're still being pummeled by enemy guns! We need to load our wounded into the tanks, but we need you to take out the rest of those guns!" Adam yelled over the radio.

10:15 HOURS. SOMEWHERE OVER THE GREAT SALT LAKE, 27 MILES AWAY FROM WENDOVER ENEMY AIR FORCE BASE - TOOELE COUNTY, UTAH:

"Heading to the enemy artillery position for another run," Dillon answered.

10:18 HOURS. SOMEWHERE IN THE GREAT SALT LAKE DESERT, 27 MILES AWAY FROM WENDOVER ENEMY AIR FORCE BASE - TOOELE COUNTY, UTAH:

Ahmad slowly and gently pulled the chunk of shrapnel from Amanda's chest, applying pressure on it to try and stop the bleeding. "Hold on! You'll be fine!" Ahmad said.

Amanda grabbed Ahmad by his clothes, her hands soaked with blood, grabbing it tightly, spurting blood into his face, while blood oozed at the edge of her lips, then suddenly slipped into unconsciousness, a lifeless gaze on her face.

"Lieutenant Taylor has been loaded safely into the tank, sir!" Lena yelled, through the constant roar of artillery shells that rained on their position, when an enemy shell came from the skies, exploding into the tank's gunnery position, where Lena manned the tank's heavy guns, completely placing the tank's gunnery position out of commission.

Eric ran over to the severely wounded gunner and pulled her out of the machine gun position, and saw that it was Lena who had been fatally wounded and yelled, "Shit! Perez is down!"

The other young soldiers watched in horror, at the injuries that she had sustained, with her face and body burnt and torn beyond recognition, her innards falling out. She grabbed onto her abdomen with both her hands, trying to keep them intact inside, clinging onto whatever life she had left, while it quickly slipped away from her.

Their eyes drowned in their tears, and frantic emotions filled their faces, at the macabre sight that laid before them, knowing that none of them would have succumbed to such a gruesome fate.

A second enemy shell exploded through the tank's burning hull, knocking them off their feet, and caused a look of concern on Adam's face. He knew that Robert was trapped inside, and had met the same fate as Lena, and said softly, "No. We lost Taylor. This can't be."

Lena soon succumbed to her fate, looking into Eric's eyes with a lifeless gaze, like many others before who had met their untimely demise, peering at the vast ocean of blue skies. Ahmad slowly closed her eyes, and gently laid her down on the scorching desert sands, with much deserved dignity, in dying a soldier's death in the line of battle.

"Keep firing!" Adam yelled. "Or it will be the rest of us! There's nothing that we can do for them, now! This is General West to flight leader! Requesting more fighter support! The enemy guns are still active, and we're still taking heavy losses! Taylor and Perez are down! I repeat! Taylor and Perez are down! And we're sustaining more casualties and need air support! We need you to take out those guns, or we will suffer total casualties!"

Despite the heavy losses, they continued to hold their ground against the enemy artillery position, with whatever long range guns they had left.

"How is your ordinance holding up, pilot?" Adam asked, breaking the silence.

10:24 HOURS. SOMEWHERE OVER THE GREAT LAKE DESERT, 27 MILES AWAY FROM WENDOVER ENEMY AIR FORCE BASE - TOOELE COUNTY, UTAH:

Dillon and the remainder of his squadron flew into the enemy artillery position and were instantly greeted by countless volleys of enemy ground fire.

They heard the roar of jet engines closing on their positions, on their final strafing run to silence the enemy guns

"The only ordinance that we have left are just a few air to ground missiles, some machine guns, and just the bullets in our side arms. But, they should be enough to silence these guns once and for all," he answered while he looked down at Adam's position, from the view of his cockpit, seeing the destruction the enemy had wrought upon them.

A bright flash of light filled his cockpit, followed by the frantic radio chatter of one of his wingmen shot down from enemy fire, quickly descending to the surface, crashing and burning near the enemy position. "Just lost another one!"

He steadied his plane while it shuddered from the thick wall of flak and anti-aircraft fire, tearing through its fuselage, while he maintained his course towards the enemy position, and quickly deployed his ordinance, with the other planes in close succession.

10:27 HOURS. SOMEWHERE IN THE GREAT SALT LAKE, 27 MILES AWAY FROM WENDOVER ENEMY AIR FORCE BASE - TOOELE COUNTY, UTAH:

The ground trembled from the explosion as a giant wall of flame quickly swept through the remainder of the enemy artillery positions, this time completely silencing their positions.

They remained fixated from a safe distance from the artillery positions, staring quietly at the towering walls of flames that devoured everyone and everything along its path, leaving behind an eerie calm that suddenly swept over the desert. Only the crackling flames broke the silence, like they had seen so many times before.

The battle was grueling and though they had won the round, the price they paid for the cost of their victory was heavy, leaving many wounded and even more dead in its wake, as the cycle of war continued to repeat itself.

"What do we do now, General?" Eric asked.

"We load as many of our troops on our helicopters and transport as we can. We head for the outpost in the mountains. Our base is too far away. And from there, we can use more of our resources, and have them airlifted to our base, so they can get proper medical attention. Honor the fallen, since there is nothing we can do for them," Adam replied, looking at the smoke that rose high into the morning skies from the enemy position, as they gained more ground from the wreckage.

They arrived at the wreckage of the enemy artillery position that once wreaked havoc on their position, now silenced, the corpses of countless enemy soldiers charred and dismembered from their barrage of ordinance. The crackling tongues of flames danced on their bodies. The fighters slowly walked through the wreckage, carefully investigating it.

The young and inexperienced soldiers continued to watch the grisly sight with horror and awe, turning their gazes away at how so many had succumbed.

"This is what war is all about. It's ugly and unsettling. There's no place for the faint of heart. This is the nature of what we do, when you see it up close. Welcome to our world. It's either us or them, Yamaguchi," Christopher said to Steven.

"E-vac is ready, sir," Eric said to Adam.

"Okay. We're done here. We can leave enough of the bloodshed for another day. Enough have died for today," Adam said softly.

"Can't there be another way to settle this, General West?" Tiara asked.

"There are no negotiations in this kind of theater. It's either you're one of them or one of us. No gray area. No in-between. Either way, it comes down to making a choice, because in a war, atrocities are inevitable, whether in the name of tyranny or freedom. Death is the only way out - for you, for me, for any of us. This is one of these things that none of us can get used to. I'm afraid that no one is exempt."

"Should the gunships stay until the evacuation comes, sir?" Steven asked.

"Yes. Get on the radio and tell them to keep an eye out until all our wounded have been evacuated. I'll stay back, to make sure that all our wounded get out," Adam responded, in a distant manner.

Eric placed his hand on Adams's shoulder, and said, "We've taken as many wounded as we can. There're more Blackhawks en-route to this position."

"Based on these circumstances, we don't have much of a choice. It can't be helped," Adam replied.

"He was one of us. We'll miss him too, General," Christopher said, placing his hand on Adam's shoulder.

"We'll stay with you," Ahmad added.

"The choice is yours to do so, as you so choose. It doesn't matter now," Adam said softly.

They heard the squawking of countless birds. Birds of prey circled high above their positions, ready to feast on the corpses that remained sprawled on the battlefield, as the final group of Blackhawk helicopters arrived to carry the rest of their wounded back to the outpost.

They remained hovering over the decimated enemy position, watching the gruesome spectacle of the corpses of enemy soldiers that laid in the desert, charred, dismembered, and mangled, bound to eternal peaceful slumber, amidst all the wreckage and flames. They moved on to circle over Adam's position, where they made their last stand, against the larger number of the enemy forces, silently paying their respects, and loaded the rest of their wounded to be transported to their outpost for treatment.

Adam boarded the helicopter, and sat quietly in his seat, in deep contemplation. He watched many of his soldiers, seasoned and inexperienced alike, meet their demise through a war that consumed the entire nation, shifting his gaze to the tank, where Robert's body remained trapped in its burning hull, while they headed back to base. As the distance grew further between them, he said, "It was an honor, my friend. It truly was."

11:32 HOURS. SECRET FREEDOM FIGHTER OUTPOST. SOMEWHERE NEAR THE DINOSAUR NATURAL MONUMENTS, 272.4 MILES AWAY FROM HILL FREEDOM FIGHTER AIR FORCE BASE, UTAH:

A number of soldiers went to and from the river gathering drinking water in large quantities to keep their bodies hydrated from the unforgiving temperature that plagued the desert, while the medical crew continued their feverish attempts to tend to all their wounded.

The freedom fighters moved through the compound, with the rest of the wounded carrying them to their makeshift infirmaries in the unforgiving wasteland, offloading the rest of the fresh batch of wounded that arrived on the Blackhawks from the battlefield.

Adam slowly walked out of the helicopter, and walked past Karen and the rest of his lieutenants towards his quarters, with a heavy heart of losing another one from his unit.

Karen ran towards Adam and called out softly, "General West."

"What's on your mind, pilot?" he asked.

"I'm so sorry for what happened to your friend. I felt like this was my fault, sir. I know how much he meant to you in the war effort. When I crashed, there was still ordinance on my gunship. Maybe these soldiers would still be alive if I had made use of all of them," she said.

"None of this is your fault, Santiago. We're at war, and this line of work has no respect for any one of us. It wasn't the unused ordinance on your gunship that caused us to lose Robert. It was the long-range guns that continued to pound our positions every chance they got. What happened to Robert could've happened to any one of us, as you can see with all the dead and wounded in the base. You don't want your wound getting infected. Go to the infirmary and get your leg checked."

"Okay, General West," she said softly, and made her way towards one of the tents for medical attention. She unwrapped the bloody cloth, dropping it to the ground, and began digging into the wound with the hunter knife that she always carried on her person, vigorously searching for the shrapnel that impaled her.

One of the medics ran over to her, grabbing her hand and said, "Without the proper tools, you're creating a crater from a pond, young lady. God knows where this knife has been. Don't want that getting infected, or you won't be able to fly your gunship ever again, at all. I may not be on Dr. Weaver's level, but it doesn't take much to see signs of infection that we may have to amputate."

"I'm no stranger to pain," she said, pausing, instantly drawn to the young medic, searching for his nametag on his uniform.

"It's Thompson. Brian Thompson. But you'll just get that wound infected if you continue, uhh," Brian said searching for her name on her nametag.

"Santiago. It's Karen Santiago. You could've just asked, you know," Karen said, looking into his eyes, and continued, "In a time like this, you're trying to sweep me off my feet, huh?"

"Sounded like a good idea at the time," he said.

"You men are so typical."

"Could you blame me?" he asked.

"I guess not," she said.

"Seeing who's in front of me gives me the perfect incentive to perform such a task," he said.

"Aren't you afraid that I may be a bit feisty? We Latina women pack quite a punch," she said.

"Well, we need as many as we can get, especially for the war effort."

"Good point."

"And with that being said, I need to take you deeper inside, so I can properly administer treatment for your leg wound. So, that means that I may literally have to sweep you off your feet," he said, carrying Karen in the operating section for treatment.

"Well, you just had to say so. You didn't have to use my injury as an excuse," she said.

"I hope to get my chance soon enough."

"Who knows?" she said.

"I'll definitely be looking forward to it," he said, walking into the infirmary to tend to her wound.

12:17 HOURS. SOMEWHERE IN THE GREAT SALT LAKE. 27 MILES AWAY FROM WENDOVER ENEMY AIR FORCE BASE - TOOELE COUNTY, UTAH:

Hours after the war had ended in the desert, Robert slowly woke from unconsciousness, completely confused about his whereabouts, looking at the dark confines of the dilapidated armored unit that remained burning from the last enemy shell that plunged into it. Slowly and painfully, he staggered into the gunner's chair, with the cloth that wrapped around his head wound drenched in his blood, trickling down his face.

He peered through the tank's scope, seeing that the battlefield had been completely deserted, and climbed out the crippled unit, dragging his weary body to its top into the gunnery position. He fell onto the unforgiving tundra from the excruciating pain from the head wound, and remained still for a brief moment as he sat on the parched earth, trying to gather whatever strength he had left.

He looked back at the enemy position, seeing that it was completely blanketed in smoke and flame, and laid on his back motionless from his waning strength. He looked at the vultures feasting on the corpses of the dead, while more circled the skies, and slowly lifted his body, falling to his knees. He saw Lena's remains, her hands clutching her innards, sand tumbled onto one of the dilapidated transports, and grabbed one of the radios. He said softly, as he tried to gather his strength, "Is anybody receiving me? Over?"

12:24 HOURS. SECRET FREEDOM FIGHTER OUTPOST. SOMEWHERE NEAR THE DINOSAUR NATURAL MONUMENTS. 272.4 MILES AWAY FROM HILL FREEDOM FIGHTER AIR FORCE BASE, UTAH:

Back at the outpost, Karen sat in the infirmary, as Brian carefully removed the piece of shrapnel from her leg, and administered antibiotics, sanitizing the wound.

She heard the distress call filled with static from the radio on the wooden table next to her, as she sat on the bed, realizing it was Robert's voice. She quickly grabbed it and limped out the infirmary towards Adam's quarters, with her hasty departure leaving a baffled look on Brian's face.

He shook his head with a hint of disappointment and said, "Just when we were getting to know each other."

She quickly made her way into Adam's quarters, and called out, "General West, I have some good news!"

"What is it?" Adam asked with a hint of surprise.

She handed him the radio in excitement, and said, "Someone's still alive from our last position. I think it's Lieutenant Taylor, sir."

He quickly grabbed the radio and answered excitedly, "Are you sure?"

"Yes, I'm sure it's him," she said, when Christopher, and a number of the other freedom fighters made their way into his quarters to tell him the news.

"We're having a chopper prepped so we can go to his location and have him extracted as we speak, sir," James added.

"Wait for my order. It might be a trap. I can't believe he's still alive," Adam said, as the radio static of Robert's voice filled his quarters. The other soldiers looked on eagerly to proceed with the rescue mission.

He held the radio and said, "This is General West. Taylor is that you?"

12:28 HOURS. SOMEWHERE IN THE GREAT SALT LAKE. 27 MILES AWAY FROM WENDOVER ENEMY AIR FORCE BASE - TOOELE COUNTY, UTAH:

"Yes, it's me, and I need a ride back to base. I'm still bleeding from my wound, and I'm being circled by vultures, and the rest are feeding on the bodies. My God, there are so many of them," Robert said, looking at the skies, watching the vultures continue to circle.

12:30 HOURS. SECRET FREEDOM FIGHTER OUTPOST. SOMEWHERE NEAR THE DINOSAUR NATURAL MONUMENTS. 272.4 MILES AWAY FROM HILL FREEDOM FIGHTER AIR FORCE BASE, UTAH:

"Are you the only survivor at your location?" Adam asked.

12:31 HOURS. SOMEWHERE IN THE GREAT SALT LAKE. 27 MILES AWAY FROM WENDOVER ENEMY AIR FORCE BASE - TOOLE COUNTY, UTAH:

"Yes. Everybody else is…" Robert said, not having the right words to respond, and continued, "Well, you were there. You should know."

12:32 HOURS. SECRET FREEDOM FIGHTER OUTPOST. SOMEWHERE NEAR THE DINOSAUR NATURAL MONUMENTS. 272.4 MILES AWAY FROM HILL FREEDOM FIGHTER AIR FORCE BASE, UTAH:

"Okay Taylor, sit tight. We're having a Blackhawk prepped, and ready to come get you. Just hold on a little longer," Adam said, with a hint of relief that Robert was still alive.

12:34 HOURS. SOMEWHERE IN THE GREAT SALT LAKE. 27 MILES AWAY FROM WENDOVER ENEMY AIR FORCE BASE - TOOELE COUNTY, UTAH:

"Do I have a choice?" Robert asked, keeping his gaze to the skies, with the scent of death attracting more vultures to corpses that lay sprawled on the battlefield.

12:32 HOURS. SECRET FREEDOM FIGHTER OUTPOST. SOMEWHERE NEAR THE DINOSAUR NATURAL MONUMENTS. 272.4 MILES AWAY FROM HILL FREEDOM FIGHTER AIR FORCE BASE, UTAH:

"Sure you do. You can hold on for a bit and wait to be evacuated from the shithole where you are, if you really want to, or you can stay there and be food for the birds, or target practice for the enemy. So if I were you, I'd keep my ass sitting tight where you are. Just you hold on. We're coming," Adam replied, with a sigh of relief.

12:34 HOURS. SOMEWHERE IN THE GREAT SALT LAKE. 27 MILES AWAY FROM WENDOVER ENEMY AIR FORCE BASE - TOOELE COUNTY, UTAH:

As Robert remained seated on the ground in the shade of the dilapidated transport, his back leaned firmly towards it, and his strength waning awaiting evacuation, he heard the engines of a small convoy of enemy transports heading towards his position.

He picked up the radio and said, "I see a group of transports approaching my position. And they're closing in fast. I'll keep an open channel so you can hear everything."

12:35 HOURS. SECRET FREEDOM FIGHTER OUTPOST. SOMEWHERE NEAR THE DINOSAUR NATURAL MONUMENTS. 272.4 MILES AWAY FROM HILL FREEDOM FIGHTER AIR FORCE BASE, UTAH:

Adam's face creased with awe, and he asked, "Other than Taylor, do we have any other personnel from our last position?"

"No, sir. We evacuated all of our wounded on our transports. It seems that Lieutenant Taylor is the only one who's alive at that location," Tiara said.

"My God, they found him. We may need to hold back on that chopper," Adam said, watching the look of concern on their faces, knowing that Robert was about to be intercepted by the enemy forces, listening helplessly on the opened channel, knowing of what was about to come to pass.

12:36 HOURS. SOMEWHERE IN THE GREAT SALT LAKE. 27 MILES AWAY FROM WENDOVER ENEMY AIR FORCE BASE - TOOELE COUNTY, UTAH:

Robert remained seated helpless on the ground, with his back firmly tucked against the crippled transport, watching the enemy transports drawing closer, then stopped.

Enemy soldiers drew nearer towards him, while they looked all around the battle area, searching for any signs of life amidst all the wreckage, until they stumbled upon him, drenched in blood from his head wound, clinging on to whatever strength he had left.

He looked up and saw the familiar face of someone he once knew. He showed a weak smile and said, "It's been a long time, Lieutenant."

12:40 HOURS. SECRET FREEDOM FIGHTER OUTPOST. SOMEWHERE NEAR THE DINOSAUR NATURAL MONUMENTS. 272.4 MILES AWAY FROM HILL FREEDOM FIGHTER AIR FORCE BASE, UTAH:

The looks on the soldiers' faces at base suddenly creased with more concern, knowing that Robert would not be taken prisoner by the enemy forces.

"We're still waiting for your orders, General," Tiara said softly to Adam.

"Does it matter now? We won't get there fast enough. By the time we get there, he'll already be dead. He's already dead. He should've died from that explosion. Damn him for still being alive," Adam said, with a look of concern on his face, while he listened to the radio.

12:42 HOURS. SOMEWHERE IN THE GREAT SALT LAKE. 27 MILES AWAY FROM WENDOVER ENEMY AIR FORCE BASE - TOOELE COUNTY, UTAH:

The enemy soldier's face remained without emotion. His eyes remained cold and calculating, showing no signs of remorse towards the wounded soldier who served with him on many of his missions in his past life - missions that had been completely purged from his memory.

He pulled out his sidearm from his holster, and pointed it at Robert's face. He paused for a brief moment, still not exhibiting any signs of remorse.

"Why don't we find out what he knows? He's worth more to us alive than dead. Don't do this. Please," Jason said, appealing to the assassin to save Robert's life.

"Everyone dies, soldier. I signed up knowing that someday, my time will come. And today, mine has. It's just a matter of time before yours does, too. All of you," Jason said, smiling, knowing that he was about to meet his demise, and added, "I'm dying. Go ahead, Lieutenant, grant me a quick mercy. Give me a soldier's death and help ease my suffering, like you did Alvarez and Collins. I can go away now knowing what it was like to walk into the light, and for that, I have no regrets. It was a great honor to have served with you, and to have a soldier's death, on the field, my friend. Until we meet again."

"Please Lieutenant," Jason continued, begging, trying to persuade the assassin to spare Robert's life, and was startled when the clamor of a gunshot rang throughout the desert, ending Robert's life, instantly stopping the transmission. Robert's body slumped onto the parched earth of the unforgiving tundra, followed by more shots, the assassin making certain that he had completed his task.

12:45 HOURS. SECRET FREEDOM FIGHTER OUTPOST. SOMEWHERE NEAR THE DINOSAUR NATURAL MONUMENTS. 272.4 MILES AWAY FROM HILL FREEDOM FIGHTER AIR FORCE BASE, UTAH:

Adam and all the others who stood next to him in his quarters listened helplessly at Robert speaking his last words to his nemesis, and were startled hearing the gunshot that ended his life, cutting off the transmission. "There'll no longer be an evacuation," Adam said. "Get all the Blackhawks you can find and bring all their bodies home. They don't deserve to be food for these vultures feeding on them. They deserve to have proper goodbyes with honor. It's the least we can do for him, and all the others."

"Was that him again? The one who murdered Lieutenant Alvarez and Collins? Was that him?" Tiara asked, with a worried look on her face.

"Yes. And the ghost still comes back to torment us," Adam said, slumping backwards on his chair.

"I'm so sorry, General West," she replied.

The other soldiers remained in shock after hearing the chilling last moments of Robert's life, looking at each other in disbelief, knowing that another one of their own had met their demise at the hand of the enemy.

12:51 HOURS. SOMEWHERE IN THE GREAT SALT LAKE. 27 MILES AWAY FROM WENDOVER ENEMY AIR FORCE BASE - TOOELE COUNTY, UTAH:

The soldier bowed his head in remorse as the assassin walked past him towards the group of transport. He slid into the driver's seat, with his usual straight face void of remorse or reasoning.

Jason exhaled sharply and walked towards the vehicle where he sat, and glanced at the assassin for a brief moment, noticing the usual the calmness in his demeanor, his gaze fixed on the endless patch of desert in front of him, and turned on the ignition, making their way to their base.

The war continues…

CHAPTER 5: OPERATION BANSHEE

10:17 HOURS. SOMEWHERE IN THE PAINTED DESERT. 170 MILES FROM MILES FROM MONUMENT VALLEY - CAMERON, ARIZONA:

The year is 2029. Four years have passed since "The Great Fall of Genesis."

The heat from the morning sun burned brightly over the unforgiving tundra of the rainbow-colored canyons of the Painted Desert, flushing out its true splendor.

A mountain lion slowly traversed through the canyons high above, tending after her cubs, suddenly alarmed by the sounds that her acute senses hearing picked up from a far distance.

A roadrunner gripped a rattlesnake firmly within its razor-sharp talons, squeezing onto its long, slender body, until it became motionless, swallowing it whole and quickly scampering away deeper into the heart of the desert.

A prairie dog and the rest of her pups happily congregated out of their burrow, and were alarmed, hearing the sounds from a distance and quickly tunneling back into their burrow.

A gray fox traversed through the desert with a rodent trapped in its jaws, suddenly stopped picking up sounds from its acute senses of movement from afar, and quickly scampered to safety.

A pack of wild burros feeding on the shrubs that sprouted defiantly in the sands of the unforgiving tundra, were suddenly alarmed and ran away from where they grazed, braying.

A flock of black necked stilts looking for food in the river that flowed through the canyon took flight together.

A group of freedom fighter scouts continued making their way to their secret outpost found deep within the heart of the desert through the sweltering heat of the merciless tundra and stopped at the salt river to catch their breaths, and quench their thirst, binging on their water supplies after their long and grueling journey.

One of the soldiers walked towards the river's edge, unzipped his trousers and began to urinate, expressing a sigh of relief, and washed his hands and face, sprinkling water all over his face and body.

He looked to the skies and felt the ground vibrating under his feet, growing stronger each passing moment. He looked in the direction of the noise, hearing the roaring of jet engines heading towards their positions and was ambushed by a lethal volley of air-to-ground fire from enemy jet fighters, heading towards Adam's position. Their transports suddenly burst into flames.

Within moments, the entire group of scouts en-route to the outpost were lying dead from the enemy planes' awesome fire power.

The enemy planes flew over their position for another strafing run, and saw the amount of destruction that had consumed the desert in such a short period of time in search of any survivors. They continued their way towards Adam's position to capture it with a blitzkrieg attack of their own.

After the enemy planes swept over their position in a single assault, a female soldier remained lying on the ground, amidst all the burning wreckage and corpses of the other soldiers, charred, and torn to pieces from the blast. She looked all around her, feeling lost and completely disoriented, struggling to make sense of the situation that had befallen her, while she laid on the desert floor.

She looked at her hands and saw they were badly burnt and disfigured by all the shrapnel from the explosion, with a number of her fingers missing from the force of the blast.

She tried standing up and screamed in pain from her stomach wound and looked down at her feet, gazing in disbelief. Her torso was completely separated from the rest of her body a few feet away, her intestines sprawled across the desert sands, with the rest of her blood slowly oozing from her body. She slowly began to lose her senses as the roar from the enemy planes' engines slowly faded in the distance. She slowly began to pass, taking her last breaths, until she finally succumbed to the extent of her injuries.

10:20 HOURS. SECRET FREEDOM FIGHTER OUTPOST. SOMEWHERE IN THE PAINTED DESERT, MORE THAN 30 MILES FROM THE HUBBELL TRADING POST NATIONAL HISTORY SITE - CAMERON, ARIZONA:

Adam abruptly woke from his sleep, like he had suffered a bad dream, and felt that something was greatly amiss.

James ran into his quarters and yelled, "We picked up enemy bogeys closing in on our positions, sir!"

"What about our reinforcements?" Adam asked.

"We lost the transmission somewhere in the desert. My gut tells me something went wrong. Maybe they were intercepted by the enemy forces, sir," James said.

"I thought I felt something was wrong. Okay, prepare for incoming enemy assault. Assume all defensive positions, and radio to our other base and call for air support," Adam answered.

"Yes, sir," James answered and ran out of the tent through the base to man his defensive position. He ran through the base yelling, "Enemy bogeys and ground units closing in! We're under attack! Assume all defensive positions!" causing the many soldiers in the outpost to scurry frantically to maintain their defensive lines from the oncoming enemy forces that converged on their positions.

10:21 HOURS. DAVIS MONTHAN FREEDOM FIGHTER AIR FORCE BASE - TUCSON. 148 MILES AWAY FROM LUKE ENEMY AIR FORCE BASE - PHOENIX, ARIZONA:

The call for air support had finally come, causing all of the ground crew and pilots to mobilize their fighter planes neatly arranged in rows throughout the base, along with dozens of gunships spearheaded by Patrick. They lifted from the base and moved in to engage the oncoming enemy ground units, while dozens of other pilots from Dillon's squadron quickly scurried to their planes under heavy enemy fire.

As dozens of gunships moved in to intercept the ground units, they were quickly swarmed by countless enemy helicopters, keeping them distracted while the enemy armored units continued to move in closer to their base.

Dillon boarded his plane, strapping himself in the cockpit after being armed and fueled, followed by a number of his wingmen, when they were swarmed by a group of enemy planes. Dillon shouted "It's a pincer attack! They're attacking on both fronts! Break and bring them within firing range of our ground troops for support! It's the only way we can decrease their numbers! This is flight leader to all available ground crew - assume all defensive positions to provide ground support! We'll be bringing all enemy craft into your firing range for assistance!"

As another one of his wingmen lifted off the runway, and just moments from taking flight, he was suddenly overcome by a volley of enemy fire. He burst into flames as he spun out of control, heading to the surface, exploding on impact.

Dillon heard the radio chatter from the pilot's frantic last words, while he remained strapped in his cockpit, before hearing the static on the other end of the transmission. He closed his eyes tightly, knowing that it could be him meeting his demise at any given moment.

A squad of enemy planes swarmed the base, intercepting whatever planes that remained as the ground troops continued to their valiant stand to provide ground support, giving their planes time to take off. They scored a few kills against the enemy, giving the other planes a chance to take flight against the enemy on the ground, severely damaging the base.

Within moments of the enemy planes' attacks on the base, the hangar erupted in a giant wall of flame, transforming into the infamous mushroom cloud that they had seen countless times before in many skirmishes past.

10:21 HOURS. SECRET FREEDOM FIGHTER OUTPOST. SOMEWHERE IN THE PAINTED DESERT. 61 MILES FROM THE HUBBELL TRADING POST NATIONAL HISTORY SITE - CAMERON, ARIZONA.

James ran back to Adam and said, "Just received news that another wave attacked our base back in Phoenix! It seems that our plans to pincer the enemy have backfired, sir!"

"Did you have time to send for support?" Adam asked.

"Yes, sir! But we still lost a lot of our planes during the assault! Captain Kim and a few other planes barely made it out alive!"

"What's the situation?" Adam called out.

"They're engaging the enemy as we speak! But it's uncertain that they'll hold out long enough to be on time and assist us with the evacuation!"

"What about the enemy ground forces?" Adam asked.

"They're still closing in! Most of our ordinance is still back at our base! It's just a matter of time before our stock is depleted from the outpost, sir! We have enough to hold out the enemy ground forces for now, and to buy us some more time at least until we evacuate!"

"How far are the ground forces?"

"A few miles and closing! Just a matter of time before they overrun our defenses and take our position!"

10:24 HOURS. SOMEWHERE OVER DAVIS MONTHAN FREEDOM FIGHTER AIR FORCE BASE - TUCSON, ARIZONA. 148 MILES AWAY FROM LUKE ENEMY AIR FORCE BASE, 341 MILES FROM SECRET FREEDOM FIGHTER OUTPOST IN THE PAINTED DESERT - CAMERON, ARIZONA:

As the battle for the skies continued, Dillon glanced from his cockpit and saw the hangar was completely destroyed. "Our hangar has been taken out by enemy forces!" he yelled. "We lost a lot of good men down there and it's up to us to protect what's left of the ground troops! All weapons hot! Break off and engage at will! To increase our firepower, bring all enemy planes in our ground troops' lines of sight! To all available gunships, our ground troops need immediate assistance! Head to their position and provide support! We'll hold out as long as we can, and try to keep the enemy fighters off your six!"

"Copy!" Patrick answered, as he flew towards Adam's position, spearheading his group of gunships.

They quickly broke from formation to split the enemy planes and weaken their numbers, bringing the enemy planes into the firing line of their ground forces.

After the enemy planes caused havoc, they broke off their attack and headed towards the outpost in the desert, where their ground troops continued their relentless assault on the freedom fighters.

Dillon and the other planes were in immediate pursuit. "They've broken off their assault and are heading towards General West's position!" Dillon said. "They're heading towards their base, and bring us in the firing line of their ground troops, since we handed them a few losses! Myself and a few others will keep them off the gunships! The rest of you, take out their hangars, fuel, ordinance, and whatever planes they may have on the ground for takeoff! We cannot allow them to take General West!"

10:42 HOURS. LUKE ENEMY AIR FORCE BASE, PHOENIX. 148 MILES AWAY FROM DAVIS MONTHAN FREEDOM FIGHTER AIR FORCE BASE - TUCSON, ARIZONA:

The smaller group of freedom fighter planes attacked the enemy base ferociously, engaging all their fuel depots, ordinance, and transports under a thick hail of enemy fire.

The thick shell of an air-to-ground missile penetrated the hull of the enemy hangar that contained a number of planes and ammunition, falling to the concrete floor of the hangar with a deafening thud, causing a number of enemy soldiers to flee for their lives.

Within seconds after the impact, the wide confines of the entire hangar was consumed by a towering wall of fire, consuming all in its deadly blast radius, dealing the enemy forces a severe blow.

Though the freedom fighters remained outnumbered, their morale hanging thin, they still fought valiantly against the enemy forces, drastically minimizing their effectiveness in air combat.

Despite the heavy losses, the enemy ground forces fought as bravely as they could to hold back the smaller wave of freedom fighters that fought through the heavy fog of anti-aircraft fire, when one of their planes was suddenly caught in the hail of bullets, crashing and burning in the base.

After the smaller group of planes had inflicted damage on the enemy positions, just as the enemy had done earlier, they made their hasty retreat to reinforce their ground troops that were pinned down by the enemy forces, engaging whatever enemy units they could find. After, they rendezvoused with Dillon and the other group of pilots in the constant struggle to attain air supremacy.

10:47 HOURS. SOMEWHERE OVER INTERSTATE 17. 5 MILES FROM THE TONITO NATIONAL FOREST, 129 MILES AWAY FROM THE SECRET FREEDOM FIGHTER OUTPOST, IN THE PAINTED DESERT - CAMERON, ARIZONA:

Karen heard the distress call and answered, "We're still engaging enemy gunships! Be there as soon as we can!"

"Okay, Santiago, here's the deal. We stay from a distance and take out as many of the enemy gunships as possible. When we bring down enough of their numbers, we move in to clean out the rest and provide support for General West. We use the same trick until it gets old," Patrick said.

"Ready whenever you are, sir," Karen answered.

"Okay, all weapons hot and engaged. Make every shot count. I don't have to remind you that it is imperative that General West has to make it out of that outpost alive," he said.

"Yes, sir," Karen answered.

The small group of gunships began hunting the larger number of enemy gunships from a distance, inflicting a number of casualties upon them and delaying them long enough from reaching Adam's position.

Karen and Gary watched the flaming wreckage of the enemy gunships plummet into the forest, setting it ablaze, drastically reducing the enemies' numbers and effectiveness.

"We've reduced their numbers drastically, sir. What's the next course of action?" Karen asked.

"The same thing we always do. Keep shooting them from the skies. But we need to act fast," Patrick answered.

"You're the most experienced pilot out of all of us, and General West needs you. I'll play the decoy. I'll draw them away from their course," Karen replied.

"Good idea, Santiago. And when we've worn down their numbers, I need you to stay on course and in one piece. Take out as many as you can and go and provide support to General West. I'll stay back and cover your rear in case any stragglers sneak up from behind you."

"Yes, sir. Understood," she said.

"If I can't take them down, the least I can do is draw them off. There's still too many of them. After you take out as many of those bastards as you can, make your way straight to General West's position, and don't look back. Am I clear?" Patrick said firmly.

"But there's still too many of them to handle by yourself, sir," Karen replied.

"You have your orders, Santiago. It's up to you now to protect General West at all costs. If anything happens to me, that means you're the new Dragonfly leader."

"Say again, Dragonfly leader," Karen said in disbelief, and added, "We need you. I need you. I can't do this by myself."

"I've been fighting all my life, so the ones like you wouldn't have to. At least, that was what I was hoping for, and look at how that turned out. My soul is weary from fighting all this conflict, and I think the time has come to pass the torch to someone else. I've been watching you for quite some time now, and you've shown great promise. More potential than I've ever seen. I know if I don't make it back today, you'll do General West and myself proud. And there's no doubt that I made a good choice in choosing you to be my successor. If I don't make it back, I just want you to know it's been a great honor to have had the pleasure of flying with you. Now, I don't want to spend all day getting teary-eyed bidding farewell to the rest of you, since we're running low on ordinance and fuel. So, it's up to us now, to make every shot count, head straight to General West's position, and don't look back."

"We'll be coming back. Just hold on as long as you can. I promise we won't let you down, sir," Karen replied, flying full speed ahead towards Adam's position, shooting down as many of the enemy gunships as she could find. Patrick stayed back to cover their rear, to guarantee them safe passage, until they had a clear path to their destination, watching them quickly vanish in the distance, as they made their desperate run towards Adam's position.

He resumed searching for any enemy stragglers, and broke radio silence once again and said, "Whatever you do, don't look back. Not even for me." He continued a relentless pursuit searching for enemy gunships, flying like he had a death wish, deliberately placing himself in the line of fire. He lined as many of the enemy in his sights, quickly deploying one lethal barrage after the next, wasting no time moving onto the next target, when he felt the shudder from a bombardment of enemy bullets riddling through the hull of his gunship, immediately damaging the guidance systems. His plane spun out of control from the enemy barrage, trailing a long line of smoke as it fell to the desert floor and he yelled, "I'm hit! I'm hit!"

10:52 HOURS. SOMEWHERE IN THE PAINTED DESERT. 40 MILES AWAY FROM THE SECRET FREEDOM FIGHTER OUTPOST - CAMERON, ARIZONA:

"Captain O'Hara, come in! Captain O'Hara!" Karen said loudly, with a look of franticness on her face.

10:53 HOURS. SOMEWHERE OVER THE PAINTED DESERT. 50 MILES AWAY FROM THE SECRET FREEDOM FIGHTER OUTPOST - CAMERON, ARIZONA:

"Don't worry about me! You have your orders, Santiago! It's up to you now! Protect General West at all costs!" he said, before crashing on the dry, parched earth of the desert that stretched past the forest with deafening clamor, snapping his shin bone and hitting his head, rendering him unconscious.

10:54 HOURS. SOMEWHERE OVER THE PAINTED DESERT. 38 MILES AWAY FROM THE SECRET FREEDOM FIGHTER OUTPOST - CAMERON, ARIZONA:

"We'll come back for you! I'll send some support your way!" she replied, waiting for a response from Patrick.

10:55 HOURS. SOMEWHERE IN THE PAINTED DESERT. 40 MILES AWAY FROM THE SECRET FREEDOM FIGHTER OUTPOST - CAMERON, ARIZONA:

Though the radio chatter sounded loudly over his headset, he remained unconscious.

10:56 HOURS. SOMEWHERE OVER THE PAINTED DESERT. 36 MILES AWAY FROM THE SECRET FREEDOM FIGHTER OUTPOST - CAMERON, ARIZONA:

"Captain O'Hara? Captain O'Hara, come in!" she said loudly, only to receive dead silence on the other end of the transmission. She feared the worst had happened to Patrick.

While they continued flying toward the freedom fighters' position, they picked up more enemy gunships in their sights and pounced upon them, delivering a hail of fire. Soon, a lot of enemy gunships burst into flames, falling out of the skies to the desert sands with a series of clamors reverberating through the vast tundra, causing the rest to disperse. Gary broke radio silence and said, "A few down. Many more to go."

"Keep it up, Santiago. All we have to do is make it to General West's position," Gary said, celebrating. "But there's so many of them."

"Then try locking on as many as you can simultaneously to save us some time!" Karen answered.

Gary locked on to another enemy unit and deployed his ordinance. He watched it burst in flames, swivel out of control, slamming into the burning desert, breaking into pieces, burning on impact.

After sustaining many casualties, the enemy gunships broke off their pursuit to evade their pursuers.

"They're breaking off! They know we're onto them!" Gary shouted.

"Choose your target, break off and engage! If any escape, it could be bad for us! We must clear the skies of all enemy gunships in order for the evacuation to succeed!" Karen ordered.

11:00 HOURS. SECRET FREEDOM FIGHTER OUTPOST. SOMEWHERE IN THE PAINTED DESERT, 61 MILES FROM THE HUBBELL TRADING POST NATIONAL HISTORY SITE - CAMERON, ARIZONA:

Adam looked to the skies and heard the engines of all the fighter planes engaging one another, unable to tell friend from foe.

He ran through a hail of enemy artillery that rained mercilessly on their positions, grabbed a radio and yelled, "flight leader, come in! I have a visual on your position! However, unable to distinguish friendly craft from foe! Give me a sign, over." He watched Dillon perform his signature barrel roll to distinguish friendly craft from the enemy.

11:02 HOURS. SOMEWHERE OVER THE SECRET FREEDOM FIGHTER OUTPOST IN THE PAINTED DESERT - CAMERON, ARIZONA:

"This is flight leader! What's your status?" Dillon replied, looking down from the view of his cockpit at all the destruction.

11:04 HOURS. SECRET FREEDOM FIGHTER OUTPOST. SOMEWHERE IN THE PAINTED DESERT, 61 MILES AWAY FROM THE HUBBELL TRADING POST NATIONAL HISTORY SITE - CAMERON, ARIZONA:

"Our base was under heavy attack! Our hands are full down here! We sustained a number of casualties, and lost most of our birds and pilots during the assault! We need air support so we can push them back!" Adam said loudly.

11:04 HOURS. SOMEWHERE OVER THE SECRET FREEDOM FIGHTER OUTPOST IN THE PAINTED DESERT - CAMERON, ARIZONA:

"We're still heavily outnumbered and don't know how long we can achieve air superiority! We're gonna need a miracle to clear the skies of the enemy forces! Our forces are spread thin, possibly beyond breaking point! We don't know how long we can hold, General! We're doing the best we can!"

11:04 HOURS. SECRET FREEDOM FIGHTER OUTPOST. SOMEWHERE IN THE PAINTED DESERT, 61 MILES AWAY FROM THE HUBBELL TRADING POST NATIONAL HISTORY SITE - CAMERON, ARIZONA:

"Bring them within our firing range so we can get you free to cover our retreat!" Adam answered.

11:06 HOURS. SOMEWHERE OVER THE SECRET FREEDOM FIGHTER OUTPOST IN THE PAINTED DESERT - CAMERON, ARIZONA:

"Trying to break free! We'll be there as soon as we can, General!"

11:09 HOURS. SECRET FREEDOM FIGHTER OUTPOST. SOMEWHERE IN THE PAINTED DESERT, 61 MILES AWAY FROM THE HUBBELL TRADING POST NATIONAL HISTORY SITE - CAMERON, ARIZONA:

"Yee, do you have a visual on enemy ground units?" Adam shouted.

"We have lots of armored units converging on our positions, and we need to counterattack, sir!"

"We have an unconfirmed number of enemy units converging on our position! Point all guns towards the oncoming ground units! We'll take whatever support you can give," Adam answered.

11:10 HOURS. SOMEWHERE OVER THE SECRET FREEDOM FIGHTER OUTPOST IN THE PAINTED DESERT - CAMERON, ARIZONA:

"Hold on! We'll be there as soon as we can!" Dillon answered.

11:11 HOURS. SECRET FREEDOM FIGHTER OUTPOST. SOMEWHERE IN THE PAINTED DESERT, 61 MILES AWAY FROM THE HUBBELL TRADING POST NATIONAL HISTORY SITE - CAMERON, ARIZONA:

The soldiers continued to run and man their defensive positions amidst the artillery that continued to rain upon them, causing mass confusion, and began their counterattack.

Steven looked through his binoculars and saw their counterattack was out of range. He yelled, "Our shells are hitting just outside the target, sir!"

"Get on the radio and relay the coordinates for our guns to counterattack! I'm counting on you!"

"Yes, sir!" Steven answered and began to relay the coordinates, inflicting casualties on the enemy ground units. "It's working!"

"Stay on that radio and keep on calling!"

Adam grabbed Tiara by her clothes and shouted, "You're a good shot! Lead a group of tanks, get into a blockade position, and provide as much defense as you could until our support gets here! We need all the defense we can get until we can evacuate!"

"Yes, sir!" she answered, when an enemy artillery round whistled through the skies, landing near their position, tossing them off their feet.

Adam opened his eyes and saw Ahmad, Christopher, and Eric standing over him, trying to revive him, as his gaze trembled from the force of the blast. He slowly recovered while they helped him back to his feet.

"You okay, General?" James asked.

"I'm fine," Adam answered weakly, still shaken from the shock from the blast. They ran over to Tiara, picking her up from the desert floor, completely dazed, tapping her face lightly to revive her, until she came to her senses.

As the volume of enemy artillery continued to intensify on their position, while enemy ground units moved in closer, they heard Steven crying in pain from the extent of wounds he suffered from the force of the blast.

They ran over to him and stared at the horror that greeted them, his body severely burnt from the force of the explosion.

Tiara stood in shock with her eyes wide open, watching Steven crying in pain from the injuries he sustained.

"Don't just stand there! Pull him out, Edwards!" Adam ordered.

Tiara ran over and grabbed him by his arm, trying to pull him out of harm's way, but only succeeded in stripping the very flesh from his arm, showing the frame of his bones, causing him to scream louder in excruciating pain.

She quickly released his arm and watched her palms, filled with the chunks of his charred flesh, confused with no sense of what other courses of action to take next.

Though Adam and the others were no stranger to the atrocities of war, they remained dumbfounded at the grisly sight that continued to face them, witnessing Steven's calamity.

Adam tried to show fortitude, yelling, "Let's get him out!"

They lifted him by the burnt and torn fibers of his clothes and carried him to another position just outside of firing range as quickly as they could, while he continued to show rapid signs of losing consciousness.

"What do we do now, sir? Our best spotter is down!" Christopher shouted.

Adam grabbed another soldier by his clothes and shouted, "Our spotter's down and we need someone to spot to hold off the enemy units long enough for air support, and for the rest of us to evacuate! Can you call the coordinates for our guns?"

The soldier nodded his head and answered nervously, "Yes."

"What's your name, soldier?" Adam asked.

"It's Reed! Anton Reed, sir!" he answered, watching Steven in pain from the grave injuries he suffered, slowly losing his fight to stay alive.

He had a tall and chiseled physique, reminiscent of how Marines were thought to look in the armed forces from their rigorous training, with short, wavy black hair, which he often groomed. He was pushing his late early 20s, and new to the addition of freedom fighters, still trying to transition into being a soldier after spending all his years in civilian life, coming straight from high school.

"Tiara, same plan! You're one of the best shooters that we have, so I want you to get in that armor, into a blockade position, and provide support! The rest of you - we're outnumbered by enemy planes, and we need to provide ground support for our planes when they get here, to help us repel the enemy forces!"

They continued to call in the coordinates on the enemy armored units, inflicting a few more casualties, wearing down their numbers.

Steven lay dying in Adam's arms, while more enemy shells continued to pound their positions. He grabbed Adam by his clothes with his charred hands, baring his teeth from the intense pain, and slowly loosened his grip, slipping into unconsciousness with a lifeless gaze.

Adam watched helplessly as Steven slipped into his final moments, and gently passed his hand on Steven's charred face, closing his eyes.

He ran over to Anton and asked, "What's the situation?"

"They're still coming in strong! We can't hold them back for too long, sir! They're just too many in numbers!"

Adam turned his attention towards another one of the soldiers on the artillery guns and asked, "What's your name, son?"

"Moscowitz! Jason Moscowitz, sir!"

"Okay, Moscowitz! You're the one keeping us alive right now! We may not be able to hold this base, but we can hold out long enough to evacuate all the remainder of our troops! Got it?"

"Yes, sir!" Jason answered nervously.

He had just transitioned into manhood, in his early 20s, with dirty blonde hair and stubbles growing on his face. He had an average build, and came straight from an Orthodox Jewish background, joining the armed forces straight from college, from the very stages of the civil war.

Adam got on the radio and called out, "We have lots of ground units converging on our position! Calling all available units! We need air support now!"

An enemy artillery rained on Adam's position, knocking him and Jason off their feet.

Jason was dazed from the blast that nearly consumed his life. He opened his eyes and saw Adam standing over him, trying to revive him, until he fully came to his senses.

Adam helped Jason to his feet and said, "I need you to stay alive and continue calling those coordinates with Reed! The only way that we're gonna get out of this alive is if you continue calling out the enemy positions, so Reed can take them out! We need you! I'm counting on you! We all are!"

"Yes, sir!" Jason answered.

"Calling all available units! We need air support now!" Adam continued over the radio, looking to the skies, watching the planes flying over his position in deadly pursuit of one another. He continued to receive dead silence on the other end of the transmission.

The enemy ground units continued to draw closer, while the enemy shells continued to rain on their positions, inflicting more casualties.

The freedom fighters fought back bravely, manning their artillery guns, trying as best they could to repel the swarm of enemy forces that attacked their position, when a blast from an enemy artillery shell rocked their position, destroying one of their gunnery positions. It scattered tons of shrapnel throughout their position, lacerating and killing a number of freedom fighters near the position.

Adam got up from the ground and saw a female soldier dragging the severely wounded soldiers to safety, while the enemy ordinance continued to harass their positions.

He ran over to her and assisted her in carrying the wounded soldiers to safety. He grabbed the female soldier by her shirt to get her attention and yelled through all the noise, "You're doing a great job, soldier! You got a name?"

"It's Janet! Janet Jackson! No relation to the Jackson 5, sir!," Janet answered.

She was a woman with a curvy but solid build a few inches past average height, and of caramel brown complexion. She was often good-natured, sometimes with a crude sense of humor even during the most crucial stages of conflict, but showed great prowess of being a great soldier.

"How are you holding up?" he asked.

"We're losing more ground, sir! Most of our guns are destroyed! And we still have more enemy forces converging on our position! We need more support, if we're going to hold!"

Adam got on one of the radios and shouted, "We're sustaining more casualties with more enemy units still converging on our positions. Our artillery guns and armored units have almost suffered total casualties! To any available air units, we need air support!"

11:17 HOURS. SOMEWHERE OVER THE PAINTED DESERT. 10 MILES AWAY FROM THE SECRET FREEDOM FIGHTER OUTPOST IN THE PAINTED DESERT - CAMERON, ARIZONA:

Karen heard the distress call, while she and the remainder of her unit continued to hold their ground against enemy forces. She answered, "Heading to your position to provide support!"

11:18 HOURS. SECRET FREEDOM FIGHTER OUTPOST. SOMEWHERE IN THE PAINTED DESERT, 61 MILES AWAY FROM THE HUBBELL TRADING POST NATIONAL HISTORY SITE - CAMERON, ARIZONA:

"Where's O'Hara? Is he okay?" Adam asked, with a hint of concern.

11:19 HOURS. SOMEWHERE OVER THE PAINTED DESERT. 9 MILES AWAY FROM THE SECRET FREEDOM FIGHTER OUTPOST - CAMERON, ARIZONA:

"He was shot down by the enemy forces, sir! He stayed back and engaged the enemy to give us a clear path to provide support! He assigned me to provide cover until he can resume command. We won't let you down, sir."

11:21 HOURS. SECRET FREEDOM FIGHTER OUTPOST. SOMEWHERE IN THE PAINTED DESERT - CAMERON, ARIZONA:

"What's your location? We won't be able to hold our position for long! We're sustaining heavy casualties and are in need of immediate assistance until we can evacuate! Even our planes are outnumbered and are doing their best to keep them off us, but we don't know how long they can last! The way I see it, you're our only hope!"

11:22 HOURS. SOMEWHERE OVER THE PAINTED DESERT. 7 MILES AWAY FROM THE SECRET FREEDOM FIGHTER OUTPOST - CAMERON, ARIZONA:

"We're almost within range of your position! We'll be there as soon as we can! Just hold on a little bit longer!"

11:23 HOURS. SECRET FREEDOM FIGHTER OUTPOST, SOMEWHERE IN THE PAINTED DESERT - CAMERON, ARIZONA:

"You don't leave me with much of a choice! I'm counting on you, Dragonfly leader!" Adam replied. "The entire outpost is counting on you!"

11:24 HOURS. SOMEWHERE OVER THE PAINTED DESERT. 5 MILES AWAY FROM THE SECRET FREEDOM FIGHTER OUTPOST - CAMERON, ARIZONA:

"We won't let you down, sir. I promise. We'll lay down as much cover fire as we can so you can begin the evacuation process, and cover your retreat. But it's a matter of time before we get spotted by enemy planes."

"What are your orders, Dragonfly leader?" Gary asked.

"General West does not have a lot of time, and neither do we. We're almost within range of his position. Dragonfly wings 2, 3, and 4 - activate all range scanners and take out as many of the enemy ground forces as possible, so General West can begin the evacuation. The rest of you - engage as many of the enemy gunships as possible to keep our flank and rear clear. After all the enemy units are eliminated, proceed to provide support to keep our evacuation a success. We can't get too close, or the enemy fighter planes will pick us off one by one. So, our best chance to inflict massive damage to the enemy ground units is to engage with long-range ordinance from a safe distance for now."

"I have a visual," Gary said, watching the enemy column on his screen, picking up the enemy heat signature.

"All weapons free, and engage," Karen answered.

Karen and the others began to engage the enemy ground units a safe distance away from their position, and watched as their long-range missiles tracked their targets on their screens, exploding into them.

11:31 HOURS. SECRET FREEDOM FIGHTER OUTPOST SOMEWHERE IN THE PAINTED DESERT, 61 MILES AWAY FROM THE HUBBELL TRADING POST NATIONAL HISTORY SITE - CAMERON, ARIZONA:

The enemy units were within striking range of their position, while the freedom fighters tried as much as they could to fend them off, when a series of explosions from their long-range missiles tore through the enemies' offensive, stopping their advance, giving Adam a window of opportunity to commence with their evacuation.

"Thanks for the assist, Santiago! We're starting the evacuation process now! Continue providing cover!" Adam said loudly.

Though they halted the enemy advance for a brief moment, they remained under heavy attack from their long-range guns.

Christopher ran over to Adam and said loudly, "We need to get you out, General!"

"I'm staying! I need to stay and help them fight!" Adam yelled back.

"We can't allow you to be in enemy hands! You have to get out! Some of us will stay back and buy time to escape! There's something that I must do! I'll be right behind you!"

"You better be! You make sure you get your ass behind me!" Adam said, grabbing him by the sleeve of his uniform.

"If you don't see me after five minutes, get out!" Christopher said, running off.

Adam and Janet, along with a number of soldiers, ran as fast as they could to the nearest transport, through the heavy volley of enemy fire still wreaking havoc on their positions, and nervously waited for Christopher.

11:33 HOURS. SOMEWHERE OVER THE PAINTED DESERT. 5 MILES AWAY FROM THE SECRET FREEDOM FIGHTER OUTPOST - CAMERON, ARIZONA:

After almost suffering total casualties in the skirmish against the enemy gunships, Karen and Gary continued engaging the enemy armored units, wearing down their numbers with the combined aid of ground troops still being met by heavy resistance.

They heard Christopher's distress call over their radios, and continued to engage the enemy ground units to ensure a clear path for Adam and the rest of the transports to make it and clear the road for much needed reinforcements.

11:35 HOURS. SECRET FREEDOM FIGHTER OUTPOST. SOMEWHERE IN THE PAINTED DESERT, 61 MILES AWAY FROM THE HUBBELL TRADING NATIONAL HISTORY SITE - CAMERON, ARIZONA:

Eric climbed into one of the tank's gunnery positions and asked Christopher, "Where the fuck are you going?"

"I'll be right behind you! I'll stay back for now to make sure the rest of the troops get out safely! You take Evans and the others and cover the General's ass! Make sure he gets out in one piece!"

James ran to Christopher while the enemy shells continued to rain on their positions, and shouted, "All the remainder of our troops are safely onboard, sir! We need to leave now!"

"I'll come back! There's something I must do first!" Christopher replied, running off.

"Okay, Yee. Get onboard the tank! Man the turret! I'll man the guns! Let's move!" Ahmad called out to James loudly, preparing to make their way out of the battle area towards safer ground.

James hopped into the armored unit, ready to evacuate, and rolled out of the base, only an arm's length away from Eric, heading out to open ground. He rammed through obstacles of burning enemy units that blocked their path.

The enemy forces overrunning their position with their sheer numbers had become inevitable, and Christopher charged into the armory, collecting as many explosive charges that he could carry, and ran to the fuel depots, ordinance, and transports, placing as many charges as he could. He quickly made his departure, as the seconds from their timers quickly ticked away, while the enemy forces continued to close in.

"What was so important?" Adam asked, and continued, "I decided to wait so you can tell me!"

"You'll see! Let's go!" Christopher answered.

As the group of transports continued to evacuate the outpost, Eric looked back, seeing all the burning enemy armored units that stopped within striking range through his binoculars.

He looked into the skies and saw an enemy plane descending rapidly on their position. "Enemy plane!" he yelled, alarming the other soldiers that manned the tank's heavy machine guns. They greeted the oncoming enemy plane with a wall of anti-aircraft fire, and saw the enemy plane trailing a long line of black smoke, crashing and burning far from their position.

The remainder of enemy gunships moved in to engage the fleeing freedom fighters, destroying one of the fleeing armored units.

"We're still sustaining casualties from the enemy artillery shells! We need air support!" Ahmad yelled, while he fired at the enemy units that continued attacking their positions.

Christopher grabbed a radio and called out, "We have a number of transports being evacuated, and one of them has General West safely onboard! We need air support to make sure he and the others get out in one piece!"

11:36 HOURS. SOMEWHERE OVER THE SECRET FREEDOM FIGHTER OUTPOST IN THE PAINTED DESERT - CAMERON, ARIZONA:

Dillon heard the distress call and quickly descended above the enemy lines, deploying a series of air to ground missiles at their defensive lines, consuming the bulk of the enemy formation in flames, and quickly flew into the skies to engage the remaining enemy planes.

11:39 HOURS. SOMEWHERE IN THE PAINTED DESERT. 5 MILES AWAY FROM THE SECRET FREEDOM FIGHTER OUTPOST - CAMERON, ARIZONA:

"I have a visual on more enemy gunships. Weapons hot! All units engage, and cover General West's retreat! Clear all enemy units so our forces can make it to the open road," Karen ordered.

11:42 HOURS. SECRET FREEDOM FIGHTER OUTPOST. SOMEWHERE IN THE PAINTED DESERT, 61 MILES AWAY FROM THE HUBBELL TRADING NATIONAL HISTORY SITE - CAMERON, ARIZONA:

The ground troops continued to make their evacuation when they saw the blinding flashes of enemy gunships that continued to move towards their positions, bursting into flames, falling onto the desert floor with deafening clamor.

The vicinity of the outpost was now completely littered with the dead and burning shells of freedom fighters and enemy units alike, along with their corpses.

They rammed through the gauntlet of more burning vehicles that continued to block their path with their armored units in a desperate race to make it to the open road that led to their base, where they could strengthen their numbers against the enemies' onslaught.

11:49 HOURS. SOMEWHERE OVER THE SECRET FREEDOM FIGHTER OUTPOST IN THE PAINTED DESERT - CAMERON, ARIZONA:

Dillon was in pursuit of the enemy plane and unleashed a volley of fire from his plane's heavy machine guns, riddling the enemy pilot's planes with countless bullets. He watched the enemy plane disintegrate from the constant bombardment as it spun out of control. It plummeted from the skies, exploding on impact in the desert.

12:03 HOURS. SOMEWHERE ON INTERSTATE 40 NEAR THE PAINTED DESERT. 337 MILES AWAY FROM DAVIS MONTHAN FREEDOM FIGHTER AIR FORCE BASE - TUCSON, ARIZONA:

After the constant moments of struggle against the enemy forces, Adam and the remaining transports had finally made it to open road, racing towards their base.

He looked to the skies with his binoculars, watching the battle for air supremacy continue to unfold, and said, "We can offer support. Bring them to the firing range of our guns."

12:06 HOURS. SOMEWHERE OVER THE PAINTED DESERT. 5 MILES AWAY FROM THE SECRET FREEDOM FIGHTER OUTPOST - CAMERON, ARIZONA:

"General West and the others have evacuated the outpost safely. Our job right now is to make sure they get back in one piece."

"What are your orders, Dragonfly leader?" Gary asked.

"Same objective. Provide cover for our ground troops, but still remain out of sight. Don't want to make easy targets for the enemy planes. Let's take advantage of the ground targets, while they're distracted by our planes."

12:09 HOURS. SECRET FREEDOM FIGHTER OUTPOST. SOMEWHERE IN THE PAINTED DESERT, 61 MILES AWAY FROM THE HUBBELL TRADING NATIONAL HISTORY SITE - CAMERON, ARIZONA:

After the intense battle, the outpost was finally overrun by the enemy forces. They scoured through the base searching for fuel and ordinance for their planes and gunships, completely unaware that they had walked into a trap.

12:15 HOURS. SOMEWHERE ON INTERSTATE 40. 334 MILES AWAY FROM DAVIS MONTHAN FREEDOM FIGHTER AIR FORCE BASE - TUCSON, ARIZONA:

Christopher continued peering through his binoculars, seeing the outpost was overrun by the enemy forces, and said to Adam, "They have taken the base, General West."

"That's the idea. They didn't exactly come to shake hands. Why are you telling me this?" Adam replied.

"Wait for it," Christopher replied.

"Wait for what?" Adam replied.

"Just a few seconds," Christopher replied.

12:16 HOURS. SECRET FREEDOM FIGHTER OUTPOST. SOMEWHERE IN THE PAINTED DESERT, 61 MILES AWAY FROM THE HUBBELL TRADING NATIONAL HISTORY SITE - CAMERON, ARIZONA:

An enemy soldier walked to the fuel depot and came across the charges planted on the ground next to the tanks, counting down its final seconds, and erupting in a giant wall of flame, consuming everyone in its wake, followed by a string of explosions all over the outpost, consuming a great number of enemy soldiers.

12:16 HOURS. SOMEWHERE ON INTERSTATE 40. 331 MILES AWAY FROM DAVIS MONTHAN AIR FORCE BASE - TUCSON, ARIZONA:

Christopher continued peering through his binoculars, seeing the chain reaction caused by the string of explosions, and handed it to Adam and said, "I told you to wait for it."

"Wait for what?"

"Just look," Christopher said to Adam, pointing back to the captured outpost.

Adam watched through the binoculars, seeing the towering wall of flames that tore through the outpost and said, "You're clever S.O.B.," patting Christopher on his shoulder. "What did you do?"

"I figured that we would be overrun by the enemy, so while you were about to evacuate, I went to the ammunition depot and took charges and placed them on all our fuel and ordinance, since they would use them against us. So if we couldn't have it, then they shouldn't either, and that goes without saying. I implemented the scorched earth policy, like what Stalin did when the Nazis invaded Russia. Take out as many of those bastards as possible. That way, we have much less to worry about and at the same time, ensure our survival, and buy us more time."

"I didn't think you'd think of that in the heat of the moment."

"You'd be surprised about all the things I can think about in the heat of the moment."

"I'm truly impressed," Adam replied, staring at Christopher, giving his nod of approval.

"Don't look at me, General. I didn't make the rules about the scorched earth policy. I'm just glad I did it."

"I was just going to say that by doing what you did back there, you saved a lot of lives. Now, all we have to do is make it back to base in one piece."

"Let's hope our planes and gunships can keep them busy long enough."

Eric heard the roaring of a plane's engines drawing closer from behind their position, and peered through his binoculars. He said softly, "It's not slowing down. Son of a bitch, they're trying to creep up from behind! Enemy plane coming in at 6 o'clock!" He quickly opened fire at the advancing enemy plane, with the entire tank column immediately following suit, causing the enemy plane to explode in flames, veering off course, trailing a long line of thick, black smoke, crashing and burning near their position, while they continued their survival run.

Within a brief moment after shooting down one of the enemy planes, more broke away from the battle area, heading for the convoy of tanks and light armored units, only to be met by more anti-aircraft fire. They continued their desperate run towards their base.

Adam grabbed the radio and called out, "We have a visual of incoming enemy planes heading our way, and in need of air support! Don't know how long we can last!"

12:22 HOURS. SOMEWHERE OVER INTERSTATE 40. 328 MILES AWAY FROM DAVIS MONTHAN FREEDOM FIGHTER AIR FORCE BASE - TUCSON, ARIZONA:

Dillon looked down at the convoy of trucks and light armored vehicles on their desperate run towards their position, and flew in to intercept the enemy planes, launching a missile, and watching it track its target. The missile exploded into it, and Dillon moved in to intercept the next with a lethal barrage of bullets from his machine guns, while his other wingmen provided support defending their ground troops from the enemies' sneak attack. Suddenly, Dillon felt a series of enemy bullets racing past him, tearing through the canopy of his plane, riddling more holes through the hull of his aircraft, and forcing him to take evasive maneuvers. He glanced behind him for a brief moment, seeing the enemy plane in deadly pursuit, and said loudly, "Enemy dead on my tail! Can't seem to shake him! In need of assistance! Over!"

12:24 HOURS. SOMEWHERE ON INTERSTATE 40, INDIAN WELLS. 335 MILES AWAY FROM DAVIS MONTHAN FREEDOM FIGHTER AIR FORCE BASE - TUCSON, ARIZONA:

"We'll provide ground support!" Adam replied, and ordered all guns to fire at the enemy plane that pursued Dillon.

12:25 HOURS. SOMEWHERE OVER INTERSTATE 40, HEADING TOWARDS ROUTE 77, HOLDBROOK. 299 MILES AWAY FROM DAVIS MONTHAN, FREEDOM FIGHTER AIR FORCE BASE - TUCSON, ARIZONA:

Dillon continued to evade the enemy's attack as long as he could, as he headed towards the convoy for ground support, leading the enemy plane into his trap. After reaching within striking distance of the convoy, he took to the skies, exposing the enemy plane to the convoys' anti-aircraft fire, causing the enemy plane to spiral out of control, crashing and burning outside of their position.

12:27 HOURS. SOMEWHERE OVER INTERSTATE 40. 10 MILES AWAY FROM THE FREEDOM FIGHTER CONVOY:

Karen and her group of gunships continued to keep a watchful eye on the fleeing convoy and saw another gauntlet of enemy armored units blocking their path. She said, "We have another gauntlet of enemy armor. We need to clear a path."

12:31 HOURS. SOMEWHERE ON ROUTE 77 HEADING TOWARDS SNOWFLAKE. 216 MILES AWAY FROM DAVIS MONTHAN FREEDOM FIGHTER BASE - TUCSON, ARIZONA:

Ahmad peered through his binoculars and saw the other gauntlet of enemy armor blocking his way. Suddenly, he felt the surface of the interstate trembling violently while in his armored unit from the volley of enemy shells that began to rain around the convoy, as they continued drawing nearer to the enemy gauntlet or armor.

"Enemy gauntlet up ahead!" James said loudly.

"Move into blockade positions!" Adam ordered, watching helplessly as they continued drawing closer towards the enemy blockade, when a volley of missiles suddenly greeted the enemy gauntlet of heavy armor, consuming them in a series of explosions.

"Ramming speed!" Adam ordered.

"All units - ramming speed!" Eric said loudly, speeding towards the burning gauntlet, ramming through it with a deafening clamor echoing loudly through the long expanse of road.

"It wasn't our plane," Christopher said softly.

"No, it was our gunships. If they get closer to our position, they could be sitting ducks for the enemy planes. While our planes are keeping the enemy busy, they're taking out the enemy armor to guarantee us safe passage." Adam replied.

"Whatever works. Sounds good to me. With all this shit going on, let's hope we get back to base in one piece."

"Me too. We still have a long way to go."

"Look. More enemy planes," Christopher said, pointing to the skies.

"We have more enemy planes closing in on our position! Requesting air support! All units, turn your guns to the enemy planes!"

As the enemy planes swarmed the fleeing convoy, they were swiftly met with a thick wall of anti-aircraft fire, trying as much as they could to repel the enemy forces before the air support arrived, causing another enemy plane to succumb to their awesome fire power.

"And if that wasn't bad enough, we have another enemy gauntlet a few miles out!" Ahmad said as they quickly closed in towards the next enemy gauntlet, maintaining their blockade position. They met them with a barrage of heavy fire, when they suddenly burst into flames from the volley of fire from their gunships that stalked them silently from miles away from the battle area.

"Brace for more impact!" Eric shouted, charging through the enemy gauntlet. They continued fending off the enemy planes that constantly swarmed their position.

While the enemy planes continued to attack the convoy under a thick hail of anti-aircraft fire, Dillon once again moved in to intercept them from behind while they remained distracted, and locked on a number in simultaneous fashion, deploying a number of their missiles all at once, watching them track their targets, exploding into them, watching their wreckage crash and burn within the vicinity of the interstate.

After a number of losses, more enemy planes descended upon the convoy, greeting the fleeing transports with a volley of fire, while the anti-aircraft guns returned fire. One of the light armored transports was suddenly struck by enemy fire, exploding on contact, causing it to run off the road.

"We just lost transport! We need more support! We can't afford to lose too many of our transports!" Adam said loudly. "They're throwing everything they have at us!"

"Our troops are being attacked! All available wings provide support for General West!" Dillon said loudly.

12:37 HOURS. SOMEWHERE OVER ROUTE 77 HEADING TOWARDS WOODRUFF, ARIZONA:

Karen continued to watch the scene unfold and said, "Oh my God. They're throwing everything at the convoy. Still a long way to go before they can make it back to base, so keep a close eye out for enemy ground troops. All we can do at this point is clear a path."

12:41 HOURS. SOMEWHERE ON ROUTE 77, HEADING TOWARDS LAKESIDE. 208 MILES AWAY FROM DAVIS MONTHAN FREEDOM FIGHTER AIR FORCE BASE - TUCSON, ARIZONA:

The battle between both sides became more ferocious, with the convoy losing another one of their transports, causing the long column to struggle to maintain control over the long stretch of road.

Adam watched as his transport charged towards the burning truck and shouted, "Grab onto something!" feeling the violent shock from his transport ramming into the burning vehicle, knocking everyone onto their beds.

12:59 HOURS. SOMEWHERE ON ROUTE 77 HEADING TOWARDS FORT APACHE INDIAN RESERVATION. 187 MILES FROM DAVIS MONTHAN, FREEDOM FIGHTER AIR FORCE BASE - TUCSON ARIZONA:

Dillon looked at his ammunition and fuel gauge, noticing that both were almost depleted, with only a small quantity of rounds from his machine guns remaining.

He quickly moved in on another enemy plane, and opened fire using his heavy guns, watching the enemy plane descend to the bottom in flames, and quickly moved in to the next, as his ammunition continued to deplete.

The battle for air and ground supremacy was as long as it was grueling, resulting in both sides sustaining heavy losses, with the constant stresses of flying taking its toll.

After an unsuccessful attempt to annihilate the remainder of the freedom fighters, the remaining enemy planes suddenly withdrew their forces and headed back to their position, leaving the convoy to travel the rest of their destination unopposed.

13:03 HOURS. SOMEWHERE ON ROUTE 77 HEADING TOWARDS FORT APACHE INDIAN RESERVATION. 184 MILES AWAY FROM DAVIS MONTHAN FREEDOM FIGHTER AIR FORCE BASE - TUCSON, ARIZONA:

"They pulled back," Christopher said, watching in disbelief, taking a huge sigh of relief.

"Our hit on their position finally worked. Must be that they're running low on fuel," Adam replied. "That scorched earth you did saved all our asses. You're partly the reason why we're still in this war. Great job."

"It's just that we lost so many back there," Christopher replied.

"They didn't die in vain, and what's more important is that we live to fight another day."

"They pulled back," James said, watching the enemy planes retreat through his binoculars.

"We have clear roads and skies all the way back to base," Ahmad said, taking a sigh of relief.

"That was a little too close. I thought we were done for, for a second," Eric added.

16:19 HOURS. DAVIS MONTHAN FREEDOM FIGHTER AIR FORCE BASE, TUCSON. 148 MILES AWAY FROM LUKE ENEMY AIR FORCE BASE - PHOENIX, ARIZONA:

Hours after their long skirmish against the enemy air and ground forces, they arrived safely at the base.

They disembarked from their transports and stared in disbelief at the destruction the enemy had wreaked upon them.

Karen walked towards Adam and the others and said, "I'm glad you're okay, General West."

"Thanks for the support, Santiago. That was a great job you did back there. Wouldn't be here if it wasn't for you and your team," Adam replied.

"Thank you, General. That means a lot."

Dillon walked towards Adam and asked, "Are you okay, General West?"

"I'm fine. Thanks," Adam replied, placing his hand on Dillon's shoulder. "You did a great job back there - all of you. I couldn't ask for better."

"I just wished there was more we could've done," Dillon replied.

"You did the best you could. I mean that. Right now, I need the damage report."

"We lost a number of personnel, planes, and more than half of our ammo and fuel reserves, but being that the enemy concentration of resources was larger, so did they. Our defenses held up. It was a miracle we were able to get any of our planes in the air at all.

I'm just glad we were able to get airborne when we did," Dillon said.

"Any word on O'Hara?" Adam asked, looking all around the base.

"We haven't heard from him since he crashed. We're fueling one of our Blackhawks to go to his last coordinates as we speak," Karen replied.

16:25 HOURS. SOMEWHERE NEAR INTERSTATE 17. 5 MILES FROM THE TONITO NATIONAL FOREST, 129 MILES AWAY FROM THE SECRET FREEDOM FIGHTER OUTPOST, IN THE PAINTED DESERT.

A transport carrying a number of enemy soldiers drove through the desert, checking for any signs of survivors, when they stumbled upon Patrick's gunship. He opened his eyes and stared straight into the eyes of the assassin, with Jason standing next to him. Jason stuck his head closer to the cockpit of his gunship and said softly, "Captain O'Hara?"

"Who wants to know? Do I know you?" Patrick replied, wincing in pain from the broken leg he suffered from the crash.

"Yes. A long time ago. I'm Jason. Jason White. We met on my first tour the first time I went to Genesis, after the war with North Korea, just before the uprising. I was trying to be a part of your unit. But the war broke out, after the uprising on Genesis. Do you remember now?" he asked, looking at the blood slowly dripping down Patrick's face from the deep lacerations that scarred his face from broken glass.

He looked at Jason's uniform and glanced back at the assassin, and said, "Not that it will do any good, but now that you mentioned it, the name does ring a bell."

"Just hold on. I'll get you out," Jason said, trying to free him from the wreckage.

Patrick glanced at the assassin and said, "I seriously doubt that. Besides, my leg is completely broken. Shattered in a few places. I can feel it. Will be a long time before I walk again, if I ever do, from the looks of it."

The assassin stepped forward, pulling out his sidearm and pointing it towards Patrick's face with a blank stare.

"Lieutenant, please don't! He's more useful to us alive," Jason called out softly.

"Save your breath, kid. It's no use. He's doing exactly what he's been programmed to do. We both know there's only one way out of this for me," Patrick said, looking into the assassin's cold and empty eyes, and added, "It's ironic that this is how you found me during our tour in Colombia chasing some of the world's most dangerous criminals, pulling me out of the wreckage similar to this one. Now, you're the one coming to put a bullet in my head. At least give me a chance to say a few last words to the others."

"It doesn't have to be this way, Lieutenant!" Jason said.

Patrick grabbed his headset and called out to Adam while he continued to remain trapped in the dilapidated confines of the wreckage of his gunship.

16:26 HOURS. DAVIS MONTHAN FREEDOM FIGHTER AIR FORCE BASE, TUCSON. 148 MILES AWAY FROM LUKE ENEMY AIR FORCE BASE - PHOENIX, ARIZONA:

"General West!" James called out. "I'm receiving a transmission. I think it's Captain O'Hara, sir."

Adam quickly grabbed the radio and asked, "O'Hara is that you?"

16:26 HOURS. SOMEWHERE NEAR INTERSTATE 17. 5 MILES FROM THE TONITO NATIONAL FOREST, 129 MILES AWAY FROM THE SECRET FREEDOM FIGHTER OUTPOST, IN THE PAINTED DESERT - CAMERON, ARIZONA:

"Yes, it's me, General West," Patrick replied.

16:27 HOURS. DAVIS MONTHAN FREEDOM FIGHTER AIR FORCE BASE, TUCSON, ARIZONA. 148 MILES AWAY FROM LUKE ENEMY AIR FORCE BASE:

"How are you holding up? What's your position? We're having a chopper prepping for extraction as we speak."

16:27 HOURS. SOMEWHERE NEAR INTERSTATE 17. 5 MILES AWAY FROM THE TONITO NATIONAL FOREST, 129 MILES AWAY FROM THE SECRET FREEDOM FIGHTER OUTPOST, IN THE PAINTED DESERT - CAMERON, ARIZONA:

"Suffered a broken leg from the crash, and a number of bruises and lacerations. But none of that matters now. Won't be coming back to join you. There's no more hope for me. That was my last fight. You must continue the fight without me."

16:27 HOURS. DAVIS MONTHAN FREEDOM FIGHTER AIR FORCE BASE, TUCSON, ARIZONA. 148 MILES AWAY FROM LUKE ENEMY AIR FORCE BASE:

"What do you mean?" Adam asked, with a sudden look of awe on his face.

16:28 HOURS. SOMEWHERE NEAR INTERSTATE 17. 5 MILES AWAY FROM THE TONITO NATIONAL FOREST, 129 MILES AWAY FROM THE SECRET FREEDOM FIGHTER OUTPOST, IN THE PAINTED DESERT - CAMERON, ARIZONA:

"Alvarez, Collins, and Taylor have been coming to visit me in my dreams for a long time now. I never wanted to say this now. But, I knew this day would come. It was just a matter of when, and it seems that today is that day. I'm sorry that you had to find out this way, General. But, my fight has ended, and yours must continue. It truly has been an honor, General. Some of the best years of my life were serving with you, under your command. Santiago is now your new Dragonfly leader. She'll make you proud, as she has done for me," he said, with his eyes clouded in tears, and continued, "I don't want to get all teary eyed having my last words with you. But if it's all the same, before I go to that other place, I could use one last shot of bourbon right about now. Just one more for that place on the other side. I'll be seeing you in the next life, General," he said to Adam, and continued to the assassin, "I think this is your cue. I've made my peace. Now do what you must."

The assassin maintained his cold, calculating stare, completely unmoved by Patrick's last words, and pulled the trigger, quickly ending his life, followed by two more into his body.

After hearing the gunshots that ended Patrick's life, a sudden look of resentment came upon Jason's face, after watching the assassin murder one of the other soldiers from his former unit, and made his way back to the transport without any shred of remorse.

He glanced at the other soldiers who took their hats off their heads, sharing a brief moment of silence out of respect for Patrick. Though he was an enemy soldier, he was a worthy adversary. They made their way back to the transport.

Jason walked towards the transport and sat next to the assassin peering helplessly, consumed with silent anger, seeing that the assassin remained straight-faced, even after murdering someone who was once one of his own.

16:29 HOURS. DAVIS MONTHAN FREEDOM FIGHTER AIR FORCE BASE, TUCSON, ARIZONA. 148 MILES AWAY FROM LUKE ENEMY AIR FORCE BASE:

The radio slipped from Adam's hand, falling on the ground after hearing the single gunshot that ended Patrick's life, with a sudden look of shock on his face, taking a number of deep breaths, knowing that Patrick had met his demise at the hands of the man that continued to hunt them ever since the civil war had begun.

He looked all around, seeing the looks of shock on their faces and said, "We just lost O'Hara. He killed O'Hara like he was nothing."

"Sorry about O'Hara, General West," Gary said softly.

"He was a great leader. It won't be the same flying without him," Karen added.

"He passed the torch onto you, Santiago. You're the new Dragonfly leader now," Adam said softly.

"I don't know if I'm ready to take on such a task," Karen replied, drowning in tears, knowing that the burden that was being placed on her shoulders was a great responsibility.

"Patrick had a lot of faith in you. So you better learn quickly. After all, what better time to do it?"

"We're sorry about Captain O'Hara, General West. But we must continue to fight and make certain that Collins, Taylor, Alvarez, and O'Hara didn't die in vain," James added.

"Could've been any one of us, sir," Ahmad replied, in anger.

"What are your orders, General?" Christopher asked.

"We find O'Hara and the others in his last position, and bring their bodies back for a proper burial. They deserve that at least."

The war continues…

CHAPTER 6: OPERATION HELLFIRE

The year was 2030. Five years have passed since "The Great Fall of Genesis."

The cool winds dissipated, as the night slowly gave birth to the dawn, causing the searing heat from the early morning sun to burn through the desert. The warm winds howled through the barren tundra in succession, tossing about the dry and withered tumbleweeds that littered the parched earth of the desert.

A black collared lizard remained still, basking in the infinite grains of desert sands, warming its body temperature, and quickly scampered away to hide.

The vibrant colors of the body of a western coral snake showed brightly under the early morning sun, while it crawled slowly through the barren tundra, hiding among the shrubs that remained defiant to the unforgiving tundra.

A pack of wild mustangs stopped from their long journey, drinking from the Pecos River, and were alarmed, with their acute senses picking up movement, and quickly galloped away from the brief sanctuary that the cool river offered.

A desert tarantula seeking shade from the burning sun, while sinking its venomous fangs into its prey, completely immobilizing it, quickly wrapped it into a cocoon, and scampered away, after sensing danger.

A pack of wild bulls stopped to graze through the shrubs and picked up movement from afar, quickly scampering away.

An eerie silence suddenly swept across the unforgiving tundra, leaving only the howling breeze to break its silence. A convoy of enemy vehicles sped away from their base on a long journey across the unforgiving plain, en-route to the freedom fighters' outpost under the cover of complete darkness.

05:21 HOURS. CANNON FREEDOM FIGHTER AIR FORCE BASE - CLOVIS, NEW MEXICO:

After many hours, the sun began to rise from beyond the horizon, and the dust from the floor of the unforgiving tundra rose into the air from a large convoy of light and heavy armored units en-route to the freedom fighters' positions under the cover of dawn.

05:22 HOURS. HOLLOMAN ENEMY AIR FORCE BASE. MORE THAN 75.3 MILES AWAY FROM, THE WHITE SANDS DESERT MISSILE RANGE IN ALAMOGORDO, NEW MEXICO:

After moments of hearing their ground troops were almost within range of the freedom fighters' position, the enemy planes mobilized from the base, bound for their strafing run.

05:23 HOURS. CANNON FREEDOM FIGHTER AIR FORCE BASE NEAR CLOVIS, NEW MEXICO:

The alarms blared through the freedom fighters' base, warning them that the enemy was approaching. The troops mobilized towards all their gunnery positions within moments, while the enemy remained totally oblivious that they had been spotted by the freedom fighters, still a distance away.

After waiting for a moment until the enemy was in striking distance, the enemy convoy was greeted by a series of artillery shells, inflicting a series of casualties on their forces, completely ruining their element of surprise.

05:24 HOURS. SOMEWHERE OVER THE CHIHUAHUAN DESERT, EN-ROUTE TO CANNON FREEDOM FIGHTER AIR FORCE BASE - CLOVIS, NEW MEXICO:

The enemy planes heard the frantic distress calls of their ground troops being engaged by the freedom fighters, and proceeded to their coordinates as planned, thrusting their afterburners on full throttle, before their troops were completely decimated, by freedom fighters.

05:25 HOURS. CANNON FREEDOM FIGHTER AIR FORCE BASE - CLOVIS, NEW MEXICO:

The battle between the forces continued to wage. After many moments, the enemy ground troops were intercepted, and the squad of enemy planes quickly flew in at low altitude, closing on the freedom fighters' position, while they remained distracted trying to repel the enemy ground forces.

05:26 HOURS. SECRET FREEDOM FIGHTER AIR FORCE BASE. A FEW MILES AWAY FROM SANTA FE, NEW MEXICO:

After hearing the distress call from Adam's position, the smaller, yet formidable resilient group of freedom fighter pilots made their way towards their planes, mobilizing off the runway towards Adam's position.

05:29 HOURS. CANNON FREEDOM FIGHTER AIR FORCE BASE - CLOVIS, NEW MEXICO:

Within moments after a group of enemy planes stormed their positions, the communications tower erupted into a giant ball of flame, followed by a volley of air to ground missiles, causing a series of chain reactions causing the grounds to rumble violently under their feet, tossing them on the floor.

"It was a distraction! We need to hold out as much as long as we can before our support gets here! I need to know their location, and estimated time of arrival!" Adam said, grabbing Ahmad by his clothes as the destruction from both sides continued to unfold all around them, with their forces answering back with a volley of anti-aircraft fire and artillery ground fire of their own.

"Yes, sir!" Ahmad answered through the thick haze of enemy artillery and missiles. "Vaughan, find out what's the status of our gunships!"

"It's too dangerous for you to be out here, General West! You get yourself to a safe place and make the call! I'll stay here to help repel the enemy forces!"

"Look all around you right now. No place is safe! Right now, we're hanging on by a string, and at risk of being overwhelmed. Now, I won't ask you again! Get on the radio, and make the call! That's an order!" Adam cried out.

"Yes, sir!" Christopher answered, running off to check on the status of their gunships.

As the combination of thick heavy machine gun fire and flak continued to fly into the skies, blanketing the crimson shade of the dawn skies, enemy fighter planes made their strafing run through the thick wall of anti-aircraft fire, engaging the ground forces with extreme prejudice.

Jason courageously jumped onto one of the tanks through the thick hail of enemy artillery that continued to pummel their positions, manning the heavy machine guns, returning fire, until one of the enemy planes burst into flames, falling from the skies, trailing a thick, long line of black smoke, crashing and burning.

While the flames consumed the enemy plane, the pilot tried as best as he could to stop it, as he saw himself plummeting to his death, crashing and burning into the vast, unforgiving tundra.

"Good kill!" Adam shouted, when another wave of flames from an explosion of an enemy plane strafing their positions tore through the armor of the tanks, scattering shrapnel in every direction.

The attack was brief, but took a devastating toll on all caught in its wake, with Adam slowly rising to his feet, completely disoriented, his ears ringing loudly from the roar of the blast.

He looked at Jason's position and saw him slumping over the tank's gunnery position, and ran over, seeing his hands completely doused in blood.

He searched for Jason's wound, and saw a thick chunk of metal lodged deeply into the flesh of his neck, and slowly, and gently pulled it out, tossing it to the ground, applying pressure, while Jason stared back frantically at Adam, his blood continuing to spurt from his fatal neck wound, feeling his life slowly slipping away.

"Someone go get the medic! Go get Thompson!" he shouted, while Jason continued to struggle to breathe, gurgling on the blood from his neck, and slowly succumbed to his fatal wound, taking his last breath.

"Moscowitz is down! I need someone to man the tank's heavy machine guns! Anyone who's able! We need to hold out until the rest of our support gets here!"

Ahmad and Christopher had arrived into one of the barracks to find out the status of the gunships and planes, en-route to their positions, breaking radio silence.

05:32 HOURS. SOMEWHERE OVER NEW MEXICO. 5 MILES AWAY FROM CANNON FREEDOM FIGHTER AIR FORCE BASE - CHIHUAHUA, NEW MEXICO:

Karen heard the call and answered, "This is Dragonfly leader, already en-route to your position. Estimated time of arrival, 18 minutes." She looked to the skies and saw Dillon and the squad of planes flying over her position, speeding off into the distance, vanishing into the horizon, and continued, "I have a visual on the flight leader, heading towards your position."

Dillon heard the radio chatter, looked downwards from the view of the cockpit of his plane, and saw the group of gunships flying below, and said, "This is flight leader to command. What's your status? Over?"

05:45 HOURS. CANNON FREEDOM FIGHTER AIR FORCE BASE - CLOVIS, NEW MEXICO:

"We're facing a two-pronged attack from enemy air and ground units, and sustaining heavy casualties! What's your E.T.A.?" Christopher answered.

05:45 HOURS. SOMEWHERE OVER NEW MEXICO. 4 MINUTES AWAY FROM CANNON AIR FORCE BASE, CLOVIS, NEW MEXICO:

"We'll be there as soon as we can! About 10 minutes!" Dillon answered.

05:46 HOURS. CANNON FREEDOM FIGHTER AIR FORCE BASE - CLOVIS, NEW MEXICO:

"We may not have that long!" Ahmad replied.

05:47 HOURS. SOMEWHERE OVER NEW MEXICO. 3 MINUTES AWAY FROM CANNON FREEDOM FIGHTER AIR FORCE BASE:

"Hold on! We'll be there as soon as we can!" Dillon answered.

05:49 HOURS. CANNON FREEDOM FIGHTER AIR FORCE BASE - CLOVIS, NEW MEXICO:

They bowed their heads after listening to the radio chatter, feeling a complete state of helplessness after hearing that their planes and gunships were still far away.

They ran back out into the open to Adam's position through the hail of enemy artillery from the air and ground units and planes that continued to pummel their positions.

"What's the status?" Adam asked, anxiously.

"It'll be a while before they get to our position!" Christopher answered.

"And what about our gunships?" Adam asked.

"They're still out of range!" Ahmad replied. "We can't evacuate and we're surrounded from all sides. There are too many enemy planes in the sky! If we make it out of the base, we'll be cut down by either enemy ground troops, or enemy planes! The way I see it, General, we have no choice but to hold on, and fight till the last man! And if we lose this position, you must see to it that none of us fall into enemy hands! And I mean none of us! We simply can't afford to be taken alive!"

Adam bowed his head and said, "We lost Moscowitz! I need you to man the guns!"

Brian arrived and saw Jason's body lying motionless on the ground, with his clothes completely soaked in blood from his fatal neck wound and asked, "Am I too late?"

"There's nothing you can do for him now!" Adam replied.

Another shell from enemy artillery guns exploded into the base, tossing them to the ground, falling over Jason's corpse.

"We have enemy tanks closing in!" Eric yelled.

"All available remaining tanks - move into blockade positions! We need to delay them long enough until our support arrives!"

05:50 HOURS. SOMEWHERE OVER NEW MEXICO. 1 MINUTE AWAY FROM CANNON FREEDOM FIGHTER AIR FORCE BASE:

Dillon continued hearing the radio chatter from the ground forces sustaining heavy casualties and said, "Our ground forces are barely holding on. We need to get there in time before General West, our forces, and the rest of our ground forces are wiped out. We can't afford to not have this mission succeed. All weapons free and engage all hostile craft with extreme prejudice. Full thrusters ahead." The group of planes kicked in their afterburners towards Adam's position, hoping they were not too late to salvage what was left of their decimated ground forces.

05:51 HOURS. CANNON FREEDOM FIGHTER AIR FORCE BASE - CLOVIS, NEW MEXICO:

The base continued to sustain heavy punishment, and was on the brink of being completely overwhelmed from the two-pronged attack from the enemy forces.

The remainder of the tanks continued moving into blockade position, trying to repel the vast number of enemy armor that continued to overwhelm their smaller numbers.

"There's just too many of them!" Tiara yelled.

"We need to hold till the enemy arrives! Continued to engage! Do the best that you can! Fong, continues manning that heavy gun," Adam called out.

The exchange from both sides of the enemy armored units continued, rendering unspeakable destruction. The freedom fighters suffered the worst of the exchange against the larger number of the enemy units, though scoring a few significant victories of their own, while repelling their forces.

"No matter how many I take out, they just keep coming!" Tiara yelled.

"We need to hold on long enough until our support comes! Take heart! If we keep losing ground units at this rate, we'll be completely overrun!" Adam cried out.

The smaller group of freedom fighter planes snuck onto Adam's position in complete radio silence, while they remained completely occupied with the enemy forces.

"Do you hear something?" Adam asked Christopher, and continued, "I think I hear something!"

06:00 HOURS. SOMEWHERE OVER CANNON FREEDOM FIGHTER AIR FORCE BASE - CLOVIS, NEW MEXICO:

The sounds of their scanners began to blare loudly, filling the confines of their cockpits, warning them of the enemy air and ground forces that continued to assault the freedom fighters' positions.

They dove towards the enemy artillery and armored units, unleashing a series of bombs on their positions, causing a giant wall of flame. The fire consumed a number of the enemy, drastically reducing their fire power, causing the ground to tremble beneath their feet. It gave them a brief, but much needed, respite, as an eerie calm swept across the battlefield for a brief moment. Their planes flew over their positions, heading straight into the skies in pursuit of their enemies.

06:00 HOURS. CANNON FREEDOM FIGHTER AIR FORCE BASE - CLOVIS, NEW MEXICO:

"Looks like that answers my question," Adam said, as he watched the planes fly into the morning skies.

The surviving ground forces cheered, seeing their planes fly into the skies after destroying a number of the enemy heavy guns.

06:01 HOURS. SOMEWHERE OVER CANNON FREEDOM FIGHTER AIR FORCE BASE - CLOVIS, NEW MEXICO:

Dillon glanced around, trying to find any signs of the enemy planes, and said "I think it's safe to say that it's okay to break radio silence, since the enemy already knows we're here. As in most cases, we're outnumbered, so we need to make every one of our shots count, and use the rest of our support we have on the ground. We still have enemy ground forces to engage, since our ground forces sustained a number of casualties. We need to clear as many of them as we can until our gunships arrive to clean out the rest. Let's break into groups and engage all ground forces. The rest of you form up on my six. All weapons are hot and engaging."

06:02 HOURS. CANNON FREEDOM FIGHTER AIR FORCE BASE - CLOVIS, NEW MEXICO:

"All tanks - maintain a blockade position, and continue to engage and provide support. Continue to engage and provide support for our planes in the sky!"

"Reading you loud and clear!" Tiara answered, scoring kills on the enemy armored units, as the rest of the units began gaining the upper ground.

06:03 HOURS. SOMEWHERE OVER CANNON FREEDOM FIGHTER AIR FORCE BASE - CLOVIS, NEW MEXICO:

The combined group of FA-18 Super Hornets and F-16 Falcons descended upon the enemy armored units without mercy, destroying many of their units in a single pass, while they held their ground against the awesome might of the fighter planes.

06:04 HOURS. SOMEWHERE OVER NEW MEXICO. 3 MINUTES AWAY FROM CANNON FREEDOM FIGHTER AIR FORCE BASE:

As the group of gunships continued closing towards the base, Karen watched from the distance, seeing the towering columns of thick smoke rising high into the clouds, hoping that Brian was still alive amidst all the destruction. "This is Dragonfly leader to command en-route to base. What is your status? Over."

06:04 HOURS. CANNON FREEDOM FIGHTER AIR FORCE BASE - CLOVIS, NEW MEXICO:

"It's our gunships! They're en-route to our position!" Eric said, while he continued to man the tank's heavy machine guns. "Tell them that our air support has inflicted massive casualties on the enemy forces, but they're still combat capable! But we can still use more support, so our planes can go and assist the others! We've sustained a number of casualties, but our defenses are barely holding! We can still use more support so the rest of our planes can repel the enemy air forces! Over!" Eric repeated.

06:07 HOURS. SOMEWHERE OVER NEW MEXICO. 1 MINUTE AWAY FROM CANNON FREEDOM FIGHTER AIR FORCE BASE - CLOVIS NEW MEXICO:

"This is Dragonfly leader to command, reading you loud and clear. Moving in to engage," Karen answered, after receiving her orders, and added, "All weapons hot, and terminate all enemy forces with extreme prejudice. I repeat, terminate with extreme prejudice, over."

The squad of Super Hornets and F-16 Falcon fighter planes withdrew their attack, flying into the skies, joining the remainder of their planes that tried to fend off the larger squad of enemy planes, leaving the group of gunships to engage the enemy ground forces from a safe distance.

06:10 HOURS. CANNON FREEDOM FIGHTER AIR FORCE BASE - CLOVIS, NEW MEXICO:

Another wave of flames tore through the enemy armored units that continued their relentless assault on the freedom fighters' positions, confusing their ranks, giving the freedom fighters a brief respite to carry their dead and wounded soldiers off the battlefield, while the others provided support for the planes from their gunnery positions against the overwhelming number of enemy ground forces.

06:15 HOURS. SOMEWHERE OVER CANNON FREEDOM FIGHTER AIR FORCE BASE - CLOVIS, NEW MEXICO:

For a brief moment, as Dillon and the rest of his planes continued to pursue the enemy planes high above the clouds, both sides locked in a stalemate, he heard the alarms in his cockpit blaring loudly, warning him of an incoming enemy attack closing in. He glanced at his scanners, seeing an enemy missile drawing nearer and made a sharp turn, deploying his countermeasures. The missile veered off its target.

"This is Comet. I have an enemy on my tail! I can't shake him and he has a missile lock! I need immediate assistance! Over!" Comet said, watching the enemy missile flying towards her, as she watched her scanners.

"Break, Comet! Break!" Dillon called out, trying to direct her from the enemy attack.

She waited until the missile drew nearer to her plane, and made a sharp turn, deploying her countermeasures. After a brief moment, she saw a blinding flash from the missile exploding, lighting her cockpit. She rested her head back on her seat, panting heavily from her close brush with death.

Dillon glanced at the blinding rays of the sun as it burned through the canopy of his plane for a brief moment, suddenly having an epiphany and said, "Comet, Flash on my six. The rest of you, continue to engage."

The trio of planes broke out of the fight, flying higher into the skies towards the sun that shone brightly high above the clouds, while the other planes kept the enemy forces entangled.

After reaching into the sun's blinding radius, they turned their planes around to engage the enemy forces, with the sun to their backs, making them completely invisible to the enemy, locking on to their planes.

Dillon locked onto one of the enemy planes and experimented his strategy, firing one of his long range missiles from high altitude and watched it track the enemy target. It was a hit, exploding into the plane, instantly breaking the stalemate. Dillon said after seeing the success of his strategy, "All weapons hot. Engage. I repeat, weapons free."

Comet deployed her missile and watched it track into its target, exploding and said, "I got one!"

"That's a confirmed kill. But we're not out of the woods yet. Too early to celebrate. Whatever you do, don't lose your concentration," Dillon said, as he locked on to another enemy plane.

The trio of planes continued to employ the same strategy from a safe distance, with the sun to their backs.

06:07 HOURS. CANNON FREEDOM FIGHTER AIR FORCE BASE - CLOVIS, NEW MEXICO:

After hearing the roar from the series of explosions that echoed in the skies, high above the clouds, Adam, Ahmad, Christopher, and Eric, remained mesmerized, looking at the air battle that continued to ensue, seeing a number of enemy planes plummet from the skies in flames, trailing the tell-tale long contrails of thick dark smoke.

"Is it just me, or do they not know where the attacks are coming from?" Christopher asked. "I sure as hell don't."

"It's like the Tuskegee airmen again," Ahmad added.

"Whatever it is, or whoever, I'm just glad he's on our side," Adam said softly.

"I second that," Eric replied.

"In the meantime, I need a damage assessment. Can someone get me a damage report while we have the chance?" Adam ordered.

"We suffered a lot of casualties. Many dead, and more wounded. There's no question that they may die from their wounds if we don't get them medical attention in time. The entire medical staff are short on personnel, but doing all they can to save them. But that's not all of it," Brian said.

"Then what's the rest of it?" Adam asked.

"Most of our armored units were lost during the assault. We may not have enough units to repel another enemy assault," Ahmad added.

"But something good came out of all this," Eric said.

"I'm all ears," Adam replied.

"Our hangars, medical facilities, and the rest of our ordinance are still intact from the assault. Including our fuel. Which means that our planes and gunships don't have to go all the way back to our secret base to reload and refuel," Christopher added.

"Well, they'll need to," Adam answered.

"What do you mean? What are you planning?" Eric asked.

"We may not be able to repel them. So, before another attack comes, we'll take the fight to them," Adam replied.

"We may not have enough ground troops, but we have enough planes and gunships wreaking on the enemy as we speak. Can you hear that up there and outside these walls? And not to mention enough ordinance and fuel to make it their base and level that piece of shit. We may not have enough troops, but considering the circumstances, they may not either."

"That may be suicide, General," Eric replied.

"Then what the fuck should I do? If we stay here, they'll pick the rest of us off. Right now, their backs are against the ropes, and we can't let them get back in the fight! Haven't you seen what's been happening? Look around you! Our lives and morale are hanging by a thread! And if we don't do something, more of us will die, and that means all that paid the ultimate price will have died for nothing! We need to make them pay!"

"I suppose it won't hurt to kill more of those fuckers," Eric replied reluctantly, shrugging his shoulders.

"Whatever we have will have to do," Adam said, when the distant roar of another enemy plane exploding echoed in the skies, high above the clouds, catching their attention.

"Our birds just keep mowing them down," Ahmad said, with his eyes fixed to the skies.

"Is it just me, or does it look like we haven't lost a single plane yet?" Christopher asked.

"No, we haven't," Eric replied.

"I don't know what it is, but they need to keep doing it if we are going to succeed in taking the enemy position," Adam replied.

"They're still carrying the wounded men back to the med bay. What do you need us to do?" Ahmad asked.

"After we're done clearing out the enemy air and ground forces, we gather every able bodied man and woman that can bear arms to march on the enemy position. But first, our planes and gunships will have to take out their defenses."

"Okay," Eric said reluctantly.

06:15 HOURS. SOMEWHERE OVER CANNON FREEDOM FIGHTER AIR FORCE BASE - CLOVIS, NEW MEXICO:

After moments of clearing out the remainder of the enemy ground forces, the gunships flew towards the beleaguered enemy forces, hovering over the dead husks of enemy light and armored units, consumed in flames, searching for any signs of pockets of resistance. The eerie silence swept across the desert, greeting the pockets of enemy resistance that remained amidst the dead and broken husks or enemy armor that littered the unforgiving landscape with a heavy volley of fire. Dillon said, breaking radio silence, "All remaining enemy personnel and armor have been neutralized. Awaiting further orders."

06:16 HOURS. CANNON FREEDOM FIGHTER AIR FORCE BASE - CLOVIS, NEW MEXICO:

"Okay. Great job, Dragonfly leader. Return to base to reload and refuel, and wait for further orders," Adam said.

06:16 HOURS. SOMEWHERE OVER CANNON FREEDOM FIGHTER AIR FORCE BASE - CLOVIS, NEW MEXICO:

"Returning to base," Karen answered, as she approached the base on Adam's orders to reload and refuel.

06:17 HOURS. CANNON FREEDOM FIGHTER AIR FORCE BASE - CLOVIS, NEW MEXICO:

While returning to base, they hovered over the enemy positions, seeing the seemingly mighty enemy forces that had finally succumbed from the combined assault from attacks of planes and gunships after their long struggle against the freedom fighters, but not without inflicting many casualties on their foes, still leaving their reputation to be feared and respected.

They hovered over the ground forces, through the dark columns of smoke that blanketed the desert, as far as the eye could see, and flew towards the base, where the others waited for their arrival.

After landing at the base, powering down her gunship, Karen jumped out of the cockpit, watching all the destruction that filled the vicinity, seeing all the other surviving soldiers carrying the dead and wounded on stretchers.

She looked all over searching for Brian, hoping he was still alive, when she felt the soft touch from someone from behind that seemed familiar. She turned, looking into Brian's eyes, in shock that his clothes were soaked in blood from the wounded. She took a sigh of relief, and hugged him tightly, dismissing his disheveled appearance, saying, "I'm so happy you're still alive."

"It'll take more than that for you to lose me," he answered.

"Don't be so sure," she replied.

"We lost a lot of men. But so did they," he said.

"I can tell. I was there. I contributed to some of it myself. I'm just glad you're okay."

"I heard General West mention that you're about to launch an assault on the enemy position."

"Why are you telling me this? Can't we stop talking about war for once?" she asked.

"I didn't mean to. Then again, you should already know by now."

"I've been doing this too long to not know what to expect. But for now, let's just share our moment together."

They held each other in a moment of warm embrace, but were distracted by the thunderous echo of another plane bursting into flames high above the clouds of the morning skies, watching the flaming wreckage plummet towards the surface.

"Do you think it's one of ours?" Karen asked.

"I don't know. I hope not. Your guess is as good as mine," Brian answered.

"Fortunate for us, it's one of them," Eric asked.

"Been going on all morning," Ahmad replied.

"Enemy planes raining from the skies. Hallelujah," Christopher said, in jest.

"Then again, that's why the rest of the men are in gunnery positions. In case all goes awry. Can't be too careful," Eric added.

06:27 HOURS. SOMEWHERE OVER CANNON FREEDOM FIGHTER AIR FORCE BASE - CLOVIS, NEW MEXICO:

The battle for control of the skies continued to wage on, with Dillon and his wingmates continuing to tally scores of kills against the larger group of enemy planes, still without sustaining a single casualty.

He looked at his scanners, seeing that his missile count was rapidly depleting, and said, "This is flight leader to Comet and Flash. What is your ammunition holding up?"

"This is Comet. A few long-range missiles and mostly guns," she said.

"This is Flash. Almost out of missiles. Mostly guns also. What are your orders, flight leader?" he said.

"I'm almost out of missiles. So, after my long-range missiles are depleted, I'll use myself as bait so you can intercept the enemy. In the meantime, continue to engage. After all our ordinance has been depleted, we switch roles and let the others do the same."

They continued to engage the enemy planes until Dillon's long-range missiles were depleted. He watched his ammunition count and switched to his guns and said, "All my long-range weapons are depleted. Switching over to guns. I'll play as a decoy so you can distract the enemy. Should be easy for you to engage since we don't have too many enemy planes left to contend with. But nonetheless, they're still combat capable. So you really need to make your shots count."

The rest of the troops on the ground continued to watch in awe at the air battle that continued to unfold high above the clouds, seeing many of the enemy planes falling from the skies in flames.

06:57 HOURS. CANNON FREEDOM FIGHTER AIR FORCE BASE - CLOVIS, NEW MEXICO:

After their long skirmish, they landed on the runway to reload and refuel, climbing from their cockpits with a sudden feeling of invincibility after achieving complete domination of the skies against a foe greater in number.

Though they had won their skirmish, the cost of their victory came at a terrible and heavy price, seeing all the carnage and destruction that was left in the wake of the enemy.

"How many did we lose?" Dillon asked, looking around, seeing the dead and injured rushed to the infirmary.

"We lost a lot of men. We may be at half strength. Maybe less. That's the bad news," Adam answered.

"What's the good news?" Dillon asked.

"We didn't lose any of our planes and gunships. Nor did we lose our hangars with our ordinance, fuel trucks and depots from the enemies' assault. So that leaves us with a plan."

"What's the plan?" Dillon asked.

"We may be cutting it a little close, but it's worth a shot. The enemy won't be attacking us, so we attack them with everything we got."

"Okay. I'm assuming that you'll elaborate," Dillon answered.

"We may not have enough ground troops to lead a ground assault, so the trick is to keep them focused on you so the gunships can come and assist in neutralizing their defenses from a safe distance. But before that's the case, it's imperative that you fly below radar to achieve the element of surprise. Only this time, we'll do something they didn't do."

"What's that?" Karen asked.

"We'll talk about their hangars, fuel depots, and trucks. That way they don't get back in the fight. Standard military tactic. Our planes go first, achieving the element of surprise, then our gunships will stay at a safe distance, to assist in neutralizing the enemy defenses, then our ground troops will do the rest. Just make sure that we hit the essentials first. Again, a standard military tactic."

"Do you think the manpower will be enough?" Dillon asked.

"Maybe it's a suicide mission. But that's exactly what they're not counting on. It'll have to be enough, until we can come up with another plan. We did it before during the war against North Korea, and it worked against incredible odds. I think it should work again, if we play it right."

"I suppose it's worth a shot," Christopher said, shrugging his shoulders.

"Fuck it. Not that you left any one of us with a choice," Ahmad said, shaking his head.

"Okay, we all know what to do. Let's roll out."

The long and tedious process of reloading and refueling their gunships and planes had begun. Adam and a number of ground troops began to make their way out of the base en-route to the enemy position, driving past all the devastation the enemy forces inflicted upon them.

With a moment to spare, they paid their respects to those who had paid their ultimate price.

He looked to the skies, seeing vultures circling high above the battle area.

After they were fully reloaded and refueled, Dillon and his squad of planes lifted off the runway, en-route on their attack run towards the enemy base, with their gunship trailing behind.

07:27 HOURS. SOMEWHERE OVER ROUTE 70. ONE HOUR AWAY FROM HOLLOMAN ENEMY AIR FORCE BASE, 74 MILES AWAY FROM THE WHITE SANDS MISSILE RANGE, NEAR ALAMOGORDO, NEW MEXICO:

Adam looked to the skies and saw the squad of planes flying high above his positions on their attack run towards the enemy position.

The planes flew high above their position in complete radio silence at low altitude.

"This is Comet to flight leader. Are you receiving me? Over."

"This is flight leader. Receiving you loud and clear."

"Just thinking about something," she said.

"What is it?" Dillon asked.

"That trick of using the sun to your back makes you invisible. Where did you learn it from?"

"That's an old trick that goes back to the second World War, when Germany tried to invade Britain. Though they were heavily outnumbered and losing a lot of their planes, one of the high-ranking British pilots came up with the idea of using the sun to their backs to make them invisible."

"How did he know it would work?" she asked.

"It was by accident, actually, while they were celebrating at an event after repelling another wave of enemy attacks from the seemingly invincible German juggernaut. By holding his pipe against one of the lights on the wall, he realized that the brightness of the light made it invisible. And after all, it made perfect sense. You can't stare directly at the sun without being blinded by it, so they decided to implement it, and because of it, they were able to hold out, beating back wave after wave of Germans, until the attack on Great Britain was postponed. From that point on, the battle of Britain was known as, "The few who held out against many." By the time the enemy learned of the strategy, it was already too late, so they implemented it in other missions during the later stages of the war."

"In that case, it made a lot of sense. Today alone, I scored eight kills," Comet replied.

"I scored seven," Flash added.

"It's unfortunate that I didn't think of it sooner. Think of all the lives that I could've saved. I suppose the use of technology has only succeeded in rendering the basic fundamentals of air combat obsolete," Dillon added softly.

"The important thing is that we've discovered an effective strategy that could make up for our loss in numbers. Today alone, we didn't lose a single plane from implementing this strategy, and that says a lot. And after what I've seen, I have faith that this could be an effective tool in the war effort against the enemy," Comet replied.

"I agree. But the day isn't over yet. Anything could happen. We're nearing the enemies' coordinates. For now, let's maintain radio silence," Dillon answered. "Our first line of attack is to take out all forms of communication, their hangars, and fuel to keep them out of the fight. Understood?"

"Understood," Comet replied.

"Understood," Flash replied.

"Approaching enemy vector. Spread out our line of attack to cover more ground and cause more damage to the enemy position. I'll go for the tower. The rest of you - go for their hangars and fuel reserves. All weapons hot, and attack with extreme prejudice. Flight leader, going dark."

They broke formation, spreading their planes apart, igniting their afterburners, and closing in on the enemies' positions. They continued to fly at low altitude to avoid detection.

07:47 HOURS. SOMEWHERE OVER HOLLOMAN ENEMY AIR FORCE BASE. 74 MILES AWAY FROM THE WHITE SANDS MISSILE RANGE NEAR ALAMOGORDO, NEW MEXICO:

Dillon carefully aimed at the enemy communications tower, and fired a long range missile. He watched it track its target, exploding on contact. The alarms on the base blared loudly, causing countless enemy soldiers to scurry about frantically from the planes that strafed their positions, destroying their hangars and fuel depots to cripple any chance they had of mounting a defensive against them.

"Now, hit their planes on the ground and gun emplacements! Don't give them a chance to mount any type of counter attack!"

The hangars and fuel depots burst into a giant wall of flame, followed by a series of merciless attacks on their gun emplacement positions.

With no possible chance of repelling the onslaught of the freedom fighters, the enemy soldiers quickly retreated from the base.

"I see a number of enemy vehicles retreating from the base! Engage any and all vehicles on sight. Let none survive!" Dillon ordered.

As a number of enemy vehicles made their desperate run to safety, the planes quickly strafed their positions, halting their retreat.

Within a brief moment, complete pandemonium had swept over the enemy position.

07:54 HOURS. SOMEWHERE OVER ROUTE 70. 3 MINUTES AWAY FROM HOLLOMAN ENEMY AIR FORCE BASE, 75.3 MILES AWAY FROM THE WHITE SANDS MISSILE RANGE, NEAR ALAMOGORDO, NEW MEXICO:

As Karen and her squad of gunships continued flying towards the enemy position, she saw the smoke from the base rising to the skies, and said, "This is Dragonfly leader to all units. The attack on the enemy position has commenced. Now, bring in a second wave of assault. All weapons hot, and engage any enemy units on sight with extreme prejudice."

08:16 HOURS. SOMEWHERE ON ROUTE 70. 20 MINUTES AWAY FROM HOLLOMAN ENEMY AIR FORCE BASE, 75.3 MILES AWAY FROM THE WHITE SANDS MISSILE RANGE, NEAR ALAMOGORDO, NEW MEXICO:

"The second phase of the attack has begun, sir," Christopher said over the radio.

"Have we lost any planes?" Adam asked.

"No, sir," Ahmad replied.

"We have succeeded in destroying all their fuel reserves, hangars, and all the other planes on the ground, including all defensive positions, just like you said. The enemy is retreating and they are sustaining casualties as well. The enemy position will be ours by the time we get to their position, sir."

"Good. We've lost enough good men for today alone. This victory is for them," Adam said.

08:32 HOURS. SOMEWHERE OVER HOLLOMAN ENEMY AIR FORCE BASE. 74 MILES AWAY FROM THE WHITE SANDS MISSILE RANGE, NEAR ALAMOGORDO, NEW MEXICO:

After the relentless bombing campaign, the gunships finally arrived, seeing that Adam's plans worked flawlessly, greeted only by devastation.

Karen looked high into the skies, seeing the squad of planes flying in a V-formation in their victory lap.

The pilots looked down from their cockpits, seeing the amount of destruction they unleashed upon the enemy, as the enemy had done to them, the dark smoke rising high into the skies as a tell-tale sign of what had just come to pass.

"All enemy defenses appear to be disabled. Moving in for a closer look," Karen said as she hovered from a distance, with her arsenal still active, ready to engage.

As they moved towards the enemy positions' dilapidated infrastructures, she heard her scanners picking up a signal followed by a number of others, and said, "I'm reading a number of signals coming from the enemy positions nearby, but I'm not seeing anything."

Dillon heard the blaring on his scanners while he remained within the confines of his cockpit, warning him of the same readings. He flew high above the enemy positions, and replied, "So am I. I'm having multiple readings, as a matter of fact."

"Don't have a visual on any enemy personnel, flight leader. Switching to infrared," she said, while she continued to scan for enemy activity from a distance.

"Do you have a visual, Dragonfly leader?" Dillon asked.

"That's a negative. But the signal is getting stronger. Whatever it is, it doesn't sound good."

The ground troops finally arrived. Adam heard the radio chatter and asked, "What's the status?"

"We're receiving a number of readings coming from a number of positions in the area, but we can't tell what it is," Karen replied.

08:34 HOURS. HOLLOMAN ENEMY AIR FORCE BASE. 74 MILES AWAY FROM THE WHITE SANDS MISSILE RANGE NEAR ALAMOGORDO, NEW MEXICO:

"Okay, our ground troops are in the area. Moving in to inspect," Adam replied.

The ground troops jumped from their transports, and slowly and cautiously moved through the area amidst all the devastation they left upon the enemy position, and were greeted by a lethal volley of machine gun fire, perched high on the roofs of some of the surviving infrastructure.

08:35 HOURS. SOMEWHERE OVER HOLLOMAN ENEMY AIR FORCE BASE. 74 MILES AWAY FROM THE WHITE SANDS MISSILE RANGE, NEAR ALAMOGORDO, NEW MEXICO:

"My God!" Karen said with a frantic look on her face, after seeing the number of ground troops quickly decimated by the enemy guns' awesome fire power. "We have multiple Hydra-6 machine gun emplacements! All units, pull back! Pull back!" A number of her gunships were locked and caught in the volley of fire crashing and burning within the enemy base.

Adam saw a number of his troops decimated by the automated guns. "The rest of our ground troops are pinned and have lost a number of our gunships!" he yelled. "Requesting air support!"

"Negative!" Dillon yelled, seeing the lethal volley of firepower that blanketed the skies. "We're facing heavy enemy resistance from those Hydras! I repeat, the sky's too hot! Can't get a clear shot! All units, break! Break!" Two of his planes were caught in the volley of enemy fire in rapid succession, causing them to crash and burn. He looked out of his cockpit and saw the wreckage from his planes and shouted, "We just lost 2 of our planes! We need to fall back and regroup!"

"Those guns are tearing our ground troops apart. All armored units, move into blockade positions and take out those guns!" Adam shouted.

Tiara led the charge as they slowly inched towards the guns to neutralize them.

"We need to destroy those guns so our troops can take the base!" Comet said, seeing all the destruction that continued to unfold on the ground.

"Facing those guns head on is suicide! The rate of fire from these guns is unlike anything that I've ever seen! If we attack, we'll lose more of our planes!" Dillon replied.

"The ground troops have taken out one of the guns!" Flash said, breaking formation, and flying head on towards one of the guns, locking onto it.

"Flash, wait! You'll get yourself killed! Everyone, let's provide support!" Dillon yelled, watching him fly towards one of the enemy gun emplacements, quickly turning his plane around.

"I have a missile lock!" Flash said, destroying another one of the gun emplacements. He flew away into the skies when he was locked on by another one of the automated guns and greeted by the inescapable volley of fire tearing through the hull of his plane, piercing through his body in the canopy, staining the entire cockpit and canopy with his blood. He lost consciousness as the flaming plane spiraled out of control, crashing and burning in the vicinity of the enemy base.

"My God, we just lost Flash!" Comet shouted.

Dillon heard his scanners beeping loudly from another enemy machine gun tracking the signal of his plane and said, "I can see that! I'm being locked on, and I can't shake it! Everyone, break! Break!" The other planes quickly dispersed, when a number of rounds from the enemy guns ripped through the hull of Dillon's plane, causing severe damage, tearing deeply into his leg. He continued to fly out of the vicinity of the base, with his plane in flames, trailing a long line of black smoke, heading in the direction of the White

Sands Desert, as he slowly lost consciousness from the rapid loss of blood from his fatal leg wound.

A look of shock came over Comet's face after seeing Dillon was intercepted by the enemy guns. She shouted, "This is Comet to flight leader! What's your status?"

"I'm wounded and my plane has sustained heavy damage! I'm losing control and don't know how much longer I can hold on!" Dillon said, looking at the gaping hole in his leg and the shattered canopy stained with his blood. The alarms blared loudly from the heavy damage he sustained from the enemy attack.

"I'm coming in to provide support," Comet yelled.

"That's a negative! You stay behind and provide support for the ground troops!" he answered, while he continued to fly away from the battle area, leaving a trail of long and dark contrails in the skies.

08:42 HOURS. THE WHITE SANDS DESERT. 20 MILES AWAY FROM HOLLOMAN ENEMY AIR FORCE BASE, ALAMOGORDO, 54 MILES AWAY FROM THE WHITE SANDS MISSILE RANGE - SOUTHERN NEW MEXICO:

After jumping in and out of consciousness and unable to control his plane, Dillon snapped himself into consciousness, seeing the entire landscape of the desert around him had changed. He gathered as much of his strength as he could, and slowly bent down towards the ejection lever, wincing in pain from the sharp sting from his wound, and pulled, catapulting out of the damaged plane, watching it freefall from the skies, while he remained dangling from his parachute. He slowly descended to the ground, while his plane continued to spiral downwards, erupting in a giant ball of flame.

After landing on the gleaming white sands of the desert, he tried to stand on his feet, only to fall back down from the crippling pain from his wound. He quickly pulled his parachute, tearing it into pieces, and tying it to his leg wound to help contain the heavy bleeding. He shivered constantly, and sat back resting in his chair, sweat dripping down his face. The energy drained from his body, as he hoped to be rescued by a search party, while he remained stranded under the blinding rays of the sun that burned brightly over the unforgiving tundra.

08:52 HOURS. HOLLOMAN ENEMY AIR FORCE BASE. 74 MILES AWAY FROM THE WHITE SANDS MISSILE RANGE, NEAR ALAMOGORDO, NEW MEXICO:

The advance of the ground troops continued to be halted by the enemy gun emplacements, when one of the armored units burst into flames from a volley of Hydra missiles, while they continued to hold their positions.

"We lost one of our tanks! These guns are decimating our troops and tanks with those armor-piercing bullets and Hydra missiles!" Tiara shouted.

"We need to destroy those guns so we can take the base!" Adam said, trying to inspire morale among the remainder of the troops.

"Locking on target!" Tiara replied, locking onto another one of the enemy gun emplacements, and was met with a volley of armor-piercing shells tearing through her tank, missing her by mere inches. She dodged the deadly attack, temporarily delaying her attack, and said, "These guns are equipped with armor-piercing shells!" She quickly fired, destroying another gun emplacement.

"We need a distraction!" Adam said, while he remained pinned behind one of the armored units.

"Not that you left any of us with a choice!" Tiara answered.

09:00 HOURS. SOMEWHERE OVER HOLLOMAN ENEMY AIR FORCE BASE. 74 MILES AWAY FROM THE WHITE SANDS MISSILE RANGE, NEAR ALAMOGORDO, NEW MEXICO:

"The enemy guns have locked on to one of our tanks. All available units, attack!" Adam ordered.

The remaining squad of planes turned back towards the enemy guns on their strafing run, locking onto them while the other guns remained distracted by the armored units.

"I have a missile lock!" Comet said, and quickly fired a missile, causing one of the guns to lock onto her plane in exchange.

Just seconds before the enemy gun burst into flames, her plane was greeted by a volley of enemy bullets, instantly ripping through the hull of her plane.

She looked all around the cockpit, seeing the amount of damage the enemy bullets had done, and frantically felt her body, searching for bullet holes, while her plane flew out of control.

"Another enemy gun destroyed, but I'm hit! I'm hit! I can't hold on!" she said, trying to control her plane flying out of the battle area, trailing heavy contrails of dark smoke.

09:04 HOURS. HOLLOMAN ENEMY AIR FORCE. 74 MILES AWAY FROM THE WHITE SANDS MISSILE RANGE, NEAR ALAMOGORDO, NEW MEXICO:

"Bail out!" Adam said loudly, watching the plane flying over the vicinity of the base.

Unable to maintain control of her plane, her alarms blaring loudly, and blinded by the smoke that filled her cockpit, Comet quickly pulled the ejection lever, watching the bullet-ridden canopy catapult into the skies carried by the winds. Her body was boosted into the skies, as her plane spun uncontrollably into the winds, while she floated slowly from the skies towards the surface, watching helplessly as her plane crashed and burned from high altitude beneath her feet.

"Do you have a visual on Comet?" Adam asked Christopher.

"Look!" Eric said, pointing in the direction of Comet's parachute slowly freefalling far from the battle area.

"Retrieval will have to wait! We can't do anything until we neutralize these guns!" Christopher added.

"Does anyone have anything on Kim's status?" Adam asked in worry.

"His plane was headed due west of our position! Shortly after all communication went out! But the transponder from his ejector seat is still active!"

The last of the enemy guns were finally destroyed, giving the freedom fighters a moment to catch their breaths from the onslaught that claimed a number of their planes, gunships, and troops.

Adam looked around, seeing the carnage the enemy guns had left in their wake, and said, "We can't get caught off our guard again. I need all available tanks to press forward to make sure that we have completely secured the enemy position. And all available planes and gunships. As of immediately, we need to go into retrieval status."

09:04 HOURS. SOMEWHERE OVER HOLLOMAN ENEMY FORCE BASE. 74 MILES AWAY FROM THE WHITE SANDS MISSILE RANGE, NEAR ALAMOGORDO, NEW MEXICO:

"I'm on it," Karen responded, heading into the direction Dillon had flown earlier after being intercepted by the enemy guns.

09:04 HOURS. HOLLOMAN ENEMY AIR FORCE BASE. 74 MILES AWAY FROM THE WHITE SANDS MISSILE RANGE, NEAR ALAMOGORDO, NEW MEXICO"

"How's your fuel?" Adam said over the radio.

09:05 HOURS. SOMEWHERE OVER HOLLOMAN ENEMY AIR FORCE BASE. 74 MILES AWAY FROM THE WHITE SANDS MISSILE RANGE, NEAR ALAMOGORDO, NEW MEXICO:

"No time. Can't think of that right now. I'll call in if I find anything," she answered.

09:06 HOURS. HOLLOMAN ENEMY AIR FORCE BASE. 74 MILES AWAY FROM THE WHITE SANDS MISSILE RANGE, NEAR ALAMOGORDO, NEW MEXICO:

"Please do. Those shells let some serious daylight into his plane. Hope he wasn't hit by any of those rounds. But right now, I need the three of you to gather as many troops that you can spare and assist the armored units in sweeping the area," Adam replied.

09:19 HOURS. SOMEWHERE IN THE CHIHUAHUAN DESERT. A FEW MILES AWAY FROM HOLLOMAN ENEMY AIR FORCE BASE - ALAMOGORDO, NEW MEXICO:

After Nicole had landed far from the battle area, she took off her head gear, exposing her shoulder-length blonde hair, and tossed it onto the unforgiving sands.

The winds blew across the sands into her piercing blue eyes, along with the blinding rays of the sun, obstructed her vision. She squinted as she began making her way towards the captured enemy position. After a brief moment of trekking through the unforgiving tundra, she stopped in her tracks, placing her hands above her head at the sight of the small group of AH-64 Apache Longbow gunships that accompanied an enemy Blackhawk transport helicopter, hoping it wasn't enemy forces.

The Blackhawk transport helicopter touched down, flinging tiny, hot grains sands in her face, while a group of soldiers jumped out of its confines onto the desert sands with their guns pointed to her face, and quickly pointed their guns downwards after noticing she was one of the pilots who had been shot down by the enemy guns while trying to engage them.

She sighed after realizing she was being transported back to the enemy base, and placed her hands down and boarded the helicopter.

09:34 HOURS. HOLLOMAN ENEMY AIR FORCE BASE. 74 MILES AWAY FROM THE WHITE SANDS MISSILE RANGE, NEAR ALAMOGORDO, NEW MEXICO:

After a long moment of flying, Nicole saw a glimpse of all the black smoke rising from the enemy base from all the destruction they had unleashed in retaliation, though their victory had come at a terrible cost. After witnessing the horrors on the ground first-hand, she hoped that Dillon was still alive.

After landing in the base, she saw a number of soldiers carrying their dead and wounded away to any of the surviving transports.

She walked over to Adam and asked, "Any word on Captain Kim's status?"

Adam looked at the physique of Nicole's slender frame, slightly below average height, along with her blonde hair that she often wore at shoulder length, straight into her piercing blue eyes with a puzzled look on his face and asked, "Who are you?" He glanced at the name on her uniform and said, "Matheson?"

"Yes. It's Nicole. Nicole Matheson. One of Captain Kim's wingmen. I was one of those who was shot down. 'Comet' is my callsign."

"Yes. I remember now. I heard that you've been racking up a number of kills on the board. Not that we're in any competition or anything. Good to finally meet you and put a face to the name. Just not under those circumstances, since you and Captain Kim were shot down. Have you heard anything about his whereabouts?"

"No. I haven't. But one of our gunships went out searching. There's still no word on his whereabouts yet, I'm afraid."

09:52 HOURS. SOMEWHERE IN THE WHITE SANDS DESERT. 54 MILES AWAY FROM THE WHITE SANDS MISSILE RANGE - SOUTHERN NEW MEXICO:

Moments after flying over the desert, still with no sign of the wreckage from Dillon's plane, Karen continued to fly until she saw a thick, dark column of dark smoke rising in the distance. She drew closer to the crash site and said, "I have a visual of smoke a few miles out. It may be Captain Kim's plane."

09:52 HOURS. HOLLOMAN ENEMY AIR FORCE BASE. 74 MILES AWAY FROM THE WHITE SANDS MISSILE RANGE - ALAMOGORDO, NEW MEXICO:

"I need a visual confirmation of Captain Kim's status from the crash site, Dragonfly leader. Please proceed with caution, as you may be flying into another enemy ambush.

And be advised that one of his wingmen has been successfully retrieved," Adam said nervously.

09:53 HOURS. THE WHITE SANDS DESERT. 20 MILES FROM HOLLOMAN ENEMY AIR FORCE BASE, 54 MILES AWAY FROM THE WHITE SANDS MISSILE RANGE - ALAMOGORDO, NEW MEXICO:

"Copy," she answered, flying towards the crash site, until she came upon Dillon still strapped in his seat under the heat of the merciless desert sun, barely clinging to life. His one leg was soaked in blood from the wound that he sustained from the enemy attack, bounded tightly in cord and fabric. "I have a visual on Captain Kim's position."

09:53 HOURS. HOLLOMAN ENEMY AIR FORCE BASE. 74 MILES AWAY FROM THE WHITE SANDS MISSILE RANGE, NEAR ALAMOGORDO, NEW MEXICO:

Adam took a sigh of relief and replied, "Excellent. Extraction team is already being prepped for retrieval. What's his status?"

09:54 HOURS. THE WHITE SANDS DESERT. 20 MILES AWAY FROM HOLLOMAN ENEMY AIR FORCE BASE, 54 MILES AWAY FROM THE WHITE SANDS MISSILE RANGE - ALAMOGORDO, NEW MEXICO:

"He's still alive, but badly wounded from-"she replied, when she was intercepted by an enemy missile from a rocket-propelled grenade, causing her gunship to spin out of control, falling onto the desert sands, instantly immobilizing her.

After a brief moment of being dazed from the fall, she opened her eyes, and found herself looking right into the eyes of the assassin. She realized that she had come face-to-face with the man that she had heard so much about, feeling a sudden surge of fear running through her body, while she remained in a frantic state of shock.

09:54 HOURS. HOLLOMAN ENEMY AIR FORCE BASE. 74 MILES AWAY FROM THE WHITE SANDS MISSILE RANGE - ALAMOGORDO, NEW MEXICO:

"Dragonfly leader, respond! What's your status?" Adam called out.

09:55 HOURS. THE WHITE SANDS DESERT. 20 MILES AWAY FROM HOLLOMAN ENEMY AIR FORCE BASE, 54 MILES AWAY FROM THE WHITE SANDS MISSILE RANGE - ALAMOGORDO, NEW MEXICO:

"It's him," Karen said frantically, staring back into the cold, calculating eyes of the assassin, his gun pointed to her face. "I've been intercepted, but I'm still alive." She watched the assassin walking towards Dillon while he remained helpless, still strapped in his ejection seat, bleeding profusely from his leg wound. She continued to struggle to break free from the wreckage of her gunship.

She paused for a brief moment, watching the assassin and Jason walking towards Dillon, and said, "My God. He's walking towards Captain Kim! He's going to kill him!"

09:57 HOURS. HOLLOMAN ENEMY AIR FORCE BASE. 74 MILES AWAY FROM THE WHITE SANDS MISSILE RANGE - ALAMOGORDO, NEW MEXICO:

A look of shock took over Adam's face after hearing the ominous response on the other end of the radio, and said, "Have a chopper prepped for retrieval." He turned to James and asked, "Did you get a lock on her transponder?"

"We do. About 20 miles from our position. Give or take," James replied.

"Are you hurt, Santiago?" Adam asked softly.

09:58 HOURS. THE WHITE SANDS DESERT. 20 MILES AWAY FROM HOLLOMAN ENEMY AIR FORCE BASE, 54 MILES AWAY FROM THE WHITE SANDS DESERT MISSILE RANGE - ALAMOGORDO, NEW MEXICO:

"No.I'm still alive. But I'm still trapped in the wreckage of my gunship trying to break free. And I'm looking right at him," she answered nervously, watching the assassin and Jason standing before Dillon in his weakened state. "He's about to kill him!"

10:00 HOURS. HOLLOMAN ENEMY AIR FORCE BASE. 74 MILES AWAY FROM THE WHITE SANDS DESERT MISSILE RANGE - ALAMOGORDO, NEW MEXICO:

"I'm already on my way. I need to know Kim's status," Adam said nervously.

10:00 HOURS. THE WHITE SANDS DESERT. 20 MILES AWAY FROM HOLLOMAN ENEMY AIR FORCE BASE, 54 MILES FROM THE WHITE SANDS MISSILE RANGE, NEW MEXICO:

"He's still alive for now. But won't be too much longer. They're still moving towards him," Karen replied, watching helplessly from the wreckage of her gunship. The assassin and Jason walked towards the wounded pilot, as if savoring the moment towards his inevitable demise, stopping before him, watching him suffer immensely from his critical leg wound.

Jason bent towards Dillon, analyzing his leg wound, while he remained strapped in his ejection seat, completely helpless, and said, "He doesn't have long before he goes into shock. We can still help him."

Dillon opened his eyes, seeing the silhouettes of Jason and the assassin standing before him, their uniforms completely disheveled from the recent skirmish from the battle to take over the base. He continued to feel his life slowly slip away while he bled heavily, feeling the sweat dripping down his face. His body began to feel cold even while surrounded by the searing heat from the sun's rays and the warm sun. He said in a soft and weak tone, "Operation Tundra, Valley of the Kings, Egypt. Remember? We were chasing insurgents, helping to overthrow the repressive regime, providing air support until I was shot down by an enemy surface to air missile. I remembered it was the same position that you found me when I was shot down. It was also in a place like this. Another barren desert when you saved my life. Once again, we've crossed paths in another barren desert worlds away. Only now that you find me in the same position only to take my life. Isn't it ironic?"

"You don't have to take his life, Lieutenant," Jason said to the assassin, pleading for Dillon's life. He tried to lift Dillon onto his feet, and continued, "We can still save him."

"Save it, kid. We both know that I'm not going anywhere. I can feel my life slipping away from me every second while I'm sitting on my ass, bleeding to death. My time has come. This is the end of the road for me," Dillon replied.

"We can still help you," Jason softly.

"I seriously doubt that. Don't be in denial. We both know I'm at my end. He's here for one reason, and one reason only. And that's to snuff me out to help weaken our resistance. It's the only opportunity he'll get to kill me. He might as well take it," Dillon replied, scoffing.

10:02 HOURS. HOLLOMAN ENEMY AIR FORCE BASE. 74 MILES AWAY FROM THE WHITE SAND MISSILE RANGE - ALAMOGORDO, NEW MEXICO:

"We have a fix on your position. We'll be there as soon as we can," Adam said frantically boarding the helicopter, heading towards Karen's position.

10:03 HOURS. THE WHITE SANDS DESERT. 20 MILES AWAY FROM HOLLOMAN ENEMY AIR FORCE BASE, 54 MILES FROM THE WHITE SANDS MISSILE RANGE - ALAMOGORDO, NEW MEXICO:

"Well, you better make it fast. It doesn't look like Captain Kim has much time left," she said nervously, still trying to break herself free from the wreckage of her gunship.

The assassin silently drew out his sidearm from its holster, pointing it at Dillon's face, bringing about a look of shock on Jason's face.

"No, Lieutenant. Please don't," Jason pleaded.

"I always knew this day would come. My fate has been written in stone, from the moment I stepped inside the cockpit of that plane. What can I say? It's been a good run," Dillon answered, softly interjecting.

"He's worth more to us alive than dead," Jason continued.

"I'd rather die than give my brothers up," Dillon replied.

"I'm trying to save you," Jason replied.

"There's no saving me at this point. Either I bleed to death, or he pulls that trigger and ends my suffering right here and now. Frankly, he'd be doing me a favor, so please stop begging to save my life. Not that I don't appreciate what you're doing. Look at those eyes. They're cold and empty. There's no reasoning with someone like him."

"You don't know that," Jason replied.

"Oh, but I do. A number of my brothers have fallen by his hand. And today, I'll be next. The truth is as clear as day. He's doing what he has been programmed to do. I'm sure you've heard that one time too many," Dillon said, looking into his eyes, smiling and continued, "It's been a real honor,

Lieutenant. I'll see you in the next life."

"My God! He's pointing his gun to Captain Kim's face! He's about to execute Captain Kim!" Karen said frantically.

10:04 HOURS. HOLLOMAN ENEMY AIR FORCE BASE. 74 MILES AWAY FROM THE WHITE SANDS MISSILE RANGE - ALAMOGORDO, NEW MEXICO:

"We'll be there as soon as we can. Just-" Adam answered, pausing when he was startled, hearing a single gunshot, ending Dillon's life, causing a frantic look of utter shock on his face.

10:06 HOURS. THE WHITE SANDS DESERT. 20 MILES AWAY FROM HOLLOMAN ENEMY AIR FORCE BASE, 54 MILES FROM THE WHITE SANDS MISSILE RANGE - ALAMOGORDO, NEW MEXICO:

After hearing the shot, Jason stood to his feet, staring at the assassin, knowing that he was completely powerless against him.

The assassin fired another two shots into Dillon's chest, startling everyone as they watched helplessly, while Karen kept the radio on her headset active. Adam continued to listen helplessly.

"My God! He just executed Captain Kim right in front of me!" Karen said in a complete state of shock while she remained trapped in the wreckage of her gunship.

After the assassin had executed his target, he turned around slowly, staring at Karen and slowly walked towards her.

"Oh no. My God. He's walking towards me," she continued frantically, as she stopped trying to break herself free from the wreckage of her gunship.

10:07 HOURS. SOMEWHERE OVER THE CHIHUAHUAN DESERT, HEADING TOWARDS THE WHITE SANDS DESERT. 73 MILES FROM THE WHITE SANDS MISSILE RANGE, SOUTHERN NEW MEXICO:

"We lost Kim. But we need to hurry to save Santiago!" Adam said loudly, watching Christopher's, Eric's, and James' faces, knowing that they may also be too late to save Karen from their nemesis.

10:11 HOURS. THE WHITE SANDS DESERT. 20 MILES AWAY FROM HOLLOMAN ENEMY AIR FORCE BASE, 54 MILES AWAY FROM THE WHITE SANDS MISSILE RANGE - ALAMOGORDO, NEW MEXICO:

"He's going to kill me," Karen said, watching the assassin walking towards her, greeting her in stone silence.

She continued to look straight into his eyes, seeing the stone look on his face, watching his sidearm pointed at her face.

She closed her eyes tightly, breathing heavily and nervously, waiting for him to end her life, like he had done to Dillon.

"You're going to kill her too?" Jason shouted, causing Karen to open her eyes, shifting her focus towards Jason, continuing to breathe nervously.

He looked at Jason for a brief moment, and glanced back at Karen for the second time, while she continued to stare back with a frightened look in her eyes. He struck her with the butt of his sidearm, placing her into a deep state of unconsciousness, and causing Jason to take a deep sigh of relief.

He walked towards their transport, and calmly sat in the passenger seat, with Jason sitting next to him, taking one last look at Dillon's bullet-ridden corpse sprawled lifelessly over his ejection seat, completely doused in blood.

He looked at the skies and saw vultures circling high above the position where Dillon's lifeless body remained sprawled. Jason turned on the ignition, driving deeper into the vastness of the unforgiving tundra.

"Look," James said, pointing at the smoke of the wreckage.

"Do you think that Kim's still alive?" Christopher asked softly.

"I don't have to think," Adam replied, pointing to the buzzards that circled the skies, and continued, "I think we all know what that means. Forget about the smoke. If we follow these buzzards, that's where we'll find Kim and Santiago."

They arrived at Karen's location, landing near the position of her gunship, and slowly walked towards her wreckage, where she remained lying unconscious with a cut on her face from the assassin's blow.

"She's still breathing," James said, nudging her until she began to show signs of consciousness, causing them to take a big sigh of relief. Slowly and carefully, they pulled her out of the wreckage.

Adam looked behind him and glanced at Dillon's lifeless corpse laid out while still seated in his ejection seat, covered in blood. Adam slowly walked towards Dillon with his eyes drowning in tears, completely consumed in anger.

He looked back at Karen and asked, "Which direction did he go?"

"I don't know. He knocked me unconscious before I could see. But why did he leave me alive?" Karen replied.

Adam grabbed an old photograph from his uniform and asked, "Can you show me the face of the man that you saw? Do you see him in this photograph?"

She looked at the old photograph, seeing them dressed proudly in their uniforms, posing together, after their tour against the North Korean occupation of the south and said, "That's him. That's definitely him. I could never forget those eyes."

Adam took a deep breath, closing his eyes, and answered, "He's not after you. He's after me, and the other lieutenants. We served together and formed an elite unit called Unit-13, after the war with North Korea, just before the Uprising of Genesis. He's targeting us to kill the resistance and win the war. Needless to say, he's no longer one of us. Right now, we need to find him and kill him before more of us die."

"We can't go after him," Ahmad answered softly.

"Why?" Adam asked.

"For a number of reasons. If we do, we may not have enough fuel to get back to base, and risk being stranded in the desert. We took out all the ammunition and fuel reserves to keep them out of the fight, and after the long bout with the enemy, our planes and gunships have barely enough fuel as it is to make it back to our base. Besides, there's no telling where he may be by now, and for all we know, we may be flying straight into another ambush. I'm sorry, General," Ahmad concluded.

"I want to kill that son of a bitch," Adam replied.

"So do we all," Eric replied. "Dillon was one of us. He served with us on many missions, including the Uprising on Genesis. And he deserves to be avenged. But we won't do him any good if we get killed or captured by the enemy. If we do, our resistance will be over for certain."

"He murdered Kim. Damn him," Adam replied.

"What are your orders, sir?" Christopher asked.

"Load his body on the chopper and bring him back to our base. We owe him a proper burial. We owe all those who gave their lives and paid the price today," Adam replied.

"Yes, sir," Christopher replied.

"Just carry him aboard with dignity. And after he's on board, secure the crash site," Adam replied.

After wrapping his body in the fabric of his parachute, they carried him on board the helicopter and returned to base.

As the helicopter lifted off the burning hot sands of the desert, the wreckage of the gunship suddenly burst into a giant ball of flames after being charged remotely from the confines of the helicopter. While they looked at it burn, as the view of the crash site slowly vanished from their eyes, they continued to open the distance between them, continuing towards the base.

10:32 HOURS. HOLLOMAN ENEMY AIR FORCE BASE. 74 MILES AWAY FROM THE WHITE SANDS MISSILE RANGE - ALAMOGORDO, NEW MEXICO:

Moments after their long flight in complete silence, after losing another one of their closest friends at the hands of their nemesis, they landed, still consumed with anger.

"Have the remainder of the troops load the injured on the transports, and bury the dead. And as for Kim, leave him on the chopper. He'll ride with us back to base."

"Yes, sir," Ahmad replied.

Karen walked around the enemy base, seeing all the destruction the enemy guns left in their wake, though it came at the high cost of losing their position to the freedom fighters, and saw the wreckage of one of the gunships from her squad that went down from enemy fire. She glanced at the pilot's corpse in his cockpit, with a gaping hole that tore into his face, protruding to the back of his head, still oozing blood into the confines.

"I take it that you knew him. You must be the Dragonfly leader. Santiago, if my memory serves me right," Nicole said, walking towards Karen.

"You must be the Comet," Karen replied.

"Nicole. Nicole Matheson. Good to finally meet you," she replied, shaking hands with Karen.

"I'm Karen. Karen Santiago. And yes, I knew him. His name was Gary Stevens. He was a great pilot. Next in rank after me. We flew a number of missions together. Unfortunately, today was our last," she replied, looking at the gaping hole from the enemy round that tore into Gary's face, placing him into a lifeless slumber.

"I lost a number of my own, too," Nicole replied. "The one I lost was Lance Coburn. He was one of many good pilots that we lost in this war. He went by the call sign Flash. Promising but stubborn. And unfortunately, it got him killed."

"We all lost a number of our friends. Not too long ago, I saw General West and the others load Captain Kim's body into the helicopter. They're taking him back to base, as we speak."

"How did he die? Was it from the crash?"

"He was executed right before my eyes. But, whoever it was that killed him left me alive. I don't know why. But I can never forget looking into those eyes. They were cold and empty. I suppose he left me alive so I can know what it's like to be hunted. And I can't stand it one bit. And that means one of you will take Captain Kim's place from this point on."

"No one can take Captain Kim's place. Not after all he's done," Nicole replied, looking at Gary's lifeless gaze from the bullet wound, while she stood alongside Karen.

"I feel the same way, since we lost Captain O'Hara last year," Karen replied, closing Gary's other eye.

Janet walked towards them and asked, "Are you both alright? I know you both have been through a lot."

"We can say the same about you," Nicole replied.

"We'll live," Karen said softly.

"It seems that you both were close," Janet said softly.

"Yes, we were," Karen replied.

"I'm sorry to hear about Captain Kim," Janet said to Nicole.

"We all are. But in a war, we pay the price, whether we live or die," Nicole replied. "So it's up to us now to live and fight for all those who've fallen today and tomorrow, and the day after that. Captain Kim and all those who've fallen today will be missed. Sadly, many more will pay the ultimate price. After all, it's the nature of what we do."

"It's strange to think that all of this came from one incident that happened years ago," Janet added.

"Situations like these begin like a tiny symptom and escalate into a virus if left unchecked. And even if it's checked, there's no stopping it, sometimes. And sadly, this is one of them," Nicole said softly.

"Sometimes, there's nothing we can do, but to let nature run its course, and join the fight," Janet replied.

"Like now. And in the midst of all of it, we lose so many of the ones we love," Karen added.

"Unfortunately, it's the price we pay for freedom," Nicole replied.

Christopher and Eric came to stand next to Janet, Karen, and Nicole, watching the gaping hole that tore through Gary's face. Christopher turned to Karen and asked, "Are you okay? You look a little shaken up."

"I'll be fine. But yes, still shaken up, considering what just happened. Who wouldn't be?" she replied, with her eyes still fixed on Gary's lifeless body.

"I know. No matter how many times you fight a war, losing the ones that you care about is a feeling that you can never get used to."

"What about you, Matheson? Are you okay?" Eric asked.

"I'd like to say I am, but I'm not," Nicole replied.

"That's an understatement, considering the recent turn of events," Eric replied. "Every time I shut that canopy over my head, I feel like I'm flying in my own coffin. I feel like the whole world is closing in on me. If anyone says they're not afraid, then that's a damn lie. Every time I see myself flying in those skies, I feel like I'm sealing my own fate."

"It's no different to us on the ground. Nowhere is safe. Just pray that you make it out alive," Christopher answered.

"Every time we set out to fight, we can only hope that our fate isn't written in stone, like the others before us," Eric said softly.

"Like Captain Kim?" Nicole asked.

"Like him, and like Alvarez, Henry, Taylor, O'Hara, and like all the others who perished for the cause in this fight to preserve our freedom. Or whatever's left of it. Or, if there's any left at all. And sadly, there'll be more to come. Then again, it's a truth that we all know too well and have grown to make peace with it," Christopher replied.

"On that, we all can agree," Janet replied.

"The way I see it, it's a price worth paying in the fight against people like the General. And as much as I wished that I wasn't at war, I'd gladly lay my life down for the cause. Because I, for one, would rather die than to be a slave," Eric replied.

Ahmad took a deep breath, breaking his silence and said, "Not that any of us on either side was given much of a choice. After all, everyone who fights believes that his cause is just. No matter how good or twisted it may be."

Anton came walking towards their position and said softly, "General West is about to return to base. He sent me to tell you, in case any of you are thinking of leaving. The chopper is prepped and ready to leave in a few minutes."

"Okay," Nicole said softly, and walked away, with the others following.

Anton stayed around for a brief moment, watching the horror that surrounded him, and fixed his gaze on Gary's lifeless face. He looked around, seeing the wounded bodies being carried into whatever transports that could be salvaged from the enemy position, back to their base.

After boarding the helicopter, en-route to their base, Adam and the others sat quietly among themselves, watching the surviving troops scurry about the base, carrying many of the dead and wounded to the transports. Amidst all the death and destruction they had wrought upon the enemy, the cost of their victory was a heavy price to pay, escorted by the remainder of planes and gunships.

12:01 HOURS. CANNON FREEDOM FIGHTER AIR FORCE BASE. 236 MILES AWAY FROM HOLLOMAN ENEMY AIR FORCE BASE - CLOVIS, NEW MEXICO:

Brian heard the planes flying over the base, quickly vanishing in the distance, and saw a helicopter flying towards the base, escorted by fewer gunships than that they had left for their attack on the enemy position, causing a sudden look of concern to crease his face.

He hurried over to the position where the helicopter landed, and saw Christopher, Ahmad, Eric, and Anton carrying Dillon's lifeless body, draped in the fibers of his parachute as a makeshift stretcher, out of the helicopter, towards the infirmary. They saw Adam slowly walking out of the helicopter with a look of sadness on his battle-weary visage, telling them that his heart was heavy from the tragic loss of his friend, with Nicole trailing behind him quietly.

Brian ran to Adam and asked, "Did she make it?"

Adam simply nodded his head and pointed to the helicopter with Karen slowly walking out of it onto the base. He ran towards her and said, "I know I saw a lot more planes and gunships left for the enemy position. What happened?"

"We took the base. But not before we walked into an ambush of Hydra-6 machine gun nests. They were ready for us."

"Who was that draped in the parachute? Was that…" Brian asked.

Karen's hand suddenly began to tremble and answered, "I saw him," with her tears running down her face.

"Who?" Brian asked with a puzzled look on his face.

"Him. The one who killed Lieutenant Alvarez, Collins, Taylor, Captain O'Hara, and now Captain Kim, our flight leader," she answered, wiping the tears off her face, and continued, "I looked right into his eyes. They were so cold and empty."

"And he let you live? Are you sure it was him?" Brian asked with a frantic look of shock on his face. "How did this happen? I'm sorry, but I'm not following you."

"After we were ambushed, Captain Kim's plane was shot down and crash landed about 20 miles from the base. I went to look for him, and that's when I was shot down. I looked right into his eyes, when he pointed his gun to my face, while I remained trapped in my gunship. He walked over to Captain Kim and just executed him. Right there on the spot, in front of me."

"While you watched?" Brian asked, still with a look of shock on his face.

Karen nodded her head. "Then he walked back to me and rendered me unconscious with his weapon. By the time I woke up, he was already gone, and General West and the others were pulling me out the wreckage. I suppose the other soldier who begged for my life saved me."

"There were two of them?"

"Yes. And I'm sure he was begging for Captain Kim's life as well. But, that didn't work too well in his favor."

"Then why did he leave you alive?"

"I don't know. All I can tell you is he left me alive so I can feel what it's like to be hunted. Or maybe tell the tale on how we crossed paths. Either way, I'm not looking forward to either happening again."

"I'm just glad that you're okay," he said, feeling the scab on the side of her eye with his fingers.

"The ambush almost wiped us out. We walked right into their trap. Straight into a hornet's nest. We lost quite a bit of good pilots, troops, and infantry," she said.

Moments later, Brian and Karen walked into the medical bay where Dillon's bullet-riddled body lay on the table, where Adam and the others were paying their respects in complete silence of their fallen comrade.

James walked towards Adam, placing his hand gently on his shoulder and asked, "Are you okay, General West? I'm sorry about Captain Kim. I know how much he meant to you. Is there anything you'd like me to do?"

"I should've listened. I should've listened when you told me not to go," Adam replied, bowing his head over Dillon's lifeless body.

"It had to be done. You made a gamble and you won, General. The day belongs to you," Eric replied.

"We took the base," Christopher added.

"But at what cost? Every time we fight, one of us dies! Whether we win or lose! Look around you! It's just hell all around! And all it's doing is consuming all of us at some point!" Adam said sharply.

"We all know the price was great, General West. But Captain Kim paid the price for doing his job. Sadly it's a price we have to pay," Nicole said.

Adam turned towards Nicole, looking into her weary blue eyes and said, "Well, in that case, you've just been promoted to captain of the fighter squadron."

A sudden look of shock creased over Nicole's face and replied, "I don't know if I'll be able to lead the fighter squadron. Captain Kim's shoes are some pretty big shoes to fill."

"The last I heard, you were the pilot who scored a number of kills next to Kim's kill ratio. So, here's your chance to prove if you're still cut out for the job," Adam answered, looking squarely into her eyes, while she stared back, with a look of total shock on her face.

The war continues…

CHAPTER 7: OPERATION ICE HAMMER.

06:16 HOURS. SOMEWHERE OVER LAKE MICHIGAN, THE GREAT EXPANSE OF WATER STRETCHING BETWEEN THE STATES OF MICHIGAN, CHICAGO, INDIANA, AND WISCONSIN:

The year 2031. Six years have passed since "The Great Fall of Genesis."

The chilling winds howled over the vast body of water that connected the states of Michigan, Chicago, Indiana, and Wisconsin, bringing forth the infinite flurries of snow that make their long and gentle descent from the gray, overcast skies as the bitter winter quickly comes into season.

A flock of barn swallows quickly mobilized to the skies in search of warmer weather after sensing the sudden drop in temperature in their habitat.

A flock of common loons swam in the great lake in search of fish, savoring the last of their moments, before their long and arduous trip in search of warmer climate, and suddenly took flight into the overcast skies, in their usual perfect V-formation.

A downy woodpecker pecked relentlessly at the trunk of a tree to build its nest for the brutal winter, as the snow slowly begins its descent from the pale gray skies.

A flock of great egrets quickly gathered around the coast of the great lake, scavenging for whatever food they can salvage before their long trip to a more hospitable climate, and suddenly took flight after their fill.

A flock of double crested cormorants soared in the skies in great numbers in search of better sanctuary from the bitter cold.

After many of the species made their sudden, but necessary departure from their natural habitat to escape the unbearable conditions of the bitter cold soon to come, the sudden eerie calm enveloped the vast expanse of the great lake, as the cold, bitter winds howled over the sheet of ice that covered its vast expanse, when the roar from the engines of a fighter plane followed by many others battling for control of the skies, suddenly zoomed across, disturbing the serenity of the frozen tundra drowning the howling of the winds.

From beneath the dark void of the great lake, the eyes of a yellow perch quickly shifted its gaze, after catching the blinding flashes high above the clouds in the dawn of the cold morning skies, while swimming in the darkness of the abyss, when the wreckage of a fighter plane crashed into the body of thin ice that blanketed the lake, with the body of a dead pilot still strapped into his cockpit.

The burning wreckage of another fighter plane, with the body of another lifeless pilot still trapped inside the cockpit, crashed into the lake, slowly sinking into the dark void.

In rapid succession, the flaming wreckage of another fighter plane quickly followed, crashing through the thin wall of ice, sinking into the abyss, her eyes staring back with a lifeless gaze while being committed eternally to the void of the deep. The lake was becoming their watery graves, like the many of the unfortunate souls before, who had met their untimely demise, with the flaming contrails of another aircraft plummeting from the skies, showing the unavoidable outcome from relentless engagements of both factions who remained in total pursuit of one another to gain total air superiority. The frantic radio chatter from the pilots who constantly defied death, always on the brink of pushing their exhausted bodies beyond their limits, stole the serenity of the great icy tundra that lay between the neighboring states.

"We're losing too many planes!" Nicole cried out nervously. "Don't know how much longer we can hold! If we continue to lose at this rate, our entire squadron and ground forces will be wiped out! We need to come up with a plan to turn this battle around!" Another blinding flash from another plane exploding lit within the confines of her cockpit, quickly plummeting to the surface, trailing a line of dark and heavy smoke, splashing into the great lake, with deafening impact. She watched as another one of her planes made its descent into the freezing waters, checking to see if the pilot had ejected from the dilapidated aircraft. "We just lost another plane! I didn't see the pilot's ejection seat. I repeat, I didn't see the pilot's ejection seat! Does anyone have a visual on the pilot's section seat?" she asked, only to receive confirmation from one of her wingman's radio chatter that another one of their pilots was killed in action.

She began exhaling heavily, resting her head against the seat of her chair, while she remained confined within the cockpit of her plane, trying to gather her thoughts, and closed her eyes tightly for a brief moment, and suddenly felt the warm rays of the blinding sun striking on the pale skin of her face, as it burned through the gray skies through the canopy of her cockpit. She opened her eyes, and suddenly had an epiphany of how to change the course of the air battle, causing her feeling of nervousness to quickly vanish. She reminisced on Dillon's tactics of using the sun to her back, making her invisible to the enemy, a year earlier before the war had claimed his life.

With her new-found courage, she keyed the radio and said with a soft hint of confidence, "Hammer and Razor, come with me. The rest of you, keep the enemy planes entangled. I have a plan."

She and her duo of wingmen flew out of the battle area towards the sun, and quickly turned their planes around, arming their weapons while they headed back to the battle, the sun to their backs, making them invisible to the enemy.

After lining up her targets with a missile lock, she fired and watched the missile track the enemy plane, exploding into it, and said, with a louder tone of confidence, "All weapons hot. Engage at will. I repeat, all weapons hot."

Her two wingmen quickly followed suit, while the others continued to distract the enemy planes, scoring a number of hits. Slowly, the balance of the battle of the skies shifted in their favor, though they still remained heavily outnumbered by the enemy forces.

After scoring a number of hits on the enemy forces, seeing them splashing into the great lake, like many of her copilots before, she looked at the bright, warm rays of the sun piercing through the gray clouds into the canopy of her plane, and said softly, "Thank you, Captain Kim. Couldn't have done it without you."

06:21 HOURS. PEDESTRIAN BRIDGE, HEADING TOWARDS THE ENEMY COMMAND CENTER, AMWAY GRAND PLAZA HOTEL - GRAND RAPIDS, MICHIGAN:

Though the freedom fighters remained heavily outnumbered against the enemy troops, they continued to hold their ground, inflicting steady losses on the enemy-armored units while suffering heavy losses in return.

"We're suffering heavy casualties! Where's our air support?" Tiara shouted, as she continued to score kills on the enemy armored units.

"There's just too many of them! We need air support now!"

06:23 HOURS. SOMEWHERE OVER LAKE MICHIGAN:

"We're still engaging the enemy forces! Just hold on a little longer! We'll be there as soon as we can!" Nicole replied.

06:24 HOURS. PEDESTRIAN BRIDGE, HEADING TOWARDS THE ENEMY COMMAND CENTER, AMWAY GRAND PLAZA HOTEL - GRAND RAPIDS MICHIGAN:

"Well, you need to hurry! Our troops are getting killed down here!" Tiara replied.

As the ground troops continued to suffer a series of casualties, James grabbed a rocket propelled grenade and fired at one of the enemy-armored units, but only slowed it down. "Direct hit! But, it's not stopping! You need to take it out!"

Tiara carefully and masterfully lined up the enemy armored unit in her sight and quickly fired into its thick armor, causing it to erupt into flames.

"That leaves me with an idea," Anton replied.

"What? We're open to any kind of suggestions right about now!" Janet replied.

"Since we're outnumbered, we can use the R.P.G.s to slow them down long enough for our tanks to hit them and push forward!" Anton answered, through the deafening roar of gunfire.

"Good idea!" James replied.

"All units come in!" Janet shouted

"Go," Eric replied.

"We need to push forward!" Janet replied.

"What else is new?"Christopher replied.

"I have a plan, sir!" James replied over the radio.

"We're all ears!" Eric answered.

"We don't have enough tanks to hold the line so we'll have to use R.P.G.s to slow them down long enough for our tanks to get their shots in!" James replied.

"We're open to any suggestions at this point!" Christopher replied.

They implemented their strategy and slowly began to gain ground on the enemy forces.

"It's working! Keep the pressure!" Eric shouted.

"Keep pushing! We need to take that command center!" Christopher cried out.

The resilience of the freedom fighters in their resolve to overrun the enemy's greater numbers while they continued inching their way into the city gradually wore their enemies' numbers thin.

06:27 HOURS, AMWAY GRAND PLAZA HOTEL ENEMY COMMAND CENTER - GRAND RAPIDS, MICHIGAN:

The hotel was once an important landmark in the city and stood as a beacon of hope, a bustling place of business that once generated a great deal of capital for the denizens in the community. It closed down during the civil war, only to be transformed into a makeshift stronghold to store ammunition, troops, and conduct all forms of military exercises in the General's ruthless ambitions to seize the entire country under his rule in imposing martial law.

The collective, thundering footsteps of the enemy forces filled the halls of the once exquisite and spacious confines of the hotel's lobby mobilizing, after hearing the frantic radio chatter of the enemy soldiers who were slowly losing their ground to the rebels gaining toward their position.

06:28 HOURS. SOMEWHERE OVER LAKE MICHIGAN:

The war for the skies continued to wage over the large expanse of the great lake, with the tide slowly turning in the favor of the freedom fighters, after causing a series of casualties on the enemy forces resulting from their clever tactics.

06:29 HOURS. PEDESTRIAN BRIDGE, HEADING TOWARDS, AMWAY GRAND PLAZA HOTEL ENEMY COMMAND CENTER - GRAND RAPIDS, MICHIGAN:

"We're pushing them back, but our progress is still too slow! We need air support! Where's our air support!" Tiara shouted, while she continued to stave off the enemy attack. She continued to score kills on the enemy units as they continued to inch their way towards the enemy command center.

06:30 HOURS. NATIONAL GUARD ENEMY AIR FORCE BASE. 105 MILES AWAY FROM THE AMWAY GRAND PLAZA HOTEL - GRAND RAPIDS, MICHIGAN:

While the snow continued to fall within the vicinity of the base, the alarms blared loudly, causing a large number of enemy fighter pilots to scurry across the base, after hearing the tide of battle for air supremacy had turned in the favor of the smaller group of freedom fighters, along with a number of enemy ground troops.

06:31 HOURS. DETROIT ARSENAL FREEDOM FIGHTER AIR FORCE BASE - WARREN, MICHIGAN:

Adam grabbed the radio and said, "This is command to the flight leader. What's your status? Over. Anyone, please respond. Over."

06:32 HOURS. SOMEWHERE OVER THE LAKE, MICHIGAN:

"We've lost a number of planes, but were able to regroup and inflict more casualties on the enemy forces in return, and have changed the course of the battle.

We're still combat capable, but we're running low on fuel and ordinance, and need additional reinforcements, so we can provide cover for the ground troops," Nicole answered softly.

06:32 HOURS. PEDESTRIAN BRIDGE HEADING TOWARDS THE AMWAY GRAND PLAZA HOTEL, ENEMY COMMAND CENTER - GRAND RAPIDS, MICHIGAN:

"We lost most of our armed units, though we've punched a hole in the enemy defenses. We're still holding on, but it's just a matter of time before we get overrun! We need air support!" James yelled.

06:33 HOURS. DETROIT ARSENAL FREEDOM FIGHTER TANK BASE, WARREN, MICHIGAN. 153 MILES AWAY FROM THE AMWAY GRAND PLAZA HOTEL - GRAND RAPIDS, MICHIGAN:

This plant was the first-ever plant built for the mass production of tanks in the United States, established in 1940 under Chrysler, and was owned by the U.S. Government until 1996. It turned to peaceful production at the end of the war, and now has been recalled into action to mass produce tanks and store ammunition and troops for the war effort against the enemy forces.

Upon hearing the plight of their ground troops, the alarms blared loudly within the vicinity of the base, with a number of pilots and ground troops quickly mobilizing to reinforce their position to keep the enemy forces at bay, as the tide of battle slowly shifted towards the freedom fighters.

"More planes and troops are being mobilized as we speak! Reinforcements will be in your position shortly! I'm about to commandeer one of our transports and head to your position! Just hold on as long as you can! I'll keep a secure channel open!" Adam replied, running out of the command center, instantly greeted by the freezing winds, quickly hopping into one of the ground transports.

06:34 HOURS. PEDESTRIAN BRIDGE, HEADING TOWARDS THE AMWAY GRAND PLAZA HOTEL, ENEMY COMMAND CENTER - GRAND RAPIDS, MICHIGAN:

"I'm picking up a transmission! No, two of them!," James said, listening to the radio chatter.

"What is it?" Christopher asked.

"I'm picking up more enemy armor and troops heading our way to reinforce their position!"

"What's next?" Eric asked.

"A large number of enemy planes are mobilizing and heading our way!"

"What's E.T.A.?" Christopher asked.

"A few minutes. About 20 minutes at most! It's not looking good, sir!" James replied.

"Since when has it?" Eric asked.

James placed the receiver of the radio down and took a deep breath and said to Janet, "You heard it yourself! It'll take some time before all our reinforcements arrive!"

"We're making ground, but our progress is still too slow! We've lost a number of our tanks and planes, but by some miracle, we're still able to hold off the enemy forces!" Tiara replied.

"But, after all this time, our planes might be running dangerously low on fuel and ordinance!" Christopher added.

"We may not have too long before more enemy units converge on our position," Ahmad replied.

"If the enemy troops get to us first, that means we'll be squeezed on both sides, and we don't have the manpower to hold out on both fronts! Our campaign will be over for sure!" Eric replied.

"The way I see it, we just have to keep on fighting and pray for a miracle!"

Ahmad added, when they suddenly heard the roaring engines of fighter planes growing louder towards their position, raining a lethal volley of air to ground missiles over the enemy position.

They watched helplessly at the volley of air to ground missiles screaming through the cold, bitter winds, free-falling towards the enemy position, consuming all the enemy soldiers and armored units alike in a giant, crimson wall of flame. The giant mushroom cloud rose over the embattled area, causing the entire bridge to shudder beneath their feet. Fragments of dust and rusted metal from the crumbling fixtures of the bridge that slowly decayed from passing of time and the elements rained upon them, as it struggled to remain intact from the awesome force of the blast, causing the deafening roar of the tanks' massive turrets to cease. They witnessed the total annihilation of the enemy forces in a complete state of awe at the awesome yet terrifying spectacle.

06:34 HOURS. SOMEWHERE OVER GRAND RAPIDS, MICHIGAN:

As Nicole flew over their position she watched from the view of her cockpit at the giant mushroom cloud of dark smoke that rose to the skies from their attack, giving the ground troops a chance to capture the enemy command center.

06:35 HOURS. PEDESTRIAN BRIDGE, HEADING TOWARDS THE AMWAY GRAND PLAZA, ENEMY COMMAND CENTER - GRAND RAPIDS, MICHIGAN:

They watched the planes fly over their position in complete silence, vanishing into the gray, overcast skies.

"Well, don't just stand there. The flames won't put themselves out," Janet said, breaking the silence, causing everyone to come to their senses.

"Through that?" Eric asked.

"Well, you did ask for a miracle. So here it is," Janet replied.

"All units - charge! All remaining personnel, take cover behind the armored units!" Christopher ordered.

"You mean if we don't get burnt alive first?" Ahmad replied.

"If we go back, it's all for nothing. Either way, we're fucked. So, I might as well do it fighting," Eric replied.

"You do have a point. I have no intention of staying back like a sitting duck, to wait for another enemy platoon to crawl up my ass."

"All units, move forward in blockade positions!" Ahmad ordered.

All the heavy armored units formed a gauntlet, moving across the burning bridge, ramming through the burning gauntlet of all the dead husks of heavy and light armored units, as they made their way towards the enemy command center. The rest of the ground troops trailed behind using the heavy armored units for cover.

06:36 HOURS. SOMEWHERE ON INTERSTATE 696. 152 MILES AWAY FROM THE AMWAY GRAND PLAZA HOTEL, ENEMY COMMAND CENTER - GRAND RAPIDS, MICHIGAN:

Adam grabbed the radio and said, "What's the situation?"

06:36 HOURS. PEDESTRIAN BRIDGE, HEADING TOWARDS THE AMWAY GRAND PLAZA HOTEL, ENEMY COMMAND CENTER - GRAND RAPIDS, MICHIGAN:

"By some miracle, the gauntlet has been neutralized and we're advancing towards the enemy position as we speak. But our progress is still slow," Eric replied.

06:36 HOURS. SOMEWHERE ON INTERSTATE 696. 152 MILES AWAY FROM THE AMWAY GRAND PLAZA HOTEL, ENEMY COMMAND CENTER - GRAND RAPIDS, MICHIGAN:

"Okay, proceed as planned. Reinforcements are already en-route to your position," Adam replied.

06:38 HOURS. SOMEWHERE OVER GRAND RAPIDS, MICHIGAN:

After sustaining a number of casualties from the enemy forces, Nicole and the remaining planes were finally able to turn the battle for control of the skies in their favor, almost completely neutralizing the enemy, at the cost of all their ammunition and fuel almost being depleted. She remained firmly in her resolve for total air supremacy of the skies against an enemy far superior in number, while intercepting more enemy planes.

She looked at her ammunition count, along with her fuel and said, "I'm running low on fuel and ordinance, and the enemy is throwing everything they have at us! We need to hold out as long as we can before our reinforcements arrive. All units with more fuel and ordinance, pull back. I'll distract them long enough so you can regroup and engage! Same plan as follows! Over!"

06:41 HOURS. PEDESTRIAN BRIDGE, HEADING TOWARDS THE AMWAY GRAND PLAZA HOTEL, ENEMY COMMAND CENTER - GRAND RAPIDS, MICHIGAN:

The remainder of the ground troops slowly began to push through the gauntlet of burning husks of enemy vehicles, lined with the charred corpses of enemy soldiers sprawled all over the streets.

As they gained more ground towards the makeshift enemy command center, they were greeted by more heavy resistance from more enemy reinforcements, who tried desperately to hold their position against the freedom fighters as they continued to gain more ground.

06:42 HOURS. AMWAY GRAND PLAZA HOTEL ENEMY COMMAND CENTER - GRAND RAPIDS, MICHIGAN:

A small group of enemy soldiers perching on the high ground spotted the column of armored units and ground troops advancing towards their position, and immediately greeted them with a volley of rocket-propelled grenades and heavy machine gun fire, claiming a number of lives, and destroying a few of their units.

Tiara aimed her turret towards where the grenades came from, and fired one of the tank's massive shells, causing the thick walls of the building to shatter from the force of the blast. A number of other armored units followed in quick succession, taking out a number of the enemy soldiers, while the heavy machine gun fire from their tanks continued tearing through the building's infrastructure, keeping the remaining enemy forces suppressed, while the ground troops moved closer to the dilapidated building.

"Take out the front door! We need to take that building!" Eric called out.

Tiara carefully aimed at the front door frame and deployed the heavy shell from the tank, causing the entire entrance to explode into fragments.

"Point all guns at that door! Light up that position!" Christopher shouted.

The enemy position was greeted with a heavy volley of heavy machine gun fire, tearing through the entire lobby and suddenly stopped, and waited for all the smoke and debris to clear in stone silence.

After the smoke and debris cleared, they waited for their orders to move in, with their weapons gripped tightly in their palms.

"Move in! There may be more enemy soldiers hiding in the rooms! We need to flush them out!" Christopher said.

The freedom fighters slowly made their way towards the gaping hole of what the front door of the enemy command center used to be, and paused for a brief moment, their eyes probing all about watching the gaping holes made from all the tank's heavy shell and heavy machine gun fire.

"Move in. Jackson, Reed, and I, and a few others will sweep the buildings and clear out whatever remaining enemy troops left. After we're done with our sweep, we'll build a perimeter, and serve as a lookout for any incoming enemy troops, and help our tanks hold out the perimeter until our reinforcements get here. Let's go," Ahmad said, leading the charge.

They slowly and cautiously continued through the lobby completely riddled with bullet holes and countless corpses of enemy troops, combing every floor, as they went along searching for more surviving enemy troops.

Ahmad, Anton, and Janet, along with a few other soldiers, continued searching through the narrow corridors of the hotel and were suddenly greeted by a barrage of enemy machine gun fire, claiming the lives of some of their troops, striking Janet in the leg, as the other survivors fell to the floor for cover.

Janet immediately grabbed her assault weapon while she remained lying on the floor, after being wounded in the exchange, and immediately returned fire, with the others following suit, riddling the door with countless bullet holes.

The gunfire ended, leaving a dead silence through the narrow corridor of the hotel with only the sounds of the hollow, spent shell casings falling on the floor.

They remained calm, listening for any sounds of any movement behind the door that separated them and the enemy soldiers.

Anton slowly picked himself from the floor, and slipped his arms around Janet's waist, lifting her to her feet, secretly fighting his emotions.

She paused for a brief moment looking into his eyes, speechless, while her arms remained wrapped around his neck, ignoring the wound that tore into her leg from the exchange.

Anton immediately turned his look of affection towards her into a look of annoyance, and asked, "How's your leg?"

"It doesn't hurt so much, now that you're here," Janet replied.

"You're bleeding out. You need to keep pressure on your wound," Anton replied.

"Do the honors, then. You're quite the gentleman, Reed, aren't you?"

"Here's a bandage for your leg," Anton said, wrapping her wound.

"It's not the time to be flirting," Ahmad said, interrupting Janet's brief moment of affection with Anton.

"It's her," Anton replied, while he continued to wrap the bandage. "Keep still, please."

"By all means, sugar. But, did I have to get a bullet in my leg to feel your touch?" she asked.

"See what I mean?" Anton said to Ahmad.

"Whatever you say," Ahmad replied.

After Anton finished, they focused their attention to the bullet-ridden door with their guns drawn.

"I'll get the door," Anton said, pulling a hand grenade from his sachet and tossing it at the door to breach into the room.

They waited for a brief moment to hear the grenade explode, and rushed through the door only to be greeted by a number of dead enemy soldiers.

Anton looked back at the soldiers who were killed by the enemy soldiers, and said, "So many of us have to die, and for what?"

"It feels more like so many of them, and so little of us. Like the bold 300 holding out against a 1,000,000 strong," Janet replied.

"Technically, that's what it is," Ahmad replied.

As the others waited patiently downstairs, Christopher grabbed the radio and said, "Evans, what's your status?"

"We've purged the other floors of any remaining, and established a look out for any signs of any other incoming enemy forces. We lost a few men, and Jackson got hit. But she'll survive. Any news of reinforcements?"

"Not as yet. What we need to do is to hold out long enough until our reinforcements come. That's if they don't get picked off by the enemy first," Eric replied.

"How's your leg, Jackson?" Ahmad asked.

"I'll be fine. It's just a flesh wound. Feels much better with Anton's magic touch though," she replied.

"There you go again," Anton replied.

"Of course. Maybe I won't get another chance to tell you, so why not now?" she said.

"I'm not interested. Not now, or ever."

"Just stop it, both of you. You need to focus on the mission instead of wondering when you're gonna be having a hot date," Ahmad added.

"Wait. Is it just me or am I hearing something? Do you hear anything?" Anton asked.

"I do. It's your heart beating next to mine," Janet replied.

"Will you stop? I meant like a fighter plane approaching on a bombing run. This is not about you trying to display your affections," Anton replied.

"I love the sound of that, too," she replied.

"Here I am fighting a war, and in the midst of it, listening to a pair of nymphos talking about hooking up," Ahmad replied.

"It's just me for now," Janet replied.

"Forget you, Jackson," Anton said scoffing, walking towards the glass window of the hotel room, over the dead enemy troops sprawled on the cold concrete floor. He followed the sound of the plane's engines as it drew nearer, and looked to the skies, seeing the tiny dot of the fuselage of the fighter plane growing larger as it drew nearer towards their position, noticing no signs of slowing down, while it continued careening towards them.

"Think it could be ours?" Janet asked.

"No signs of slowing down," Anton replied and saw the enemy plane quickly take to the skies, vanishing into the dark, gray, overcast clouds.

"This is not good. Doesn't make any sense. Why would the plane suddenly fly towards our position and take to the skies?" Ahmad said, watching the fighter plane vanish.

Anton looked closely and saw the enemy missile coming closer towards them and shouted, "We have incoming! Get down!" pushing Janet out of the way, falling on top of her to shield her from the awesome force of the blast. The countless wreckage and debris fell on top of him, burying them beneath.

Ahmad slowly arose from the wreckage, completely disoriented, his ears ringing loudly from the force of the blast. He coughed from the smoke, and looked all around him, noticing that the deadly explosion had consumed more of their ground forces to the assault.

He walked over to Anton who was covered with debris, clearing it, only to find him lying on top of Janet, unconscious.

He slowly opened his eyes, as he remained on top of Janet, looking into her eyes. She looked back into his, immediately placing all the calamity that had befallen them out of her thoughts, and he slowly lifted her to her feet.

The brief moment of silence was interrupted by the crackling sounds of heavy machine gun fire and the clamor of more explosions.

They walked towards the gaping hole that ripped through the building from the awesome blast from the enemy attack, and looked down to the streets where all their tanks and light armored units were positioned. They watched helplessly in horror at the series of air to ground missiles plummeted towards their vehicles, engulfing many of their units into a giant sea flame, causing the entire building to shudder beneath their feet, while the anti-aircraft from the surviving units fought valiantly to repel the onslaught of the enemy fighter planes.

"Let's go! We need to leave now!" Anton said, grabbing Janet, carrying her on his shoulder.

With most of the ground units destroyed, Tiara braved the enemy fire fighting back valiantly at the enemy, trying to stave their assault, when an explosion from an air to ground missile exploded near her position, causing her tank to shudder, temporarily knocking her from her tank's gunnery position.

She quickly came to her senses and resumed her position on her tank's gunnery position, while they desperately waited for their reinforcements to arrive.

Seeing the hopelessness in their fight against the enemy, Eric grabbed the radio and said, "General West, come in!"

06:55 HOURS. SOMEWHERE OVER ON INTERSTATE 696 HEADING TOWARDS AMWAY GRAND PLAZA HOTEL ENEMY COMMAND CENTER - GRAND RAPIDS, MICHIGAN:

"This is General West. What's your status? Over."

06:56 HOURS. AMWAY GRAND PLAZA HOTEL ENEMY COMMAND CENTER - GRAND RAPIDS, MICHIGAN:

"We're being engaged by enemy forces, and we're falling less than half strength. We need air support now!" Eric called out.

06:57 HOURS. SOMEWHERE OVER GRAND RAPIDS, MICHIGAN:

Nicole heard the frantic call for air support, and briefly glanced at her ammunition and fuel gauge. "Reading you loud and clear! Coming in to provide support! This is flight leader to General West! Come in! Over!"

06:58 HOURS. SOMEWHERE ON INTERSTATE 696, HEADING TOWARDS THE AMWAY GRAND PLAZA HOTEL ENEMY COMMAND CENTER - GRAND RAPIDS, MICHIGAN:

"This is General West. Reinforcements are already en-route to your position! Hold on as long as you can! The rest of our ground troops are depending on you!"

07:00 HOURS. SOMEWHERE OVER GRAND RAPIDS, MICHIGAN:

"We're running dangerously low on fuel and ordinance, but don't know how much longer we can hold out!" Nicole called out.

07:00 HOURS. SOMEWHERE ON INTERSTATE 696, HEADING TOWARDS GRAND RAPIDS, MICHIGAN:

"I know what you're going through! Hold on as long as you can! Reinforcements will be in your position shortly!" Adam replied.

07:02 HOURS. SOMEWHERE OVER GRAND RAPIDS, MICHIGAN:

Nicole and the remainder of her planes flew closer to engage the enemy planes to help divert their attention off the ground forces, and heard the alarms blaring in her cockpit, warning her of approaching enemy planes.

She glanced at her radar for a brief moment, and quickly switched to her guns as she continued to fly towards the enemy planes. She squeezed the trigger, unleashing a series of heavy rounds from the awesome force of her plane's lethal machine guns, lodging into the enemy planes, causing them to take evasive action, breaking their formation.

After noticing one of the enemy planes had been severely damaged from the barrage of bullets from the heavy machine guns, she switched to her long range missiles and fired it at the enemy plane. She watched it track the enemy plane, exploding into it, and watched it plummet to the surface, trailing a line of thick, dark smoke, crashing and burning at the bottom.

She heard the alarms blaring in the cockpit once again, and saw enemy bullets racing past her, tearing through the hull and canopy of her plane, forcing her to take evasive maneuvers, quickly performing a barrel roll, as she flew high into the skies, while the alarms continued to blare in the cockpit of her plane, warning her of an incoming enemy missile that continued its relentless pursuit.

She watched on her scanners as the enemy missile continued to draw nearer to her plane. She tried as much as she could to evade the enemy attack, and quickly deployed her sunbursts, causing the enemy missile to suddenly veer off its target, exploding into them.

She glanced behind her seeing the enemy plane was still in hot pursuit and said, "Enemy on my six, and I can't shake him! I can't shake him! I need immediate assistance! Over!"

She continued to evade the enemy plane for as long as she could when she saw a blinding flash suddenly burning through the cockpit of her plane.

She glanced to her back for a brief moment and saw the enemy plane plummeting towards the surface in flames, crashing and burning into one of the towering skyscrapers. Nicole took a big sigh of relief and glanced to her side, seeing her reinforcements flying beside her, watching the pilot sticking his thumb up and saying, "Thanks for the assist." She rested her head back on her seat, taking off her oxygen mask, trying to catch her breath, exhaling sharply with many sighs of relief.

She glanced back at her wingmen and said, "Running low on fuel, and heading back to base to reload and refuel. Provide air support as long as you can until myself and the others return."

As the battle continued to wage in the skies, the enemy planes that remained far greater in number divided their forces in two separate groups, heading towards the remainder of the ground forces that guarded the front door who tried to gain a brief respite from the constant enemy attack, their strengths drastically falling from the constant strain that came from the barrage of the enemies' merciless onslaught.

07:05 HOURS. AMWAY GRAND PLAZA MOTEL, ENEMY COMMAND CENTER - GRAND RAPIDS, MICHIGAN:

Tiara continued to man the tank's heavy machine guns, and heard the roar of a plane's engines growing increasingly louder as it drew nearer towards her position, and yelled, "We have incoming!" She immediately opened fire.

Though many of their ground forces had succumbed from the enemy attack, they continued their valiant struggle to stave off the enemy assault as long as they could until their reinforcements arrive, greeting the enemy plane with a thick wall of anti-aircraft bullets, causing it to burst into flames, trailing a line of smoke, crashing and burning near their position, and were instantly greeted by another volley of enemy fire, as James and Tiara returned fire unflinchingly from their position, and was dazed from the sudden force of the blast, from enemy fire.

"We are still being attacked by enemy planes! We need more support!" Christopher cried out.

07:35 HOURS. SOMEWHERE ON INTERSTATE 696, HEADING TOWARDS THE AMWAY GRAND PLAZA HOTEL ENEMY COMMAND CENTER - GRAND RAPIDS, MICHIGAN:

"All available ground units provide support for our ground troops until our gunships and the rest of our ground troops arrive!" Adam said in a slightly frantic tone.

07:47 HOURS. SELFRIDGE FREEDOM FIGHTER AIR FORCE BASE, MOUNT CLEMENS, 21 MILES FROM DETROIT ARSENAL TANK BASE - WARREN, MICHIGAN:

Nicole and the rest of the surviving planes landed on the base to reload and refuel, as Karen watched, noticing that they were fewer in numbers than when they had left. She said her final goodbyes to Brian, while the other helicopter pilots rushed to their gunships, after the long and tedious process of loading on the stockpile of their deadly arsenal.

"Remember what happened the last time. Just come back," Brian said, holding her close.

"I will. I'll see you when I get back," she replied

"You better," he said.

She hurried towards her gunship, and strapped herself in the cockpit. She turned on the ignition, and glanced at Brian one last time before lifting off to her destination.

Brian simply watched and waved back half-heartedly as the squad of AH-64 Apache Longbow gunships lifted off towards their destination, and as always was the case, not knowing if Karen would make it back alive, leaving him in more state of worry, ever since her close encounter with the assassin in New Mexico the year earlier.

After the long and tedious process of reloading and refueling their planes, Nicole and the few other planes that made it back to base, completely ignoring the damage done to their planes, riddled with constant bullet holes from the constant enemy assault, battling through the skies, while exposed to the extreme elements.

After moments of waiting for the ground crew to reload and refuel her plane, Nicole watched as the ground crew gave their thumbs up indicating that she was ready for lift off and gave the thumbs up before driving the plane towards the runway, awaiting confirmation to take off.

Immediately after receiving confirmation to take off, she and her small squad of planes lifted off the runway, en-route to the enemy command center in Michigan.

07:49 HOURS. SOMEWHERE OVER INTERSTATE 696, HEADING TOWARDS THE AMWAY GRAND PLAZA HOTEL ENEMY COMMAND CENTER - GRAND RAPIDS, MICHIGAN:

Nicole looked down from the view of her cockpit and saw the formation of AH-64 Apache gunships flying below their position.

She broke radio silence and said, "This is flight leader to all wings. We are outnumbered by the enemy forces by at least three to one. Many of our ground troops are pinned down, so we need to make all our shots count, so our gunships can swoop in on the enemy ground forces and provide support. The sun is still up so remember to attack with the sun directly to our backs, to make us invisible to the enemy. Our ground troops are counting on us, so we need to keep them busy long enough so we can evacuate them from the battle area."

As Karen and her squad of gunships listened to the radio chatter, making their way towards the city, she looked to the skies and saw the smaller, but more formidable squad of planes flying high above her position, quickly heading towards the battle area.

07:54 HOURS. AMWAY GRAND HOTEL PLAZA - GRAND RAPIDS, MICHIGAN:

The enemy planes continued to pummel the ground troops who tried as valiantly as they could to hold out long enough for their reinforcements to arrive, when one of their armored units sustained a critical blow, once again temporarily knocking Tiara off her seat.

Tiara began to cough nauseatingly, as the smoke quickly engulfed the confines of her armored unit and the heat from the flames filled its interior, causing her to abandon the cover of her armored unit engulfing the tough shell of its exterior.

Unable to mount a counter assault of her own, she quickly made her way into the hotel through the storm of enemy ordinance that continued to rain upon their position mercilessly.

"We're losing ground units fast. We need air support!" Eric shouted, as he continued to return fire at the enemy planes that continued to wreak havoc on their positions from above.

07:55 HOURS. SOMEWHERE OVER INTERSTATE 696, 5 MINUTES AWAY FROM GRAND RAPIDS, MICHIGAN:

Nicole heard the distress call and replied, "E.T.A. 5 minutes!" and looked down from the view of her cockpit. She saw the ground troops and saw their reinforcements heading towards their location and continued, "Hold on as long as you can! More reinforcements are on the way!"

07:56 HOURS. SOMEWHERE ON INTERSTATE 696, HEADING TOWARDS THE GRAND PLAZA HOTEL ENEMY COMMAND CENTER - GRAND RAPIDS, MICHIGAN:

Adam heard the roar of the jet engines flying high above his position and said, "I have a visual on more air support over my position heading to provide more support! Hold on as long as you can!"

07:56 HOURS. AMWAY GRAND PLAZA HOTEL, ENEMY COMMAND CENTER - GRAND RAPIDS, MICHIGAN:

"They're picking us off out here! We really need air support!" Ahmad cried out.

"We just lost another plane!" Christopher shouted through the hail of gunfire.

"No matter how many planes we shoot down, they just keep coming. There's just too many of them," James said loudly.

"If we lose all our ground forces, we will be overrun by the enemy forces. If we have any chance of surviving this at all, you need to hurry with the air support," Eric said loudly.

07:57 HOURS. SOMEWHERE OVER INTERSTATE 696, 1 MINUTE AWAY FROM AMWAY GRAND PLAZA HOTEL, ENEMY COMMAND CENTER - GRAND RAPIDS, MICHIGAN:

Nicole watched on her radar and saw they were coming within range of the battle area and said, breaking radio silence, "Heading towards the battle area. E.T.A. in 60 seconds. All weapons hot and prepared to engage."

She looked into the direction of the glaring light of the sun and said, "All wings on my six," and flew towards the direction of the sun.

07:57 HOURS. SOMEWHERE ON INTERSTATE 696, HEADING TOWARDS THE AMWAY GRAND PLAZA ENEMY HOTEL PLAZA ENEMY COMMAND CENTER - GRAND RAPIDS, MICHIGAN:

Adam heard the radio chatter from Nicole's position and said, "This is command to flight leader. All weapons hot and engaging. Our ground troops are counting on you. Over."

07:58 HOURS. SOMEWHERE OVER GRAND RAPIDS, MICHIGAN:

"This is flight leader to command. All weapons hot and engaging the enemy. We'll do the best we can," she replied, as she continued flying towards the sun, and quickly turned back to engage the enemy.

07:58 HOURS. SOMEWHERE OVER INTERSTATE 696, HEADING TOWARDS THE AMWAY GRAND PLAZA HOTEL ENEMY COMMAND CENTER - GRAND RAPIDS, MICHIGAN:

Karen came within visual range of the ground convoy heading to reinforce their position against the enemy forces, as she flew towards their position.

08:00 HOURS. SOMEWHERE ON INTERSTATE 696, HEADING TOWARDS THE AMWAY GRAND PLAZA HOTEL ENEMY COMMAND CENTER - GRAND RAPIDS, MICHIGAN:

Adam looked up from the view of his transport and saw the group of gunships flying overhead and said, "This is command to all troops. Gunships are en-route to your position to engage the enemy ground forces."

08:00 HOURS. AMWAY GRAND HOTEL PLAZA, ENEMY COMMAND CENTER - GRAND RAPIDS, MICHIGAN:

"Well, they better hurry! Because we're losing men and units like flies!" James replied.

08:01 HOURS. SOMEWHERE OVER GRAND RAPIDS, MICHIGAN:

Nicole and her squad of planes flew toward the enemy planes with the sun to their backs, making them invisible, their weapons armed, and locking onto the enemy, firing their long-range missiles. She watched them track their targets, exploding on impact, and broke radio silence, and said, "We have visual confirmations on multiple kills. Still engaging the enemy forces."

08:03 HOURS. AMWAY GRAND PLAZA HOTEL, ENEMY COMMAND CENTER, COMMAND CENTER - GRAND RAPIDS, MICHIGAN:

The enemy planes suddenly stopped attacking the ground forces and quickly took to the overcast skies, vanishing into the gray clouds, after leaving the ground units completely demoralized from constant attack, with their surviving ground troops seeking refuge in the dilapidated confines of the enemy command center.

They remained tightly in a group, their weapons drawn facing the outside, waiting nervously for signs of the enemy troops, hoping their reinforcements would arrive on time.

The silence became deafening while they nervously anticipated any signs of movement that would come through the door, and saw a cloud of smoke slowly making its way through the space of the hotel towards them, growing thicker every passing moment, completely shrouding them.

"Jackson, remember what you said about the brave 300?" Ahmad asked.

"I do," she replied.

"You do know they all died, right?" he asked.

"I do," she replied.

"And this feels like the very same situation," Ahmad said softly.

"Well it seems a little obvious, doesn't it?" Anton replied.

The wall of smoke quickly filled the spacious lobby of the makeshift enemy command center, completely obstructing their view.

"I know that I'm going to die. I might as well go down fighting," Eric said, opening fire through the thick fog of smoke, causing the roar of machine gun fire to fill the spacious lobby of the hotel, and came to a sudden stop.

"Is everyone okay?" Christopher asked.

"Quiet. Let's retreat to higher ground," Eric replied.

As they began to retreat, through the thick wall of smoke, they were suddenly attacked, and began firing wildly at the mysterious, and unseen figure that engaged them swiftly through the hail of gunfire, resulting them being swiftly disarmed, and quickly incapacitated from his deadly techniques.

08:05 HOURS. SOMEWHERE ON INTERSTATE 696, HEADING TOWARDS THE AMWAY GRAND PLAZA HOTEL ENEMY COMMAND CENTER - GRAND RAPIDS, MICHIGAN:

"What's your status?" Adam asked.

08:05 HOURS. AMWAY GRAND PLAZA HOTEL ENEMY COMMAND CENTER - GRAND RAPIDS, MICHIGAN:

"We're being engaged! It's him! It's him!" Eric shouted, as they tried to repel the elusive and deadly assassin through the deafening hail of gunfire that roared through the thick screen of smoke.

08:07 HOURS. SOMEWHERE ON INTERSTATE 696, HEADING TOWARDS THE AMWAY GRAND PLAZA HOTEL ENEMY COMMAND CENTER - GRAND RAPIDS, MICHIGAN:

A sudden look of franticness came upon Adam's face hearing of the frightening event of the other soldiers suddenly became swiftly engaged by the assassin, almost on the verge of being wiped out single handedly.

08:09 HOURS. SOMEWHERE OVER INTERSTATE 696, HEADING TOWARDS AMWAY GRAND PLAZA HOTEL, ENEMY COMMAND CENTER - GRAND RAPIDS, MICHIGAN:

A sudden look of shock came over Karen's face hearing the frantic message of the soldiers who came under direct attack by the assassin, through the deafening clamor of gunfire, forcing her to relive the moment that they crossed paths, before helplessly witnessing Dillon's assassination in the unforgiving tundra of the White Sands Desert in New Mexico the year earlier.

She broke radio silence and said, "Heading towards your position to provide support! Estimated time of arrival: 2 minutes! This is the Dragonfly leader to all wings. Our ground troops are being engaged and are almost overrun by enemy forces, and they're depending on us to keep them alive! All weapons free and engage with extreme prejudice! I repeat engage with extreme prejudice!" she said, flying towards the location of the ground troops, hoping they would still be alive, and exact her vengeance on the assassin for Dillon's murder.

08:10 HOURS. AMWAY GRAND PLAZA HOTEL ENEMY COMMAND CENTER - GRAND RAPIDS, MICHIGAN:

The assassin continued to engage the remaining ground troops through the thick cloud of smoke, while the constant clamor of gunfire continued to persist.

As Christopher continued to do everything in his might to stave off the assassin with the others, he suddenly felt the cold steel of the assassin's knife grazing the flesh of his gut, after quickly being disarmed, while a crushing blow quickly came across Eric's face, from the assassin quickly incapacitating him.

After incapacitating Eric, he quickly switched his focus to Ahmad, slicing deeply through the flesh of his thigh, causing him to fall to the floor, grabbing his wound from the pain that followed.

The engagement was long and brutal, leaving many of the troops fatally wounded from the attacks that followed.

08:12 HOURS. SOMEWHERE ON INTERSTATE 696, HEADING TOWARDS THE AMWAY GRAND PLAZA HOTEL, ENEMY COMMAND CENTER - GRAND RAPIDS, MICHIGAN:

"Anyone, come in! What's the status?" Adam said with a look of concern on his face, after learning about the assassin's presence.

08:13 HOURS. AMWAY GRAND HOTEL PLAZA ENEMY COMMAND CENTER - GRAND RAPIDS, MICHIGAN:

"We're still being engaged! Lieutenants Fong, Vaughan, and Evans are down!" Janet shouted through the hail of gunfire, while they desperately tried to fend off the lone assassin from his lethal attacks.

08:13 HOURS. SOMEWHERE ON INTERSTATE 696, HEADING TOWARDS THE AMWAY GRAND PLAZA HOTEL ENEMY COMMAND CENTER - GRAND RAPIDS, MICHIGAN:

"My God," Adam said softly, with a frantic look on his face. "This is command to Dragonfly leader! What's your position? Over!"

08:14 HOURS. SOMEWHERE OVER INTERSTATE 696, 30 SECONDS AWAY FROM THE AMWAY GRAND PLAZA HOTEL, ENEMY COMMAND CENTER - GRAND RAPIDS, MICHIGAN:

"Estimated time 20 seconds! What are your orders, sir?" Karen asked.

08:14 HOURS. SOMEWHERE ON INTERSTATE 696, HEADING TOWARDS THE AMWAY GRAND PLAZA HOTEL ENEMY COMMAND CENTER - GRAND RAPIDS, MICHIGAN:

"By the time you arrive, our troops may already be dead, so I want you to unload everything you got into that building!" Adam said with a frantic look on his face. "If our troops don't make it out alive, neither should the enemy. Am I clear, Dragonfly leader?"

08:14 HOURS. SOMEWHERE OVER MICHIGAN, HEADING TOWARDS THE AMWAY GRAND PLAZA HOTEL ENEMY COMMAND CENTER:

Karen closed her eyes gently, knowing that there were a number of their troops still trapped inside the enemy makeshift command center, and said, "Understood."

08:14 HOURS. AMWAY GRAND PLAZA HOTEL ENEMY COMMAND CENTER - GRAND RAPIDS, MICHIGAN:

The hail of gunfire continued as the assassin engaged them through the thick cloud of smoke until all their ammunition became expended.

The smoke from the grenade canisters slowly dissipated, leaving a number of soldiers dead and wounded from his attack, leaving Anton and Janet the only ones standing, pointing their weapons towards the assassin with their weapons still drawn, but their clips empty from firing wildly through the thick cloud of smoke, in their the skirmish with the assassin.

The assassin stood before them quietly, facing them as they stared back nervously, feeling a chill of fear surging through their bodies, knowing that they were all that stood between them and him completing his objective.

He slowly took off his gear, exposing the youthful brown skin of his face, and dropped it to the floor while maintaining his cold and calculating stare at the group that was fortunate enough to have survived his onslaught.

He turned his focus on Ahmad, Christopher, and Eric, who lay severely wounded, bleeding on the floor. He pulled his knife from its sheath, gripping it tightly in his palm, ready to strike at any given moment.

They watched as the assassin walked closer towards the wounded soldiers with his knife gripped firmly, coated with the blood of its victims, knowing that they were no match for his superior skills, but were completely up to them to hold out until their reinforcements had arrived.

"Jackson, no!" Anton said, as Janet ran carelessly towards the assassin, swinging her rifle wildly, striking him to the side of his face, causing him to stop.

He looked at Janet with a straight face, as she stared back into his cold, calculating eyes with a look of fright on her face. She remained helpless standing in front of him, and suddenly felt the thundering smack to the side of her face, throwing her to the floor, knocking her unconscious.

Seeing that Janet was unconscious, from the assassin's blow, Anton suddenly became enraged, and without any regard for his life, ran towards the assassin, only to feel the brunt of his attack causing him to fall to the floor, laying almost motionless, with his entire face bloodied from the assassin's lethal skills in hand-to-hand combat.

Anton grabbed the assassin's leg as he walked past, trying as much as he could to delay him, until reinforcements could arrive, only to receive the assassin's boot to his face, completely incapacitating him, rendering him completely helpless to the assassin's mercy.

Anton gathered as much strength as he could, trying to crawl after the assassin, who continued to walk towards the others to complete his task, and grabbed his leg once more with all the strength he had left, still clinging on to hope that their reinforcements were close.

08:20 HOURS. SOMEWHERE OVER MICHIGAN, HEADING TOWARDS AMWAY GRAND PLAZA HOTEL ENEMY COMMAND CENTER - GRAND RAPIDS, MICHIGAN:

"This is Dragonfly leader to command! I'm getting thermal reading readings at the enemy command center! Requesting permission to engage! Over!"

08:21 HOURS. SOMEWHERE ON INTERSTATE 696, HEADING TOWARDS AMWAY GRAND PLAZA HOTEL ENEMY COMMAND CENTER - GRAND RAPIDS, MICHIGAN:

"Permission granted, Dragonfly leader! Hit that enemy command center with everything you got! If none of our troops make it out alive, then neither should the enemy! Got it?"

08:23 HOURS. SOMEWHERE OVER MICHIGAN, HEADING TOWARDS THE AMWAY GRAND PLAZA HOTEL, ENEMY COMMAND CENTER - GRAND RAPIDS, MICHIGAN:

Immediately after receiving Adam's orders, Karen and the other gunships unleashed a deadly payload of ordinance upon the hotel's beleaguered infrastructure, where the others laid unconscious and Anton was doing the best he could to delay the assassin until reinforcements arrived.

08:24 HOURS. AMWAY GRAND PLAZA HOTEL ENEMY COMMAND CENTER - GRAND RAPIDS, MICHIGAN:

After his long ordeal of receiving punishment from the assassin, Anton was barely clinging on to life, his face bruised from the deadly skills of his nemesis, crawling on the floor, heaving from all the pain, as the assassin walked towards Christopher and the others to end their lives.

Christopher slowly opened his eyes and saw the dark silhouette of the assassin walking towards him as he lay helpless on the floor, bleeding profusely from the wound that sliced into his abdomen.

The assassin raised his knife to deal the final blow, as if savoring the moment of his victory over his enemies, when a series of explosions from the gunships' payload began tearing through the building's beleaguered infrastructure, causing tons of debris and rubble to rain on top of him.

Noticing that the debris would fall over Janet as she lay unconscious from the assassin's attack, Anton quickly flew on top of Janet, shielding her from further harm.

Moments after the intense bombing from the gunships' payload, the attack stopped, leaving an eerie calm and silence through the dilapidated confines of the hotel with the crackling sounds of the flames and fragments of debris falling to the floor, filling the void of the silence.

08:24 HOURS. SOMEWHERE OVER GRAND RAPIDS, MICHIGAN:

The group of gunships continued to hover over the city. after watching the destruction they had just unleashed upon the makeshift enemy command center, watching the thick wall of dark smoke rising to the skies in complete radio silence.

"Target neutralized. Awaiting further orders," Karen said, flying away, in search of enemy forces to engage.

08:27 HOURS. SOMEWHERE ON INTERSTATE 696, HEADING TOWARDS THE AMWAY GRAND PLAZA HOTEL ENEMY COMMAND CENTER - GRAND RAPIDS, MICHIGAN:

"Search for any signs of enemy activity and engage on sight. We'll be there as soon as we can," Adam said, with his face creased in worry.

08:40 HOURS. AMWAY GRAND PLAZA HOTEL ENEMY COMMAND CENTER - GRAND RAPIDS, MICHIGAN:

After moments of lying unconscious beneath all the debris from all the fallen wreckage, Christopher fought to free himself, completely covered in dust, still dazed from the punishment that he had sustained from the assassin. He tried to gather his thoughts, still feeling the shock of being alive while he continued bleeding profusely from his wound.

He looked all around the hotel floor for any signs of the assassin and quickly began to scavenge through the rubble for more signs of survivors, momentarily coming across Anton's unconscious body, while he remained sprawled over

Janet, pulling him away, while she slowly began to regain consciousness.

She rolled over to Anton nudging him, searching for any sign of life, until he responded. Janet said, taking a sigh of relief, "Thank God. I thought I lost you."

"He took quite a beating. It's a miracle he's still alive," Christopher said, clutching his stomach from the pain in his wound.

"It's a miracle that we're still alive after we got our asses whooped by yours truly, and had an entire goddamn building falling on top of us. Come on, I need you to help me move him," Janet replied.

"We need to see if we can find more survivors."

"You're bleeding," she said, looking at his clothes soaked in blood.

"I could say the same about you, Jackson. But no time for that now. We need to search for the others before more enemy troops make their way to our position."

They continued digging through the rubble, uncovering the others, leaving the assassin's body nowhere to be found, only finding the gear that concealed his face.

"What the fuck? Where is he?" Janet asked, with a sudden look of shock on her face.

"How the hell should I know? Last I checked, I was buried beneath the rubble just like you. What we need to do is get the fuck out while we have a chance," Christopher answered.

Wounded and exhausted from the assassin's onslaught, they cautiously made their way out of the enemy command center in search of any able transport they could find, hoping they wouldn't be spotted by any of the enemy forces. They stepped into the streets filled with the countless corpses from their unit, along with countless husks of burning vehicles.

They looked to the overcast skies and saw the fighter planes still battling for supremacy high above the dark gray clouds and quickly continued making their way through the streets in search of an escape vehicle, until they came across a group of enemy vehicles.

"Can you drive, Jackson?" Christopher asked.

"I'll manage. My leg is fine. It's Anton and the others that I'm worried about," she said.

"Okay, let's get everyone aboard before the enemy regroups and gets to our position," Christopher replied after loading all the wounded and injured aboard the transports.

Janet turned on the ignition, ready to make her hasty departure, when Eric looked through the ranks of soldiers, noticing that James was missing and said, with a sudden burst of energy, "Yee!"

"What about him?" Ahmad asked.

"Stop the truck! I'm going back! I need to find him. Think of what they'll do to him if they find him," Eric said, hopping out of the truck.

"And if the enemy sees you, they'll kill you on sight," Christopher replied.

"Think of what they'll do to him if they find him. You know that as well as I do. He's one of us, and it's our code to never leave a man behind. And I'm going to find him," Eric said.

"I'll come with you," Ahmad replied.

"No, you go on without me," Eric said.

"What's taking you so long? We have a lot of people in need of medical assistance," Janet said.

"You go on without me. I'm going back to get Yee," Eric replied.

"You're bleeding like a tap. And you're telling me that you're going back there alone? He's still out there, wherever the fuck he is," Christopher replied.

"I know. But I'm not leaving James behind. He is one of us. He put his ass on the line no different from the rest of us. You go on without me. Take the others back to base. I'll be right behind you."

"Okay," Janet replied, running into the truck, and turning on the ignition.

"You better be right behind the rest of us," Christopher replied.

"I'll be. I promise. Now all of you get the fuck out before the enemy forces get here. Notify General West that you're heading back to base in enemy transports, before your asses get lined up with bullets."

"Okay. Just make sure that you're right behind me," Janet said.

"Just go. I'll be right behind you. I promise," Eric said, and began running towards the enemy command center.

He heard the trucks driving away and turned back for a brief moment watching them head back to base, and continued to make his way to the enemy command center. After making his way into the enemy command center filled with debris, he began to search frantically for James's body. He stumbled upon James still unconscious from his bout with the assassin, combined with the falling debris, and tapped his face to revive him, until he showed signs of life.

James opened his eyes and asked, "What the fuck happened?"

"Everything. It was him. After the thick wall of smoke came through the building, the next thing I remembered was all of us getting our asses kicked, and after that, all I remember was the entire building falling on top of us. I think it was from our gunships. They wanted to make sure if we didn't survive, then neither did he. It's a miracle we're still alive, even after all this."

"Where are all the others?" James asked.

"They already left. I came back for you when I realized that you're the only one of us who was missing."

"Thanks. I owe you one," James said.

"I know. We need to go."

"Where is he?" James asked.

"I don't know. And frankly, I don't care. That makes my job of getting you out of here a whole lot easier. But what I do know is that we need to leave before more troops come back. Including him."

"You're bleeding."

"And right now, you have a face that only a mother could love," Eric answered, looking at James's battered face.

"Now, we can stay here all day admiring eachother's faces, or we can get the fuck out."

"Okay, you made your point. Let's go," James said, struggling to get on his feet.

08:45 HOURS. SOMEWHERE IN GRAND RAPIDS, MICHIGAN:

They quickly made their way out of the enemy command center running through the empty streets, heading towards the abandoned enemy transports parked in the distance, Eric supporting James on his shoulder.

He shoved James into the passenger seat of an enemy transport, and rested his head onto the steering wheel, trying to recuperate from the pain of the wound he sustained from his bout of the assassin. Eric turned on the ignition, when in a split second, he saw an enemy transport careening towards them, giving him no time to react. It crashed into him with a deafening impact, shattering his windshield and the side windows, and pinning him into the wall of a nearby building, completely dazing him.

After a brief moment, Eric opened his eyes and looked outside of the window at the enemy vehicle that pinned them to the wall through the passenger side of his commandeered transport. He glanced at James, who had instantly bled to death from the severity of the gaping wound that tore deeply into his side from the impact of the truck, staring down with a lifeless gaze. Eric nudged James gently to receive any response, but to no avail.

The inevitably of Eric's death had become clear as he watched helplessly at the shadowy figure slowly walking towards him, his vision still blurred from the impact. It slowly became clearer, as Eric saw it was the assassin that stood before him, staring back with a straight face. He instantly recalled the very same man that had once saved his life during one of their missions in their early days in Brazil, who was now the very same one who had come to claim it.

The assassin stood calmly and silently, watching the blood dripping down Eric's face from the lacerations from the shards of broken glass from the shattered windows.

Eric smiled timidly and said, "It's strange that this was the same way you found me on our mission in Brazil, chasing a war criminal, when you cut my restraints and pulled me out of the truck and saved my life, before another one crashed into me. I remember all of it like yesterday, only to see that you're the one who crashed into me just to take my life. It's strange how everything comes full circle."

The assassin remained unmoved by his last comment, and slowly pulled out his sidearm, pointing it to his victim's temple, ready to execute him.

Jason walked towards the truck where James remained seated, his eyes staring down in a lifeless gaze, the entire interior of the transport covered in blood from the gaping wound that tore into his side from the impact of the crash, and looked at Eric's bloody face, bleeding profusely from the broken glass that lacerated his face, while he remained trapped in the transport. Jason said, "He's already dying, Lieutenant. You don't have to do this. Or we can still save him and find out what he knows. But you don't have to kill him. You already made your point. Please."

But to no avail, Jason's plea to save Eric's life fell upon deaf ears, as the assassin remained still with his sidearm pointed to Eric's face, ready to execute his victim.

"Forget it. We both know this is the end for me," Eric said, awaiting his fate.

"Don't do this, Lieutenant. Please."

The assassin paused for a brief moment, as he watched Eric pick up the radio to relay his final words to Adam with the assassin's sidearm still pointed to his face, and said, "Come in, General West."

09:03 HOURS. SOMEWHERE ON INTERSTATE 696. 20 MINUTES AWAY FROM THE GRAND HOTEL ENEMY COMMAND CENTER - GRAND RAPIDS, MICHIGAN:

"This is General West. Who is this?" Adam replied, with a sudden look of shock on his face, not recognizing the voice on the other end.

09:04 HOURS. SOMEWHERE IN GRAND RAPIDS, MICHIGAN:

"It's Fong. Just wanted to tell you that I won't be making it back. It's been a great honor serving under your command. But like everything else, it has an end. And today marks mine," Eric said, trying to maintain his strength.

09:04 HOURS. SOMEWHERE ON INTERSTATE 696. 20 MINUTES FROM AMWAY GRAND HOTEL PLAZA ENEMY COMMAND CENTER - GRAND RAPIDS, MICHIGAN:

"What are you talking about?" Adam asked, with a sudden look of concern on his face.

09:04 HOURS. SOMEWHERE IN GRAND RAPIDS, MICHIGAN:

"I won't be making it back. This is the end of the line for me."

09:05 HOURS. SOMEWHERE ON INTERSTATE 696. 19 MINUTES AWAY FROM AMWAY GRAND HOTEL PLAZA ENEMY COMMAND CENTER - GRAND RAPIDS, MICHIGAN:

"I'm not reading you! Say again, Fong! Say again!" Adam said, with a frantic look on his face, knowing that Eric was about to meet his demise at the hands of his nemesis.

09:06 HOURS. SOMEWHERE IN GRAND RAPIDS, MICHIGAN:

Eric watched as the assassin remained standing with his sidearm drawn to his bloody face, blood obstructing his vision and said, with a timid smile, knowing that he was about to meet his demise, "It's your cue. Go ahead. Put me out of my misery. It's what you're here for, isn't it? I'll be seeing you in the next life."

"Don't do it, Lieutenant. Please. He was one of us before. You can still save him. We can still use him," Jason said, while he continued to beg for his life.

The assassin remained standing before Eric with a straight face, his weapon still drawn, unmoved from Jason pleading for Eric's life, and fired a single shot, ending his life, followed by three more to make certain that his task was complete.

09:08 HOURS. SOMEWHERE ON INTERSTATE 696. 15 MINUTES AWAY FROM AMWAY GRAND ARMY HOTEL PLAZA - GRAND RAPIDS, MICHIGAN:

Adam was startled after hearing the single gunshot that ended Eric's life, knowing that Eric had met his demise at the hands of the assassin, and said, "This is command to all wings. We just lost Fong. It was him. Make a sweep of the area and find him or anyone that doesn't look like one of us. When you do, you know what to do."

09:09 HOURS. SOMEWHERE OVER GRAND RAPIDS, MICHIGAN:

A sudden look of shock came across Karen's face, and asked, "Who got Lieutenant Fong?"

09:10 HOURS. SOMEWHERE OVER INTERSTATE 696. 12 MINUTES AWAY FROM THE AMWAY GRAND HOTEL PLAZA - GRAND RAPIDS, MICHIGAN:

"I think it was him. I'm certain it was. I'd bet my life that it was him. You and the others, keep the lookout for any signs of enemy activity, and engage all hostiles. We'll be there shortly," Adam replied softly.

09:15 HOURS. SOMEWHERE OVER GRAND RAPIDS, MICHIGAN:

Karen and the group of gunships made their search all over the city in a frantic search of Eric's whereabouts. After a brief moment of searching, she came to a sudden stop, hovering over his position, where his commandeered transport remained pinned, and said, "I found him. I'm relaying his coordinates to you."

09:22 HOURS. SOMEWHERE IN GRAND RAPIDS, MICHIGAN:

Adam had finally arrived into the city, and stopped and ran out of his transport to where Eric's truck was plowed by the assassin's. He came to a sudden stop, seeing all the blood from Eric's and James's wounds smeared throughout the entire interior of the transport, spread all over the shards of broken glass from the shattered windows.

He peeped slightly into the passenger side of the transport, seeing the gaping hole that tore into James's side that caused him to bleed to death, and shifted his gaze to Eric, seeing the bullet hole that tore into his skull, along his lacerated face, staring back with a lifeless gaze, his face and rest of his body riddled with bullet holes.

He ordered the truck to be removed, freeing Eric's transport, and pried the passenger side where James's body lay lifeless with a gaping hole to his side, gently pulling his corpse out of his seat, laying his body on the road.

He leaned over Eric's body, staring back at his lifeless gaze, and gently passed his palm over his face, closing his eyes. Adam was completely consumed with anger that he had lost another one of his lieutenants who was crucial to their war effort, as he and all the others paid their respects in silence.

09:26 HOURS. SOMEWHERE OVER GRAND RAPIDS, MICHIGAN:

Karen broke radio silence and asked, "What are your orders, sir?"

09:27 HOURS. SOMEWHERE IN GRAND RAPIDS, MICHIGAN:

"There's been enough killing. Too many people have died today. Let's head back to base. Take their bodies to whatever transports we have available."

09:35 HOURS. SOMEWHERE OVER GRAND RAPIDS, MICHIGAN:

After loading their bodies on the transports, they began their long journey back to the base, when Karen's scanners began blaring loudly, warning her of an incoming enemy missile quickly closing in towards her position and shouted, "We have incoming! All units take evasive maneuvers!" as she skillfully dodged the incoming enemy missile. She shouted, "Protect General West at all costs!"

"Enemy on the rooftops!" Nicole shouted, dodging another enemy missile, and responded, pounding their positions with a lethal volley of fire.

"General West should get back to base at all costs! All units, get to higher altitude!" Karen said loudly.

09:36 HOURS. SOMEWHERE IN GRAND RAPIDS, MICHIGAN:

The ground troops began to make their departure when a number of enemy ground troops blocked their path and erupted in flames from their gunships' awesome arsenal of long range ordinance.

The group of transports continued to make their way out of the city towards the open road, where they were blocked by another gauntlet of enemy vehicles. A shell from an enemy tank exploded within close proximity, causing the group of transports to shudder with great force.

"We have enemy armor at 12 o'clock!" Adam yelled, as they continued dashing towards the gauntlet of enemy transports, when Karen swooped in to provide protection, deploying her hellfire missile at the enemy armored units, reducing them to into blazing husks, providing Adam and the rest of the convoy a chance to continue their escape run.

09:39 HOURS. SOMEWHERE OVER GRAND RAPIDS, MICHIGAN:

"Get to the open road as quickly as you can!" Karen said as she and the rest of the gunships continued to stave off the relentless enemy attacks.

"There're too many of them!"

Every inch of distance the fleeing convoy of soldiers traveled was fraught with the constant danger of them being killed or captured by the enemy forces.

09:41 HOURS. SOMEWHERE IN GRAND RAPIDS, MICHIGAN:

"This is command to flight leader! We're experiencing heavy resistance from the enemy! We don't know how long our gunships can hold off the enemy ground assault! We need immediate air support! What is your status? Over!" Adam shouted.

09:44 HOURS. SOMEWHERE OVER GRAND RAPIDS, MICHIGAN:

"We are still facing enemy resistance! We've managed to destroy a number of the enemy planes, but they're still combat capable! We'll be there as soon as we can!" Nicole replied.

09:45 HOURS. SOMEWHERE IN GRAND RAPIDS, MICHIGAN, HEADING TOWARDS INTERSTATE 696:

They suddenly came under attack from another enemy blockade, while they continued to make their escape run. The gunships unleashed another volley of fire, causing the enemy vehicles to burst into flames, while the fleeing convoy of freedom fighters continued to advance towards them.

"Ram it!" Adam said, as they continued driving towards it, ramming into it, feeling the impact from the collision. They continued to escape the elaborate lines of enemy gauntlets, while they made their escape towards the blast into the seemingly endless interstate, as their gunships continued to provide cover.

"We have more enemy armor up ahead! There's so many of them!" Karen shouted as she continued to cover the ground troops' escape to the long stretch of road to their freedom. "Open road just ahead! We'll hold them off for as long as we can!" she continued.

They continued to drive towards the interstate under heavy enemy assault, while advancing towards another enemy gauntlet of light and armored units, and were quickly disposed of by the lethal payload from their gunships, until they finally began to traverse the endless stretch of road.

For a brief moment, an eerie silence could be heard as they continued to traverse the long stretch of road to their destination.

They watched in stunned silence at all the destruction they wreaked upon the enemy, though it came at a heavy cost of losing so many of their own.

As the infinite flurries of snow continued to fall from the overcast, gray skies, they continued to watch the red flames consume the husks of armor that remained motionless on the stretch of road, with the giant plumes of smoke rising to the skies, telling the gruesome tale of the great calamity that had come to pass, slowly fading away as they gained more distance every passing moment.

Thinking that they were completely free from the enemy forces, their brief moment of peace was interrupted when they suddenly came under fire from another enemy gauntlet that blocked their path.

09:49 HOURS. SOMEWHERE OVER INTERSTATE 696, HEADING TOWARDS, SELFRIDGE FREEDOM FIGHTER AIR FORCE BASE - WARREN, MICHIGAN:

Karen and her group of gunships immediately began to engage the enemy ground troops under heavy ground fire and shouted, "There's too many to take on at once! We need air support!"

After the long skirmish, the skies were now clear of enemy planes over the city and Nicole heard the distress call. She responded, "Reading you loud and clear! Coming in hot! All units, stay clear!"

She armed her weapons as she continued to fly closer to the enemy position, as the fleeing group of transports made their way closer towards the enemy gauntlet that blocked their path.

The roar from the engines of the F-15 Strike Eagle fighter planes filled the skies over the long stretch of interstate, growing louder as they swooped over the enemy ground units that blocked their path deploying their deadly payload and quickly flying back into the overcast skies, vanishing into the gray clouds, with the roar of their engines fading into the distance.

09:51 HOURS. SOMEWHERE ON INTERSTATE 696, HEADING TOWARDS SELFRIDGE FREEDOM FIGHTER AIR FORCE BASE - WARREN, MICHIGAN:

A towering wall of flame swept through the walls of enemy ground units that blocked their path of escape, consuming all in its wake, causing the very ground beneath them to shudder with much force, causing them to pause for a brief moment to watch all the destruction their planes had left in their wake.

"Drive through it," Adam said softly.

The convoy of vehicles drove through the burning wreckage of enemy vehicles sprawled across the interstate, and once again looked back at more of the destruction their planes and gunships had left in their wake in complete silence, as they sped away to safety.

Moments after they had cleared the enemy gauntlet, the assassin freed himself from the wreckage, dusting off his battle-ridden clothes, and pulled Jason's unconscious body out of the burning vehicle, checking for his pulse until he came conscious shortly after.

The assassin slowly walked through the burning husks of transports amidst all the dead and injured soldiers clinging to life, and watched the convoy of trucks vanishing in the distance on the long stretch of road with his usual cold and uncompromising stare. Jason, who suffered a series of bruises from the attack on his face, slowly trailed behind, still suffering from the shock from his near-death experience from the air strike that consumed the bulk of their ground forces.

12:13 HOURS. SELFRIDGE FREEDOM FIGHTER AIR FORCE BASE, MOUNT CLEMENS. 21 MILES AWAY FROM DETROIT ARSENAL TANK BASE - WARREN, MICHIGAN:

They had arrived at the base and began to disembark from their transports shortly after Janet's arrival.

Adam slowly stepped out of his transport, watching their faces showing heavy signs of being weary from battle and said, "We lost Yee, and Lieutenant Fong. He got to them before I could. How could this have happened? Why does this always have to happen?"

"We were heading towards the base, and the next thing we knew, we were under enemy attack. It seems that we were spotted by an enemy patrol," Christopher replied softly.

"We were hoping to avoid any confrontation with the enemy by trying to get to the base under the cover of darkness. It was a good thing we had time to get our call in for air support, or else we would have surely been wiped out," Ahmad replied.

"We were outnumbered by at least three-to-one. We would've lost all our planes if it weren't for what Captain Kim had taught me and the others. The ground troops would have suffered the same as well," Nicole added.

"How much ordinance do we have left?" Adam asked.

"We lost a lot of planes and used a lot of ordinance against the enemy forces. It's not looking good. And as for the ground troops, this is all we have left until we get more troops. With our current numbers, we won't be able to hold off another enemy attack. Let's pray all our reinforcements come soon enough," Nicole concluded.

Adam watched as they carried Eric's and James's lifeless bodies out of the transports with the sheets shrouding over them, stained heavily in their blood and said, "He got to Fong and Yee before we did. How could he have survived that assault? How is that even possible?"

"I don't know. I unloaded quite some ordinance on that building," Karen replied with a look of shock on her face, after hearing that the assassin had survived, and continued, "It's impossible for anyone to have survived that assault. It was a Hellfire missile that I unloaded into that building. He should've been killed during that assault. It just isn't possible."

"I should've stayed with him," Christopher added.

"And you would've gotten killed if you had stayed with him, along with Fong. And you would only add to the tally of all the others he killed before," Adam replied.

Janet pulled the assassin's gear closer to her face and said, "This belonged to him."

"How did you get it?" Christopher asked.

"He made it quite simple, really. After the smoke had cleared, he dropped it on the floor, and all he did was stand there, waiting for us to make a move, which I did, and look and look where it got me. Although Anton suffered the worst of it. It's a miracle he's still alive. He did as much as he could to hold him off until you arrived. The strange thing about all this is I looked right into his eyes. They were cold and empty. There was nothing in them. No soul. Just dark and empty."

"But I don't understand. Why didn't he just kill you?" Nicole asked.

"Because he wasn't after you. He's after the ones he served with. He's after us. And today alone, all of us were this close to being wiped out. He almost succeeded. And as for the both of you on the other hand, he wanted to make you feel what it's like to be hunted. I suppose it was his way of saying that you were not worth the time or energy to be pursued. You were not worthy adversaries, or worth killing," Adam replied.

"I could live with that. If that's what it's like to be hunted, I'd hate to be in your shoes, Lieutenant Vaughan, and Evans. No offense," Janet replied.

"None taken, Jackson," Christopher replied.

"Better us than you, I suppose," Ahmad added.

"No arguments there. Besides, I was just bitch-slapped by an angry assassin for charging like I was stupid and paid for it. Come to think of it, that was one time too many. But to be fair, that was some of the best offensive and disarming skills I've ever seen. All of us for that matter," Janet said.

"True. If the General has more men like him, then we're finished. I wouldn't want to be on the receiving end of those skills," Nicole replied

"Too bad he's not on our side. We can use those skills right about now," Janet replied.

"Are you okay, Reed?," Adam asked, watching Anton's battered face with a look of concern on his face

"I'll be fine, General West," Anton replied, clutching his side from the pain that he endured from the assassin's deadly skills.

"As I said before, he got the worst of it," Janet replied.

"It was Jackson and myself standing in his way, after he'd taken everyone else out, when we ran out of bullets and he was about to kill Lieutenant Vaughan and Evans. I couldn't stand by and let it happen. I know I couldn't beat him, so I delayed him for as long as I could until our reinforcements came. I suppose he was telling me that I wasn't worth killing. Considering that I'm still alive, it worked out pretty good for me, don't you think?"

"He was just this close to completing his task, and by some miracle, that's when the gunships came, leveling the enemy command center. Couldn't have come at a better time," Janet said, as she continued holding him up on his feet.

"You did that for me? For us?" Christopher asked, with his eyes drowning in his tears, showing his gratitude for Anton who risked his life to save his, and the others.

"I couldn't stand back and let it happen. I just had to do something," Anton replied.

"When the bombing came, he laid on top of me, protecting me from the falling debris," Janet added.

"We both owe you our lives," Ahmad said.

"We're all on the same side," Janet replied.

"Don't kid yourself, Reed. Those men are in your debt," Adam answered, and looked all around watching all those who were fortunate to survive the onslaught from the assassin, and all the other faces that stood around him, and said, "We've lost so many, today alone. Lieutenant Fong and James Yee were among those we lost today. They will surely be missed. Whatever happened to all the ones who didn't come back, could've happened to any one of us standing at this moment. But, unfortunately, fate chose them. Sadly, there'll be more of us who will make the ultimate sacrifice, pay the ultimate price in our fight for freedom. All those who have fought and still continue to fight and die for the greater good and for a cause greater than themselves knew the risks, and accepted the consequences. They were only more than happy to pay with their lives, in hopes that one day, this once great country of ours will once again be united." He paused for a brief moment from giving his speech, looking into their sad and weary faces, the strength completely drained from their bodies, and courage drawn from their faces from their long and exhausting campaign against the enemy forces, like he had seen many times before, and continued, "But before we drag our exhausted souls to arms against the enemy, we take on that burden knowing that the hopes of an entire nation rests on our shoulders, and that we're all that stand between tyranny and freedom. We've come so far. And no matter how difficult the road may be, we can't give up the fight. Even if it means the death of all of us, like those before us who made the ultimate sacrifice. We must continue to fight."

The war continues…

CHAPTER 8: OPERATION SNOWBLIND.

15:27 HOURS. SOMEWHERE NEAR INTERSTATE 79. THE TOWN OF BRIDGEORT, WEST VIRGINIA:

The year was 2032. Seven years have passed since "The Great Fall of Genesis."

A white-tailed deer with her fawn slowly trekked through the snow in search of food, and came to a sudden stop. They immediately made their hasty retreat.

A stray dog walked through the small town, and came to an abrupt stop and quickly scampered away.

A cardinal chirped on a naked tree branch through the blinding storm, and suddenly flew away into the winds.

The hulking physique of a moose walked through the small town, crossing the street in search of food, and suddenly stopped, hearing the noise from afar, drawing nearer, and suddenly ran away.

A Virginia opossum slowly traversed through the naked branches of the trees, in constant sniffing through the winds for the scent of prey.

A snowshoe hare slowly and calmly walked through the snow, through the sparse vegetation, in search of food in the harsh winter, and suddenly became distracted with its antennae-like ears picking up noises from afar.

As the cold, bitter winds grew stronger, sweeping through the snow-filled streets, a convoy of light and heavy armored vehicles containing troops and supplies steadily made its way through the town, en-route to the state capital, when one of the enemy tanks suddenly erupted in flames from the surprise attack from an ambush, followed by another in quick succession, causing the entire enemy convoy to come to a complete stop.

The enemy soldiers jumped out of their transports, assuming defensive positions, searching nervously for the origin of the attacks, as the snow storm gained more momentum, while they remained exposed in the open from more attacks.

While the blinding snowstorm continued to persist, they remained frozen in their tracks, their eyes probing nervously about, and their weapons gripped tightly in the grip of their palms.

From behind the old husks of abandoned vehicles strewn on one side of the streets, a group of freedom fighters ambushed the enemy soldiers, opening fire. They were flanked from the other side, resulting in a pincer attack on the enemy troops.

After a carefully laid-out strategy, the enemy convoy was completely cleared of enemy troops, leaving only a trail of lifeless bodies from the carnage that lasted only brief moments.

The freedom fighters came out of their hiding places, and quickly cleared the streets of the lifeless bodies. They climbed onto the armor of the heavy units, pulling the bodies off the heavy machine gun positions and piling them in the streets.

"Is anybody hurt? Is everyone fine?" Adam asked loudly, trying to catch his breath after the assault.

"Everyone is fine. We're ready to go. Just give the word," Christopher answered.

Adam grabbed the radio and said, "Come out."

Adam waited for a brief moment until the formidable group of gunships came out of hiding, and flew towards their position, and hovered above them, awaiting their orders.

"What are your orders, General West?" Karen asked, as she continued to hover above them.

"Scout ahead and see if there's any more enemies. Make sure there are no more surprises."

Ahmad watched the gunships fly away and asked, "Why are we doing this again?"

"Because we're facing a force more seasoned, and in far greater numbers than ourselves, in every respect. That means more planes, and more resources. And I mean a whole lot more. The purpose of our attack is to create a ruse, to get their planes away from their positions, leaving them exposed, so we can weaken their fire power. While they fly towards our position to attack us, they'll be burning precious fuel and using precious ordinance in the process. Either they split their forces, or they completely abandon their pursuit on us, while we make our run towards the enemy command center in the capital so we can either take control of it and use it as our base, or bomb the shit out of it. Either our planes succeed, or we do. The whole point is to divide the enemy forces so it could be easier to score a decisive battle," Adam said.

"So, basically we're bait?" Ahmad asked.

"Deception is the key to victory. I learned that during the war of the North Korean occupation. So, yes, we are. And basically, it's what they would do, and have done in the past. It's payback and it's a bitch," Adam answered.

"How certain are you that this is going to work?" Ahmad asked.

"Well, considering how far our base is, I'm not. Our best chance of completing this mission is to survive long enough until they abandon their pursuit. It's a long shot, but it's all we have to work with."

"I hope you know what you're doing," Ahmad replied.

"It's a calculated risk." Adam said, and turned to Christopher and said, "Keep an open channel and keep me updated. Come on. Let's go."

15:29 HOURS. SHEPHERD FIELD FREEDOM FIGHTER GUARD BASE. 192.5 MILES AWAY FROM THE STATE OF PENNSYLVANIA, 309 MILES FROM CHARLESTON ENEMY AIR NATIONAL GUARD BASE -CHARLESTON, WEST VIRGINIA:

While howling winds of the snow storm continued to grow louder as the overcast skies continued to grow darker, Nicole and a number of the pilots raced towards their planes, while the ground crew scurried all about, arming and fueling them.

After the long and tedious task of arming and fueling them, the roar from all their engines filled the vicinity of their base, quickly lifting off the runway, embarking on the long and dangerous flight towards the enemy position through the blinding storm.

15:29 HOURS. CHARLESTON ENEMY AIR NATIONAL GUARD BASE. 3 AND 1/2 HALF MILES AWAY FROM THE STATE CAPITOL BUILDING ENEMY COMMAND CENTER - CHARLESTON, WEST VIRGINIA.

After receiving a transmission from the beleaguered convoy, a number of enemy pilots scurried through the base heading towards their planes, en-route to the position where they were intercepted by Adam and his band of soldiers, starving them of their reinforcements and supplies.

15:30 HOURS. SOMEWHERE NEAR INTERSTATE 79, NEAR THE SMALL TOWN OF BRIDGEPORT, WEST VIRGINIA:

Christopher pressed the headphone harder to his ear, listening closely to all the chatter, and said, "I've intercepted a transmission. We have incoming, General West. The enemy took the bait. They're on their way."

"Is the channel secure?" Adam asked.

"Yes, sir," Christopher answered.

"Are you sure they're on their way?" Adam asked.

"Yes, sir. During the assault on the convoy before we seized it, they had enough time to send a transmission to the enemy base. Just got confirmation that they lifted off. We need to move, sir, because we have a lot of enemy bogeys heading straight for us. And they'll be here soon."

"Here goes nothing," Ahmad answered.

"Have faith," Adam answered.

"Do I have a choice?" Ahmad asked.

"We all have a choice."

"What the hell? Why do I always listen to you? We're already up to our eyeballs in this shit anyway. Might as well."

Adam sat in the driver's seat, grabbed the radio, and said, "We have enemy bogeys heading towards our position. Engage all hostile craft at will. For this mission to succeed, we need to hold out long enough for our planes to strike deep in the heart of the enemy forces. The success of this mission solely depends on us surviving long enough for them to complete their mission. Let's mobilize."

The convoy of trucks and heavily armored units began to make their way towards the enemy command post situated in the capital, through the cold and slippery streets.

Adam grabbed the radio and broke radio silence and said, "This is command to Dragonfly leader. I need a report."

15:31 HOURS. SOMEWHERE OVER INTERSTATE 79, NEAR THE SMALL TOWN OF BRIDGEPORT, WEST VIRGINIA:

"Visibility is low, but no more signs of the enemy. The coast is clear. I repeat the coast is clear. Over."

"Vaughan, what's the status?" Adam asked.

"Enemy bogeys are airborne and closing in fast. No telling how soon they'll be here. We need to have weapons hot right now."

"What are your orders, sir?" Karen asked.

15:31 HOURS. SOMEWHERE NEAR INTERSTATE 79, NEAR THE SMALL TOWN OF BRIDGEPORT, WEST VIRGINIA:

"The enemy planes will be at our positions soon. You and your squad wouldn't be able to escort the convoy to the capital without the enemy planes picking you up and cutting you down."

15:33 HOURS. SOMEWHERE OVER INTERSTATE 79, NEAR THE SMALL TOWN OF BRIDGEPORT, WEST VIRGINIA:

"Are you sure?" Karen asked with a sudden look of shock on her face.

15:34 HOURS. SOMEWHERE NEAR INTERSTATE 79, NEAR THE SMALL TOWN OF BRIDGEPORT, WEST VIRGINIA:

"You have your orders, Santiago. From this point out, it's up to us. There's nothing you can do to assist the war effort from this point. All that will happen from this point out, is your entire outfit will be picked off by the enemy firepower. Your gunships are no match for these planes. Now return to base."

15:34 HOURS. SOMEWHERE OVER INTERSTATE 79, NEAR THE SMALL TOWN OF BRIDGEPORT, WEST VIRGINIA:

"Reading you loud and clear. Returning to base," Karen replied, breaking off her advance, making the long trip back to their position through the blinding storm.

15:35 HOURS. SOMEWHERE NEAR INTERSTATE 79, NEAR THE SMALL TOWN OF BRIDGEPORT, WEST VIRGINIA:

They watched the squad of gunships flying over their heads, heading back, abandoning them to their fates that lay ahead on their arduous tasks.

"Okay, this is it. Operation Snowblind has officially just begun," Adam said, taking a deep breath.

"It sure has," Ahmad answered nervously.

"Pray this works."

"God damn right," Ahmad said, shaking his head.

"What's the status of the enemy planes, Vaughan?"

"Closing in fast. They'll be here soon. We need to get ready."

15:40 HOURS. SOMEWHERE OVER INTERSTATE 79. 10 MILES AWAY FROM THE FREEDOM FIGHTER CONVOY, HEADING TOWARDS THE STATE CAPITOL BUILDING ENEMY COMMAND CENTER - CHARLESTON, WEST VIRGINIA:

The squad of enemy planes flew towards Adam's position, through the blinding storm, picking up multiple contacts on their radars, priming their weapons for their assault.

15:43 HOURS. SOMEWHERE OVER WEST VIRGINIA. 250 MILES AWAY FROM CHARLESTON ENEMY AIR NATIONAL GUARD BASE - CHARLESTON, WEST VIRGINIA:

The formidable group of freedom fighter planes continued making their way on their attack run towards the enemy base through the blinding storm.

Nicole felt the hull of her plane shuddering constantly from the heavy bombardment of the violent snowstorm.

She took her view off and glanced at the skies for a brief moment, searching for the sun, noticing the skies were getting darker, rapidly diminishing their chances of achieving invisibility on the enemy forces, and said, "We need to hurry, if General West is to survive on his raid towards the capital. We are in the winter months, and won't have the advantage of the sun for achieving total surprise for too much longer. If our ground troops suffer too many casualties, our mission will be a total failure. In order for our mission to succeed, General West and the ground troops must survive at all costs."

15:46 HOURS. SOMEWHERE ON INTERSTATE 79, HEADING TOWARDS STONEWOOD, HEADING TOWARDS THE STATE CAPITOL BUILDING ENEMY COMMAND CENTER - CHARLESTON, WEST VIRGINIA:

"Two miles and closing! Coming from due west of our position!" Christopher shouted nervously.

Ahmad heard the distant roar of the jet engines growing louder, and looked all around the skies searching for the enemy planes, unable to see them through the dark, stormy skies, and said, "I can't see shit through this storm! We need to get to them before they get to us!"

"I agree!" Adam replied.

"Attention all units, we have multiple enemy bogeys coming from due west of our current position! Engage at will! I repeat, all weapons hot and engage!"

While they remained seated firmly in their transports, listening to the direction of where the sounds of the enemy planes were coming from, they opened fire, greeting the enemy planes in a thick wall of anti-aircraft fire.

As the enemy planes descended the convoy through the gray clouds, and were immediately greeted by the barrage, one of the enemy planes was hit by anti-aircraft fire, causing it to burst into flames, its flaming wreckage careening from the skies.

Christopher saw the flaming wreckage falling from the skies and said, "Concentrate all firepower in that direction!"

"Let's hope that this operation hasn't ended before it has begun," Ahmad said softly to himself.

In retaliation for losing their convoy from their well-planned ambush, the enemy planes returned a volley of fire through the thick hail of ground fire, causing one of the ground units to burst into flames, while countless enemy bullets and heavy ordinance continued to rain all over their position.

"We just lost another one of our transports!" Ahmad yelled.

"I can see that!" Adam yelled through the hail of gunfire.

15:59 HOURS. SOMEWHERE OVER WEST VIRGINIA. 150 MILES AWAY FROM CHARLESTON, ENEMY AIR NATIONAL GUARD BASE -CHARLESTON, WEST VIRGINIA:

The group of planes continued on their way towards the enemy base, through the blinding storm. Karen glanced at the sun, hoping that they would still have the element of invisibility, and said, "We're about halfway to the enemy position. The first thing we need to do is to draw attention long enough for them to establish contact with their planes, and then sever all communications. Hopefully that'll draw them away from our ground troops, and by the time they get here, their positions will be reduced to rubble. They'll have no place to land, refuel, or rearm. Maintain radio silence, and get ready to arm weapons on my mark."

16:01 HOURS. SOMEWHERE ON INTERSTATE 79, NEAR LOST CREEK, HEADING TOWARDS THE STATE CAPITAL BUILDING ENEMY COMMAND CENTER - CHARLESTON, WEST VIRGINIA:

The ground troops continued to maintain their valiant efforts to try and repel the enemy planes amidst all the enemy fire that continued to rain upon them.

From the unwavering exchange from both sides, another enemy plane succumbed to the thick hail of ground fire, causing it to plunge from the gloomy skies, crashing and burning near their position.

"Good hit!" Adam said, while he continued driving, trying to maintain his control on the icy, slippery road, when a sudden, blinding explosion from one of the transports, causing him to make a sharp turn to evade the burning wreckage sprawled about the long stretch.

"We're taking more casualties!" Ahmad yelled.

"I can see that!" Adam said, while he tried to maintain control of his transport.

"Can't this thing go any faster?" Ahmad yelled nervously.

"I'm trying, but the road is too slippery! It could cause a major pile up, and that'll be the end of our mission!"

"What's the status on our planes?" Ahmad asked impatiently.

"They're halfway across the state! They need to maintain radio silence until they're in attack range of the enemy!" Christopher answered.

Another transport from the convoy slid off the road after erupting into flames, missing Adam narrowly, causing him to make another sharp turn.

"They're picking us off one by one!" Ahmad yelled frantically, seeing all the destruction the enemy planes continued to leave in their wake.

"I can see that!" Adam answered.

"We should do something!" he cried out.

"We are!" Adam answered.

"At this rate, we'll never reach the capital!"

Another transport from the constant enemy barrage temporarily obstructed the view of the convoy, as they continued to move forward.

Adam saw the flaming wreckage in the road, knowing the only way forward was to go through the fiery obstacle, gripped the steering wheel tighter and said, "Hang on to something!" He pressed the acceleration with all his might, causing his vehicle to go into ramming speed, and rammed into the obstacle, clearing it out of their path, causing his transport to shudder violently from the awesome force of the impact.

He grabbed the radio and said, "We need to hold out long enough for our planes to hit the enemy position, and continue our assault on the capital! To have a better chance of repelling the enemy planes, move in closer to support to keep a heavier concentration of fire!"

The transports huddled closer to create a stronger wall of firepower to repel the relentless enemy planes that continued to strafe their positions.

Christopher spotted another enemy plane rapidly descending upon them and shouted, "We have incoming!"

The enemy plane was immediately greeted with a thick hail of anti-aircraft fire from all the transports huddled together closely, riddling the body of the enemy pilot with a number of hits, causing him to instantly lose consciousness, slumping over the controls covered in blood, causing the plane to dive from the skies, leaving a trail of smoke, crashing and burning.

"Aren't we a little too close? What if they dropped a bomb? They could wipe us out!" Ahmad cried out over the radio.

"Isn't that what they're trying to do in the first place? Look behind you! I've lost track of how many of our transports we've lost since we've been attacked! It's a 50-50 chance! The closer we are, the stronger the defense. The farther we are, the weaker the firepower! Won't have the same effect! If you have any other suggestions, I'm open to hear it!"

"Let's go back home!" Christopher said.

"Not an option!" Adam said.

"Exactly!" Christopher replied.

16:04 HOURS. SOMEWHERE OVER THE WEST VIRGINIA. 50 MILES AWAY FROM CHARLESTON ENEMY AIR NATIONAL GUARD BASE - CHARLESTON, WEST VIRGINIA:

The squad of fighter planes continued their attack run towards the enemy base through the blinding storm under complete radio silence.

Nicole glanced at the sky, staring at the sun for a brief moment, and stared at the canopy of her plane, seeing the constant accumulation of ice being swept away from the strong currents of the stormy winds, feeling the constant shudder, struggling to maintain control.

16:05 HOURS. SOMEWHERE ON INTERSTATE 79, JANE LEW, NEAR ROUTE 19, HEADING TOWARDS THE STATE CAPITOL BUILDING ENEMY COMMAND CENTER - CHARLESTON, WEST VIRGINIA:

The gun fire continued to echo loudly on the long stretch of road between the convoy and the enemy planes that continued to terrorize their position, with both sides sustaining a number of casualties.

"I need an update on our planes!" Adam said.

"They're almost within range!" Christopher said, as he continued to monitor their movements on his portable device. "They can't afford to break radio silence yet! We need to hold on a little longer!"

"If we keep on losing transports at this rate, there won't be a we!" Ahmad replied.

16:07 HOURS. SOMEWHERE OVER WEST VIRGINIA. 10 MILES AWAY FROM CHARLESTON ENEMY AIR NATIONAL GUARD BASE - CHARLESTON, WEST VIRGINIA:

Nicole checked on her radar, seeing that they were almost within range and broke radio silence, and said, "Nearing the enemy vector. Weapons are hot. Break formation and engage with extreme prejudice. I repeat, engage at will. Leave the communications tower long enough to get their transmissions out to call for reinforcements, and then we sever all communications to blind them. We need to hurry. The sun won't be up much longer to achieve total invisibility."

16:09 HOURS. SOMEWHERE ON INTERSTATE 79, JANE LEW, NEAR ROUTE 19, A FEW MILES AWAY FROM WESTON, NEAR ROUTE 19, HEADING TOWARDS THE STATE CAPITOL BUILDING ENEMY COMMAND CENTER - CHARLESTON, WEST VIRGINIA:

The convoy of ground units continued to hold the ground valiantly, while the enemy planes continued their relentless assaults, as they struggled to maintain control of their vehicles, countering with anti-aircraft fire.

"It won't be long now!" Christopher said over the radio.

"Not long now, is still too long!" Adam replied.

16:09 HOURS. SOMEWHERE OVER WEST VIRGINIA, HEADING TOWARDS CHARLESTON ENEMY AIR NATIONAL GUARD BASE - CHARLESTON, WEST VIRGINIA:

The group of planes were on the final phase of their assault, deliberately flying towards the enemy position from high altitude to be detected by the radars in the enemy position.

Karen broke radio silence and said, "All weapons hot, and engaging! I repeat, all weapons are hot!"

The alarms of the enemy base echoed through the vicinity, causing all the enemy personnel to scurry towards their defensive positions.

The formidable squad of planes flew boldly towards the enemy position, and were quickly greeted by a sky full of flak, and anti-aircraft fire.

She watched as the other planes flew past her, when a blinding flash of light suddenly flashed through the confines of her cockpit.

She glanced from the view of her cockpit, seeing one of her wingmen flying towards the surface in a heap of flaming wreckage, and said, "We're in enemy range, and heavy taking fire! We just lost Razor! I repeat, we just lost Razor!"

16:10 HOURS. SOMEWHERE ON INTERSTATE 79, WESTON, NEAR ROUTE 19 HEADING TOWARDS THE STATE CAPITOL BUILDING ENEMY COMMAND CENTER - CHARLESTON, WEST VIRGINIA:

"They made it! They're attacking the enemy positions!" Christopher said, listening to the radio chatter.

"And we're still getting our asses kicked down here!" Adam replied, still struggling to maintain control of his transport on the slippery road covered thickly in ice.

16:11 HOURS. SOMEWHERE OVER CHARLESTON ENEMY AIR NATIONAL GUARD BASE - CHARLESTON, WEST VIRGINIA:

The squad of planes continued to inflict heavy damage on the enemy positions through the thick wall of enemy anti-aircraft fire.

Nicole broke formation and flew towards the communications tower, locking it into her cross hairs, and fired her missile. She watched it track its target, erupting into flames, severing all communications with their planes that continued to attack the convoy relentlessly, and took another glance at the sun, while she soared high above the enemy position, listening intently for the enemy planes to break off their assault from the ground troops.

16:14 HOURS. SOMEWHERE ON INTERSTATE 79, NEAR BURNSVILLE, HEADING TOWARDS THE STATE CAPITOL BUILDING ENEMY COMMAND CENTER - CHARLESTON, WEST VIRGINIA:

After their long-standing battle against the resilient ground troops, the enemy planes finally broke off their assault after hearing the radio chatter from their position turning into static, realizing that they had been deceived, and headed back to the base, leaving the remainder of the convoy to make their run towards the capital unopposed.

"We did it! They're breaking off! It's working! They took the bait!" Christopher celebrated.

"Oh thank God," Adam said, taking a huge sigh of relief.

"You can say that again," Ahmad answered, resting his back against the seat, taking a deep breath.

"What are your orders?" Christopher asked.

"We lost a number of transports all across the interstate. Dispatch whatever available units that we have to search the wreckage for any survivors."

16:15 HOURS. SHEPHERD FIELD FREEDOM FIGHTER GUARD BASE, MARTINSBURG, WEST VIRGINIA. 192.5 MILES AWAY FROM THE STATE OF PENNSYLVANIA, 309 MILES AWAY FROM CHARLESTON ENEMY AIR NATIONAL GUARD BASE - CHARLESTON, WEST VIRGINIA:

A number of pilots began to scurry across the base towards the Blackhawk helicopters after receiving Adam's orders to search for any remaining survivors who may have been in the wreckage that littered the long stretch of the interstate.

Within just moments of arriving at the base, Karen began towards her quarters, and saw a number of helicopter pilots mobilizing through the base to their helicopters, and headed back to her gunship to provide support, after the Blackhawks lifted off the base.

16:20 HOURS. CHARLESTON ENEMY AIR NATIONAL GUARD BASE, CHARLESTON, WEST VIRGINIA. 309 MILES AWAY FROM SHEPHERD FIELD FREEDOM FIGHTER GUARD BASE, 608 MILES AWAY FROM THE STATE OF PENNSYLVANIA:

Nicole and her squad of planes continued to wreak havoc on the enemy position when she heard the transmission from Adam that the enemy planes were en-route to intercept them.

She looked at the skies staring at the sun and said, "The enemy will be within range soon. Form up on my order," and flew up into the sun to achieve invisibility for their surprise attack.

16:20 HOURS. SOMEWHERE ON INTERSTATE 79, A FEW MILES AWAY FROM GASSAWAY, HEADING TOWARDS WEST VIRGINIA STATE CAPITOL BUILDING ENEMY COMMAND CENTER - CHARLESTON, WEST VIRGINIA:

"What's the status?" Adam asked.

"The enemy had no choice but to withdraw from our pincer attack, and have lost a number of their planes. Some by us, the rest by our planes, and partly because they have no place to land and have run low on fuel and ordinance, and do not have the sufficient numbers to hold out against ours. We've dealt a heavy blow to the enemy, leveling out the playing field. And at this point, all they can do is fight until the rest of their ordinance and fuel run out, or abandon their planes, which leaves our run to the capital unopposed," Christopher said.

"Well played, General West," Ahmad said, after listening to the transmission.

"If only so many didn't have to pay the price. Their sacrifice won't be in vain. I promise you," Adam replied.

"I know," Ahmad replied.

"Now, after they finish off the enemy planes, the next step is to level the enemy command post, when we get to the capital, if we can't seize it."

"The enemy still has a lot of fight in them. In case you haven't noticed, we may be running low on fuel and ordinance too. But knowing our lead pilot, she's proven to be very resourceful. She's proven herself more than I care to remember after being under Captain Kim's tutelage. May God rest his soul."

16:30 HOURS. SOMEWHERE OVER WEST VIRGINIA, HEADING TOWARDS CHARLESTON ENEMY AIR NATIONAL GUARD BASE, CHARLESTON, WEST VIRGINIA. 306 MILES FROM SHEPHERD FIELD FREEDOM FIGHTER AIR NATIONAL GUARD BASE- MARTINSBURG, WEST VIRGINIA:

The enemy planes were almost within range of the capital. They noticed the flickering lights in their cockpits warning them that they were running low on fuel and ordinance.

They watched the flames that consumed their positions from the view of their cockpits, from high above in the stormy skies, with no place to land and rearm, left with no other alternative, but to fight to the bitter end.

Nicole looked at her scanners, picking a large number of contacts quickly closing in on their position. She looked at the sun and said, "Falcon, Executioner, and Stallion, form up on my six. The rest of you, weapons hot, and engage and eliminate all hostiles with extreme prejudice. I repeat, eliminate all hostile craft. The goal is to distract the enemy, and wear them down as much as possible, while we still have total invisibility to our advantage. I can't stress how important it is for us to clear the skies for General West and the rest of our troops who are paying the ultimate price at this very moment. Their sacrifices will not be in vain. We need to clear those skies of enemy bogeys. General West and the others are depending on us."

She watched as the group of planes flew into the enemy numbers head on, engaging one another, and said, "We're in the winter months, and the sun won't be up much longer. We have a limited window of opportunity to attack from it."

She flew into the sun with her wingmen, and quickly turned around using the sun to her back to make her invisible to her enemies and locked on to one of the enemy planes, firing her missile, and watching it track the enemy exploding into it, while the others continued to keep the enemy planes distracted.

16:35 HOURS. SOMEWHERE ON INTERSTATE 79, GASSAWAY, HEADING TOWARDS THE WEST VIRGINIA STATE CAPITOL BUILDING ENEMY COMMAND CENTER - CHARLESTON, WEST VIRGINIA:

"I need a status report," Adam said softly.

"Our planes are still engaging the remainder of the enemy planes. It seems that the enemy had more fight than we expected. But it would seem that the plan worked," Christopher said over the radio.

"It would seem that way," Adam answered.

"Let's hope that's all the fight they have left."

"But we have them on the run. What could they possibly do?" Ahmad asked.

"You would be surprised to see what you're capable of when your back is against the wall. Didn't you learn anything during the North Korean occupation of the south, when we were outnumbered more than 20 to 1? I don't know about you, but that's something that I could never forget, and I don't envy anyone who was a general at the time, to send his troops on a suicide mission. But in all fairness, our flight leader did an excellent job to help us contain the threat."

16:37 HOURS. SOMEWHERE OVER CHARLESTON ENEMY AIR NATIONAL GUARD BASE - CHARLESTON, WEST VIRGINIA:

They continued to pursue the enemy planes relentlessly through the gray, overcast skies, as they tried to make their desperate run towards the capital for ground support from their troops.

Nicole was able to lock on to another enemy plane in her sights and deployed another long range missile, and watched it track its target.

The enemy soldier heard his alarm blaring into his cockpit, warning him that he was being pursued by an enemy missile, after he was out of missiles and quickly running low on fuel after their long skirmish against the convoy over the interstate. He pulled the ejection lever, quickly causing the canopy of his plane to fly off, thrusting him out of his cockpit into the stormy skies.

He watched as his plane descended uncontrollably from the skies towards the surface, crashing and burning, while remaining strapped to his seat.

Nicole watched from the view of her cockpit at the enemy pilot's parachute heading towards the surface, and continued to pursue the other enemy planes.

She broke radio silence and said, "Don't let them escape to the capital! Not even a single enemy plane! If they do, they'll have ground support, and make our mission a lot more difficult to accomplish!"

After a long period of engaging the rebel forces, the enemy forces were beginning to run dangerously low in fuel, while they made their desperate attempt to reach the capital for additional ground support.

She watched another missile cruise past her, exploding into another enemy plane, while she continued her silent pursuit of the enemy planes, undeterred from running low on fuel and ammunition, lining them in her sights, wearing their numbers thin.

16:43 HOURS. SOMEWHERE ON INTERSTATE 79, HEADING TOWARDS CLENDENIN, NEAR ROUTE 19, WEST VIRGINIA:

"What's the status on our planes?" Adam asked calmly.

"They've almost cleared the skies of enemy planes. But the enemy is still heading towards the capital for support. As for our planes, they're running dangerously low on fuel at this point. If they don't finish off the enemy forces before we get there, there's a chance that our mission could fail."

"We need to get to the capital as quickly as we can," Christopher answered.

Adam took a deep breath after listening to Christopher on the radio and said, "If it's not one thing, it's another."

16:47 HOURS. SOMEWHERE OVER WEST VIRGINIA, HEADING TOWARDS THE STATE CAPITAL BUILDING ENEMY COMMAND CENTER - CHARLESTON, WEST VIRGINIA:

After a carefully laid-out strategy to maintain supremacy of the skies, the enemy planes were now completely outnumbered. They continued to hold valiantly against the freedom fighters, while they were almost within reach of the capital, where a number of their ground forces were stationed.

16:51 HOURS. STATE CAPITOL BUILDING ENEMY COMMAND CENTER - CHARLESTON, WEST VIRGINIA:

The enemy soldiers heard the frantic radio chatter from their planes, and searched in all directions for the noise of their engines, waiting nervously to fire their weapons.

16:53 HOURS. SOMEWHERE OVER THE STATE OF WEST VIRGINIA. 2 MILES FROM THE CAPITOL BUILDING ENEMY COMMAND CENTER - CHARLESTON, WEST VIRGINIA:

The freedom fighter continued to pursue the enemy towards the capital, straight into the trap that awaited them, after the warnings from the surviving enemy planes.

Within moments of being in range of the capital, the enemy ground troops saw the flashing of the beacon lights heading closer to their direction.

Unable to tell friend from foe, the planes were immediately greeted by a volley of anti-aircraft fire.

Nicole was immediately surrounded by a number of blinding flashes from enemy flak and more anti-aircraft fire burning through her cockpit, as she and her planes flew right into the heart of the enemies' defenses, in relentless pursuit of the surviving enemy planes.

The flak from an enemy shell exploded within reach of her plane, severely damaging her canopy, while she and her squad of planes continued their relentless pursuit of the remainder of the enemy planes that made it towards their position for much needed ground support.

16:57 HOURS. SOMEWHERE ON INTERSTATE 79, CLENDENIN, HEADING TOWARDS THE STATE CAPITOL BUILDING ENEMY COMMAND CENTER - CHARLESTON, WEST VIRGINIA:

"What's the status?" Adam asked, breaking radio silence.

Ahmad fixated his gaze, seeing a series of bright flashes that rose to the skies, with a sudden look of shock on his face, knowing that it was anti-aircraft fire, realizing that their planes were in the hailstorm of enemy fire, and said, nudging Adam, "Look over there."

"What is it?" Adam asked.

"Just look," he answered, pointing his finger in the direction of the anti-aircraft fire brightening the dark skies.

"My God. The enemy made it to the capital, and our planes are now in the thick of it." Adam said in disbelief. He grabbed the radio and said, "Vaughan. Find out what's the status of our planes."

16:58 HOURS. SOMEWHERE OVER THE STATE CAPITOL BUILDING ENEMY COMMAND CENTER - CHARLESTON, WEST VIRGINIA

"We're in the heart of the hornet's nest and being engaged! And we're running dangerously low on fuel and ordinance," Nicole answered, while she flew through the thick wall of enemy flak. A blinding flash suddenly lit through the cockpit of her plane. She continued, "Damn it, we just lost another plane! We don't know how long we can last! What are your orders? Over!"

16:59 HOURS. SOMEWHERE ON INTERSTATE 79, CLENDENIN. 7 MILES FROM STATE CAPITOL BUILDING ENEMY COMMAND CENTER, WEST VIRGINIA:

"Split your forces and engage the enemy gun emplacements!" Adam answered nervously, looking at the bright crimson burst of flak that filled the night skies from afar, while they continued to race towards the enemy command center, in the capital.

The howling winds suddenly calmed, improving their visibility, and making their travels to the capital less difficult.

They heard an explosion from a plane high above their position and looked to the skies, seeing the flaming wreckage free falling to the surface.

Ahmad broke radio silence and asked, "What's your status, flight leader?"

17:00 HOURS. SOMEWHERE OVER THE STATE CAPITOL BUILDING ENEMY COMMAND CENTER - CHARLESTON, WEST VIRGINIA:

"That was a confirmed enemy kill," she said as she flew through the thick haze of enemy flak, switching to her heavy machine guns, while she continued to gain closer ground towards the enemy plane. She quickly greeted it with a thick barrage of machine gun fire, until it exploded, spiraling out of control, crashing and burning on the surface near the capital.

After shooting down the enemy plane, she felt her own plane suddenly shake violently from the burst of enemy flak, tearing through the hull of her plane.

Noticing the hull of her plane was badly damaged from the burst, she quickly performed her evasive maneuvers through the thick wall of flak, heading higher into the evening skies, quickly turning her plane for another strafing run, watching the bright muzzle flashes from the enemy gun emplacements from the view of her cockpit, locking on to them, firing at their positions, until she saw a crimson burst of flame consuming them on the surface, and took to the skies, while the other enemy anti-aircraft positions continued to try to repel the planes that swarmed their positions mercilessly.

She looked at her scanners, seeing that her fuel and ammunition was almost depleted, and said, "We've caused significant damage to the enemy position, but they're still combat capable and still putting up heavy resistance! We've sustained more casualties!" She paused, listening to the radio chatter from one another of one of the other pilots shot down from enemy ground fire, crashing and burning and continued, "We've just lost Executioner! I repeat, we just lost another one of our planes! I'm down to mostly guns, and a few missiles, and my fuel supply is running dangerously low. And for us to seize the capital, we need an immediate ground assault! Over!"

17:01 HOURS. SOMEWHERE ON INTERSTATE 79 CLENDENIN. 6 MILES AWAY FROM THE STATE CAPITOL BUILDING ENEMY COMMAND CENTER - CHARLESTON, WEST VIRGINIA:

"Hold the enemy off for as long as you can! We'll be there as long as we can to offer ground support! E.T.A. 15 minutes!"

17:02 HOURS. SOMEWHERE OVER THE STATE CAPITOL BUILDING ENEMY COMMAND CENTER - CHARLESTON, WEST VIRGINIA.

"We may not have 15 minutes!" Nicole yelled as she continued to navigate through the thick haze of enemy anti-aircraft fire.

17:03 HOURS. INTERSTATE 79 CLENDENIN. 4 MILES AWAY FROM THE STATE CAPITOL BUILDING ENEMY COMMAND CENTER - CHARLESTON, WEST VIRGINIA:

"If we don't get there in time, our squad will be slaughtered, and our mission will be a total failure. We need to get there quickly, before we're too late," Ahmad said, softly.

"I know. I hope it isn't too late already," Adam replied softly, with his optimism fading.

17:07 HOURS. SOMEWHERE ON INTERSTATE 79 – WESTON, WEST VIRGINIA:

The helicopters scoured through the entire interstate in search of anyone who may have survived the enemy onslaught, while Karen and her squad of gunships continued to provide reconnaissance in search of more crash sites littered all over the interstate.

She intercepted Nicole's frantic call for ground support and immediately headed towards the location of the capital, where the last enemy stronghold made their last stand.

17:15 HOURS. INTERSTATE 79, CLENDENIN. 2 MILES AWAY FROM THE STATE CAPITOL BUILDING ENEMY COMMAND CENTER - CHARLESTON, WEST VIRGINIA:

While Adam and the others made their way towards the capital, they heard the engines from the gunships flying over their positions.

"Do you hear something?" Ahmad asked, popping his head out to see where the noise was coming from.

"I do," Adam answered, looking in the skies, seeing the squad of gunships flying over the convoy, and continued with much jubilation, "It's the cavalry. I'll be damned. It's Dragonfly squad."

17:15 HOURS. SOMEWHERE OVER INTERSTATE 79, CLENDENIN. 2 MILES AWAY FROM THE STATE CAPITAL BUILDING ENEMY COMMAND CENTER, WEST VIRGINIA:

Karen watched from the view of her cockpit, seeing the convoy of transports containing troops making their way towards the capital and said, "This is Dragonfly leader to Command, what's your status, over?"

"Our planes are running low on fuel and ordinance, and taking heavy hits from the enemy ground forces, and need immediate assistance. Can you provide until we get there?"

17:16 HOURS. SOMEWHERE OVER INTERSTATE 79, CLENDENIN. 2 MILES AWAY FROM THE STATE CAPITOL, WEST VIRGINIA:

"This is Dragonfly leader, reading you loud and clear. Heading to provide assistance," Karen said, heading towards the enemy anti-aircraft positions.

17:16 HOURS. SOMEWHERE ON INTERSTATE 79. 1 MILE AWAY FROM THE STATE CAPITAL BUILDING ENEMY COMMAND CENTER, CHARLESTON, WEST VIRGINIA:

Adam watched as the squad of helicopters flew towards the capital, vanishing into the night in their quest to quell the enemy positions that continued their valiant stand to turn the tables against the freedom fighters.

17:17 HOURS. SOMEWHERE OVER INTERSTATE 79. 1 MILE AWAY FROM THE STATE CAPITOL BUILDING, WEST VIRGINIA:

As Karen flew towards the capital to engage the enemy forces, her face creased into a sudden look of shock, seeing the bright crimson bursts of enemy flak brightening the dark skies. The giant walls of flames and countless chaos consumed the vicinity of the capital.

She activated her infra-red sensors, monitoring all the activity near the anti-aircraft guns, and said, "We have a visual of all the enemy anti-aircraft positions, permission to engage? Over."

17:18 HOURS. SOMEWHERE ON INTERSTATE 79. 1 MILE FROM THE STATE CAPITOL BUILDING, CHARLESTON, WEST VIRGINIA:

"Permission granted, flight leader. You are free to engage."

17:18 HOURS. SOMEWHERE OVER INTERSTATE 79. 1 MILE AWAY FROM THE STATE CAPITOL BUILDING, CHARLESTON, WEST VIRGINIA:

The squad of gunships hovered from afar, analyzing the anti-aircraft positions through the thick, blinding clouds of dark smoke on their infra-red sensors, and greeted the enemy anti-aircraft positions with a lethal barrage of fire.

Within moments of Karen deploying her long range missiles, a series of explosions rocked their positions, quickly overwhelming them and drastically decreasing their volume of firepower against the remaining planes that continued their skirmish high above the dark skies.

Nicole stared down from the view of her cockpit, seeing a number of the enemy anti-aircraft positions were in flames, while she continued to engage the remainder of the enemy planes.

Adam finally arrived at their destination to assist on the attack on the capital, and stopped to watch from a safe distance, seeing all the destruction the group of gunships continued to unleash on the enemy ground units.

He paused for a brief moment after hearing the planes' engines that continued to soar high above his position, while they still battled for supremacy of the skies. He turned his attention back to the beleaguered enemy units and said, "I didn't come all the way here just to be a witness. All units, move into position and fire at will at anyone or anything that's not one of us."

The tanks moved into position to combine their firepower with their gunships, decimating more of the enemy anti-aircraft positions, until the clamor of the fire suddenly stopped, leaving behind only the eerie silence of the crackling of flames that consumed the enemy anti-aircraft positions. The corpses of the dead were sprawled all about, telling the gruesome tale of what had just come to pass, and the distant buzzing of fighter planes high above their positions were in search of one another, catching their attention once again, when the sudden echo from an enemy plane bursting into flames, and plummeting towards the surface.

They watched helplessly as the burning wreckage arrowed towards the surface, crashing and burning, leaving the skies clear of all remaining enemy planes.

Adam grabbed the radio and asked, "This is command to flight leader. What is your status? Over."

17:27 HOURS. SOMEWHERE OVER THE STATE CAPITOL BUILDING ENEMY COMMAND CENTER, CHARLESTON, WEST VIRGINIA:

"The skies are finally clear of enemy bogeys. I've taken a few hits, but I'm still holding. Running dangerously low on fuel and my ordinance is almost completely depleted, not to mention we've lost a number of our planes. It was a good thing you arrived here when you did. Sorry it took so long. But, the enemy had more fight than we expected," she replied.

17:28 HOURS. NEAR THE STATE CAPITOL BUILDING ENEMY COMMAND CENTER, CHARLESTON, WEST VIRGINIA:

"No need to apologize, flight leader. You performed admirably. Such resistance was to be expected from engaging an enemy far more superior in numbers. We all know how capable the enemy is. Couldn't have asked for a better job. Job well done," Adam replied.

He climbed his transport, watching all the destruction in front of the state capital building, and looked at Ahmad and Christopher. He stared at the young and frightened faces of the ones who were fortunate to make it all the way to the steps of the state capital, and said reluctantly, "We need a clean sweep of the enemy position to see if we can salvage anything that may be of use, or any survivors."

Ahmad grabbed a flare gun and tucked it firmly into his pants and said, "This might come in handy."

"How so?" Christopher asked.

"He might be in there waiting on us. And if he is, I'll call an airstrike on his ass."

"Look around you. No one or nothing could've survived that."

"Can't be too careful, Vaughan," Adam answered.

"Okay. You win," Christopher replied.

"Let's roll out," Adam softly, leading the charge.

The dark smoke filled the vicinity of the capitol building, completely obstructing their view, as they moved forward in search of anything that they can use to their advantage in the future episodes to come.

They continued to walk through the wreckage from all the anti-aircraft guns that lay burning, and the countless corpses of enemy soldiers sprawled all across their positions, with their weapons clutched tightly in their palms in case of any surprises from any surviving enemy troops.

"Keep your eyes open. We may have taken the enemy position, but it doesn't mean that we're out of the woods yet," Adam said, shifting his head from side to side, trying to see through the smoke.

Though they saw no signs of any more enemies, they still continued, as the assassin laid in wait, hidden below the wreckage as they walked past him.

The canister of a smoke grenade silently rolled to their feet, as they continued to walk through the embattled capital, instantly enveloping their entire position.

A sudden look of concern creased over Adam's face, seeing the thick cloud of smoke that quickly enveloped them, knowing that they had walked into the assassin's trap. He shouted, "Retreat! Everyone, pull back!"

Just as they were making their way through the blinding smoke, Janet felt a sudden and crushing blow to her face, throwing her to the floor, dazing her, while the others were suddenly and quickly disarmed by the unseen enemy who greeted them with a swift and lethal barrage of punishment.

A hail of gunfire suddenly echoed from the soldiers who were trapped deep within the thick wall of smoke, trying to detect the elusive enemy while he continued to engage them swiftly, facing a series of punishment from his unmatched skills, causing a number of the troops to retreat into clearer ground.

"It's him!" Ahmad shouted, warning Adam and Christopher, while he tried to fend off the assassin single handedly, sustaining a series of blows.

"General West, pull back!" Christopher shouted as he joined the fight to assist Ahmad in trying to slow the assassin, but to no avail, only to sustain more punishment.

"Protect General West at all costs! Go! "Don't worry about me!" Ahmad said to Christopher.

17:29 HOURS. SOMEWHERE OVER INTERSTATE 79. 1 MILE AWAY FROM THE STATE CAPITOL BUILDING, CHARLESTON, WEST VIRGINIA:

Karen saw the assassin engaging the soldiers on her infrared scanners, trying to get a clear shot while she listened to the frantic screams that filled the radio and said, "I have a visual, but I can't get a clear shot! I can't risk friendly fire! Can't risk hitting General West!"

17:31 HOURS. NEAR THE STATE CAPITOL BUILDING ENEMY COMMAND CENTER - CHARLESTON, WEST VIRGINIA:

After receiving a lot of punishment, Christopher was pulled from the thick cloud of smoke to safety by another soldier, totally abandoning Ahmad to his fate, while Ahmad continued to fight the assassin valiantly, clinging to the assassin as tightly as he could, grabbing onto his wrist, after suffering a fatal blow to his chest from the assassin's knife, placing an instant halt to his courageous efforts.

Ahmad watched the others escaping to safer ground, and watched the blood from his fatal wound trickle to the ground. He slowly loosened his grip on the assassin's arm, and fell to the ground.

He reached into his pants, grabbing the flare gun, firing a shot into the dark skies, marking the spot for the air strike, knowing that he was about to lose his life for the sake of his mission.

"Everyone, pull back!" Adam shouted.

"No," Christopher said frantically, knowing that Ahmad was about to pay the ultimate price for the sake of their mission, like many others before.

The assassin, who looked completely disheveled from the constant bombardment from the air attacks, pulled his sidearm from his holster, and pointed it at Ahmad. He watched the flare traveling high into the dark skies, marking their position.

Ahmad chuckled, gurgling on his blood, and said, "I brought this just in case our paths would cross. Clever huh? It's just you and me now, bitch."

Adam grabbed the radio reluctantly and said, "This is Command to flight leader. Come in."

17:33 HOURS. SOMEWHERE OVER CHARLESTON, WEST VIRGINIA:

"This is flight leader. What are your orders? Over," Nicole asked, watching her ammunition and fuel gauge, nearly depleted.

17:34 HOURS. NEAR THE STATE CAPITOL BUILDING ENEMY COMMAND CENTER - CHARLESTON, WEST VIRGINIA:

Adam closed his eyes and said, "We've just received coordinates to purge the area of any enemy activity. The red flare is the mark. How's your ordinance holding up?"

17:36 HOURS. SOMEWHERE OVER CHARLESTON, WEST VIRGINIA:

"Fuel and ordinance are almost depleted. We may need to reload and refuel soon, or I'll risk crashing. Whatever you have planned, you need to say it now, before my fuel runs out. What are your orders?" she asked, the alarms in her cockpit blaring loudly.

17:37 HOURS. NEAR THE STATE CAPITOL BUILDING ENEMY COMMAND CENTER - CHARLESTON WEST VIRGINIA:

Adam closed his eyes, and answered, "We've just confirmed the area still has pockets of enemy resistance, and have sent you the coordinates to purge the area of any remaining enemy activity. If you can see the red flare, then that's the mark."

17:38 HOURS. SOMEWHERE OVER CHARLESTON, WEST VIRGINIA:

Nicole closed her eyes, being painfully aware of the difficult task that she was asked to perform, after listening to all the frantic distress calls from their brief skirmish with the assassin who laid to ambush. Her gaze was fixed on the bright glow of the flare shooting high into the dark skies, falling back towards the surface, and she replied, "But sir, Lieutenant Evans is still in the area. We can kill our troops with friendly fire."

17:40 HOURS. NEAR THE CAPITOL BUILDING ENEMY COMMAND CENTER - CHARLESTON, WEST VIRGINIA:

"Goddamn it, flight leader! You have your orders, do you hear me?" Adam replied with his eyes filled with tears, knowing that he was about to lose another one of his closest friends, and added, "Red flare's the mark."

17:41 HOURS. SOMEWHERE OVER CHARLESTON, WEST VIRGINIA:

"Orders received. Red flare's the mark," Nicole replied. "Coming in for the final bombing run," she said, flying towards the coordinates where the red flare was fired, arming the remainder of her ordinance. She rapidly reduced her altitude, but was completely reluctant to deploy her payload on Ahmad's position, followed by a squad of planes.

17:41 HOURS. NEAR THE STATE CAPITOL BUILDING ENEMY COMMAND CENTER - CHARLESTON, WEST VIRGINIA:

The assassin looked to the skies, hearing the roar of the engines getting louder as they drew nearer. He turned back to watch Ahmad, while he continued to lay bleeding on the ground, the knife wound deep in his chest.

Jason ran over to his position and said, "We don't have to kill him! We need to leave now!" Jason grabbed Ahmad, trying to drag him away to safety, while the assassin remained stationary with his sidearm pointed. Jason said, "We need to leave now! They're on final approach on their bombing run!"

A shot suddenly rang out, ending Ahmad's life, startling Jason, stopping him in his tracks. The shot was followed by a number of others for good measure to make certain that the assassin's task of eliminating another of the president's high-ranking lieutenants to bring their rebellion to a halt, came one step closer.

Though they were far from the bombing zone, Adam and the others were startled from the shots that echoed loudly, claiming the life of one of his closest friends, who had gladly sacrificed his life for the sake of theirs and their mission.

With not being able to sway the assassin from sparing Ahmad, Jason began to make his desperate run to safety, and was suddenly swooped off his feet when the ground rumbled from the shockwave caused by the violent impact of the blast from the bombing run.

Adam and the others watched as the giant wall of flames spread through the enemy position, consuming everything in its path in complete silence. The fighters stood frozen in their tracks, as if mesmerized by the amazing yet awesome power from all the destruction. Adam's eyes quietly drowned in tears, trying as best as he could to maintain his shell-like exterior, consumed with mixed emotions of anger and remorse from the loss of his friend.

17:43 HOURS. SOMEWHERE OVER THE STATE CAPITOL BUILDING ENEMY COMMAND CENTER - CHARLESTON, WEST VIRGINIA:

Nicole watched the flames that continued to consume the enemy position as she flew over, resting her head against her seat, trying to come to peace at what she'd just done, knowing that Ahmad's sacrifice was the only way to complete their mission.

She broke radio silence and said, "I'm running low on fuel, and out of ordinance. Heading back to base."

Adam ignored the radio chatter, while he continued to maintain his gaze on the flames that continued to ravage the enemy position in stunned silence while Christopher stood by his side, taking notice of the radio chatter, watching the planes fly over his position, heading back to base.

He grabbed the radio from Adam and answered softly, "Permission granted, flight leader. Return to base."

17:45 HOURS. SOMEWHERE OVER INTERSTATE 79. 1 MILE AWAY FROM THE STATE CAPITOL BUILDING - CHARLESTON, WEST VIRGINIA:

Karen and the rest of the gunships continued to hover from a safe distance, watching the giant wall of flame that continued to consume the enemy position, and said, "Requesting permission to return to base."

"Permission granted, Dragonfly leader. Return to base. You're done for tonight."

17:48 HOURS. NEAR THE STATE CAPITOL BUILDING ENEMY COMMAND CENTER - CHARLESTON, WEST VIRGINIA:

"Why did he have to do it?" Adam asked.

"Because he knew it was the only way to complete our mission. He knew it. I know it. We all did at the time," Christopher answered, placing his hand on Adam's shoulder.

"Keep telling yourself that."

"I'm trying not to. But from the look on your face, you know that I'm right. We both do," Christopher replied, and added, "Take a good look at our faces. We barely survived. We wouldn't be breathing if it weren't for Ahmad's sacrifice. We were almost wiped out. Our mission almost failed. He was the reason why we succeeded."

"But at what cost?" Adam asked. "Every time we go out. I lose the ones closest to me. And that's wearing down our resistance."

"It could've been any one of us in there. Who knows? The next time, it might be me. But until that day comes, we must keep on fighting. He gladly made the sacrifice, because he knew the day would come, like I know mine will come someday if not for old age. But I can't afford to worry about it now. Not with so much hanging in the balance. The fight must continue and if I must give my last breath for the sake of my mission, then so be it. But till then we must fight. All of us must live with losing the ones that we've become close to. It's a price we have to pay."

Adam turned his head and watched the flames that continued to consume the enemy position for a brief moment and silently boarded the rear of one of their transports, bound for their base.

The troops remained frozen in their tracks, glancing at the towering walls of flame that continued to consume the enemy anti-aircraft position with their hearts heavy from losing another soldier who had proven to be vital to the war effort.

Christopher paused for a final moment and said, "Let's roll out."

He boarded the transport, sitting directly in front of Adam, who continued to glance back at the towering flames, as they drove away back to their base, seated quietly until the view of all the destruction had completely vanished from their sights under the cover of the night.

21:59 HOURS. SHEPHERD FIELD FREEDOM FIGHTER AIR GUARD BASE - MARTINSBURG, WEST VIRGINIA. 306 MILES FROM CHARLESTON ENEMY GUARD BASE, 192.5 MILES FROM THE STATE OF PENNSYLVANIA:

They arrived at the base and silently disembarked from the transports in complete silence, their hearts heavy from losing another one of their friends, and high-ranking lieutenants.

Karen walked towards Christopher and asked, "How's he doing?"

"We went way back together, so naturally he took it pretty hard. And who could blame him after all we've been through just to take the capital? What's the head count on the survivors?" he asked.

"We suffered quite a number of casualties. Most were dead from the enemy assault. The ones who survived are barely clinging on to life. It's a miracle we made it this far at all."

Adam quietly disembarked from the transport and slowly began making his way back to his quarters. He stopped to look at his battered face in the window of one of the vehicles parked in the base, with the reflection of his face staring back, and cried out, "Goddamn it!" He slammed his fist into the glass, shattering it into many pieces, ignoring the pain from the shards of broken glass that sliced through the flesh of his fist.

Christopher and the others quickly ran to his aid, restraining him and yelled, "Calm down! Calm down! Ahmad was my friend too, and none of this will bring him back! I'll miss him too! We all will!" He felt a sudden calm from Adam and watched Adam's fist trickling blood on the ground. Christopher continued softly, "It's been a long day for all of us, but we can't do anything with you in this state. We need you to focus."

"What do you want me to do?" Karen asked.

"Take him to the infirmary, and have Brian to stitch him up."

"Okay," Karen answered softly, walking him to the infirmary.

"How are you holding up?" he said to Nicole.

"How do you think? General West just asked me to kill one of our own," Nicole answered.

"None of this was easy for us. Imagine how Adam feels knowing that he had to sacrifice Ahmad. We've been through a number of missions together, up until the Fall of Genesis, when we defied the General's orders and were branded as traitors, almost becoming soldiers without a country. We were cleared by Dr. Weaver, after making it to the mainland, pleading his case to the president to remove all troops from Genesis indefinitely. Look at my face. Myself, along with a number of soldiers, were on the verge of being wiped out by him alone. Not to mention the others who didn't make it. And who perished at his hands. We were almost wiped out, and our mission almost failed. Believe it or not, it was Ahmad that saved us from him, because he knew it was the only way. He knew that one day, his time would come, like mine undoubtedly will someday. What happened out there could've happened to any one of us, and we only succeeded because of him."

"But I was ordered to kill one of ours. There had to be another way. There just had to be. I'm the one who depleted what was left of my ordinance on his position. I'm the one who has to live with what I've done."

"If you feel the way you feel, think of how Adam feels. Like you, he has to live with sacrificing his friend that he spilled blood with on the battlefield through many missions. Think of how I feel. Like you, I too have to live with this and so will Adam, and all those who were there, as long as we continue to draw breath. You did your job, Captain. And if it makes you feel any better, I'd rather have him here with us than to win this damn war. Can't put a price on friendship, or a life."

"Well, it doesn't."

"I know. And believe me, I feel the same. But we're at war and all that means is that at some point, it'll consume us, one way or another. I, too, must live with standing by and watching my friend sacrifice himself for the sake of this damn mission. And Adam has to live with making the hard choices that send hundreds and thousands of young men and women to their deaths today alone, including Ahmad. It's a sacrifice that he was more than happy to make at the time that it presented itself, to save the rest of us. It's been a long day full of unexpected twists and turns. And although we succeeded in taking the state capital, we suffered a major blow. Sadly, there'll be more of us to follow, and more difficult choices will have to be made. Now, go on and get some rest. You need it, after all that happened today."

22:05 HOURS. NEAR THE CAPITOL BUILDING ENEMY COMMAND CENTER - CHARLESTON, WEST VIRGINIA:

After the bombing run on the enemy position, an eerie silence swept over the capital, accompanied by the crackling flames that still consumed all the destroyed anti-aircraft emplacements. The assassin slowly rose from beneath the wreckage, dusting off his clothes, completely disheveled from the carnage and destruction the freedom fighters had unleashed upon them. He looked around him, and slowly walked through the wreckage and corpses that littered the front of the capitol building.

He saw some of the wreckage fidgeting and walked closer to inspect it, clearing it, and saw Jason lying beneath it. Jason stared back in a state of shock that the assassin came to his rescue.

He gently grabbed Jason by his clothes, and lifted him to his feet. He stared with his usual cold stare that came along with his straight and chiseled face.

Jason dusted his clothes and looked all around him with a look of shock, seeing all the dead soldiers who littered the ground, wondering how he could survive such an assault and asked "Am I dead?" only to be greeted by the usual stone silence.

Jason continued walking amidst all the destruction until he stumbled on Ahmad's charred and lifeless corpse, stopping abruptly in his tracks, and turned back and glanced at the assassin who continued to greet him with the usual stone silence that matched his cold demeanor. Jason quickly came to the grim realization, like many times before, that his skills and lack of remorse were merely the outcome of the programming that suppressed all of his humanity only to carry out the General's bidding.

22:17 HOURS. SHEPHERD FIELD FREEDOM FIGHTER AIR GUARD BASE - MARTINSBURG, WEST VIRGINIA:

A woman walked towards Christopher, noticing his distress over losing one of his closest friends, and asked, "are you okay, Lieutenant Vaughan?" She held the slim physique of a woman with a tad less of average height, and dark hair, with slanted brown eyes. Though her exterior looked frail, her resolve was deceptively firm, rivaling that of any soldier, male or female, on the field.

"I'll live," Christopher answered, and asked, "Who are you?"

"I'm Chan. Jacqueline Chan. But they call me Jacky for short."

He stared at her bruised face and answered, "I take it that you were in the smoke getting your ass kicked like the rest of us."

"That's a good way to put it," she answered.

"I take it that you're the one who saved my ass back there."

"Yes, I pulled you out. There was no need for any more of us to be in there, so I just grabbed the nearest person I could find. It just happened to be you."

"You're got more guts than you look, Chan. That took a lot of guts putting your life on the line back there. I suppose that I'm in your debt."

"No need. I just wanted to say that I'm sorry about your friend, sir."

"Thank you, Chan. But we all did our jobs. And we have to make sure that his sacrifice wasn't in vain."

"I'll be around if you need me, sir."

"Thank you."

"You're welcome, sir," she said softly.

Christopher was about to walk to his quarters, when he saw the heavy bruises on Janet's face, and asked, "Are you okay?"

"Do I look okay? For a few years in a row now, I've been bitch slapped by the same angry assassin. Now, I'm beginning to think that me and this guy are married in some toxic relationship. I mean, look at my damn face. It's like this has become a common occurrence, and from the looks of you, it looks like the both of you have been scrapping it out just like me. No offense." she answered.

"None taken. You'll live," Christopher replied.

"I hope so. Let's hope that's all he does, because I wouldn't be able to take anything else he could throw at me. Just being honest."

"Let's hope so. Let's hope we got him this time."

She gently grabbed him by his arm and said, "There was no other way. It had to be done. With Lieutenant Evans, sacrificing himself for us, I mean."

"Since that time it happened, it's what I've been trying to tell myself. And I'm sure Adam is too."

The war continues…

CHAPTER 9: OPERATION BLOCKADE.

05:27 HOURS. FORT BRAGG FREEDOM FIGHTER AIR FORCE BASE, NORTH CAROLINA:

The year is 2033. Eight years have passed since "The Great Fall of Genesis."

A flock of northern bobwhite quails grazed the snowy ground in search of whatever food they could scavenge, and quickly took flight.

The sounds of a cockaded woodpecker pecking echoed through the deep woods while pecking into the thick trunk of the tree to build its nest.

A group of wild turkeys gobble in unison, while grazing through the snowy grounds in the thick foliage of the dark woods.

A squirrel fox slowly walked through the foliage, sniffing the snow-covered ground, scavenging for prey.

A striped skunk slowly traversed through the woods, leaning against one of the lumbering trees that towered above the undergrowth, marking its territory, its pungent body fluids secreting from its glands.

The ever watching great horned owl quietly perched on a snow-covered branch of a tree, scanning through the darkness spotting prey, and suddenly took flight.

The temperature through the base plummeted, as the cold winds suddenly swept through the compound, with the tiny flakes showering from the skies, blanketing the ground into a thick white sheet.

"Hi," Jacqueline said, startling Anton.

"Goddamn it, Chan. Don't sneak up on me like that. I could've knocked you out. Even worse, I could've shot you."

"Well, you didn't. And if I were the enemy, I would've picked you off from afar. "

"Well, don't sneak up on me like that, anyway. Bad things happen. Especially since I've been feeling jumpy these days. And I can say the same for a lot of other people in this place."

"I'm sorry. But, it's really cold, and I could really use someone to talk to and pass the time," Jacqueline answered.

"Well, I can use someone to talk while sitting next to a bonfire."

"That'll do, too."

"Hi," another soldier said, startling them.

"My God. The both of you are so jumpy all of a sudden," the soldier said.

"In case you haven't noticed, there's a civil war going on. And we're in its crosshairs," Anton replied.

"And you are?" Jacqueline answered.

"Sorry to startle you. I'm Jill. Jill Nicoletti. Just thought it would be a good idea to pass the time since it's so cold outside. A fire wouldn't hurt," she answered, with the frigid winds passing through her dark brown hair.

"Funny. We were just talking about the same thing. I'm Chan. Jacqueline Chan. But you can call me Jacky. And this is Anton. Nice to meet you."

"The pleasure is mine," Anton answered.

"Likewise," Jill answered.

A raven landed on one of the transports, suddenly interrupting their conversation, cawing loudly, causing a sudden look of shock to take over Jacqueline's and Jill's faces. They remained frozen, watching the raven still cawing, peering as it stood before them, like it was making a brazen attempt to warn them of a series of unfortunate events to come.

Anton watched the looks of shock on their faces, and remarked, "The both of you look like you've seen ghosts."

"You will be if you don't sound the alarm. All of us, for that matter," Jill answered, looking at the ominous messenger.

"What are you talking about? It's just a damn crow," Anton replied.

"It's a raven," Jacqueline answered, still with a look of shock on her face, still keeping her gaze on the raven.

"Not that much of a difference," Anton said.

"We need to sound the alarm now," Jill said.

"That's a first. Seasoned soldiers shitting in their pants at the signs of a damn bird," he said.

"Anton, listen to me well. We've been at war for a long time now. And we need to take everything into consideration. The enemy may be at our gates right now, and I can't shake the feeling that something bad is about to happen," Jacqueline said, panting nervously.

"She's right, Anton. They always say that when something bad is about to happen, a raven comes as a messenger! As a warning! And as of this moment, we're being warned!

You need to make the call! You must sound the alarm! Please!" Jill added.

"Funny. It never came before after all these years we've been fighting this war," he replied.

"Well, it's here now, and we need to do something. Make the call. Please," Jill replied.

"I won't place the base under high alert because of some superstition about some damn crow, raven, or whatever the fuck you think it is."

After cawing four times, the raven suddenly took to the frigid snow-filled skies, quickly vanishing into the night.

"No more crow, no more attack. See? It's gone. Now, if you don't mind, this time, I'd like to complete my rounds uninterrupted, without the both of you telling me about any more bird talk. Top of the morning to y'all."

"Anton, please," Jill pleaded.

"If you feel so strongly about it, then be my guest. It's all on both of you."

"I'll do it," Jill said to Jacqueline.

"I'm with you," Jacqueline answered. "Let's go."

Adam slept soundly in his quarters and suddenly awoke from all the memories of the others in the unit who paid the ultimate price over the past years, during the course of the war, that continued to haunt his dreams.

He walked slowly towards the window, stepping into the beam of the bright moonlight, watching the large, silver moon that remained motionless in the dark, snowy skies, maintaining his gaze, when an enemy shell suddenly screamed through the snowy skies, exploding in front of his quarters, shattering the walls and quickly turning windows into projectiles of broken glass falling on top of him, while tossing him on the floor, dazing him.

Christopher and Nicole quickly ran into his quarters, searching frantically for him, and saw that he laid on the floor, barely conscious, trying to regain his senses from the shock he absorbed.

"Are you okay, General West?" Nicole asked.

Adam simply nodded his head, while he arose from the floor, still dazed and disoriented, trying to come to his senses. "Matheson, you need to get our planes in the air. Don't worry about me. I'll be fine."

"But first, we need to get you out of here!" she replied.

"Come on, let's go!" Christopher yelled, carrying Adam's semi-conscious body out of the burning building.

They ran out of the house as quickly as they could, when they heard another enemy shell whistling through the cold, unforgiving breeze, exploding into his sleeping quarters, tossing them to the ground.

"Looks like we were just in time," Nicole said, breathing heavily, from her near brush with death.

"You need to get moving! Go! If we don't get our planes in the air, we're done for! I'll take care of General West!" Christopher shouted.

"Okay!" Nicole answered, running towards the hangar with a few other pilots through the thick hail of enemy shells that continued to pummel their positions to try and mobilize their planes to counter the enemies' attacks.

They paused for a brief moment, seeing a number of enemy planes flying over their positions on their bombing run to destroy a number of their positions, while they continued to make their way towards the hangar, hoping they wouldn't be caught in the wake of the enemies' attack.

Adam had regained his senses and said, "Tell all armored units to move into blockade positions! And any and all remaining air personnel to provide support!"

Within moments of Adam's orders, a massive wall of anti-aircraft fire immediately brightened the dark skies, as Tiara spearheaded the ground attack against the enemy armored units, blocking their path. They moved into position, while shells from the enemy artillery and tanks continued to rain mercilessly upon them.

"Anton!" Jacqueline said, tapping him on his cheek, while he laid unconscious on the snowy ground, until he slowly came to his senses.

"What happened? Where am I?" he asked in a confused state.

"We're being attacked. You are on the ground," Jacqueline replied.

Jill took a deep sigh of relief, and said softly, "I thought we'd lost you."

Anton looked all around him, seeing all the carnage that continued to unfold, realizing that the omen Jill and Jacqueline had predicted had come to pass.

"Now do you believe?" Jacqueline asked.

"I guess we must be careful about what we really asked for. We wanted a fire. Well, there it is," Jill said, picking Anton's tall and lumbering physique from the ground.

"Not funny, Nicoletti. And it's not that I'm saying that I believe anything either, Chan," Anton answered.

"I was just saying," Jill answered.

"We need to help with the ground support! Man whatever defensive positions we can find, so we can buy our planes enough time to get in the air! And provide some cover," Jacqueline answered.

The alarms continued to blare loudly in the vicinity of the base, as more soldiers moved to their defensive positions, while the enemy air and ground forces continued to press their attack.

"We need to block all enemy personnel from entering the base!" Tiara yelled, while she continued to engage the vastly superior amount of enemy ground units that continued to press their attack, slowly overwhelming the freedom fighters. "We need to hold on long enough until our planes can get airborne! If they don't, we may not be able to hold out much longer!"

The anti-aircraft fire against the enemy planes became stronger, as the ground troops tried as much as they could to stave their attacks to stop them from destroying the hangars, along with the other planes that were arranged neatly in their designated areas.

Nicole and the others continued running towards their planes as quickly as they could, when a sudden blast from an enemy shell exploded near their position, tossing them to the snow-covered ground.

They looked all around them, while they laid on the ground, and suddenly made their desperate dash towards their planes, hoping they wouldn't be intercepted.

Nicole quickly jumped into the cockpit of her plane and strapped herself in, turning on the ignition, taxiing off the runway, followed by the other planes, when a blinding flash from an explosion suddenly lit through the cockpit of her plane.

She glanced back for a brief moment, seeing the hangar that contained a number of their planes quickly transformed into giant plumes of flame, and said frantically, "We're being attacked and need ground support until we can get airborne! We need support for the rest of our planes to get airborne!"

"There's too many of them! We're being hit from all sides! We're doing the best we can! Don't know how much longer we could hold! Just a matter of time before we were overwhelmed by the enemy forces! You need to get your planes in the air as quickly as you can! Over!" Tiara replied, while she and the others continued to hold off the enemy attack.

An enemy plane suddenly burst into flames after being hit from a constant barrage of ground fire, spinning out of control, crashing and burning into the base. "Got one!" Janet said, celebrating. "And a lot more to go!"

05:44 HOURS. SOMEWHERE OVER FORT BRAGG FREEDOM FIGHTER AIR FORCE BASE, NORTH CAROLINA:

After their desperate dash, Nicole and the surviving fighter pilots were now completely airborne. She looked around her, seeing all the destruction the enemy had unleashed upon them within their brief moments of their attack.

She closed her eyes, trying to regain her concentration, and said, "Form up on me!

We're outnumbered and need all the ground support we can get! We need to wear them down enough so we can engage them head on! The only way we can do that is to bring them within range of our ground support! Engage if you can, but if you're being engaged, bring them into range of our ground units! Break off and engage at will!"

05:44 HOURS. FORT BRAGG FREEDOM FIGHTER AIR FORCE BASE, NORTH CAROLINA:

"We're being overwhelmed and don't know how long we can hold out!" Tiara yelled frantically while she continued to hold back the enemy armored units. "All available air units in the area, please send immediate support! Over!"

05:44 HOURS. SOMEWHERE OVER FORT BRAGG FREEDOM FIGHTER AIR FORCE BASE, NORTH CAROLINA:

Nicole heard the distress call and quickly turned her plane around, heading towards Tiara's position, flying through the thick hail of anti-aircraft fire from the ground units.

She flew higher into the cold, dark skies, and turned around, heading towards the surface atop the enemy position, and was instantly greeted by a thick barrage of enemy ground fire.

She quickly armed her ordinance, as she continued to descend unflinchingly towards their positions through the thick sheet of enemy ground fire, watching helplessly as the bright flashes of flame raced past the canopy of her plane, waiting for the right moment to release her payload upon the enemy forces and suddenly felt the round from an enemy anti-aircraft round tear through her plane's armor, grazing her leg, staining the interior of the cockpit with her blood, penetrating through the canopy, leaving a gaping hole.

She quickly released her payload and leveled her plane after taking back to the skies. She watched all around the cockpit, seeing the heavy blood spatters that stained its confines, and quickly glanced at the enemy position, hearing the impact of the explosions after her bombs hit their mark. The giant wall of crimson flames consumed a number of the enemy armored units that tried to push their forces deeper into the base.

She glanced at her wounded leg, gushing blood on the floor of her plane, as she flew off to engage the other enemy planes, while their ground troops continued their attempts to stave off both the remaining enemy ground troops and planes that continued to pummel their positions.

05:49 HOURS. FORT BRAGG FREEDOM FIGHTER AIR FORCE BASE, NORTH CAROLINA:

Tiara saw the number of enemy armored units destroyed from the bombing run and said, "All remaining units move in to engage the enemy! I repeat, move in to engage! What is your status, flight leader?"

05:49 HOURS. SOMEWHERE OVER FORT BRAGG FREEDOM FIGHTER AIR FORCE BASE, NORTH CAROLINA:

Nicole watched her leg wound continue to bleed profusely, and shifted her gaze to the shattered canopy, stained with her blood, and answered calmly, "My plane took a hit. But, I'm still combat capable. We're still outnumbered by the enemy planes, and requesting ground support. Over."

"Reading you loud and clear. Providing support."

The alarms in the cockpit of her plane suddenly began blaring, warning her of an imminent attack from an enemy, causing her to quickly resort to her evasive maneuvers, deploying her countermeasures, and watched the enemy missile follow it, exploding, causing the blinding flash to fill the cockpit of her plane.

She glanced to her back for a brief moment after seeing a number of blinding flashes racing past her plane, and the enemy plane still in hot pursuit, and said, "This is flight leader to all ground units! Enemy plane is on my tail and I can't shake him! I need immediate support! Over!"

05:50 HOURS. FORT BRAGG FREEDOM FIGHTER AIR FORCE BASE, NORTH CAROLINA:

"Reading you loud and clear! Head to my position! I'll provide support!" Tiara replied, watching Nicole heading towards her, as she looked at the skies, ready to press the trigger to dispose of the enemy plane that continued its relentless pursuit of Nicole.

05:51 HOURS. SOMEWHERE OVER FORT BRAGG FREEDOM FIGHTER AIR FORCE BASE, NORTH CAROLINA:

She quickly headed towards the ground troops for support with the enemy plane still continuing its relentless pursuit, and was greeted swiftly by a thick volley of anti-aircraft, and suddenly burst into flames, falling from the skies.

She glanced behind her for a brief moment, watching the burning wreckage of the enemy plane falling from the skies, crashing and burning as it plummeted to the surface, and immediately set her sights on one of the enemy planes that continued to pursue one of her wing mates. She quickly moved into pursuit, trying to lock on the target, as the enemy plane continued to evade, unable to get a missile lock, while it maneuvered skillfully. She quickly switched to her guns, and opened fire with short bursts, wearing down its armor, until it rapidly disintegrated from the barrage, and quickly moved on to the next target.

She glanced at her leg for a brief moment, and saw her trousers now completely soaked with her blood from the wound that she sustained from the enemy bullet, with the pain beginning to take its toll.

05:53 HOURS. FORT BRAGG FREEDOM FIGHTER AIR FORCE BASE, NORTH CAROLINA:

Adam and Christopher watched their planes engage the enemy planes from below, while they assisted the ground units, providing much needed support.

He took the radi and said, "This is General West to flight leader, what's your status? Over!"

05:53 HOURS. SOMEWHERE OVER FORT BRAGG FREEDOM FIGHTER AIR FORCE BASE, NORTH CAROLINA:

"Still outnumbered, and encountering heavy resistance," Nicole answered. "What's your status? Over!" The sweat dripped down her face, while she continued to brave the pain from her wound that was slowly beginning to take its toll.

05:53 HOURS. FORT BRAGG FREEDOM FIGHTER AIR FORCE BASE, NORTH CAROLINA:

"We've lost most of our tanks from the enemy assault, but our defenses are still holding in blockade positions! Don't know how much longer we can last!
How's your ordinance holding up?" Adam asked.

05:53 HOURS. SOMEWHERE OVER FORT BRAGG FREEDOM FIGHTER AIR FORCE BASE, NORTH CAROLINA:

"My ammo count is holding out for now! What are your orders? Over!" Nicole said over the radio, her sweat slowly dripping down her face as she grew more despondent every passing moment from losing blood from the tear in her leg.

05:53 HOURS. FORT BRAGG FREEDOM FIGHTER AIR FORCE BASE, NORTH CAROLINA:

A young soldier, with a slender physique of a little past average height came running towards Adam and Christopher and called out, "General West!"

"Yes!" Adam answered, seeing the frantic look on his face. As he looked into his eyes, he realized the situation was grave, and asked, "What's the situation? And who are you?"

"Min! Jonathan Min, sir!"

He was a fifth generation Korean, in his early 20s, like a number of the fresh recruits who had just poured into the war effort, with short, dark hair and a tall and slender build.

"What's the report, Min?" Adam replied, preparing himself to receive bad news.

"We've made a number of successful kills against the enemy armored forces, but there's still too many to push back! We don't know how much longer we can last! Just a matter of time before our defenses are overrun, sir!"

Adam grabbed the radio and said, "This is command to flight leader! Our defenses are still suffering heavy casualties, and have more enemy ground units converging on our position! We need more assistance!Can you provide support? Over!"

05:57 HOURS. SOMEWHERE OVER FORT BRAGG FREEDOM FIGHTER AIR FORCE BASE, NORTH CAROLINA:

While receiving the distress call, Nicole was still in hot pursuit of her target, and quickly opened fire with her heavy machine guns until the enemy planes completely disintegrated into a bright ball of flame. She replied, "Reading you loud and clear! Heading over to provide support! This is flight leader to any available craft in the area! We have more of the enemy ground units converging our position! Our ground units are being overwhelmed and requesting immediate support! I repeat, we are being overwhelmed by enemy units, and they need ground support! Over! Weapons hot and engaging! I repeat, all weapons hot!"

06:01 HOURS. FORT BRAGG FREEDOM FIGHTER AIR FORCE BASE, NORTH CAROLINA:

Adam stared at Jonathan's face, still frantic, and asked, "Is there anything else?"

"We've lost a number of our troops, sir! Many more seriously injured during the assault! Compared to the manpower that we had before, we're just a handful! If we continue at this rate, we will be overrun for certain! We have to do something quickly with the numbers that we have left! Our hangars are completely destroyed, along with most of our planes and ordinance! We only have a few transports left, and we may not have enough resources or manpower to repel another enemy assault, sir! If worst comes to worst, our only option may be to evacuate!"

"Goddamn it!" Adam answered, closing his eyes.

"What are your orders, General?" Christopher asked.

Adam looked all around him, seeing all the destruction that continued to unfold, and the enemy shells continued to pummel the base, and answered, "We're not left with much of a choice! We may have to evacuate! Get as many of the wounded as you can on the transports! Take Min with you! Go on!"

"Yes, sir!" Christopher replied, and left to help evacuate the wounded.

A series of explosions suddenly tore through the enemy armored formations, completely decimating their lines, while their smaller number of armored units continued to stave them off, startling Adam as the ground beneath his feet shook violently, temporarily throwing him off his balance.

An eerie silence suddenly swept over the compound, and he slowly stumbled to his feet, and watched in shock seeing the giant explosion. After seeing that the brunt of the enemy attack was broken in one single swoop, he picked up the radio and said, "This is command to flight leader, what's your status? Over."

06:05 HOURS. SOMEWHERE OVER FORT BRAGG FREEDOM FIGHTER AIR FORCE BASE, NORTH CAROLINA:

Nicole watched the blood flowing from her wound, as the pain grew stronger, taking its toll, feeling the chills in her body as sweat ran down her face and answered, "I'm doing fine. What are your orders, sir?"

06:06 HOURS. FORT BRAGG FREEDOM FIGHTER AIR FORCE BASE, NORTH CAROLINA:

"How's your ordinance holding up?" Adam asked.

06:07 HOURS. SOMEWHERE OVER FREEDOM FIGHTER AIR FORCE BASE, NORTH CAROLINA:

"A few long range missiles. But mostly guns. But I'm still combat capable," she said softly, trying to hide the pain in her voice.

06:09 HOURS. FORT BRAGG FREEDOM FIGHTER AIR FORCE BASE, NORTH CAROLINA:

"We've lost most of our hangar with most of our planes and ordinance, along with most of our tanks and transports. We may have more enemy reinforcements closing in. I need you and your team to do some recon. Engage if you see any sign of enemy activity, and hit their positions with everything you have. I know it's a lot to ask, but we have a lot more wounded, and our forces are stretched very thin. We may not have the manpower to hold out against another assault. We need to get the wounded out, and we need you to buy us as much time as you possibly can. Can you provide assistance?"

06:10 HOURS. SOMEWHERE OVER FORT BRAGG FREEDOM FIGHTER AIR FORCE BASE, NORTH CAROLINA:

"We'll do the best we can," Nicole said softly, while she and the small squad of planes continued to stave off the larger number of enemy planes, with their combined support from the remainder of their ground forces.

She closed her eyes tightly as the excruciating pain in her leg grew stronger, and did as much as she could to ignore it, engaging the enemy forces, as her fuel and ordinance began to deplete.

She glanced at the horizon and saw the crimson glow of the morning sun that slowly gave birth to the dawn of a new day.

The sweat continued dripping down her face and her senses continued to fade from the wound bleeding profusely, forming a puddle on the floor of the cockpit of her plane.

She took a deep breath, gathering as much strength as she could, and said, "I need a few wingmen to form up on me. The rest of you, continue to engage."

She took another glance at the horizon and flew towards the direction of the rising sun. She quickly turned her plane in the direction of the enemy planes, with the sun to their backs, making her completely invisible to the enemy, helping to turn the battle of the skies in their favor, until it was clear of all the enemy planes.

For the second time, another eerie calm swept over the compound, with only the flames crackling over all the burning wreckage from all the friend and enemy units alike, littering the ground, along with countless corpses that paid the ultimate price for their cause.

06:15 HOURS. FORT BRAGG FREEDOM FIGHTER AIR FORCE BASE, NORTH CAROLINA:

Adam and the rest of the survivors looked all around them, laying their eyes on all the destruction the enemy had unleashed upon them. The eerie calm had swept over their position, seeing a number of wounded soldiers being loaded on the surviving transports, as they prepared their mass evacuation, filling them with a sudden feeling of rage and remorse.

He watched the small group of planes circle over his position, picked up the radio, and said, "This is flight leader. What's your status? Over?"

06:16 HOURS. SOMEWHERE OVER FORT BRAGG FREEDOM FIGHTER AIR FORCE BASE, NORTH CAROLINA:

Nicole heard the call, and closed her eyes, feeling her strength continuing to drain from her body, as sweat continued to drip down her face, and took a deep breath and answered, "My plane took a few more hits, lost a few more of our planes, but our numbers are still strong. We're still combat capable."

06:16 HOURS. FORT BRAGG FREEDOM FIGHTER AIR FORCE, BASE, NORTH CAROLINA:

"How's your ammo count?" he asked.

06:17 HOURS. SOMEWHERE OVER FORT BRAGG FREEDOM FIGHTER AIR FORCE BASE, NORTH CAROLINA:

"Mostly guns. Just a few long-range missiles left," she said.

06:17 HOURS. FORT BRAGG FREEDOM FIGHTER AIR FORCE BASE, NORTH CAROLINA:

"The plan is still the same. We need you to hit them as hard as you can. Cripple their ability to keep on coming at us. Can you handle it? Do you have enough ordinance to complete the mission?" Adam asked, suddenly having an epiphany.

06:17 HOURS. SOMEWHERE OVER FORT BRAGG FREEDOM FIGHTER AIR FORCE BASE, HEADING TOWARDS SEYMOUR JOHNSON, ENEMY AIR FORCE BASE:

"If we combine all our ordinance and hit all the vital areas, we can complete the mission. Heading over to mission directives. We'll contact you as soon as we've completed the mission. Over and out," Nicole replied softly, as she felt her strength continue to drain from her exhausted body from the pain of her leg wound.

06:47 HOURS. SEYMOUR JOHNSON ENEMY AIR FORCE BASE. 68 MILES AWAY FROM FORT BRAGG FREEDOM FIGHTER AIR FORCE BASE, NORTH CAROLINA:

As the sun rose higher into the skies, the activity on the enemy base became more intense, with more of their planes mobilizing, when the enemy watchtower suddenly burst into a giant ball of flame.

Nicole and her small formidable squad of planes quickly swarmed the enemy planes as they lined up on the runway about to take flight, causing complete chaos and confusion in their lines, after greeting them with a constant barrage of heavy machine gun bullets and all their combined resources at their disposal.

She watched one of the enemy planes try to take off from the runway, and quickly pursued, greeting it with a heavy volley of fire until it exploded, falling back to the surface, and said to her other wingmen, "Don't let a single one get off the ground! Hit the fuel trucks! Destroy all their fuel supply! Hit them hard like they did us!"

The smaller group of planes continued to harass the enemy positions, attacking all their fuel supplies, including a number of their vehicles.

She saw a few transports trying to escape through all the chaos and immediately descended upon them without mercy, until they became a flaming pile of metal on the road.

After they had destroyed many of the enemy planes and fuel supply, unable to continue, she looked at the gaping wound in her leg, feeling the deep and excruciating pain. She looked to the direction of the hangar and said softly, "Split up in teams, and reduce those hangars to flaming rubble. The rest of you, make sure those gunships don't get off the ground."

As she flew over the enemy position, she saw the signal warning her that her fuel and ammunition were completely depleted, and said, "Our mission is complete. All units return to base. This is flight leader to command, are you receiving me?"

06:48 HOURS. FORT BRAGG FREEDOM FIGHTER AIR FORCE BASE, NORTH CAROLINA:

"This is command. What's your status? Over.?"

06:52 HOURS. SEYMOUR JOHNSON ENEMY AIR FORCE BASE. 68 MILES, AWAY FROM FORT BRAGG FREEDOM FIGHTER AIR FORCE BASE, NORTH CAROLINA:

"Mission complete. All remaining hostile forces were neutralized. Returning to base. Over."

06:53 HOURS. FORT BRAGG FREEDOM FIGHTER AIR FORCE BASE, NORTH CAROLINA:

"Job well done, flight leader. Permission to return to base," Adam answered, taking a deep breath, and watched as the others continued to load their wounded soldiers into the surviving transports.

Christopher walked over to Adam and said, "We've loaded all the wounded in the transports. Fortunately, we had enough transports to get the wounded out. There's no point in staying here. You need to secure a spot on one of the transports. I'll be right behind you."

"My place is here," Adam answered.

"And so is mine," Christopher answered. "I understand how you feel. I really do. But we've lost most of our friends in this war. And all that's left of our hierarchy to keep our resistance alive is you and me. And right now, our main priority is to keep you safe at all costs. We've lost the base, and our birds have bought us enough time to evacuate, and all we can do at this point is to live and fight another day. Now, if I were you, I'd get my ass into one of those transports. I'll attend the others. I'll be right behind you."

Christopher escorted Adam to one of the few remaining transports, about to leave with a number of wounded soldiers, along with Anton, Jill, Jacqueline, and Janet, and were suddenly attacked by the assassin.

"What the hell?" Christopher shouted, watching the assassin with awe, realizing that he was still alive, after the bombing run that claimed Ahmad's life. "He just won't die!"

The attacks were quick as they were deadly, landing a shattering blow to Janet's jaw, knocking her unconscious. He was swiftly attacked by the others, trying to delay him long enough to give Adam time to get to one of the transports.

Though they had numbers to their advantage, they continued to suffer from his quick and deadly attacks.

Adam suddenly felt the powerful and sudden grip from his nemesis grabbing onto his collar, pulling him back, tossing him to the ground, while the others remained dazed and unconscious from the attacks they suffered at his hands.

The assassin quickly pulled his knife from its holster, and rushed towards Adam, as he lay helpless on the ground, and raised his hand to deliver the final blow to end his life, only to thrust it deeply into Christopher's shoulder, as he shielded Adam from the assassin's deadly blow.

Christopher grabbed the assassin's hand tightly, feeling his knife penetrating deeper into his shoulder, and yelled, "Go! Don't worry about me! Just go!"

They quickly boarded the transport and drove away, after narrowly escaping their deaths at the hands of the assassin, while they watched Christopher who remained totally at his mercy.

The assassin watched as Adam drove away to safety with his usual cold stare, as Adam stared back helplessly, knowing that Christopher would meet his inevitable demise at the hands of his nemesis.

Christopher watched as the transports sped away until they were at a safe distance and slowly loosened his grip on the assassin's wrist. He fell on the snowy ground, with his body slumping, grabbing his shoulder wound, as he bled profusely from the injury he sustained, with his hand completely soaked in his blood.

He stared at the assassin, as he was completely disheveled from the intense battle they had fought, and said with a weak smile, "Looks like you'll have to wait a little longer before you get to meet General West. And as long as he's still alive, we live to fight another day. The resistance continues."

The assassin stared at Christopher's battered face with a blank expression, and pulled out his side arm, ready to execute him, when Jason quickly came forward and pleaded, "You don't have to do this, Lieutenant. We can use him. Please."

"It's no use. There's no reaching him. You're wasting your time. Your words are falling on death ears. Haven't you learnt anything over all these years? This is what he has been programmed to do. Besides, I knew this day would come. This is the end of the road for me. My soul is weary from all this conflict. I need to rest. All that matters now is the mission. It's now up to General West," Christopher answered.

The assassin watched the column of fleeing transports, knowing how close he'd come to completing his objective to eliminate Adam to put an end to the resistance, as Jason's words continued to fall on his deaf ears. He looked back at Christopher, who lay helpless on the ground.

Christopher looked at the assassin's cold and empty stare, knowing his life was about to come to an end, and said smiling, "See you in the next life, my friend."

"Lieutenant, no!" Jason pleaded, when he heard the sudden gunshot, ending Christopher's life, followed by two more in quick succession, to make certain that he had completed his task.

Jason bowed his head and walked away, realizing that his attempts to reach the assassin were futile in saving Christopher's life.

Adam and the others heard the shots echo in the distance, knowing that Christopher had paid the ultimate price for saving Adam from certain death at the hands of the assassin, and bowed their heads in a moment of silence at the loss of their fallen comrade.

07:01 HOURS. 3 MILES AWAY FROM SEYMOUR JOHNSON ENEMY AIR FORCE BASE, NORTH CAROLINA:

After moments of attacking the enemy positions, Nicole and her squad of planes had left the enemy position in piles of flaming wreckage, and headed back to their position.

The sweat continued to fall down her face as she continued to feel her life slowly draining away from her body. The blood continued to gush from her leg wound, causing her to fall in and out of consciousness.

She quickly came to her senses, opening her eyes, and looked back from the view of her cockpit, taking her final glance at the destruction they had left behind in their wake, after paying a heavy price.

07:27 HOURS. SOMEWHERE OVER FORT BRAGG FREEDOM FIGHTER AIR FORCE BASE, NORTH CAROLINA:

After their successful bombing run, they flew over their position, seeing all the destruction the enemy had left in the wake of the attack, seeing the dark, towering columns of smoke rising into the morning skies.

07:27 HOURS. FORT BRAGG FREEDOM FIGHTER AIR FORCE BASE, NORTH CAROLINA:

Jason and the assassin watched as the squad of planes flew over their position, knowing all too well that they had come from their bombing run on their position, heading towards the columns of fleeing transports that had recently evacuated the base.

07:28 HOURS. SOMEWHERE OVER FREEDOM FIGHTER AIR FORCE BASE, NORTH CAROLINA:

Nicole broke radio silence and said weakly, "This is flight leader to command. Are you receiving me? Over."

07:44 HOURS. A FEW MILES AWAY FROM FORT BRAGG, NORTH CAROLINA, HEADING TOWARDS INTERSTATE 66:

Adam and the others contemplated Christopher meeting his demise, and were suddenly interrupted by the sudden incoming transmission.

Adam grabbed the radio and responded, "This is command. Receiving you loud and clear."

"What is your status? Over."

"We've lost the base, and have evacuated all wounded personnel. We narrowly escaped with our lives. How's your fuel holding up? Are you hurt?"

07:49 HOURS. SOMEWHERE OVER FORT BRAGG FREEDOM FIGHTER AIR FORCE BASE, NORTH CAROLINA, HEADING TOWARDS INTERSTATE 66:

Nicole watched her leg wound that continued to bleed profusely, and circled her eyes around the cockpit of her plane, glancing at the heavy blood stains and bullet holes that tore into the canopy, feeling her strength of her body, as the sweat continued to drip down her face.

07:50 HOURS. A FEW MILES FROM FORT BRAGG, NORTH CAROLINA, HEADING TOWARDS INTERSTATE 66:

Adam heard the dead silence on the other end of the transmission, and said, "Come in, flight leader. Are you receiving me?"

He heard the roaring of the planes' engines heading closer to their position, causing a deep sigh of relief.

07:51 HOURS. SOMEWHERE OVER FORT BRAGG, NORTH CAROLINA, HEADING TOWARDS INTERSTATE 66:

Nicole heard the radio chatter with her eyes closed, and her strength almost completely drained. She glanced out of the view of her cockpit, seeing the column of transports making their way towards the interstate, while she continued to listen to the radio chatter, jumping in and out of consciousness.

07:52 HOURS. SOMEWHERE ON INTERSTATE 66, HEADING TOWARDS VIRGINIA:

Adam continued listening to the complete silence on the other side of the transmission, while he watched the plane fly above his position, knowing that something was wrong, and said, "We have a visual on your position."

07:53 HOURS. SOMEWHERE OVER INTERSTATE 66, HEADING TOWARDS VIRGINIA:

She suddenly opened her eyes, jumping back into consciousness, and for the final time, looked all around the cockpit, wondering where she was in total delirium, checking for the ejection lever, and gathered whatever strength she had left. She pulled onto the lever as hard as she could, while she rested her back firmly into her seat.

She felt the sudden force of being catapulted from the cockpit of her plane, closing her eyes tightly, feeling the cold, morning breeze of winter confronting her wounded body.

The peace of the cold morning breeze seeming like an entire world away, with only the sounds of her deep muffled breaths within the tight confines of her oxygen mask breaking the silence. She continued free falling from the skies, helplessly watching her plane plummet to the surface, crashing and burning, and finally slipping into unconsciousness, completely oblivious to her final destination, after contact on the surface.

07:54 HOURS. SOMEWHERE ON INTERSTATE 66, HEADING TOWARDS VIRGINIA:

Jonathan saw the parachute falling from the skies and said pointing, "Look."

"She's alive. Thank God," Adam said, taking a sigh of relief.

"We can't leave her out there, General West," Janet suggested.

"We won't. We'll get her."

Moments after retrieving Nicole, they continued embarking on the long journey quietly in the transports, still deeply within their thoughts after losing Christopher who had willingly given his life to save them.

Anton remained quietly in his thoughts, shifting his gaze to Jill and Jacqueline, in deep regret of not heeding their warning, and bowed his head.

Their concentration was disturbed after hearing Nicole slowly regaining her consciousness, and surrounded her.

She opened her eyes, seeing the blurred silhouettes of all the faces that surrounded her, until her vision came into focus, staring right into their bruised faces, and asked, with her eyes probing all around her, searching for Christopher, and asked, "Where am I?"

"You're safe," Adam answered.

"Where's Lieutenant Vaughan?"

Adam shook his head and answered, "Unfortunately, he didn't make it. We lost him during the evacuation. He gave his life for us. For me. I narrowly escaped. We all did."

After hearing the tragic news, she closed her eyes, tears streaming down her face, and replied, "I'm so sorry. I know how much he meant to you."

"He meant something to all of us," Adam replied, smiling timidly at his loss.

"I'm sorry. I wish there's more that I could've done."

"None of that was your fault. You did the best that you could've done. What you did saved a lot of lives today. Because of what you did, we live to fight another day. No one could ask more of you."

"Where are the other pilots?" she asked

"They're safe. They ran out of fuel shortly after you ejected."

"When am I going to be back in the fight?"

"There'll be time for you to fight. For all of us. You shouldn't worry about anything else right now. You've lost a lot of blood. And it's a miracle you're still alive. Just rest. You need to rest for now."

The war continues…

CHAPTER 10: OPERATION BOMBSHELL.

18:58 HOURS. FORT STORY FREEDOM FIGHTER AIR FORCE BASE - CHESAPEAKE BAY, VIRGINIA:

The year is 2034. Nine years have passed since "The Great Fall of Genesis."

The flurries of snow fell slowly from the night skies, completely shrouding the entire ground in white, as the sudden gust of freezing winds swept across the base, scattering the countless flakes in every direction.

19:00 HOURS. SOMEWHERE ON INTERSTATE 495, HEADING TOWARDS FORT MYERS ENEMY AIR FORCE BASE - ARLINGTON, VIRGINIA:

A large convoy filled with freedom fighters made their way towards the enemy base under complete radio silence.

19:01 HOURS. FORT STORY FREEDOM FIGHTER COMMAND CENTER - CHESAPEAKE BAY, VIRGINIA:

Adam slowly and nervously walked through the base in the thick snow that blanketed the ground, braving the frigid winds that continued to howl through the night, as all the other soldiers stood in salute as he walked through their ranks.

He saluted nervously in response, and slowly walked into the command room.

19:02 HOURS. SOMEWHERE ON INTERSTATE 95, HEADING TOWARDS FORT BELVOIR ENEMY AIR FORCE BASE - FAIRFAX, VIRGINIA:

Another convoy of freedom fighters rode quietly in their transports en-route to their destination under the cover of darkness, watching the snow shower blanketing the long stretch of road behind them, with their weapons clutched tightly in their grasps, soon to carry out the orders that will be given to them in the later course of their mission that awaited them.

19:03 HOURS. FORT STORY FREEDOM FIGHTER COMMAND CENTER - CHESAPEAKE BAY, VIRGINIA:

Adam gently and nervously grabbed the microphone, and glanced at Brian, who nodded his head giving him the nod of approval to commence his speech.

Adam took a deep breath and grabbed the microphone tighter, and said softly, "To all my soldiers who still fight. We bear the scars of a long and terrible war, after toiling through a bloody conflict that seems to have no end, for so long. We were once a nation united through brotherhood, forged by the fires of our forefathers, now broken and dispirited through years of turmoil and conflict that has taken away so many of our loved ones. So many lives, young and old, vanished in an instant."

19:03 HOURS. SOMEWHERE ON INTERSTATE 64, HEADING TOWARDS FORT LEE, ENEMY AIR FORCE BASE - PRINCE GEORGE COUNTY, VIRGINIA:

BROADCAST CONTINUED:

"The ugly truth remains that the scars that we bear from this long and terrible war could never be healed. All we could do is to keep all the memories of all our fallen comrades alive. We're outnumbered and outgunned by the enemy forces, and still we fight, carrying the hope of an entire nation on our shoulders."

A soldier pulled out a photograph from the pocket of her uniform, gazing at a loved one lost during the war, tears rolling down her cheeks, pondering deeply on Adam's words.

19:04 HOURS. SOMEWHERE ON INTERSTATE 64 HEADING TOWARDS FORT EUSTIS ENEMY AIR FORCE BASE - NEWPORT NEWS, VIRGINIA:

The soldiers laid their backs against the interior of their transports in deep contemplation, nodding their heads at one another, as their morale slowly boosted.

19:04 HOURS. FORT STORY FREEDOM FIGHTER COMMAND CENTER - CHESAPEAKE BAY, VIRGINIA:

BROADCAST CONTINUED:

"Though many of us have paid the ultimate price, and sadly, many more will in this long and costly conflict."

Karen and her gunship squad listened closely to Adam's morale-boosting speech, as they remained in their transports parked in the bitter cold, covered in snow, along with Jonathan, Janet, Jill, and Anton.

19:05 HOURS. U.S.S. HARRISON AIRCRAFT CARRIER FLEET, STATIONED 20 MILES IN THE ATLANTIC OCEAN, FROM FORT STORY FREEDOM FIGHTER COMMAND CENTER - CHESAPEAKE BAY, VIRGINIA:

Nicole and the other F-22 Raptor pilots remained still, listening to Adam's speech with their head gears tucked firmly to their sides, ready for their daunting task ahead at any moment's notice.

19:06 HOURS. FORT STORY FREEDOM FIGHTER COMMAND CENTER - CHESAPEAKE BAY, VIRGINIA:

BROADCAST CONTINUED:

"Though we continue to pay the ultimate price against an enemy ever determined and far greater in number, we still search deeper within ourselves to find the courage to drag our battle-weary souls to the battlefield."

19:06 HOURS. U.S.S. SINGER AIRCRAFT CARRIER FLEET, STATIONED 23 MILES AWAY IN THE ATLANTIC OCEAN, FROM FORT STORY FREEDOM FIGHTER COMMAND CENTER - CHESAPEAKE BAY, VIRGINIA:

The entire crew that stood on the aircraft carrier deck, braving the bitter cold, near the squad of F-35 Lightning fighter planes, listened attentively to Adam's inspiring words, as they continued to boost their morale.

19:07 HOURS. FORT STORY FREEDOM FIGHTER COMMAND CENTER - CHESAPEAKE BAY, VIRGINIA:

BROADCAST CONTINUED:

"We make that sacrifice, and we do so proudly, because we are all that stands between total freedom and absolute tyranny, and will not stop until this war is won."

19:08 HOURS. SOMEWHERE ON INTERSTATE 564, HEADING TOWARDS ROUTE 60, TOWARDS LANGLEY, ENEMY AIR FORCE BASE - LANGLEY, VIRGINIA:

The group of transports that carried freedom fighters heading towards the enemy position listened to the broadcast, feeling inspired by Adam's profound speech that inspired morale in them, making them find the courage to continue to fight the long and consuming war that has ravaged the entire country for the past nine years, heading into an entire decade.

19:09 HOURS. FORT STORY FREEDOM FIGHTER COMMAND CENTER - CHESAPEAKE BAY, VIRGINIA:

BROADCAST CONTINUED:

"Time and time again, they've driven us back, and time and time again, we've defeated them. We've shown that no matter how great the fight, the harder we find the resolve to win. There's another dark cloud brewing on the horizon, and once again, we're called upon to look into our souls and dig deeper to weather the destruction about to be wreaked upon us if we stand idly by, and watch the tyranny take its evil root."

19:09 HOURS. U.S.S. HANLEY AIRCRAFT CARRIER FLEET, STATIONED 22 MILES AWAY IN THE ATLANTIC OCEAN, FROM FORT STORY FREEDOM FIGHTER COMMAND - CHESAPEAKE BAY, VIRGINIA:

A number of high-ranking officials remained still in the command tower of the carrier fleet, listening to the message, before they scrambled their FA-18 Super Hornet fighter planes to attack the enemy positions.

19:10 HOURS. FORT STORY FREEDOM FIGHTER COMMAND CENTER - CHESAPEAKE BAY, VIRGINIA:

BROADCAST CONTINUED:

"We're resilient people. And we have no choice but to be for those whom we've lost. And for those yet to come, that they may not suffer a fate worse than death. We have survived much. And what we survived in the past, only made us stronger. No matter how hard the enemy fights, or how great their numbers, our resolve and determination will show that our voices will never be silenced. Nor our will to be extinguished, or go quietly into the night, because we fight for a cause greater than ourselves. We fight for future generations, so they won't have to endure the ugliness left behind from all this endless war and conflict."

19:11 HOURS. U.S.S. BLAKELY AIRCRAFT CARRIER FLEET, STATIONED 21 MILES IN THE ATLANTIC OCEAN, FROM FORT STORY FREEDOM FIGHTER COMMAND CENTER - CHESAPEAKE BAY, VIRGINIA:

The entire ground crew remained still near the F-16 Falcon fighter planes as the message of hope continued to echo through the speakers of the aircraft carrier fleet.

19:12 HOURS. FORT STORY FREEDOM FIGHTER COMMAND CENTER - CHESAPEAKE BAY, VIRGINIA:

BROADCAST CONTINUED:

"There's no doubt in our minds that we'll continue to engage an enemy far more superior in numbers. Which is why tonight, from this very moment, we take the fight to them."

19:12 HOURS. U.S.S. BANNER AIRCRAFT CARRIER FLEET, STATIONED 25 MILES AWAY IN THE ATLANTIC OCEAN, FROM FORT STORY FREEDOM FIGHTER COMMAND CENTER - CHESAPEAKE BAY, VIRGINIA:

The entire crew on the aircraft carrier fleet began to cheer loudly, as their morale began to skyrocket.

19:13 HOURS. FORT STORY FREEDOM FIGHTER COMMAND CENTER - CHESAPEAKE BAY, VIRGINIA:

BROADCAST CONTINUED:

"Tonight, we fight for all our loved ones that we've lost! Who willingly laid down their lives in the name of freedom! In the name of courage! In the name of duty for their country, for the ones they loved and hold dear, and for a better tomorrow! Tonight, we will fight!"

19:13 HOURS. U.S.S. MASTERSON AIRCRAFT CARRIER FLEET, STATIONED 24 MILES IN THE ATLANTIC OCEAN, FROM FORT STORY FREEDOM FIGHTER COMMAND CENTER - CHESAPEAKE BAY, VIRGINIA:

The carrier fleet roared loudly from Adam's message of hope, in their fight to the enemy in the long bitter struggle that awaits them.

19:15 HOURS. FORT STORY FREEDOM FIGHTER COMMAND CENTER - CHESAPEAKE BAY, VIRGINIA:

BROADCAST CONTINUED:

"No matter how long it takes, we will continue to fight! And we will win!" Adam said, feeling a great sense of honor in raising their morale.

19:17 HOURS. THE ENTIRE AIRCRAFT CARRIER FLEET, SOMEWHERE IN THE ATLANTIC OCEAN, MORE THAN 20 MILES FROM FORT STORY FREEDOM FIGHTER AIR FORCE BASE - CHESAPEAKE BAY, VIRGINIA:

The entire aircraft carrier fleet, stationed in the Atlantic Ocean, and the ground troops en-route to all the enemy positions, including all the remainder of the personnel at the base, cheered loudly and quickly scrambled to their positions to take the fight to the enemy with their new found courage.

19:17 HOURS. FORT STORY FREEDOM FIGHTER COMMAND CENTER - CHESAPEAKE BAY, VIRGINIA:

Adam gently placed down the microphone on the desk, and slowly walked out of the command center into the bitter and cold winds, taking a huge sigh of relief, relieving his nervousness after his inspiring speech that boosted up the morale of all his troops, when he heard Jonathan called out to him.

Jonathan walked towards him and said, "We have a slight change of plans."

"What do you mean?" Adam asked.

"We need you to stay and relay the commands from here."

"But, I'm the General. I'm supposed to be on the frontlines with my troops."

"Not tonight," Anton answered.

"He's still out there and you know it," Janet answered.

"If we lose you, then the fight is over," Jill added.

"She's right, General West," Janet answered.

"You're the only one left. It's better if you stay here, and leave the fighting to us," Anton said.

"I suppose you've made your point," Adam answered.

"You know we're right about this. We can't afford to lose you," Anton replied.

"Okay," Adam said softly.

Jonathan and the others began walking towards their transport column, when they saw Brian and Karen sharing tender moments, kissing each other passionately.

Janet wrapped her arms around Anton's neck and rested her head on his chest, and asked, "When are we gonna get to that point?"

Anton gently pushed her away and said, "That's enough, Jackson. You play too damn much."

"God, you're so feisty. I like it. Rrrrrrrrrr," Janet said, purring at Anton.

"But you must admit, that was a good question," Jacqueline added.

"That's enough. All of you. We have a war to fight," Anton answered.

"So feisty. I see why you like him so much," Jill remarked.

"I know. It turns me on," Janet answered smiling, watching him walk away.

"I think it's safe to say, she likes you, Reed," Jonathan said, smiling.

"Are you gonna be entertaining her too, Min?," Jonathan asked, turning back.

"Hey, I'm just saying," Jonathan answered, laughing.

"Well, stop saying," Anton said.

"You know you like her. Quit playing around," Jonathan answered.

"I'm hoping it will get to that point when this is over," Janet said, looking at Anton.

"Will all of you stop acting like children, and stop worrying about Reed getting laid," Jacqueline remarked sarcastically.

"You're all hopeless," Anton said, doing a double take at Janet, as she smiled back at him quietly, feeling deep affection towards him, and walked away to his transport.

After their long and passionate kiss, Brian rested his forehead onto Karen's and said, "I can't wait for us to really be together."

"If all goes well tonight, we will," Karen answered.

"I'm sick of fighting this stupid war. I don't want to spend all my life fighting this stupid war."

"You won't," she answered.

"I wanna have kids and settle down somewhere, and live out the rest of my days in a quiet place, somewhere."

"We will, when this is all over. I promise you."

"I wish you didn't have to go."

"Me too. But I must. The others are waiting. I'll talk to you when I get back," she said.

"Okay," Brian answered, following Karen near her gunship, with her fingers trailing in his hands. He stopped, and watched her climb into the front seat of her gunship, telling him goodbye, kissing her fingertips, and gently resting them on the canopy of her cockpit, and turned on the ignition.

The blades of the gunships began to spin, turning the snow that covered the ground into mist, scattering in every direction as Brian watched from a safe distance, and watched them take flight.

Jill and the others walked past him, patting him on his shoulder, as they walked towards their transports to attack the enemy positions.

19:18 HOURS. THE ENTIRE CARRIER FLEET, IN THE ATLANTIC OCEAN, MORE THAN 20 FROM FORT STORY FREEDOM FIGHTER COMMAND CENTER - CHESAPEAKE BAY, VIRGINIA:

The entire ground crew scurried all about the deck, arming all their planes, waiting for the lead pilot to spearhead the assault.

19:20 HOURS. U.S.S. HARRISON AIRCRAFT CARRIER FLEET, STATIONED 20 MILES IN THE ATLANTIC OCEAN FROM FORT STORY FREEDOM FIGHTER COMMAND CENTER - CHESAPEAKE BAY, VIRGINIA:

Nicole calmly walked across the fly deck into her F-22 Raptor fighter plane, with the cold breeze that swept across the ocean blowing through her blonde hair, with the headgear that bore her insignia tucked firmly under her arm, climbing into the cockpit of her plane. She strapped herself firmly inside, and raised her thumb after turning on the ignition, giving the ground crew the signal that she was ready for lift off to spearhead the charge on the enemy positions.

The winds continued howling, and the snow from the skies began to fill the runway of the fly deck of the fleet. The ignition of her plane roared loudly, drowning the sounds of the howling winds that continued its relentless passing across the seas, until she finally received the signal for departure.

After receiving confirmation from the tower, her plane quickly sped off the fly deck, taking off into the cold, night skies, with the others following shortly after, giving the other fleets an indication that their assault on the enemy strongholds had begun.

19:21 HOURS. U.S.S. SINGER AIRCRAFT CARRIER FLEET, STATIONED 23 MILES IN THE ATLANTIC OCEAN, FROM FORT STORY FREEDOM FIGHTER COMMAND CENTER - CHESAPEAKE BAY, VIRGINIA:

The squad of F-35 Lightning fighter planes quickly made their ascent off the runway of the aircraft carrier, following the squad of F-22 fighter planes that soared high above their position, as they flew towards the command center on their attack run on the enemy positions.

19:22 HOURS. U.S.S. BLAKELY AIRCRAFT CARRIER FLEET, STATIONED 21 MILES, IN THE ATLANTIC OCEAN, AWAY FROM THE FREEDOM FIGHTER COMMAND CENTER - CHESAPEAKE BAY, VIRGINIA:

The squad of F-16 Falcon fighter planes immediately sped off the runway of the aircraft carrier in quick succession, joining the ranks of F-22 Raptor fighter planes and F-35 Lightning fighter planes in quick succession.

19:23 HOURS. U.S.S. HANLEY AIRCRAFT CARRIER FLEET, STATIONED 22 MILES IN THE ATLANTIC OCEAN, FROM THE FREEDOM FIGHTER COMMAND CENTER - CHESAPEAKE BAY, VIRGINIA:

The squad of FA-18 Super Hornet fighter planes flew off the fly deck, following the squad of F-22 Raptor fighter planes, F-35 Lightning fighter planes, and F-16 Falcon fighter planes, flying towards the mainland.

19:24 HOURS. U.S.S. BANNER AIRCRAFT CARRIER FLEET, STATIONED 25 MILES IN THE ATLANTIC OCEAN, FROM THE FREEDOM FIGHTER COMMAND CENTER - CHESAPEAKE BAY, VIRGINIA:

An entire squad of F-15 Strike Eagle fighter planes took off the aircraft fleet, joining the squad of F-22 Raptor fighter planes, F-35 Lightning fighter planes, F-16 Falcon fighter planes, and FA-18 Super Hornet fighter planes, heading towards the mainland.

19:25 HOURS. U.S.S. MASTERSON AIRCRAFT CARRIER FLEET, STATIONED 24 MILES IN THE ATLANTIC OCEAN, FROM THE FREEDOM FIGHTER COMMAND CENTER - CHESAPEAKE BAY, VIRGINIA:

The large number of F-14 Tomcat fighter planes lifted off the aircraft carrier fleet, joining the ranks of planes that flew towards the mainland.

19:26 HOURS. SOMEWHERE OVER THE ATLANTIC OCEAN HEADING TOWARDS FORT STORY FREEDOM FIGHTER, COMMAND CENTER - CHESAPEAKE BAY, VIRGINIA:

Nicole watched the constant flurries of snow falling atop the canopy of her plane from the dark, winter skies, and felt the hull of the entire plane suddenly shudder violently from a great gust of wind that swept across the entire ocean, seeing the flakes that covered the canopy of her plane being quickly being blown away.

She broke radio silence and said, "This is flight leader to command. All planes have been mobilized, and headed towards your position."

19:27 HOURS. FORT STORY FREEDOM FIGHTER COMMAND CENTER - CHESAPEAKE BAY, VIRGINIA:

Adam received the message and checked on the radar, and saw a number of contacts heading towards his position. He answered, "I read you loud and clear, flight leader. Receiving confirmation of you heading towards my position."

He stepped out of the command room into the blistering cold and saw the large squad of planes flying over the base.

19:34 HOURS. SOMEWHERE OVER FORT STORY FREEDOM FIGHTER COMMAND CENTER - CHESAPEAKE BAY, VIRGINIA:

Nicole looked downwards from the safe view of the cockpit of her plane, staring at the bright lights that gave away the position of the command center.

Adam and Brian watched as the large squadron of planes continued to fly over their position, vanishing into the night skies.

He walked back into the warm confines of the command center and said to Brian, "And so it begins."

19:44 HOURS. SOMEWHERE OVER INTERSTATE 564, HEADING TOWARDS FORT MONROE ENEMY AIR FORCE BASE - HAMPTON, VIRGINIA:

Karen looked up in the dark skies, as she sat in the cockpit of her gunship and saw the blinking lights of the entire fighter plane squadron flying over her position. She said to her squad, "This is Dragonfly leader 1 to all crew. I've received confirmation of all fighter planes heading towards our present vector. Reduce altitude, maintain radio silence, and break off to designated vector, over."

Upon her instructions, the large formation of gunships quickly broke off to their designated positions, while the large number of fighter planes continued soaring over their position on their attack run on the enemy positions.

Nicole saw the readings of all the gunships on her radar and looked down from the view of her cockpit and saw the blinking lights. She said, "This is flight leader to Saber wing. Come in."

"This is Saber wing. What are your orders, flight leader?"

"Second wave is in position. Weapons hot, reduce altitude, maintain radio silence, and engage with extreme prejudice, over."

"This is Saber wing to flight leader, reducing altitude, maintaining radio silence, and engaging enemy vector with extreme prejudice, over."

19:44 HOURS. SOMEWHERE OVER INTERSTATE 564. 7 MINUTES AWAY FROM FORT MONROE ENEMY AIR FORCE BASE - HAMPTON, VIRGINIA:

The squad of F-14 Tomcat fighter planes quickly descended upon the unsuspecting enemy base, flying over the squad of gunships as they continued to decrease their altitude flying over the column of transports that were still en-route towards the enemy position.

They felt their transports suddenly shuddered from the noise of the fighter planes' engines, and stopped, warning them that their attack on the enemy position was imminent.

They prepared their assault weapons for the final wave of their assault on the enemy positions as they continued moving into striking range.

19:51 HOURS. FORT MONROE ENEMY AIR FORCE BASE - HAMPTON, VIRGINIA:

The howling winds grew fiercer, scattering the flurries of snow in all directions. The enemy communications tower that stood defiantly through the snow storm suddenly burst into flames, with a sudden flurry of attacks from F-14 Tomcat fighter planes descending upon the enemy positions without warning, achieving total surprise.

19:52 HOURS. SOMEWHERE OVER FORT MONROE, ENEMY AIR FORCE BASE - HAMPTON, VIRGINIA:

Nicole saw the giant ball of flame consuming the enemy communications tower, followed by a series of explosions from their strafing run and said calmly, "This is flight leader to command. Come in."

19:52 HOURS. FORT STORY FREEDOM FIGHTER COMMAND CENTER - CHESAPEAKE BAY, VIRGINIA:

"This is command," Adam answered, looking at Brian nervously.

19:54 HOURS. SOMEWHERE OVER INTERSTATE 564, HEADING TOWARDS FORT MONROE ENEMY AIR FORCE BASE - HAMPTON, VIRGINIA:

"We've begun our assault on the enemy vector and have achieved complete surprise. I repeat, we've achieved complete surprise. Heading towards the next vector, over."

19:55 HOURS. FORT STORY FREEDOM FIGHTER COMMAND CENTER - CHESAPEAKE BAY, VIRGINIA:

The loud cheers of people celebrating filled the command room, after hearing the news of achieving total surprise on the enemy position.

Adam maintained his resolve as he watched the others celebrate their success and answered, "Outstanding, flight leader. Proceed to the next vector."

19:58 HOURS. SOMEWHERE OVER INTERSTATE 64, HEADING TOWARDS LANGLEY ENEMY AIR FORCE BASE - LANGLEY, VIRGINIA:

As the squad of planes flew towards their next objective, Nicole glanced at her radar, and picked up the signal from a large number of gunships en-route to the enemy base, and said, "This is flight leader to Thunder wing, come in, over."

"This is Thunder wing. What are your orders? Over."

"We're approaching the enemy vector. Second wave already in position, weapons hot, reduce altitude, maintain radio silence, and engage with extreme prejudice, over."

"Reading you loud and clear, flight leader. Weapons hot, going dark, and engaging."

The squad of F-16 Falcon fighter planes quickly broke formation, flying past her, quickly descending upon the enemy position under the complete cover of the darkness.

She watched as the planes flew past her and vanished into the stormy night on their attack run on the enemy positions.

20:00 HOURS. SOMEWHERE OVER INTERSTATE 64. 3 MINUTES AWAY FROM LANGLEY ENEMY AIR FORCE BASE - LANGLEY, VIRGINIA:

The squad of F-16 Falcon fighter planes flew over the squad of gunships that hovered at low altitude, as they continued their attack run towards the unsuspecting enemy position in complete radio silence, under the cover of darkness.

20:01 HOURS. SOMEWHERE INTERSTATE 64, ROUTE 70. 7 MINUTES FROM LANGLEY ENEMY AIR FORCE BASE - LANGLEY, VIRGINIA:

The convoy of freedom fighter trucks suddenly felt their transports begin to shudder from the loud vibrations from the roar of the fighter planes' engines, warning the ground troops that their attack on the enemy position was imminent, and did their ammunition count, and prepared their assault rifles for the final phase of the attack on the enemy position.

20:03 HOURS. LANGLEY ENEMY AIR FORCE BASE - LANGLEY, VIRGINIA:

The blinding snow continued to fall mercilessly, as the winds grew stronger, scattering the flurries in every direction.

A missile suddenly exploded into the enemy communications tower, followed by an immediate succession of attacks from the squad of F-16 Falcon fighter planes, causing complete pandemonium in the enemy position.

As Nicole and the remainder of her squadron flew towards their next objective, they saw the bright flashes from the chain of explosions from all the destruction of their squadron of F-16 fighter planes wreaking havoc on the enemy base.

She broke radio silence and said, "This is flight leader to command. Come in, over."

20:04 HOURS. FORT STORY FREEDOM FIGHTER COMMAND CENTER - CHESAPEAKE BAY, VIRGINIA:

"This is command to flight leader," Adam responded softly, staring at Brian with a nervous look on his face.

20:05 HOURS. SOMEWHERE OVER INTERSTATE 64, HEADING TOWARDS FORT EUSTIS ENEMY AIR FORCE BASE - NEWPORT NEWS, VIRGINIA:

"We have commenced our attack run on the next enemy vector, and have achieved complete surprise. I repeat, we've achieved complete surprise. Moving on to the next vector, over."

20:05 HOURS. FORT STORY FREEDOM FIGHTER COMMAND CENTER - CHESAPEAKE BAY, VIRGINIA:

"Roger that, flight leader. Good job. Proceed to the next vector," Adam answered, maintaining his resolve, while the others cheered loudly.

20:12 HOURS. SOMEWHERE OVER INTERSTATE 64, HEADING TOWARDS FORT EUSTIS ENEMY AIR FORCE BASE - NEWPORT NEWS, VIRGINIA:

As the group of fighter planes continued to fly towards the next enemy position, Nicole saw a number of contacts on her radar from the large squad of gunships that moved towards the enemy position.

She broke radio silence and said, "This is flight leader to Blaster wing, come in, over."

"This is Blaster wing. What are your orders, over."

"We're approaching the enemy position. The second wave is already in position. All weapons hot, reduce altitude, and engage with extreme prejudice. I repeat, engage with extreme prejudice."

"Reading you loud and clear, flight leader. All weapons hot, engaging with extreme prejudice, and going dark. Blaster wing, out."

Nicole watched from the view of her cockpit as the squad of F-15 Strike Eagle fighter planes broke their formation, commencing their attack run towards the enemy position.

20:13 HOURS. SOMEWHERE OVER INTERSTATE 64, HEADING TOWARDS FORT EUSTIS ENEMY AIR FORCE BASE - NEWPORT NEWS, VIRGINIA:

They were spotted by the squad of gunships that hovered from a safe distance, and heard the engines from the F-15 Strike Eagle fighter planes fighting high above their positions rapidly descending towards the unsuspecting enemy forces on their attack run.

20:14 HOURS. SOMEWHERE ON INTERSTATE 64, ROUTE 105. 15 MINUTES AWAY FROM FORT EUSTIS ENEMY AIR FORCE BASE - NEWPORT NEWS, VIRGINIA:

The F-15 Strike Eagle fighter planes continued their rapid descent upon the enemy position under strict radio silence, under the cover of darkness, soaring over the convoy of ground troops.

The ground troops felt the hull of their transports suddenly shudder from the noise of the fighter planes' engines, and stopped, warning them that their attack on the enemy position was imminent.

They immediately made their weapons check for the final phase of their assault.

20:16 HOURS. FORT EUSTIS ENEMY AIR FORCE BASE - NEWPORT NEWS, VIRGINIA:

The snow storm continued to progress, leaving a few enemy soldiers to continue braving the cold of the frigid winds to patrol the area, when a sudden explosion erupted into the communications tower, immediately followed by a series of explosions wiping out all those who were caught unaware in the wake of the aftermath.

Within moments, the squad of F-15 Strike Eagle fighter planes descended upon the enemies' position, wreaking untold havoc.

Nicole watched the destruction unfold from high altitude from the view of her cockpit, broke radio silence, and said, "This is flight leader to command. Are you receiving me? Over."

20:16 HOURS. FORT STORY FREEDOM FIGHTER COMMAND CENTER - CHESAPEAKE BAY, VIRGINIA:

"This is command. What is the situation? Over," Adam answered nervously, taking a deep breath in hopes of not receiving bad news.

20:16 HOURS. SOMEWHERE OVER INTERSTATE 64, HEADING TOWARDS FORT LEE ENEMY AIR FORCE BASE - PRINCE GEORGE COUNTY, VIRGINIA:

"We've begun an aggressive approach on the enemy position, and achieved total surprise. I repeat, we have achieved total surprise. Moving to the next coordinates. Over."

20:17 HOURS. FREEDOM FIGHTER COMMAND CENTER - CHESAPEAKE BAY, VIRGINIA:

"That's outstanding, flight leader. Move on to the next vector," Adam answered, and watched the crowd in the command room continue to cheer after receiving the news, nervously maintaining his resolve hoping his plans of attack on the enemy positions didn't go awry.

20:18 HOURS. THE ENTIRE CARRIER FLEET STATIONED MORE THAN 20 MILES IN THE ATLANTIC OCEAN FROM FORT STORY FREEDOM FIGHTER COMMAND CENTER - CHESAPEAKE BAY, VIRGINIA:

The entire fleet celebrated after hearing the news of their achievements of total surprise on the enemy positions.

20:27 HOURS. SOMEWHERE OVER INTERSTATE 95, HEADING TOWARDS FORT LEE ENEMY AIR FORCE BASE - PRINCE GEORGE COUNTY, VIRGINIA:

Nicole continued to fly towards the next enemy way point and picked up the signals of another large number of gunships on her radar.

She broke radio silence and said, "This is flight leader to Vulcan wing. Are you reading me? Over."

"This is Vulcan wing. What are your orders, flight leader?"

"We're almost within range of the next enemy way point. Second wave of assault is in position. All weapons hot, maintain radio silence, reduce and engage with extreme prejudice, over."

"This is Vulcan wing, reading you loud and clear. Weapons hot, reducing altitude, and engaging."

The pilots of the squad of gunships saw the squad of FA-18 Super Hornet fighter planes flying above their heads, rapidly descending towards the enemies' position under the complete cover of darkness of the raging storm.

20:28 HOURS. SOMEWHERE ON INTERSTATE 95. 8 MINUTES FROM ROUTE 36, HEADING FOR FORT LEE ENEMY AIR FORCE BASE - PRINCE GEORGE COUNTY, VIRGINIA:

The ground troops heard the roar from the planes growing louder, as the squad of FA-18 Super Hornets soared over their transports, causing a shudder for a brief moment, and stopped, warning them that an attack on the enemy position was imminent, and immediately made their weapons check for the final phase of their assault.

20:31 HOURS. FORT LEE ENEMY AIR FORCE BASE - PRINCE GEORGE COUNTY, VIRGINIA:

The strong, howling winds continued to sweep across the enemy base, as the snow continued falling mercilessly, making the visibility almost impossible to see through.

The enemy communications tower suddenly blew into flames, followed by a number of attacks completely overwhelming the enemy base in rapid succession.

The squad of FA-18 Super Hornets quickly stormed the base, unleashing the ordinance from their deadly payload, destroying everything in the wake of their attack.

20:32 HOURS. SOMEWHERE OVER INTERSTATE 95, HEADING TOWARDS FORT BELVOIR ENEMY AIR FORCE BASE - FAIRFAX, VIRGINIA:

Nicole watched the destruction unfold from above and in the cockpit of her plane and said, "This is flight leader to command. Are you receiving me? Over."

20:33 HOURS. FORT STORY FREEDOM FIGHTER COMMAND CENTER - CHESAPEAKE BAY, VIRGINIA:

Adam took a deep breath and answered, "This is command. What is your status, flight leader?"

20:34 HOURS. SOMEWHERE OVER INTERSTATE 95, HEADING TOWARDS FORT BELVOIR ENEMY AIR FORCE BASE - FAIRFAX, VIRGINIA:

"We've began aggressive approach on the enemy position, and have achieved complete surprise. I repeat, we've achieved complete surprise."

20:34 HOURS. FORT STORY FREEDOM FIGHTER COMMAND CENTER - CHESAPEAKE BAY, VIRGINIA:

Adam took a deep sigh of relief and answered, "Excellent, flight leader. Proceed to the next vector."

The cheering once again began, while Adam nervously kept his resolve, looking at the others around him.

20:42 HOURS. SOMEWHERE OVER INTERSTATE 95, HEADING TOWARDS FORT BELVOIR ENEMY AIR FORCE BASE - FAIRFAX, VIRGINIA:

As Nicole continued flying towards the next objective, her radar picked up another large number of contacts from another squad of gunships flying in the same direction. She broke radio silence and said, "This is flight leader to Rhino wing. Are you receiving me? Over."

"This is Rhino wing. What are your orders, flight leader?"

"All weapons hot. Reduce altitude, maintain radio silence, and engage with extreme prejudice. Over."

"Reading you loud and clear, flight leader. All weapons hot, reducing altitude, and engaging. Over."

The squad of F-35 Lightning fighter planes immediately broke formation and began their descent upon the enemy position.

The gunship pilots heard the sounds of the planes' engines directly above their position, and saw them flying towards the enemy position, while they continued their rapid descent.

20:42 HOURS. SOMEWHERE ON INTERSTATE 95. 13 MINUTES AWAY TOWARDS ROUTE 1, HEADING TOWARDS FORT BELVOIR ENEMY AIR FORCE BASE, VIRGINIA:

The convoy of transports filled with ground troops heard the screams of jet engines growing louder as they drew nearer above their positions, causing their transports to shudder for a brief moment, and suddenly ceased, warning them that their attack on the enemy was imminent.

They made their weapons check on the assault rifles for the final phase of their assault.

20:44 HOURS. FORT BELVOIR ENEMY AIR FORCE BASE - FAIRFAX, VIRGINIA:

The squad of F-35 Lightning fighter planes continued their descent under complete radio silence under the cover of night, lining up the enemy communications tower in their sights to commence the first phase of their attack, and deployed a missile and watched it find its way into the tower, exploding into it.

Within moments, the squad of fighter planes descended upon the enemy positions, causing total destruction.

20:45 HOURS. SOMEWHERE OVER INTERSTATE 95, HEADING TOWARDS FORT MYERS, ENEMY AIR FORCE BASE - ARLINGTON, VIRGINIA:

Nicole and her squad of F-22 Raptors fighter planes flew over the enemy base, watching the destruction that continued to unfold from the view of her cockpit high above, broke radio silence, and said, "This is flight leader to command. Are you receiving me? Over."

20:45 HOURS. FORT STORY FREEDOM FIGHTER COMMAND CENTER - CHESAPEAKE BAY, VIRGINIA:

"This is command. What is your status, flight leader?" Adam asked, peering nervously at Brian.

20:46 HOURS. SOMEWHERE OVER INTERSTATE 95, HEADING TOWARDS FORT MYERS, ENEMY AIR FORCE BASE - ARLINGTON, VIRGINIA:

"We've begun our descent on the enemy position, and have achieved complete surprise. I repeat, we have achieved complete surprise. Moving on to the next vector."

20:47 HOURS. FORT STORY FREEDOM FIGHTER COMMAND CENTER - CHESAPEAKE BAY, VIRGINIA:

"Outstanding, flight leader. Proceed to the next vector," Adam answered, nervously maintaining his reserve, hoping his attack plans would continue to go smoothly, while the others in the command room cheered loudly.

20:57 HOURS. SOMEWHERE OVER INTERSTATE 495, HEADING TOWARDS FORT MYERS, ENEMY AIR FORCE BASE - ARLINGTON, VIRGINIA:

As Nicole drew closer towards the enemy position, she picked up a large number of gunships on her radar, broke radio silence, and said, "This is flight leader to command. Are you receiving me? Over."

20:58 HOURS. FORT STORY FREEDOM FIGHTER COMMAND CENTER - CHESAPEAKE BAY, VIRGINIA:

The command room suddenly grew quiet, as Adam picked up the microphone and answered, "This is command. What's your status? Over."

21:00 HOURS. SOMEWHERE OVER INTERSTATE 495, HEADING TOWARDS FORT MYERS, ENEMY AIR FORCE BASE - ARLINGTON, VIRGINIA:

"We're almost within range of the designated enemy vector. All weapons hot, maintaining radio silence, reducing altitude, and engaging with extreme prejudice. Over."

21:00 HOURS. FORT STORY FREEDOM FIGHTER COMMAND CENTER - CHESAPEAKE BAY, VIRGINIA:

"Reading you loud and clear, flight leader. All weapons hot, maintain radio silence, and course to the current vector. You have the green light to engage, over."

21:04 HOURS. SOMEWHERE OVER INTERSTATE 495, HEADING TOWARDS FORT MYERS ENEMY AIR FORCE BASE - ARLINGTON, VIRGINIA:

"This is flight leader to all remaining planes. We're maintaining a present course towards the enemy vector. All weapons hot, reduce altitude, maintain radio silence, and engage with extreme prejudice. I repeat, all enemies are to be engaged with extreme prejudice."

Nicole led the charge on the final stage of the assault, towards the enemy stronghold, quickly descending upon them, and saw a number of contacts of gunships on her radar.

The F-22 Raptor fighter planes continued their quick descent towards the enemy position under complete darkness of the stormy skies, soaring over the convoy of trucks that carried their ground troops.

21:05 HOURS. SOMEWHERE ON INTERSTATE 495. 6 MINUTES FROM ROUTE 258, HEADING TOWARDS FORT MYERS ENEMY AIR FORCE BASE, VIRGINIA:

They heard the loud roar of the planes' engines passing over the canopies of their transports, feeling the violent shudder that suddenly stopped, warning them that an attack on the enemy position was imminent, and did the weapons check on their rifles to the final phase of their attack.

21:06 HOURS. FORT MYERS ENEMY AIR FORCE BASE - ARLINGTON, VIRGINIA:

The snow continued to fall through the howling winds, completely masking the enemies' presence, when the enemy communications tower suddenly erupted into a giant ball of flame, followed by a series of attacks from the other fighter planes that followed.

Within moments, all the defensive and flight capabilities of the enemy forces were completely neutralized from the lethal precision of their assault.

After her first bombing run, she took to the dark, stormy skies, and glanced from the cockpit of her plane for a brief moment, at the devastation that she and her squad of planes had unleashed, and said breaking radio silence, "This is flight leader to command. Are you receiving me? Over."

21:06 HOURS. FORT STORY FREEDOM FIGHTER COMMAND CENTER - CHESAPEAKE BAY, VIRGINIA:

"This is command. What is your status? Over," he asked, looking at Brian nervously.

21:07 HOURS. SOMEWHERE OVER FORT MYERS ENEMY AIR FORCE BASE - ARLINGTON, VIRGINIA:

"We have commenced our attack run on the enemy position and engaged with extreme prejudice. We have achieved total surprise. I repeat, we have achieved total surprise. Do you read?" Nicole asked.

21:07 HOURS. FORT STORY FREEDOM FIGHTER COMMAND CENTER - CHESAPEAKE BAY, VIRGINIA:

Adam released a big sigh of relief, and answered, "That's outstanding, flight leader. Commence the second phase when ready."

The people in the command center cheered loudly after receiving the news that their mission to achieve complete surprise on the enemy was a great success.

21:08 HOURS. THE ENTIRE CARRIER FLEET STATIONED MORE THAN 20 MILES IN THE ATLANTIC OCEAN, FROM FORT STORY FREEDOM FIGHTER COMMAND CENTER - CHESAPEAKE BAY, VIRGINIA:

The entire crew aboard all the ships celebrated loudly after receiving their news about their success on attacking the enemy forces.

21:09 HOURS. SOMEWHERE OVER FORT MYERS ENEMY AIR FORCE BASE - ARLINGTON, VIRGINIA:

After a series of strafing runs on the enemy position, Nicole broke radio silence, and called out, "This is flight leader, to Saber wing. What is your status? Over."

21:11 HOURS. SOMEWHERE OVER FORT MONROE ENEMY AIRFORCE BASE - HAMPTON, VIRGINIA:

"This is Saber wing, and all enemy defenses have been neutralized. I repeat, all enemy defenses have been neutralized. Over."

21:11 HOURS. SOMEWHERE OVER FORT MYERS ENEMY AIR FORCE BASE - ARLINGTON, VIRGINIA:

"This is flight leader to Thunder wing. What is your status? Over."

21:12 HOURS. SOMEWHERE OVER LANGLEY ENEMY AIR FORCE BASE - LANGLEY VIRGINIA:

"This is Thunder wing. All enemy defenses have been neutralized. I repeat, all enemy defenses have been neutralized. Over."

21:13 HOURS. SOMEWHERE OVER FORT MYERS AIR FORCE BASE - ARLINGTON, VIRGINIA:

"This is flight leader to Blaster wing. What is your status? Over."

21:13 HOURS. SOMEWHERE OVER FORT EUSTIS ENEMY AIR FORCE BASE - NEWPORT NEWS, VIRGINIA:

"This is Blaster wing to flight leader, and all enemy defenses have been neutralized. I repeat, all enemy defenses have been neutralized."

21:14 HOURS. SOMEWHERE OVER FORT MYERS ENEMY AIR FORCE BASE - ARLINGTON, VIRGINIA:

"This is flight leader to Vulcan wing. What is your status? Over."

21:15 HOURS. SOMEWHERE OVER FORT LEE ENEMY AIR FORCE BASE - PRINCE GEORGE COUNTY, VIRGINIA:

"This is Vulcan wing to flight leader. All enemy defenses have been neutralized. I repeat, all enemy defenses have been neutralized. Over."

21:16 HOURS. SOMEWHERE OVER FORT BELVOIR ENEMY AIR FORCE BASE - ARLINGTON, VIRGINIA:

"This is Rhino wing to flight leader. All enemy defenses have been neutralized. I repeat, all enemy defenses have been neutralized."

21:17 HOURS. SOMEWHERE OVER FORT MYERS, ENEMY AIR FORCE BASE - ARLINGTON, VIRGINIA:

"This is flight leader to command. Come in."

21:17 HOURS. FORT STORY FREEDOM FIGHTER COMMAND CENTER - CHESAPEAKE BAY, VIRGINIA:

"This is command," Adam answered, taking a deep breath, and asked, "What's your status? Over."

21:18 HOURS. SOMEWHERE OVER FORT MYERS ENEMY AIR FORCE BASE - ARLINGTON, VIRGINIA:

"All enemy defenses have been disabled. Requesting permission to sanitize. Over."

21:19 HOURS. FORT STORY FREEDOM FIGHTER COMMAND CENTER - CHESAPEAKE BAY, VIRGINIA:

"Permission granted, flight leader. You are a go to sanitize. Over. I repeat, you have a green light."

21:20 HOURS. SOMEWHERE OVER FORT MYERS ENEMY AIR FORCE BASE - ARLINGTON, VIRGINIA:

"Roger that, command. Receiving you loud and clear. We are proceeding to sanitize. This is flight leader to Dragonfly leader 1. Are you receiving me? Over."

21:21 HOURS. SOMEWHERE OVER FORT MONROE, ENEMY AIR FORCE BASE - HAMPTON, VIRGINIA:

"This is Dragonfly leader 1. What are your orders, flight leader?" Karen asked, as she continued to watch the destruction upon the enemy position continue to unfold, seated from the view of the cockpit of her gunship from a safe distance.

21:22 HOURS. SOMEWHERE OVER FORT MYERS ENEMY AIR FORCE BASE - ARLINGTON, VIRGINIA:

"All enemy defenses are disabled. You are a go for phase 2. I repeat, you have a green light to sanitize."

21:23 HOURS. SOMEWHERE OVER FORT MONROE ENEMY AIR FORCE BASE - HAMPTON, VIRGINIA:

"Reading you loud and clear, flight leader. Commencing next phase of operations," Karen said, moving closer to the beleaguered enemy position.

21:23 HOURS. SOMEWHERE NEAR FORT MONROE ENEMY AIR FORCE BASE - HAMPTON, VIRGINIA:

The ground troops heard the transmission from Nicole and immediately rushed from their transports storming the enemy position in a hail of gunfire to clear out the pockets of enemy resistance that remained.

21:23 HOURS. SOMEWHERE OVER FORT MYERS ENEMY AIR FORCE BASE - ARLINGTON, VIRGINIA:

"This is flight leader to Dragonfly leader 2, what is your status? Over."

21:24 HOURS. SOMEWHERE OVER LANGLEY AIR FORCE BASE - LANGLEY, VIRGINIA:

"This is Dragonfly leader 2. What are your orders, flight leader?"

21:24 HOURS. SOMEWHERE OVER FORT MYERS ENEMY AIR FORCE BASE - ARLINGTON, VIRGINIA:

"If all enemy defenses are disabled. You have a green light for phase 2. I repeat you have a green light to sanitize."

21:25 HOURS. SOMEWHERE OVER LANGLEY ENEMY AIR FORCE BASE - LANGLEY, VIRGINIA:

"Reading you loud and clear, flight leader. Moving in to sanitize," the gunship pilot answered, moving in to provide support for the ground troops who waited for the signal to move in to clear out the remaining pockets of enemy resistance.

21:25 HOURS. SOMEWHERE NEAR LANGLEY ENEMY AIR FORCE BASE - LANGLEY, VIRGINIA:

The soldiers heard the transmission and quickly moved through the enemy base, engaging the remainder of surviving enemies.

21:25 HOURS. SOMEWHERE OVER FORT MYERS ENEMY AIR FORCE BASE - ARLINGTON, VIRGINIA:

"This is flight leader to Dragonfly leader 2, are you receiving me? Over."

21:26 HOURS. SOMEWHERE OVER FORT MYERS ENEMY AIR FORCE BASE - ARLINGTON, VIRGINIA:

"This is Dragonfly leader 3. What are your orders, flight leader? Over."

21:27 HOURS. SOMEWHERE OVER FORT MYERS ENEMY AIR FORCE BASE - ARLINGTON, VIRGINIA:

"All enemy defenses are neutralized. You have permission to sanitize. I repeat, you have permission to sanitize."

21:28 HOURS. SOMEWHERE OVER FORT EUSTIS ENEMY AIR FORCE BASE - NEWPORT NEWS, VIRGINIA:

"Orders received, flight leader. Moving in to sanitize. Over," the pilot said, moving in to provide aerial support greeting the enemy positions in a hail of fire.

21:28 HOURS. SOMEWHERE NEAR, FORT EUSTIS ENEMY AIR FORCE BASE - NEWPORT NEWS, VIRGINIA:

After receiving the signal, the ground troops moved in to purge the enemy pockets of enemy resistance, greeting them with a thick hail of gunfire.

21:28 HOURS. SOMEWHERE OVER FORT MYERS ENEMY AIR FORCE BASE - ARLINGTON, VIRGINIA:

"This is flight leader to Dragonfly leader 4. Are you receiving me? Over."

21:31 HOURS. SOMEWHERE OVER FORT EUSTIS ENEMY AIR FORCE BASE - NEWPORT NEWS, VIRGINIA:

"This is Dragonfly leader 4. What are your orders? Over."

21:31 HOURS. SOMEWHERE OVER FORT MYERS ENEMY AIR FORCE BASE - ARLINGTON, VIRGINIA:

"All enemy defenses are neutralized, you are a go to sanitize. I repeat you are a go to sanitize."

21:32 HOURS. SOMEWHERE OVER FORT LEE ENEMY AIR FORCE BASE - ARLINGTON, VIRGINIA:

"Reading you loud and clear, flight leader. We are moving in to sanitize, over," the gunship pilot answered.

The squad of gunships quickly swarmed towards the dilapidated enemy positions to provide cover, greeting them with a thick volley of fire through the blinding storm.

21:32 HOURS. SOMEWHERE NEAR FORT LEE ENEMY AIR FORCE BASE - ARLINGTON, VIRGINIA:

The ground troops quickly jumped from their transports, and ran into the enemy position, searching for whatever pockets of resistances in a hail of gunfire.

21:33 HOURS. SOMEWHERE OVER FORT MYERS ENEMY AIR FORCE BASE - ARLINGTON, VIRGINIA:

"This is flight leader to Dragonfly leader 5, are you receiving me? Over."

21:33 HOURS. SOMEWHERE OVER FORT BELVOIR ENEMY AIR FORCE BASE - FAIRFAX, VIRGINIA:

"This is Dragonfly leader 5. What are your orders? Over."

21:34 HOURS. SOMEWHERE OVER FORT MYERS ENEMY AIR FORCE BASE - ARLINGTON, VIRGINIA:

"All enemy defenses are neutralized. You are free to sanitize. I repeat, you are a go to sanitize. Over."

21:34 HOURS. SOMEWHERE OVER FORT BELVOIR ENEMY AIR FORCE BASE - FAIRFAX, VIRGINIA:

"Roger that, flight leader. Moving in to sanitize. Over," the pilot said, moving to provide support, greeting the dilapidated enemy positions with a massive volley of fire.

21:34 HOURS. SOMEWHERE NEAR FORT BELVOIR ENEMY AIR FORCE BASE - FAIRFAX, VIRGINIA:

The troops quickly moved into the enemy position to clear out the remaining pockets of enemy resistance in a hail of gunfire.

21:35 HOURS. SOMEWHERE OVER FORT MYERS ENEMY AIR FORCE BASE - ARLINGTON, VIRGINIA:

"This is flight leader to Dragonfly leader 6," Nicole called out, watching the destruction that she and the rest of her wing had unleashed upon the enemy forces from the view of her cockpit.

"This is Dragonfly leader 6. What are your orders, flight leader?"

"We've neutralized all enemy defenses, and you are a go to commence the final phase of the assault. Over."

"Receiving your orders, flight leader. Moving in for the final assault."

The squad of gunships quickly swarmed into position to provide cover fire for the ground troops, who quickly rushed into the beleaguered enemy base to clear out whatever pockets of enemy resistance that remained.

21:45 HOURS. FORT MONROE ENEMY AIR FORCE BASE - HAMPTON, VIRGINIA:

After the ground troops had cleared the enemy base of all remaining troops, they fired a flare into the skies to confirm that it was completely sanitized of enemy troops.

21:46 HOURS. SOMEWHERE OVER FORT MONROE ENEMY AIR FORCE BASE - VIRGINIA:

Karen broke radio silence, and said "This is Dragonfly leader1 to flight leader, come in."

21:46 HOURS. SOMEWHERE OVER FORT MYERS ENEMY AIR FORCE BASE - ARLINGTON. VIRGINIA:

"This is flight leader. What is your status? Over."

21:47 HOURS. SOMEWHERE OVER FORT MONROE ENEMY AIR FORCE BASE - HAMPTON, VIRGINIA:

"All hostiles are completely neutralized, and all ground troops are completely accounted for. Requesting further orders, over."

21:47 HOURS. SOMEWHERE OVER FORT MYERS ENEMY AIR FORCE BASE - ARLINGTON, VIRGINIA:

"This is flight leader to Saber wing, come in."

21:48 HOURS. SOMEWHERE OVER FORT MONROE ENEMY AIR FORCE BASE - HAMPTON, VIRGINIA:

"All enemy positions are completely neutralized and all ground troops are accounted for. You and Dragonfly leader 1 are ordered to return to base."

"Orders received, flight leader. Returning to base," the pilot radioed. "This is Saber wing to command, are you receiving me? Over."

21:48 HOURS. FORT STORY FREEDOM FIGHTER COMMAND CENTER - CHESAPEAKE BAY, VIRGINIA:

"This is command. What's your status?" Adam asked.

21:48 HOURS. SOMEWHERE OVER FORT MONROE ENEMY AIR FORCE BASE - HAMPTON, VIRGINIA:

"All enemy hostiles are neutralized, and all ground troops are accounted for. Returning to base, over."

21:49 HOURS. FORT STORY FREEDOM FIGHTER COMMAND CENTER - CHESAPEAKE BAY, VIRGINIA:

"Outstanding, Saber wing. You and Dragonfly leader 1 are free to return back to base, over."

21:50 HOURS. SOMEWHERE OVER FORT MONROE ENEMY AIR FORCE BASE - HAMPTON, VIRGINIA:

After receiving Adam's command, the squad of F-14 Tomcat fighter planes turned their planes and flew over the dilapidated enemy positions at low altitude, peering down at the squad of gunships from the view of their cockpits, after achieving total victory over the enemy in their surprise attack, en-route to the aircraft carrier fleet stationed in the Atlantic Ocean.

21:50 HOURS. FORT MONROE ENEMY AIR FORCE BASE - HAMPTON, VIRGINIA:

The troops cheered loudly as the group of F-14 Tomcat fighter planes, along with the group of AH-64 Apache Longbow gunships, flew over their position.

21:50 HOURS. LANGLEY ENEMY AIR FORCE BASE - LANGLEY, VIRGINIA:

After the area had been completely neutralized of all remaining pockets of enemy resistance, the ground troops fired a flare into the skies indicating that the area was completely secured.

21:50 HOURS. SOMEWHERE OVER LANGLEY ENEMY AIR FORCE BASE - LANGLEY, VIRGINIA:

The lead gunship pilot saw the flare shoot into the dark stormy skies and said, breaking radio silence, "This is Dragonfly leader 2 to flight Leader, come in."

21:51 HOURS. SOMEWHERE OVER FORT MYERS ENEMY AIR FORCE BASE - ARLINGTON, VIRGINIA:

"This is flight leader to Dragonfly leader 2. What is your status? Over."

21:51 HOURS. LANGLEY ENEMY AIR FORCE BASE - LANGLEY, VIRGINIA:

"All remaining enemy resistance neutralized, and all ground troops are accounted for. What are your orders, flight leader?"

21:52 HOURS. SOMEWHERE OVER FORT MYERS ENEMY AIR FORCE BASE - ARLINGTON, VIRGINIA:

"This is flight leader to Thunder wing. Come in, over." Nicole answered.

21:54 HOURS. SOMEWHERE OVER LANGLEY ENEMY AIR FORCE BASE - LANGLEY, VIRGINIA:

"This is Thunder wing. All enemy troops have been neutralized, and all ground troops are accounted for. Awaiting your orders, flight leader."

21:54 HOURS. SOMEWHERE OVER FORT MYERS, ENEMY AIR FORCE BASE - ARLINGTON, VIRGINIA:

"Thunder wing, you and Dragonfly leader 2 are ordered to return to base. I repeat, you are ordered to return to base."

21:57 HOURS. SOMEWHERE OVER LANGLEY ENEMY AIR FORCE BASE - LANGLEY, VIRGINIA:

"Receiving you loud and clear, flight leader. Thunder wing returning to base," the pilot said. "This is Thunder wing to command, are you receiving me? Over."

21:58 HOURS. FORT STORY FREEDOM FIGHTER COMMAND CENTER - CHESAPEAKE BAY, VIRGINIA.

"This is command. Come in Thunder wing. What is your status? Over."

21:59 HOURS. SOMEWHERE OVER LANGLEY ENEMY AIR FORCE BASE - LANGLEY, VIRGINIA:

"All enemy defenses are destroyed, and all ground troops are accounted for. Requesting permission to return to base."

22:00 HOURS. FORT STORY FREEDOM FIGHTER COMMAND CENTER - CHESAPEAKE BAY, VIRGINIA:

"Permission granted. Return to base, Thunder wing."

22:02 HOURS. SOMEWHERE OVER LANGLEY ENEMY AIR FORCE BASE - LANGLEY, VIRGINIA:

After receiving permission to return to base, the squad of F-16 Falcon fighter planes turned their planes around and flew over the beleaguered enemy position, heading back to the aircraft carrier fleet stationed in the Atlantic Ocean.

22:02 HOURS. LANGLEY ENEMY AIR FORCE BASE - LANGLEY, VIRGINIA:

The ground troops cheered loudly as the planes flew over their positions, headed towards the aircraft carrier fleet stationed in the Atlantic Ocean.

22:05 HOURS. SOMEWHERE OVER FORT MYERS ENEMY AIR FORCE BASE - ARLINGTON, VIRGINIA:

"This is flight leader to Dragonfly leader 3. What is your status? Over."

22:06 HOURS. FORT EUSTIS ENEMY AIR FORCE BASE - NEWPORT NEWS, VIRGINIA:

After completely neutralizing the remaining pockets of enemy resistance, the ground troops fired a flare into the skies, to tell their support that the area was completely purged of all enemy activity.

22:06 HOURS. SOMEWHERE OVER FORT EUSTIS ENEMY AIR FORCE BASE - NEWPORT NEWS, VIRGINIA:

The gunship pilot saw the flare, and called out, "All enemy positions have been neutralized, and all ground troops are accounted for. What are your orders, flight leader?"

22:07 HOURS. SOMEWHERE OVER FORT MYERS ENEMY AIR FORCE BASE - ARLINGTON, VIRGINIA:

"This is flight leader, to Blaster wing. What is your status? Over."

22:07 HOURS. SOMEWHERE OVER FORT EUSTIS ENEMY AIR FORCE BASE - NEWPORT NEWS, VIRGINIA:

"All enemies neutralized. What are your orders, flight leader?"

22:08 HOURS. SOMEWHERE OVER FORT MYERS ENEMY AIR FORCE BASE - ARLINGTON, VIRGINIA:

"Upon completion of your mission, you and Dragonfly leader 3 are ordered to return to base, over."

22:09 HOURS. SOMEWHERE OVER FORT EUSTIS ENEMY AIR FORCE BASE - NEWPORT NEWS, VIRGINIA:

"Reading you loud and clear, flight leader. Returning to base," the pilot said.

"This is Blaster wing to command. Are you receiving me? Over."

22:09 HOURS. FORT STORY FREEDOM FIGHTER COMMAND CENTER - CHESAPEAKE BAY, VIRGINIA:

"This is command, Blaster wing. What is your status? Over."

22:10 HOURS. SOMEWHERE OVER FORT EUSTIS ENEMY AIR FORCE BASE - NEWPORT NEWS, VIRGINIA:

"All enemy defenses have been neutralized. Requesting permission to return to base, over."

22:10 HOURS. FORT STORY FREEDOM FIGHTER COMMAND CENTER - CHESAPEAKE BAY, VIRGINIA:

"Permission granted, Blaster wing. You and Dragonfly leader 3, return to base," Adam answered.

22:11 HOURS. SOMEWHERE OVER FORT LEE ENEMY AIR FORCE BASE - NEWPORT NEWS, VIRGINIA:

After receiving permission to return to base, the squad of F-15 Strike Eagle fighter planes turned their planes around and flew over the burning enemy position, watching all the destruction they had wreaked upon the enemy.

22:12 HOURS. FORT LEE ENEMY AIR FORCE BASE - NEWPORT NEWS ,VIRGINIA:

The ground troops cheered loudly as the squad of planes flew over them, heading toward the aircraft carrier fleet stationed into the Atlantic Ocean, after achieving total success of their mission to liberate the enemy position.

22:13 HOURS. SOMEWHERE OVER FORT MYERS ENEMY AIR FORCE BASE - ARLINGTON, VIRGINIA:

"This is flight leader to Dragonfly leader 4. What is your status? Over."

22:14 HOURS. FORT LEE ENEMY AIR FORCE BASE - PRINCE GEORGE COUNTY, VIRGINIA:

After the enemy positions were neutralized, the troops fired a flare into the dark and stormy skies to signal as a sign that all the remaining pockets of enemy resistance had been neutralized.

22:15 HOURS. SOMEWHERE OVER FORT LEE, ENEMY AIR FORCE BASE - PRINCE GEORGE COUNTY, VIRGINIA:

The gunship pilot saw the flare flying into the skies and said, "This is Dragonfly leader 4. All enemy personnel have been neutralized, and all remaining ground troops are accounted for. What are your orders, flight leader?"

22:15 HOURS. SOMEWHERE OVER FORT MYERS ENEMY AIR FORCE BASE - ARLINGTON, VIRGINIA:

"This is flight leader to Vulcan wing. Are you receiving me? Over," she said to the other pilot.

22:15 HOURS. SOMEWHERE OVER FORT LEE ENEMY AIR FORCE BASE - PRINCE GEORGE COUNTY, VIRGINIA:

"This Vulcan wing. What are your orders, flight leader?"

22:16 HOURS. SOMEWHERE OVER FORT MYERS ENEMY AIR FORCE BASE - ARLINGTON, VIRGINIA:

"You and Dragonfly leader 4 are ordered to return to base. I repeat, return to base."

22:16 HOURS. SOMEWHERE OVER FORT LEE ENEMY AIR FORCE BASE - PRINCE GEORGE COUNTY, VIRGINIA:

"Read you loud and clear, flight leader. Returning to base," the pilot said. "This is Vulcan wing to command. Are you receiving me? Over."

22:17 HOURS. FORT STORY FREEDOM FIGHTER COMMAND CENTER - CHESAPEAKE BAY, VIRGINIA:

"This is command. Receiving you loud and clear, Vulcan wing. What is your status?"

22:17 HOURS. SOMEWHERE OVER FORT LEE ENEMY AIR FORCE BASE - PRINCE GEORGE COUNTY, VIRGINIA:

"Mission accomplished. And requesting permission to return to base, over."

22:17 HOURS. FORT STORY FREEDOM FIGHTER COMMAND CENTER - CHESAPEAKE BAY, VIRGINIA:

"Permission granted. Return to base," Adam said, with a sigh of relief.

22:18 HOURS. SOMEWHERE OVER FORT LEE ENEMY AIR FORCE BASE - PRINCE GEORGE, VIRGINIA:

After receiving orders to return to base, the formidable group of FA-18 Super Hornet fighter planes turned around and flew over all the destruction they left in their wake.

22:18 HOURS. FORT LEE ENEMY AIR FORCE BASE - PRINCE GEORGE COUNTY, VIRGINIA:

The ground troops cheered loudly as the planes flew over their positions heading toward the aircraft carrier fleet stationed in the Atlantic Ocean, after achieving total success.

22:18 HOURS. FORT BELVOIR ENEMY AIR FORCE BASE - FAIRFAX, VIRGINIA:

After the enemy position was completely cleared of the last pockets of enemy resistance, the troops fired a flare into the skies to confirm that the enemy position had been completely secured.

22:19 HOURS. SOMEWHERE OVER FORT BELVOIR ENEMY AIR FORCE BASE - FAIRFAX, VIRGINIA:

The gunship pilot saw the flare burning into the dark, stormy skies and said, "This is Dragonfly leader 5 to flight leader, are you receiving me? Over."

22:19 HOURS. SOMEWHERE OVER FORT MYERS ENEMY AIR FORCE BASE - ARLINGTON, VIRGINIA:

"This is flight leader, Dragonfly leader 5. What is your status? Over,"

22:20 HOURS. SOMEWHERE OVER FORT BELVOIR ENEMY AIR FORCE BASE - FAIRFAX, VIRGINIA:

"All enemy resistance have been neutralized. What are your orders? Over."

22:20 HOURS. SOMEWHERE OVER FORT MYERS ENEMY AIR FORCE BASE - ARLINGTON, VIRGINIA:

"This is flight leader to Rhino wing. Are you receiving me? Over."

22:20 HOURS. SOMEWHERE OVER FORT BELVOIR ENEMY AIR FORCE BASE - FAIRFAX, VIRGINIA:

"This is Rhino wing. What are your orders, flight leader?"

22:21 HOURS. SOMEWHERE OVER FORT MYERS ENEMY AIR FORCE BASE - FAIRFAX, VIRGINIA:

"You and Dragonfly leader 5 are ordered to return to base."

22:21 HOURS. SOMEWHERE OVER FORT BELVOIR ENEMY AIR FORCE BASE - FAIRFAX, VIRGINIA:

"Reading you loud and clear, flight leader. Returning to base," the pilot said, and added, "This is Rhino wing to command. Are you receiving me? Over."

22:22 HOURS. FORT STORY FREEDOM FIGHTER COMMAND CENTER - CHESAPEAKE BAY, VIRGINIA:

"This is command, Rhino wing. What's your status? Over."

22:22 HOURS. SOMEWHERE OVER FORT BELVOIR ENEMY AIR FORCE BASE - FAIRFAX, VIRGINIA:

"All enemy positions neutralized, and requesting permission to return to base, over."

22:23 HOURS. FORT STORY FREEDOM FIGHTER COMMAND CENTER - CHESAPEAKE BAY, VIRGINIA:

"Permission granted Rhino wing. Return to base."

22:23 HOURS. SOMEWHERE OVER FORT BELVOIR ENEMY AIR FORCE BASE - FAIRFAX, VIRGINIA:

After receiving permission to return to base, the group of F-35 Lightning fighter planes turned around and flew over the beleaguered enemy position.

22:24 HOURS. FORT BELVOIR ENEMY AIR FORCE BASE - FAIRFAX, VIRGINIA:

The ground troops cheered loudly as their planes flew over their positions, enroute to the aircraft carrier fleet, stationed in the Atlantic Ocean.

22:25 HOURS. SOMEWHERE OVER FORT MYERS ENEMY AIR FORCE BASE - ARLINGTON, VIRGINIA:

After the enemy position was completely neutralized by all pockets of enemy resistance, Nicole saw the flare burning into the night skies.

The gunship pilot broke radio silence and said, "This is Dragonfly leader 6 to flight leader. Are you receiving me? Over."

"This is flight leader. What's your status, Dragonfly leader 6?"

"All remaining resistance has been neutralized. What are your orders? Over."

"Return to base. I repeat, return to base."

"Reading you loud and clear, flight leader. Returning to base."

"This is flight leader to command. Are you receiving me? Over."

22:26 HOURS. FORT STORY FREEDOM FIGHTER COMMAND CENTER - CHESAPEAKE BAY, VIRGINIA:

"This is command to flight leader. What's your status? Over."

22:26 HOURS. SOMEWHERE OVER FORT MYERS ENEMY AIR FORCE BASE - ARLINGTON, VIRGINIA:

"All enemy positions were completely neutralized. Requesting position to return to base, over "

22:26 HOURS. FORT STORY FREEDOM FIGHTER COMMAND CENTER - CHESAPEAKE BAY, VIRGINIA:

"Any casualties, flight leader?" Adam asked in concern.

22:27 HOURS. SOMEWHERE OVER FORT MYERS ENEMY AIR FORCE BASE - ARLINGTON, VIRGINIA:

"All ground and air personnel are safe and accounted for," Nicole replied.

22:28 HOURS. FORT STORY FREEDOM FIGHTER COMMAND CENTER - CHESAPEAKE BAY, VIRGINIA:

Adam took a big sigh of relief and answered, "Job well done, flight leader. Come on home."

They once again began to celebrate their mission being a total success, without sustaining a single casualty, causing Adam to simply sit in his chair, slumping his back in his seat, in total disbelief, that he had finally achieved the impossible in all of military history.

22:29 HOURS. SOMEWHERE OVER FORT MYERS ENEMY AIR FORCE BASE - ARLINGTON, VIRGINIA:

"This is flight leader. Returning to base," Nicole said for the last time, watching the destruction they had wreaked upon the enemy, from the view of her cockpit, as she headed back to the carrier fleet.

The ground troops cheered loudly as they saw their planes flying over their positions.

22:29 HOURS. FORT STORY FREEDOM FIGHTER COMMAND CENTER - CHESAPEAKE BAY, VIRGINIA:

Adam took another deep breath,slowly rose from his seat, and walked out of the command center into the freezing winds of the blinding storm, searching for their planes.

He heard the screaming of the planes' engines and saw the first squad of planes flying above his position, heading towards the aircraft carrier fleet stationed in the Atlantic Ocean.

Brian walked towards Adam while he watched the skies, seeing their fighter planes heading towards the aircraft carrier fleet, and said, "You did it, General West."

"What do you mean?" Adam asked.

"It's over. You pulled it off without a single casualty. No one has ever done that in military history."

"I really don't know, Thompson. I sense this is only the beginning. For a strike of this magnitude. I feel we stirred up a hornet's nest. Besides, he may still be out there."

"What are you talking about? That son of bitch is dead. No one could've survived that assault. No one, you hear me? Tonight, we've completely immobilized the bulk of the General's forces. The next stop is the Nation's Capital. It's over, General West, so if I were you, I'd be basking in the glory. You practically single handedly wiped out the opposition.

No one would have planned a better surgical strike in hitting the enemy."

"I hope that you're right, Thompson," Adam answered, with a look of worry on his face.

"I am right, and you know that."

"We'll see."

"You just tipped the entire balance of the war in our favor. You just gave the resistance hope."

As another wave of planes flew over their position, en-route to the carrier fleet. Brian pointed to the skies and asked, "Do you hear that? That's the sound of freedom. The chance for a better tomorrow, and a brighter future. The chance of a new hope. And you're the one who did that."

He heard the sounds of the gunships flying in and said, "Our gunships are rolling in, and it's about that time to get that quality time in, if you know what I mean. I'll see you around."

Brian ran over to where the gunships had landed, and waited for them to power down, looking for Karen.

After they had powered down, he saw Karen running towards him, hugging him tightly, and kissing him passionately.

He rested his forehead on top of hers and said, "I was worried that I'd never see you again."

"I was worried too. Now, all we have to do is move forward, and do what we always planned. It's finally over and we have a lot to look forward to. It's a new beginning for us now."

22:50 HOURS. AIRCRAFT CARRIER FLEET STATIONED MORE THAN 20 MILES IN THE ATLANTIC OCEAN, FROM CHESAPEAKE BAY, VIRGINIA:

The crew aboard the entire fleet cheered loudly as the fighter planes landed on the fly decks covered with snow from the raging storm.

The morning sun rose slowly from beyond the horizon, as the freezing storm winds slowly subsided, leaving only the snow to fall gently from the skies.

Nicole climbed from the cockpit of her plane, watching the crew aboard the aircraft carrier running all about, celebrating their victory over the enemy forces.

She walked closer to the edge of the aircraft carrier, and remained standing by herself, as the time steadily passed, completely resigned to her thoughts. She watched the endless ocean until the morning sun rose over the horizon with a renewed sense of optimism and hope of a possible future. The cold and subtle breeze whistled through her long, blonde hair, that she had grown after often wearing it at shoulder length.

She watched the skies seeing a flock of loons migrating in a V-formation in search of warmer climate.

An osprey glided gracefully through the skies freely, high above their positions, cawing in search of food.

A flock of seagulls flew high above, and dove head first into the frigid ocean, in search of fish.

A pod of dolphins traveled in search of warmer climate, proudly displaying their acrobatics at the sights of the vast carrier fleet.

A bald eagle descended from high above, gliding towards the ocean, clutched a fish in the deadly grip of its razor sharp talons, and flew away, vanishing into the distance with its prize.

05:37 HOURS. FORT STORY FREEDOM FIGHTER COMMAND CENTER - CHESAPEAKE BAY, VIRGINIA:

Hours after all the ground transports containing the ground troops had arrived safely back at the base, the other remaining ground troops continued to celebrate.

Shortly after arriving at the base, Jonathan and Anton ran into the command center, where Adam sat back down savoring the moment of his victory, and grabbed him from his seat, and carried him on their shoulders in a victory lap around the base.

Another soldier walked towards them and said, "General West, I presume," causing the celebration to come to an abrupt stop.

"Who wants to know?" Anton asked, walking towards the strange soldier.

They looked at the stranger square in his eyes, as he stared back.

"I'm Frank Hoshi. But everyone calls me "Ho," for short. No relation," the soldier said.

He was of a long line of Japanese background, with a slightly stocky build, and past average height. He was one of the few soldiers that survived from the beginning of the war, and continued, "I heard it was you who planned this entire mission. You practically single handedly broke the enemies' back."

"And they are?" Jonathan asked, stepping in front of Adam.

"No need to be alarmed. We're on the same side here. And these two fine people are my colleagues. We only came to join the festivities, after hearing of your victory."

"Do your other fine colleagues have names? I'm sure they can speak for themselves," Janet answered..

"I'm Kathy Silverman. We just came to do our part," she said, shrugging her shoulders, smiling nervously, with a half-smile, at the troop's reaction. She was of an orthodox Jewish background, with a slender build and dirty blonde hair, nearing her 30s. She was the one before the last of many siblings who joined in the late stages of the war, against the wishes of her family who were completely opposed to fighting, but out of being rebellious, she chose to pick up arms against the General.

"Matthew Masaquela. Nice to meet all of you," who was nearing the 30-year mark, with a background from the African Diaspora, whose parents were survivors of civil war during their early years. They fled to the United States like many others in search of a better life.

When he came of age, he joined the later stages of the war, where he met and bonded with Frank and Kathy, and have been inseparable since then.

"Good for you," Anton replied.

"In case you didn't notice, this is a victory lap. Where you come from, or your family tree, has nothing to do with us. Then again, welcome the war effort," Janet replied plainly.

"We didn't mean to alarm you, General West. It's just that we heard so much about you, and always wanted to meet you in person. Proud to be serving under your command, sir," Frank said, extending his hand.

"What you did was nothing short of a miracle, and even without sustaining a single casualty. No one in the history of any military has ever done something as complex as this surgical strike without sustaining a single casualty. The most remarkable achievement to date," Matthew said.

"It's a true honor to finally meet you, General West," Frank said, shaking his hand.

"The pleasure is mine," Adam replied.

"So why don't we continue to celebrate? Don't let us stop you," Frank said.

"I'm with you on that one," Janet answered.

They resumed their celebration of their victory over the enemy forces, parading Adam on their shoulders throughout the base.

07:02 HOURS. SECURE LOCATION, SOMEWHERE IN RICHMOND, VIRGINIA:

Dr. Alexander Weaver was tall, with a youthful visage, and dark hair lined with shades of gray, as a tell-tale sign that he had slowly began to age, along with a graceful physique though he was of a gentle nature, his resolve and principles remained true, even in the face of adversity.

Three decades earlier, by some twist of fate, he crashed into the jungles of the Ivory Coast after parachuting from his burning plane, suffering a number of serious injuries to his body, and was rescued by the natives, shortly after being attacked by rebel forces from a tiny air strip at an outpost in Liberia, while providing relief for refugees who had survived their long standing civil war.

During the Ivory Coast's dark period of civil unrest that claimed the lives of 100,000 people, and the Chimera strain that continued to ravage the country, claiming the lives of 350,000 people, he became greatly renowned for his work after finding the cure to the deadly epidemic, only to relive another dark chapter of his life, being one of the few sole survivors from another rebel attack on the outpost, that claimed the lives of many more civilians.

Even after three decades, history came to remember the darkest moment of the country's chapter as The Ivory Coast Massacre.

And after 2 decades of his experiences in the Ivory Coast, he built the Genesis fortress, far from the prying eyes of the world in the frigid and remote tundra of Antarctica, becoming its founding father. He vowed to use his work to help those in need, from war-torn countries around the world, passing his work as his legacy in genetic engineering on to his only daughter, Kassandra, before she was captured by the General's forces just before the beginning of the decade-long civil war, that resulted shortly after The Great Fall of Genesis.

He touted many groundbreaking achievements in the field of medicine, as well as established world peace that earned him the humanitarian award. His daughter earned the Nobel peace prize and the title of one of the world's greatest scientific minds upon arriving in the United States after The Great Fall of Genesis, after Dr. Weaver lost his wife, Jane during the evacuation.

Though decades have passed since The Ivory Coast Massacre and The Great Fall of Genesis, the memories of all his loved ones who perished during these events still continue to haunt his dreams.

He was sworn in to take the line of succession of the president before he went missing, in hopes that he could reunite the entire country, because of his capacity to lead and unite all others like he did during his tenure on Genesis, only to spend the entire decade of the civil war trying to locate his daughter's whereabouts, ever since her abduction by the enemy forces.

He stood in the middle of the room, watching and listening quietly for news of his daughter's whereabouts.

He looked at the senior analyst and asked, "Any new developments, Celina?"

Celina was a young brown-haired and hazel-eyed woman in her late 20s, who was one of the most gifted hackers in the entire country. She was drafted by the government straight out of high school for her great skills during her early teens, along with a few others, during the eve of the civil war, under the leadership of Dr. Weaver, to help him locate his long-lost daughter.

She stood up and said, "They've made a series of strafing runs on all the enemy positions. And all were successful. They didn't seem to sustain any casualties. Possibly, this could mean the end of the war."

"That's wonderful, Celina. But do you have any news on my daughter's whereabouts?"

"No, not yet, Mr. President. We've been trying but still no success. If we try to breach their firewalls, our position could be compromised. But we'll continue to try."

"That's fine. Keep listening, and see what you can come up with. Something will come up eventually."

"We're trying the best that we can, sir."

"I know."

07:34 HOURS. FORT MYERS ENEMY AIR FORCE BASE - ARLINGTON, VIRGINIA:

Hours had passed since the attack on the enemy position, which left many dead in its wake.

The assassin slowly dug his way from beneath the rubble, pulling Jason from beneath, and dragging him away, dropping his body on the snow-filled ground, causing the cold that peppered his skin to revive him.

The assassin looked disheveled from his close encounter with death, dusted his clothes, and slowly walked around the beleaguered base, seeing the number of corpses that the freedom fighters' surgical strike had left in its wake, consuming him in total anger.

Jason walked alongside the assassin, trying as best he could to control his emotions, and knelt to the snowy ground. His tears tracked down his face from his close encounter with death and seeing all those who were unfortunate to be claimed by the carnage.

They thought the war had ended. But it has only just begun…

CHAPTER 11: VIPER.

The year is 2035. Ten years have passed since "The Great Fall of Genesis."

The bombing campaign was thought to have wiped out the enemy forces brought about the prospect of hope and as a result, the morale of the freedom fighters had sky rocketed.

And as result of their success, many more freedom fighters joined the fight against the remaining pockets of the enemy forces believed to be holding out against them to put a swift end to the war.

They were wrong. What they thought was the end, was only the beginning…

06:02 HOURS. ENEMY COMMAND CENTER, PENTAGON – WASHINGTON D.C. – THE NATION'S CAPITAL:

As the infinite flurries of snow continue to fall from the dark morning skies, the enemy forces secretly amass the largest strike force ever assembled in the history of the armed forces.

A heavily armored transport suddenly stopped at the entrance of the Pentagon, deploying a number of armored troops who guarded the General under heavy detail, their heavy boot steps echoing through the brightly lit narrow halls of the Pentagon, silently being escorted into the command room.

General Bradley Woodruff was once a noble man who served his country proudly, and with great distinction. He was also a great friend and ally of Dr. Alexander Weaver when they met in the armed forces, up until the dark era of the civil war and the Chimera outbreak at the Ivory Coast, with the Ivory Coast massacre that soon followed, causing them to go separate ways.

After serving his country proudly for many years, overseeing many tours from Ukraine to the reunification of Korea under southern rule, up until the Great Fall of Genesis, he had fallen out of grace, and was responsible for committing many war crimes in Peru, against the rebels of the Peoples' Liberation Front that sparked another global incident, marking one of the most controversial periods in history.

He was sentenced to life in a military prison, but because of his influence of serving his country by many of the other inmates and other soldiers, he was still able to seize power, even from within the prison walls.

He bore a tall and imposing physique, with his dark hair lined with shades of gray, neatly dressed in a trench coat that covered his uniform. Four stars lined the bands on his shoulders that he displayed with great pride, a sign of his overall rank of absolute power, equipped with his trusty sidearm tucked firmly in its holster. He walked into the command room, nodding his head, instructing his guards to stand at the door.

The other high-ranking soldiers stood from their seats as he walked in, out of respect for his rank.

General Woodruff nodded his head and said, "As you were, gentlemen."

The high-ranking officers continued to stand at attention, quietly waiting for the general to relay his commands.

The General stood quietly for a brief moment and said, "The venom from the bite of the viper is already underway. And today is the day that we inject that venom into the heart of the resistance. And with our pincer strategy, it should put a squeeze on General West and his band of misfits. But, make no mistake. He was a worthy adversary, but it all ends today. It has to. We will show them that there's no winning against our forces. That attack against us the year before was the single biggest mistake he ever made, and that was the beginning of the end of their rebellion. We lead our Washington strike force due west and circle east to Chesapeake Bay, where the main command post is located, rendezvousing with our Maryland strike force to place the finishing blow, to sink their entire fleet. And we need to do so under the cover of darkness. Our ground troops are already on the way to all the rebel strongholds as we speak so all we have to do is achieve surprise like they did to us. You may commence all operations."

06:03 HOURS. ANDREWS ENEMY AIR FORCE BASE, MARYLAND:

A large number of enemy pilots and crew men scurried across the compound, fueling and arming all their planes for their task ahead. After they were completely armed and fueled, they lined up on the runway, waiting for confirmation to take off.

06:04 HOURS. BOLLING ENEMY AIR FORCE BASE - WASHINGTON D.C., THE NATION'S CAPITAL:

The crew and pilots continued to scurry across the base, still arming and fueling all the planes for the long and arduous task of purging and retaking all the freedom fighters' strongholds like they did the year before.

After the planes were loaded with fuel and armed with ordinance, the pilots sat in their cockpits, waiting for their lead pilot to lead the charge on all the freedom fighters' positions.

The infamous pilot who went by the moniker, "Viper," was of slim and graceful physique, caramel brown in complexion, with dark, curly hair. She calmly walked through the base with her head gear that bore her infamous insignia clutched tightly to her side.

In the past years of the war, her aerial fighting skills had come to be known by both her colleagues and freedom fighters alike. She was known as one of the best pilots in the skies after inflicting a number of kills on the freedom fighters, rivaling Nicole.

She slowly and calmly walked through the base after the ground crew had readied their planes for the assault on the freedom fighters, and climbed into the cockpit of her plane, turning on the ignition, slowly taxiing on the runway for lift off, with a number of the other enemy planes trailing from behind.

She patiently waited for the confirmation to lift off the tarmac, and upon receiving it from the tower, when the sounds of the engines revving, filled the entire vicinity of the base, she taxied on the runway, drawing more speed, until she was airborne.

The roar of all the other enemy planes' engines filled the vicinity of the base, as they waited for their turn to be airborne, for their attack run on the freedom fighters' positions, taking to the skies after receiving confirmation from the tower.

06:07 HOURS. ANDREWS ENEMY AIR FORCE BASE, MARYLAND:

A vast number of enemy planes consisting of F-15 Strike Eagles, F-16 Falcons, FA-18 Super Hornets, and A-10 Warthogs lifted off the runway, making their way to the carrier fleet stationed in the Atlantic Ocean.

06:08 HOURS. SECURE LOCATION, SOMEWHERE IN RICHMOND, VIRGINIA:

"Dr. Weaver, Dr. Weaver," Celina called out in haste. "We've picked up something."

"What did you get?" he asked eagerly.

"We've just intercepted another transmission. Another war is about to break out. It sounds like the enemy is attacking General West's positions."

"Which one?" he asked, with a look of concern on his face.

"All of them. It seems that the General has amassed a much bigger army than General West did the year before. This is by far the biggest force ever amassed. And from the looks of it, it seems they're on a path to wipe out the resistance once and for all. And that was just one squadron."

"What do you mean?" Dr. Weaver asked.

"We've just intercepted another transmission from Andrews Air Force Base, in Maryland. I think they are attacking simultaneously. While one attacks the bases, the other is en-route to the aircraft carrier fleet stationed in the Atlantic. Looks like the General might have pincered General West from both fronts, sir."

"How could this happen? Can't we send a distress call to warn them?"

"If we do, they may be able to track us. And that means our location will be at great risk of being compromised. And the first priority is to keep you safe at all costs."

"My God. Let's pray for a miracle," he said, with a sudden hint of nervousness on his face.

06:10 HOURS. ENEMY COMMAND CENTER, PENTAGON - WASHINGTON D.C. - THE NATION'S CAPITAL:

Colonel Maxwell Radcliffe was a few years past middle age, with average build and height, blonde hair lined with streaks of gray, and like the General, spent a number of his years in the armed forces and was fiercely loyal.

He stood up from his seat and said, "The attack is about to begin, General. Our Maryland strike force is already en-route to the carrier fleet, and will be making radio contact soon."

"Excellent," the General answered.

06:12 HOURS. SOMEWHERE OVER THE NATION'S CAPITAL, HEADING TOWARDS FORT MYERS FREEDOM FIGHTER BASE - ARLINGTON, VIRGINIA:

An entire squad of planes consisting of F-22 Raptors, F-14 Tomcats, F-15 Strike Eagles, F-16 Falcons, and FA-18 Super Hornet F-35 Lightning fighter planes made their way towards the unsuspecting freedom fighters' positions.

06:15 HOURS. SOMEWHERE OVER INTERSTATE 64, 1 MILE AWAY FROM FORT STORY FREEDOM FIGHTER COMMAND CENTER - CHESAPEAKE BAY, VIRGINIA:

"I'm impressed with the level of activity with so many freedom fighters rolling in to join the movement against the enemy forces," Frank said, as he sat next to Adam.

"It's a wonderful feeling. But somehow, my instincts tell me that it's not over. As a matter of fact, something tells me it hasn't even begun. It's been too quiet. Way too quiet."

"And what makes you say that?" Matthew asked.

"I've been fighting this war too long. And this marks 10 long years now. An entire decade. And every time we hit the enemy, they just come back stronger. And after what we did, I can't shake the feeling that they'll come back with a vengeance to annihilate all of us, once and for all. I once served under the General's command, and believe me, he's not one that'll go without a fight. Let's not forget the devil was a saint before he became a fallen angel, just like I was one of his own before I switched my allegiances."

"We'll see how much fight he has left once we're done with cleaning out the rest of the remaining resistance," Kathy answered.

"I'm hoping we won't. I've been fighting for too long. My soul is weary from all this conflict, and for all we know, they could be on their way right now," Adam answered.

"I don't mean to be biblical, General West, but the words you said could have a lot of devastating consequences behind them," Matthew said.

"Well, it's a feeling that I just can't shake. Besides, I've just received word that the enemy forces have amassed, and just seized the Pentagon right under our noses, since we spent so long repairing the other enemy bases we seized."

06:18 HOURS. SOMEWHERE OVER MARYLAND, HEADING TOWARDS THE FREEDOM FIGHTER AIRCRAFT CARRIER FLEET, STATIONED MORE THAN 20 MILES IN THE ATLANTIC OCEAN, FROM FORT STORY FREEDOM FIGHTER COMMAND CENTER - CHESAPEAKE BAY, VIRGINIA:

"This is Saber wolf Leader to command. Come in, over."

06:18 HOURS. ENEMY COMMAND CENTER - PENTAGON, WASHINGTON D.C., THE NATION'S CAPITAL:

"This is command, Saber Wolf, Leader. What is your status? Over."

06:19 HOURS. SOMEWHERE OVER MARYLAND, HEADING TOWARDS THE FREEDOM FIGHTER AIRCRAFT CARRIER FLEET, STATIONED MORE THAN 20 MILES IN THE ATLANTIC OCEAN, FROM FORT STORY FREEDOM FIGHTER COMMAND CENTER - CHESAPEAKE BAY, VIRGINIA:

"Heading towards the aircraft carrier fleet. What are your orders? Over."

06:19 HOURS. ENEMY COMMAND CENTER, PENTAGON - WASHINGTON D.C. - THE NATION'S CAPITAL:

"All weapons hot, and maintain radio silence towards the current vector. Break silence after bombing run has commenced, over."

06:19 HOURS. SOMEWHERE OVER MARYLAND, HEADING TOWARDS THE FREEDOM FIGHTER AIRCRAFT CARRIER FLEET, STATIONED MORE THAN 20 MILES IN THE ATLANTIC OCEAN, FROM FORT STORY FREEDOM FIGHTER COMMAND CENTER - CHESAPEAKE BAY, VIRGINIA:

"Reading you loud and clear. Maintain radio silence. Over and out."

06:19 HOURS. SOMEWHERE OVER THE NATION'S CAPITAL. 5 MINUTES AWAY FROM THE STATE OF VIRGINIA, HEADING TOWARDS FORT MYERS FREEDOM FIGHTER AIR FORCE BASE - ARLINGTON, VIRGINIA:

"This is Viper to command. Are you receiving me? Over."

06:20 HOURS. ENEMY COMMAND CENTER, PENTAGON - WASHINGTON D.C. - THE NATION'S CAPITAL:

"This is command. Come in flight leader," the General said.

06:20 HOURS. SOMEWHERE OVER THE STATE OF VIRGINIA, HEADING TOWARDS FORT MYERS FREEDOM FIGHTER COMMAND CENTER - ARLINGTON, VIRGINIA:

"We're heading towards the enemy vector on aggressive approach. Maintaining radio silence, over."

06:20 HOURS. ENEMY COMMAND CENTER, PENTAGON - WASHINGTON D.C. - THE NATION'S CAPITAL:

"Maintain radio silence and engage with extreme prejudice, over," he said calmly, expecting the outcome.

06:20 HOURS. SOMEWHERE OVER THE STATE OF VIRGINIA, HEADING TOWARDS FORT MYERS FREEDOM FIGHTER COMMAND CENTER - ARLINGTON, VIRGINIA:

"Reading you loud and clear, command. Commencing aggressive approach."

"This is flight leader to Python wing. Are you receiving me? Over."

"This is Python wing. What are your orders, flight leader?"

"Maintain present course on aggressive approach. All weapons hot maintain radio silence, reduce altitude, and engage with extreme prejudice, over."

"This is Python wing to flight leader. Reading you loud and clear. All weapons hot, maintaining current vector and engaging," the pilot said and broke formation from the large group of planes.

The lead pilot watched as the large group of F-15 Strike Eagle fighter planes broke formation, quickly reducing altitude, rapidly descending onto the freedom fighter's position under complete radio silence.

06:23 HOURS. SOMEWHERE ON INTERSTATE 495, HEADING TOWARDS FORT MYERS FREEDOM FIGHTER AIR FORCE BASE - ARLINGTON, VIRGINIA:

The enemy soldiers felt their transports suddenly began to shudder violently for a brief moment, from the roar of the planes' engines, as they flew over their positions and suddenly stopped, as it had begun, warning them that the attack on the freedom fighters' positions was imminent.

The sounds of them cocking their assault rifles immediately filled the confines of their transports, as they prepared to sanitize the freedom fighters' positions on the second phase of their mission.

06:24 HOURS. SOMEWHERE OVER FORT MYERS FREEDOM FIGHTER AIR FORCE BASE - ARLINGTON, VIRGINIA:

The winds blew gently over the base, scattering the tiny, infinite flurries that continued to fall from the skies, shrouding the ground into a thick blanket of gleaming white.

The enemy pilot deployed one of his missiles, and watched it travel, while he remained seated in the cockpit of his plane. He moved towards the freedom fighters' position on his attack run, and watched it explode into the freedom fighters' communications tower, cutting them off from all communications with the other outposts.

Within moments, an entire squad of F-15 Strike Eagle fighter planes descended upon them, annihilating without mercy.

The lead pilot saw the destruction had begun to unfold and broke radio silence, and said, "This is flight leader to command."

06:25 HOURS. ENEMY COMMAND CENTER, PENTAGON - WASHINGTON D.C. - THE NATION'S CAPITAL:

"Come in, Viper. What is your status? Over," the General asked.

06:26 HOURS. SOMEWHERE OVER INTERSTATE 495, HEADING TOWARDS FORT BELVOIR FREEDOM FIGHTER AIR FORCE BASE - FAIRFAX, VIRGINIA:

"Python wing have commenced their strafing run on the enemy position, and we have achieved total surprise. I repeat, we have achieved total surprise."

06:26 HOURS. ENEMY COMMAND CENTER, PENTAGON - WASHINGTON D.C. - THE NATION'S CAPITAL:

"Outstanding, Viper. Continue towards the next enemy vector," the General answered, while he remained standing calmly in the room, waiting to hear results from his other pilots.

06:26 HOURS. SOMEWHERE OVER INTERSTATE 495, HEADING TOWARDS FORT BELVOIR FREEDOM FIGHTER COMMAND CENTER - FAIRFAX, VIRGINIA:

"Roger. Heading towards the next objective," the lead pilot answered, as she and the remainder of planes continued to fly towards the remainder of their objectives.

She broke radio silence and said, "This flight leader to Saber Wolf, are you receiving me? Over."

"This is Saber Wolf. What are your orders, flight leader?"

"Approaching the next enemy vector. All weapons hot, reduce altitude, maintain radio silence, and engage with extreme prejudice. Over."

"All weapons hot, reducing altitude, maintaining radio silence, and engaging. Saber Wolf, out."

She watched as the group of F-14 Tomcat fighter planes broke formation and quietly descended upon the unsuspecting freedom fighters' position under complete radio silence.

06:27 HOURS. SOMEWHERE ON INTERSTATE 95 HEADING TOWARDS FORT BELVOIR FREEDOM FIGHTER AIR FORCE BASE - FAIRFAX, VIRGINIA:

The group of transports filled with enemy troops racing towards the unsuspecting freedom fighters' positions suddenly began to tremble uncontrollably for just a brief moment from the noise from the planes' engines gliding over them. The planes quickly descended towards their objectives and stopped as the roars of their engines faded with distance, warning them that an attack on the freedom fighters' position was imminent.

The enemy soldiers immediately made the weapons check to prepare for the second phase of their assault to rid the position completely of freedom fighters.

06:29 HOURS. SOMEWHERE OVER FORT BELVOIR FREEDOM FIGHTER AIR FORCE BASE - FAIRFAX, VIRGINIA:

The winds continued to blow lightly throughout the compound, sweeping the light flakes of snow all about while the soldiers who patrolled remained totally oblivious to the impending attack.

The enemy pilot fired his missile and watched it track its target, while they continued their bombing run on the freedom fighters' position, and watched it transform the communications tower in an infernal ball of flame.

Within moments, the group of F-14 Tomcat fighter planes swarmed their positions, quickly neutralizing all their defenses, causing havoc.

Viper watched as their planes continued to wreak havoc on the freedom fighter outpost and said, breaking radio silence, "This is the Viper to command. Are you receiving me? Over."

06:39 HOURS. ENEMY COMMAND CENTER, PENTAGON - WASHINGTON D.C. - THE NATION'S CAPITAL:

"This is command to Viper. What is your status? Over," the General asked.

06:40 HOURS. SOMEWHERE OVER FORT BELVOIR FREEDOM FIGHTER COMMAND CENTER - FAIRFAX, VIRGINIA:

"Saber Wolf wing has begun an aggressive approach on the enemy position and has achieved total surprise. I repeat, we have achieved total surprise."

06:40 HOURS. ENEMY COMMAND CENTER, PENTAGON - WASHINGTON D.C. - THE NATION'S CAPITAL:

"Outstanding, Viper wing. Proceed to the next vector."

06:45 HOURS. SOMEWHERE OVER INTERSTATE 64, HEADING TOWARDS ROUTE 36 TOWARDS FORT LEE FREEDOM FIGHTER COMMAND CENTER - PRINCE GEORGE COUNTY, VIRGINIA:

"Maintaining radio silence until the next vector. flight leader out," she said, switching back to radio silence.

Moments later in flight, she watched her radar as she drew nearer towards their next objective. She broke radio silence and said, "This is flight leader to Black Mamba wing. Are you receiving me? Over."

"This is Black Mamba. What are your orders, flight leader?"

"All weapons hot. Maintain radio silence towards the present course of the enemy vector. Reduce altitude and engage with extreme prejudice. I repeat - engage with extreme prejudice, over."

"This is Mamba Wing. All weapons hot, reducing altitude and engaging."

She watched as the squad of F-16 Falcon fighter planes quickly broke formation and rapidly descended upon the unsuspecting freedom fighters.

The squad of enemy planes flew over the group of enemy transports, causing the hull of their transports to shudder violently for a brief moment from the deafening roar, after gliding over them towards their target, and suddenly stopped.

06:46 HOURS. SOMEWHERE ON INTERSTATE 64, HEADING TOWARDS ROUTE 36, TOWARDS FORT LEE FREEDOM FIGHTER COMMAND CENTER - PRINCE GEORGE COUNTY, VIRGINIA:

The enemy troops saw their squad of planes flying above their position, warning them that an attack on the freedom fighter position was imminent, and immediately prepared their weapons for the final phase of their assault to clear the base of all remaining resistance.

06:49 HOURS. SOMEWHERE OVER FORT LEE FREEDOM FIGHTER AIR FORCE BASE - PRINCE GEORGE COUNTY, VIRGINIA:

The flurries of snow continued falling through the base as the winds continued to howl softly, scattering the tiny flakes of snow, as they continued falling from the skies.

The lead enemy plane of F-16 Falcons deployed one of his missiles from a low altitude, and watched it track its target as he sat in the cockpit, heading towards the freedom fighters' position.

The communications tower exploded into a giant ball of flame, placing the entire vicinity into high alert.

Within moments, the squad of F-16 Falcon fighter planes stormed the vicinity of the beleaguered base, setting off a trail of carnage in their wake.

The Viper watched as the tall, dark columns of smoke quickly began to fill the skies and said, breaking her silence, "This is flight leader to command. Are you receiving me? Over."

06:50 HOURS. ENEMY COMMAND CENTER, PENTAGON - WASHINGTON D.C. - THE NATION'S CAPITAL:

"This is command. Come in Viper wing."

06:51 HOURS. SOMEWHERE OVER INTERSTATE 64, HEADING TOWARDS FORT EUSTIS, FREEDOM FIGHTER AIR FORCE BASE, NEWPORT NEWS, VIRGINIA, HEADING TOWARDS LANGLEY, FREEDOM FIGHTER AIR FORCE BASE:

"Black Mamba wing has begun an assault on the enemy position and has achieved complete surprise. I repeat, we have achieved complete surprise. Moving towards the next vector, over."

06:51 HOURS. ENEMY COMMAND CENTER - PENTAGON, WASHINGTON, D.C., THE NATION'S CAPITAL:

"Excellent, Viper wing. Move towards the enemy vector."

07:01 HOURS. SOMEWHERE OVER INTERSTATE 564, HEADING TOWARDS FORT EUSTIS FREEDOM FIGHTER AIR FORCE BASE - NEWPORT NEWS, VIRGINIA:

"Reading you loud and clear. Moving on towards the next vector," she said. "This is flight leader to Firefly wing, are you receiving me? Over."

"This is Firefly wing. What are your orders, flight leader?"

"All weapons hot, reduce altitude, maintain radio silence, and engage with extreme prejudice, over."

"Weapons hot and engaging."

She watched as the group of FA-18 Super Hornet fighter planes broke formation, heading towards the next freedom fighter position on their attack run, and waited for the grisly outcome of what was about to be another moment of baptism of fire and death for their unsuspecting enemies.

07:03 HOURS. SOMEWHERE ON INTERSTATE 564, HEADING TOWARDS ROUTE 105, TOWARDS FORT EUSTIS FREEDOM FIGHTER AIR FORCE BASE - NEWPORT NEWS, VIRGINIA:

A convoy of enemy transports hurried towards the freedom fighters' positions and felt the violent shudder from the hulls of their transports, from the roar of the fighter planes' engines. They stopped, knowing that the attack on the freedom fighters position was imminent.

They made their weapons check of their assault rifles to prepare for the final phase of their assault to rid the freedom fighter positions of all remaining hostiles.

07:07 HOURS. SOMEWHERE OVER FORT EUSTIS FREEDOM FIGHTER AIR FORCE BASE - NEWPORT NEWS, VIRGINIA:

The howling winds grew colder, as the snow continued to rain harder upon the tranquil vicinity of the base.

The lead of the FA-18 Super Hornet pilots fired his missile to initiate the beginning of their attack on the freedom fighters' position and watched the missile follow its target, exploding into the communications tower, unleashing a giant ball of flame. They instantly disturbed the tranquility that once filled the base, causing total panic among the freedom fighters.

The group of FA-18 Super Hornet fighter planes quickly descended upon the freedom fighters' position without mercy, causing total death and destruction in their wake after being caught by their surprise attack.

07:08 HOURS. SOMEWHERE OVER INTERSTATE 564, HEADING TOWARDS LANGLEY FREEDOM FIGHTER AIR FORCE BASE - LANGLEY, VIRGINIA:

"This is flight leader to command. Are you receiving me? Over," she said, breaking radio silence, staring at the crimson flames, turning into a thick, dark fireball of smoke rising to the skies, knowing they had succeeded in achieving another surprise attack on the enemy.

07:09 HOURS. ENEMY COMMAND CENTER - PENTAGON, WASHINGTON, D.C., THE NATION'S CAPITAL:

"This is command. Come in, Viper wing. What is your status? Over."

07:10 HOURS. SOMEWHERE OVER INTERSTATE 64, HEADING TOWARDS LANGLEY AIR FORCE BASE - LANGLEY, VIRGINIA:

"Firefly wing has converged on the enemy vector, and engaged with extreme prejudice. We have achieved total surprise on the enemy position. I repeat, we have achieved total surprise."

07:10 HOURS. ENEMY COMMAND CENTER - PENTAGON, WASHINGTON, D.C., THE NATION'S CAPITAL:

"Very good, Viper. Head to the next vector."

07:18 HOURS. SOMEWHERE OVER INTERSTATE 64, HEADING TOWARDS LANGLEY FREEDOM FIGHTER AIR FORCE BASE - LANGLEY, VIRGINIA:

"This is flight leader to Cobra wing. Are you receiving me? Over."

"This is Cobra wing. What are your orders, flight leader?"

"We're almost within range of the next enemy vector. All weapons hot, maintain radio silence, and engage with extreme prejudice, over."

"Weapons hot and engaging. Firefly out."

She watched as the squad of F-35 Lightning fighter planes quickly broke formation and rapidly descended unto the freedom fighters' position.

07:20 HOURS. SOMEWHERE ON INTERSTATE 64, HEADING TOWARDS LANGLEY ENEMY AIR FORCE BASE, HEADING TOWARDS ROUTE 70 - LANGLEY, VIRGINIA:

The convoy of enemy transports that raced towards the freedom fighters' position felt their transport shuddering from the deafening roaring effects of the planes' engines and stopped, warning the enemy soldiers that the attack on the freedom fighters' position was imminent, and quickly made their weapons and ammunitions check for the final phase of their attack to clear out the remaining pockets of enemy resistance.

07:21 HORUS. SOMEWHERE OVER LANGLEY FREEDOM FIGHTER AIR FORCE BASE - LANGLEY, VIRGINIA:

The howling winds continued to grow stronger through the compound, scattering the tiny flurries in all directions.

The enemy pilot aimed at the communications tower and deployed a missile and watched it track the communications tower exploding into it, cutting them off from all communications to the other outposts. Immediately, the entire base was placed on high alert.

Within moments, the group of F-35 Lightning fighter planes immediately swarmed the base causing much havoc in their wake.

07:22 HOURS. SOMEWHERE OVER INTERSTATE 64, HEADING TOWARDS FORT STORY, FREEDOM FIGHTER COMMAND CENTER - CHESAPEAKE BAY, VIRGINIA:

"This is flight leader to command. Are you receiving me? Over?," she said, breaking radio silence after seeing the destruction her squad of F-35 Lightning fighter planes began to wreak on the freedom fighters' positions.

"Cobra wing has commenced attack on the enemy position, and has achieved total surprise. I repeat, we have achieved total surprise. Over."

07:22 HOURS. ENEMY COMMAND CENTER - PENTAGON, WASHINGTON, D.C., THE NATION'S CAPITAL:

"That's excellent news, flight leader. Proceed to the next vector."

07:22 HOURS. SOMEWHERE OVER INTERSTATE 64, HEADING TOWARDS FORT STORY FREEDOM FIGHTER COMMAND CENTER - CHESAPEAKE BAY, VIRGINIA:

"Reading you loud and clear. Heading towards the next vector."

07:25 HOURS. FORT STORY FREEDOM FIGHTER COMMAND CENTER - CHESAPEAKE BAY, VIRGINIA:

The crimson glow of the sun had begun to show from rising from beyond the horizon, giving birth to the new day.

Brian and Karen walked through the base holding hands, heading towards the squad of gunships that remained motionless, all covered with the falling snow, watching the sunrise in close and warm embrace, when she felt nauseous and began to vomit.

A sudden look of concern came over Brian's face, as he watched her continue vomiting, and asked, "Are you okay?"

"Just an upset stomach. Must've been something that I ate. Been feeling a bit nauseous all day. But, I'll be fine."

"You sure you're okay?"

"I'll be fine. Don't worry," she said.

"Okay. If you say so," Brian answered, looking back at her, with a sudden look of concern on his face. Anton walked through the base, entered one of the transports, sitting down in the driver's seat, and rested his back, and took a deep breath from being exhausted from his long trip, rubbing his tired eyes, turning heavy from sleepiness.

He closed his eyes for a brief moment, and was suddenly awakened by a raven landing on the trunk of the transport.

His eyes opened wide, with a sudden look of shock showing on his face, watching the raven staring back, cawing for a brief moment, and they suddenly flew away.

He quickly arose from his seat, and jumped out of the truck, watching the raven fly away, triggering premonition of something catastrophic about to happen, like a repeat of what happened 2 years before, and said softly to himself, "We are under attack. My God, they're coming." He ran towards the command center, looking for Adam to sound the alarm to mobilize all personnel to thwart the enemy onslaught that rapidly advanced towards their position, bouncing into Jonathan.

"What happened? You look like you've just seen a ghost," Jonathan said.

"If General West doesn't sound the alarm, we'll all be ghosts," he said, in haste, trying to get to Adam to warn the others.

"What the hell are you talking about? You're not making any sense," Jonathan said.

"We're under attack, Min! We're being attacked as we speak! And every moment that we're here wasting time talking, the closer they are to wiping us out! We need to warn General West fast!"

"How do you know that?" Jonathan asked.

"You won't understand if I told you! Let's go! I'll tell you later!"

Anton ran into the command center with Jonathan trailing behind, and called out nervously, "General West! General West, I know this sounds crazy, but we're under attack!"

"What do you mean? How do you know?" Adam asked calmly.

"There's no time to explain. It's complicated. I'll tell you later, but for now, get in touch with the other bases to see if you can get a signal out."

Adam tried contacting their other bases, and received only the sound of static on every channel, and stared at Anton with a look of shock on his face, and stared at Jonathan, watching him shrugging his shoulders.

Please listen to me, General West. We're being attacked! Sound the alarm!" Anton said loudly.

"How do you know? And what if you're wrong?" Adam asked.

"Then I'll take full responsibility. Right now, it's time to be safe rather than sorry. But something tells me that I'm right. An attack is imminent. I just know it. I'll explain later. But first make the call. Please," he begged.

Adam grabbed the microphone and said with a hint of apprehension, "Attention all crew. An attack from the enemy is imminent from positions unknown. I repeat, an attack on our position is imminent from positions unknown. This is not a drill," Adam said, as Anton and Jonathan watched.

07:28 HOURS. A FEW MILES OFF THE COAST OF MARYLAND, HEADING TOWARDS THE FREEDOM FIGHTER AIRCRAFT CARRIER FLEET, STATIONED MORE THAN 20 MILES IN THE ATLANTIC OCEAN, FROM CHESAPEAKE BAY, VIRGINIA:

The other squad of enemy fighter planes continued making their way towards the freedom fighter aircraft carrier fleet on their attack run, under complete radio silence, priming their weapons.

07:30 HOURS. FREEDOM FIGHTER AIRCRAFT CARRIER FLEET, STATIONED MORE THAN 20 MILES IN THE ATLANTIC OCEAN FROM CHESAPEAKE BAY, VIRGINIA:

Nicole heard the alarms blare loudly and quickly moved in to mobilize, along with a number of other pilots.

07:33 HOURS. SOMEWHERE OVER THE ATLANTIC OCEAN, HEADING TOWARDS THE FREEDOM FIGHTER AIRCRAFT CARRIER FLEET, MORE THAN 20 MILES FROM CHESAPEAKE BAY, VIRGINIA:

The enemy planes were almost within range of the aircraft carrier fleet, ready to commence their assault on the freedom fighters.

07:34 HOURS. ENEMY COMMAND CENTER - PENTAGON, WASHINGTON, D.C., THE NATION'S CAPITAL:

"General," Maxwell called out softly, and said, "Our Maryland strike force is almost within range of General West's fleet in the Atlantic. It appears we still have the element of surprise."

"Outstanding. All is going as planned. This will make the rebels tremble at our might," the General said.

07:37 HOURS. SOMEWHERE OVER THE ATLANTIC OCEAN, 47 SECONDS FROM THE FREEDOM FIGHTER AIRCRAFT CARRIER FLEET, MORE THAN 20 MILES OFF THE COAST OF CHESAPEAKE BAY, VIRGINIA:

The radars in the enemy planes began to blare loudly, telling them of their close proximity to the aircraft carrier fleet, and broke off into a number of groups in their attack run.

07:38 HOURS. ENEMY COMMAND CENTER - PENTAGON, WASHINGTON, D.C., THE NATION'S CAPITAL:

"They've broken off into groups and on their attack run on the fleet," Maxwell said softly.

"Good. I want that entire fleet at the bottom of the ocean," the General answered.

07:40 HOURS. FREEDOM FIGHTER AIRCRAFT CARRIER FLEET, STATIONED IN THE ATLANTIC OCEAN, MORE THAN 20 MILES AWAY FROM CHESAPEAKE BAY, VIRGINIA:

Nicole and a number of planes were quickly airborne, while a number of the crew saw tall columns of dark smoke rising from the distance, and flew towards their position as quickly as they could, to give cover to the other planes that tried to take off from the fly decks to strengthen their numbers to repel the enemy assault.

She broke radio silence and shouted, "This is flight leader to command! Are you receiving me? Over!"

07:40 HOURS. FORT STORY FREEDOM FIGHTER COMMAND CENTER - CHESAPEAKE BAY, VIRGINIA:

Adam heard the frantic distress call from Nicole and answered, "This is command. What's happening out there?"

07:40 HOURS. FREEDOM FIGHTER AIRCRAFT CARRIER FLEET, STATIONED IN THE ATLANTIC OCEAN, MORE THAN 20 MILES AWAY FROM THE FREEDOM FIGHTER COMMAND CENTER - CHESAPEAKE BAY, VIRGINIA:

"We're under heavy enemy attack, and have sustained a number of casualties. A number of our ships and carriers are severely damaged, and still sustaining heavy punishment! We've also lost a number of our planes on takeoff. We need more air support and moving in to provide support so we can give the others a chance to get airborne! My God! There's so many of them stranded in the water!" Nicole said frantically.

07:41 HOURS. FORT STORY FREEDOM FIGHTER COMMAND CENTER - CHESAPEAKE BAY, VIRGINIA:

Adam placed his hands on his face in a sudden state of complete shock, and said, looking at Anton, "My God. I knew this wasn't over. It's starting all over again. All personnel assume defensive positions! We're under attack! I repeat we're under attack! This is not a drill! I repeat - this is not a drill!"

07:42 HOURS. SOMEWHERE OVER INTERSTATE 64 HEADING TOWARDS FORT STORY FREEDOM FIGHTER COMMAND CENTER - CHESAPEAKE BAY, VIRGINIA:

"This is flight leader to command, are you receiving me? Over."

07:43 HOURS. ENEMY COMMAND CENTER - PENTAGON, WASHINGTON, D.C., THE NATION'S CAPITAL:

"This is command. What is your status? Over."

7:44 HOURS. SOMEWHERE OVER INTERSTATE 64, HEADING TOWARDS FORT STORY FREEDOM FIGHTER COMMAND CENTER - CHESAPEAKE BAY, VIRGINIA:

"Approaching the last enemy vector. All weapons hot reducing, altitude, maintaining radio silence, and engaging with extreme prejudice. Over."

07:44 HOURS. ENEMY COMMAND CENTER - PENTAGON, WASHINGTON, D.C., THE NATION'S CAPITAL:

"Very well, Viper wing. All weapons hot and engage. I repeat, weapons hot and engage with extreme prejudice. Over."

07:46 HOURS. SOMEWHERE OVER INTERSTATE 64, HEADING TOWARDS ROUTE 13. 7 MINUTES AWAY FROM FORT STORY FREEDOM FIGHTER COMMAND CENTER - CHESAPEAKE BAY, VIRGINIA:

Upon receiving the General's final orders, she and the squad of F-22 fighter planes quickly descended toward Adam's position, flying over the group of transports that raced to be in position to commence the second phase of their operation, causing the hull of their transports to suddenly shudder for a brief moment, from the deafening roar of all their engines, and suddenly stopped, warning the ground troops that the attack on the base was imminent. They did their weapon's check for the final phase of their assault to clear out any pockets of enemy resistance that survive after their bombing run.

07:46 HOURS. SOMEWHERE ON INTERSTATE 64, HEADING TOWARDS ROUTE 13. 20 MINUTES AWAY FROM FORT STORY FREEDOM FIGHTER COMMAND CENTER – CHESAPEAKE BAY, VIRGINIA:

After the deafening roar of all the planes' engines had subsided from the distance that separated them, Jason turned to the assassin who sat quietly next to him, and said, with a sinking feeling of doubt on his face, "I guess this is it."

The assassin simply remained calm, a blank expression on his face, while remaining in deep contemplation of executing his objective of finally eliminating Adam to crush their resistance once and for all, as he had proven to be a worthy, but elusive adversary.

07:50 HOURS. FORT STORY FREEDOM FIGHTER COMMAND CENTER – CHESAPEAKE BAY, VIRGINIA:

Adam, Anton, and Jonathan ran out of the command center, looking in the direction of where their aircraft carrier fleet was stationed in the Atlantic Ocean. Through their binoculars, Adam saw the thick, dark smoke from the smoldering ruins of the burning aircraft carriers and ships, and said softly, "My God," with a look of frantic on his face, seeing the amount of devastation the enemy continued to wreak on their fleet. "Spread out and search where the next wave of attack is coming from!"

The base was on sudden high alert, as the personnel scurried about to their defensive positions in nervous anticipation.

Anton searched in all directions and saw the tiny specs approaching from afar. He said, "I see them! They're coming from over there!" pointing in the direction where the enemy planes were coming from.

Karen saw the quick mobilization of all the soldiers in the base, and asked, with a sudden look of shock on her face, "What the hell is going on?"

"Your guess is as good as mine. But whatever it is, it can't be good," Brian answered, looking all around him in a total look of shock, realizing that Adam's premonition about an imminent enemy had finally come true.

Adam watched through his binoculars as the enemy planes continued to draw closer and said, "Point all surface to air missiles in that direction and fire at will."

08:01 HOURS. SOMEWHERE OVER INTERSTATE 64, HEADING TOWARDS FREEDOM FIGHTER COMMAND CENTER - CHESAPEAKE BAY, VIRGINIA:

The lead enemy pilot deployed a missile at the communications tower, and watched it fly towards its target.

08:02 HOURS. FORT STORY FREEDOM FIGHTER COMMAND CENTER - CHESAPEAKE BAY, VIRGINIA:

The communications tower suddenly burst into a giant ball of crimson flame, after the missile slammed into it from an enemy plane.

"They just took out the communications tower!" Jonathan yelled.

"I can see that!" Anton answered, looking in a state of panic.

"Oh no. This is not happening," Brian said, watching all around in total shock.

"It's happening all over again. Only this time, we're on the receiving end of it," Karen answered.

A number of surface to air missiles were quickly deployed in quick succession, to try and thwart the enemies' imminent attack.

08:03 HOURS. SOMEWHERE OVER INTERSTATE 64, HEADING TOWARDS FORT STORY FREEDOM FIGHTER COMMAND CENTER - CHESAPEAKE BAY, VIRGINIA:

As the sun continued to rise beyond the horizon, giving birth to the new day shining through the canopy of her plane, Viper had a sudden look of shock on her face. The alarms in the cockpit of her plane suddenly began blaring, warning her of a number of surface to air missiles advancing towards their position, and said softly, "What the hell?"

She watched ahead in the distance and saw the contrails of a number of surface to air missiles closing in on her position, suddenly realizing that their element of surprise had been compromised, and shouted, "We have incoming! I repeat, we have incoming! Take evasive action and activate all countermeasures!"

The fighter planes immediately took evasive action trying to avoid the group of surface to air missiles that tracked them relentlessly through the skies, with a blinding flash from one of the planes from her squad exploding, quickly filling the confines of her cockpit.

She heard the alarms in her plane continued blaring loudly, warning her of more missiles closing in from behind, and quickly took evasive action, deploying sunbursts, to lead the missile off its course, as she still continued to fly towards the command center.

Her alarms continued to blare loudly as she continued her strafing run, and saw the ranks of gunships parked neatly in rows and deployed a missile destroying a number all at once. She was instantly greeted by a sky filled with flak and ground fire.

She flew towards the burning wreckage of the gunship, as the missile followed the heat of her plane, leading it into the flaming wreckage, and quickly pulled to the skies, causing the missile to explode into it.

Matthew watched in great awe, seeing how brilliantly the enemy pilot showed great skill at evading an attack, and said, "Well, I'll be damned. Whoever is in that plane is one hell of a pilot," and remained distracted for a brief moment, seeing the plane continuing to perform a series of expert maneuvers to escape the missile attacks.

The enemy pilot glanced at her back for a brief moment and broke radio silence, and said, "This is flight leader to command! Are you receiving me? Over!"

08:04 HOURS. ENEMY COMMAND CENTER - PENTAGON, WASHINGTON, D.C., THE NATION'S CAPITAL:

The General noticed the sound of urgency and panic in her voice, along with the others, causing a sudden look of shock on their faces, realizing that they had lost the element of surprise and answered, "This is command. What is your status, flight leader?"

08:05 HOURS. SOMEWHERE OVER FORT STORY FREEDOM FIGHTER COMMAND CENTER - CHESAPEAKE BAY, VIRGINIA:

"The rebels have mounted a counter attack! We have lost all elements of surprise! I repeat, we have lost all elements of surprise! Over!"

08:05 HOURS. ENEMY COMMAND CENTER - PENTAGON, WASHINGTON, D.C., THE NATION'S CAPITAL:

"That's impossible, flight leader! How could this have happened?" the General asked.

08:05 HOURS. SOMEWHERE FORT STORY FREEDOM FIGHTER COMMAND CENTER - CHESAPEAKE BAY, VIRGINIA:

"I don't know, sir! They were ready for us by the time we arrived!" she said.

08:06 HOURS. ENEMY COMMAND CENTER - PENTAGON, WASHINGTON, D.C., THE NATION'S CAPITAL:

"What is the status of the mission, flight leader?"

08:06 HOURS. SOMEWHERE OVER FORT STORY FREEDOM FIGHTER COMMAND CENTER - CHESAPEAKE BAY, VIRGINIA:

"We've lost a number of our planes, and are still encountering heavy resistance!" she answered nervously, as the constant burst of flak and the blinding streaks of bullets surrounded her plane.

Another bright light from one of their planes bursting into a ball of flames exploding shone, as she said, "We've lost another plane! We're almost down to half strength! Over!"

08:07 HOURS. ENEMY COMMAND CENTER - PENTAGON, WASHINGTON, D.C., THE NATION'S CAPITAL:

"Reading you loud and clear, flight leader. But your orders still remain the same. Do not deviate from your mission. I repeat, do not deviate from the current mission. Over."

08:08 HOURS. SOMEWHERE OVER FORT STORY FREEDOM FIGHTER COMMAND CENTER - CHESAPEAKE BAY, VIRGINIA:

A sudden fit of anger came over her, causing her to close her eyes, after realizing that she was now leading the charge of a suicide mission. She answered, "Yes, sir."

08:10 HOURS. FORT STORY FREEDOM FIGHTER COMMAND CENTER - CHESAPEAKE BAY, VIRGINIA:

After the communication's tower was destroyed, Adam ran towards one of the surviving transports, grabbed the radio and yelled, "We've lost all of our gunships, and most of our transports to help evacuate the wounded. We're still sustaining heavy damage and more casualties, and our defenses are almost overwhelmed. We have another wave of enemy assault converging on our current position as we speak! We need air support! Over!"

08:11 HOURS. SECURE LOCATION - SOMEWHERE IN RICHMOND, VIRGINIA:

"They've lost the element of surprise. General West's forces are fighting back," Celina said to Dr. Weaver, listening to the radio chatter.

"What do you think just happened? How did they know an attack was coming?" Dr. Weaver asked.

"It seems that a miracle came after all, sir."

"Any other news?"

"The fleet received the message in time to mobilize their planes. It seems the resistance won't be wiped out after all."

"Let's hope so," Dr. Weaver answered.

08:12 HOURS. SOMEWHERE OVER THE FREEDOM FIGHTER AIRCRAFT CARRIER FLEET STATIONED MORE THAN 20 MILES IN THE ATLANTIC OCEAN, FROM FORT STORY FREEDOM FIGHTER COMMAND CENTER - CHESAPEAKE BAY, VIRGINIA:

The entire carrier fleet, along with all the warships that surrounded them, remained afloat, still burning in flames, from the heavy punishment they had sustained from the enemies' onslaught, while they still continued to maintain the gargantuan task of trying to repel the large squad of enemy planes. Frantic crew aboard scurried all about to contain all the damage they sustained, clearing as much of the damage from the debris as they could, to allow more planes to take off to engage the enemy fighters.

Nicole received the distress call and answered, "This is flight leader to command! Our entire fleet has sustained heavy damage, but we're still combat capable, but don't know how long the fleet can stay afloat! We're heavily outnumbered, but I can see a number of our planes taking off some of our carriers! I can see a number of our crew dead in the water! Just floating, while the others are swimming towards whatever they could find to stay afloat! Oh my God!"

08:13 HOURS. SOMEWHERE ON INTERSTATE 64, HEADING TOWARDS FORT STORY FREEDOM FIGHTER COMMAND CENTER - CHESAPEAKE BAY, VIRGINIA:

The enemy ground troops listened to the transmission, hearing that they had finally lost their element of surprise on the freedom fighters' position, causing them to question how their strategic plan had been compromised.

"My God. We're heading right into it. I just knew something would go wrong. I just knew this was too good to be true," Jason said, frantically.

08:15 zHOURS. FORT STORY FREEDOM FIGHTER COMMAND CENTER - CHESAPEAKE BAY, VIRGINIA:

The base had suffered heavy damage with all of their gunships and most of the surface to air missile platforms, and all their hangars containing a portion of their planes and more heavy ordinance, lay in a burning wreck, though they continued to fight valiantly against the enemy forces whatever weapons they had left.

Brian and Karen ran in search of Adam amidst all the destruction, when one of the transports exploded, knocking them to the ground.

Janet and Jill picked them off the ground, while they were running towards the same direction in search of Adam, and asked, "Where's General West?"

"I don't know!," Karen answered.

"We need to find him! We won't be able to hold out much longer!" Jill answered.

They arrived at one of the transports where they saw Adam continue making distress calls to Nicole from the transport's radio.

Amidst all the destruction, Adam turned towards the direction of their aircraft carrier fleet in the far reaches of the ocean, and stared through the thick lens of their binoculars, seeing the giant clouds of smoke rising to the skies.

"We're blocked either way! What are your orders, sir?" Jonathan asked.

"We fight or we die!"

08:17 HOURS. SOMEWHERE OVER THE FREEDOM FIGHTER AIRCRAFT CARRIER FLEET STATIONED MORE THAN 20 MILES IN THE ATLANTIC OCEAN, FROM FORT STORY FREEDOM FIGHTER COMMAND CENTER - CHESAPEAKE BAY, VIRGINIA:

"Oh, my God!" Nicole yelled, seeing a giant ball of red flame suddenly erupting from one of the aircraft carriers, slowly transforming into thick, black smoke. "We just lost one of our carriers! I repeat, we just lost one of our carriers!"

08:18 HOURS. FORT STORY FREEDOM FIGHTER COMMAND CENTER - CHESAPEAKE BAY, VIRGINIA:

"We have enemy ground troops converging on our position! Assume defensive positions! We need to hold on long enough for air support to come!" Adam ordered.

08:20 HOURS. SOMEWHERE OVER THE FREEDOM FIGHTER AIRCRAFT CARRIER FLEET, STATIONED MORE THAN 20 MILES IN THE ATLANTIC OCEAN FROM THE FORT STORY FREEDOM FIGHTER COMMAND CENTER - CHESAPEAKE BAY, VIRGINIA:

"This is flight leader to any available units! Are you reading me? Over! If you're receiving me, form up on my six!" she said, as she continued to score as many kills, trying to turn the vicious air battle in their favor.

"This is Saber!"

"This is Vulcan!"

"This is Thunder!"

"This is Blaster!"

"This is Rhino! What are your orders, flight leader?"

"We have enemy ground troops converging on General West's position and we need to keep him alive! There's no way we can make a run for it without being engaged! We need to clear the skies of enemy planes as much as we can!"

Another explosion suddenly echoed through the vast expanse of the ocean, scattering burning shrapnel and debris, tossing away all those who were unfortunate to be caught in its wake into the seas, startling Nicole and the other pilots that followed her command.

"This is Blaster! What are your orders, flight leader?"

"Oh my God!" Nicole yelled, watching the terrifying explosion of another aircraft carrier, seeing more dead and injured members of the crew floating in the ocean, trying to maintain her focus, and said, "We're outnumbered on both fronts, so we have to make all our shots count for General West's sake! All weapons hot, and engage at will! We can't afford to miss any of our shots! So we need to attack using the sun at our backs to make us invisible, and maybe get more of our planes in the skies! We need to clear the skies of these enemy planes so we can make our attack run towards General West's position! Now, all weapons hot, and engage at will!"

08:24 HOURS. FORT STORY FREEDOM FIGHTER COMMAND CENTER - CHESAPEAKE BAY, VIRGINIA:

Adam and the others heard another clamor from the explosion in the distance, and watched in total sadness and shock, after losing another aircraft carrier that was vital to their war effort.

08:27 HOURS. ENEMY COMMAND CENTER - PENTAGON, WASHINGTON, D.C., THE NATION'S CAPITAL:

"This is command to Python wing. What is your status? Over."

08:27 HOURS. SOMEWHERE OVER FORT MYERS FREEDOM FIGHTER AIR FORCE BASE - ARLINGTON, VIRGINIA:

"This is Python wing. All enemy defenses have been neutralized. Awaiting further orders. Over."

08:29 HOURS. ENEMY COMMAND CENTER - PENTAGON, WASHINGTON, D.C., THE NATION'S CAPITAL:

"Commence the second phase of operations. You are free to sanitize, over."

08:29 HOURS. SOMEWHERE OVER FORT MYERS FREEDOM FIGHTER AIR FORCE BASE - ARLINGTON, VIRGINIA:

"Reading you loud and clear. Commencing the second phase of operations. Python wing out. Python Wing to all ground personnel. You are clear to sanitize. I repeat you are free to sanitize, over."

The enemy ground troops quickly ran out of their transports through the beleaguered freedom fighters' position, greeting the surviving troops with a hail of gunfire.

08:30 HOURS. ENEMY COMMAND CENTER - PENTAGON, WASHINGTON, D.C., THE NATION'S CAPITAL:

"This is command to Saber Wolf. What is your status? Over."

08:30 HOURS. SOMEWHERE OVER FORT BELVOIR FREEDOM FIGHTER AIR FORCE BASE - FAIRFAX, VIRGINIA:

"This is Saber Wolf. All enemy defenses have been neutralized. Awaiting further orders, over."

08:31 HOURS. ENEMY COMMAND CENTER - PENTAGON, WASHINGTON, D.C., THE NATION'S CAPITAL:

"Commence the second phase of operations. I repeat you are you a go to sanitize, over."

08:32 HOURS. SOMEWHERE OVER FORT BELVOIR FREEDOM FIGHTER AIR FORCE BASE - FAIRFAX, VIRGINIA:

"Reading you loud and clear. We are moving in to sanitize. This is Saber Wolf to all ground personnel. You are clear to commence phase 2 of operations." The enemy ground troops quickly climbed from their transports and rushed through the beleaguered freedom fighters' position, greeting the remaining pockets of resistance with a hail of gunfire.

08:33 HOURS. ENEMY COMMAND CENTER - PENTAGON, WASHINGTON, D.C., THE NATION'S CAPITAL:

"This is command to Black Mamba wing. Are you receiving me? What is your status? Over."

08:34 HOURS. SOMEWHERE OVER FORT LEE FREEDOM FIGHTER AIR FORCE BASE - PRINCE GEORGE COUNTY, VIRGINIA:

"This is Black Mamba wing. All enemy defenses are neutralized. What are your orders? Over."

08:34 HOURS. ENEMY COMMAND CENTER - PENTAGON, WASHINGTON, D.C., THE NATION'S CAPITAL:

"You have a green light to sanitize. I repeat, you are clear to sanitize, over."

08:34 HOURS. SOMEWHERE OVER FORT LEE FREEDOM FIGHTER AIR FORCE - WASHINGTON D.C., THE NATION'S CAPITAL:

"Reading you loud and clear. Commencing phase 2 of operations. This is Black Mamba to all ground personnel. You have permission to commence phase two of operations. I repeat, you are a go to sanitize."

The enemy troops quickly sprang into action, rushing out of their transports, and into the burning compound, greeting the remaining freedom fighters with a deadly barrage of machine gun fire.

08:35 HOURS. ENEMY COMMAND CENTER - PENTAGON, WASHINGTON, D.C., THE NATION'S CAPITAL:

"This is command to Firefly. What is your status? Over."

08:36 HOURS. SOMEWHERE OVER FORT EUSTIS FREEDOM FIGHTER AIR FORCE BASE - NEWPORT NEWS, VIRGINIA:

"All enemy defenses neutralized. Awaiting further orders, over."

08:37 HOURS. ENEMY COMMAND CENTER - PENTAGON, WASHINGTON, D.C., THE NATION'S CAPITAL:

"You have a green light to commence the second phase of operations. I repeat, you are a go for second phase of operations, over."

08:38 HOURS. SOMEWHERE OVER FORT EUSTIS FREEDOM FIGHTER AIR FORCE BASE - NEWPORT NEWS, VIRGINIA:

"Reading you loud and clear. Commencing the second phase of our assault. This is Firefly to all ground troops. We are a go for phase 2 of operations. I repeat we have a green light to sanitize."

Upon receiving their signal, the enemy ground troops stormed into the freedom fighters' position, greeting the remaining survivors in a hail of gunfire.

08:39 HOURS. ENEMY COMMAND CENTER - PENTAGON, WASHINGTON, D.C., THE NATION'S CAPITAL:

"This is command to Cobra wing. What is your status? Over."

08:39 HOURS. SOMEWHERE OVER LANGLEY FREEDOM FIGHTER AIR FORCE BASE - LANGLEY, VIRGINIA:

"This is Cobra wing. All enemy defenses have been neutralized. What are your orders? Over."

08:39 HOURS. ENEMY COMMAND CENTER - PENTAGON, WASHINGTON, D.C., THE NATION'S CAPITAL:

"You have permission to commence phase 2 of operations. I repeat, you are a go for phase two, over."

08:40 HOURS. SOMEWHERE OVER LANGLEY, FREEDOM FIGHTER AIR FORCE BASE - LANGLEY, VIRGINIA:

"Reading you loud and clear, Command. About to commence the second phase of our assault. Cobra wing out. This is Cobra wing to all ground personnel. You are clear to sanitize. I repeat, commence phase 2 of assault."

The enemy soldiers rushed into the burning compound, to clear out the remaining pockets of resistance, greeting them with a hail of gunfire.

08:41 HOURS. ENEMY COMMAND CENTER - PENTAGON, WASHINGTON, D.C., THE NATION'S CAPITAL:

"This is command to Viper wing. What is your status? Over."

08:42 HOURS. SOMEWHERE OVER FORT STORY FREEDOM FIGHTER COMMAND CENTER - CHESAPEAKE BAY, VIRGINIA:

"Most of the enemy defenses have been neutralized. But the enemy is not letting up! They're still combat capable! We've sustained more casualties, and are less than half strength! I repeat, we are less than half strength! Over!"

08:43 HOURS. ENEMY COMMAND CENTER - PENTAGON, WASHINGTON, D.C., THE NATION'S CAPITAL:

"Your orders are to neutralize that position, and break the back of their resistance once and for all, Viper wing. This resistance ends today. Am I clear, flight leader?"

08:43 HOURS. SOMEWHERE OVER FORT STORY FREEDOM FIGHTER COMMAND CENTER - CHESAPEAKE BAY, VIRGINIA:

"Reading you loud and clear! Viper out!," she answered, closing her eyes tightly in a sudden fit of rage, when another blinding flash from another plane exploding, lit through the confines of her cockpit.

She glanced from the view of the cockpit of her plane, and saw another one of their planes descending towards the surface in flames, trailing a long line of dark smoke, crashing with deafening impact.

CHAPTER 12: DRONE.

"We still have one of the rebel strongholds still putting up resistance. And at this rate, we might lose the entire Viper squadron, since we lost all elements of surprise. We need a contingency plan to take control of the situation immediately. Those rebels are cornered, and desperate. Your adversary becomes more dangerous. We can't let any escape. Not even one. They must be crushed once and for all. So I propose that we send in the Drone."

Colonel Warren Davidson, like the other senior ranking officers, was past middle age who was very proud and opinionated, and one of the many high ranking officers who spent all his life serving his country alongside the General since the beginning of the civil war.

He stood from his seat and with a look of sudden shock on his face, after hearing the General's orders, said, "With all due respect, General, the Drone is the most valuable asset we have at our disposal, even more than all the others combined. Surely, you don't think of sending him and our troops right into the bombing campaign. They'll be caught in the blast. They'll be killed by friendly fire, and we may not be able to complete our objective."

"We have lost the element of surprise and that position must be pacified of all remaining rebel activity, one way or another. And in war, we must make sacrifices. Some of those sacrifices must be paid in the lives and blood of our brothers," the General replied.

"But General, this is madness! You can't do this!" Warren answered back loudly, when a single gunshot suddenly rang out loudly through the confines of the command room, startling all the other high ranking officers, causing the rest of the guards who guarded the front door of the command room to rush in.

He glanced at the guards with a straight look on his face and nodded his head once again to signal them to go back to their posts, and turned his attention to the other remaining high-ranking officers.

The scent of the gun smoke filled the command room as it slowly rose from the barrel of his gun, while he paused keeping it pointed towards the direction, where Warren's lifeless body slumped over the controls, and slowly holstered his side arm, and asked with a firm tone of voice, "Is there anyone else who wishes to challenge me?"

The other remaining officers looked at the dead corpse of their fallen comrade slumped over the controls, with a gaping hole in his head, gushing blood onto the floor and nodded their heads.

"I thought so. Now, before we go any further, let me say that if I were to be challenged, it would be as respectfully as possible. I will not tolerate any kind of defiance or insubordination from anyone, in any way, shape, or form. But before we go any further, first, get someone to clean this mess, and out of respect to our fallen comrade, he is to be committed with full military honors. He has served his purpose. It was regrettable he had to go this way. But from this point on, if my orders are questioned, my personal guards that you see standing outside the door will do the honors, as regrettable as my actions may be," he said, pointing at the door in the command room.

09:00 HOURS. SOMEWHERE OVER THE FREEDOM FIGHTER AIRCRAFT CARRIER FLEET, STATIONED MORE THAN 20 MILES IN THE ATLANTIC OCEAN, FROM THE FORT STORY FREEDOM FIGHTER COMMAND CENTER - CHESAPEAKE BAY, VIRGINIA:

Nicole and her few wingmen lined up as many enemy planes in their cross hairs as they could, scoring a number of kills, steadily wearing down the number of enemy planes with their tactics of using the sun behind them to make them invisible to the vast number of enemies.

Another enemy plane snuck through their defenses completely undetected on a strafing run towards one of the remaining aircraft carriers that remained afloat. It was completely consumed in flames from the constant enemy bombardment, while it continued to hold out against the enemy with its remaining anti-aircraft guns. The plane deployed its bomb straight into the aircraft carrier's deck, penetrating through its hull, heading straight into the ammunition storage compartment, when it suddenly exploded, tearing the aircraft carrier in half with a giant ball of crimson flame, scattering many of the crew and shrapnel high into the air in all directions.

Though the volley of anti-aircraft fire was still high on the entire fleet of warships, they continued to sustain heavy damage, from constant barrage from the enemy.

Another enemy plane on a strafing run was caught in the thick wall of anti-aircraft fire and burst into flames, with the enemy pilot unable to maintain control, crashing into the warships, triggering another giant ball of flame.

"Oh my God!" Nicole cried, looking down from the view of her cockpit, seeing the entire fleet burning and knowing that it was only a matter of time before the remaining ships and aircraft carriers would succumb to enemy attacks. She felt the overwhelming state of helplessness from not being able to help all the unfortunate crewmen who met their fate from the enemy.

"We must protect the rest of the fleet at all costs! And provide support for General West! Oh my God! There are so many of them!"

"This is Saber to flight leader. General West needs support, and they may not have much time left. You go on and give them support. Take a few others with you. Blaster, Thunder, and the rest of us will stay back and hold them off as long as we can. If we're done repelling the enemy, we'll come by and provide assistance. General West must live for this resistance to continue. He's our only hope. Now go. And if I don't make it back, I just want you to know that it's been a real honor," the pilot said, his eyes filled with tears, knowing that there's a great chance that he may not survive.

"You just come back in one piece, you hear me?" Nicole answered softly, with her eyes filled with tears.

Another aircraft carrier burst into flames from constant enemy fire, while they continued to repel the enemy forces.

Hearing the collective roar of the planes exploding, and the aircraft carrier burst into flames as their anti-aircraft guns returned fire, she closed her eyes, as her tears rolled down her face, and answered, "Heading over to our next objective. This is flight leader to command! What's your status? Over."

09:06 HOURS. FORT STORY FREEDOM FIGHTER COMMAND CENTER - CHESAPEAKE BAY, VIRGINIA:

"This is command! Our defenses are almost overwhelmed! And we have enemy troops inbound at any second! Don't know how much longer we could hold! We need air support now!" Adam yelled

09:07 HOURS. SOMEWHERE OVER THE ATLANTIC OCEAN, HEADING TO THE FORT STORY FREEDOM FIGHTER COMMAND CENTER - CHESAPEAKE BAY, VIRGINIA:

"Reading you loud and clear! We'll be there as soon as we can! Over!"

09:07 HOURS. FORT STORY FREEDOM FIGHTER COMMAND CENTER - CHESAPEAKE BAY, VIRGINIA:

"We may not be able to hold out that long!" Adam yelled when a bomb hit the communications center, along with a few of the other remaining transports, causing an enormous explosion that tossed them to the snowy ground, dazing them and severing all communications.

09:08 HOURS. FREEDOM FIGHTER AIRCRAFT CARRIER FLEET STATIONED MORE THAN 20 MILES IN THE ATLANTIC OCEAN FROM THE FORT STORY FREEDOM FIGHTER COMMAND CENTER - CHESAPEAKE BAY, VIRGINIA:

Nicole heard the static over her radio from the transmission suddenly cut off, causing her face to crease in a sudden look of shock, thinking of the grim reality that their resistance would come to an end if Adam had met his demise at the hands of the enemy, and pressed the afterburner, hoping that she was not too late.

09:10 HOURS. ENEMY COMMAND CENTER - PENTAGON, WASHINGTON, D.C., THE NATION'S CAPITAL:

A group of soldiers walked into the communications room and looked at Warren's dead body sprawled over the control table, a gaping bullet wound in his head. Blood was on one of the consoles and on the floor. They looked with shock on their faces at the General's ruthlessness, though it should be of no surprise given his reputation during the course of the long war that plagued the nation.

Maxwell nodded his head, giving them the sign to carry the dead soldier's body out of the command room, and glanced at the other who stood at the door, silently consumed with anger.

Though he did so with a heavy heart, losing one of his friends at the General's hand, his blinding loyalty towards the General overshadowed his friendship towards the others.

They looked at the corpse for a brief moment, and glanced at the General, as he stared back with a blank expression on his face, and slowly carried Warren's corpse out of the command room.

The General waited for them to leave, and said without a shred of remorse, "Now that we've gotten that out the way, give the order to have the ground troops to sanitize, whether their defenses are neutralized or not."

Maxwell nodded his head and grabbed the radio, and said, "This is command to flight leader. What is your status? Over."

09:11 HOURS. SOMEWHERE OVER FORT STORY FREEDOM FIGHTER COMMAND CENTER - CHESAPEAKE BAY, VIRGINIA:

"This is flight leader! We're less than half strength, but their defenses are almost completely neutralized! Where is our support?" she asked.

09:11 HOURS. ENEMY COMMAND CENTER - PENTAGON, WASHINGTON, D.C., THE NATION'S CAPITAL:

"Commence the second phase of operations. I repeat, send in the Drone," Colonel Maxwell said.

09:11 HOURS. SOMEWHERE OVER FORT STORY FREEDOM FIGHTER COMMAND CENTER - CHESAPEAKE BAY, VIRGINIA:

A sudden look of shock frowned over her face after hearing her orders. She answered, "Enemy defenses are still active! I repeat, the enemy is still combat capable!

Our troops will be hit by friendly fire! Over!"

09:12 HOURS. ENEMY COMMAND CENTER - PENTAGON, WASHINGTON, D.C., THE NATION'S CAPITAL:

After hearing the pilot's voice, the General grabbed the radio, and answered, "You have your orders, flight leader. It would be wise at this point to not challenge my authority, since you've proven to be incapable of neutralizing the enemy despite all your accomplishments. Today was supposed to be the most defining moment of your career, but turned out to be a disaster. Now, you're ordered to commence the second phase of operations, or you'll be answering me, personally. And believe me, you don't want that."

09:12 HOURS. SOMEWHERE OVER FORT STORY FREEDOM FIGHTER COMMAND CENTER - CHESAPEAKE BAY, VIRGINIA:

After listening to the General's orders, she was suddenly consumed by more anger, closing her eyes, silently trying to contain her emotions, and answered, "Copy that. Commencing phase 2. This is Viper wing to all ground personnel. The area is still hot and the enemy is still combat capable.

You have a green light. I repeat, you are clear for the next phase."

09:12 HOURS. FORT STORY FREEDOM FIGHTER COMMAND CENTER – CHESAPEAKE BAY, VIRGINIA:

Jason heard the transmission and replied, "My God. They're sending us in there to be slaughtered."

The assassin walked through the front gate without any hesitation, remaining unflinching in his resolve of eliminating Adam to finally put a swift end to their resistance, through the thick exchange of fire that raged between the ground forces of the freedom fighters and the enemy planes that continued to terrorized the remainder of their units on the ground.

Only a few of their defenses remained intact, and the enemy soldiers began charging through the base greeting the survivors with a hail of gunfire.

The smoke from all the husks of burning transports and gunships, along with the wreckage of all that was caught in the wake of the destruction, swept across the area like a dark cloud of mist, hiding the terrors that lurked within, while it concealed either friend or foe.

Adam heard the constant cracking of gunfire drawing louder, as the enemy soldiers made their way deeper within the base. He saw a mere glimpse of someone who he thought was the assassin, and saw the smoke quickly shrouding the image he thought he'd just seen.

He stared slowly downwards, with a sudden look of awe, and saw a knife protruding into his chest, just a few inches above his heart, and slowly fell to the ground.

Anton got up from the ground dazed and disoriented from an explosion, and saw Adam with a knife sticking out of his chest, and ran over to him, lifting up, struggling to carry him towards one of the surviving transports.

Frank, Kathy, and Matthew made their way in search of another transport, when a group of enemy soldiers came charging through the smoke that shrouded the base from all the burning wreckage, greeting them with a barrage of fire.

They hid behind the transports and returned fire through the thick cloud of smoke, while Anton and Jonathan loaded Adam's wounded body into one of their transports to make their escape. They suddenly felt the assassin pulling them off the truck, as Adam landed safely within its confines, with the assassin's knife still buried deeply on his chest.

Janet fired her weapon wildly through the smoke, hoping to hit the elusive assassin, while the others remained incapacitated from the flurry of his attacks, and suddenly felt a crushing blow to her jaw, causing her head to bounce off the hull of the transport, falling on top of Anton, as he laid on the snowy ground.

She looked into his eyes for a brief moment and quickly came to her senses. After a moment of unconsciousness, she quickly stood to her feet, while he stared back, as Anton lay helpless on the ground.

Without a moment of hesitation, Janet and Jacqueline ran to the driver's seat of Adam's transport and turned on the ignition, with Adam's wounded body, in their desperate attempt to escape through the blinding wall of smoke that shrouded the base, while the others continued to suffer tremendous punishment at the hands of the assassin, unknowingly leaving Jill behind.

The assassin watched for a brief moment, seeing the transport with Adam's wounded body hurrying from the vicinity of the base, and turned back hearing another transport coming from behind, leaving him with no moment to react, slamming into him, tossing him away with much force, causing him to be motionless on the ground.

Frank and the others quickly ran out of the transport, staring frantically in the assassin's direction, hoping he wouldn't revive from the impact of the truck, while he continued to load as many of the troops into their transport, quickly making their escape.

Jill slowly opened her eyes after being unconscious from an explosion that rocked the base near her position, and felt herself being hoisted over Matthew's shoulder, and quickly being tossed at the back of the transports.

Kathy banged the interior of the transport loudly, warning Frank that Jill was on board, and called out, "Let's go! Let's go!"

Frank heard the loud banging and charged through the thick, blinding wall of smoke, making their desperate run out of the battle area.

The assassin slowly rose from the snowy ground, dusting off his uniform, and saw one of the transports making their escape, and ran towards one of the surviving transports in immediate pursuit.

Janet grabbed the radio and shouted, "This is transport one to any and all available craft! Are you receiving me? Over!"

09:13 HOURS. SOMEWHERE OVER THE ATLANTIC OCEAN HEADING TOWARDS FORT STORY FREEDOM FIGHTER COMMAND CENTER - CHESAPEAKE BAY, VIRGINIA:

"This is flight leader!" Nicole answered, with a frantic look on her face, seeing the thick dark fog of smoke from the distance where the command center was located. "What's your status? Over!" she asked, immediately turning her plane towards the direction of the base to give her support to the survivors.

09:13 HOURS. FORT STORY FREEDOM FIGHTER COMMAND CENTER - CHESAPEAKE BAY, VIRGINIA:

"We've lost the entire base from the enemy attack, with only a few survivors left!

General West has been seriously injured and enemy troops are in pursuit, and need immediate support! Over!" Janet yelled, frantically looking for air support.

09:13 HOURS. SOMEWHERE OVER THE ATLANTIC OCEAN, HEADING TOWARDS FORT STORY FREEDOM FIGHTER COMMAND CENTER - CHESAPEAKE BAY, VIRGINIA:

"Oh no," she answered softly in a state of panic, witnessing all the destruction as she continued closing the distance. She was suddenly alarmed after her radar picked up a number of enemy contacts and said, "This is flight leader to any and all available craft in the area. We have lost the base from enemy attack! General West is reported to have been seriously injured from the assault, and is being evacuated, and is now being pursued by the enemy! No matter the circumstances, General West is to be protected at all cost! I repeat, General West is to be protected at all costs! We are heavily outnumbered, and our best chance of survival and to protect General West is to stay invisible! All weapons hot and engage! I repeat, all weapons hot!"

She skillfully maneuvered her plane using the sun to her back, lining up her sights on the enemy planes, and fired her missile from long distance. She watched them explode into her enemy, and quickly made her way towards Adam's position as some of the other planes entangled the other enemy planes, giving her time to slip away to provide support to the survivors who evacuated the base.

09:14 HOURS. SECURE LOCATION, SOMEWHERE IN RICHMOND, VIRGINIA:

Celina looked at Dr. Weaver with a sudden look of distress on her face hearing the disturbing news and slowly removed her headphones, placing them on the desk near the monitor.

"What is it?" Dr. Weaver asked softly.

"General West's position has fallen. All their defenses are overwhelmed. They tried to hold out as long as they could, but the air support never arrived in time. General West has been seriously wounded, and is being evacuated, along with a few of the surviving troops, and now being pursued by the enemy forces, sir. I'm so sorry."

"My God. How could it come to this? At this rate, the resistance will be wiped out," Dr. Weaver said.

"That wasn't all."

"There's more?" Dr. Weaver asked with a frantic look on his face.

"The second wave of planes that attacked the aircraft carrier fleet suffered total casualties."

"That's good news."

"But the entire navy was lost. Only a few surviving planes left, and running low on ordinance and fuel, but heading towards General West's position, and pray they're not too late. Just a matter of time before they run out of fuel or get intercepted by the enemy forces. I'm so sorry, sir."

"Then the resistance is finally over. After all this time, it all finally came crashing down," Dr. Weaver said, nervously.

09:14 HOURS. FORT STORY FREEDOM FIGHTER COMMAND CENTER - CHESAPEAKE BAY, VIRGINIA:

The lead enemy pilot intercepted Nicole's radio message, flew over the fog of dark smoke, and broke radio silence.

09:14 HOURS. ENEMY COMMAND CENTER - PENTAGON, WASHINGTON, D.C., THE NATION'S CAPITAL:

"This is command. What is your status? Over."

09:14 HOURS. SOMEWHERE OVER FORT STORY FREEDOM FIGHTER COMMAND CENTER - CHESAPEAKE BAY, VIRGINIA:

"I've intercepted a transmission that General West has been seriously wounded during the assault, and fleeing from the base."

09:14 HOURS. ENEMY COMMAND CENTER - PENTAGON, WASHINGTON, D.C., THE NATION'S CAPITAL:

"Do you have a visual, Viper wing?" the General asked with a sudden look of shock on his face.

09:15 HOURS. SOMEWHERE OVER INTERSTATE 64, A FEW MILES AWAY FROM FORT STORY FREEDOM FIGHTER COMMAND CENTER - CHESAPEAKE BAY, VIRGINIA:

"That's affirmative! I have a visual on General West's position!" she said, closing her eyes from a blinding flash in her cockpit from the remainder of her planes being hit from ground attacks.

She heard the alarms of her radar blare loudly, warning her of an impending missile attack, and glanced to her back for a brief moment, seeing it coming closer to her. She immediately took evasive maneuvers, and deployed her countermeasures, leading the missile away from her plane, watching them explode into the heat of her sunbursts.

09:16 HOURS. FREEDOM FIGHTER AIRCRAFT CARRIER FLEET, STATIONED MORE THAN 20 MILES IN THE ATLANTIC OCEAN FROM THE FREEDOM FIGHTER COMMAND CENTER - CHESAPEAKE BAY, VIRGINIA:

Though the enemy planes continued to inflict heavy damage on the aircraft carrier fleet, they continued to sustain heavy casualties from the formidable squad of surviving freedom fighter aircrafts, until another aircraft carrier erupted into a giant ball of flame.

09:17 HOURS. ENEMY COMMAND CENTER - PENTAGON, WASHINGTON. D.C., THE NATION'S CAPITAL:

"What's your status, Viper?" the General asked.

09:17 HOURS. SOMEWHERE OVER INTERSTATE 64, A FEW MILES AWAY FROM FORT STORY FREEDOM FIGHTER COMMAND CENTER - CHESAPEAKE BAY, VIRGINIA:

"I've lost my entire squad from enemy fire, and I'm still in pursuit of General West! I'm all alone, and in need of reinforcements! Over!"

09:18 HOURS. ENEMY COMMAND CENTER - PENTAGON, WASHINGTON, D.C., THE NATION'S CAPITAL:

"You are to complete your objective at all costs, Viper. I repeat, by any means necessary. I will send in reinforcements as soon as possible."

09:18 HORUS. SOMEWHERE OVER INTERSTATE 64, A FEW MILES AWAY FROM FORT STORY FREEDOM FIGHTER COMMAND CENTER - CHESAPEAKE BAY, VIRGINIA:

"Reading you loud and clear," she answered, looking behind her, checking to see if she was being pursued, while she continued her pursuit.

09:19 HOURS. ENEMY COMMAND CENTER - PENTAGON, WASHINGTON, D.C., THE NATION'S CAPITAL:

"This is command to Python wing. What is your status? Over."

09:19 HOURS. SOMEWHERE OVER FORT MYERS FREEDOM FIGHTER AIR FORCE BASE - ARLINGTON, VIRGINIA:

"This is Python wing. All defenses have been neutralized, but still in phase 2. What are your orders?"

09:19 HOURS. ENEMY COMMAND CENTER - PENTAGON, WASHINGTON, D.C., THE NATION'S CAPITAL:

"We have a confirmed visual of General West's last position. You are to head to that position to intercept immediately. We're sending in coordinates."

09:20 HOURS. SOMEWHERE OVER FORT MYERS FREEDOM FIGHTER AIR FORCE BASE - ARLINGTON, VIRGINIA:

"Coordinates received. Reading you loud and clear. Heading out to engage," the enemy pilot said, and radioed the ground troops to pull out.

09:20 HOURS. FORT MYERS FREEDOM FIGHTER AIR FORCE BASSE - ARLINGTON, VIRGINIA:

The ground troops suddenly pulled out from clearing the base of all remaining freedom fighters, heading towards their transports bound for Adam's positions.

09:20 HOURS. ENEMY COMMAND CENTER - PENTAGON, WASHINGTON, D.C., THE NATION'S CAPITAL:

"This is command to Saber Wolf. What is your status? Over."

09:21 HOURS. SOMEWHERE OVER FORT BELVOIR FREEDOM FIGHTER AIR FORCE BASE - FAIRFAX, VIRGINIA:

"This is Saber Wolf to command. Enemy position completely neutralized. Still in the second phase of assault. What are your orders? Over."

09:21 HOURS. ENEMY COMMAND CENTER - PENTAGON, WASHINGTON D.C., THE NATION'S CAPITAL:

"We have confirmation on General West's position. Abort mission and intercept immediately. We're sending in coordinates."

09:21 HOURS. SOMEWHERE OVER FORT BELVOIR FREEDOM FIGHTER AIR FORCE BASE - FAIRFAX, VIRGINIA:

"Coordinates received. Read you loud and clear. Heading out to engage. Saber Wolf, out," the pilot said and relayed the General's orders to the ground troops.

09:21 HOURS. FORT BELVOIR FREEDOM FIGHTER AIR FORCE BASE - FAIRFAX, VIRGINIA:

The enemy soldiers continued to purge the freedom fighter's positions of the remaining soldiers, and suddenly stopped, heading back to their transports, in pursuit of General West.

09:22 HOURS. ENEMY COMMAND CENTER - PENTAGON, WASHINGTON D.C., THE NATION'S CAPITAL:

"This is command to Mamba. What is your status? Over."

09:22 HOURS. SOMEWHERE OVER FORT LEE FREEDOM FIGHTER AIR FORCE BASE - PRINCE GEORGE COUNTY, VIRGINIA:

"All enemy defenses have been neutralized, and still in phase two. I repeat, we're still in phase two. What are your orders? Over."

09:22 HOURS. ENEMY COMMAND CENTER - PENTAGON, WASHINGTON, D.C., THE NATION'S CAPITAL:

"I've received confirmation of General West's current location. I am ordering you to abort the mission and head to his vector. I'm sending you coordinates."

09:22 HOURS. SOMEWHERE OVER FORT LEE FREEDOM FIGHTER AIR FORCE BASE - PRINCE GEORGE COUNTY, VIRGINIA:

"Coordinates received. Reading you loud and clear. Moving in to engage. Mamba, out," the pilot said, and relayed the General's orders to the ground troops.

09:22 HOURS. FORT LEE FREEDOM FIGHTER AIR FORCE BASE - PRINCE GEORGE COUNTY, VIRGINIA:

While purging the freedom fighters' position, the enemy soldiers suddenly turned around to head out to engage General West.

09:23 HOURS. ENEMY COMMAND CENTER - PENTAGON, WASHINGTON D.C., THE NATION'S CAPITAL:

"This is command to Firefly. What is your status? Over."

09:23 HOURS. SOMEWHERE OVER FORT EUSTIS FREEDOM FIGHTER AIR FORCE BASE - NEWPORT NEWS, VIRGINIA:

"All enemy defenses are neutralized and still in phase 2. What are your orders? Over."

09:23 HOURS. ENEMY COMMAND CENTER - PENTAGON, WASHINGTON, D.C., THE NATION'S CAPITAL:

"We have a confirmed visual on General West's location. Abort mission and engage. I repeat, about mission and engage. Sending you coordinates of General West's vector. Over."

09:23 HOURS. SOMEWHERE OVER FORT EUSTIS FREEDOM FIGHTER AIR FORCE BASE - NEWPORT NEWS, VIRGINIA:

"Reading you loud and clear. Heading to the next vector."

09:24 HOURS. ENEMY COMMAND CENTER - PENTAGON, WASHINGTON, D.C., THE NATION'S CAPITAL:

"This is command to Cobra wing. What is your status? Over."

09:24 HOURS. LANGLEY FREEDOM FIGHTER AIR FORCE BASE - LANGLEY, VIRGINIA:

"This Cobra wing. All defenses are neutralized, and still in phase 2 of assault. Awaiting further orders. Over."

09:24 HOURS. ENEMY COMMAND CENTER - PENTAGON, WASHINGTON, D.C., THE NATION'S CAPITAL:

"We have visual confirmation of enemy transports evacuating the base. One of them contained General West. You are ordered to head to his location and intercept. We're sending in the coordinates. Over."

09:24 HOURS. SOMEWHERE OVER LANGLEY FREEDOM FIGHTER AIR FORCE BASE - LANGLEY, VIRGINA:

"Coordinates have been received. Heading over to engage the target. Cobra wing, out," the enemy pilot said, and relayed the General's orders to the ground troops that continued to purge the base.

09:25 HOURS. LANGLEY FREEDOM FIGHTER AIR FORCE BASE - LANGLEY, VIRGINIA:

While the enemy troops continued to purge the base of pockets of resistance, they suddenly turned back and headed to their transports in pursuit of General West and the other survivors.

09:33 HOURS. FREEDOM FIGHTER AIRCRAFT CARRIER FLEET STATIONED MORE THAN 20 MILES IN THE ATLANTIC OCEAN FROM FORT STORY FREEDOM FIGHTER COMMAND CENTER - CHESAPEAKE BAY, VIRGINIA:

After the long and hard air and sea war that ensued the vast ocean of the North Atlantic, the enemy planes had suffered total casualties at the combined fire power of the aircraft carrier fleet, and the few surviving fighter planes that methodically used the blinding tactics with the sun to their backs, making them invisible from the other enemy planes, that gradually helped shifting the balance of the war in their favor, though the entire aircraft carrier fleet had also suffered total casualties from the enemies' surprise attacks.

Left with no alternative, the surviving pilots, in their desperate stand against the vast enemy, continued to push their exhausted bodies to their limit, until all their fuel and ammunition were on the verge of depletion.

They flew over the flaming ships and aircraft carriers that slowly sunk in the ocean to their watery graves, and watched helplessly as a number of their crew men and women floated lifelessly in the frigid waters, while some of the survivors clung on whatever debris they could find to stay afloat amidst the destruction in a state of total helplessness, knowing there was nothing that could save them. The last surviving aircraft carrier that still remained defiant, even after being totally consumed in flames from the heavy punishment it endured from the enemy attacks, suddenly erupted into a giant ball of flames, scattering chunks of debris in all directions, ending its defiance.

After the explosion, the last defiant aircraft carrier, slowly sunk to the bottom to its watery grave that will soon become its eternal resting place.

09:35 HOURS. SOMEWHERE ON INTERSTATE 64, HEADING TOWARDS, RICHMOND, VIRGINIA:

The fleeing transports continued driving as quickly as they could, fleeing from enemy soldiers, when they heard the loud clamor of the last defiant aircraft carrier erupt in a giant ball of crimson flame, turning into a giant mushroom cloud of dark smoke, rising into the skies far from their position.

They watched in total silence, with the grim realization that their entire resistance was now leaderless and on the brink of collapse, seeing what was left of their once mighty fleet now instantly reduced to smoke and rubble, about to be committed to eternal void of the abyss, with so many of their comrades who paid the ultimate price, and many more trapped inside, with some of their survivors, stranded in the deep, frigid waters, waiting to meet their gruesome fate as the ones before them.

Adam slowly began to fidget with the assassin's knife stuck deeply in his chest and murmured, "Elaina. We must find Elaina. Everything is lost, and no one will be safe. They will find her. We need to find her."

"Who's Elaina? What the hell is he babbling about?" Brian asked.

"How the fuck should I know?" Anton answered.

"Get a secure channel. I'll give you the coordinates where we should meet."

"Be still, General West. I need you to hold him still," Brian said as he tried to keep Adam still, and keep pressure on his wound to help stop the bleeding.

"We're about to pull this knife from your chest, and it'll hurt a bit. But first, we need you to be still. Someone, get something to staunch the bleeding."

"There has to be a kit somewhere," Karen said.

"Just get it over with," Adam answered.

"Okay," Brian answered, quickly pulling out the assassin's knife from his chest, while Adam yelled loudly in pain, causing his entire body to fidget, feeling the serration of the assassin's knife slicing through his flesh.

Janet saw a blockade of the enemy blocking their path, deploying a number of enemy troops and said, "We have an enemy blockade up ahead!"

She looked in the side view mirror, and saw a tiny dot growing larger as it quickly descended towards them, and shouted, "We have an enemy plane on our ass too! And another transport on our tail! Get on the radio and call for air support!"

Jacqueline picked up the radio, and called out, "This is transport one to any available air units in our position! We're being pursued by enemy forces on all sides and in need of air support! I repeat, to any and all aircraft in the vicinity, we need immediate assistance! Over."

The enemy pilot intercepted the transmission and continued to descend upon them, priming her weapons, when she was suddenly once again from her alarms blaring, warning her that her fuel was running low, and broke radio silence and said, "This is Viper to command. Are you receiving me? Over."

09:36 HOURS. ENEMY COMMAND CENTER - PENTAGON, WASHINGTON, D.C., THE NATION'S CAPITAL:

"This is command. What is your status? Over."

09:36 HOURS. SOMEWHERE OVER INTERSTATE 64, HEADING TOWARDS RICHMOND, VIRGINIA:

"I have a visual on General West's position. The Drone is in pursuit. I repeat, the Drone is in pursuit. Running low on fuel and ordinance, requesting permission to reload and refuel, over."

09:36 HOURS. ENEMY COMMAND CENTER - PENTAGON, WASHINGTON, D.C., THE NATION'S CAPITAL:

"You are ordered to engage and neutralize the enemy target at all costs. I repeat, General West is to be neutralized at all costs. Take the shot with whatever ordinance you have at your disposal," the General ordered.

09:36 HOURS. SOMEWHERE OVER INTERSTATE 64, HEADING TOWARDS RICHMOND, VIRGINIA:

"But the Drone is in pursuit!" she said loudly, and added, "I repeat, the Drone is in full pursuit! If I engage, it may result in friendly fire! Over!"

09:36 HOURS. ENEMY COMMAND CENTER - PENTAGON, WASHINGTON, D.C., THE NATION'S CAPITAL:

"We both know that the success of this mission is more important than the Drone or your life itself, flight leader. Drone or no Drone, I order you to take the shot, even if it means all your ammunition and fuel gets depleted. Sacrifices must be made for the cause under the circumstances, and if necessary, ram your plane into the target. This resistance ends today. Am I being clear?" the General said, firmly.

09:37 HOURS. SOMEWHERE OVER INTERSTATE 64, HEADING TOWARDS RICHMOND, VIRGINIA:

After hearing the General's orders on the other end of the receiver, she was instantly consumed with rage, and watched her fuel gauge continue to blink. She flew past the duo of fleeing transports, heading towards the enemy blockade, deploying one of her remaining missiles, destroying them, clearing the path for the fleeing transports, and quickly took to the skies.

09:37 HOURS. SOMEWHERE ON INTERSTATE 64, HEADING TOWARDS RICHMOND, VIRGINIA:

Matthew watched the plane flying into the skies after her bombing run, as he sat at the front passenger side of the transport next to Frank and said, "That's not ours. That's one of the planes that attacked us."

"How do you know?" Frank asked.

"Because I saw it when the base was attacked. Those skills are a dead giveaway."

"I'm confused. Then why is he helping us?" Frank asked.

"Don't ask me. Then again, based on the circumstances, I don't care, and neither should you."

"On that, we both agree," Frank answered, as he continued to drive through the long stretch of the interstate, fleeing the enemy forces that continued their relentless pursuit.

"Damn, he's good, whoever he is. Looks like someone up there still loves us. It's not our time to go yet," Matthew answered.

"I hope so," Frank answered.

Jason heard the General's chilling message over the radio and sat next to the assassin, who remained calm and consumed with anger, and said, "My God. They're trying to kill us," with a sudden look of shock on his face, and asked, "What are we going to do?"

The assassin quickly abandoned his pursuit of Adam, when a number of enemy transports pulled in from behind in hot pursuit driving past him, ramming into the fleeing transports, trying to ran them off the road, while

Brian, Anton, and Jonathan continued to struggle taking out the serrated blade buried deep within Adam's chest.

Janet struggled to maintain control of her transport, while the enemies continued ramming into them.

"We need to get those enemy vehicles off our tails! I need you to hold him down!" Anton said, grabbing a rifle from the bed of the truck.

"Okay," Karen answered.

"Min, you're with me."

"Okay, what do you need me to do?" Jonathan asked.

Anton immediately opened fire at the enemy vehicle, trying to fend off the relentless enemy transports that harried them.

"Okay," Jonathan said, following Anton's lead, with their combined fire power causing one of the enemy vehicles to run off the road, crashing on the side.

They continued to fend off as many of the enemy vehicles as they could, while Janet continued to struggle to maintain control. Anton shouted, "It's no use! There's too many of them!"

Brian and Karen continued to hold Adam's body to the floor of the transport, still trying to pull the knife from his chest. But all the disturbance drove the knife deeper into Adam's wound.

Jill and Kathy sat in the other transport, feeling the clash from the enemy transports, tossing them to the floor.

They grabbed their weapons from the floor and immediately opened fire at the pursuing enemy transports, hitting the driver, causing it to veer out of control, crashing into another transport.

Janet saw the flaming wreckage of another enemy blockade and yelled, "We have another enemy blockade!"

"Just go through it!" Jacqueline answered.

"Hang on!" Janet replied, pressing the acceleration as hard as she could, charging through the burning gauntlet, throwing Brian, Karen, Jonathan, and Anton off balance, while they struggled to maintain Adam's safety.

They continued to greet the pursuing soldiers with fire.

"There's too many of them!" Jacqueline yelled.

"Get on the radio, and call for air support! And continue calling until we get it!"

"This is Foxtrot 1! This is Foxtrot 1 to any and all available craft in the area! We are being engaged by enemy units and need immediate support! Over!Any available aircraft in the area, please respond! Over!"

09:39 HOURS. SOMEWHERE OVER INTERSTATE 64, HEADING TOWARDS RICHMOND, VIRGINIA:

Nicole heard the distress call and answered, with a huge sigh of relief, "Reading you loud and clear, heading to your position." She looked from the cockpit of her plane, seeing the fleeing transports, and said, "All wings form up on me. I have a visual on General West's position."

09:40 HOURS. SOMEWHERE ON INTERSTATE 64, HEADING TOWARDS RICHMOND, VIRGINIA:

"Foxtrot 1?" Janet said to Jacqueline.

"Had to say something. Figured it was a good idea at the time," Jacqueline answered.

"Oh no," Janet said softly, with a sudden look of shock coming on her face, seeing a number of enemy planes flying towards their position. "This is it. We're done." She saw a few planes bursting into flames, falling from the skies, causing the other enemy planes to break off their attack. She flew over the small group of transports, causing their hulls to shudder greatly from the noise.

One of the enemy pilots caused a glimpse of the plane that engaged them and broke radio silence in his frantic call to the General.

"What the hell just happened?" Jacqueline asked.

"What does it look like? She turned, isn't that obvious?" Janet replied.

"I'm so confused. Just happy we're not dead. Thank God."

"I think it's safe to say that for now."

09:44 HOURS. ENEMY COMMAND CENTER - PENTAGON, WASHINGTON, D.C., THE NATION'S CAPITAL:

A sudden look of disbelief came over their faces as they sat in the command room hearing the frantic call to the General.

The General picked up the radio and answered, "This is command. Who is this and what is your status?"

09:45 HOURS. SOMEWHERE OVER INTERSTATE 64, HEADING TOWARDS RICHMOND, VIRGINIA:

"This is Cobra. We're being engaged! I repeat, we're being engaged by flight leader! We've lost two of our planes."

09:45 HOURS. ENEMY COMMAND CENTER - PENTAGON, WASHINGTON, D.C., THE NATION'S CAPITAL:

"From this moment on, Viper is considered a traitor and should be considered as one of General West's. All available crafts, pursue and terminate Viper with extreme prejudice. I repeat, engage with extreme prejudice."

09:45 HOURS. SOMEWHERE OVER INTERSTATE 64, HEADING TOWARDS RICHMOND, VIRGINIA:

Nicole intercepted the radio message from the enemy pilot and saw one of the enemy planes suddenly racing towards her, racing over her canopy, causing her plane to shudder for a brief moment, and looked behind her, trying to make sense of what she'd just heard.

The enemy pilot broke radio silence and said, "This is Viper to flight leader, are you receiving me? Over."

"What do you want?" Nicole answered sharply.

"For now to unite our skills," the enemy pilot answered, closing her eyes in a confused state, trying to come to terms with what she had just done to her fellow pilots.

"You led an assault on us, and now you demand an alliance? You murdered so many of my friends. Many of whom are lying in their graves at the bottom of the ocean."

"As did you, when you led an assault on all our positions the year before, and all the years before that. All of us at this very moment are guilty of all those sins. It's the price we pay in this perpetual game of war."

"What made you do it? Why did you change sides?"

The enemy pilot closed her eyes, as her tears ran down her face, and answered, "That's not important now. What's more important is keeping General West alive so you can continue your precious resistance."

"Our resistance is indeed precious. On that we both agree," Nicole responded.

"Your entire fleet was destroyed, along with most of your planes."

"And who's fault was that?"

"You, along with General West and what's left of your forces, are heading into a hornet's nest. You're completely outnumbered, and after all the planes that you've shot down, we both know that you're low on ordinance and fuel, and will eventually be overwhelmed by the enemy forces"

Nicole looked at her gauge, seeing her ammunition count, and saw she was indeed running low on fuel. "You made your point. What do you propose?"

"We join forces," the enemy pilot said.

"How do I know that I can trust you?"

"You don't. But as I mentioned, General West is your first priority. And the best that we can do for the moment is to hold out long enough against the others to buy your ground troops enough time to escape. After we've done our jobs, we can kill each other if you want. Just you and me, so we can have our revenge for our friends that we've both lost."

"Wouldn't have it any other way," Nicole answered.

"I've heard a lot about you, and I must say, I'm impressed by your skills. They are extremely commendable. They were not exaggerated at all."

"The same could be said of you, I suppose," Nicole replied.

"The trick with you using the sun to your back to make you invisible to the naked eye was very impressive. If I don't make it back, I'd just like to say that you were a worthy opponent fighting this war all these years."

"The sentiment is well shared. Thank you for the motivational speech. But after we complete our mission, I'm still going to kill you," Nicole replied.

"I respect that. But first, let's get to the job at hand."

"Agreed," Nicole replied, heading towards the transport and continued, "I read enemy planes at 12 o'clock. Vulcan and Rhino, we need to break the enemy formation, and protect General West at all costs. All weapons hot, and cover our asses. We use the same formation to engage the enemy forces. And as for you, Viper. You're not getting out of my sight. If I go, you go down with me."

"Understood. What are your orders, flight leader?"

"Break their formation and engage the stragglers. Wear them down. The more we wear them down, the longer we have a chance of coming out alive, and our ground troops surviving." The remainder of enemy planes had reformed their ranks and descended on the transports on their strafing run. They were suddenly greeted by a volley of missiles coming from the direction of the sun, causing them to once again disperse, giving Nicole and the rogue pilot enough time to engage the stragglers.

09:47 HOURS. SOMEWHERE ON INTERSTATE 64, HEADING TOWARDS RICHMOND, VIRGINIA:

"Who is that woman?" Kathy said, listening to the radio chatter.

"Well, well, well. Today's just full of surprises," Matthew said, watching the fighter planes battle for supremacy in the skies.

Janet heard the loud clamor in the skies from the explosion and saw the enemy plane burst into flames, falling from the skies, with the wreckage falling onto the interstate, causing them to swerve their transport to avoid the searing heat from the wreckage scattered all about the long stretch of road from the blast.

"What the fuck was that?" Janet asked nervously.

"What does it look like? It's enemy planes falling from the skies! Hallelujah!" Jacqueline answered.

"Is it me, or you're just crazy!? We're dodging planes on the damn road!" Janet yelled.

"Better them than us!" Jacqueline answered.

"If we get hit, then it will be us! And we have bigger problems!" Janet answered.

"What now?" Jacqueline asked.

"They're still coming! And they're trying to ram us off the road! Don't know how much longer we can hold! Call for air support!"

The assassin continued to trail from behind. He drove beside one of the enemy transports and rammed into one of them, separating them from the group.

"Are you seeing this?" Kathy asked Jill.

"I am," Jill answered, in a state of shock, seeing the assassin separating the enemy soldiers away from their transport.

09:51 HOURS. SOMEWHERE OVER INTERSTATE 64, HEADING TOWARDS RICHMOND, VIRGINIA:

"I'm seeing multiple contacts! Please identify your position! Over!" Nicole said, watching her radar.

09:51 HOURS. SOMEWHERE ON INTERSTATE 64, HEADING TOWARDS RICHMOND, VIRGINIA:

Matthew grabbed the radio and answered, "She's isolating the target for engagement! I repeat, go for isolated targets! Over!"

09:51 HOURS. SOMEWHERE OVER INTERSTATE 64, HEADING TOWARDS RICHMOND, VIRGINIA:

Nicole looked down from the view of her cockpit and saw the assassin isolating the enemy transports, and answered, "All air units, continue to engage all enemy forces."

09:52 HOURS. SOMEWHERE ON INTERSTATE 64, HEADING TOWARDS RICHMOND, VIRGINIA:

As the assassin continued to isolate the enemy transports, the duo of planes descended upon the enemy ground troops without mercy.

As Janet led the charge at the front, she saw another enemy gauntlet and yelled, "We have another enemy roadblock! We need support!"

Jacqueline grabbed the radio and yelled, "Enemy roadblock at 12 o'clock! We need support!"

09:52 HOURS. SOMEWHERE OVER INTERSTATE 64, HEADING TOWARDS RICHMOND, VIRGINIA:

The duo of planes quickly descended upon the enemy roadblock of enemy transports, and greeted them with a barrage of heavy machine gun fire, until they erupted into flames, clearing the way for the duo of transports to continue their desperate run.

09:53 HOURS. SOMEWHERE ON INTERSTATE 64, HEADING TOWARDS RICHMOND, VIRGINIA:

Jacqueline saw the lethal barrage of bullets from their planes' heavy machine guns raining from the skies, tearing into the armor of the enemy vehicles and said softly, "Oh shit."

"What do you mean? They just saved our asses."

"It's just that it would suck being on the receiving end of those bullets right now."

"Ain't that the shocking truth?" Janet replied.

10:01 HOURS. SOMEWHERE OVER THE ATLANTIC OCEAN, HEADING TOWARDS FORT STORY FREEDOM FIGHTER COMMAND CENTER - CHESAPEAKE BAY, VIRGINIA:

The surviving squad of planes flew towards the position of the command center, seeing the smoke rising from the flaming husks of all the rubble, friend and foe alike, knowing that many more of their comrades had paid the ultimate price in the attack.

The grim reality of what they had just witnessed instantly caused mixed emotions of anger and sadness, as they continued flying, looking for any signs of Nicole, or any of their pilots.

One of the pilots broke radio silence and said, "This is Machete to any available craft in the area. Come in. Over."

10:02 HOURS. SOMEWHERE OVER INTERSTATE 64, HEADING TOWARDS RICHMOND, VIRGINIA:

"This is flight leader to Machete. Are you receiving me? Over."

10:02 HOURS. SOMEWHERE OVER FORT STORY FREEDOM FIGHTER COMMAND CENTER - CHESAPEAKE BAY, VIRGINIA:

"Receiving you loud and clear, flight leader. What are your orders?"

10:02 HOURS. SOMEWHERE OVER INTERSTATE 64, HEADING TOWARDS RICHMOND, VIRGINIA:

"What is your status, Machete?"

10:02 HOURS. SOMEWHERE OVER FORT STORY FREEDOM FIGHTER COMMAND CENTER - CHESAPEAKE BAY, VIRGINIA:

"The enemy forces have suffered total casualties, but we still lost the entire carrier fleet. So many trapped in the water, and so many more dead. Only a handful of us remain."

10:03 HOURS. SOMEWHERE OVER INTERSTATE 64, HEADING TOWARDS RICHMOND, VIRGINIA:

"How's your ammunition count and fuel holding up?" she asked.

10:03 HOURS. SOMEWHERE OVER FORT STORY FREEDOM FIGHTER COMMAND CENTER - CHESAPEAKE BAY, VIRGINIA:

"Just a few hundred rounds and long range missiles left, and running low on fuel. What are your orders, flight leader?"

10:04 HOURS. SOMEWHERE OVER INTERSTATE 64, HEADING TOWARDS RICHMOND, VIRGINIA:

"General West has been wounded from the assault, and is on the run. He must be protected at all costs! We're surrounded by enemy air and ground forces, and still engaging, and need immediate assist, over! Our current vector is northwest of your position, do you read? Our top priority is protecting General West! Even at the cost of our lives! Over!"

10:04 HOURS. SOMEWHERE OVER FORT STORY FREEDOM FIGHTER COMMAND CENTER - CHESAPEAKE BAY, VIRGINIA:

"Reading you loud and clear. Heading towards your current vector."

10:04 HOURS. ENEMY COMMAND CENTER - PENTAGON, WASHINGTON, D.C., THE NATION'S CAPITAL:

"Any available units report status, over," the General said, breaking radio silence, growing impatient for news since the recent turn of shocking events.

10:05 HOURS. SOMEWHERE OVER INTERSTATE 64, A FEW MILES FROM RICHMOND, VIRGINIA:

"This is Firefly. We have a visual on General West's position, and we've lost another convoy."

10:05 HOURS. ENEMY COMMAND CENTER - PENTAGON, WASHINGTON, D.C., THE NATION'S CAPITAL:

"And what of the Drone and traitor craft?" he asked.

10:05 HOURS. SOMEWHERE OVER INTERSTATE 64, A FEW MILES AWAY FROM RICHMOND, VIRGINIA:

"We're still being engaged. I repeat, we're still being engaged! And sustaining casualties! Still no visual of the drone or traitor craft!"

10:05 HOURS. ENEMY COMMAND CENTER - PENTAGON, WASHINGTON D.C., THE NATION'S CAPITAL:

"These enemy crafts should be destroyed at all costs. They are disorganized and leaderless. Their resistance is on the fringe of collapse. It ends today," he said calmly, in a fit of rage.

10:05 HOURS. SOMEWHERE OVER INTERSTATE 64 - RICHMOND, VIRGINIA:

"Reading you loud and clear, command. Engaging all hostiles!"

10:06 HOURS. ENEMY COMMAND CENTER - PENTAGON, WASHINGTON, D.C., THE NATION'S CAPITAL:

"We have no visual on the Drone or Viper, and we're still taking measures."

"What do you have in mind, General?" Maxwell asked.

"We need to monitor all movement. In case of times like these, I had a contingency plan in place to keep track of anyone who may have strayed from your flock, including the traitor craft and the Drone. Activate all tracking beacons."

10:10 HOURS. SOMEWHERE ON INTERSTATE 64, A FEW MILES FROM RICHMOND, VIRGINIA:

The group of transports continued making their way through the long stretch of road, battling countless enemy ground troops as they tried to take Adam to a safe place to tend to his injury.

Brian continued to struggle to pull the knife out from Adam's chest, until he had finally succeeded. He put the knife closer to his face and said, "This blade was designed to kill. My God, he's really out to kill him. It's a miracle General West is still alive," and threw it on the bed of the transport.

"We need to keep pressure on his wound to contain the bleeding," Karen said.

"How did you know we would be attacked?" Jonathan asked.

"It was the raven," Anton answered.

"What do you mean?" Brian asked.

"Remember Fort Bragg, a couple of years ago?" Anton asked.

"Can't imagine anyone who was there could forget. Why?" Jonathan asked.

"Jill, Jacky, and myself, along with a few others, were out on patrol that night, and the raven landed on one of the transports, right in front of us. They told me to call it in, but I didn't listen, no matter how much they begged me. And that's when the enemy attacked us."

"You're kidding, right?" Jonathan asked.

"They always say that when something bad is about to happen, the raven comes. Just like what you see in the movies. And the night the enemies attacked, and after, I'd seen the raven. I made a promise to myself that I'd never doubt that omen again."

"Go on. I'm listening," Brian added.

"Think of the number of lives that I could've saved if I had called it in that night back at Fort Bragg," Anton said softly.

"Well, you called it in and we still lost a lot of lives," Jonathan answered angrily.

"Take it easy, Jonathan," Karen said. "All of us could've gotten killed in the assault. It's because he called it that we have some of our planes in the skies right at this very moment covering our asses, and keeping General West and the rest of us alive."

"For how long?" Jonathan asked.

"Does it matter? Haven't you been looking outside lately? There's still a war going outside in case you didn't notice," Brian answered. "Our birds got free from the carriers just in time before the enemy attacked, and are still getting killed out there trying to keep us alive. That call that Anton made gave us a fighting chance, because all of us could've been wiped out, along with the resistance."

"After we came from Langley, I was exhausted and sat in one of the trucks to rest my eyes for a moment. There it was, looking right at me, like it was talking to me, trying to tell me something was about to happen and it just flew off. And that's when I knew something was wrong. Something bad was about to happen. So, I called it in. And just when I had doubts, the communications tower went up in flames. To a certain degree, I was right when it happened, but mostly I wished I wasn't seeing so many of us losing our lives. I really wished I wasn't."

"Well, we could've been wiped out if it weren't for that warning," Brian answered.

"The resistance is still alive because of you. Or what's left of it, anyway," Karen answered.

"She's right, Min, and you know it," Brian answered.

"I apologize for being hard on you. You're right. We still have a fighting chance to salvage what's left of the resistance. I hope it'll be enough," Jonathan answered.

"It's okay. If I were you, I wouldn't believe you either," Anton replied.

"Now that that's out the way, we need to get somewhere safe to attend to General West," Brian added.

"Where do you think we can go?" Anton asked.

"There's an abandoned base a few miles from here, and our best chance of survival is to take advantage of the situation while the enemy planes are distracted by ours. Let's hope we don't have any enemy roadblocks," he answered.

10:17 HOURS. SOMEWHERE OVER INTERSTATE 64 - RICHMOND VIRGINIA:

Nicole picked up the contacts from a number of planes moving closer to her position, and said, "This is Comet to all oncoming craft. Identify yourselves over."

"This is Bulldog."

"This Hyena."

"This is Scorpion."

"This is Mustang."

"This is Machete."

"This is Black Jack."

"This is Havoc. What are your orders, flight leader?"

Nicole took a sigh of relief and answered, "I'm so glad you made it. Our orders are still the same. Protect General West at all costs. We're completely outnumbered and running low on ordinance and fuel. Don't know how long we'll be able to fight. So, we need to make all our shots count. We need to keep on clearing the path for our troops to get General West to safety no matter the cost. Myself, Viper, Vulcan, and Rhino will strafe the ground troops, and the rest of you, use the same tactics to keep you invisible for as long as you can, until the coast is clear. Our best chance is to combine our fire power. Now break. Weapons free and engage at will."

The other planes broke formations upon Nicole's orders, while she continued to fly over the ground troops with the other remaining planes, scanning for more enemy roadblocks, and picked up a large number of enemy contacts heading towards their direction. She said to the other planes, "I'm reading a large number of enemy contacts. You have your orders."

10:20 HOURS. SOMEWHERE OVER INTERSTATE 64 - RICHMOND, VIRGINIA:

The planes waited patiently, trying to line up their targets with the sun to their backs, making them completely invisible to the enemies, until they locked into their targets, and deployed their long-range missiles, before the enemy planes had a chance to engage. They watched the missiles follow their targets, exploding into them, causing the other enemy planes to disperse.

10:25 HOURS. SOMEWHERE ON INTERSTATE 64 - RICHMOND, VIRGINIA:

The small group of fleeing transports of freedom fighters were once again intercepted by a number of enemy transports, slowly being overwhelmed by their sheer numbers.

Matthew grabbed the radio and called out for air support, while Frank struggled to maintain control of their vehicle, with Jill and Kathy returning fire in the rear to try and repel the pursuing enemy forces.

The assassin pulled in from behind, and rammed into one of the enemy transports, throwing it off the road.

10:27 HOURS. SOMEWHERE OVER INTERSTATE 64 - RICHMOND, VIRGINIA:

Nicole and a few of her wingmen heard the distress call and immediately dove towards their position to engage, while the assassin continued to isolate them from the fleeing transports to avoid friendly fire.

10:29 HOURS. SOMEWHERE OVER INTERSTATE 64 - RICHMOND, VIRGINIA:

Jill and Kathy suddenly stopped firing their weapons and watched with a sudden look of awe on their faces as the assassin rammed the other transports away from theirs, isolating them for their air units to engage, as he drove right past them, staring directly into Matthew's eyes.

Matthew stared into his eyes, with a look of shock, as the assassin stared back coldly, while he slowly drove past them, and asked, "Are you seeing this, Frank?"

"Yes I am," Frank answered, watching the assassin drive past their vehicle, with a sudden look of shock and nervousness on his face, staring into the assassin's eyes.

"I'm so confused right now."

"Better them than us. He's making our job a whole lot easier," Frank replied, keeping his gaze fixed.

The assassin continued to drive past them, maintaining his cold calculating stare, as they stared back helplessly, making his way towards Adam's transport.

"Look," Brian said, watching the assassin drive past him, maintaining his cold, calculating stare, while all the others froze, once again coming face to face with the man that pursued them for so long, with Jason at his side.

He continued driving past their transport, and peered into Jacqueline's eyes while Janet continued to maintain her course at the wheel, with the bruises on their faces that spoke volumes of their ordeal from the punishment they sustained from the assassin's deadly skills, and continued driving past them.

Jacqueline continued maintaining her look of shock on her face, and asked, "Uhh, Janet, are you seeing this?"

Janet, briefly distracted, watched their would-be nemesis driving past them without engaging, also with a sudden look of franticness on her face. "Yes, I did. I'd be a liar to say that I'm not scared shitless. But I'm still trying to understand what the fuck just happened."

"Who cares? He just left us alone, didn't he? Just don't do anything to antagonize any kind of situation."

"You don't have to tell me twice. Besides, if there's anything that would be antagonizing any situation, it's that enemy roadblock up ahead," Janet replied.

"He'll clear it for us, I hope, if our planes don't get to it first."

10:34 HOURS. SOMEWHERE OVER INTERSTATE 64 - RICHMOND, VIRGINIA:

Nicole flew towards the enemy roadblock and fired a missile, forming a giant wall of flames, completely obliterating it, clearing the path for the ground transports. They were suddenly swarmed by enemy planes, when a blinding flash suddenly lit into her cockpit after losing one of her planes.

She listened to the pilot's distress call as the plane went down in flames and called out, "This is flight leader to Machete, do you read? Machete, come in!"

She heard the static from the dead radio silence, followed by the loud clamor of the explosion after the plane crashed, and saw the black smoke from the wreckage. She closed her eyes in a brief moment of silence, after losing one of her own who made the ultimate sacrifice.

"This is Scorpion! This is Scorpion! Enemy on my tail and I can't shake him! Need immediate assist!" the pilot said and was suddenly riddled by a number of heavy enemy machine gun fire, tearing through the controls, scattering his blood throughout the confines of the cockpit, killing him instantly, causing the plane to plummet to the surface, crashing and burning, while Nicole and the other planes took evasive maneuvers.

10:39 HOURS. SOMEWHERE ON INTERSTATE 64 - RICHMOND, VIRGINIA:

The assassin continued to drive past them, charging through the gauntlet of enemy vehicles that were turned into flaming wreckage Nicole and the other planes left in their wake from clearing a path for the fleeing ground troops.

10:41 HOURS. ENEMY COMMAND CENTER - PENTAGON, WASHINGTON, D.C., THE NATION'S CAPITAL:

"Give me a report," the General demanded.

"It's the drone, sir," Colonel Maxwell answered.

"What about him?"

"He's no longer engaging. And he's moving at an incredible speed," Colonel Maxwell answered.

"He's heading out of the battle area."

"Do you know where he's headed?" the General asked.

"Judging from the speed and direction," Maxwell said, pausing nervously, "I think he's coming here, sir."

The General smirked wickedly and answered, "If that's the case, we won't be disappointing our guest."

They simply stared at one another in disbelief, after witnessing that the General showed no fear of the assassin.

10:45 HOURS. SOMEWHERE OVER INTERSTATE 64 - RICHMOND, VIRGINIA:

The enemy planes adapted their tactics, as they continued to overwhelm the smaller group of planes with their sheer numbers and combined firepower.

The sudden explosion once again lit through Nicole's cockpit from the missile impact of the enemy, causing her to lose another one of her pilots. She watched the plane fly down into flaming wreckage and said, "I just lost Mustang! There's just too many of them!" She glanced for a brief moment to her back and saw another enemy plane pursuing her and quickly turned watching her radar, seeing the enemy was in hot pursuit. She shouted to the rogue pilot, while she tried to maneuver her plane, "I can't shake him!" She flew ahead of the rogue pilot, while the bright flashes of enemy bullets continued to fly past her, and quickly turned around. Nicole said, "I'm about to lose him! Get ready!"

"If you're going to do something, now is the time!" the rogue pilot yelled back, while she continued to evade enemy attack, watching Nicole closing the distance towards her.

"Just get ready to bank on my mark!" Nicole answered.

"Okay!" the rogue pilot answered, waiting nervously for Nicole's signal.

Nicole timed the distance from the rogue pilot's plane, and shouted, "Break!" swinging her plane in one direction, while the rogue pilot went in the other direction, causing the enemy planes to crash into one another, falling into the skies in a burning heap of rubble.

10:47 HOURS. SOMEWHERE ON INTERSTATE 64 - RICHMOND, VIRGINA:

They watched the entire scene unfold, as the planes continued to battle for total supremacy of the skies, and were amazed at how Nicole and her wingman stave off the enemies' attacks.

"We need to make our move while those planes are distracted," Anton suggested.

10:50 HOURS. SOMEWHERE OVER INTERSTATE 64 - RICHMOND, VIRGINIA:

"This is Rhino to flight leader! What's your status? Over!"

"Viper Wing and myself are low on ordinance and fuel!"

"What are your orders, flight leader?"

"Continue to engage, while I maintain my visual on General West's location to provide support! Over!"

"What's your status, Rhino?"

"Our ordinance and fuel are almost depleted also. Don't know how much longer we can hold out! We'll try to maintain it as long as we can!"

"This is Black Jack to flight leader. Do you read?" the pilot said softly.

"This is flight leader," Nicole answered softly, knowing what the pilot was about to say from the soft tone in his voice.

"I know that you heard this before, but in case any of us don't make it back, I just want you to know that Lieutenant Kim taught you well, and he would be proud of you. You were the best I ever had the pleasure of working with. It was a pleasure serving with you, and in General West's command," the pilot said, listening to his alarms blaring, warning him that his fuel and ordinance were almost depleted.

"Don't say that. You will make it back. The fight is not over yet. We'll get through this," Nicole answered.

The rogue pilot closed her eyes, being suddenly overwhelmed by a sudden feeling of guilt and sadness, knowing that she had been the cause of so many lives being extinguished in an instant, as she listened quietly over her channel.

Nicole's eyes filled with tears, knowing that all of them were on the verge of paying the ultimate price, and continued, "In case I don't make it back, I just want you to know, the pleasure was all mine serving with you. All of you. But we can't worry about that now. This fight is far from over. We still have some fight left. General West and the others are depending on us. So, let's just do our jobs."

11:07 HOURS. SOMEWHERE ON INTERSTATE 64, A FEW MILES AWAY GLENROY ABANDONED AIRFIELD, WEST OF RICHMOND, VIRGINIA:

The group of transports began to make their way towards the abandoned base to take Adam to safety, while evading the enemy forces.

11:09 HOURS. SOMEWHERE OVER INTERSTATE 64 - RICHMOND, VIRGINIA:

As the intense air battle continued between the enemy forces, Nicole monitored her scanners, seeing her ammunition and fuel continue to deplete, and said to the rogue pilot, "My ordinance and fuel are almost depleted. How's your ordinance and fuel holding up?"

"I'm low on fuel as well. Just a few rounds. We need to hold out long enough to see your General to safety."

"Agreed. But just so you know, this doesn't change anything between us. I will kill you when this is over."

"As I said earlier, we can kill each other after we complete our objective. For now, let's complete the task at hand."

"Agreed. We need to keep these planes distracted for General West's sake. The future of the resistance depends on it," Nicole answered.

"Understood."

They heard their pilots' distress call, and flew high into the skies to engage the enemy planes to keep them distracted for General West and the remaining ground troops to escape. The battle continued to high above the clouds, while they continued their journey on the long stretch of the interstate.

CHAPTER 13: ROGUE.

The battle for the skies continued to wage with both factions being locked in merciless skirmish for total supremacy.

Nicole watched her fuel gauge and ammunition as it continued to deplete with every passing engagement. She radioed the rogue pilot and asked, "What's your ammunition count, Viper?"

"Just a few rounds of ammunition left. All my missiles are depleted. After that there's nothing I can do. What do you suggest that we do in the meantime?" she asked.

"There's only one thing that I can do," Nicole answered.

"I'm listening," the rogue pilot answered.

"This is flight leader to all planes. Come in, over."

"This is Bulldog!"

"This is Havoc!"

"This is Black Jack!"

"This is Vulcan!"

"This is Rhino!"

"This is Hyena! What are your orders, flight leader?"

"I'll play the decoy, while the rest of you engage, over!"

"Are you sure about this?" the rogue pilot asked.

"It's the only thing left to do at this point. Without any kind of ordinance, our planes are useless. And our job is to make sure that General West gets to safety. Even at the cost of our lives."

"Understood," the rogue pilot answered.

11:23 HOURS. SOMEWHERE ON INTERSTATE 95 - ARLINGTON, VIRGINIA:

They watched from the view of their transports as the war for total control of the skies continued to escalate, with them hearing the constant roar of the fighter jet engines flying over their positions.

11:24 HOURS. ENEMY COMMAND CENTER - PENTAGON, WASHINGTON, D.C., THE NATION'S CAPITAL:

"This is command to all wings. Give me a report, over."

11:24 HOURS. SOMEWHERE OVER INTERSTATE 95 - ARLINGTON, VIRGINIA:

"This is Cobra! Traitor craft is still being engaged, over!"

11:24 HOURS. ENEMY COMMAND CENTER - PENTAGON, WASHINGTON, D.C., THE NATION'S CAPITAL:

"Your orders are still the same. Engage and kill the traitor craft and all other enemy personnel. Do not leave the battle area until all enemies are neutralized. I repeat, do not leave the vicinity until all enemy personnel are neutralized," the General said.

11:25 HOURS. SOMEWHERE OVER INTERSTATE 95 - ARLINGTON, VIRGINIA:

One of the General's men stood and said softly, "We have some news, General."

"What news do you have?"

"We've received confirmation that our package is now coming from due west as we speak."

"What is the estimated time of arrival?"

"About an hour. 2 at the most."

"Excellent. Right on schedule," the General answered.

11:27 HOURS. SECURE LOCATION, SOMEWHERE IN RICHMOND, VIRGINIA:

"Dr. Weaver," Celina called out softly to Dr. Weaver.

"Yes, Celina?" he answered.

"I think we may have something."

"What did you find?"

"We've just intercepted a message from the Pentagon, mentioning something coming from due west. They called it "The Package," if I heard correctly."

"Package. The Package," Dr. Weaver said, repeating to himself, wondering what the message had meant, pondering deeply, until he put all the pieces together, finally decoding the message and saying, opening his eyes wide. "You did hear right."

"Do you have any idea what it means?" Celina asked.

"Yes. It's a way of describing a high valued hostage, or something of great value. My God. It's… It's my daughter being shipped from one facility into the capital. It has to be. I'm sure of it. Do you have a fix on their location?" he asked, with a sudden look of shock on his face.

"We're trying to get a fix on any radio frequency we can get, from the convoy."

"Good work. Try and see if you can give a live feed. I know it can be a little difficult. Let me know if anything else surfaces."

"Yes, Mr. President."

11:33 HOURS. SOMEWHERE OVER INTERSTATE 95 - ARLINGTON, VIRGINIA:

Nicole was down to her last few rounds of ammunition, with all her long range missiles completely depleted, and decided to put them to use, before the last stores of her fuel had become completely spent.

She was suddenly greeted with a heavy volley of machine gun fire ripping through the hull of her plane, severely damaging it, and skillfully flew vertically in the skies, maneuvering it, positioning herself behind the enemy plane, and unleashing the last of her heavy bullets, tearing through the enemy pilot's body, until the body of the enemy pilot slumped over the controls of the plane. It disintegrated into flames, and began to plummet to the surface, trailing the tell-tale signs of dark smoke, crashing and burning.

"This is Firefly to command! Are you receiving me? Over!"

11:33 HOURS. ENEMY COMMAND CENTER - PENTAGON, WASHINGTON, D.C., THE NATION'S CAPITAL:

"This is command. What is your status? Over."

11:34 HOURS. SOMEWHERE OVER INTERSTATE 95 - ARLINGTON, VIRGINIA:

"We've just lost Cobra! And the enemy flight leader is still combat-capable! Enemy flight leader still-" the enemy pilot yelled and was suddenly cut short.

11:35 HOURS. ENEMY COMMAND CENTER - PENTAGON, WASHINGTON, D.C., THE NATION'S CAPITAL:

The General and the others listened to the static on the other line of the transmission that was suddenly cut short, knowing that another one of his pilots had met their grim fate at the hands of the pilot turned traitor.

The other high-ranking officers simply watched one another in a state of disbelief, seeing the sheer will and courage of the freedom fighters, and how much they were willing to fight to the end.

11:36 HOURS. SOMEWHERE OVER INTERSTATE 95 - ARLINGTON, VIRGINIA:

The rogue pilot watched as the enemy pilot barrel rolled from the skies, trailing crimson flames and the tell-tale line of dark smoke, knowing what it meant, and said softly, with a hint of remorse, "I'm so sorry."

"That was a good kill," Nicole responded, knowing how difficult it was for the rogue pilot to engage one of her own planes.

"There's no need to celebrate yet. We still have a job to do."

"Understood," Nicole answered, when she suddenly came under heavy enemy fire, piercing through the plane's hull into the controls, setting the entire cockpit ablaze, and yelled, "I'm hit! I'm hit! I can't maintain control of my plane! Bailing out!"

She quickly pulled the ejection lever and saw the canopy of her plane flying off, with the ejection seat following in rapid succession, as the burning plane quickly plummeted, the cold winds blowing in her face. She remained trapped in her seat, breathing heavily in her mask, closing her eyes tightly. She had flashbacks to the years before in New Mexico and Fort Bragg, North Carolina, reliving the moments when she was seriously wounded from an enemy bullet that tore through her leg, causing her to eject from her plane, while on the brink of unconsciousness, after losing so much blood, and quickly came back to her senses,watching her plane descend to the surface in flames trailing smoke, while she remained helpless dangling from her parachute, slowly descending towards the surface.

The rogue pilot watched as Nicole made her slow descent towards the surface, and took a quick glance at her fuel gauge, knowing that she may have to do the same.

11:37 HOURS. SOMEWHERE ON INTERSTATE 95 - ARLINGTON, VIRGINIA:

Janet saw the parachute falling from the skies and said to Jacqueline, "Look."

"What is it?" Janet asked.

"A parachute."

"Who do you think it could be?" Jacqueline asked.

"It's one of ours. It's her. I know it's her. She made the call before she bailed out."

"What are you going to do? She put her ass on the line for us. We can't leave her out there."

Jacqueline grabbed the radio and said, "We have a visual on flight leader. Moving in for pick up."

Brian peeped outside and saw the parachute falling from the skies and said, "I know where that is. It's not too far from where we're going."

"Okay," Janet answered.

"Let's just hope there won't be any enemy roadblocks."

"What about support?" Jacqueline asked.

"If we radio for support, they might get a fix on our location. And we don't have enough numbers to hold off another enemy ground assault."

11:38 HOURS. SOMEWHERE OVER INTERSTATE 95 - ARLINGTON, VIRGINIA:

The rogue pilot suddenly came under attack by one of her former allies until her plane suddenly caught ablaze. She quickly ejected, while remaining intact to her seat, spiraling uncontrollably into the skies, feeling the violent turbulence of the frigid winds against her face and body while struggling to regain control. Her eyes closed tightly, and the heavy sounds of her breaths filled the tight confines of her mask, while she remained strapped in her seat, when her parachute suddenly opened, rapidly slowing her descent to the surface.

"This is Python to command. Over."

11:38 HOURS. ENEMY COMMAND CENTER - PENTAGON, WASHINGTON, D.C., THE NATION'S CAPITAL:

"This is command. What is your status? Over."

11:38 HOURS. SOMEWHERE OVER INTERSTATE 95 - ARLINGTON, VIRGINIA:

"Traitor craft has been neutralized. I repeat, traitor craft has been neutralized."

11:38 HOURS. ENEMY COMMAND CENTER - PENTAGON, WASHINGTON, D.C., THE NATION'S CAPITAL:

"Do you have a visual on any survivors? Over," the General asked in suspense.

11:39 HOURS. SOMEWHERE OVER INTERSTATE 95 - ARLINGTON, VIRGINIA:

"Affirmative. I have a visual. What are your orders? Over."

11:40 HOURS. ENEMY COMMAND CENTER - PENTAGON, WASHINGTON, D.C., THE NATION'S CAPITAL:

"Your orders are to engage. You are to tear the traitor pilot to pieces before she hits the ground, over."

11:40 HOURS. SOMEWHERE OVER INTERSTATE 95 - ARLINGTON, VIRGINIA:

As the rogue pilot slowly descended to the surface, still strapped to her seat, she saw an enemy plane racing towards her on its attack run to engage her, as she watched helplessly.

The enemy plane lined up its sight, switching to its machine guns, taking aim at her parachute, when a missile suddenly exploded into it, leaving her to continue her slow descent to the surface unharmed. She watched the plane that saved her from her ultimate demise flying over her position, as she slowly continued her descent, taking a deep sigh of relief, as she continued to slowly plummet to the surface, strapped in her parachute.

11:40 HOURS. SOMEWHERE IN ARLINGTON, VIRGINIA:

Nicole had landed safely, and looked all around her trying to find her bearings, and saw a parachute falling to the surface, unable to tell friend from foe.

11:40 HOURS. SOMEWHERE ON INTERSTATE 95 – ARLINGTON, VIRGINIA:

"Look. Another one," Jacqueline said, pointing to the skies, watching the other parachute making its descent from the skies.

"When it rains, it pours," Janet answered.

"Maintain course. We'll find out who that other pilot is," Brian added.

11:41 HOURS. ENEMY COMMAND CENTER - PENTAGON, WASHINGTON, D.C., THE NATION'S CAPITAL:

"The traitor pilot is still alive, sir," one of his senior officers said.

"How is that even possible?"

"Our plane was engaged before it could get a lock on the target, sir."

"Where was the traitor pilot's last location?"

"We're tracing her signal. It's somewhere in Arlington, sir."

"How far is the convoy with the package?"

"Somewhere on Interstate 66, heading into Arlington, as we speak, sir."

"And what of the asset? Where is he?" the General asked.

"He's somewhere in the area as well. Still moving at an incredible pace towards our position a few miles from where the traitor pilot is still transmitting."

The General grabbed the receiver and said, "Attention all units. We are in pursuit of the traitor pilot and 0-7 who have gone rogue. You are ordered to engage all rogue agents on sight with extreme prejudice. I repeat, terminate all rogue agents with extreme prejudice, And, bring 0-7 back to me dead or alive. Good luck to you all," he said, turning off the radio, and softly added, "Because you'll need it."

11:43 HOURS. SOMEWHERE ON INTERSTATE 66, HEADING INTO ARLINGTON, VIRGINIA:

Kassandra sat quietly in the transport, dressed neatly in her usual gleaming white lab coat, guarded tightly by the General's heavy security detail of elite and heavily armed soldiers. She heard the radio chatter from the General's voice issuing orders to terminate all the rogue subjects, with the troops responding to him, causing her face to turn into a sudden look of shock, knowing that something had gone awry.

11:43 HOURS. SECURE LOCATION, SOMEWHERE IN RICHMOND, VIRGINIA:

"I think we found something, Mr. President," Celina said softly.

"What is it?" Dr. Weaver asked eagerly.

"We've just intercepted a transmission. A pair to be exact."

"From where?"

"One from the Pentagon. And the other from Interstate 66. My guess is the convoy carrying one of the assets, which is believed to be your daughter, sir. They also said something about pursuing a traitor pilot to be eliminated on sight, and 0-7 going rogue and wanted dead or alive. I get the part about the traitor pilot. But who or what exactly is 0-7?" Celina asked.

"0-7?" Dr. Weaver said in surprise.

"Yes. If my hearing didn't fail me, that's what I heard. Does that mean anything?"

"That means it's about to get messy. Very messy."

"What do you mean, sir?"

"0-7 is the code name for the government's deadliest assassin."

"Really?" she asked, with her face suddenly awestruck.

"And if what you're telling me about him going rogue is true, then, no matter how big the clean-up crew is, it won't be enough to clean up the number of dead bodies that he'll be leaving in his wake. He was the youngest and most decorated marine in the entire corp. Even surpassing the General in medals, himself. Don't let his calm demeanor fool you. Beneath that calm exterior is a killing machine. He's proven to be a natural born leader. Even more efficient than the General himself. Which is why he was chosen by the General over all the others to lead the unit. During my stay on Genesis, the General had introduced us, and told me that he was looking into making him into an elite 7-man team. He was the last to complete the squad. And when North Korea invaded the South, uniting the entire Korean Peninsula under their repressive rule like they tried in 1950, even the Chinese warned their former ally to stop the invasion. So out of retaliation, they waited until our forces met with the Chinese and launched a series of coordinated attacks on the Chinese air force bases, wiping out a number of their forces, bringing their army less than half strength. Some of our troops were also stationed there. We both suffered a lot of casualties, but the Chinese had suffered more. It was very strategic how the North Koreans thought out and executed their plans against their former ally. The Chinese never saw that coming. From that point on, the press dubbed it The Shattered Alliance, being decades of peace had just been shattered in an instant, after the Americans and Chinese had separated the Korean Peninsula under their separate rules, after the Korean War in 1950. So, left with no other alternatives, the Chinese became our allies. The attack had instilled so much fear in China's other allies, that even they didn't want to spear troops for an assault on the North Koreans."

"Okay, but where does this 0-7 fit in all this?" Celina asked.

"From that point, the mission to liberate South Korea became a suicide one. They were desperate for revenge on the former ally, the Chinese General, and this power hungry dictator of ours turned to him for answers."

"So that's what happened during the war? I was just in my teens when it happened," Celina replied.

"Then a few days later, despite being outnumbered by more than 20 to 1, they were able to thwart the North Koreans, and place the entire peninsula under southern rule. And after that came the uprising on Genesis, and from there our civil war on the mainland. And after the General rose to power, he charged 0-7 for treason, but had other plans for him instead."

"What plans?"

"He and my daughter were captured. And they did this to him," Dr. Weaver said, pausing.

"Did what?"

"They wiped out his memories. All of them. They turned him into the killing machine he now is, and used him to snuff out the other lieutenants in General West's resistance. In our resistance. Now, all that's left to do is to eliminate General West himself, to crush the entire resistance, once and for all, and he was just that close. Unfortunately for them, that was the biggest mistake they made, because it looks like that mistake came back to haunt them, with him leaving a trail of bodies all across the state. And he hasn't even started."

"My God," Celina answered, with a sudden look of shock on her face.

"Someday, I'll tell you all you need to know. But for now, let's see what happens. Because from this point, a lot more of the General's bodies are about to pile up. Just watch."

"My God."

"That's a good way to put it. Because God won't be able to do anything for them. God would have mercy, but 0-7 won't. I can promise you that much," Dr. Weaver said.

"Is he as good as you say he is?"

"I guess you'll have to wait and see. From the looks of it, he's about to show us."

11:46 HOURS. SOMEWHERE IN ARLINGTON, VIRGINIA:

The rogue pilot had landed, with her parachute trapped in the branches of the trees at her location, and quickly struggled to free herself from the straps before the enemy troops could close in on her position.

She looked in the skies and saw the planes still battling each other for control and looked all around her, trying to get her sense of direction, and ran towards the coordinates of Nicole's last location using all the parked vehicles and other obstacles strewn on the streets that she could find to avoid enemy detection, until she arrived at the exact coordinates, looking all around searching for Nicole, and was suddenly attacked from behind.

With the fighting for aerial supremacy continuing to ensue high above their position, they continued to exchange blows, tumbling vigorously on the snow-filled earth, until they became separated, drawing their sidearms, them at each other's faces.

"Who are you?" Nicole asked, breathing heavily, trying to catch her breath from her brief scuffle with the rogue pilot.

"That look in your eyes," the rogue pilot answered.

"What about it?" Nicole answered.

"It's a look I've seen too many times to not know what it means."

"What do you mean?"

"I think you know exactly what I mean. I think we both know that you know who I am. Your eyes are bearing witness against you."

"I'm not here to go biblical on my eyes or any of my body parts bearing witness against me or anybody else. But if it makes you feel any better, I recognize your voice. You're the Viper. You're the one who led the attack against us. Our ships are now at the bottom of the ocean because of you, along with a number of good servicemen and women."

"Among other things, unfortunately. And you're the Comet. And I would like to say that I'm very pleased to finally meet you. Just not under those circumstances at least, pointing guns in each other's faces."

"Not that you left me or any one of us with a choice."

"I wasn't left with much of a choice, either."

"Really? If there's one thing I do know about vipers, is that you can raise and feed them, but they'll still come back to bite you. And for the amount of people that you've killed today alone, I can tell that your venom is the most lethal. Which goes without saying that snakes have no loyalty. From the looks of it, we would know. After all, you turned against your master, didn't you?"

"We are all vipers to a certain degree, my friend. When self-preservation comes knocking, we are forced to take whatever measures to survive. Even if it means going against our own, or going against the codes that make us who we are."

"I beg to differ, and I'm not your friend. And I should just kill you right now," Nicole said sharply.

"As should I. So, here's a thought. Either we can work together to survive this, or we can pump holes into each other. The choice is entirely yours. But the fact remains that I have valuable information that your resistance can use, that can change your fortunes in this war."

"You just killed your own. Who's to say that you won't do the same to me? How do I know that I can trust you?" Nicole asked.

"I see that look in your eyes again. I think we both know the answer to that. The answer to the question is, where else can I go? And if I go back, we both know what'll happen to me, and I'm not prepared to face my maker. yet. So, as I said earlier, it's either we can kill each other right here and now, or put our differences aside, at least, for the time being, and work together. After all, I almost became easy pickings dangling from the end of my parachute trying to find you."

"And I guess that's where I say it suits you right. I'm Nicole. Nicole Matheson," Nicole said, shrugging her shoulders.

"I'm Wells. Nina Wells. But I still can't say whether or not I'm pleased to meet you, especially under these circumstances pointing guns at each other. But I'll take what I can get at this point."

"I'm just curious. Why did you do it?"

"Do what?" Nina asked.

"I see that look in your eyes. It's a look that I've seen too many times to not know what it is. Your eyes are bearing witness against you. I think you know exactly what I'm talking about."

"Touché. Well played. That was a nice throwback. Since the both of us have gotten somewhat religious towards each other, I take it that we're getting off to a good start."

"I suppose we are. But I wouldn't get too comfortable if I were you," Nicole said in caution.

"To answer your question, the way I see it is that no one or any mission is worth more than my life. And when I'm ordered to sacrifice myself, or be used or discarded like I was nothing, doesn't sit too well with me. I'm a living breathing life form. A human being. Not a machine or something that you use and toss away like the General thinks we are. And because of that, there may be a lot more people from the other side that may come to be sympathetic to your cause. Of that I have no doubt. Beginning with myself and 0-7, as he's so-called. Just so you know, I'm not proud of the course that I've taken. But I've lived under the rule of tyranny for a little too long now. And the rest is personal. Are you satisfied?"

"Can't say I am. But I'll roll with it if that's all I can get."

"Also, I would like to commend you on your skills. You would've made a worthy adversary over the course of all these campaigns."

"The feeling is mutual, though I wished that I'd killed you earlier."

"Now that we have that out of the way, I need to tell you the enemy knows the coordinates of my last position, but I'm sure that you already know that. So, it's safe to say that we should get moving, preferably with us not pointing guns at each other's faces."

"Don't know if I can do that. Vipers strike when you least expect."

"I assure you that won't be the case."

"I see that look in your eyes that you're telling the truth. The thing is, I don't know if my colleagues will believe it."

"I think that we'll find out, one way or another. Not that I have a choice in the matter. The way I see it is either way, I'm screwed. I just prefer taking my chances on the other side."

"Considering the amount of people that you've placed at the bottom of the ocean today alone, and those without a pulse all over the country, I doubt that either side you take will make a difference."

"Well, I suppose that you'll have to use your rank to persuade them otherwise, since General West is indisposed at the moment, flight leader."

"No thanks to your mindless pet, I might add."

"He's not entirely to be blamed for it. And we both know that."

"I suppose not."

"But if it makes you feel any better, he's on his way to kill the General at this very moment."

"What do you mean?" Nicole asked in surprise.

"Why do you think that he was isolating the target so you wouldn't have any friendly fire?"

A sudden look of awe took over Nicole's face, causing her to ponder on the strange course of events that took place while providing air support for their ground units.

"Not only was I asked to sacrifice myself to kill General West, I was also asked to kill him in the process. And believe me when I say that he heard it loud and clear too, and that didn't sit well with either of us. I guess you missed that part of the radio chatter, didn't you?"

The other transports carrying the remainder of the freedom fighters had arrived at their location. They immediately disembarked. and quickly surrounded Nina, pointing their guns to her face.

Nina knelt, slowly placing her sidearm on the snow-covered ground, and placed her hands at the back of her head, interlocking her fingers in total surrender, waiting for Nicole to intervene. Jacqueline ran towards her, pressing the nozzle of her rifle firmly to the back of her head and said, "Let's put a bullet in her head and call it a day."

Nicole slowly walked towards Nina's sidearm, and picked it up from the ground, looking into her eyes, sensing her sincerity, while Nina stared back and said, "Wait."

"What do you mean wait?" Janet asked. "She killed thousands of us today alone. She's the enemy."

"I know that. But she has valuable intel that could change the course of this war. We can't get any intel from her if we kill her."

"Do you believe this bitch? She's trying to bide her time!" Jill shouted

"Today, I saw an enemy become an ally. And after seeing that, I believe that I'm willing to believe that anything is possible."

"Are you fucking stupid?" Kathy asked.

"I have an idea. Why don't we get all the information we can get, and put a bullet in her head, anyway," Jacqueline asked, pressing the muzzle of her rifle firmly against the back of Nina's head, jerking it.

Nina looked at Karen bowing her head towards the snowy ground, retching and said, "Ahh, morning sickness. Trust me, I would know."

"What? What do you mean, morning sickness?" Brian asked in shock.

"None of your business, bitch. Just an upset stomach," Karen answered.

"If I'm not mistaken, I'd say that you're lying. Assuming that you didn't get pregnant on your own. Why don't you tell your significant other what's really happening to you? Or better yet, why don't you make him feel the swelling in your breasts, assuming that he already made good use of them in your tender moments of pleasure. You've gained weight, and your face is pale, but there's that glow in your cheeks and your skin. The morning sickness, and constant cravings. The signs are all there," Nina said looking at Karen.

"What's she talking about, Karen?" Brian asked with a sudden look of shock on his face.

"I found out this morning at the base," Karen replied.

"And I had to find out this way?" Brian replied.

"I didn't want to worry you. Besides, I thought the war was over. We all did. I was waiting for the right time to tell you. I'm sorry you had to find out this way. Damn you, bitch," Karen answered.

"Oh," Brian answered softly, still in shock.

"How could you put me on the spot like that?" Karen asked.

"I didn't mean to," Nina answered, and added, "You see, the thing is that you have a new addition to the resistance. And it won't do any of us good if we get intercepted by the enemy. They won't care if you're pregnant or not. For all they know, a pregnant woman is a threat, because she is the one carrying the next future resistance fighter, or leader, or what have you. And it won't matter whether or not it's true. All they want is blood. And they'll stop at nothing to get it."

"Then why the fuck did you turn?" Janet asked.

"That's a good question," Jill added.

"With good reason," Nina answered.

"We're listening," Frank asked.

"The thing is that both of us came across a transmission that specifically stated that I'm supposed to kill this drone, or 0-7, or whatever you call him, and sacrifice myself in order to kill General West to end your precious resistance once and for all. And I had a problem with that. I still do actually, because I'm not ready to go just yet. And as I said, no mission is more important than my life. And to add insult to injury, I don't have anything to show for all my accomplishments fighting for the General."

"No shit. Join the club," Anton answered.

"Needless to say that General West's would-be assassin heard the conversation between myself and yours truly, and from what I saw, he wasn't too happy about it either. So, it propelled him to launch his own personal crusade to fight his one-man war against the one man that turned into my enemy from that moment. Why do you think he was isolating the targets? It was to avoid friendly fire."

"That was a close call, to be fair," Janet answered.

"It's strange how the others don't share your enthusiasm," Nina said to Janet.

"Don't get it twisted, bitch," Janet answered, squeezing the muzzle of her rifle to Nina's temple.

"I'm not. But, I do know this - other than myself, you know that you can afford to have the 0-7 as a very valuable ally, since we're on the same side. His skills are second to none, and judging from the heavy bruises on your faces, and the few times that he's let you live, you know I'm telling the truth. He could've wiped all of you out, just like that. Like you were nothing. Then again, you were nothing."

"Then why didn't he?" Nicole asked.

"Because he simply didn't want to. He wanted to make you feel what it was like to be hunted. It was just his way of telling you that fighting you would be wasting his time. You simply were not worth killing, like General West was. Or still is. Now that's a man worth killing, considering how long he has survived all these attacks, don't you agree?"

"I hate to say it, but she has a point. I've been bitch slapped by this guy for quite some time now, and I'm still breathing. and I speak for all the others when I say that," Janet replied.

"But I still say let's put a hole in her head when we're done," Jacqueline added.

"Since you're still eager to put a bullet in my head, let me add that if anything happens to me, the 0-7 will pay you a personal visit. And if you think what happened to your other lieutenants was something, wait until he pays you another personal visit. And this time, we all know it won't be good.

Whatever happened to you previously will be welcomed compared to what he will do to all of you this time. Him saving your lives all the times that your paths were crossed is as friendly as he will ever get. And this time, being bitch slapped will be the least of your worries," Nina concluded watching their bodies slump in worry, after fooling them into saving her life.

"But, I still say we put a bullet in her head. How would he know it was us?" Jacqueline answered.

"Hold it, Chan!" Nicole intervened.

"She's not one of us!" Jacqueline answered.

"I said hold it! That's an order!" Nicole yelled. "She was ordered to kill General West, but she didn't."

"Just like she was ordered to kill all those people on the carrier fleet," Brian replied.

"Believe me, there's nothing more that I want than to pump a few holes inside her right now. But, I do know for a fact, that captured enemies can provide valuable information."

"Well, she did save General West, and in doing so, she gave our resistance a second chance. I suppose that counts for something," Anton added.

"So what do we do with her in the meantime?" Matthew asked.

"For now, tie her up and take General West to somewhere safe, and tend to his wound," Nicole answered.

"The old base is not far from here. About a mile and a half," Brian answered.

They loaded Nina in the back of the transport and headed to the abandoned base, hoping they wouldn't be intercepted by any enemy forces.

After moments of engaging the enemy forces on the interstate, the assassin drove quietly through the city, when he and Jason were suddenly ambushed by a number of rebels, greeting them with a hail of bullets from the cover of all the decaying vehicles parked in the streets.

The assassin calmly walked out of the transport through the thick hail of machine gun fire, climbing through the back, after still being greeted with an endless barrage of machine gun fire, tearing through the fabric that lined the rear of the transport, and suddenly stopped.

The streets suddenly grew silent, after the sounds of spent shells casings falling on the streets from every direction.

Jason remained lying on the front seat, completely covered in shards of broken glass from the shattered windows of the transport, peeped slightly through the window, and saw a number of resistance fighters closing in on his position. He quickly bowed his head, hoping that he wouldn't be spotted.

The freedom fighters slowly walked towards the truck with their weapons drawn, and were suddenly greeted with a hail of bullets from the rear, wiping out a number of soldiers within mere seconds of his ambush.

He climbed from the back of the truck with a giant cartridge filled with ammunition strapped to his back, the spinning turret of a gatling gun gripped tightly in the heated grip of his palm. He quickly decimating the number of the remaining soldiers, while he continued to walk through the hail of bullets from the resistance fighters who fought back valiantly against the awesome firepower that he wielded.

While he continued exchanging against the resistance fighters through the blinding exchange of gunfire, one the bullets struck the armor plate that protected his chest, temporarily pushing him off balance, damaging the tracking device lodged deeply within his sternum, instantly causing it to stop transmitting.

11:57 HOURS. ENEMY COMMAND CENTER - PENTAGON, WASHINGTON, D.C., THE NATION'S CAPITAL:

"General," Maxwell called out softly.

"What's the situation?" the General asked.

"It's 0-7, sir."

"What's going on?"

"His tracking beacon just went offline."

"What do you mean?"

"He was still for just a moment, and it just went offline."

"I watched her place that tracking beacon inside him myself. How is that even possible?"

"We have no way of tracking him now. He could be anywhere. He could be right under our noses, and we wouldn't even know."

"Yes, we would. All we have to do is wait," the General replied.

"How do you mean?"

"You'll see. Split the convoy into two teams. Send a team to where the coordinates of the traitor were last tracked, and the other where our asset was last transmitted. In the meantime, radio for more reinforcements to his position. He's a greater priority at this point."

12:04 HOURS. SOMEWHERE IN ARLINGTON, VIRGINIA:

The enemy convoy continued to drive on the long stretch of the interstate, with Kassandra seated among them under heavy security detail, as she listened quietly to the radio chatter of the General's high-ranking officers relaying orders to the other soldiers. They continued driving through the snowy streets, until they stumbled upon Nina's parachute trapped in the branches of a tree. They picked up her headgear, bearing the bold insignia of the dreaded viper, and noticed a fresh set of footprints, and boarded their transports, following the signal of her tracking beacon towards the direction of the abandoned base.

12:15 HOURS. ARLINGTON VIRGINIA AIR FORCE BASE - ARLINGTON, VIRGINIA:

They had arrived at the abandoned base and gently lifted Adam's wounded body from the truck, rushing him into the abandoned building, when Brian said, "Stop. We can't go inside."

"Why?" Nicole asked.

"Maybe it's just me, but they may be onto her, and they'll kick that door in for sure."

"But we need to take General West somewhere," Nicole answered.

Brian walked through the snow and saw the large metal cover of the manhole, and said, "Here we go. We go in there."

"How do you know this place so well?" Janet asked.

"When I was a student doctor, this was one of the places that I came to practice with the other senior medics. Needless to say, it was before the war."

They quickly opened the hatch of the sewer and climbed down into the dark hole with Adam's wounded body, hoping to evade enemy capture.

Frank drove the truck over the opening and climbed down the long dark hole, sealing the hatch behind them with the thick metal cover, and waited silently and nervously, with their weapons drawn.

12:16 HOURS. ENEMY COMMAND CENTER - PENTAGON, WASHINGTON, D.C., THE NATION'S CAPITAL:

"General we've lost the signal of the traitor pilot."

"Where was her last position?"

"We were able to track near an old, abandoned base in Arlington. A few miles from where she landed."

12:18 HOURS. SOMEWHERE IN ARLINGTON, VIRGINIA:

The battle between the lone assassin and the resistance fighters continued to wage in the streets while he continued to suppress their attacks with the awesome might of his firepower.

The projectiles from the assassin's awesome weapon flew across the streets, and tore through the vehicles, triggering a series of explosions.

Jason peeped from the passenger seat of the truck, and saw the carnage that the assassin had left in his wake, in just a few moments, with a sudden look of shock.

The assassin caught a mere glimpse of a few people running into a building from the view of his peripheral vision, and followed the trail of footsteps embedded deeply in the snow, until he came to a thick, wooden door. He immediately opened fire with a lethal volley of rounds, tearing through the wooden door and walls.

He kicked the door open and slowly walked into the old decrepit structure, stopping dead in his tracks, seeing all the corpses of the innocent civilians that lay at his feet, lifeless in pools of their own blood, causing him to be slowly consumed by a strange and alien feeling of remorse.

A young girl suddenly arose from beneath the pile of corpses, completely drenched in their blood and in deep shock from the ghastly events. She saw his sidearm being pointed to her face, and stared deeply into the cold and empty stare of his eyes, while he continued to pause, slowly pulling away the gear that concealed the brown skin of his entire face, that shielded it from the bitter cold, watching her face all covered in the blood of her loved ones, when the sudden image of a young woman's battered face suddenly flashed vividly in his mind. He contemplated deeply, his face slowly creasing with a sudden look of confusion, as the image of the young woman continued to torment his memory, while the frightened child continued standing before him, waiting for fate to deal its final blow.

Jason slowly walked through the streets among all the dead corpses of the resistance fighters, heading in the direction of the assassin, until he came across the old decrepit structure of a building with its door and walls completely riddled with bullet holes. He slowly walked inside, only to be greeted by the heavy stench of gun smoke filling the dark confines of the sanctuary, and saw the assassin standing before the frightened child, who remained still, completely frozen with terror.

He looked at all the bodies lying on the floor, with a frantic look on his face and said softly, "My God. What did you do?"

He watched the mixed emotions of confusion and remorse on the assassin's face, as he tried to make sense of the images that continued to haunt his memories and said, "I've seen that look more times than I care to remember. You remembered something, didn't you? It's all coming back to you, isn't it?"

He watched the frightened child and said, "She's just a child. She poses no threat. Let's just leave before the others get here."

The other half of the enemy convoy had arrived near the assassin's location, and disembarked from their transports. stepping into the streets, and saw the carnage that greeted them. They slowly trekked through the pile of corpses of the resistance fighters sprawled all about, and saw the set of footprints that led to the decrepit foundations of the sanctuary, until they stumbled upon a wooden door and walls, riddled with countless bullet holes.

"Please Lieutenant," Jason begged, and added, "For ten long years, I've had to stand idly by and watch you kill your friends. But a helpless child? There's no honor in this. That's not what we are. That's not who you are. Please!" he concluded loudly.

An enemy soldier slowly walked into the sanctuary, and saw a number of dead bodies on the floor in pools of their own blood and broke all radio silence, calling their chain of command.

12:30 HOURS. ENEMY COMMAND CENTER – WASHINGTON, D.C., THE NATION'S CAPITAL:

"General, 0-7 has been spotted."

"Where?"

"Somewhere in Arlington, sir. It appears he was engaged by some of General West's men during his travels."

"If our asset is still alive, then he's the one who engaged them. No one who has engaged our asset has lived to tell the tale. Maybe, except General West, or anyone else not worth the time and effort," the General said.

"There's another report from our troops in the area, sir," Maxwell said.

"Speak," the General said firmly.

"Our troops just reported that he just snuffed out an entire sanctuary filled with civilians."

"Any survivors?" the General asked.

"Yes. A little girl," Maxwell answered.

The General grabbed the radio and said, "This is the General to all available personnel in the area. You are authorized to eliminate any survivors at your current location. I repeat, eliminate all targets at your current location." He placed the radio down, watching the faces of his high-ranking officers and said, "I take no pleasure doing this. But right now, my main objective is to make sure that there can be no form of future resistance of any kind."

"Yes, General," Maxwell answered, softly in total submission, with his allegiance to the General slowly beginning to wane.

12:31 HOURS. SOMEWHERE IN ARLINGTON, VIRGINIA:

The enemy soldier received orders and said to the assassin, "You are ordered to eliminate the target," while he remained frozen in front of the child, his sidearm pointed to her face, while the images from his past continued to torment his memories.

Sensing the worst, Jason immediately placed his hand on his sidearm in defense of the helpless child, hoping he won't have to use it.

The enemy soldier pulled his sidearm from his holster, causing the assassin to slowly shift his focus towards him, and point his sidearm to the enemy soldier's temple. He pulled the trigger, causing Jason to immediately take a sigh of relief, seeing that there was still some humanity left inside him, and that he wouldn't have to face the impossible task of engaging him in combat, knowing that he would face sudden death.

After the shot rang out loudly within the dark confines of the sanctuary, exploding into the temple of the enemy soldier, completely sweeping him off his feet, the other enemy soldiers ran inside to investigate, and were swiftly engaged by the assassin, using the deadly skills of hand-to-hand combat at his disposal, quickly disposing them.

12:36 HOURS. ARLINGTON VIRGINIA AIR FORCE BASE - ARLINGTON, VIRGINIA:

The other half of the convoy had arrived at the location where they last picked up Nina's signal within the vicinity of the abandoned base, and looked at the tire tracks imprinted in the deep snow, noticing they were fresh, and followed them.

12:38 HOURS. SOMEWHERE IN ARLINGTON, VIRGINIA:

After the assassin left the enemy soldiers lying lifeless on the floor among all the corpses of the civilians, a young woman who suffered great shock from her near brush with death, after the tragedy that had befallen the sanctuary ran forward, grabbing the frightened child, holding her tightly, shielding her with her back facing the assassin's sidearm, while she remained helpless with her face all covered in blood.

She looked into the assassin's eyes, while he maintained his cold and distant stare at the frightened child, and the other corpses of the enemy soldiers lying on the cold floors of the sanctuary and asked, "Who the hell are you people? You just walked into houses, and murder people indiscriminately?"

"He's not going to hurt you," Jason answered.

She looked all around her seeing all the lifeless corpses and answered, "You sure about that? Could've had me fooled. Look all around you and tell me what you see."

"I know this may not bring any comfort to you. But it was an honest mistake. He thought these people were enemy soldiers. He didn't mean for any of this to happen."

"And that makes me feel all warm and fuzzy inside, doesn't it?" she said, switching her focus to the assassin, watching him strap the cartridge filled with heavy bullets to his back and turning abruptly to exit into the streets that remained consumed with death, and immediately opened fire on the remaining convoy of enemy soldiers, quickly decimating their numbers.

A soldier broke radio silence while being engaged by the assassin and called out for reinforcements during the firefight.

12:40 HOURS. ENEMY COMMAND CENTER - PENTAGON, WASHINGTON, D.C., THE NATION'S CAPITAL:

The General and the others received the distress call, and listening to the machine gun fire in the background, answered, "This is command! What's status? Respond!"

12:40 HOURS. SOMEWHERE IN ARLINGTON, VIRGINIA:

"It's 0-7! We're being engaged! I repeat, we're being engaged by the-" the dying soldier said, while meeting his demise.

12:40 HOURS. ENEMY COMMAND CENTER - PENTAGON, WASHINGTON, D.C., THE NATION'S CAPITAL:

"Respond! Respond! What is your status? Over!" the General asked, only to be met with static on the other end of the transmission, knowing what the outcome was.

12:43 HOURS. ARLINGTON VIRGINIA AIR FORCE BASE - ARLINGTON, VIRGINIA:

The enemy convoy continued driving until they saw the other transports belonging to the freedom fighters, completely battered, and climbed from their vehicles, walking towards them to investigate, following a set of footprints in the snow. They received a call from the General to abandon their search for the fugitives and pursue the assassin.

The freedom fighters listened nervously to the enemy soldiers walking about on the surface while hiding underground, and breathed sighs of relief, listening to them pulling out, after receiving their orders from the General.

While Kassandra remained seated under heavy security detail, she heard the General issuing his orders to head to the designated area, where the assassin was last spotted, sensing that something tragic had happened to the other troops while on mission.

12:45 HOURS. ENEMY COMMAND CENTER - PENTAGON, WASHINGTON, D.C., THE NATION'S CAPITAL:

"The other half of the convoy is headed to his current position."

"How long will it take them?" the General asked.

"They'll be there in the next half hour. Give or take."

"Let's hope they don't get there too late," the General said softly.

12:45 HOURS. SECURE LOCATION, SOMEWHERE IN RICHMOND, VIRGINIA:

"They keep mentioning something about being engaged by "The Drone." Does that mean anything? Is this making any sense to you?" Celina asked.

"It's 0-7. 0-7 is the Drone who has gone rogue. He is the one who is causing all this mayhem. He goes by a number of names, I'm afraid. And what you heard was only a couple," Dr. Weaver said.

"My God," Celina answered with a sudden look of shock on her face. "But why do they call him that?"

"The name is most appropriate for someone who was captured, lobotomized, controlled, and used to wipe out most of his entire former unit with no shred of remorse, and now he's engaging the enemy, so I think it's safe to say that the Drone has officially gone rogue. You're perfectly aware of all the lives lost in this civil war, aren't you?" he asked.

"Yes, Mr. President," Celina replied.

"Well, it's nothing compared to what's about to happen, now that he's been unleashed. There's about to be a trail of bodies all over this state. Even all over this country, the likes of which you have never seen. And he hasn't even begun yet. I hope you have a strong stomach. Because you'll need it. I know I will."

Celina simply watched Dr. Weaver with a look of shock on her face.

12:48 HOURS. SOMEWHERE IN ARLINGTON, VIRGINIA:

The assassin walked through the streets, filled with more corpses from dead enemy soldiers, who had joined the numbers of resistance fighters.

Jason searched through the enemy transports to salvage whatever means of escape he could find from all the damage that he had unleashed from his attacks, and said, "Everything has been shot to hell."

They heard the sound of the next enemy convoy approaching from afar and hid behind one of the armored transports.

The enemy soldiers slowly stepped out of their transports into the streets filled with death, checking the long trail of corpses of their allies and foes alike.

After checking all the bodies of the soldiers that littered the streets in search of the assassin, they were greeted by a sudden barrage of machine gun fire, until all the assassin's rounds were depleted, alarming Kassandra inside the truck, painting the grim realization of what had happened to those who came before.

12:49 HOURS. ENEMY COMMAND CENTER - PENTAGON, WASHINGTON, D.C., THE NATION'S CAPITAL:

The General's high-ranking officers continued to look at the screen, seeing a number of tracking beacons that within just seconds after another, staring at one another with looks of shock on their faces.

"What's wrong?" the General asked.

"The entire convoy has been wiped out, sir. They're all gone. The only one left is the asset and his subordinate, Sergeant White."

The General grabbed the radio and said, "Attention all units. We have a situation. Code Red. I repeat we have a situation, Code Red. 0-7 has gone rogue and is now considered hostile, and completely dangerous, and is now responsible for the deaths of a number of my troops. You are ordered to engage on sight. Subject is to be terminated on sight. I repeat, the subject is to be terminated on sight, with extreme prejudice, and secure the asset at all costs."

He placed the radio on the desk and said, "Even after all these years, my demons have finally come back to torment me. I always knew this day would come. Was just a matter of when. And now, it finally has."

12:50 HOURS. SECURE LOCATION, SOMEWHERE IN RICHMOND, VIRGINIA:

Celina heard the radio chatter from the dying enemy soldiers screaming, and said, with a look of shock on her face, "My God. He did it again. He killed them like they were nothing."

"Which means that he's all alone with my daughter, and he's the only one standing in their way of taking her prisoner," Dr. Weaver said.

CHAPTER 14: THE ROGUE AND THE PACKAGE.

13:04 HOURS. SOMEWHERE IN ARLINGTON, VIRGINIA:

After his ammunition was completely spent, the assassin quickly rummaged through all the corpses of the enemy soldiers sprawled across the streets to replenish his supplies.

He looked at one of the transports, and noticed a tiny space through its door and slowly walked towards it, his weapon drawn. He swung it open, and quickly stepped back, seeing Kassandra seated in the vehicle. Kassandra quickly placed her hands up and shouted, "Don't shoot! Don't shoot! It's me! It's me, Kassandra!"

The assassin looked back with a sudden look of shock on his face, glancing deeper into the vehicle, noticing a number of the enemy soldiers laying lifeless in pools of their own blood, and slowly pointed his weapon downwards.

She noticed the assassin and said softly, "It's you. I'm so glad to see you."

The assassin continued to glance back with an alien gaze on his face, watching her quickly making her way closer to him.

She hugged him tightly and said, "I know that you don't remember me. But I'll tell you everything you need to know. The General just called for more reinforcements. They'll be here soon, so we need to leave now."

The assassin peered back with a cold stare. He turned his back and began walking away, when she gently grabbed him, causing him to quickly turn towards her with his rifle pointed to her face, still maintaining his usual cold and calculating stare.

She quickly put her hands up and said, "Please take me with you. I won't get in your way. I promise. I just can't stand being a prisoner any longer. I need to find my father, and you're the only one who could take me to him. Please. I really need your help."

"She's right," Jason said to the assassin, and said to her, "It's nice to see you again. What are the odds of finally seeing the Rogue and the Package back together again?"

The assassin once again slowly pointed his rifle downwards, while he continued to maintain his usual cold stare and simply walked away.

"The Rogue and the Package? Have we met?" she asked.

"More or less. You're Kassandra Weaver, the acting president's daughter. I'm Jason. Jason White."

"I remember you now. You were the soldier that froze in court and lied to our faces, helping them seal his fate."

"And every day, I wished I hadn't. Then again, I was young and afraid."

Jason was soon distracted seeing the survivors from the sanctuary and walked towards them with his hands up and said, "Please, don't be afraid. I know that you are," he said to the young frightened woman, all covered in blood.

She looked all around her, seeing all the dead bodies and asked, "Is he afraid?"

Jason glanced at the assassin for a brief moment and answered, "Probably not. Just a little shocked at what just happened."

"I see that you got yourself a doctor. What's she gonna do? Try and bring them back to life?"

"No. It's nothing like that. I know that it won't make you feel any better, but I'm sorry for what just happened back there. He thought these people were enemy soldiers," Jason answered.

"That's easy for you to say, considering the fact that you're still breathing, after seeing all my friends that I've lived with for so long, and not to mention her entire family, were wiped out like they were nothing. That makes me feel a whole lot better. Thank you so much for mentioning it, sir."

"I'm only trying to tell you that I'm sorry for your loss, and hers as well," Jason replied.

"Well, you're quite apologetic for someone who didn't do anything," she said.

"With good reason. It was a tragic situation," he answered.

"What's wrong with him? Why isn't he apologizing? After all, he's the one who murdered all those people. Did someone get his tongue?" Arianna asked.

Jason glanced at the assassin for a brief moment, and replied, "He doesn't talk too much. As you can see, he lets his guns do all his talking for him."

"Well, considering the nature of what I just witnessed, I wouldn't be doing any more talking either. As you can see, we're still trying to cope from all the shock. Who's he? What's his angle?"

"Let's just say it would be wise to remain on his good side," Jason said.

"And who's the broad in the white lab coat?"

"I'm Jason White. And this is the acting president's daughter."

"I'm Kassandra. Pleased to meet you," Kassandra said.

"I'm Arianna. Arianna Martinez. And this is Susan, who just witnessed her entire family get slaughtered, by the way, and my friends, included by your silent pet. So what now?"

"Getting acquainted will come later. I'll tell you everything you need to know. But first, we need to get moving," Kassandra said.

"Why? How come you're in so much of a hurry to leave after all this? Aren't you supposed to have a moment of silence for all the people who were just massacred by your personal hitman?"

"Because we have more enemy troops on their way, and this time, you may not be so lucky," Kassandra replied.

Arianna looked all around the streets for the second time, seeing all the bodies sprawled in pools of their own blood, and asked, "Do I really have a choice?"

"Yes. The both of you can stay here and be target practice for the other enemy soldiers on their way here as we speak. And believe me, they won't share the same sentiment that the both of us are sharing towards the both of you right now," Jason answered

"It's not that you left me with much of a choice."

"From what I can see, it's the only choice the both of you have," Jason answered.

"Please, come with us," Kassandra added.

"Say no more," Arianna replied.

"Wait. I hear something. We have more coming," Jason said, watching nervously.

"Hurry back into the sanctuary. You can't afford to be spotted. Get inside as fast as you can," Kassandra added.

As Arianna hurried back to the sanctuary, they smelled the heavy scent of fuel that leaked from the transports that lay crippled from the assassin's flurry of attacks from his gatling gun that was once strapped to his back.

The assassin walked away from the transport that once carried Kassandra and placed charges to ambush the enemy transports. He positioned Jason and Kassandra in the middle of the street at a safe distance and walked away, hiding behind one of the heavily armored transports.

"What's he doing?" Kassandra asked.

"I think it's safe to say that he's using us as bait. A distraction, putting it mildly," Jason said.

The assassin moved towards one of the decaying vehicles parked near the sidewalk and waited for the convoy of armored transport to draw nearer, while Kassandra and Jason continued to wait in the street to distract the enemy soldiers.

As the enemy armored transports drew nearer, they stopped, seeing their targets standing in the streets, waiting for them to be taken.

They stepped out of the safety of their armored transports, and slowly walked towards them with their weapons drawn, seeing a great number of their soldiers along with freedom fighters sprawled throughout the entire streets, when a number of the charges placed on the streets exploded, consuming the enemy armored units, cutting off all their means of escape, causing Kassandra and Jason to run for cover behind the decrepit civilian transports.

From a safe distance, the assassin took out a smoke grenade and gently tossed in towards their position. He watched it hiss into a thick cloud of smoke to obscure their field of vision, while they remained confused.

The enemy soldiers who had survived the series of blasts, still dazed and confused from the shock, stumbled to their feet, completely unaware of the assassin stalking them through the thick wall of smoke that covered the streets.

The assassin grabbed his sidearm and attached a silencer. He took aim at the enemy soldiers who were completely clueless of his presence, and silently disposed of them.

The remaining enemy soldiers heard the bodies of their comrades falling heavily on the road, and began to fire at random in every direction, and broke radio silence to call for more reinforcements.

Arianna and Susan were startled after hearing the gunfire while they remained hidden within the walls of their compromised hideout, hoping that they wouldn't be discovered by the enemy forces.

13:07 HOURS. ENEMY COMMAND CENTER - PENTAGON, WASHINGTON, D.C., THE NATION'S CAPITAL:

They listened to the frantic screams of their soldiers calling for more reinforcements, through the crackling blasts of gunfire, while being hunted by the assassin who swiftly disposed of them.

13:08 HOURS. SECURE LOCATION, SOMEWHERE IN RICHMOND, VIRGINIA:

Dr. Weaver and the others heard the frantic screams of the enemy soldiers through the roar of gunfire, while the assassin continued to engage them.

They stared at one another with shock on their faces, hearing the assassin unleashing his deadly skills, eliminating at will through the noise of all the gunfire while Dr. Weaver listened to the disturbing transmission with a blank expression on his face, hoping his daughter wouldn't be recaptured by the enemy forces.

Celina gently placed her headphone on the desk and sat down on the chair, still with the look of shock on her face, and asked, "That's the man you trust to protect your daughter?"

"Do you have a better idea?" Dr. Weaver asked.

"His tactics seem a bit too extreme," she said.

"And so was the General when he kidnapped my daughter in the first place. Do you think for a second that you could negotiate with people like that? The only way that you can get through with people like him is through force. And as much as I hate it, if that's what it takes to be reunited with my daughter again, then so be it. And it looks like he hasn't even begun yet. As I told you before, I hope you have a strong stomach because what you've just heard is nothing compared to what's about to happen soon."

Celina simply stared back with a frightened look on her face.

13:10 HOURS. SOMEWHERE IN ARLINGTON, VIRGINIA:

The lone assassin continued to engage the enemy forces through the hail of gunfire, until it suddenly stopped, and the cold, bitter wind slowly swept across the streets, blowing the crimson colored smoke away.

Jason and Kassandra saw the smoke slowly clearing, seeing the assassin to be the only one left standing among all the fresh batch of corpses that he had laid to waste. The assassin walked over to the bodies to replenish his supplies.

She watched Jason in a state of shock, after having a rare opportunity to witness the sheer cunning from the assassin's deadly skills firsthand, while Jason stared at the assassin with an expression of total disbelief.

They ran into the sanctuary and saw Arianna and Susan hiding and quickly gestured for them to come out of their hiding places.

Arianna looked at Jason with a frantic look in her face and asked, "What the hell just happened?"

Jason watched as the assassin walked inside with a blank expression on his face and answered, "That. That's what just happened. And I don't have to stress on how important it is for us to hurry right now."

"Yeah, no shit," Arianna answered, watching the assassin, with the blood of the enemy soldiers on his face and clothes.

"We can't leave them here," Kassandra said.

"She's right. I know it's a lot to ask, but I'll give you all the help I can. Please," Jason said to the assassin

The assassin simply stared back at Arianna and walked out of the sanctuary into the streets filled with corpses of the enemy soldiers.

"He didn't say anything," Arianna said with a frightened look on her face.

"He didn't say no either," Jason answered.

"Are you sure? Don't want to end up like one of them," Arianna said.

"I'd advise you to just stay on his good side," Jason said.

"Don't have to tell me twice."

They walked through the streets, and saw one of the bodies of the freedom fighters fidgeting on the road in close proximity from where the assassin committed the total massacre of the enemy troops, and ran towards him to investigate his vital signs.

Jason saw his uniform and said, "He's a freedom fighter. He survived. He's lost a lot of blood and is barely conscious."

"There's a name on his uniform. It's Jacobs. We need to get him to a hospital," Kassandra said, trying to keep pressure on his wound to help contain the bleeding.

"There's a hospital a few miles from here," Arianna replied.

"We can use one of the armored cars, that's if they're not pumped with holes inside of them," Jason answered.

"If we can't find one, we can use the next alternative," Arianna suggested.

"Which is?" Kassandra asked.

"We can carry him, if we can't get an able transport," Jason said.

"And we both know what's going to happen if we do," Kassandra said.

"I'm just saying," Arianna replied.

"I'll be right back," Kassandra said, running off.

"Where are you going?" Jason asked.

"Going to see if I can get a transport to get us out before more enemy soldiers come," she said, running away.

"Good idea," Jason answered.

They searched through the streets of corpses and burning transports, until Jason stumbled onto one still in good condition and said, "Found one."

"Oh, thank God," Arianna said, with a huge sigh of relief.

They carried the wounded soldier's body into the armored transport and boarded, en-route to the nearest hospital.

"I'll drive, you shoot," Kassandra said.

"Wouldn't have it any other way," Jason answered.

13:15 HOURS. ENEMY COMMAND CENTER - PENTAGON, WASHINGTON, D.C., THE NATION'S CAPITAL:

"The package is on the move, General, in one of our armored units," Maxwell said softly.

"And what of 0-7?"

"Still no transmission. Possibly he may still be with her."

"He is. Of that I have no doubt. In case you haven't noticed, our men didn't die of natural causes. Wherever the rogue is, the package won't be too far away," the General said. "The orders are the same. No harm comes to the Package, and terminate the rest on sight."

"Yes, sir."

13:34 HOURS. MID-ATLANTIC URGENT CARE - ARLINGTON, VIRGINIA:

They stepped out of the transport, when they heard someone lifting the thick, heavy cover of a manhole cover, silently signaling them to come forward.

The assassin quickly pointed his rifle towards the manhole, as he watched the cover being dragged further from the deep, dark hole and a tall, brown-haired young man with piercing blue eyes and a dirty blonde-haired female with green eyes and average height climbed through the hole with their hands up.

The mysterious young man walked towards them and said, "You're Kassandra. The president's daughter. Or should I say, the acting president. We know who you are."

"And I know who he is," the young woman said, pointing to the assassin.

"Who are you?" Jason asked.

"The underground resistance. Or what's left of it. My name is David. David Berenger," the mysterious young man answered.

"And I'm Stephanie. Stephanie Walker."

"We're not posing any threat to any of you. We mean you no harm," David said softly, with his hands still up.

"Good luck trying. It'll be the last thing you ever do. I can promise you that," Arianna remarked.

"As I said, I know who he is. And to be fair, we could use someone like him," David said.

"Well, you do have a point there," Kassandra said.

"We can help each other out," David answered.

"What can you do?" Jason asked.

"I'm a hacker. I can hack into the most complex programs ever made by man. Hence the reason for the resistance. Or what's left of it," he said.

"And what does she do?" Arianna asked.

"She's my lovely assistant. Any other questions?"

"Maybe we can use someone like you. The problem is, there's nothing to hack," Jason answered.

"Maybe not yet. But trust me, it will come in handy. How do you think we found you? We heard every broadcast during the air strike. And what happened when the General wanted him dead. Every bit of information from the entire war. Everything. Information is power. So we have to be prepared," Stephanie replied.

"Well, in that case, she does have a point, you know," Kassandra replied.

"We don't have much time for niceties now. We'll tell you all you need to know. But, for now, we need to get moving," David answered.

"Funny you said that. That's exactly what they said to me," Arianna added.

The assassin listened quietly and switched his focus from David's blue eyes to Stephanie's green eyes, with his usual cold stare, as if he was gazing deeply into her soul, instilling a sudden feeling of fear into her.

"I hate to break up the social circle. But we need to get him inside if we'll have any chance of saving him at all," Kassandra said.

"She's right. We need to leave now," Jason answered.

"I won't get in your way. I promise," David replied, watching the assassin, switching his focus to his rifle pointed towards his face, with his hands still up.

"Let's see what he has to say about it," Arianna commented.

The assassin slowly pointed his weapon downwards and silently walked towards the front doors of the hospital.

"That's as any response that you'll get. The only one actually," Arianna said.

"But he didn't say anything," David replied.

"Exactly. He didn't say no either. And it's a good idea not getting in his way and all. It's the same thing they told me. So, just get used to the silent treatment. Trust me, the others learned the hard way," Arianna whispered.

"We'll keep that in mind," Stephanie answered.

"Your life depends on it. Trust me. So, forget what you think you know. I just saw the horror show first-hand," Arianna remarked.

They walked slowly through the door and were greeted by the cold, discolored, and decrepit walls, and dimmed lights that constantly flicker after many years of abandonment and neglect.

"It doesn't look too equipped to operate on someone," Stephanie remarked.

"What did you expect after surviving a civil war after 10 years?" Arianna asked.

"It'll have to do. We need to try if we're going to save him. We need to take him to the operating room," Kassandra answered.

"We'll stay here and watch the door," Arianna said, sitting on the chair, holding Susan closely to her.

"Well, I hope the both of you can bounce bullets off your skins," Kassandra replied, as she and Jason carried the wounded soldier to the operating room.

"Just lead the way," David said, pulling on Stephanie's arm to the operating room.

They quickly walked into the operating room and flipped the switches on the wall, turned on the light, and laid the wounded soldier on the bed. They cut off the section of his blood-stained clothes, and dropped it on the floor.

Kassandra examined the gaping wound that tore through his deltoid, causing heavy bleeding, and said, "The bullet from that mini gun went right through. Fortunately, no vital organs were hit. Considering that he's lost so much blood, think of what would have happened if he were hit somewhere else."

"What do you need?" Jason asked.

"Some antiseptics to clean the wound."

After a few moments of searching, Jason brought the antiseptic and placed it next to the wounded soldier and said, "This is what I found."

"It'll have to do," she said.

"Do you need any thread?"

"No," Kassandra answered.

"Then how are you going to close the wound?"

"I have my ways," she said, cleaning the soldier's wound, while he continued to cling to life, and continued, "He's lost a lot of blood. The serum that I have is very fast-acting. If I administer it, it might put him in shock, and may kill him. He needs a blood transfusion. Fortunately for us, after running his blood analysis, it concluded that he's a universal recipient. And that makes the job a whole lot easier."

After careful searching in the blood issue room, Jason arrived with a blood pack, and handed it to her.

She connected the blood pack to a long tube, and punctured his arm with a needle. She watched the blood travel through his vein, as Jason applied pressure on his wound.

After a brief moment of the blood transfusion, she reached her hand into her pocket and took out a syringe-like shaped vial and injected some of its contents into his arm near the wound, placing the wounded soldier into a very deep state of comatose.

They became startled, seeing how quickly the medicine began to take its course after closing the wound.

"No way," Arianna said, with a sudden look of surprise on her face.

"Who are you, really?" Stephanie asked.

"I'm the president's daughter. Or acting president. Whichever you want to call it."

"It looks to me like you're a little more than that," Stephanie answered.

"And it looks like this is the reason why you're so important to the government," Arianna added.

"Wait a minute. Since you're so important, that means you're being tracked. And it'll lead them here," David said, placing his hand on his head, in a state of nervousness.

"I knew you'd say that," Arianna said with a worried look on her face.

"That means you're being tracked. How do you think they sent all those reinforcements straight to your position? You're a high valued hostage. And there's no way that they won't use a contingency plan to keep watching you, and risk coming after you. It makes sense, doesn't it?" David answered.

"I figured that out when they were sending more meat to the grinder," Kassandra answered, pointing to the assassin.

"Well, I hope he recovers really quickly, because we'll need all the guns we can get," Stephanie replied.

"He's right," Jason replied.

David reached into his packet, taking out a portable x-ray machine, and turned it on, hovering it over the assassin's body and heard it chiming loudly, as it reached over the assassin's chest and said, "We have a winner here."

"Are you going to take it out?" Jason asked.

"Nope. Don't want to end up like those guys back there," Jason answered.

"Good point. Doesn't look like he likes watching you strip his armor off and shit," Arianna commented.

"Here's an idea, *chica*, why don't you try?"

"The name is Arianna, *gringo*."

"Let me know when the both of you stop fighting like a married couple," Kassandra said, intervening.

She walked towards the assassin and said, "I need to take your gear off so I could take off your tracking beacon."

The assassin pointed his weapon downwards and slowly stripped his battle-ridden gear off his body, and calmly dropped it to the floor.

She placed a metal detector over his chest, and saw the tiny device hidden deeply within the fibers of the muscles of his chest.

She grabbed a tiny operating knife off the table and created a tiny incision, while the assassin remained unflinching from the sting, and used a tweezer, dipping into the tiny incision and gently pulling out the tracking device. She dropped it on the table near the bed.

They were surprised at how he ignored the pain from the sharp sting of the incision, and said, "This was supposed to be a fail-safe device. They placed that beacon inside him in case he didn't comply, even if his memory came back even after being wiped out all this time. They placed it on his heart to provide a painful electric shock to keep in line. To keep him controlled. They couldn't risk him going against them. If the government can't have him, then no one can. Well, you get what I'm talking about," Kassandra said.

"What happens if he continues to disobey orders?" Arianna asked.

"If the General couldn't contain him, then eventually they would kill him. They programmed it to self-destruct. Remotely of course. The General knows that his troops can turn against him at any given moment, so he planted a tracking device, only under the false pretense of it being a tracking device. But what it really is, is a bomb. It's his fail-safe mechanism inside them."

"So he planted a bomb inside you?" David asked.

"No, not me. What I have is just a tracking beacon, because the General would never dream of killing me. Besides, he needs me alive. But, I can't say the same for him or the others. For the numbers of soldiers under his command, he has to keep some kind of contingency plan in place to keep them in line," she said, taking a clean piece of gauze and gently resting it against the tiny incision on the assassin's chest to soak the dripping blood.

She reached into her pocket and took the vial, injecting a tiny dose of its contents into his veins to help accelerate the healing process.

"His body armor must've reduced the impact of the bullet, damaging the tracking device in his chest. Could've happened at a better time too," Stephanie said.

"Maybe we can use that against the General. Maybe I can tap into the main source of their power and disable all the tracking beacons and turn the troops against him. I'll have to examine it closer to see what I can come up with," David said, watching the damaged device closely.

"Why isn't he going to sleep?" Stephanie asked, as she and the others remained in shock, seeing how the assassin bore incredible resilience to the drug's effects.

"I suppose during his conditioning in being programmed to kill, it came with losing some feelings in his nerves," Kassandra answered. "It might take more than a small dose to put him to sleep. Or it appears that his body has instantly bonded with the serum on a cellular level. Thus far, I've never seen anyone bear such resilience to it like he has."

"Although it was damaged from a hit, it's still in good condition," David said, looking at the damaged device closely.

"It is," Jason said.

"Oh no," David said, suddenly having an epiphany. "There's good news and bad news. Which one do you want first?"

"I can use some good news after seeing all this shit that went down," Arianna replied.

"The good news is that the interference within the walls of the hospital is jamming the signals of all your tracking beacons. And that's just the good news."

"What's the bad news?" Stephanie asked.

"Your tracking beacon was active long enough to lead them here. And considering the nature of all the bad people that we're up against, that's some really bad news."

"Not again. I knew you'd say that," Arianna replied.

"Which means that they'll be here any minute," David concluded.

The assassin quickly grabbed Jason's assault rifle and handed it to him and walked out of the operating room into the corridors, through the glass doors, into the streets and saw an enemy convoy approaching from afar.

He looked all around the area, and saw the old abandoned building and hurried into its hollow shell, placing a number of explosives all about. He saw a number of rats scurrying across the floors of the decrepit structure in search of food, and turned on the damaged tracking beacon, and tied it to one of the rodents. He watched it scurry about, deeper into the old decrepit structure, and hurried back outside, using all the parked vehicles as cover to not be spotted by the enemy soldiers.

14:06 HOURS. ENEMY COMMAND CENTER - PENTAGON, WASHINGTON, D.C., THE NATION'S CAPITAL:

"General," Maxwell called out softly. "We have a location on the target. His tracking beacon just went active."

"Is it still or moving?" the General asked.

"It's moving, sir."

"The subject must be pacified at all costs. This is our top priority. Divert as many of the personnel to his location as possible. As for the remaining few, to the Package."

"We've just received word from one of our planes en-route to the base, sir."

"What's the status of the mission?" the General asked.

"The squad from the Maryland strike force suffered total waves. Though they were able to sink the entire aircraft carrier fleet. As for the squad from our base, they suffered heavy casualties, but were still able to repel the enemy."

"I don't know what alarmed them. But whatever it was, it saved the entire resistance from being wiped out. At least for now."

"Then again, to be fair, General West once served under my command, and I don't expect anything less. And for someone who once served proudly under my command, he's proven to be a worthy adversary. Outnumbered and outgunned, and yet they were able to put up a good fight. It simply means that I did my job. Couldn't have asked for a more worthy opponent, except maybe for 0-7 under different circumstances. And now that our most valuable asset has deflected on the side of the resistance, all that's left to do is to kill him first, before he gets his mind back. And it's no surprise to see that he's more difficult to kill than all my elite soldiers put together in all the armed forces."

"What do you suggest, sir?" Maxwell asked.

"Activate the other six, and use her work to improve their abilities."

"As you wish, General."

"But for now, let's see if we can make any progress in eliminating the 0-7."

"Yes sir."

14:10 HOURS. SECURE LOCATION, SOMEWHERE IN RICHMOND, VIRGINIA:

"They're going after him," Celina said to Dr. Weaver.

"Indeed they are. Hope it goes well for them. And check to see if we can get a live feed from the satellite, and check to see if we can get the safest route to that location. I'm going to find my daughter," Dr. Weaver answered.

"It may be too dangerous, sir. We run a high risk of being captured."

"I haven't seen my daughter in 10 years and I'm not waiting for another second before it happens again. Am I clear?"

"Yes, Mr. President," Celina answered softly.

"We move in 10."

"Yes, sir," she said reluctantly.

14:11 HOURS. SOMEWHERE IN ARLINGTON, VIRGINIA:

The enemy soldiers quickly moved in the direction of the assassin's tracking beacon, and rushed into the dark and decrepit confines of the building, while the others moved towards the hospital, where Kassandra and the others waited, hoping not to be discovered by the enemy.

As the enemy soldiers moved into the abandoned structure, following the signal of the tracking beacon, they immediately opened fire in all directions, seeing they were close to the source of the signal. They stopped, seeing no sign of the assassin, and looked all around them, seeing the walls riddled with bullet holes, with many charges placed all around the abandoned structure, and looked at their feet, seeing a rat quickly scurrying by, with the assassin's tracking beacon and a charge tied to its body, causing them to realize they had walked into the assassin's trap. They made a desperate attempt to vacate the old abandoned structure, and were consumed by a giant wall of flame, causing the entire spacious confines of the hospital to shudder violently from the shock wave of the blast, as the structure crumbled to the ground. This caused the remaining enemy soldiers to abandon their search in the hospital, and ran back to the door in the direction of the blast, when they were swiftly engaged by the assassin, who silently snuck up from behind, using his deadly techniques of hand-to-hand combat, quickly disarming them, and using their weapons against them.

They remained quiet inside, listening to the roar of the gun fire and screams of dying soldiers echoing through the walls of the hospital, covering their ears tightly. "Hope the both of you have strong stomachs for the horror show," Arianna said to David and Stephanie.

"Why do you say that?" David asked.

"Because knowing about him is one thing. But seeing what he can do is something else entirely. And believe me, I have. Right?" Arianna said to Jason.

"No comment," he replied.

"See?" Arianna said.

"He just said no comment," Stephanie answered.

"You don't believe me? Take a look, and see for yourself," she said.

They slowly made their way through the corridors of the hospital filled with flickering lights, until they arrived at the glass doors and peeped outside. They saw a number of bodies sprawled in front of the entrance, and saw the assassin standing among them, watching back with his usual cold and intimidating look.

Arianna looked at them and said, "I'd hate to say that I told you so. But I told you so. The guy inside needs to get well and I mean fast. He needs to rest some more."

"There's no time. The longer we stay, the more we risk being compromised. The top brass already knows what happened, and will be sending more troops to this position. If we must leave, then now's the time," Jason answered.

"How's he doing anyway?" David asked.

"He's coming along slowly. Vital signs stabilizing," Kassandra answered.

Arianna looked through the glass doors and saw a number of enemy transports approaching and said, "Oh shit. Looks like we're about to have more company."

"Right now, the only way for us to move undetected is to go underground," David said.

"I agree. And from the looks of it, we need to do it fast," Arianna answered.

The assassin threw more charges in the road, while the others hurried back into the emergency room where the wounded soldier laid, and waited at the entrance quietly to detonate them.

As the unsuspecting transports approached, the assassin waited until they were within range, and quickly detonated the charges, causing a series of explosions. The transports crashed into one another, as the assassin tossed a few smoke grenades into the streets to create a giant wall of smoke to cover his advance, and quickly moved in to dispose the enemy soldiers, while they were dazed from the blast laid from the charges, switching techniques between his knife and sidearm.

The remaining enemy soldiers, hearing the sounds of someone fighting through the thick cloud of smoke, opened fire in all directions in a desperate attempt to repel who was hunting them through the cloud, but to no avail, and stopped as quickly as it had begun.

They stared at one another, wondering what the outcome was, knowing that enemy soldiers had met their demise from the assassin's skills, while they remained confined within the cramped interior of the operating room.

14:20 HOURS. ENEMY COMMAND CENTER - PENTAGON, WASHINGTON, D.C., THE NATION'S CAPITAL:

After moments of constant vigilance of the monitor, seeing all the tracking beacons that transmitted all the vital signs of all the soldiers suddenly stopped transmitting, they watched the General with a look of hopelessness on their faces, and nodded their heads, telling him that all the soldiers sent in as reinforcements were killed in action.

The General took a deep breath and said, "We'll keep on sending as many troops until we get him. But for now, let's head for the base and hear from our pilots. Keep all channels opened."

14:23 HOURS. SOMEWHERE IN ARLINGTON, VIRGINIA:

The assassin calmly walked into the operating room and glanced at all the others with his usual cold gaze, and quickly walked back out.

"I think it's safe to say, this is our cue to leave," Arianna said.

"I'd hate to say I told you so. But I told you so," Jason replied.

"He's still unconscious. What are we supposed to do with him?" David asked.

"We can't just leave him here," Kassandra said.

"I'll go check to see if I could find something," Jason replied.

"Hope they're not shot up like the last time," Arianna said.

Jason walked through the streets filled with corpses of enemy soldiers and husks of burning transports, until they stumbled upon one of the transports still in good condition. They opened the door and carefully inspected the vehicle. Jason nodded his head and said, "This will do nicely. I'll go and get the others." He walked into the emergency room while the assassin continued to stand guard outside and asked, "How's he holding up?"

"He's stable. He's beginning to come around," Stephanie answered.

"We found a transport. We're getting out."

"Finally," Arianna said, taking a sigh of relief.

They carried the wounded soldier to the armored vehicle and laid him on the floor, with the blood pack still attached to his arm.

"We're still being tracked. So, we need to get as far as we can. Give him enough time to recover at least," Jason said.

"True. You can always use one more gun," Arianna said.

"You drive. We'll shoot," Jason said Kassandra.

They began to drive out of the city with the wounded soldier, as he slowly regained consciousness.

15:17 HOURS. BOLLING ENEMY AIR FORCE BASE - WASHINGTON, D.C., THE NATION'S CAPITAL:

The General arrived at the base to greet the pilots who had survived the onslaught against their enemies.

He waited from a safe distance until the planes powered down, with his hands behind his back, and watched one of the surviving pilots approach.

As the pilots slowly approached, he stood at attention, noticing the

General who had come to greet them personally.

The General nodded his head, and said softly, looking at the moniker of the giant snake on his plane, "At ease, Python,"

"Yes, sir," the pilot answered.

"What happened out there? How did she lose the element of surprise?"

"We don't know, sir. I'm afraid only Viper knows the answer to that question. And I speak for the others when I say that they achieved total surprise and supremacy."

"What was the status of the entire mission? My colonels told me. But I need to hear it from you personally."

"All the enemy positions were neutralized, including the entire aircraft carrier fleet. But the entire squad from Maryland suffered total casualties. We're all that's left. I'm sorry, sir."

"There's no need to be sorry. There's no victory without sacrifice. You went out and did your jobs, and paid a hefty price at the hands of our enemies, although they're still our countrymen. They put up a good fight, and I didn't expect any less of them. The cost was heavy, but we still pulled it off. Great job, pilot. Now get yourself some rest. You're dismissed for now."

"Thank you, sir," the weary pilot said.

Maxwell came forward and said, "Permission to speak, General."

"Granted," the General answered.

"We have movement. The Package is on the move, along with his subordinate."

"Let's head back. Keep me posted."

"Yes, sir."

"Send in more troops to her location. Wherever the Rogue is, the Package isn't far behind. 0-7 isn't far behind."

CHAPTER 15: RONIN.

15:35 HOURS. SOMEWHERE ON INTERSTATE 64, RICHMOND, VIRGINIA, HEADING TOWARDS ARLINGTON:

Dr. Weaver and his assistants drove as quickly as they could on the long stretch of road, and looked all around them, seeing the towering columns of thick, dark smoke in the distance from some of the wreckage of allied and enemy planes alike that were destroyed in the skirmish that once ensued in the skies, finally realizing just a tiny fraction of what had come to pass, and looked ahead seeing the burning husks of a number of enemy vehicles scattered every inch of the roads.

"My God. Doesn't take much to see what happened here. Some things you should never have to see," Celina said, staring in disbelief.

"I'd go through anything to see my daughter again. The pain of not holding my daughter all this time is far worse than anything that I've had to endure. Believe me when I say that I take no pleasure putting you through this. I don't want anything for you that I don't want for myself."

"Yes sir, I understand," she said.

"Just keep on finding other routes around any other enemy troops that may be in the area."

"But how will we know if she was present, anyway?"

"It's simple. We follow a trail of bodies. That was another thing that I hoped you'd never have to see," Dr. Weaver replied.

"Me too."

They continued driving and saw a gauntlet of burning enemy vehicles stretched and scattered across the road.

"What do I do?" Celina asked nervously as they came closer to it.

"Ramming speed. Go through it!"

"Are you sure?"

"It's the only way!"

"Hold on to something!"

She slammed her foot on the acceleration and charged through the burning gauntlet, feeling the violent impact from the crash, causing the entire transport to shudder, throwing the others off their balance.

"They left a trail of destruction. How are we going to find her if we're going at this rate?"

"As I said. We follow a trail of bodies and burning vehicles. If she's there, she won't be hard to find."

"I hope so."

"Trust me."

15:46 HOURS. SOMEWHERE IN ARLINGTON, VIRGINIA:

As they continued to drive through the streets, the wounded soldier slowly opened his eyes and asked, "Who are you? Where am I?" looking all around and quickly jumped to his feet, seeing the assassin staring back with a straight face.

"It's okay. It's okay. You're with friends now," Arianna said, trying to calm him down.

"Well, the last time I checked, our friend here wiped out my entire squad with a damned mini gun."

"You forgot to mention a lot of enemy troops too. And there were a lot more of them than you and your friends," Arianna said.

"I'm sure," he said looking into the assassin's eyes, while he continued staring back silently, with a straight face. "I bet he's been mowing everything down with a pulse."

"I'm Arianna. And this is Susan."

"I'm Jason, and this is Kassandra."

"Nice to meet you," the wounded soldier replied.

"Good to see you're okay. Seems like the serum really worked," Kassandra replied.

"I guess it's safe to thank you for saving my life. I'm Daniel Jacobs," he replied.

"I guess," Arianna replied.

"I'm Stephanie."

"I'm David."

"What's going on here?" Daniel asked, looking at the assassin.

"Still saving your ass. The last we checked," Arianna replied.

"You're safe. He's not going to hurt you," Jason answered.

"I hope not. He won't gain anything from it. He already did it once," Daniel answered, not taking his eyes off the assassin.

"He's the reason why you're still alive, so show some gratitude. Most of us anyway. We need him," Arianna answered.

"Right now, we're on the run and we need all the guns and bodies that we can get," David added.

"Welcome to the resistance," Stephanie added.

"Do I have a choice?" Daniel asked.

"Sure you do. You can get off here and go at it alone, and eventually get your head blown off. Or you can stay here with us, and try and stick it out. It's entirely up to you," Stephanie replied.

"I can use some numbers right now," Daniel answered, as he continued to watch the assassin, who stared back with the same blank expression on his face.

"That's more like it. Good choice," David said.

Dr. Weaver and his assistants had arrived at the first location of where they had received the transmission where his daughter was traced, climbed down from their transports, and saw a number of corpses of enemy soldiers and freedom fighters alike, sprawled all about the streets.

"He was here?" Celina asked.

"Yes. He was most definitely here. As I said before, check the trail of bodies. Only he could've done that much damage. These soldiers are the best of the best, the bad of the bad, or the worst of the worst, or whatever point of view you'd like to use, and being that he's at the top of the list in being the best, it's safe to say that he's the one he's the one responsible for laying waste to an entire battalion of soldiers."

Celina slowly walked through the door riddled with bullet holes and came to a sudden stop after seeing one of the enemy soldiers with a gaping hole from a single gunshot wound to his temple lying in a pool of his own blood, along with a number of civilians who were massacred, and quickly turned her head facing Dr. Weaver, unable to fathom all the grisly sights that she'd just witnessed.

The others watched the horrific scene, wondering how someone was capable of committing such atrocities against human beings like himself.

"We need to leave. It hasn't even begun yet I'm afraid," Dr. Weaver said.

"I don't want to see what the rest of it looks like," Celina said, walking out of the sanctuary in great haste, with her eyes filled with tears from the savage nature of the atrocities that were committed.

She looked at the road completely blanketed in snow and saw the tire impressions heading away. "It looks like they went in that direction."

"Then that's where we go," Dr. Weaver said.

Kassandra continued to drive through the city in the armored transport, when it suddenly stopped.

"Why did we stop?" Arianna asked, with a sudden look of nervousness on her face.

"It wasn't me. We're out of fuel. The fuel gauge is on empty," Kassandra replied.

They walked out of the armored transport, and smelled the heavy scent of fuel and looked under the vehicle, seeing that the fuel line was ruptured from the explosion of the charges that had caused all the fuel to leak.

"How are you feeling?" Stephanie asked.

"My legs are still asleep. They feel like jello," Daniel answered.

"There's a number of vehicles parked on the streets. Maybe we can hot wire one," Stephanie said, waiting for a response, only to receive none, as they stared back.

"Looks like we'll have to go on foot, and hope we don't get spotted," Arianna answered.

"It looks that way," David answered.

They walked through the city streets with Daniel clinging onto David and Stephanie, feeling total paralysis from his legs from the temporary side effects of the medicine, as it ran its final course through his body, while Jason and the others remained vigilant.

The glass doors of an old cell phone store that went out of business during the civil war suddenly swung open, alarming them, causing them to point their weapons in that direction.

An old Chinese man came out with an old shotgun and yelled, "Freeze!" He froze after seeing the amount of guns pointed at his face, with the assassin pointing the red dot to his forehead, and quickly dropped his gun, putting his hands up.

His grandson came running out with his hands up and said, "We don't want any trouble. We're just trying to survive."

"So are we," Jason answered.

"What do you want?" the old man asked.

"One of us is injured. We just need a little time for him to recover. And we'll be out of your way as soon as possible. I promise," Arianna answered.

"Who's she?" the old man asked, looking at Kassandra. "She's very pretty. Maybe one day you can be my grandson's girlfriend. Please come in," he said, winking, and smiling.

They walked into the store, laughing at what the old man had suggested about Kassandra.

"Here's a gift for you. Maybe you can call each other," the old Chinese man said, handing the cell phone to Kassandra.

"Thank you," Kassandra said softly, smiling, gently grabbing the phone from the elderly man.

"Not that it'll work. Cell phones went out of business after the civil war began. But he can make it happen. He can make a cell phone completely untraceable. That's his area of expertise," his grandson replied. "I apologize for my grandfather's behavior. We don't get visitors often, so I suppose he's very happy to see you."

"It's quite alright. No apologies required," she answered, and suddenly felt the cell phone vibrate in her pocket.

"I can hook up a cell phone for you. With firewall encryption. The works. So they can't intercept all your messages," the elderly Chinese man said, winking at Kassandra.

"You might as well give them out since you have no use for them. And since you have no use for them, what are we going to do?" Stephanie asked.

"It might come in handy," Kassandra said.

"She's right. You never know. Everything is high-tech. They won't count on us being conventional. Never know when it can come in handy," Jason answered.

"I suppose you're right. Until now, I never had one. I suppose it can't hurt," Stephanie replied.

"So, will you be my grandson's girlfriend?" the old man asked, winking at her again.

"Again, I apologize for my grandfather's behavior. I'm Brandon. Brandon Tang. And this is Grandpa Tang, as you have met."

"My name is-" Kassandra answered, before she was suddenly interrupted by a hail of enemy gunfire tearing through the store, fatally wounding Brandon's grandfather, causing him to fall to the floor, lying in a pool of his own blood.

"Let's go to the store room!" Brandon yelled.

The assassin quickly pulled out a smoke grenade, tossing it on the floor, forming a wall of smoke to cover their escape while he stayed behind to engage them.

The enemy soldiers pursued the others through the blinding smoke and were introduced to the assassin's deadly skills in disarming and turning their weapons against them.

The screams of agony quickly began to fill the confined area of the store, as the group of elite enemy soldiers fell to his unmatched skill, with the loud blasts of gunfire causing the others to relive the frightening moments they had endured before.

After a brief moment of engaging the enemy soldiers, the gunfire suddenly stopped, and the smoke from the grenade slowly slipped through the bullet holes in the glass windows into the streets.

Another group of enemy soldiers slowly walked into the store with their weapons drawn, and were greeted with the lifeless bodies of their comrades. They saw the assassin laying on the floor, covered in blood.

One of the enemy soldiers slowly and cautiously walked towards him to investigate, kneeling closely towards him and nudged him, and saw that he remained lifeless. He signaled to the others that the assassin was killed in action, causing the enemy soldiers to drop their guard.

The enemy soldier turned back once again to face the assassin, and saw him opening his eyes, catching him by surprise, and quickly felt the assassin's knife in the flesh of his throat, causing him to bleed profusely.

The assassin quickly opened fire at the remaining enemy soldiers, using the enemy soldier's corpse as a shield, while the other soldiers continued to return fire, tearing through the armor on the enemy soldier's back.

He tossed a hand grenade at the remaining enemy soldiers, while he continued to shield himself with the corpse, and quickly made his departure after tossing it away, seriously wounding them as they tried to retreat to a safer distance.

After the explosion, he slowly brushed the debris from his clothes, and walked in the direction of the door, ending the suffering of the enemy soldiers that lay inside of the store wounded from the blast of the grenade, placing the final shots in their bodies.

He walked towards the door and stepped into the open streets, where he was suddenly greeted with a hail of enemy bullets, causing him to delay his offensive.

The remaining enemy soldiers stayed near the transports for cover, in fear of advancing towards the assassin's position, while they waited nervously outside, and saw an object flying towards them, causing them to scramble for cover, deceiving them into thinking that he'd tossed a grenade at their positions.

The assassin tossed another cell phone at them, while they remained stationary, checking the previous cell phone he had tossed at them.

They walked towards the other cell phone, picking it up to examine it, and were suddenly swept away by a giant explosion, killing a number of the enemy soldiers.

The fighters struggled to get on their feet as they were completely shaken from the shock of the explosion, wobbling towards the transport for support.

The assassin, sensing the enemy soldiers were still recovering from the shock of the blast, tossed a smoke grenade to cover his advance, as he quickly and quietly moved through the streets, silently engaging the enemy soldiers.

The enemy soldiers, seeing they were slowly being consumed by the wall of smoke, knew this was a sign that the assassin was near. They opened fire, shooting in all directions, and stopped as quickly as they began.

"What do you think happened to him?" Stephanie asked.

"You mean them?" Jason answered.

"That was a lot of guns to neutralize," Arianna added.

"I wouldn't worry about that," Kassandra answered.

"Is he that good?" Brandon asked.

"The best. And he's the only reason why I'm still not captured by them, and why the rest of you are still alive," Kassandra answered.

"I don't like it. It's a little too quiet," Daniel added.

"There's nothing to like about dodging bullets. But given the circumstances, I say we don't have much of a choice in the matter either," David answered.

"True. Because I can tell you there's some other place I'd prefer to be right now, and it's anywhere but here," Stephanie answered.

"Yeah. As for me, it's counting sheep. Being any place is better than being here right now," Arianna answered.

"See? There's someone who agrees with me. But this is what I have to deal with now," Stephanie answered.

"What do you think is going on outside right now?" David asked.

"You don't seem to be fazed by any of this," Arianna said to Kassandra.

"Should I be? Better them than you, myself, or any of the others," she answered. "And believe me, you don't want him to come after you."

"Can someone go and see what's happening outside?" Arianna said, whispering.

"You first," David replied.

"I'm taking care of Susan," she replied.

"Why don't you hand Susan over to me and you go check since you suggested it?" Stephanie answered.

"I would, but my feet hurt," Arianna replied back.

"I bet," Stephanie said back.

"It's okay to admit that you're too afraid to move. We all are," David remarked.

"That too," Arianna replied.

Daniel peeped his head slightly from the warehouse, only seeing signs of all the bloodshed and destruction the assassin had left in his wake. He saw the thick, black smoke coming from outside.

He turned back and said to the others, "There's no sign of him. Just a trail of dead bodies inside leading to the door."

"Think they got him?" Arianna asked, with a look of concern on her face.

"I seriously doubt that," Kassandra replied.

"What makes you so sure?" Brandon asked.

"Because he was the best soldier in the entire corp, and still is. He was engineered to be a total killing machine, and trained in the arts. All of them."

"So, you're saying he left us to go settle a personal vendetta? I knew it," Arianna replied.

"I'm saying he left to keep you alive. All of you, and his main directive is to make sure that I don't fall back into enemy hands. And based on the circumstances, you'll need these skills to keep all of you breathing. For a very long time," Kassandra said.

"Then where is he?" Daniel asked, and took a peep back outside, suddenly seeing the assassin standing before him, all covered in blood. "Never mind."

The assassin calmly walked into the store room and glanced at Kassandra. He strolled back out, as they watched in total silence and awe.

"See? I told you so," Kassandra remarked.

"I'm feeling a little weak. I feel like my whole life is draining from my body," the grandfather said, feeling his blood flowing from the wounds he sustained during the attack.

"Oh no. Grandpa," Brandon said, running to the front, checking on his grandfather, who laid in a pool of his own blood.

The sudden look of horror quickly creased on Brandon's face, seeing the extent of his grandfather's injuries from his body completely filled with enemy bullets. The grandfather slowly took his final breath, releasing Brandon's hand.

"They just killed him. For no reason. They just… killed him," Brandon said, with his eyes filled with tears.

"I'm sorry about your grandfather," Kassandra said, gently placing her hand on Brandon's shoulder. "You're welcome to come with us if you want. You can choose to stay here, too. But if you do, the same thing will happen to you. And you won't be any good to him. If you loved your grandfather, then come with us and avenge him."

"I suppose you're right," Brandon replied, with his eyes clouded in tears.

"David's hit!" Stephanie yelled.

"Oh no," Kassandra said softly, running towards David.

"It came through the walls," Jason said, watching the bullet hole filled with David's blood. "He didn't even know he was hit."

"The bullet didn't go all the way through. But, it's still inside him. The walls must've minimized the impact," Kassandra answered.

They tried lifting David to his feet, and heard him wince in pain from the sharp sting of the wound.

The assassin took out his knife and pitched it into the floor, startling the others, and quietly walked out of the storeroom to the streets to watch out for more enemy activity.

Kassandra dug into David's wound with the razor-sharp knife, while the others held him down. He writhed in constant pain, until she pulled out the bullet from his back, causing the wound to gush out more blood.

16:02 HOURS. MID-ATLANTIC URGENT CARE – ARLINGTON, VIRGINIA:

Dr. Weaver and his agents arrived at the hospital and saw the grisly sight that awaited them.

"I smell something," Celina said.

"Me too. I recognize that smell anywhere."

"It's coming from that burning building over there. But is it what I think it is?"

They followed the trail of countless footsteps towards the burning building, as the stench grew stronger.

Dr. Weaver took one last glance at the snowy streets filled with the enemies' footsteps and answered, "It's burning flesh. It's a smell that I became very familiar with during my time on the Ivory Coast. I'd recognize it anywhere. He lured them from outside into that building over there, and took out the entire building with them inside it. And judging from the smell, it seems there were quite a number of them. He's as clever as he's deadly. He's not the kind you'd want to have as your enemy. He may be only a single man. But if you're not careful, he could take out an entire army."

"Where do we go now?" Celina asked.

"We go inside. And something tells me it won't be pretty either."

They followed another trail of corpses that led deeper into the hospital, and slowly opened the door with their weapons drawn, only to be greeted by decrepit walls filled with bullet holes and decorated with heavy smears of blood from more dead enemy soldiers. They saw tiny droplets of blood on the floor leading into the emergency room.

"Do you think he was hurt?" Celina asked nervously, looking everywhere.

"Judging from all the carnage, I seriously doubt that. I'm 100% certain this blood belongs to someone else. We'll find out when we get to the emergency room. Just be on your guard."

"Not that any of us are left with a choice," she replied.

They continued to trail tiny specs of blood leading to the emergency room, and slowly opened the door. The operating equipment was stained heavily with blood.

Dr. Weaver picked up a piece of clothing stained heavily with blood, and looked at the pattern on the uniform. "Whoever was here was one of General West's men. One of ours."

"How do you know?" Celina asked.

"Because the patterns on this piece of clothing are almost identical to yours."

"I see."

"The enemy soldiers are dressed like the ones outside. Look. Those footprints are fresh. And the tracks vary. They're not all wearing military issued gear. Must've picked up more people other than this soldier."

"Very perceptive," she said.

"That means my daughter's chances for not falling back into enemy hands has just increased by more than 50%."

"How do you guess that?"

"Because that means that 0-7 has help. Even if he doesn't need it. Or, at least I don't think he does."

"I'm confused."

"How so?" Dr. Weaver asked.

"If 0-7 was fighting against the freedom fighters, and now there's a freedom fighter along with him and your daughter, do you think it's possible that he regained all his memories?"

"I seriously doubt that. When you looked around you, you saw both the General's men, along with those from our side. For now, he's like a rabid animal who suddenly recognized who the enemy is, and from that point, went on a killing spree, fighting on both fronts. Now there's a freedom fighter in the midst. It almost makes no sense," Dr. Weaver said.

"What do you think happened?" she asked.

"It's been 10 years since his memories were wiped out. Something must've triggered some kind of memory inside him. I'm certain of it."

"Do you think it could've been someone?"

"Quite possibly. But whatever it was that did it, I'm glad. Though, I wished it was without all this bloodshed."

"What do we do now?" Celina asked.

"We continue to follow the trail."

"There may be more enemies en-route."

"It's a chance I'm willing to take. I've been waiting in the shadows long enough. I'm not leaving without my daughter. It's just that simple. How's the feed from the satellite coming along?"

"We're trying as much as we can, but there's too much interference."

"Well, in the meantime, trace whatever transmissions we get from the enemy, and search for alternate routes to avoid them at all costs. Let's move."

"Yes, sir," Celina said reluctantly.

They hurried outside into their vehicles, saw the direction where the tracks led, and continued to pursue them in hopes of finding Dr. Weaver's daughter.

16:07 HOURS. ENEMY COMMAND CENTER - PENTAGON, WASHINGTON, D.C., THE NATION'S CAPITAL:

"They found her, sir. but were engaged."

"If you want something done right, you have to do it yourself. Any movement on our asset?" the General replied.

"Somewhere in Arlington. It's an old cell phone store, the last we checked."

"Something's holding her back. Or maybe someone."

"Do you think that it may be 0-7? Do you think he could've been wounded in the fight?" Wilson asked.

"Possibly. But I seriously doubt that. Not from the amount of my men that he's just killed. It's someone else they're helping. I'm quite sure of it. I'm so sure of it, I'd bet my life on it."

"What do you propose?" Kurt asked.

"As I said earlier, if he wants me so badly, then it's rude to keep the man waiting," he answered, looking at Kurt squarely in his eyes, while they stared back in surprise at his bold remark.

"Prepare a helicopter. I'm going to pay him a visit personally."

"Yes, sir," Kurt said, with a look of shock on his face.

16:12 HOURS. SOMEWHERE IN ARLINGTON, VIRGINIA:

After numerous attempts of trying to contain the bleeding from David's wound, they had finally succeeded.

"We need to close the wound," Stephanie said.

"They'll be here soon," Arianna said nervously.

"Just keep him still," Kassandra answered, reaching into her pocket for the vial- shaped syringe, shooting some of its contents into his veins, instantly healing the wound at the cost of placing him in deep unconsciousness.

"We need to get moving now," Jason said, while he and Daniel lifted David off his feet.

"Way ahead of you," Arianna said, running out in the open, and quickly stopped in her tracks seeing all the carnage the assassin cast all over the store. She glanced at the savage sight at one of the enemy soldier's body completely filled with bullet holes after being used as a human shield, along with Brandon's grandfather, who laid lifelessly in a pool of his own blood.

She looked at Brandon and said, softly, "I'm truly sorry about your grandfather."

"I appreciate it. But there's nothing we can do about that now. I've already shed my tears. And all that's left to do now is to keep on moving."

They began making their exit out of the store slowly and cautiously through the string of grisly murders of countless enemy corpses lying on the floor, heading into the streets, seeing a number of burning armored vehicles consumed in flames, with more enemy soldiers sprawled all over the streets at their feet.

They gazed at each other once again in complete bewilderment, at how much carnage one man was capable of leaving in his wake.

Arianna and Stephanie checked all around the streets filled with burning transports to evacuate the area, when they were met with total misfortune.

"All the transports are too damaged to go anywhere," Arianna said with a hint of anger.

"Maybe that's not too bad," Stephanie replied.

"What do you mean?" Arianna asked.

"What she's saying is if we go by road, we risk being spotted by the enemy," Stephanie replied.

"So what do we do?" Arianna asked.

"We go underground," Kassandra answered.

"They're expecting us to use the open road. So, we sneak around them using the underground passages. That'll buy us enough time for David to recover and throw them off our scent. At least for the time being. The point is I'm being tracked. And as long as I'm being tracked, they'll keep finding us. We need to hold on long enough for me to remove the tracking device, so we can move undetected."

"She's right," Jason answered.

They hurried through the streets, frantically looking for an escape route, until they stumbled upon the large metal cover of a manhole.

"I need help to open this," Jason said, handing David's unconscious body over to Kassandra, while they tried to pry the metal cover open.

Stephanie and Arianna hurried to assist while Daniel held on to David's body, slumping over, as the assassin remained on guard.

After moments of trying to pry the heavy lid from the hole, they finally succeeded. They slowly began their descent into the deep dark hole, carefully lowering David's body below, and sealed off the hole behind them.

Moments after they made their departure, Dr. Weaver and his small group of hackers had arrived where their transport had run out of fuel.

He ran out of the transport towards the armored truck to inspect it, and watched the transport, still leaking drops of fuel, with its engine still warm from recent use.

He inspected inside to see if there was any trace of his daughter or anyone who was with her, and checked the fuel gauge. He said, "This belonged to them. They were definitely in here. They ran out of fuel. A ruptured line leaked all the fuel out. And it wasn't long ago they were here," he said, inhaling the strong scent of fuel.

"How do you know?" Celina asked.

"They didn't get far before. And the scent of fuel is strong. That fuel line might've been damaged from the explosion. And they're on foot right now. We may still be able to catch them."

They drove slowly through the snow-filled streets, following the footprints until they saw the smoke from all the wreckage of burning enemy vehicles.

Dr. Weaver quickly ran out of his vehicle and ran over the burning wreckage. He looked at the number of dead enemy troops sprawled on the streets, lacerated from the blast that tore through the thick armor of the transports.

Celina picked up an object from the streets, noticing it was a cell phone and said, "I'm confused. It's a cell phone. It's still in good condition near a bombing. What does that mean?"

"Doesn't it make any sense to you?" Dr. Weaver asked.

"No. I'm afraid not. I can't imagine how a cell phone near a bombing makes any sense at all."

Dr. Weaver picked some of the parts and analyzed them closely and said, "He's clever. Ingenious way of deceiving the enemy."

"I'm afraid you're losing me. But I suppose this is where you're going to clarify all this to me."

"The cell phone is on the floor. There's no reason for it to be on the floor, except it might've been a diversion."

"I'm listening," she said.

"They ran for cover thinking it was a bomb that would detonate, but didn't. So, they regrouped."

"He played a prank on them. A prank turned deadly."

"And when they regrouped, he placed a charge on another cell phone, and used all the transports filled with fuel to maximize the explosion. And when the transports exploded, the burning metal became razor sharp projectiles of flying shrapnel, impaling and killing those in its path. And then thinking it was another prank, they paid for it with their lives. He took those men down without lifting a finger. Can't say I feel sorry for them."

"The government created a monster and now they want to destroy it," Celina said.

"It appears that someone's demon has come back to torment them," Dr. Weaver answered.

Dr. Weaver glanced all around him for a brief moment and saw that the glass windows of the cell phone store and metal framing of the doors were completely shattered and riddled with bullet holes. He slowly stepped into the store, stepping over a number of other enemy corpses.

He analyzed the scene and said, "This is where they were," and slowly walked through the door, stepping on all the razor sharp shards of broken glass, and saw the body of Brandon's grandfather, riddled with bullet holes, laying in a pool of his own blood, next to a soldier who had suffered the same fate.

He analyzed the soldier's lifeless corpse and said, "0-7 used him as a human shield."

"How do you figure?" Celina asked.

"If there's one thing that I've learned, and one day you'll learn, is that eventually, deception is the key to victory. To overcome your opponent, you have to deceive him."

"This just keeps getting more complicated."

"It's easy to comprehend, actually."

"Enlighten me. Or, rather, should I say ``us."

"There's the empty shell of a smoke grenade on the floor."

"I'm listening."

"The walls are filled with bullet holes."

"That's obvious."

Dr. Weaver contemplated the scenario, and answered, "I think I know how all this went down."

"We're all ears," Celina answered, a look of intrigue on her face, though she was frightened of all the carnage and destruction that the assassin had left in his wake, but remained greatly impressed by his resourcefulness.

"After 0-7 and my daughter made it here on foot, they tracked her here, opened fire, killing the old man. As you can see by the empty canisters, he used a smoke grenade to blind the enemy so he could cover their retreat, and engaged them through the smoke. Not knowing where he was attacking from caused them to be shooting everywhere in a frenzied attack trying to fend him off, judging from all the bullet holes inside the store. These unfortunate souls didn't see it coming. None of them did. And that's what makes him so dangerous. The fact that he can think on his feet in situations like these. The assassin definitely left his mark. That much is obvious. I can't say for certain if I'm right about everything, but I'm sure I'm damned close to it."

"Wow," Celina answered softly.

"And judging from the damage at the entrance, it could only mean that he tossed a hand grenade to take the others out," he said, backtracking towards the door. "Judging from all the angles of the bullet holes outside, they were firing at him, so he used the cell phone as a diversion, only this time, the prank proved fatal the second time."

"I'm not for violence, but I'm impressed that one man could be so resourceful," Celina replied, causing Dr. Weaver to gaze at her in awe.

"Sorry, sir. I didn't mean it that way," she said.

"Don't be. It's okay to say that you're impressed. After all, 0-7 is impressive. And the best that I've ever seen. As much as I don't approve of using force myself, I've grown to be very impressed by his resourcefulness as well. Especially against insurmountable odds like the ones against them. He's the reason why the entire Korean Peninsula was under our rule, after turning a desperate suicide mission into one of hope. Now he's using the same skills against the very man who turned him into the monster he is. And doing a really good job of it. So, I share your sentiment, Celina."

Dr. Weaver walked over the debris that littered the floor into the store room, and saw blood stains dripping from a bullet hole on the wall. He looked on the floor, seeing blood spatters, along with a bullet covered in blood, and picked it up from the floor. He said, holding the bullet up to his face, "Someone else was injured. And it looks like the wall minimized the impact."

"Do you think it could've been your daughter?"

"No. God forbid that happens. But I think it was her who was resourceful enough to take it out."

"Is it still fresh?"

"Yes. And it wasn't long ago they left. I was right. The question is where did they go?"

"Do you think that 0-7 could really be our ally based on all that's happened? Especially in those circumstances?"

"0-7 became a Ronin from the moment he turned against the General, breaking free from being the government's mindless assassin," he said.

"What's that?" Celina asked.

"A renegade. A warrior without a master. Bound to no one. Fights for no one's honor or cause but his own. And just so we're clear, Celina, 0-7 is fighting to keep my daughter out of enemy hands. He just doesn't know it.

He's running purely on instinct, or whatever memory that came back to him. And right now, he's the only means to my daughter not falling back into enemy hands. But to her, he's much more than that, and I don't blame her since he was the one who stuck his neck out to rescue her during the uprising on Genesis. And still is."

"Conflicting interest," Celina answered.

"That's a good way to look at it," Dr. Weaver answered.

"But he just doesn't know it yet. But still, a Ronin in every aspect, in the event he doesn't know he has loyalties to no one but her. At least for now."

He hurried outside, yelling his daughter's name as loudly as he could, hoping to get a sign that she was close.

As they slowly made their way through the long, dark sewers beneath the streets, Kassandra heard the faint echo traveling towards their position, and asked, "Did you hear something?"

"What do you think it is?" Arianna asked.

"You mean who?" Stephanie answered.

"Shhh," Kassandra pondered, and said, "Oh my God. It's him. He came. He was able to track me down all this way."

"Who is it?" Jason asked.

"My father," she answered in surprise.

"I can barely hear it. How do you know it's him? How do you know it's not a trap?" Stephanie asked.

"I'd know my father's voice anywhere," she said, running back towards the hole.

Dr. Weaver saw a trail of footprints leading towards the large metal cover of the manhole and said while he continued to grunt, "I need you to help me with this."

Celina and Dr. Weaver started to lift the heavy cover of the manhole, when Celina heard an echo from a distance growing louder as it drew nearer. "Wait. Someone's coming. It's a helicopter," she said.

"I need to see my daughter! I'm not leaving until I see my daughter!"

"More enemy troops are on their way! We need to leave now!"

"You're much too important to the resistance! You're no good to her if you get caught! We need to get going!" she said, pulling on his arm.

He finally relented and listened to the sound of the helicopter. He nodded his head in anger and told them to board the transports.

Kassandra began climbing the ladder leading towards the surface, and heard the group of transports quickly driving away.

She tried as hard as she could to lift the heavy cover by herself, but was quickly overwhelmed by its weight.

Stephanie came running towards her and said, "We need to keep moving."

"I missed him. I just missed him," she answered.

"And you'll keep on missing him if you get caught. And I don't need to tell you what'll happen to us if we get caught. Are you sure it was him?"

"I've lived with my father for most of my life. I think I should know his voice by now," Kassandra said.

They heard a helicopter landing on the streets, along with a number of armored transports deploying troops.

"See? I told you so," Stephanie said to her, pulling onto Kassandra's coat.

She quickly jumped from the ladder, and followed Stephanie through the dark and stench-riddled confines of the underground passageways, trying to place more distance between themselves and the fresh group of enemy soldiers about to pursue them, with David's unconscious and heavy body hampering the speed of their movements.

The General climbed from the helicopter and slowly walked over to where the bodies of his dead soldiers were sprawled all over the streets. He picked up the cell phone and walked over to the pieces of the assassin's charges. He walked into the store, seeing more corpses that the assassin had left in his wake, and continued walking deeper into the store, stepping over the shards of debris and broken glass, breaking under the thick and heavy sole of his boots. He saw one of his soldiers lying face-down with his back filled with bullet holes, alongside the corpse of Brandon's grandfather, and followed the trail of footsteps into the warehouse at the back of the store, seeing a bullet on the floor doused in blood. He slowly made his exit, knowing all the carnage was the work of the assassin, and walked over to where all the other corpses lay sprawled out on the streets.

He walked over to one of his high-ranking officers, and softly called out, "Colonel Danvers."

"Yes, General?" Kurt answered, looking at the general with a straight face, knowing that he would be given the tremendous task of pursuing the assassin. "What are your orders, sir?"

He stared at the General who he had served with his entire life, with blue eyes bearing a constant look of contempt towards him.

"Are you sure this is where the Package was last transmitted?"

"Yes, sir. Apparently, they've left the area," Kurt answered.

"I can see that. But being that this was her last position, they couldn't just vanish into thin air. People don't just disappear. Which means they couldn't have gone far. And judging from the looks of those footprints, they look recent."

The General followed the footprints to the cover of the sewers and said, "Which means that if we can't track her, then she and the others are underground. Clever girl. She's truly her father's daughter, and that means she's a lot tougher than she looks. Do not underestimate her. Never underestimate her. Since I'm a bit disappointed in not being able to give 0-7 a proper welcome, I'm charging you with finding her, and eliminating the Ronin who has laid waste to many of my men, at all costs."

"What's a Ronin, sir?" Kurt asked.

"A warrior without a master. A renegade. Bares no allegiances to anyone but himself. Fights for his own cause. And in my case, settles his vendetta against me for making him into what he is."

"And how am I supposed to complete this task of eliminating this Ronin?"

"0-7 made it this far because he was able to adapt, like he was trained to do, and as you can see, he has proven to be the best at it. It appears that she is learning to do the same as well. My men paid the price because they couldn't. And in our line of business, we both know that to survive, you must adapt. And we both know what happens when you can't. He may be the best soldier to date in the entire corp. But, it doesn't make him invincible. As much as this is a great challenge, look at it as an opportunity of a lifetime to test your leadership skills, although to be frank, you may lose a lot of men just to get the Ronin. That's if you ever do. I'll leave it all to you. Take as many men as you want. But it has to be done today."

"Understood, General," Kurt answered, feeling his anger mounting deep inside, trying to contain himself, with the demise of his close friend at the hand of the General still burning freshly in his mind.

"I can't be a general forever. I'm looking for a worthy successor. And possibly you could be the one to take my place."

"I'll do my best, sir."

"I'm sure you will. Success is paramount. Or you'll die trying."

"Yes, sir," Kurt answered.

The General looked into his eyes, and walked towards him smiling, while he remained staring back with a straight face, and said, "I recognize that look of contempt that you feel towards me. I'd recognize it anywhere. And believe me, I understand why.

But just so you know, just like you, I have a job to do. I wish I hadn't done what I did at the Pentagon. But this is not a popularity contest and I didn't get this far by being underestimated, nor do I appreciate anyone questioning my authority. I bear no qualms of anyone speaking his mind or sharing his opinion, but do so with respect and discretion, as we were all men before Lieutenants and Generals at the end of the day. If one person gets so bold and continues to do so, it means the rest will follow suit, and I can't allow it to happen under my command. I'm not asking you to like me, nor do I care. But all I ask for is a little respect and your loyalty."

"I understand, sir," Kurt answered.

"Now that that's out the way," the General said, placing his hand on Kurt's shoulder, "Let me reiterate that you're free to use everything you need at your disposal, including the chopper. I feel a little bit too confined at the Pentagon. I can use a drive and enjoy the fresh air of my country. Call in if you need anything. Let's hope you won't run out of men in this task in apprehending the target."

"Yes, General."

"Take care," the General said, as he was driven away in one of his light armored transports

Kurt looked at the soldiers and nodded at them to pursue the assassin and Kassandra, who continued to traverse through the dark recesses of the underground.

They quickly uncovered the heavy lid on top of the deep, dark hole, and rapidly descended into the sewers in hot pursuit of their targets, causing their tracking beacons to go offline, blinding the surveillance team that kept track of their movements.

The others continued walking through the tunnel as quickly as they could to widen the gap from their pursuers, when the assassin suddenly stopped and looked back.

"Why is he stopping?" Stephanie asked.

"Isn't it obvious? We're being followed," Kassandra replied.

Arianna paused for a brief moment, seeing a red dot on Stephanie's chest, followed by a number of red dots pointed on them, while they remained frozen with fear, causing Daniel to open fire. The enemy soldiers exchanged, while the others scrambled for cover.

The assassin waited in the dark confines of the underground, waiting for the enemy soldiers to walk past his position, while they slowly overwhelmed Daniel and Jason with their firepower.

He equipped his night vision goggles and slowly emerged from the dark and confined space that he'd carefully hidden from the enemy soldiers and attacked, causing confusion in the ranks, as he disposed of them with his deadly skills, until the gunfire suddenly stopped.

Kurt and the remaining soldiers heard the echo of the gunfire travel through the dark and narrow passages of the underground, heading towards their position, and suddenly stopped, knowing that their troops had met their grim fates at the hands of the assassin and took a deep breath, bowing his head, and closing his eyes.

He quickly shook his head at the other wave of soldiers that were about to descend into the dark confines of the underground, stopping them saying, "No. Don't. We'll only be sending more to die needlessly. It's too dark there. It's exactly what he wants. The same will just happen to you, like the others. They'll come to the surface eventually. It'll be a lot easier to track them in the open."

After the assassin had finished eliminating the pursuing enemy soldiers, he calmly walked past them like they didn't exist.

They looked at one another, mumbling among themselves, while the assassin continued his path.

Daniel ran towards the dead soldiers to replenish his supplies, while Jason and Stephanie continued to carry David's unconscious body through the long, dark passage of the sewers, to wherever the path led them.

CHAPTER 16: GATES OF OLYMPUS.

After moments of traversing underground, they climbed from the hole and into the opened streets, trying to find their bearings.

"Where are we?" David said, as he slowly regained consciousness, startling the others.

"You're awake," Stephanie said in surprise.

"I can't feel my legs."

"It'll wear off. You'll feel your legs soon enough," Kassandra replied.

Jason looked all around him and said, "We're in Springfield."

"What makes you so sure?" Arianna asked.

"Take a good look at the uniform. It has taken me all over the country. The last place worthwhile was Genesis, before the great fall, as we so call it."

"Good point," Arianna replied.

"And if my memory serves me right, the metro station is just about a mile up ahead."

"How far?" Daniel asked.

"Just a few minutes walk. That means they'll be having enough time to lock on to you tracking beacons, and come at us with everything they have."

"There may be more enemy soldiers coming. We can't take a chance to go on foot," Arianna said nervously.

"The metro station may be the only place where you can rest for a moment, until he gets his legs back," Jason said. "I got a plan."

"What are you thinking?" Stephanie asked.

"I was thinking that we can slow them down," Jason answered.

"How?" Daniel asked.

"Make him rough me up a little. Then they would track me here, take me back to base, and from there, I can work from the inside, and warn you about enemy troop movements."

"Are you crazy?" Kassandra asked.

"It's the only way," he replied.

"What if they kill you?" Arianna asked.

"It's a chance I'm willing to take. For a long time, I've been trying to live with myself, knowing that I was fighting on the wrong side. Like it or not, we're the resistance now, and we have to use everything at our disposal. Our best weapon at this point is information, other than him, of course. It's either I succeed, or die trying," Jason said.

"Well, I hate to say it, but he does have a point," Daniel answered.

"You have to let me do this, Kassandra. If they get me all bruised up, they'll take me to the General, and I deliver a message from yours truly. He lets me go, I'll be free to roam the base, and feed you information from the inside. It's much more difficult than it sounds, but you get the idea," Jason said.

Kassandra glanced at the assassin, and looked at Jason and asked, "You do know that he could kill you with one blow, right?"

"I know. Let's just get it over with," Jason answered.

"Before we do that, let's just say that the enemy picks you up. What will you tell the General?" Stephanie asked.

"I'll just tell him that 0-7 couldn't be stopped and that he spared me so I can tell the General he's coming for him. I'll think of something."

"I hate to say it, but he does have another good point," Arianna replied.

"On that, I think all of us agree. But know this - it's your funeral," Kassandra added.

Jason looked at the assassin and said nervously, "Take it easy. I need to be delivered in one piece." He quickly said, "Wait," taking off his gear and dropping it on the ground. "I need to be restrained so it can look like I am a prisoner."

"We'll do it after. In the meantime, get it over with. They'll be here at any time. You need to hurry," Daniel replied.

"Okay. "It's your show now," Jason said to the assassin.

"You know this is going to hurt, right?" Stephanie said, watching Jason acting nervously.

"It's going to be painful, but quick," Kassandra said.

"Will you stop?" Jason yelled back, and said to the assassin, "Go ahead. I'm all yours."

The assassin quickly thrusted his fist into Jason's gut, forcing the air out of his lungs, and quickly followed with a flurry of combinations to his face, restraining his full power, causing Jason to fall onto the snow-filled streets, laying on his back, with his face all bruised.

Jason nodded his head and said, "That'll do it."

"You're right about that," Daniel answered.

"Better you than any one of us," David said, watching the bruises on Jason's face form.

"Now you can put on the restraints," Kassandra said to the assassin.

After placing the restraints on his wrists, Jason said, "The metro station is just up ahead. You need to hurry before more come to our position. Go on, get out of here."

"Just be careful. Good luck," Stephanie said.

"After all this time, it's the least I can do. It's necessary," Jason said

"I'll see you soon," Arianna said, grabbing Jason's gear and hurrying to the metro station.

17:08 HOURS. SOMEWHERE IN ARLINGTON, VIRGINIA:

The enemy soldier picked up the signal from Kassandra's and Jason's tracking beacon, while another soldier walked towards Kurt and said, "We've picked up the signal from the Package. She's moving. We also have a fixed location on Sergeant White."

"Where are they?" Kurt asked.

"They're in Springfield. Moving towards the rail station, sir."

"And as for Sergeant White, he's a few blocks away from their current location."

"He's not mobile like the others, but his transponder is still active. He may be immobilized. Probably hurt from either when we engaged 0-7, or 0-7 might've been the one to deal the fatal blow," the enemy soldier said.

"And what about 0-7? What's his status?"

"Still no sign of him, sir."

"Which means he's still with her. Let's head to Sergeant White's location and move on to her."

17:22 HOURS. FRANCONIA-SPRINGFIELD METRO RAIL-STATION - SPRINGFIELD, VIRGINIA:

After arriving at the rail-station, they slowly walked through the metal doors and were greeted by the eerie silence, along with dust and debris strewn all about from the many years of abandonment, since the civil war began.

The assassin watched as they walked through the entrance, and placed a charge on the door to ambush the unsuspecting enemy soldiers. He crawled under one of the stationery vehicles sprawled throughout the streets, patiently waiting for the enemy soldiers to arrive.

David slowly arose from the floor, sat upright, and said, "I'm beginning to get the feelings in my legs back."

"Good. Because you'll need them in case we need to get running," Kassandra answered.

"You're quite the optimist, aren't you?" Stephanie answered.

"She's right. We're out in the open, and we'll need to use our legs as much as we can," Daniel said.

17:24 HOURS. SOMEWHERE IN SPRINGFIELD, VIRGINIA:

Kurt had arrived at the location where Jason's beacon was still active, and saw him lying unconscious on the snowy streets, his face severely bruised from the assassin's punishment, while the helicopter hovered over his position. Kurt ordered the other soldiers to move to Jason's position to secure him and ordered the pilot to land the helicopter.

The enemy soldiers quickly moved towards Jason's unconscious body and nudged him to see if he was still alive.

Jason slowly opened his eyes and saw the enemy soldiers standing over him, while he remained lying on the snow-filled streets.

They slowly picked him up and stared at his bruised face in disbelief, seeing that he was the only one who had survived the assassin's onslaught.

Kurt arrived at his location, saw his bruised face, stared at his hands tied in restraints, and ordered the soldiers to cut them off his wrists. Kurt asked, "What happened to you?"

"Isn't it obvious? He did this to me," Jason replied.

"Why?" Kurt asked. "You've been assigned to him since the beginning of the war."

"I tried to stop him. But he just can't be stopped. I guess we both know that by now. I saw what he did to those soldiers. He's like a rabid animal. He's beyond saving. Ever since Arlington, he just changed. I don't know what came over him. He just went out of control, and did this to me. I'm lucky he even left me alive."

"Why did he leave you alive?" Kurt asked.

"He left me alive to deliver a message to the General."

"What message might that be?"

"To tell him that he's coming for him."

"And that's exactly what you'll do. I suppose someone has to," Kurt answered. He nodded to the soldiers and said, "Take him to the General. The rest of you, apprehend the Package at all costs."

17:30 HOURS. FRANCONIA-SPRINGFIELD METRO RAILSTATION - SPRINGFIELD, VIRGINIA:

After moments of patiently waiting for the enemy troops to arrive, laying still under the decaying transport sprawled all about the streets, the assassin noticed a number of enemy vehicles arriving near his position, deploying a number of enemy troops.

He remained still under the stationary vehicle, observing the movement of the enemy troops, as they continued to lock onto the signal of Kassandra's tracking beacon. THey quickly rushed towards the doors of the rail-station, totally unaware that they had walked into the assassin's carefully laid trap, and slowly pulled the door, expecting resistance.

They heard the deafening roar from the explosion from deep inside the station, feeling the violent tremor from the building's entire foundation, causing dust and debris to shower over them, after the assassin quietly set off the detonator. The charge caused a giant explosion to rock the entire foundation of the building, shuddering violently, with the burning shards of glass and shrapnel from the metal instantly killing the enemy soldiers, startling Kurt as he waited for their report.

He quickly rose from the seat of the transport, watching the carnage that the assassin had caused effortlessly in just one attempt.

The assassin continued to observe the movements of the remaining enemy soldiers, and silently crawled from beneath his hiding place and slowly disposed of the stragglers, until there were no more enemy troops left alive.

Kurt suddenly felt the cold steel of the assassin's sidearm pointed to his temple, and slowly sat down in his seat.

The assassin grabbed him by his collar, gently pulling him out of his seat, leading towards the gaping hole where the doors made of glass and metal once stood, and paused at seeing the remaining enemy soldiers who were silently disposed, sprawled on the streets near the transport. He made his way into the dark confines of the rail-station, impaled by the countless projectiles of glass and shrapnel.

Kurt paused one more time for a few seconds, looking at the bodies of the soldiers, and said to the assassin, "More will be coming. You don't have much time."

The assassin simply nudged him to walk into the rail-station with his rifle pointed firmly into his back.

He continued into the rail station and stopped, seeing the civilians, along with one of General West's troops, and Kassandra, slowly being overcome with a look of shock and remorse on his face. He glanced at Susan being held tightly in Arianna's arms, and asked, "Aren't you going ask me to put my hands down?"

"Should I?" Kassandra asked.

"It's not that I can go anywhere, or do anything. Your bodyguard here will make sure that I don't succeed," Kurt replied.

"He's more than that. He's a true friend. I owe him my life. We all do. Including you, considering the fact that he hasn't killed you yet, since he doesn't take any prisoners," Kassandra replied.

"I suppose you're right," Kurt answered, slowly placing his hands down.

"I didn't say you could put your hands down."

"I don't need your permission. But if it pleases you to kill me, then go ahead. You're a fugitive, the acting president's daughter, who's also a brilliant scientist like her father before her, who can change the world like her father dedicated his life to do, or destroy it. And I've looked into the eyes of many souls over these years, and have been in this business long enough to know that you're not a murderer like the General. I don't see anything in these eyes that says you're a murderer. Clever and resourceful like your father, maybe, but it's not like you to kill a defenseless man. You carry your father's name, and with that name comes much honor. To kill me right here in front of all these people would be staining the honor of what the Weaver name stands for."

"Technically, you're the enemy so he should kill you. And frankly, I don't think anyone would disagree, or lose a good night's sleep over it."

"Believe me, I know how you feel," Kurt answered. "Technically, as you so put it. But you think that I was given much of a choice?"

"Then why are you following me?"

"It's obvious, don't you think?" Kurt asked. "The daughter of the world's most renowned scientist and philanthropist, who is also the acting president's daughter, must be apprehended at all costs, since she is valuable to the General's war effort. And we're the ones getting slaughtered in the process, so one man can live out his ruthless ambition."

"Well, I'm not going back," she said sharply.

"Frankly, I don't care what you do, or where you go at this point, Kassandra."

"That's enough information about me or my father," Kassandra answered, with a look of total surprise on her face, looking all around her suspiciously, still trying to keep the real reason why she was abducted from the enemy forces from the others.

"The entire chain of command knows who you are. Including that you're being held against your will. What they don't know is why. Or at least all of it."

"As long as they come after us, this is what will continue to happen," she answered.

"So many have to die for one man's ambition. It just never makes any sense."

"No, it doesn't. After 0-7 did everything he was told, the General wanted him killed. Just tossed to the side like garbage, after serving his purpose."

"Do you know why he thinks I'm important to the war effort? Did he ever tell you?" she asked. "So I can help him win the war by helping him to create abominations, and help him place the entire country under his control. But that much you already know, I'm sure."

"I don't have the slightest idea of what you're talking about," Kurt replied with a total look of shock on his face. "I'm not always given all the details. His intentions are his own. He gives me enough information and the rest he keeps to himself. All I do is follow orders, and all I'm ordered to do at this point is to bring you back, because you were important to his plans. Then again, I thought you said that it was enough information about you and your father."

"Well, that still stands. And you can try to take me back if you want to. But I don't have to tell you that it won't end well for you," Kassandra answered

"I don't want to. And if it makes you feel any better, I want to kill the son of a bitch myself," Kurt said.

"Well, here's a pleasant surprise. What do you mean you want to kill him?" she asked. "And here I was, thinking both of you were on the same side."

"It's not all of us who fight for the General means that we're on the same side. Not all of us were given much of a choice," he said.

"I'm listening," she answered.

"I've spent most of my entire life serving my country, like my father before me, and his father before him. I was just this close to being a General, myself, and after my soul became weary, live out the rest of my days quietly watching my children grow up to be men and women and follow the right path. After all that, we've suffered fighting this damned war, I pray that my children don't fight for a cause like the General's. Frankly, I'm tired of fighting. My soul lost the will to fight a long time ago, simply for the fact that we didn't uphold the prestige of who we once were of being the good guys that some thought we once were, and making so many enemies in the process. And when I saw the country came under his control, I knew what was about to happen. And every day, I kept on saying to myself that I should've left a long time ago. Then it came to me, that the only way you could leave from the General's service was in a box, covered in dirt, 6 feet under. I was just a senior lieutenant when the North Koreans attacked the South, and saw how they dealt with all their enemies with brutal efficiency, until I saw the same man who fought the North Koreans take his ruthlessness to another level. I had never seen so much apathy in my life, until today at the Pentagon."

"What do you mean?" Kassandra asked.

"After one of our Washington strike force had lost the element of surprise in attacking General West's last position, he ordered our troops to move into the base and sanitize it, even while our planes were still on their bombing run. Fortunately for them, it didn't result in any friendly fire."

"I heard. I heard everything while I was under the security detail heading towards the capital. But I still never fully understood what really happened," Kassandra said.

"When one of the others protested, the General put a bullet in his head, and acted like it was nothing. He didn't shed an ounce of remorse. Nothing. I saw another good man die for no reason. Like a number of other good men before him. And as much as we considered the rebels our mortal enemies, it made me really realize that the real enemy all along was the General. I've been on the wrong side all this time and was too blind to see it. Or maybe too afraid to tell you the truth. But sometimes, when you fight, it's not always about your allies or enemies. It's about self-preservation, so you join the side that you think is going to win. General West was on the verge of being wiped out when our lead pilot was asked to fly her plane, and make the ultimate sacrifice into 0-7's transport if necessary. But the problem is, she wasn't ready to meet her maker, and frankly I don't blame her. Then the next thing I remember was she was going crazy, turning on her own, picking off a number of pilots, including some of our ground troops, and is now in hiding like the rest of you."

"Whatever it was, she had her reasons. And judging from what she had to deal with, I don't blame her either," Arianna added.

"I suppose," Kurt answered.

"I saw a number of the General's men walk into a sanctuary and put a gun to a child's face. They were ready to snuff her out on his orders. If it weren't for 0-7, they would have succeeded."

"Welcome to the human race. It appears that our infamous assassin has a conscience after all."

"Well, he could've killed you, but he didn't. So, that should count for something, right?" Kassandra added.

"I suppose it does. I know about the massacre at the sanctuary. I was there when the General relayed the instructions to kill her. And you wouldn't believe the reason why he said to silence that little girl."

"What did he say?" Kassandra asked.

"He couldn't afford her growing up to be a resistance fighter."

"Are you serious?" Arianna answered.

"Yes," Kurt answered.

"Well, I'm glad they're all dead. That means they would have snuffed me out if they had the chance as well," Arianna said.

"That's basically what he said. But still, in the same breath, he told me that he took no pleasure in doing it. It just didn't seem that way to me. I don't take pleasure in sending young men and women to their deaths. But as I said, I wasn't given much of a choice."

"There's always a choice," Daniel answered.

"We left another soldier about a mile back. Did you find him?" Kassandra asked.

"Yes. He's on his way to the General even as we speak. No doubt that it was your assassin's handiwork," Kurt said, gesturing to the assassin.

"That was just a little something to let the General know what's in store," Arianna remarked.

"It sounds like you're having a change of heart," Kassandra said.

"The truth is, I had one a long time ago. Just waiting for the right time to defect, I suppose," Kurt said

"Well, it's either you do, or end up like them," Stephanie remarked.

"What do you need me to do?" Kurt asked.

"You do know that you could be charged with treason for disobeying the General? Don't you?" Stephanie asked.

"I committed treason a long time ago against myself, when I didn't have the courage to do what's right. The way I see it, either way I'm screwed. Better the General putting a bullet in my head, than him slitting my throat. I've seen enough to know that this is not where I want to live out the rest of my days fighting. The funny thing is, I've been looking for every excuse to defect, for quite some time now. And when I heard him order our troops to sanitize General West's position while our planes were still bombing the position was one thing. But what he did at the Pentagon to one of my friends and when he ordered the execution of an unarmed civilian - a child, for that matter - was something else entirely. By no means the General should be the one to lead us in the president's stead."

"Wise choice," David answered.

"My career was over a long time ago, when I wasted all my years fighting on the wrong side. And I know that I'll get pumped up with a lot of holes for this. But whatever it is, I'm willing to do. If 0-7 is the one to kill the bastard, then by all means let him do it."

"Amen to that," Arianna replied.

"What do you need me to do?" Kurt asked.

"We need to get to the nation's capital."

"But you're being tracked even as we speak right now. They'll see you coming more than a mile away," Kurt answered.

"Exactly. All attention on me, while 0-7 slips into the Pentagon, and kills the General," Kassandra answered.

"With him at large, the Pentagon has to be on high alert. Security and all surveillance have been increased by more than double."

"True. But the thing is, 0-7 is no longer being tracked. So, I'm sure there has to be a way that he can get inside undetected."

"And what if he fails?" Kurt asked.

"He won't. He never has. He's in a better position to succeed than all of us combined."

"You really think so?" Kurt asked.

"I know so. Haven't you looked outside?"

"I suppose there's no changing your mind."

"It's not about that."

"Then tell me what it's about?"

"My father's work," she said.

"The General thought the war would've ended in a few years, since the freedom fighters were outnumbered by more than 20 to 1, but he was wrong. At first, he had me kidnapped to lure my father out and seize his work. But, as the war went on, he wanted me to use my father's work as a weapon. And if he does, then all hope is lost."

"What do you mean?"

"It's a little more complicated than what it seems. I wasn't kidnapped for my good looks. As I told you before, I was kidnapped because I'm my father's daughter. I know about my father's research, and I'm the only one other than him who can use it. And right now, I can't let them use my father's research as a weapon. Because if they do, all of those who made the ultimate sacrifice fighting this war will be for nothing. More people will die. It won't matter who you are, whether you're a civilian or freedom fighter. And I said that I didn't want to divulge any more information about my father, but you don't leave me with much of a choice."

"We all have a choice. And you have my undivided attention once again. I didn't know it was that bad," Kurt said, with a tiny hint of shock on his face once again.

"It's worse than what I told you. But I can't afford to get into the details right now, and the more we stand here talking about it, the more time we waste. We need to get going."

"There's only one problem," Kurt said.

"What's that?" Kassandra asked.

"The chopper won't fly itself."

"Problem solved," Kassandra said, raising her hand.

"You?" Kurt asked in surprise.

"Exactly. Where's the chopper?" she answered

"I left it a mile back from here."

"Let's go."

They made their way through the entrance, where all the dead soldiers laid, slowly stepping over their corpses as they made their way to the helicopter.

After moments of trekking through the war-torn streets, they reached the helicopter, sat inside, and turned on the ignition.

"Are you sure you can fly? I hope you know what you're doing."

"Just relax. My father used to fly," she said, struggling to lift the helicopter off the ground.

"For someone who spent most of her time in captivity, how did you learn how to fly?" Kurt asked.

"I didn't. It's my first time," she answered, causing a sudden look of shock on their faces.

"Put the chopper down now!" Kurt demanded.

"Too late. You'll have to jump if you want to get out," Kassandra answered, and swerved the helicopter in the direction of the nation's capital, as Kurt and the others held on for their lives.

17:42 HOURS. SOMEWHERE IN ARLINGTON, VIRGINIA. A FEW MILES AWAY FROM THE NATION'S CAPITAL:

After a brief ride out of the embattled area, the General stopped the vehicle and stepped out, pausing for a brief moment, enjoying the brisk climate, inhaling the frigid winds deep within his lungs, while admiring the dense vegetation of the peaceful wilderness that lined both sides of the long stretch of road, covered thickly with the gleaming white snow that blanketed the entire country. He peered at the giant dome of the Capitol Building that remained as a symbol of the nation's capital since it was founded.

He walked back slowly to his transport, bound for the capital, and suddenly spotted one of his transport helicopters flying over his position.

He grabbed the radio and said, "This is command to Colonel Danvers, do you read? What is your status? Over."

17:42 HOURS. SOMEWHERE OVER ARLINGTON, VIRGINIA, A FEW MILES AWAY FROM THE NATION'S CAPITAL:

Kassandra heard the General's voice with a sudden look of shock on her face and asked, "What do I do? It's him. I think he's seen us."

"Whatever you do, don't key that headset. Just fly," Kurt answered.

"I think the General is onto us," Daniel answered.

"Well, the last I recalled, you had a plan to sneak us into the capital," Kurt said.

"I still do. It hasn't changed. It'll just have to wait a little longer. All we have to do now is to get to the capital. And then I'll figure what to do," Kassandra answered

17:43 HOURS. SOMEWHERE IN ARLINGTON, VIRGINIA, A FEW MILES AWAY FROM THE NATION'S CAPITAL:

The General watched the helicopter continue to fly over his position and said to the soldier in the driver's seat, "None of my men would ignore my call. It's him. 0-7 is on board that chopper. And they're heading towards the capital. And it seems he wants to make good on his promise. And wherever he is, she isn't far behind."

He grabbed the radio and said, "Attention all units. We have a visual on the Package and 0-7 moving towards the capital. All units converge to his position, seal off the capital, and neutralize all opposition. Apprehend the Package at all costs. I repeat, apprehend the Package at all costs. Do not let them breach the Gates of Olympus under any circumstances. I repeat - do not let them breach the gates. You will engage the targets or die trying," he said, and placed the radio on its box. He said to himself, "If he breaches the Gates of Olympus, then God help you all."

17:43 HOURS. BOLLING ENEMY AIR FORCE BASE - WASHINGTON, D.C., THE NATION'S CAPITAL:

Immediately after receiving the General's orders, a number of enemy troops mobilized in pursuit of Kassandra, the assassin, and the others heading to the capital.

17:57 HOURS. THE WHITE HOUSE - WASHINGTON, D.C., THE NATION'S CAPITAL:

The helicopter landed on the lawn filled with grass that was always well trimmed and constantly maintained by the many custodians who were once employed to oversee its safekeeping, now transformed into towering blades and thick weeds anchoring firmly into the soil.

They climbed out of the helicopter, stepping into the tall blades of grass, filled with weeds and looked at the grand structure of the building, once thought to be the most powerful house in the entire world, with its once gleaming walls. Now, it has become a shadow of itself, decrepit and decayed, after many years of abandonment.

Arianna looked at the grand infrastructure of the building and said in amazement, "Wow. I've always wanted to come to the White House. I remembered when this place was all they talked about. Now it's just a shadow of its former glory."

"You can thank the General for that," Stephanie answered.

"I hope we didn't just come here to admire the architecture. In case you didn't notice, the General has ordered more troops to our location. So, what's the plan?" Kurt asked.

"We can't stay outside. That's for sure," David answered.

"We need to get inside," Arianna said, grabbing Susan tightly, heading into the building.

The assassin walked calmly past them, heading towards the front gate, walking into the streets.

"Where's he going?" Kurt asked.

"To keep the rest of you breathing. He knows what he's doing," Kassandra answered.

"We need to move quickly. They'll be here soon," Daniel said, nervously.

"We've been spotted coming in. What's plan B?" Kurt asked.

"Hide the others to keep them safe, and draw all the attention to myself, since the both of us are the only ones being tracked, giving 0-7 enough time to make his way to the General."

"And if that doesn't work?"

"We have an experienced soldier inside. We'll try and hold them off and wear them down as much as possible. And pray for a miracle. If there's any at all. Either way, the entire mission hinges upon 0-7 succeeding. And the best way we can do so is to work together and move undetected. If we move undetected, all of us have a better chance of succeeding. And makes it a whole lot easier for 0-7 to carry out his mission."

They walked into the dark recesses of the building, pausing for a brief moment, marveling at its grand architecture, and continued scurrying about, looking for a place to hide.

"We need to hide quickly," Arianna said.

"That's the plan," David answered.

"You know this place as much as they do," Arianna said to Kurt.

"Yes, I do. And with my tracking beacon online, they'll be able to track me just like her," Kurt answered, looking at Kassandra.

"Where are the best places to hide?" Arianna answered.

"There's one way they'll be able to find you," David answered.

"The clock's ticking," Kurt said, suggesting that he makes his point quickly.

"The elevator. This place has an elevator. But, normally any form of electronics shuts down once we're on the inside," David answered.

"Or the hospital," Stephanie answered.

"Or underground," Kassandra said, interrupting, and said, "Wait a minute. cell phones can also jam electronics. I remember on my way to Europe, to receive my Nobel prize for genetic engineering, they always said to shut down all electronics because they said it could interfere with the navigational systems of the flight."

"Good idea," Kurt answered.

"When he said he was going to come in handy, he wasn't kidding," Arianna said softly.

They ran deeper into the White House, towards the elevator to jam the signals of their tracking beacons.

After moments of waiting for the enemy reinforcements lying beneath the parked vehicles on the streets, a number of enemy transports suddenly pulled in, deploying enemy troops, securing the entire perimeter with their weapons drawn.

The assassin slowly and quietly rolled from his position under the vehicle, and moved silently towards one of the enemy transports, placing a charge under it, and crawled to the next one, placing another charge.

He continued to move through the column of transports undetected, placing more charges, until he saw the one soldier seated with his wrists bruised from the restraints, knowing it was Jason.

He took out a pebble and tossed it at Jason, signaling him of his presence, showing him the charge, and slowly vanished to not arouse any suspicion.

Jason slowly stepped out of the vehicle, and walked closer to the other soldiers, as the assassin continued to place more charges on the remaining enemy transports to cut them off from all the means of pursuing them.

After he had placed all the charges on the enemy vehicles, he began contemplating how to move through the gauntlet of enemy soldiers undetected, as he glanced at the heavy stains of blood on his clothes from all those that had met their untimely demise from his deadly skills, and quickly contemplated about what David mentioned about the tracking device going offline if the host had been killed in action.

He silently crept behind one of the unsuspecting stragglers, grabbing him from behind, and quickly dragged him away, silently cutting off his air supply, until he went into total unconsciousness, and quickly dressed into his clothes. He disposed of his bloody clothes under one other vehicle and made his way to where the other soldiers had gathered at the front gates, staying out of sight, monitoring all enemy activity. He watched as the first wave of enemy soldiers prepared themselves to go through the front gates to continue the hunt for Kassandra and the others.

He walked past Jason, deliberately bumping into him, to catch his attention, warning him that he was about to make his entrance into the White House, in his directive to protect Kassandra, and the others.

Jason turned around and watched silently at the assassin walking past him in the midst of the enemy soldiers, hiding plainly in their sights, neatly dressed in one of their uniforms, and walked towards the White House. The other enemy soldiers stayed behind, watching them go through the front door, and went to the monitor where another group of enemy soldiers remained, to track the signals of their tracking beacons, as they opened the towering doors of the building.

Meanwhile, near the column of enemy transports, another soldier made his way from the group, and stumbled upon the unconscious soldier, sprawled on the snowy road, completely stripped of his clothes, and saw the bloodstained gear of the assassin close to his position, firmly tucked under one of the vehicles. He sounded the alarm, warning the others that 0-7 had made his way into the building with them.

They watched with a sudden look of shock on their faces, after seeing a number of the tracking beacons suddenly went offline almost simultaneously, knowing that the assassin was the one responsible for their untimely demise, after hiding within their ranks in plain sight.

After quickly disposing of the enemy soldiers, the assassin watched from within the darkness of the White House's grand hall through the windows, seeing the enemy soldiers go on high alert, after listening to their frantic radio chatter, and saw a second wave approaching the building, in larger numbers.

He waited until they entered and gently rolled a smoke grenade on the floor, and watched it explode into a giant wall of smoke to ambush his enemies. As they slowly walked deeper into the grand hall of the building, he quickly and silently disposed of them with his deadly skills, as the smoke covered his advance.

Shots suddenly echoed through the grand hall of the building, shattering the windows, and tearing through the doors, alarming those that waited outside, that they were once again being engaged by the assassin, and suddenly stopped.

After hearing the shots, Jason quickly made his way into one of the communications posts, and witnessed a number of tracking beacons that monitored their vital signs went offline. He was astonished at how quickly the assassin had neutralized the enemy soldiers, and said softly, "My God."

He listened to one of the high-ranking officers asking to breach the White House from the roof, and slowly walked away from the mobile command post. He sent a text message to Kassandra, warning them of the enemies attacking from the roof.

Kassandra heard her phone alarm from the incoming message and read it, and said, "Oh my God."

"What is it? I thought you couldn't get a signal underground. What does it say?" Kurt asked.

"Me too. It says that 0-7 has neutralized all the enemy soldiers. And they're planning on breaching the roof to flush us out. I need to warn him."

"And who sent you that information? It's him, isn't it? It's the one we found with his hands tied in Springfield, isn't it? He's working on the inside? Him being found and being beaten up was just a ruse to slow us down and to get inside wasn't it?" Kurt asked.

Kassandra shrugged her shoulders and answered, "Yes. I didn't tell you, because I didn't know if I could trust you."

"Based on the circumstances, what do you think now?" Kurt asked.

"I know I can trust you now. I'm sorry that I misjudged you," she answered.

"And what if your informant gets killed?" he asked.

"It was his idea. We tried to talk him out of it," Kassandra said.

"As much as I think he was an ass for coming up with a reckless and dangerous plan, it was absolutely ingenious that you went low tech."

"Thank you, Colonel. But the cell phone idea was Brandon's grandfather in the hope that I'd be his girlfriend, right before they killed him, not that it was a bad idea though."

"He was smart for thinking about that too. And just so you know, I'm sorry for what happened to your grandfather, Brandon. He didn't deserve that."

"Thank you, Colonel. Me too," Brandon answered.

"Wait a minute. I just received a message from this phone," Kassandra said, in a sudden state of shock.

"So?" Arianna asked.

"We're underground. We're not supposed to have signals. Which means that Colonel Danvers and myself are still transmitting. Which means that we're not deep enough underground."

"Which also means that your tracking beacon will lead them to our position," David answered.

"This is not good," Stephanie said.

"Yeah. No shit," Arianna replied.

"Our only hope now is 0-7," Kassandra answered.

"There's no way I can hold all those soldiers off all at once. I'm not that skillful," Daniel added.

"He'll be here. I know he will," Kassandra replied.

"You really have faith in him, don't you?" Stephanie asked.

"Yes. And considering how far that the rest of you have come, all of you should too. He's never let me down before. And he won't do it now."

"I believe you," Kurt answered.

The assassin continued standing in the smoke that clouded the grand hall confidently, as it slowly cleared. He heard the radio chatter from the enemy soldiers' mobile command post, giving orders to breach the White House through the roof, on the radio attached to the uniform that he'd stolen from the enemy soldier. He quickly made his way to the roof planting charges, and hurried back to the lower level, patiently waiting in the darkness to ambush the unsuspecting enemy soldiers.

The helicopter carrying a number of enemy troops hovered over the White House, rappelling into the building, running through the dark corridors with their footsteps pounding on the floors, echoing through the halls.

The assassin watched in the dark as they ran past him, rushing towards their tracking beacons and waited for the last of the soldiers. The assassin quickly snatched the last soldier from behind, quickly disposing of him, and making his escape, placing the enemy mobile unit stationed outside on high alert once again, warning them of his presence.

The enemy soldiers instantly reacted, knowing that he was in the area, splitting up into groups, as the assassin watched all activity in the darkness, silently stalking for signs of any stragglers that continued their pursuit.

While they continued to pursue him, they were distracted by the pounding footsteps of a soldier running towards them, acting erratically and immediately opened fire, riddling the soldier with bullets, until he fell to the floor in a pool of his own blood, his hands tied and gagged.

They watched for a brief moment, and saw that it was one of their own who had fallen to friendly fire, and shed their remorse for a brief moment, knowing that the assassin was nearby, stalking them, slowly and silently wearing down their numbers. Suddenly, they were enveloped by a wall of smoke, and felt their weapons quickly being snatched away from them, while being swiftly engaged.

The radio chatter quickly filled enemy mobile units outside of the gates, as they heard the frantic distress call from a group of their dying soldiers. The chatter suddenly became static, as the other group of soldiers who had gone a separate route hurried to their previous position through the thick cloud of smoke that concealed them. The assassin quickly and silently engaged them, until they met their demise like their comrades sprawled on the dusty floors of the White House.

Kassandra grew impatient, wondering about the assassin's status and said, "I have an idea."

"With all that's going on, what are you planning this time?" Kurt asked.

"They're after me. Which means that if I play the bait, that will lead them away from you, and at the same time flush them out, so 0-7 could snuff them out," Kassandra replied.

"You're truly your father's daughter. You're a lot tougher than you look. You got nerves of steel. I'll give you that. But the last thing that you want is to fall back into enemy hands, or be killed by mistake," Kurt said.

"I won't. He'll save me. I know he will," she answered

"Be careful," Stephanie said.

"I will," Kassandra answered and slowly walked out of her hiding place nervously.

The enemy soldiers remained in shock observing all the activities in their mobile units after seeing all their soldiers' tracking beacons stop transmitting, after listening to their distress calls, and being called in for more reinforcements. They suddenly stopped after they picked up the signal from Kassandra's tracking beacon moving closer to the door, and sent another wave of soldiers to retrieve her, and neutralize the assassin.

She slowly walked through the dark corridors, and continued to walk, looking for the assassin, when she suddenly came upon a number of flashlights from the enemy soldiers coming in her direction, obstructing her view. She slowly raised her hands to the top of her head, as she walked closer to them, with her eyes probing all about, hoping for the assassin to come to her rescue.

As Jason watched Kassandra's tracking beacon in the enemy mobile unit, he saw them moving closer towards Kassandra, causing him to express silent signs of frustration.

18:22 HOURS. ENEMY COMMAND CENTER - PENTAGON, WASHINGTON, D.C., THE NATION'S CAPITAL:

Colonel Wilson Sanders was an African-American high-ranking soldier who had spent most of his years serving his country, like the General, Colonel Danvers, and the others. He was past middle age, with his dark hair lined with shades of gray, from all the stresses that the civil war had produced throughout the entire decade.

And unlike Maxwell, he had now begun to question his allegiance to the General from the recent turn of events. He stood from his seat, and said softly, "General, we have a visual on the Package."

"Really?" the General asked.

"Yes. She's moving into their custody right now," Colonel Sanders answered.

The General pondered for a moment and asked, "Where is 0-7? It's a trap! Pull out! Pull out now!"

18:23 HOURS. THE WHITE HOUSE - WASHINGTON, D.C., THE NATION'S CAPITAL:

The assassin stayed a distance in the darkness, and fired a number of shots with his silenced weapon, quickly disposing of enemy soldiers, until Kassandra was the only one left standing.

She took a deep sigh of relief, and said, "There are more of them moving towards Colonel Danver's position."

He stared at the corpses of the dead soldiers sprawled on the floor, and stripped the clothing from their lifeless bodies, shoving them into Kassandra's hands to take to the others, and moved on to engage the others who may be on the way to intercept them.

18:23 HOURS. ENEMY COMMAND CENTER - WASHINGTON, D.C., THE NATION'S CAPITAL:

Colonel Sanders stared at the monitor, seeing all the beacons of their soldiers suddenly offline, and stared back at the General with a look on his face, as he continued witnessing firsthand how proficient the assassin was, which had made his reputation as the government's number one killing machine.

The General looked back calmly, with a blank expression on his face, and said to Colonel Sanders, "This is just a taste of what he can do. Today alone, he's laid waste to a number of my men. He's very shrewd and cunning. And sadly for those men, there'll be more to come. As I said earlier, my demon has come to torment me."

18:24 HOURS. THE WHITE HOUSE - WASHINGTON, D.C., THE NATION'S CAPITAL:

The assassin made his way to the others as they waited for Kassandra to return, only to be greeted by more enemy soldiers.

Kurt watched as the flashlight of the enemy soldiers drew closer towards them, and immediately opened fire, causing Daniel to follow suit.

Within a brief moment, the firefight between both sides had ensued. The others covered their ears tightly, cowering from the deafening roar of the machine gun blasts that echoed through the lower levels of the White House, when the assassin suddenly snuck up from behind. He silently snatched the last unsuspecting soldier, and plunged the long serrated blade of his knife deeply into his neck, until he stopped breathing. The assassin dropped his lifeless body on the floor without a shred of remorse before the others, and grabbed the lifeless soldier's weapon, quickly disposing the others, and quickly stripped their bodies of their clothes and threw it at their feet, and walked away, the same direction he came.

Kassandra dropped the remainder of the enemy soldiers' uniforms at their feet and said, "There'll be more coming. Then again, I'm sure you already know that."

"And right now is our best chance to make our escape. But we must use the enemy uniform as disguises. Brilliant," Kurt answered.

"And if we're lucky, make it as far as the front door," Arianna replied.

"Either way, we have to try," Kassandra answered.

"The best chance for all of us to come out alive is to leave by air, in a helicopter. But how can we get remotely close to getting one, with all the troops posted outside?" Stephanie asked.

"I have an idea. But it's 50-50," Kassandra replied.

"None of us have a choice right now. At this point, we're open to just about anything. And I speak for all of us when I say that," Arianna answered.

"Anything beats staying here, and being a walking target for those assholes," Kurt answered.

"Our plan of getting into the nation's capital didn't go so well," Kassandra said.

"I think we can all attest to that right about now," Kurt answered.

"So since Kurt and I are being tracked, we can't take the one we have outside, so why not have Kurt radio for one, and Kurt, you and the others pretend that you've taken me hostage, since you're the highest ranking officer, and all the rest of you are dressed in the enemy uniform. Then we use the helicopter out there and get us somewhere safe. Anywhere."

"And what do we do with the pilot after?" David asked.

Kassandra shrugged her shoulders and answered, "I don't know. I'll leave it to 0-7."

"Quite an ambitious plan. Very clever. But the problem is that our choppers are equipped with a tracking beacon. Won't matter which one we leave in. But it's worth a try. I'll radio for one just to make sure," Kurt answered.

"Well, none of us have much of a choice right now, given the circumstances," Kassandra replied.

"What about Susan? There's no way she can sneak by without being noticed. The last I checked, these clothes couldn't fit," Arianna added.

"We have to keep her hidden. Stay in a tight formation to keep her out of sight," Kassandra replied.

"This is too risky," Daniel added.

"If we stay here, they have a better chance of overwhelming us. and if they do, we know what will happen to the rest of you. 0-7 may be the government's best assassin, but he's far from being invincible. He gave those clothes to you because he knows that our best option for all of us to stay alive is to get out of here and go somewhere else, and regroup and come up with another plan to secure my father's research."

"You made your point. Lead the way. Either way, there must be another one coming as we speak." Kurt answered.

Kassandra grabbed Daniel's sidearm, placing it into his hand, pressing it to her back, and said, "After me. Remember to stay as close, tightly as possible to keep Susan from being spotted."

"I admit, you're by far more clever than I give you credit for. But I pray it works," Kurt said.

"Thank you, Colonel Danvers. But it's the best way for us to get out. We don't have much time."

"The rest of you need to get dressed now."

"Beats staying here and getting killed. I can tell you that much," Stephanie remarked.

After they got dressed in the enemy uniforms, they walked towards the front doors of the building, walking over the trail of dead corpses the assassin left in his wake.

"My God," Kurt said, looking at the carnage that was left before him in total shock.

"Don't act like you've never seen dead bodies before," Kassandra answered.

"Not like this," Kurt answered.

"Better them than you. And if you don't worry, that's exactly what's going to happen to the rest of you."

They arrived in the hallway, seeing more corpses sprawled on the floor. "I prefer him being for us than against us. I can tell you that," Daniel remarked.

"On that, we both agree," Kassandra answered.

She walked towards the front door and said, "Wait," taking a deep breath.

18:35 HOURS. ENEMY COMMAND CENTER - PENTAGON, WASHINGTON, D.C., THE NATION'S CAPITAL:

"General," Wilson called out softly.

"Yes, Colonel Sanders," the General answered.

"We have something."

"What is it?"

"I'm receiving a couple of transmissions."

"From who?"

"One is from her."

"And who's the other?"

"Colonel Danvers. He's still alive."

The General remained silent in thought, trying to evaluate the entire scenario.

18:37 HOURS. THE WHITE HOUSE - WASHINGTON, D.C., THE NATION'S CAPITAL:

Kassandra slowly walked out of the door with her hands up in surrender, with the others' weapons pointing to her back, as they remained closely together, trying to conceal Susan's presence.

Jason and the other enemy soldiers watched Kassandra waved at one of the helicopters, signaling it to pick her up.

As the helicopters landed on the towering blades of grass on the lawn in front of the White House, they boarded as quickly as they could, staying together tightly, trying to conceal Susan to not arouse any suspicion.

18:37 HOURS. ENEMY COMMAND CENTER - PENTAGON, WASHINGTON, D.C., THE NATION'S CAPITAL:

The General maintained his silence for a brief moment, still assessing the recent turn of events and asked, "How many tracking beacons are still active?"

"Just her and Colonel Danvers, sir."

"Radio the position and ask if there are any more troops with them," the General said, with a puzzled look on his face.

18:38 HOURS. THE WHITE HOUSE - WASHINGTON, D.C., THE NATION'S CAPITAL:

After boarding the helicopter, the enemy pilot turned around and saw Susan, and quickly realized they were impostors. He quickly reached for the radio, and suddenly felt the cold steel of the assassin's sidearm to his temple, causing him to pause with his hand over the radio.

"I'd do what she says if I were you," Kurt said.

They heard the radio chatter from the other soldiers outside asking for confirmation of the other identities of the other soldiers, who sat with Kassandra and Kurt.

The enemy pilot paused, listening to the radio chatter with the assassin's gun still pointed to his temple, contemplating if he should risk his life to alarm the others outside. "Don't even think about it, son. If you pick up that radio, you'll be breathing through a hole other than your nostrils," Kurt said, looking into the enemy pilot's eyes through the lens of his glasses, as the enemy pilot stared back, contemplating his next course of action.

"Trust me," Kassandra said. "We've been seeing bodies piling up all day. And if you don't want the same to happen to you, just do what you're told. Now, I want you to carefully lift the helicopter off the ground. And just go. It doesn't matter where. Let's just go."

The enemy pilot looked into the assassin's cold stare, feeling his gun pointed to his temple, realizing that he had come face to face with the nemesis of many of the troops who were unfortunate to have crossed his path, and slowly lifted the helicopter from the premises of the White House, en-route to nowhere in particular.

Jason listened to the high-ranking soldier still calling out for confirmation, only to receive dead silence.

They looked on the monitor and saw only 2 transmitters active, along with the pilot's, and radioed the Pentagon.

18:41 HOURS. ENEMY COMMAND CENTER - PENTAGON, WASHINGTON, D.C., THE NATION'S CAPITAL:

"Only 2 transmitters, sir, not including the pilot. The others are unaccounted for."

"I knew it. Just as I thought. They're working together."

"What are you saying, General?"

The General looked into his eyes and replied, "I know that look well enough to know that you know exactly what I mean. Based on the evidence, we have come to realize that Colonel Danvers has switched sides."

"With all due respect, sir. Colonel Danvers is a proud man. And a man of great integrity. And his character is above reproach. There's no way that could be possible."

"You mean beyond reproach, up until now? Isn't it obvious? Only two tracking beacons, while everybody else is unaccounted for. Which means that

0-7 is on board, and with our pilot's two hands on the controls, he is no match for him. Even with his hands not on the controls," the General said, and pointed at the console, with the stains of blood on it. "This was where Colonel Davidson stood right before I killed him, for not following orders. I didn't take pleasure in doing it. But unfortunately, it had to be done. And if necessary, I'd do it again. And ever since then, from that moment on, when I looked into Coronel Danvers's eyes, I saw his hatred and resentment towards me. And I knew deep down that my alliance with him had come to an end, and it was just a matter of time before he went over to the other side, to get back at me. And what better opportunity to do so if he teams up with 0-7? I know that Colonel Davidson was also a close friend of yours. And there's no question in my mind that the rest of you hold a grudge against me. I expect that much. But, I respect it. I really do. But until then, as long as you're dressed in that uniform, you will follow my orders. No ifs, ands, or buts about it. No 2 ways about it. It's either your alliances are with me, or with them. And we both know what happened, and what's about to happen to them. All of them. Just a matter of time before the rest are found and dealt with. Now, I want you to radio our troops at the White House and tell them to bring that chopper down, or they'll be brought down the hard way, even with her on board. This may be the only opportunity we have to capture the Package and eliminate 0-7, once and for all, unless he has already found a way out, which I'm sure he has. You are also under strict orders to find and eliminate Colonel Danvers, and all other personnel not one of us."

"Yes sir," Wilson answered.

18:42 HOURS. THE WHITE HOUSE - WASHINGTON, D.C., THE NATION'S CAPITAL:

The troops surrounding the White House along with the other helicopters hovering around them received strict orders to shoot them down if they didn't comply in landing their commandeered helicopter, causing them to react nervously, causing the enemy pilot to laugh hysterically, thinking they had no means of escaping.

"Shit, I knew this wouldn't work!" Daniel said, in a fit of anger.

"What now?" Arianna asked, grabbing Susan tightly.

"Does your bodyguard have a way out of this now? Did he bother to cover his escape this time?" Stephanie yelled, and said softly, "We're so dead."

Kassandra took a deep breath in a state of total defeat, watching the looks of total hopelessness, and said, looking at the assassin, "I'm sorry."

The enemy pilot began laughing louder in the cockpit of the helicopter and began to land the helicopter, when he suddenly felt the cold steel of the assassin's sidearm pressed harder against his temple, quickly delaying his descent.

"I really didn't think I'd go like this. But it looks like there's nothing any of us can do at this point," David said sadly.

"It was a good run. It was a real honor, at least for a short time," Kurt said, in a state of hopelessness.

The assassin calmly pulled out the detonator from his sachet and looked all around him, seeing the other enemy helicopters that hovered over the White House, and watched the countless enemy soldiers near the perimeter at the front gate as he listened to the constant warnings from the radio chatter to land. He looked into the pilot's eyes, bringing the detonator closer to his face.

"What the hell is he doing?" Stephanie asked, with a hint of worry on her face.

Kassandra recognized the device and answered, with a sudden look of hope, "It's going to be rough. Hold on to something as tightly as you can."

"Do what she says," Kurt answered, grabbing on to whatever he could find.

The assassin pressed the trigger, causing a series of explosions at the front gates, with the shock of the blast dazing them.

Moments after, the roof of the White House erupted into flames, towering up to the helicopters that hovered over it, causing them to veer out of control after being struck by flaming debris, crashing and burning into it, completely wiping the smile from the enemy pilot's face.

"You're the best," Daniel said, patting the assassin on his shoulder. He turned to the enemy pilot and asked, "Your ass is quiet now, huh?"

"Today, while we're still young, please," Kassandra remarked at the enemy pilot.

The enemy pilot quickly made his way out of the area, in fear of meeting his demise at the hands of the assassin.

18:44 HOURS. ENEMY COMMAND CENTER - PENTAGON, WASHINGTON, D.C., THE NATION'S CAPITAL:

Wilson looked at the monitor and saw a number of the tracking go offline, causing a sudden look of shock on his face. He stood from his seat, faced the General, and said, "We have a problem, sir."

"I'm listening"

"We've lost a number of troops from the perimeter at the front gates, including the rest of our choppers. We have more reinforcements moving in. But by the time we get there, it may be too late. The only one that made it out has the package and Colonel Danvers in it."

"Are there any survivors, at all?" the General asked.

"Just Sergeant White and a few other soldiers, sir."

"Where are they headed?"

"They're heading west, towards Virginia. The exact destination is unknown at this point, sir."

"Mobilize gunship support immediately," the General said firmly.

18:46 HOURS. BOLLING ENEMY AIR FORCE BASE - WASHINGTON, D.C., THE NATION'S CAPITAL:

A number of enemy gunship pilots immediately scurried across the base heading towards their gunships in pursuit of the rogue helicopter, with 0-7, Kassandra, and Colonel Danvers moving west.

They powered up their engines and immediately lifted off from the base, through the low visibility of the falling snow, after receiving immediate confirmation to lift off in pursuit of the fugitives.

18:49 HOURS. SOMEWHERE OVER WASHINGTON, D.C., THE NATION'S CAPITAL:

"Where to? Where are we going?" Kurt asked, taking a huge sigh of relief.

"Anywhere. Nowhere. Anywhere is better than here. We need to find someplace where we can lay low. Somewhere with a lot of vegetation where we can hide. I'll figure it out. For now, let's just fly," Kassandra answered.

"Well done, Kassandra. You truly are your father's daughter. He would be proud," Kurt said, smiling.

"Thank you, Colonel Danvers. But the one you should be thanking is 0-7. He's the reason why you're still alive, and me still not back into enemy hands," Kassandra answered.

"And he has done a wonderful job in keeping you out of enemy hands."

"He means a lot to me. He's more than just a friend. He's like my sword and shield. My guardian angel."

"I know what happened. I see why he means so much to you now."

"Let's not celebrate yet. We're not home free yet," Stephanie said, still trying to catch her breath from the excitement of almost being captured by the enemy forces.

Daniel stuck his head out of the helicopter, and saw a number of AH-64 Apache Longbow gunships coming in quickly in hot pursuit, closing in on their positions. "We have incoming!"

"They just don't quit!" Arianna said, holding Susan tightly.

"The rest of you, hold on to something!," Kurt said, mounting one of the machine guns, opening fire to keep them at bay.

"We can't let them get close!" Kassandra shouted.

Brandon mounted the other machine gun and immediately opened fire at the enemy units, as they quickly closed the distance.

As the enemy units continued to draw closer, they immediately returned fire, causing the enemy to take evasive maneuvers from the enemy gunships' lethal front mounted cannons, riddling their helicopter with a number of bullet holes, tearing through Brandon's shoulder, throwing him to the floor.

Kassandra quickly ran to him to examine his wound. She tore a piece of her clothing and made a tourniquet to help stop the bleeding, and quickly injected the serum into his veins.

Daniel immediately took his place and returned fire unflinchingly, until the bullets from the machine gun he fired found its way into the cockpit of one of the enemy gunships, causing it to plummet from the skies, crashing and burning on the surface.

A series of enemy bullets continued to tear through the hull of their helicopter, causing the fuel tank to rupture, discharging a thick cloud of smoke, with Kurt sustaining a series of hits to his chest, pushing him away from the mounted gun to the floor, killing the enemy pilot who manned their controls, causing their helicopter to slowly veer out of control.

The assassin opened the door, and tossed the body of the dead pilot out, as Kassandra quickly took over the control. SHe regained control of the helicopter, and moved on to man the machine guns, and immediately opened fire at the pursuing enemy gunships.

She watched the fuel gauge and saw how rapidly the fuel began to dwindle, and yelled, "We're losing a lot of fuel and altitude! We'll have to make an emergency landing somewhere!"

They continued trying to repel the enemy units as much as they could, but to no avail.

The assassin continued returning fire unflinchingly, as the enemy bullets flew all around him, until he finally brought down another one of the enemy gunships.

After sustaining a series of critical hits from the enemy attacks from the pursuing enemy units, the alarms in the cockpits began blaring loudly, as their fuel continued to dwindle, while the helicopter continued to trail the thick cloud of dark smoke, trying to evade the pursuing enemy gunships.

David and Stephanie attended to Kurt, applying pressure on his wounds, while he continued to bleed profusely, as his senses slowly slipped away, from the extensive damage that he sustained from the relentless barrage from the enemy units.

The cockpit of the helicopter instantly filled with smoke, obstructing Kassandra's view, causing them to cough hysterically as the thick, dark cloud filled their lungs.

"I'm losing control! I can't see anything!" Kassandra shouted.

"What do we do?" Arianna yelled, hugging Susan tightly.

"Hold on to something! We'll have to do an emergency landing!" Kassandra yelled, looking at the fuel gauge pointing towards empty, as the hull of the helicopter suddenly erupted in flames, while Daniel and the assassin valiantly tried to continue repelling the enemy gunships' onslaught on their battered helicopter.

18:53 HOURS. ENEMY COMMAND CENTER - PENTAGON, WASHINGTON, D.C., THE NATION'S CAPITAL:

"General," Wilson called out softly. "We have a visual on her current position."

"Where are they headed?" the General asked.

"Still heading west. Towards the Appalachian Mountains."

"What's her status?"

"Still transmitting."

"Colonel Danvers?" the General asked.

"Still transmitting as well, sir."

"Have a few of our Blackhawks prepped with an extraction team and ready immediately."

"Yes, sir."

18:55 HOURS. BOLLING ENEMY AIR FORCE BASE - WASHINGTON, D.C., THE NATION'S CAPITAL:

A number of heavily armed soldiers ran towards the Blackhawk helicopter, and mobilized, in pursuit of Kassandra, after they crashed in the mountains.

19:00 HOURS. SOMEWHERE OVER VIRGINIA, HEADING TOWARDS THE APPALACHIAN MOUNTAINS:

After constant punishment from the enemy gunships, their helicopter suddenly lost control, as it headed towards the deep undergrowth of the mountains. Kassandra tried to maintain control as much as she could, but to no avail and shouted, "We're gonna crash! Brace yourselves!"

The flaming helicopter plummeted towards the thick, dark undergrowth, crashing through the trees, with its propeller slicing through them, impacting the undergrowth with a monstrous thud, tossing them out their positions, causing them to slam into one another, with the shock from the impact temporarily immobilizing them.

19:19 HOURS. SOMEWHERE IN THE APPALACHIAN MOUNTAINS, VIRGINIA:

The flames from the wreckage continued to fill the insides of the helicopter, as the rest of them lay unconscious from the crash.

The assassin slowly opened his eyes, noticing the others were unconscious from the crash, and smelled the heavy scent of fuel. He saw it leaking slowly onto the thick foliage of the forest's undergrowth towards the flames, and quickly sprang into action, pulling Kassandra and the others from the wreckage as quickly as he could before it could be set ablaze.

After a brief moment, of being unconscious from the shock of the crash, Kassandra slowly opened her eyes, seeing the blurred silhouette of the assassin standing over her.

She sat upright, shaking her head, still trying to recover from the impact of the shock, and ran to the others to revive them.

After reviving them, she ran over to Kurt, where he laid on the ground, his uniform that was always properly groomed completely soiled in his blood, taking his final breaths.

Kassandra quickly reached into her pocket to take out the serum to heal his injuries, and felt Kurt gently grabbing her hand, with his hands soaked in his blood, staining the sleeves of her lab coat, soiled from the earth from the undergrowth, shaking his head.

"But I must heal you," Kassandra answered.

"There's no time. My injuries are too severe. Those bullets went right through me. Struck a few of my vital organs. I'm bleeding internally. I can feel it pouring from inside me. We both know that I won't make it. My fight was over from the moment I joined you. I knew this day would come."

"I'm sorry. I never meant for any of this to happen," she replied.

"I'm not. It was worth it. I wanted to see my last moments fighting. Fighting for a cause bigger than myself. My only regret is I didn't do it sooner. It felt good staying at the back of a machine gun, squeezing off those rounds again. It's just like the old days. Brought back that fire again. Too bad it was short lived. I can say that I've regretted so many things that I've done in my career working for the government, but I can't say I have any regrets about today. It felt good taking the fight back to the son of a bitch."

Kurt tightened his grip on Kassandra's arm with one hand, and grabbed the assassin's hand with the other, and said, "Before I take my last breath, I just want to thank all of you for helping me find my way again. To find the courage to do what's right. For so long, I was in the darkness. Just this once, it felt good being in the light. My fight is over now. But yours is beginning, I'm afraid. You must stop him at all costs. He has to face justice for all he's done. He has to pay."

"He will," Kassandra said softly, with her tears rolling down her cheeks.

"Don't feel sad. In this line of business, dying is a part of it. I'm sure you've seen that by now. I can feel my senses slipping away from me. I can't tell if my eyes are open or closed. I can't feel anything."

"Just rest, you'll be fine," she answered.

"I'll see you on the other side," Kurt said, taking his last breath.

After moments of flying over the forest, unable to find Kassandra and the others, the enemy gunships spotted them and opened fire.

The assassin quickly ran back to the dilapidated helicopter, manning its heavy machine guns and fired at one of the enemy units, causing it to burst into a ball of flame, falling into the foliage that blanketed the mountains, setting it ablaze, and quickly locked on to the other firing, causing it to meet the same fate as the first one before, causing the flames to spread through the undergrowth, quickly consuming the dense and lumbering vegetation that shrouded the mountain.

19:25 HOURS. ENEMY COMMAND CENTER - PENTAGON, WASHINGTON, D.C., THE NATION'S CAPITAL:

"We've lost all our gunships, General," Wilson said softly.

"And what of the Package and Colonel Danvers?"

"They both stopped transmitting. But we can only assume that they're still alive, since we lost both of our gunships near the crash site. That location is dense with vegetation. And makes any form of transmission and communication difficult or impossible to detect."

"How far are the reinforcements?"

"A few minutes away."

"And as for the attack at the White House, we have a few survivors, Sergeant White being among them."

"Bring him to me."

"Yes, General," Wilson said.

19:27 HOURS. THE WHITE HOUSE - WASHINGTON, D.C., THE NATION'S CAPITAL:

Another team of soldiers converged onto the White House, and combed through all the wreckage and dead soldiers from the assassin's wake, recovering Jason's unconscious body, along with a few other survivors.

Jason opened his eyes, seeing the blurred images of the soldiers' silhouette standing above him, and slowly staggered to his feet with his ears ringing loudly from the roar of the explosion.

He turned around and saw the burning wreckage from the enemy helicopters that crashed and burned into the roof of the White House and said, "My God."

19:32 HOURS. SOMEWHERE IN THE APPALACHIAN MOUNTAINS, VIRGINIA:

Shortly after Kurt had taken his last breath, the group began walking further into the mountains. Brandon was beginning to show signs of recovery from the numbing effects of the serum, but still not fully responsive.

"What's that smell?" Arianna asked, looking all around her, seeing fuel leaking downwards towards the burning wreckage where the enemy gunships remained totally consumed in flames, and said, "We need to leave now! It's about to blow!"

Stephanie and Daniel lifted Brandon on his feet, and made a hasty retreat, as quickly as they could, deeper into the forest. More fuel from their helicopter made its way towards the flames, causing the helicopter to erupt. The fuel spill continued making its way to the other burning enemy gunships, quickly engulfing all the wreckage into a giant wall of flame, interacting with the remainder of the volatile ordinance that was attached to the wreckage, exploding into a towering wall of fire, making its way back towards their dilapidated helicopter, causing it to erupt into a ball of flame, scattering shrapnel and burning debris all about. The flames consumed the foliage of the undergrowth, quickly rushing towards them, while an enemy helicopter arriving with a fresh squad of enemy troops circled above their position.

After a brief moment of trying to escape from the inferno, Arianna felt a sharp pain tearing deep into the flesh of her back, and felt a sudden drop of energy level. She leaned onto one of the trees, slowly releasing Susan's hand and said weakly, "I don't feel so good. Something's wrong."

"We need to keep moving!" Stephanie yelled.

Kassandra ran over to her and placed her hand on Arianna's shoulder, and felt the chunk of debris pinching the palm of her hand, and said, "Oh no."

She tilted Arianna's body forward and saw the chunk of shrapnel that tore deeply into the body armor that protected her body.

"What's wrong?" David asked.

"She's impaled by the shrapnel. We need to take it out as soon as possible," Kassandra replied.

"We may not have time. We're being pursued by more enemy troops, and a raging inferno. We have to take her with us!"

"If we don't get it out now, the shrapnel will dig deeper into her body, sever vital organs, and kill her! Causing tissue and nerve damage could be the outcome at least. But either way, I need to get it out!"

"We need to hurry! They're coming!" Daniel shouted.

"I need a knife to take it out!" Kassandra yelled.

"Here! We need to hurry," Daniel said nervously, handing her his knife.

She grabbed the knife and dug into Arianna's wound, removing the piece of shrapnel that impaled her. Covered in Arianna's blood, Kassandra analyzed it closely, throwing it away, and said, "The vest reduced the impact. If it had gone one inch closer, she would've been dead."

"I don't mean to be rude, Doc, but we don't have time for the diagnostics right now," Stephanie said nervously, feeling the intense heat of the flames that continued to rush towards them.

Kassandra quickly reached into her pocket and took out the serum, injecting some of its contents into Arianna's veins and said, "I'm done. Let's go."

Daniel quickly lifted Arianna onto his shoulder as she remained unconscious from the powerful effects of the drug, while Kassandra carried Susan to safety, and David carried Brandon on his shoulders, making their hasty retreat, while the flames raged through the darkness of the undergrowth.

While they were trying to evade the raging inferno, they heard the enemy helicopters flying above their positions, deploying a number of enemy troops.

After landing on the ground, the troops immediately began their pursuit of Kassandra and the assassin, as they slowly closed the distance towards their positions, with the speed of their retreat constantly hampered, carrying Brandon and Arianna who remained paralyzed from the serum's powerful effects.

As the enemy soldiers continued to gain ground on their position, the assassin stopped and placed a charge on the ground, covering it with the leaves of the foliage, while the others continued to run away, trying to evade the enemy forces, and quickly made his way towards Kassandra and the others.

The enemy soldiers continued to pursue them through the dark forest when the deafening roar from the blast suddenly echoed, killing a number of the enemy troops, delaying the others' advance, giving them enough time to place distance between themselves and the pursuing enemy troops.

"What the hell just happened?" Stephanie asked.

"What the hell do you think?" Kassandra answered back, as she continued running through the foliage.

The assassin paused for a brief moment, realizing there would be no end to the enemy soldiers' pursuit, and looked all around him, staring at the trees that towered high above the understudy, looking for the perfect vantage point to spring his ambush.

Daniel turned around for a brief moment, seeing no sign of the assassin, continued running, and said, "He left us!"

"I seriously doubt that!" Kassandra answered, while she continued running through the mountains.

"Then where is he?" David asked.

"He stayed back to keep the rest of you breathing! And me from falling back into enemy hands, like many times before!" she answered, while she continued running, trying to evade the enemy forces.

"Say no more!" David answered, while he continued running as fast as he could, feeling Brandon's weight on his shoulder hampering his movement.

The remainder of the enemy soldiers continued to pursue, totally oblivious to the assassin's presence, as he waited from his vantage point for them to run past him. He jumped from the top of the tree with all his might onto one of the unsuspecting enemy soldiers, snapping the bones in his shoulders and neck, killing him in an instant, and quickly moved on to engage the others, as the echo of gunfire suddenly rang through the forest, and after a brief moment of engagement, suddenly stopped.

"What the fuck just happened?" Daniel asked, with a hint of shock.

"What do you think? He just took care of your problem. Our problem," Kassandra said, trying to catch her breath.

The feeling in Brandon's legs slowly came back, while Arianna slowly regained her consciousness, as they laid on the foliage of the undergrowth.

They looked in the skies and saw the enemy helicopters circling over their position and suddenly withdrew, after not seeing any signs of Kassandra and the others.

"Where am I?" Brandon asked.

"The Appalachian Mountains," Kassandra answered.

"What happened?" he asked.

"We crashed trying to evade the enemy forces. And they're still after us."

He looked all around him and asked, "Where's Colonel Danvers? Where's 0-7?"

"Colonel Danvers didn't make it. As for 0-7, he'll be back soon."

After a brief moment, the assassin calmly walked past them, looking straight ahead, with his usual calm demeanor and straight face like nothing happened, even after engaging the enemy soldiers that continued their relentless pursuit.

"And there's 0-7," Kassandra said, smiling. "And he just took care of our problem. For the time being, at least."

"Help me up. I can't feel my legs," Arianna said, trying to get up.

"Just lie back for now, until you get your strength. The effect will pass soon. Good to have you back."

"You could've left me back there. But you didn't. You saved me. Thank you."

"You're welcome. We're all in this together," Kassandra said.

20:03 HOURS. ENEMY COMMAND CENTER - PENTAGON, WASHINGTON, D.C., THE NATION'S CAPITAL:

The General's troops escorted Jason into the command room where the General stood patiently in anticipation of any news on the assassin's status.

He stared at Jason's bruised face and shifted his eyes down at his disheveled appearance, and asked, "What happened?"

"I was attacked by 0-7, after he went on a rampage murdering your troops."

"Then why did he leave you alive?"

"To tell you that he was coming after you. And if we ever meet again, I won't be coming back alive. There was no stopping him. I was lucky he didn't kill me. I'd never been so afraid in my life. I was praying to get out of there. And based on the circumstances, there's only one thing left to do."

"What's that?" the General asked.

"Either you kill me or let me join the General population."

"And why would I have you executed?" the General asked.

"Because I was unsuccessful in capturing 0-7. I know you made it clear that either we succeed or die trying."

"Don't worry, Sergeant. I'm sure you did your best. You've been through enough for today. Get some rest. You earned it," the General said, smiling.

"Thank you, General."

"Any news on the wreckage, Colonel Sanders?"

"No sir. We deployed a number of our troops, but haven't received any word yet. As I said, there's no telling what might've happened. From the moment they hit the ground, their tracking beacons went offline from all the interference in the area. We're running blind at the moment."

"Commit more troops to the area. I need confirmation as soon as possible. If 0-7 is alive, then she should be as well."

"Is there anything else you'd like me to do, General?" Jason asked.

"No Sergeant. That'll be all for today. Get some rest. Glad to have you back in one piece."

"Thank you, sir."

"Colonel Sanders," the General called out softly.

"Yes, sir."

"I need a tanker prepped and headed to that location. Send as many troops as you need to get results. This ends tonight. Am I clear?"

"Yes, General. Right away, sir."

20:09 HOURS. BOLLING ENEMY AIR FORCE BASE - WASHINGTON, D.C., THE NATION'S CAPITAL:

A tanker completely filled with flame repellent fueled and took off from the base, while a number of soldiers scuttled towards their transports, bound for the crash site.

CHAPTER 17: INTRODUCTION.

20:29 HOURS. SOMEWHERE IN THE APPALACHIAN MOUNTAINS, NEAR INTERSTATE 81, VIRGINIA:

The constant flurries of snow continued to fall from the dark skies, blanketing the entire undergrowth of the deep dark forest.

The assassin checked his ammunition supplies and calmly sat on an old log, completely covered with snow, looking at the long stretch of road that lay before them at the bottom of the mountain in constant vigilance for any signs of enemy activity, where they viewed the burning wreckage from a safe distance.

Kassandra calmly sat a few feet behind him on the snow covered undergrowth, gazing quietly at him, pondering all the calamities he suffered since they crossed paths.

Stephanie looked all around her and said, "It looks like we're right back to where we started."

Arianna sat next to her and remarked, "For someone who is the acting president's daughter, and not to mention the most reckless pilot I've ever seen, you sure know so much about miracle medicine. Who are you really? Is your name even Kassandra? Or are you bullshitting us about that, too? You're full of surprises. And just when I think I've seen it all, you keep on surprising the rest of us. I've never seen anything like what I've just seen, or what you have in your possession. And I do know for a fact that no known cooperation or even the F.D.A., or what it used to be, would approve this shit since it works so well. Too well, for that matter. And from what all of us have seen with this miracle cure, you are more than who you claim to be. No medicine known to man can do what we've just seen. None that I know of, at least."

"I suppose this is as good as any time to provide some kind of explanation," David added.

"I suppose this is as good a time as any to make an introduction," Kassandra answered, and continued, "My name really is Kassandra, with a K. I didn't want to tell you because I figured you have enough to worry about. Or wasn't sure if I could trust anybody at the time. Being in captivity for so long does that to you. I'm sorry."

"We already figured that out back in Springfield. What we need to figure out is why those troops are going through so much trouble just to capture you. I mean, we can see some things, but why do they really need you, and want to put us in the ground so much?" Stephanie asked.

"Kassandra Weaver," she replied.

"Weaver?" Arianna asked, and said, "That name rings a bell. You mean you really are the daughter of the late Dr. Alexander Weaver, who is the acting president? Was he also the founding father of Genesis? I thought Jason was exaggerating when he said it. I'm a little slow on all the family history. Besides, I lost track of a lot of things since this civil war broke out."

"Yes," Kassandra answered, contemplating. "Well I did tell you that I was the president's daughter. And also, the sole heir of the Weaver legacy. Or what's left of it, anyway."

"I'm Arianna Martinez. You already met Brandon, Daniel, David, Stephanie, and this young lady here is Susan. Susan Hasagawa."

"I figured there was more to you than being the acting president's daughter. We all did," David answered.

"That serum is a little too high-tech for just a president's daughter to have. That alone is too much power for one person to have at their fingertips. Other than that serum, there has to be more of a reason why the military is after you so much," Brandon added.

"Not to mention a high tally of fresh enemy corpses left all over the place. Not that I feel sorry for any of them, considering all the things they have done," Stephanie said.

"Since you know me so well, and I don't know any of you, I suppose that it's not too much of a good thing to be popular under those circumstances," Kassandra replied.

"On that, we all can agree," David answered.

"The General said that I was important to his war effort," Kassandra answered.

"Yeah, no shit. We all figure that from all the bodies that your bodyguard has been stacking up. And from the looks of it, he hasn't even started yet," Arianna said, plainly.

"You don't know him like I do. He's not just a bodyguard. He's my friend. A great friend. I owe my life to him. You all do," Kassandra replied.

"How could you call him that after all the freedom fighters he murdered today alone? God knows how many he's killed before that," Daniel answered.

"I know that it's difficult to grasp. But people like him are not born. They're made," Kassandra answered.

"And I suppose that you're going to tell us his whole life story," Daniel remarked.

"What better time to do it?" Kassandra answered softly.

"Okay," Stephanie said softly. "You were not who you claimed to be at first, and now you claim that your bodyguard is a saint. The way we see it is we have two for the price of one."

"It's your show," Arianna said softly.

"My father was a doctor, like his father before, and his father's father before. So, it's safe to say that I come from a long line of doctors."

"What does that have to do with anything?" Daniel asked.

"My father wasn't fulfilled and tried to break the cycle by being something else. I suppose he was tired of being the son of a doctor. He loved flying. His father taught him to fly with an old crop duster that was in his family for generations, so he practiced constantly, and later on joined the armed forces to continue to pursue his love of flying. I don't know much of what happened during his time as a soldier. He never really talked about it much. But during my stay on Genesis, I learnt of his time on the Ivory Coast. Some of it, at least."

"What happened on the Ivory Coast?" Brandon asked.

"I don't know all the details. But if my memory serves me right, he saved an entire country from being wiped out from a deadly epidemic."

"How so?" Stephanie asked.

"About 2005. 30 years ago. At the time of the civil war in the war-torn country, after completing a few missions in the line of duty, and for a much-needed break, he put in a request with the chain of command using his father's credentials to help provide relief for survivors of war and disaster. Then one day, while he was stationed in Liberia, providing relief, they suddenly came under attack by the local militia, raiding all the local villages for ammunition, supplies, food, slaves, or whatever they could find. It was just a few against so many, but their numbers were too great, so they fled. And even as they fled, their plane came under heavy attack, and his co-pilot was fatally wounded, after the plane had sustained heavy enemy fire."

"What happened after that?" David asked.

"His co-pilot later succumbed to his wounds, and the plane burst into flames in mid-flight while he was trying desperately to get out of the area and found himself in Ivorian airspace. He tried to make an emergency landing. But the plane was severely damaged and couldn't hold on long enough to do it. Then, not too long after he had gotten into Ivorian airspace, he parachuted and landed somewhere in the jungle. The plane crashed a few miles from his location. He sustained a broken leg and a few ribs, and was unconscious from the fall, but was rescued after dangling for hours on a tree by a woman who lived in a nearby village. After battling the fires of the crash site for hours, they were able to salvage as much as they could from the wreckage of the plane, and the body of his co-pilot, who was burnt beyond recognition."

"And then what happened?" David asked.

"After being unconscious for days, he awoke in a strange place. Plagued by civil war and disease, like many other places before on the African continent. If my memory serves me correctly, about 100,000 perished in the civil war alone. Then the war suddenly stopped."

"How come?" Daniel asked.

"They thought the war had ended, but another enemy far worse than the war itself had taken hold of the country."

"What was it?" Brandon asked.

"People were dying at an alarming rate from the mysterious outbreak. It was called the Chimera strain, I believe, if my memory serves me right."

"How did it take form?" Brandon asked.

"If my memory serves me right again, they said that one person was infected with the strain by a mosquito bite, and from that point, it went airborne. From the hospital, he was transported to a tiny fishing village near the coast by some of the natives, just after the war had ended, or was delayed courtesy of the strain. It was there he learnt of the strain and knowing the kind of person he really was, he couldn't stand by and do nothing. Out of gratitude for saving his life, he put in an inquest to the U.S. Government to provide relief for the survivors while they were stationed near the coast. That tiny fishing village became a haven while he searched tirelessly for a cure to combat the deadly strain. And it was just a matter of time before the strain made its way to the sanctuary in that small fishing village. More people and livestock were dying at an alarming rate, and the time was running out to find a cure."

"How did he find the cure?" Arianna asked.

"It appeared that some of the livestock bore an amazing resilience to the strain. So, he theorized that maybe if he extracted blood samples from the animals, he could use the antibodies to create a cure against the disease."

"Did it work?" Daniel asked.

"After all the failed attempts of finding a cure, he had finally done it. And all those who had made it to the outpost were inoculated against the strain. With no regard for his life, he traveled through the disease zones to plead to the local government to stop burning the infected alive, and to tell them that he'd found a cure. But the disease was so deadly and was killing at such an alarming rate, that no one believed him. So they threatened to throw him out of the country if he continued to interfere."

"So, what did he do afterwards?" Arianna asked.

"So, he and a few soldiers who were stationed at the haven went deep into the heart of the disease-infested zones, trying to inoculate as many of the sick and dying as they could, and take them into a safe zone to receive more treatment."

"And what would happen to the ones that he couldn't save?" Stephanie asked.

"After the strain had run its full course, I suppose it was impossible to save them. The ones that couldn't be saved were often abandoned to their fate and met their slow and painful demise at the hands of it. So, to help contain the disease, they were burnt in the villages, even though they were still clinging to life. They would meet a fate far more cruel than death itself. Imagine all these sick men, women, and children who knew they were left back to die from that dreadful disease. The thing is, the Ivory Coast was once colonized by the French. So the government turned to them to help contain the threat."

"What did the French do?" Daniel asked.

"There was a base stationed in the region. So, they launched a squad of fighter planes to bomb all the infected villages, wiping out all those infected people. They called the containment procedure The Hellfire Campaign. These protocols to contain the threat were not the most honorable courses of action, but considering the pain and suffering that those natives endured from the disease, I suppose it was a mercy killing of all of those who were infected. But my father could only do so much, even with finding a cure for this disease."

"What happened after?" Brandon asked.

"Despite the civil war, due to the lack of health insurance, Africa has one of the highest populations of those infected with AIDS, so he tested the vaccine on the virus and it worked with flying colors. And in the history of modern medicine, he was the first in history ever to create the world's first U.A.V."

"What does that mean?" Brandon asked.

"Universal Antidote Vaccine. With one vaccine, he had found a cure for a number of diseases. Even for some of the worse ones that the human race has come in contact with, like AIDS and Ebola. One thing myself and everyone here knows for a fact is that the Food and Drug Administration, or the pharmaceutical companies, would never approve it, for the simple fact that there is more profit in death than life to them. It's all a business to them. But nonetheless, that tiny fishing village on the coast became the salvation for an entire country. Or so, it would seem."

"What do you mean?" Arianna asked.

"Even after the Hellfire Campaign, hundreds more fled to the outpost.

Then hundreds became thousands. And it just continued to grow from there. And after all they had endured, there was finally hope. Or so it would seem."

"What happened after that?" David asked.

"They had finally begun to flourish, and they were happy. That small fishing village on the coast felt like that Garden of Eden to all those who had made it there. And that's when the unthinkable happened."

"What happened? What took place?" Stephanie asked, with a sudden look of intrigue on her face.

"An old enemy had come back to cast its shadow. Only this time, they were destroying everything that my father had worked so hard to build. It was in the wee hours of the morning, and everyone was all about their duties in the outpost. And from nowhere they came."

"Who came?" Daniel asked.

"It was the rebels. Many had lost their lives from war against the national army, and starvation, but most had died from the strain. So, those who had survived had grown desperate and raided the outpost for whatever food and supplies they could get, to sustain themselves, killing indiscriminately as they went along. Fortunately, there was a carrier fleet stationed a few miles near the coast, but unfortunately, there weren't enough soldiers to defend the outpost. The marines were fewer in number, but were organized and had that special training, whereas, the rebels were far greater in numbers, but were desperate and disorganized, ready to overwhelm at any given moment. No matter how many were killed, their greatest weapon was desperation in their moment of self-preservation. They just kept coming. So, left with no other alternative, they called in an airstrike, and what happened after would shake the most seasoned soldier, and from what I gathered, it shook the entire world to its core."

"What happened next?" Arianna asked.

"All the rebels were wiped out," Kassandra answered.

"How's that so bad?" Daniel asked.

"At the expense of a number of civilians losing their lives. All those men, women, and children who had made it to the outpost in search of hope, were wiped out from the so-called precision bombing, leaving only a handful of survivors. My father was one of those people who had survived and still bears the scars that remind him of that fateful day he lost everything he worked so hard to build. Most of the others who died from the bombing were burnt beyond recognition, and torn apart from the force of the blast. All rebel activity was completely neutralized. I'm thankful that I wasn't there to witness all these horrific images that those people went through during the civil war in the Ivory Coast, when I was on Genesis. I could only imagine what they went through. I'm sure there's no words to describe their ordeal. But what haunts me most was the image of a woman who was caught in the bombing holding on to her son and pregnant with another child. I can remember clearly when I was in Genesis, doing research on the Ivory Coast, and the Hellfire Campaign. I can never forget seeing the look on my father's face. It's like I was making him relive all those dark times in that country all over again. Whenever I had asked him about it, he always seemed withdrawn or evasive. But I was always very angry, because I do remember clearly when he scolded the General about some incident that had taken place, during his first visit with 0-7. Maybe it was about the bombing or something else. There must've been something that he'd lost, or someone. I wasn't there so I can't tell you all the details about the Ivory Coast. Maybe someday if, or whenever we get reunited, he can tell me. But, all I can do is tell you everything that really happened in Genesis. I remember all of it like yesterday. So, is it beginning to make sense why the General wants me so badly?"

"Other than the fact that you're the daughter of a brilliant scientist who took the place of the actual president after he went missing? No," David answered.

"Why does he want you so badly?" Brandon asked.

"The thing is my father and the General were best friends. They were stationed in the Ivory Coast. That much you might have figured out by now. It was the General who called the air strike that killed all those civilians and the rebels, and later took all the credit. I believe it was from that moment, they went their separate ways. After finding the cure for the Chimera strain, my father came up with another idea."

"What was that?" Stephanie asked.

"He was always heartbroken seeing people die from hunger and disease, so he theorized about tapping into the human genome, to strengthen the immune system against disease and provide more endurance against disease and all the pain that went along with it. So, since he and the General were close, the General knew of that research, and that incident that killed all these people halted his plans, so he moved to the mainland and later married my mother, shortly after. Although he had suffered a great loss, the government was so impressed with what he had achieved in Africa, that they proposed he build another Genesis some place far from the rest of the world."

"The south pole," Arianna answered.

"In all, it took about 20 years to complete the project. And in that time, so many countries around the world poured resources into making it a reality. Even North Korea. Just this once, the whole world came together in peace, despite all their differences they had from the past. And that tiny fishing village off the coast was the first Genesis that inspired the Genesis that you came to know in Antarctica. My father had unknowingly inspired what every other world leader would never achieve. And building a bigger and better Genesis was the first step. I didn't move to Genesis until I was 17. And before that, I won the peace prize for genetic engineering in Sweden. That was the only place I ever went to before I came to Genesis. It wasn't until I witnessed the war against the North Koreans that I realized that human civilization had nothing to offer but death and destruction, and that he was protecting me from the outside world. And it was there that I met him," she said, motioning to the assassin.

"And what happened?" Arianna asked.

"He was tasked with killing an enemy soldier."

"An enemy soldier on Genesis?" Brandon asked in surprise.

"She was a young girl. They once met on one of his previous missions, before either came to Genesis. She was orphaned from the war and moved to Genesis in search of a better life. To start over. She was like a sister that I never had, and my family became the family she always wanted. And from that point we were inseparable."

"And what happened after?" Daniel asked with a sudden look of intrigue.

"She attacked one of the troops stationed at Genesis, and during that period, he was on his way to Genesis for some time off, after the war against North Korea, when it happened. He was the General's most trusted lieutenant, and the most decorated in the entire corps, and most naturally was charged with finding and executing her."

"Did she do it? Did she attack the soldier I mean?" Arianna asked.

"No. They said that she had attacked one of the troops, but I knew better. And from that point, my father came to her defense, and he shifted his allegiance to my father. And that was the beginning of the end of Genesis. For all those in the unit."

"How so?" David asked.

"It became 13 against an entire army. Who would've thought that one infraction would shake the whole world to its entire core? So many lost their lives for one man's dreams and ambitions," Kassandra said.

"What happened after that?" Brandon asked.

"The citizens rose against the military, and from that point the fall of Genesis was all but certain. Undeniably inevitable.

The next thing we know, the entire world went up in flames, and from that point it was total anarchy. The freedom fighters were outnumbered even before the war started. It was 13 soldiers against an entire battalion of soldiers. We couldn't hold on to Genesis, so my family was led back to safety back to the mainland. It was during the evacuation I lost my mother. And If it weren't for the assassin, I would've never made it this far."

"How come?" David asked.

"The uprising had begun to take its course, and there was no stopping it. People were dying like flies at the hands of the military, and there were troops everywhere. I was trapped inside. He had already made it out of Genesis with the others, and risked his life coming back for me. We cut off all their means of following us, or so we thought. And when we had made it out, they were all over us. We held out for as long as we could. Time was running out and the enemy troops were gaining on my father's position. It was just a matter of time before they were overrun, so left with no other alternative, they began to make their way to the mainland. The plane began to taxi off the runway for takeoff, and we followed as fast as we could, but the entire area was covered thickly with snow. We were barely able to see anything, but kept on pursuing and for just one brief moment, it was beginning to pay off. I was at arm's length of being rescued, but the ice on the runway was too slippery, causing us to crash. When we got out of the wreckage, all we could do from that point was to see the planes take off, and I remembered staring right into my father's eyes while he stared back. and all I could do was to watch him leave without me. That moment was the last time I saw him."

"And what happened after?" Stephanie asked.

"And from 13, it became just him against the entire corp. Or should I say just the 2 of us."

"How's that even possible?" Daniel asked.

"It's not. After the plane took off, we were completely surrounded, and they swarmed on our positions like a pack of rabid wolves. He didn't have a chance. We didn't have a chance," Kassandra said.

"We?" Arianna asked.

"He fought tooth and nail, holding out as long as he could, while I tried giving him whatever support that I could. Though it wasn't too much help. But based on the circumstances, anyone would agree I did well enough. I may be the daughter of a brilliant scientist, but it doesn't mean I can't hold my own. I've been resourceful so far. We had a few significant victories, we held out for as long as we could, but eventually we were overwhelmed by many of the General's forces. They descended upon him without mercy, and took us back to Genesis, where the General stripped him of his rank, after disgracing him."

"And what happened after?" David asked.

"The uprising came to a standstill after many were lost. More civilians than soldiers. It had seemed for that one moment that the soldiers had gained the respect of the citizens, and the General was losing his allies fast."

"What did the General do after?" Stephanie asked.

"We fled Genesis, bound for the mainland, and were running low on fuel. We landed in Peru to refuel so we could continue to the mainland, and of course, what happened on Genesis didn't sit well with the peoples' liberation army, who demanded our release. And then a repeat of Genesis happened. Only this time, after the skirmish, the survivors were rounded up and executed. Only they didn't stay dead. Not all of them, anyway."

"What do you mean?" Arianna asked.

"They thought they had killed all the survivors. But two had survived to tell the tale."

"Do you know who they were?" Brandon asked.

"One was a soldier. The other was a high-ranking lieutenant in the army. The daughter of the late President Jorge Ramos, who was executed by guerillas, about 30 years ago, about the same timeline with the civil unrest in the Ivory Coast. If my memory serves me right, she is the sole survivor of his entire legacy. She lost her 2 older brothers in the fight."

"I think I remember something like that going down before the entire country went into civil war," Daniel added.

"Did the General know they had survived?" Stephanie asked.

"Not until he came to the mainland. I could only imagine seeing the look on his face. He knew he was in for a rude awakening. We all did. After the survivors gave their testimony on the atrocities the General's forces had committed, the entire Latin American country went into unrest. And soon after, the whole world followed. It was like a powder keg waiting to explode. And it was from that moment that I realized what my father was trying to tell me all this time. That all civilization has to offer is death and destruction. And when civilization came to Genesis, that's exactly what happened. I supposed that my father made the same mistake that his father had always warned him about. It didn't make sense until that moment. None of it did. As long as the human race exists, civilization flourishes only so it can crumble in the end. Create things so they can be destroyed. After all, it makes sense that it's the natural order of things. We are born so we can die and fill in the great circle of life. The only thing is that sometimes we get to choose how we live, but sometimes we don't get to choose how we die. And the lesson that all this taught me is that there's no escaping who or what we really are or destined to be. I should know. Look where it got me. Anyway, when we arrived on the mainland, the General, much to his surprise, was arrested for war crimes and taken into custody. And I was finally reunited with my father."

"Then how did the General get so powerful?" Daniel asked.

"It appears that since the General left Genesis before the uprising had really taken form, he was found not guilty. But the witnesses' accounts of all the atrocities sealed his fate. And he was sentenced to life in a military prison. It appeared that his status grew even stronger on the inside, because it seemed that his troops were still loyal to him. And one night, my father and best friend were out discussing the withdrawal of all military personnel, after what had happened, and the possible future of Genesis. She escaped with Adam and my father, and the next thing I remember, we were taken hostage. It appears that the General had people working on the inside for him all along."

"How did he get out?" Brandon asked.

"He managed to secure the allegiance of every convict and war criminal who was only happy to get out and kill again. The next thing we knew, every other convict from civilian and military prisons were set free, making his army the largest in the world. It was either fighting for the General or being a freedom fighter. No in-between."

"What happened when you both were kidnapped?" David asked.

"The assassin was given a second chance to take command of the General's special unit, and I was given the option to use my father's research in the General's war effort. And we both refused," Kassandra said.

"And what did the General do?" Stephanie asked.

"They beat him so badly, that I often wondered how a man could endure so much punishment, and still live after that. And after all they did to him, his face was completely disfigured and his eyes were completely swollen shut. I wondered how much more punishment he could endure, with a number of his ribs cracked in more places than I care to remember. When I looked into his face, I could barely recognize him. Despite all the punishment he suffered, he continued to fight and continued to refuse. I'd never seen anyone with so much courage. But, ultimately, fighting was futile. I had no choice but to relent."

"What happened?" Arianna asked.

Kassandra paused for a brief moment and answered, with her eyes drowning in tears reliving all the painful memories of his torture and answered, "I killed him. And now my demons have tormented me every single night, keeping me awake when I close my eyes to sleep. For every day, over the past 10 years."

"What do you mean? How is that even possible?" Brandon asked, with a look of shock on his face.

"The man that you see before you is just a shadow, a shell of his former self, a walking corpse. He's alive but he's not living. He's completely numb to all emotion. He's like a machine only programmed to destroy. To kill. I was the one who took away everything that made him human. I was the one that made him into the monster that he is. I took him away from his brothers that he once fought and bled with on the battlefield and the woman who loved him so much. I took everything away from him. And I know that someday, I have to answer for what I did to him."

"What did you do?" Stephanie asked with a cryptic look on her face.

Kassandra wiped the tears from her eyes and answered, "In exchange for saving his life, I agreed to do what the General asked, although at the time, it was too much."

"What did he want?" David asked.

"He had suffered too much at the hands of the General, so I agreed to make him lead the General's army, one way or another."

"And how did you do that?" Stephanie asked.

"To make him more manageable, I wiped out his entire mind. Before I pulled the switch, even when he begged me not to. He wanted me to give him death instead of eternal servitude to the General. He really was ready to die, instead of the next alternative. But, I had no choice. What was I supposed to do?" she continued while tears rolled down her cheeks. "I couldn't watch him die. Not after all he did for me. If I had let him die, I felt like I was just standing by, and I couldn't let it happen. I just couldn't. That night, we were together in enemy hands witnessing all the moments of him being tortured, was the longest and hardest moment of my life. So, I finally did what they told me to do, to save his life. I pulled that switch that took his mind away, and programmed him into believing the other lieutenants of his former unit, who fought for my father, were his enemies. And we all know how that turned out. The thing is he only pulled the trigger. I was the one that killed those men. The very same men that put their lives on the line to save my father and fight for him. For 10 long years, I had to stand by and listen to those men taking their last moments at the hands of the monster I made. And for 10 long years, it's been tearing me apart. This is one of the effects of the General altering my father's research from the Ivory Coast and forcing me to use it for the war effort."

"If your father's research was for good, how could the General use it for war?" Stephanie asked.

"There's 2 sides to this story, like every other story," Kassandra answered. "Look at him. A shadow of himself. And yet his skills as an assassin are the deadliest anyone of us has ever seen. My father's research was to tap into the human genome and help strengthen the immune system to repair itself against disease, or any other foreign agents. But to save him, I agreed to use my father's research of tapping into the human genome and do just that and more. So multiply his skills to that of a soldier that can instantly heal from sustaining fatal and life-threatening injuries on the tour of duty. Imagine a squad of seven other soldiers like him."

"Imagine an entire army of super soldiers. My God," Daniel answered.

"The other side to all this is that the rebels are heavily outnumbered, and the General didn't count on the war lasting this long, so he made me to hasten those plans to put a swift end to it. And not to mention that this serum still contains the strain of the Chimera. If the strain was to be completely isolated, think of the effects of if they made it into a biological weapon. Countless dead, or one generation after the next, deformed from the effects. The prospect of leaving my father's work in the wrong hands is simply unacceptable."

"So, what you're saying is that you hold the key that could save or destroy the human race in the palm of your hands? Those blueprints that you researched for the General hold the key to our country's future?"

"Yes. I'm afraid so. What became a cure for mankind could end up being a potential biological weapon, or helping to create a race of super soldiers, and could potentially be used to destroy all of humanity. The possibilities are endless. Whatever the outcome, if the General turns my father's research into a weapon that won't be good for anyone, anywhere," Kassandra answered softly. "That's why I can't allow him to use it. I suppose things start one way and end another."

"How far did you get with those blueprints?" Arianna asked.

"Far enough I suppose. So, I stalled for as long as I could, after drawing all the blueprints. I only did the project in theory. It seemed accurate to me at the time. Practical application was yet to be introduced. And hope it still is."

"You said it was a cure. If it really is a cure like you say it is, then why would you use a strain of the virus to make it?" Arianna asked.

"Think of being bitten by a snake, or any foreign agents that attack the immune system for that matter. The most logical thing to do is to create an antidote that could harness itself in the immune system, or be dispersed into the lymphatic system just as quickly to deliver a cure. In other words, the best course of action is to create a vaccine using the same foreign agents to travel just as quickly into the bloodstream, only this time manipulating the foreign agents into delivering the cure to the disease or poison in question. If you get my meaning."

"Similar to that of the flu shot or an antidote of snake venom traveling through your body, or AIDS in this case, since we're talking about the Chimera disease," Stephanie added.

"Yes. The same rules apply in any cure, or most. All of them it seems," Kassandra replied softly.

"Makes sense I suppose, since your father's breakthrough in modern medicine saved an entire country from being wiped out by the virus," David added.

"Maybe a little too much. All that knowledge came with a price. A very heavy price that I couldn't afford to pay, but I did nonetheless. For so long, I kept on hoping and praying that something would happen soon enough. And thank God it did when it did," Kassandra replied.

"How so?" Brandon asked.

"Because something unexpected happened. The war took a different turn. I was under heavy security detail when I heard he and one of the General's pilots had gone rogue over the transmission, and at the same time, he rescued me. It's strange how he tried to rescue me from Genesis, and 10 years later he's doing the same, only this time, leaving a number of corpses in his wake."

"Well, I hope these theories of yours will never become practical applications," Arianna added.

"Either way, I must secure them. They must never be in the wrong hands."

"Okay, we get that. But why does the General want him to lead his forces?" Daniel asked.

"It was during the time when South Korea came under attack from their cousins from the north, and China had protested against the north attacking the south unprovoked, uniting the country under their repressive regime. At the time, they had the biggest army in the world. In retaliation for China's protest, and being alongside the Americans, the North Koreans bombed China, rendering their army less than half strength. I suppose it was by a strange twist of fate the Americans were stationed there. And even they too suffered a number of casualties. The North Koreans waited for a number of troops on both sides to meet and planned their attack. It was very strategic the way they did it. I remembered seeing the footage on television, and no one else, wanted to spare any troops for the assault on the North Koreans. In short, it was a suicide mission, and the morale of the combined forces of Chinese and American forces had plummeted. But being that he was the corps' most decorated soldier, both Generals turned to him to help turn the war in their favor against the North Koreans, and made him spearhead the assault. After hours of heavy resistance against the enemy, they had finally succeeded in driving them back to the north, all the way past the capital, almost to the Chinese border, until the entire country was united under the southern rule. It was because of his ability to lead, especially under those circumstances, that they won the war for the south. And since he didn't want to lead the General's army in this war, he suggested that he use 0-7 to weaken the resistance of the freedom fighters. Only this time, he wasn't himself, like he was against the North Koreans. So I don't have to stress why he is important to the General. And that's both our stories put together. Despite the fact that you've seen him as an assassin, if you look close enough, you'll see there's still something left. I know there is. He was my guardian angel in Genesis. And after all this time, he came back to me. Contrary to what you believe. I owe him my life. You may not agree with his methods, but he's the reason why all of you are still alive, and are forever in his debt."

"That's true. There's still something human. After all, he could've killed Susan and myself in the sanctuary but he didn't. When I looked into his eyes, I thought it was just me, but it seemed like he actually felt remorse. He felt pity for all those people. Almost like something clicked," Arianna replied.

"I didn't know. None of us did. I'm sorry if we judged him wrong. I see why now you're close to him," Daniel replied.

Brandon grabbed her hand gently and said softly, "You're right. We're all his debt, just like I'm forever in yours for saving me. If your father were here now, he'd be proud of you."

"Thank you," Kassandra answered, grabbing his hand, smiling.

Arianna rested her head on the tree trunk, took a deep breath, and said softly, "I never thought that I'd live to see the day that I would be pursued by people looking to kill me all across the country for no damn reason. My mother passed away while giving birth to me. And I was very young when I lost my father in a drug deal gone to shit. I'm supposed to be angry at him but I'm not. I suppose he did whatever he had to do to keep clothes on my back and food on the table. But, it's as you said - sometimes, we get to choose how we live but not always how we die. And that couldn't be more true. So, I moved in with relatives and that didn't work out too well to help take care of an orphan, so I ended being owned by the state, moving from one foster home to the next, until I was 17 and got fed up and left and been on my own ever since, until today. I discovered a passion for the medical field, and was studying to become a registered nurse, and then this war broke out, dividing the entire country, extinguishing all my dreams along with it. So, like some people, I wanted no part of it. I decided to wait it out, and it did for a while, until the day it came to my doorstep. Now it seems that a war I wanted nothing to do with follows me everywhere I go. It's uncertain how my life will play out after this. But I have no choice but to stay and wait and see what the future holds."

"Fredericksburg is just a few miles away from here. My old neighborhood," David said softly, and added, "I always wanted to visit someday, and possibly start over. Just not under those circumstances. I was in Richmond when the civil war broke out, from when the very first shot was fired, until it continued to sweep across the entire nation. They often say that information is power, so to stay ahead of current events, myself and a bunch of techies hacked into the government's mainframe, listening to every transmission being broadcasted. It wasn't difficult to hack in. But it wasn't difficult to track us either. We got a little too comfortable trying to stay ahead of current events. Little did we know, that would be our undoing. One day, the door of our hideout was breached, and all I remember seeing were bright flashes from guns, and bullets flying right past me, into everyone and everything. It all happened so fast, and it suddenly sank in that I was being shot at. One tore right into my shoulder, knocking me to the floor, and I felt like I was paralyzed, laying in a pool of my own blood. The pain was unbearable. Just as quickly as it had begun, it was over. The next thing that I realized, I had lost everyone that I cared about. I'd lost everything. Everyone all around me was dead and I was the only one who survived. My entire family and all my friends paid the price. They thought that we were rebels, and I suppose due to our activities, we were since we hacked into the government, and after acquiring all the sensitive information we had to be silenced. As an experienced hacker, I should've kept it at the back of my mind that we were being tracked. But I didn't. And I ask myself everyday why I'm the only one still standing. That scar from the bullet that tore into my shoulder is a grim reminder everyday of how close I came to being wiped out along with the others, and after all this time thinking that I'd be fighting alone, I'm being hunted once again with a number of people I never knew who existed before today. Not knowing that I was still alive the first time was the biggest mistake that the General's forces made. And they'll pay for it, I promise you. Come to think of it, they're paying right now. The funny thing is, I'm enjoying every moment listening to their screams, seeing all the bodies piling up, making all of them pay in blood for every inch of land they step foot on. I just wished I was the one doing it."

"Well, I'm originally from Charlottesville. It's the next lovely town on this long and lonely interstate," Stephanie said. "I used to go hiking with my old man, and one day he just upped and vanished. And why? I don't know. It's a question that I've been asking myself ever since. On the surface, he appeared to be happy, but behind closed doors was a different story I suppose. As for my mother, she had me straight from high school. Couldn't make ends meet, working in those fast-food joints, so she joined the armed forces and took a chance to be a helicopter pilot, and succeeded with flying colors. Her skills took her to a number of places like the Ukraine, Kyrgyzstan, Colombia, Tunisia, and France, more than 10 years ago. And it was there I lost her. So, officially, I became an orphan. Fortunately, I was able to fend for myself, though it never made it any easier. I had just moved to Fredericksburg, and that's when the war broke out. The next thing I knew was, things went from bad to worse. I was dodging enemy soldiers and bullets and was all alone doing it, hoping that I won't be captured by enemy forces or worse yet, get killed. And one day, by some strange turn of events, while scavenging for food at an abandoned supermarket, I met David doing the same. And we've been together ever since. The family that runs and hides together stays together, I suppose. Or should I say the couple. I always wanted to go back home and try and find my place, and it looks like I'll finally get my wish, since I'm on the run with all of you. It seems quite a few of us have found just that. And now that I'm about to find it, I wished I never did. I suppose being careful what you ask for, because one day you'll get it really rings true," she concluded.

Daniel took a deep breath and said while resting his head on an old tree trunk, "I was on my way to meet General West when all hell went from bad to worse. Our convoy was only a few miles from the base when we heard about the enemy surprise attack. Can't say I knew it was coming. Can't say I was looking forward to it either. But, truth be told, I thought the war was this close to being over, and looking to celebrate our victory lap across the country. As we drove through the streets, all we saw were a number of bodies scattered all about, and they were not ours. We were confused at first, and then it all began to make sense, seeing that he was the only one left standing. So naturally, we saw the enemy uniform and thought there were more of us who had stacked those bodies, and that's when we intercepted your bodyguard, but it was more like he intercepted us, and the next thing we knew we were dying like flies. The next thing I remembered was that I was hit by one of those bullets and with every second passing, I can feel my life pouring out of me, causing me to slowly slip away. So out of desperation, I commandeered any transport that I could find and drove as far and as fast as I could, looking for someplace to get some medical attention, before my senses completely ran out. I believe that's when you found me. And when I came to my senses, it had finally occurred to me that he was the one stacking all those bodies, before he wiped out my entire platoon. It always comes down to the power of the human spirit. In one day, I saw one man fight a war on both sides and lived to tell the tale, or in this case, fight another day. In all my years of fighting, I admit these are the best skills I've ever seen any one soldier possess. I've never seen anyone with such potential. The irony is that now I am in an alliance with the very same man that wiped out my entire team. I'm fighting by his side, piling more bodies everywhere we go. Can't say I hate him for it, though. What else is there to do, under the circumstances? After all, it's what I signed up for. I just wished that he was on our side sooner," Daniel concluded.

"You people are the closest thing to family I ever had," Brandon said softly, and added, "I can't say that I'm not happy to see you though. Just not under those circumstances. My mother was a cop and lost her life in the line of duty and a few years later, I lost my father in a car accident. Family curse, I suppose. The rest of the family was a little too busy to care for another mouth to feed, so I ended up in the care of my grandfather. The way I saw it, I had nothing to worry about. He had his own business, so I didn't have to worry about looking for a job or anything. I figured, what's the point of looking for one, since I can run the store with my grandfather. And then we went out of business when the war broke out. And if that wasn't bad enough, they killed him for no reason. And from that point they took everything from me, seeing that he was all I had left. And someday I'll make them pay. I never wanted to have anything to do with war. But I suppose at some point we all have to choose a side. And it looks like I chose mine.

The next order of business is to give them a taste of their own medicine."

"We'll be fine. We've made it this far," Kassandra said softly, grabbing Brandon's hand.

"I know it will," Brandon answered.

"Not all is lost after all. There's still some fight left in us, while we're still alive, and we have him and myself. 2 soldiers are better than 1. That should make our jobs a lot easier, and increase our chances of survival. Though he doesn't look like he needs my help at all," Daniel said.

"The only thing left to do is to stay alive, until our numbers get stronger," Stephanie answered.

"Well, that settles it. Now that we've had proper introductions, I think that it's safe to say that there was a reason why all of our paths crossed," Arianna added.

"There's no such thing as coincidences," Brandon remarked, looking into Kassandra's eyes. "Everything happens for a reason at precisely the time it's supposed to happen."

"I suppose you're right," Kassandra answered softly, staring back.

"All of us have lost loved ones before or after this war. And despite all that has happened in the past, we all have to survive together. That much we have in common," Daniel added.

"The rest doesn't matter now," Kassandra said.

"Welcome to the new underground resistance," David remarked.

"So, what now?" Stephanie asked.

"Hope we can get some sleep while we can. I'm feeling sleepy," Arianna replied, resting her back on the snowy undergrowth.

Kassandra heard the distant buzzing of a plane drawing nearer and said, "Shh."

"What is it?" David answered.

"Just a second. I hear something. And it's coming closer. Oh my God," she said.

"What is it?" Arianna asked.

"It sounds big and hollow, like a cargo plane, or something."

"I can hear it, too," Brandon answered.

"Oh no. It's a tanker," she said, softly.

"What kind of plane is that?" Brandon asked.

"The kind that they use to put out forest fires, and they're headed straight for the crash site. Which means there'll be a lot more enemy soldiers swarming that crash site to look for us soon. Which also means they'll be following the trail of bodies he left behind, and that'll bring them right to us. So we need to act fast," Kassandra said.

"Do those guys never quit?" Arianna asked out of frustration.

"Looks like you'll have to put counting sheep on hold for a little longer," Kassandra answered. "Because we're about to have more serious company."

The massive hull of the tanker flew towards the position of all the flaming wreckage of the helicopters that consumed a large portion of the forest in the mountains, and quickly doused the flames and continued its course, heading back to base after the flames were extinguished.

The assassin continued to keep watch, and saw the tiny specs of light in the far distance converging onto the position of the crash site.

After stopping near the crash sites, the enemy troops carefully combed through the wreckage, searching for any signs of Kassandra and the assassin, only finding signs of Kurt's corpse, completely charred from the raging fire that once engulfed the forest.

They continued following the trail through the undergrowth of the dark forest, stumbling onto the bodies of a number of their soldiers, lying lifeless on the foliage.

The assassin glanced for a brief moment, observing ground enemy troops converging towards the crash site through the thick lens of his binoculars, and quickly traversed down the hill towards the enemy positions.

"Where's he going?" Stephanie asked.

"I think it's pretty obvious, don't you? Looks like we won't be having company soon after all. We just found our way out. Let's go wait near the road," Kassandra said, watching the assassin quickly descend down the hill, towards the interstate.

After moments of trekking the interstate under the cover of darkness, the assassin had finally arrived at the enemy position, analyzing the troop movements to figure out his best course of action, and quietly moved through the column of enemy transports. He carefully and stealthily engaged the remaining stragglers, placing them into states of unconsciousness so their tracking beacons won't go offline to arouse suspicion, and placed explosive charges under their transports, should he need to cover his escape. He quietly commandeered one of the enemy transports, making his way back to the others slowly fading into the distance under the cover of complete darkness.

An unsuspecting enemy soldier slowly traversed down the hill to report his findings to the General, and saw one of the transports speeding away under the complete cover of darkness. He fired his weapon in the air to signal the other soldiers.

The assassin had arrived at Kassandra's position, where they waited anxiously and quietly for his return, and quickly made their way towards the next town, a few miles from their position.

21:27 HOURS. SOMEWHERE ON INTERSTATE 81, HEADING TOWARDS FREDERICKSBURG, VIRGINIA:

They continued to speed on the long stretch of the interstate, hoping to remain undetected in evading the enemy forces, when the bright lights from the other enemy transports suddenly flashed into their rear view window, followed by a lethal barrage of machine gun fire.

"Can't this thing go any faster? They're turning this transport into Swiss cheese!" Arianna shouted under the hail of enemy gunfire.

"I'm going as fast as I can!" Kassandra replied.

"That's the least of our worries! They're gaining on us!" Brandon answered

"If that's not bad enough, I see contacts coming from the skies!" Stephanie added.

A series of enemy bullets tore into the thick armor of their transport, while the pursuing enemy forces continued to close the distance.

"Someone man the machine gun! It's the only way we'll get out in one piece!" Kassandra shouted.

"What's he doing?" Daniel asked, watching the assassin.

"Don't worry! He's got a plan!" she answered, and said softly, "I think."

"I'll man the guns," Daniel said, manning the transport's heavy machine guns, opening fire on the enemy ground.

He focused his attention briefly on the enemy gunships that flew quickly towards their positions exchanging rounds, striking one of the enemy pilots, causing him to crash and burn into some of the pursuing enemy transports, and looked for cover from the overwhelming barrage of enemy fire from the combined efforts of air and ground units.

The assassin patiently waited for the enemy transports to surround them, and watched as they tried ramming them off the road, while another enemy gunship flew over the canopy of their transport.

"If you have a plan, now's the time!" Kassandra shouted, while trying to stay on the road from their constant assault.

He calmly reached into his sachet and took out a detonator for all the charges that he had placed in their transports, waiting for the right moment to trigger the explosions.

"What the hell is he doing?" David yelled.

"Taking care of our problem!" Kassandra answered back.

"It's taking him long enough!" David said.

"He knows what he's doing!" Kassandra answered confidently.

"We'll see!"

"We sure will!"

He slowly and calmly pressed the button of the detonator, triggering a series of explosions, with the force of the blast scattering countless pieces of razor sharp debris and shrapnel in all directions. It shattered the windows of their transport, while he remained unfazed as the shards of razor sharp glass raced past his face, pounding missiles of the gunships relentlessly, causing them to explode, the force of the blast forcing them to swivel out of control, falling onto the interstate, exploding, scattering more shrapnel and debris in every direction.

"There's debris everywhere and there's no escaping! What do I do?" Kassandra asked frantically.

"Go through it!" Daniel shouted.

A sudden clamor echoed through the interstate as Kassandra charged through the burning wreckage from the blast, causing their transport to shudder violently, almost causing her to lose control of the vehicle.

Stephanie suddenly felt a sharp stabbing pain in her side and dipped her finger into a wound, seeing it was thickly covered in her blood, and watched the chunk of glass protruding into her side, saying softly, "Oh my God."

"My God! Stephanie is hit! And she's bleeding badly!" David said in shock.

"Brandon, take the wheel!" Kassandra yelled.

The road was completely blanketed in ice from the falling snow, causing them difficulty in maintaining control of their vehicle, while Kassandra tried to pull out the shard of broken glass from Stephanie's side, with her hands completely soiled in blood.

"We have more incoming!" Daniel yelled.

Brandon pressed the acceleration as hard as he could on the snow-covered road, causing the bloody shard of glass to slip from Kassandra's fingertips, going deeper into Stephanie's wound.

"I can't get it out! There's too much commotion! We need to get those enemy transports off our tail!" Kassandra shouted.

"I'm doing the best I can! How's your bodyguard going to get us out of this mess?" Brandon asked frantically.

"He's your bodyguard too!" she answered. She turned to Daniel as he continued to man the transport machine gun and said, "We need to lose those transports before we get to the next town! The road is slippery! Take out the driver. Maybe, it can cause a pileup!"

"The road is slippery and I can't really get a clear shot. I need to stay straight long enough to line up my shots!" Daniel replied.

The assassin carefully lined up his shot as their transport maintained control on the slippery road and fired a shot at one of the enemy transports, eliminating the driver, causing the transport to drive off the road crashing into the guard rail, as more enemy transports continued to pursue.

"They're still coming!" Arianna yelled.

"It's working! Continue aiming for the driver!" Kassandra answered, while she continued to try pulling the bloodstain shard of glass from Stephanie's side.

The assassin carefully continued to line his shots, eliminating the drivers one by one until a monstrous impact from a number of enemy vehicles crashing into one another filled the streets, giving a brief respite as they continued to make their escape unchallenged into the next town.

"How's she doing?" David asked in concern.

"She's losing a lot of blood. If we don't get her to the next town soon, she could bleed to death," Kassandra answered.

"The next town is up ahead," David answered.

21:47 HOURS. SOMEWHERE IN FREDERICKSBURG, VIRGINIA:

They arrived at the city with the transport severely damaged from the heavy barrage of enemy bullets they sustained.

"We need to get rid of this transport," Brandon said.

"But first, we need to take her to a hospital," Kassandra answered, while she continued to try and control the bleeding.

"No time. One place is as good as another. This piece of junk has run its course. Can't get too far in this. There's a library not too far from here. It'll have to do," David answered.

21:56 HOURS. SALEM CHURCH PUBLIC LIBRARY - FREDERICKSBURG, VIRGINIA:

The damaged vehicle continued to limp deeper into the city, leaking heavy fuel and smoke, stopping directly at the entrance of the library, with its engine catching ablaze.

"Nick of time," Arianna remarked.

"Come on, let's take her in," David said, grabbing her, holding her tightly in his arms, rushing towards the entrance.

"We must hurry. They'll be here soon," Kassandra answered, following behind.

Brandon tested the door and said, "It's opened."

"Let's hurry," Kassandra said.

They rushed into the library with Stephanie still held tightly in David's arms, leaving a long trail of tiny droplets on the floor.

"The enemy soldiers will be here soon. We need to take her all the way to the back. The deeper we go, the more time it'll take for them to find us. But we must hurry. These shelves will provide some good cover."

"What about your ninja over here?" Arianna asked.

"Don't worry about him. He knows what to do," Kassandra said, running to the back.

"Okay, I'll help suppress enemy fire as long as I can, before he gets here."

They ran deeper into the library as far back as possible, with the tall shelves fully stocked with dusty books providing cover.

David gently laid Stephanie on the cold concrete floor of the library, while he looked into her eyes, seeing life slowly slipping away from them, with a look of fright on his face. Her wound continued to bleed profusely from the shard of glass that penetrated deeply into her stomach. He held her hand tightly while she held him back timidly, her energy rapidly depleting. She grimaced from the sharp stabbing pain from the wound that tore into her side. David said, "You need to hurry if you're going to save her."

"I know. It's a delicate procedure," Kassandra answered.

"Wait," Stephanie called out softly, and grabbed David's hand as tightly as she could, and nodded her head back to Kassandra, indicating that she was ready.

"The glass has gone very deep, and I must dig it out. It's going to hurt a bit, okay?" Kassandra said nervously.

"I'm ready. Let's get this over with," Stephanie replied, while she continued to grab David's hand tighter.

"Your move, Doctor," David said with a hint of worry on his face.

"Here it goes," Kassandra said softly, as she commenced the delicate procedure, dipping the knife slowly into Stephanie's wound to dig out the shard of broken glass that sliced into her gut, while she continued to grimace in pain. "Just a little longer."

"How long will it take?" David asked in concern.

"Can't tell for sure. The glass is very deep. If I'm not careful, it can damage vital organs, and cause her to bleed internally. But, I'm working as fast as I can. She'll be fine, I promise," Kassandra answered and continued digging into Stephanie's wound that found its way deeper inside of her.

Moments after digging, she slowly pulled out the glass and said, "Got it," analyzing it closely, completely doused in Stephanie's blood, and threw it to the floor.

"You need to contain the bleeding. She's still losing a lot of blood," David said, with a hint of concern in his voice.

"I need you to keep pressure on the wound," Kassandra answered, dipping her blood-soaked hands into the pocket of her once gleaming white lab coat, taking out the syringe laced with the serum and injecting it into Stephanie's veins.

She felt the immediate effects of the medicine traveling through her blood stream, placing her into instant comatose, while it helped her healed.

"The serum is taking its course now. Though she has lost a lot of blood. She'll be fine."

"Thank you, Dr. Weaver," David said.

"Don't mention it. Just take care of her. Now, I need to get all this blood off my hands," Kassandra said, searching for a place to wash the blood off.

As the assassin waited outside under one of the abandoned vehicles parked near the sidewalk, he saw a number of enemy soldiers heading into the entrance of the library.

The enemy soldiers carefully walked into the hall of the library, scanning all about for any sign of enemy activity, and saw a trail of tiny droplets of blood leading to the back, and followed the direction.

Kassandra went on a frantic search for the restroom when she noticed a number of enemy soldiers walking into the library. She peered through the shelves of dusty books, advancing to the back and said, "They're coming. Get ready," and ran in hiding.

Daniel waited for the enemy soldiers to draw nearer, and quickly opened fire, ambushing and killing a few in number, with the others responding in swift retaliation.

Within moments after the first shots were fired, the library had become completely consumed in gunfire, as the exchange of bullets tore through the old dusty books that lined the tall wooden shelves, gaining quick ground on the few who made their desperate attempt to hold the enemy soldiers at bay, before they were completely overwhelmed.

Brandon and David joined the fight and opened fire on the enemy forces, until their ammunition were depleted, while Daniel continued his desperate attempt in fending them off single handedly.

David took one last look at Stephanie lying unconscious on the floor from the effects of the serum running its course inside her and looked at Brandon with a sudden look of desperation on his face, knowing what he would have to do to save her life.

He took out the clip of his rifle, seeing it was completely depleted, and threw it to the floor and looked in the direction of the enemy soldiers who were quickly gaining ground towards their position.

"What are you doing?" Brandon yelled through the hail of gunfire.

"Whatever I must!" David answered back.

David began to make a suicidal run through the hail of enemy bullets, when a giant cloud of smoke suddenly blanketed the interior of the entire library, completely enveloping the enemy soldiers, stopping them completely in their tracks. David took cover behind the shelves, waiting for the carnage that was about to be unleashed at the hands of their protector.

As the smoke continued to envelop the enemy soldiers, the deafening roar of gunfire filled the halls of the library, as the assassin quickly engaged them with cunning and stealth, while the bullets continued flying, tearing the shelves of old dusty books that lined the shelves. The enemy soldiers fired in all directions trying to locate their nemesis, while the others continued to scramble for cover.

David lay on top of Stephanie through the thick hail of enemy bullets, protecting her from any further harm, while she laid unconscious on the floor, recuperating from the serum's paralyzing effects.

The screams of the enemy soldiers continued to echo loudly through walls of the library, amidst the deafening roar of machine gun fire, and suddenly stopped.

The thick cloud of smoke slowly cleared and the torn and bullet-riddled pages that once lined the old dusty books of the library slowly fell to the floor.

They slowly came out of their hiding places, and saw the assassin standing amidst all the corpses of dead enemy soldiers, sprawled on the cold floor of the library, replenishing his supplies, and tossing the rest to the others.

They watched in a complete state of disbelief, seeing the carnage the assassin continued to leave in his wake, looking at all the dead soldiers that he disposed of single handedly.

"They'll be more coming. We need to get new supplies," Kassandra said.

"What we need to do is get out. I'll go get Stephanie," David said, running to the back.

"They won't be bothering us anymore. A few less enemy soldiers to worry about," Kassandra remarked, watching the dead soldiers on the floor.

"You're not fazed by any of this?" Arianna asked.

"Should I be? No time to reminisce. We need to keep moving. What we need to do is restock on whatever we could find, beginning with those. And as much as we can carry," she said, pointing to all the ammunition the assassin salvaged from the corpses of the dead enemy soldiers, and began collecting as many of the charges from their inventory as she could carry.

"Where to?" Arianna asked.

"The next city, town, or wherever, so we can find a hospital. I'm being tracked. And as long as I have that tracking device inside me, they'll know where to find us and keep on sending more troops. I must find a hospital or a clinic. Anywhere with medical supplies that we can use for surgical purposes," Kassandra answered.

They rushed outside of the library and saw no sign of enemy activity, and laid Stephanie's unconscious body into one of the enemy soldier's transports. They headed towards the next city in search of more supplies, while continuing to evade the enemy soldiers.

22:27 HOURS. SOMEWHERE ON INTERSTATE 81, HEADING TOWARDS CHARLOTTESVILLE, VIRGINIA:

Shortly after they left the library, heading towards the next city, Stephanie was slowly regaining consciousness, while her body still remained paralyzed from the effects of the serum.

She slowly opened her eyes and looked all around her, feeling she was moving and asked, "Am I dead?"

"Not your time to go yet," David answered.

"Are we still being followed?" she asked.

"We're in the clear for now," he answered, holding her tightly in his arms.

"Where are we?"

"Heading towards the next city. Where we can salvage fresh clothes, food, and more supplies," Kassandra answered.

"Where are the others?"

"They're in the other transport right behind us. If we load up on supplies, we'll need the extra space," Kassandra said.

"Okay good. I know where we can find a weapons store. We can stop there," Stephanie said.

CHAPTER 18: CARNAGE.

22:57 HOURS. SOMEWHERE IN CHARLOTTESVILLE, VIRGINIA:

After trekking through the interstate a while longer, they arrived at the weapons goods store and cautiously walked through the door, in anticipation of an enemy ambush, noticing the eerie silence from the constant years of abandonment, and began running through the entire store gathering as many supplies as they could carry, before they could be intercepted by the pursuing enemy forces. David ran to the back of the store, carrying Stephanie tightly in his arms, and gently laid her to rest on the cold pavement, and said softly, "Rest here for a moment. You'll be safe."

"We need to get as many supplies as we can carry. They'll be here soon," Kassandra said.

"I'll go keep watch," Daniel said, running outside.

The assassin calmly walked through the aisles, and suddenly came to a stop, gazing at a samurai blade tucked firmly into its sheath, and gently grabbed it from the shelf. He unsheathed the dull blade, watching it shimmer in the light, with much admiration.

He grabbed the sharpening stone off the shelf, and sharpened the dull blade after a number of strokes, and grabbed a shirt from the aisle. He tossed it in the air and watched it fall slowly onto the blade, slicing through the fabric.

He looked at the blade one last time, placed it back into its sheath, and strapped it onto his back.

Daniel stood guard outside and watched as the light flurries of snow slowly continued to fall from the skies. He looked into the distance, saw the lights from the enemy helicopters quickly approaching, and ran back into the store and yelled, "Enemy helicopters approaching! Everybody get cover! They'll be here soon! You need to hurry!"

"We need to leave now!" David yelled.

"We don't have time! If we drive out into the open, we'll be sitting ducks! If we run, they'll find me and kill all of you for sure. Including Susan," Kassandra said nervously.

"Then what do we do?" Brandon asked.

"We do the only thing left to do. We fight and buy ourselves more time. It'll be a while before the next group of soldiers arrive. By then, we'll be long gone. Trust me. We've gotten this far," she answered softly, grabbing his hand.

"Let me know when you lovebirds are finished making out! Didn't you just hear what he said? We need to hurry!" Daniel said.

The assassin calmly walked by the others and headed out of the store into the falling snow, to assess the situation.

"Where the hell is he going?" Arianna asked.

"What's he doing this time?" David asked.

"The same thing he always does. Snuff them out so he can keep the rest of you breathing," Kassandra answered. "Let's move."

"Don't have to tell me twice," Arianna said, running to the back of the store, holding Susan tightly in her arms.

The assassin walked out of the store into the snow and saw the enemy helicopters drawing nearer.

He handed Daniel a grenade launcher and raised his finger to gesture when to fire. He signaled him to use the abandoned vehicles for cover, and laid in wait under one of the vehicles, watching the enemy soldiers scurry through snow covered streets into the store, watching the glass door swing back and forth after the last enemy of the soldiers had entered.

The enemy soldiers waited quietly at the front of the store with their guns drawn, waiting for the hulking mass of the highest ranking soldier to give his orders to sweep the store in search of Kassandra.

The thumping of his boots sounded loudly on the floor, as he walked forward and yelled, "We know you're here! You're completely surrounded!

There's no escape! Surrender peacefully and you will not be harmed!"

"Where is he?" Arianna whispered.

"He's here. Just be quiet," Kassandra answered softly.

"Feel like wasting those fuckers," David said softly.

"You can't handle them alone. There's too many of them," Kassandra answered.

"Then what do we do in the meantime?" Brandon asked softly.

"I'll try to buy us some time," she answered.

"What the fuck are you going to do?" Arianna answered.

"I'll turn myself in."

"Are you crazy?" Brandon asked.

"It's not me they want to kill. They want me alive. It's you that I'm worried about."

"Don't do this, Kassandra. Please," Brandon begged.

"I'm just trying to buy us time till he gets here."

Kassandra sprang to her feet from the back of the store, with her hands up, slowly walking towards the squad of enemy soldiers, her eyes probing all around nervously, looking for any sign of the assassin, and said softly to herself, "I need a sign. If you're here, now is a good time."

"Where are the others?" the high-ranking soldier asked firmly.

"0-7 and the others left. I'm the only one here. He just wants to be alone. And the others are just innocent civilians. They have nothing to do with this. It's me that you want."

"I'll be the one to figure out who's innocent or guilty."

"Let them go. The only thing they're guilty of is just trying to survive."

"I'll ask again, and won't do it a second time. Where's 0-7?"

Kassandra remained silent with her eyes wide opened, watching a smoke grenade slowly rolling on the floor towards the squad of enemy soldiers, and answered nervously, knowing of the carnage that was about to unfold and said softly, "Be careful what you wish for," and watched it stopped just a few feet away from them, while they remained unsuspecting of it.

"Secure the Package. And kill the others on sight," the high-ranking soldiers ordered.

As the enemy soldiers quickly moved in to search for the other civilians, a giant cloud of smoke quickly shrouded the area, blanketing the interior of the entire store, quickly confusing them.

Kassandra caught just a mere glimpse of the thin, shiny blade slicing through the smoke, slicing through the flesh of the soldier's wrist, completely severing it, disarming him, causing him to scream loudly in pain.

The roar of gunfire filled the confines of the store, as the enemy soldiers fired wildly through the blinding smoke at their elusive nemesis, who moved as swiftly as the wind, engaging them.

Kassandra scrambled for cover after hearing the roar of machine gun fire, covering her ears, while the others in the back of the store laid firmly on the floor, hearing the haunting screams of dying enemy soldiers from the assassin's vicious onslaught.

The deafening roar of gunfire had suddenly stopped, and the smoke slowly cleared through the bullet holes that riddled the glassed doors, leaving the spent shell casings of countless enemy bullets littering the cold and bloody floor.

They slowly came out from their hiding places and much to their horror, witnessed the grisly site of the slaughter the assassin left in his wake, after being the last man standing through the hail of enemy bullets.

They slowly walked towards the grisly scene, and saw the enemy soldiers laying in pools of their own blood from his deadly skills, clutching his blade tightly in his fist, completely appalled by the carnage they had just witnessed.

"My God," Arianna said softly.

"Could people really be capable of such savagery?" David asked.

"Yes," Kassandra answered. "Apparently so."

"It's like they were just slaughtered. Just massacred. It's just a massacre. Just pure carnage. I liked him better when he used guns," Brandon added.

Kassandra slowly walked towards the wounded top-ranking soldier, through the sea of dead enemy soldiers, who lay lifeless in pools of their own blood, walking past his severed hand on the blood-soaked floor, and stooped towards him, kneeling.

She took a deep breath, and paused for a moment, watching the extent of his injuries, with the long and deep laceration from the assassin's blade that ran from his hip, moving all the way up to his chest, slicing through his collar bone, spewing blood heavily.

She looked at his name tag on his uniform and said softly, "Lieutenant Richardson. I told you to be careful what you ask for."

The wounded soldier peered back at Kassandra with the helpless look of a dying soldier on his face, while he continued to take his last breaths, until he finally succumbed to his wounds.

Susan slowly came walking from the back of the store, walking towards the others, with her hands covered in blood, and slowly fell to the floor.

"My God, Susan's hit!" Arianna shouted, running towards her, picking her up from the floor.

"We need to get the bullet out! I need a knife!" Kassandra yelled, applying pressure on her wound.

The assassin took out his knife and gently placed the hilt in Kassandra's palm, while she prepared Susan for surgery.

Daniel came running into the store and said, "We have two-" and stopped abruptly, seeing the carnage the assassin had left in his wake, with the aid of his new weapon, with a sudden look of fear and awe on his face, and continued, "What the hell happened here?"

"What does it look like? Any idea when you'll be getting to the point?" Kassandra asked, while she continued to prep Susan for surgery.

"Looks like we found our means of escape. There are 2 choppers parked outside. The only thing is that we have 2 pilots sitting in the front."

"Handle it! Take him with you! My hands are full, as you can see!" she answered.

The assassin calmly walked past Daniel, while Kassandra continued to tend to Susan.

"This should be easy," Daniel said softly, watching the assassin walk past him.

"I need someone to apply pressure on the wound to help stop the bleeding!" Kassandra yelled.

"Okay," Arianna said nervously, applying as much pressure as she could on Susan's wound. "Hang in there, baby, you'll be fine."

Moments after digging into Susan's shoulder wound with the assassin's knife, taking out the bullet, she threw the bullet to the floor, and reached into her pocket, taking out the syringe and injected it into Susan's arm, placing her into an instant comatose.

The assassin calmly walked out of the store and saw the duo of helicopters from a safe distance, and handed Daniel a rocket propelled grenade and raised his finger, gesturing to him to wait for the right moment to fire.

They moved silently through the snow filled streets using the abandoned civilian transports for cover, until they were at a striking distance, and watched the assassin closely, until the assassin gave him the signal to fire, while he was within striking distance of the next enemy helicopter.

Daniel calmly aimed at one of the helicopters and fired a single shot, causing it to burst into flames, suddenly catching the attention of the other enemy pilot.

The other enemy pilot tried to make a hasty retreat, trying to climb from the cockpit of his helicopter, and suddenly felt the cold, bloody steel of the assassin's blade resting firmly on his neck.

A sudden look of shock creased his face, seeing that he had come face to face with the assassin, with his eyes probing all about nervously, seeing the assassin's clothes were completely drenched in the blood of his victims, knowing those that had walked into the store had met a grim fate at his hands.

He slowly placed his hands up and said nervously, "Don't kill me. I have a wife and a daughter. I have a family."

"So did all the people that you killed," Daniel answered.

"I'm just a pilot. I just do what I'm told. I just follow orders just like you."

"The same orders that made you murder innocent men, women, and children. It's never good when the shoe is on the other foot, now is it? Well, just so you know, I hope when you walk through that door, you're ready for a rude awakening. I sure as hell wasn't," Daniel said, pointing his gun at the pilot's temple.

The assassin grabbed the enemy pilot by the collar of his uniform and dragged him out of the cockpit, into the store, and tossed him onto the bloodstained floor, littered with the corpses of his fellow soldiers, who had met their untimely fate at his hands.

The pilot looked all over, seeing the countless spent casings from all the bullets that had missed their mark, littering the bloody floor, and saw the spent shell of the canister of a smoke grenade, making him come to the chilling realization that they had fallen into the trap of the assassin's deadly ambush.

His face suddenly creased into more shock, watching the highest-ranking soldier of their unit sitting on the bloody floor with a lifeless gaze, his wrist completely severed, and a long, gaping wound that tracked from his pelvis all the way to his collarbone, and suddenly began to vomit.

"Yeah. My thoughts exactly," Arianna said, with a hint of sarcasm.

Kassandra grabbed a blade from the shelf and pulled it from its sheath. She walked towards the enemy pilot and pressed it firmly against his neck, and looked at the name on his uniform, and said, "Consider this a warning, Crawford. Tonight is the most important night of your life. It seems that God has smiled upon you this time. You've been spared for the specific purpose of telling the others that if they continue to pursue us, this is exactly what will happen to them, and believe me, this is nothing compared to what will happen if they don't heed the warning. This was only scratching the surface. Consider yourself lucky that God has mercy on you, because I assure you that the next time the both of you meet, our friend here will not. Got it?"

The sweat dripped down the strands of his straight brown hair, down the stubbles of hair on his cheeks, as he closed his green eyes tightly, nodding his head, indicating that he agreed to Kassandra's terms.

She dropped the blunt blade on the floor and said, "I always wanted to do that."

"Are you enjoying this?" Arianna asked.

"Should I feel sorry for them?" she answered.

"Don't you feel fazed by all this?" David added.

"Should I be?" Kassandra asked.

"Considering what just went down, don't you feel a little?" Brandon asked.

"No, I'm not! If it were up to me, I'd do the same to all of them any chance that I got!" she yelled. "Have you become so naive? Haven't you been listening? They came to kill you! All of you!" she said, pointing to Susan, as Arianna held her tightly to her chest while she slept in her comatose state.

"But this," Jacob said, pointing to their mutilated corpses.

"But this? What about "this"? What do you think they came to do? Shake hands? Their sole purpose was to kill all of you, and not to lose a single night's sleep after doing it!"

"I don't know if we have the stomach for this," Stephanie added.

"Well, I suggest you get used to it, because this is just the beginning, because he hasn't even begun stacking bodies," Kassandra answered softly. "What you've just seen, and what you're about to see is not for the faint of heart. So unfortunately, that doesn't leave you with much of a choice. Any of you. But they have a choice on whether they should live past tonight, or die young prematurely. And this is it. I suggest that they choose quickly, because there won't be any more second chances, because this warning of what we've all just witnessed was crystal clear! And it doesn't get any clearer than that!" she said, showing the assassin's blood-stained blade.

"All I'm saying is I like it better when he uses guns. This course of action was a bit too extreme," Brandon answered.

"So is trying to kill innocent civilians! So was trying to murder Susan! So, tell me, does it even matter what any of you like at this point? Or how he stacked these bodies? Or how effective his methods are? His methods may be brutal, but effective! All that matters is that all of you are still alive because of his methods, no matter how brutal they are! In case all your thick skulls have gone hazy, we're all in danger, and you're worrying about which course of action to take? Seriously? Clearly, I saw they didn't come here to be friends, and I know you saw that too, and the message was as clear as day! For them, it's business as usual, and for us, it's all about survival, and right now, his course of action is the only thing keeping me from being captured, and the rest of you breathing! So whatever the course of action he takes, I really don't care, and judging from the looks on your faces, you know I'm right! Susan right now is in a coma, with a hole in her shoulder, and was just this close to bleeding to death, courtesy of yours truly!" she said, pointing at the corpse of the high-ranking soldier sprawled lifelessly on the floor. "They won't stop until you're dead! All of you! So, here's a thought - if all of you don't have the stomach for all this! Why don't the rest of you go on your own, and see how far you'll get without him! Any volunteers?" she asked, looking at the others, who quietly pondered on what she said, looking at one another. "You're all free to go! Well?"

"I wouldn't even wish this on my enemy," Brandon said softly.

"Well, I would!" Kassandra said loudly. "It's because of them that my father lost everything! Everything he worked so hard to build! And all he was trying to do was save them from themselves! I lost my mother! They killed her for no reason! I lost my entire family! They forced me into all this after they kidnapped me, and sacrificed my youth to help with this stupid war effort! They sacrificed the only ones who I cared about, and who cared about me! Well, I say they all deserved it, and tonight was a clear warning to those that follow! So, I ask again, any volunteers?"

They continued to ponder silently among themselves, after Kassandra had finished making her comments.

"I didn't think so," she answered softly.

They looked at all the dismembered and mutilated corpses of all the enemy soldiers laying in pools of their own blood, with a hint of remorse after witnessing first-hand the savagery of the assassin's methods.

"Let's stock up on as many supplies as we can carry aboard the helicopter. It looks like we'll be flying out military style," Kassandra said softly.

"Where to?" Brandon asked.

"I need to get to the nearest hospital or clinic, so I can take this tracking device out of me. As long as I have it, they'll keep on finding us. It's the only way we can move undetected."

"I'm sure there's one nearby," Arianna said softly.

"There'll be more coming to this position since we're keeping him alive. His tracking device must be transmitting to this location right now, so we need to move quickly. How's Susan?" Kassandra asked.

"She's still asleep. The effects of the serum are still strong. Her immune system is still young. Her resistance is low. There's no telling how long she'll be out," Arianna asked.

"How are you holding up, Stephanie?"

"Still a little drowsy from the effects. But it's beginning to wear off."

"Okay let's go."

As the others made their hasty departure from the store, the assassin turned back one last time, staring at the enemy pilot, with a cold, stern look on his face, serving as a warning that if their paths were to cross, he would pay the ultimate price, while the pilot stared back nervously, and watched the assassin and the others walk away.

23:29 HORUS. MARTHA JEFFERSON HOSPITAL LABORATORY - CHARLOTTESVILLE, VIRGINIA:

They landed on the street a few yards in front of the hospital, and hurried through the glass doors of the entrance.

They cautiously opened the front door, their weapons drawn, expecting to be greeted by enemy soldiers, but instead saw the dimmed flickering lights and the cold discolored walls marred with countless mold, after years of abandonment and neglect.

Though being greeted with the deplorable conditions of the hospital, they remained reluctant to venture further into the building, thinking there were enemy soldiers lurking in ambush.

Kassandra suddenly ran through the dimly lit corridors in search of an operating room to remove the tracking device buried deep inside her, totally ignoring any security protocols.

"What the hell are you doing? Are you crazy?" Brandon yelled.

"Looking for the operating room!" she answered back, as she continued to run through the dimly lit corridors.

"What if there are enemy soldiers?" David asked.

"No time! We must hurry! There'll be more coming!" she yelled back.

They continued to walk cautiously through the dimly lit corridors of the dilapidated structure, checking all the rooms for any signs of enemy activity, when Kassandra suddenly stuck her head out of the doors of the operating room, startling the others yelling, "All clear!"

"You sure?" Arianna asked nervously.

"No one here! Just us!"

"Well, stop yelling. You're making the rest of us more nervous than we already are," Stephanie answered.

"I swear this bitch is getting crazier every second," Arianna said softly.

Brandon looked at Arianna and answered, "For once, we both agree on something."

"I'll stand watch in case more show up," Daniel said.

"They will. You can count on that. The rest of you, go inside. It's about to get messy. Really messy. Don't want to be around seeing the freak show," Daniel said.

"Say no more," David said, staring at the assassin, and walked away.

Daniel walked towards the reception desk, assuming defensive position, while the assassin patiently waited near the entrance to ambush the unsuspecting enemy soldiers.

Kassandra and the others walked into the x-ray room, and immediately scanned for the hidden device.

Arianna placed Susan on a bed in the dimly lit room, covering her body with a sheet, and walked towards Kassandra.

They took the diagrams from the machine and analyzed them carefully in search of the tracking device.

Arianna looked closely and asked, "What's that?"

"It's like a tiny dot, or it looks like one," she answered.

"Can't see anything," Stephanie answered.

"Me either," David answered.

"I see it. It's right near my brain stem, to the back of my neck," Kassandra answered.

"What if it's not?" Arianna asked in concern.

"It's a chance we may just have to take."

"We?" Arianna asked.

"I've got a bad feeling about this," David added.

"It's either we take a chance, or have more enemy troops chasing us in every corner of the country. Do you have the detector?" Kassandra asked.

"No. Lost it back in Arlington, when we were being chased underground. Sorry," David replied.

"Then it's settled. It's a chance I'll just have to take," Kassandra said and walked over to the table lined with a number of operating knives, and sat on the bed. She grabbed one, handing it to Arianna, and said, "Take it."

"I said I was practicing to be a nurse. I never said I was one," Arianna said, reluctantly grabbing the blade from Kassandra.

"Well, here's your chance."

"That tracking device is next to your brain stem. If anything goes wrong, that means instant and permanent paralysis. What do I do then?" Arianna asked.

"No time to think. Just do it. They'll be here soon," Kassandra said.

"Wouldn't even know where to begin. It's like I'm treating you like a guinea pig."

"Based on the circumstances, neither of us have a choice in the matter. Now, what I need you to do is calm down and create a tiny incision at the back of my neck with the knife. After you've done that, get a tweezer, and pull it out," Kassandra said, bowing her head forward, raising her long, dark hair over her face, exposing the naked skin at the back of her neck.

"It's easier said than done. Okay, here goes," Arianna said, injecting the anesthetic into Kassandra's neck to numb her muscles from the sharp pain of the incision.

Kassandra slowly succumbed to the paralyzing effects of the tranquilizer, slumping on the bed with her face hitting the mattress.

Arianna gently created a tiny incision with the sharp knife, and carefully probed deeper into the back of her neck, searching for the tiny device embedded deeply into her flesh.

Moments after Arianna had commenced the delicate procedure, a group of enemy soldiers had arrived at the hospital, and slowly walked through the revolving doors made of glass and metal.

Daniel waited nervously in hiding for a considerable amount of time before they walked through the door, and took a deep long breath, closing his eyes, and waited for them to draw nearer to his location, listening to their footsteps growing louder. The assassin quietly pulled out a smoke grenade, gently pulling out the pin as they walked past him, as he hid behind the door.

As the enemy soldiers' footsteps grew louder as they walked deeper into the hospital's corridors, Daniel quickly opened fire, bringing down the number of advancing soldiers.

In the midst of exchanging fire with the enemy soldiers, he saw a giant wall of smoke clouded the corridor, completely shrouding them from behind, and quickly went for cover behind the reception desk, and said to himself, "Here we go again."

Arianna and the others were immediately startled at the sudden roar of the all the machine gun fire, while she continued to the delicate procedure of searching for the device buried deeply into Kassandra's neck, while her hands continued to tremble uncontrollably, causing her to pause taking deep breaths, while the sweat began dripping down her face, from all the commotion that continued to ensue within the narrow dimly lit corridors of the dilapidated building which was once a proud institution.

The thick cloud of smoke continued to shroud the long and narrow corridors of the hospital, covering the assassin's advance, as he continued to swiftly engage the enemy soldiers, quickly and silently disposing of them with his deadly skills in close quarters combat.

Arianna and the others did their best to remain calm, while she continued her search for the elusive tracking beacon under the intense pressure of trying to ignore the screams of the assassin's victims being slaughtered by his deadly skill, drowned by the constant clamor of machine gun fire, while David, Stephanie, and Brandon nervously monitored the door of the operating room, with their weapons drawn, posing as the last line of defense, in case the assassin had failed to neutralize any of the remaining enemy soldiers.

Daniel remained covered behind the reception desk, as the bullets continued to penetrate through its wooden structure that shielded him from the enemy fire, covering his ears firmly from the noise, coming from the deadly encounter that continued to ensue at close range.

After a brief moment, the deafening roar of gunfire had suddenly stopped, with only the sounds of the empty spent casings from the enemy bullets rolling on the cold, concrete floors of the hospital.

After the assassin had quickly disposed of the enemy soldiers, Daniel watched quietly, while he remained behind the makeshift barricade of the reception desk riddled with enemy bullets, watching the assassin standing among the dead enemy soldiers with his weapon still tightly clutched in his palm, with a stunned look on his face.

After moments of exhaustive searching, Arianna had finally recovered the device that was buried deep in Kassandra's neck, and slowly pulled it out, examining it, as she pulled it to her face, completely doused in Kassandra's blood, and gently pressed its top, switching it off, and laid it in the tray next to the bloody scalpel that she used to create the tiny incision at the back of her neck.

As the enemy soldiers remained posted outside behind their transports, with their weapons pointed nervously towards the entrance of the hospital, they heard the agony of the other troops, drowned by the deafening roar of machine gun fire from within its walls, knowing that the others had met their fate at the hands of the assassin, after listening to the eerie calm that suddenly swept through the bullet-ridden corridors of the hospital.

Moments after the skirmish, they waited nervously outside, staring at one another, to see who would go in next, when the door suddenly swung opened, causing the thick fog of red smoke to rush out into the streets, and saw a soldier staggering through the door, his clothes drenched in blood, falling heavily onto the snowy pavement, just past the door, leaving it opened, as the crimson smoke continued to rush out, masking his presence.

The enemy soldiers quickly dropped their guards and rushed towards the dying soldier into the crimson colored cloud of smoke that continued to rush through the door, slowly concealing them in the wall of fog.

One of the enemy soldiers took off the dying soldier's face mask, catching just a mere glimpse of the assassin's face, causing a sudden look of shock on his face, realizing that he was about to face his inevitable demise after falling into the assassin's carefully laid trap. He felt the cold steel of the assassin's knife slicing deeply into his neck, killing him, after being completely shrouded by the crimson wall of smoke, using the cloud to conceal his presence, as the street was about to become his hunting ground, like the cold decrepit corridors of the hospital, and many other places before.

Within moments, the screams of dying men echoed through the hail of gunfire, completely shrouded by the cloud of crimson smoke that seemed eerily familiar like the hospital corridors just moments before. Daniel remained in the confines of the hospital, listening helplessly to the troops who were unfortunate to cross paths with the assassin, only to meet their untimely demise, as the assassin quietly continued hunting through the thick wall of smoke, strategically thrusting his blade through the back of one of the enemy soldiers, forcing him to scream from the pain, diverting the other enemy soldiers to his position, frighteningly greeting the dying soldier with a constant barrage of bullets. The assassin quickly silenced him, as he fired frantically in all directions. They remained completely unaware of the assassin's position, while he continued in quickly disposing of them with the use of his trusty blade, with lethal precision through the thick fog.

Daniel continued to stay out of harm's way, as he lay hidden behind the reception desk completely riddled with bullets, hearing the constant screams of the assassin's victims being butchered by their nemesis's deadly skills, amidst the constant crackling of machine gun fire, laying completely frozen in fright, knowing of the horror of the atrocities the assassin was yet to leave in his wake, when the gunfire had once again ceased, along with the screams of dying soldiers and machine gun fire.

Daniel slowly arose from behind the reception desk, cautiously peeking from behind it, his eyes probing in all directions, seeing the decrepit walls of the hospital from time and neglect completely stained in their blood and riddled with bullet holes.

He slowly walked through the carnage the assassin had left inside, heading towards the exit, amidst empty smoke grenade canisters, and spent shell casings that littered the floor, beneath the thick soles of his heavy boots, following the trail of bloody footprints that led to the front glass doors, completely riddled with countless bullet holes.

He slowly opened the door, peeping through the tiny gap to make sure the front was clear of enemy soldiers, after the smoke had cleared, and saw more of the carnage the assassin had left in his wake.

The heat of his breath fogged his face as it mingled with the cold, subtle winds that swept through the entrance of the hospital that became another one of his killing fields, as he breathed nervously, while he continued through the sea of dead enemy soldiers, until he finally came up to the assassin being the only man standing, his blade gripped tightly in his palm, covered in their blood, dripping off its tip onto the snowy ground, staring back into his eyes with his usual cold and calculating stare, his face completely absent of remorse and emotion, as he had done many times before.

He looked all around him, seeing that the once gleaming white snow that covered the ground became a crimson glow with the blood of the enemy soldiers, with a sudden look of horror and disbelief on his face. He turned back, slowly walking to the doors of the hospital, absent any words like he had been completely entranced at what he had just witnessed, and slowly made his way to the operating room.

He walked slowly into the operating room, with the others quickly drawing their weapons drawn to his face without reacting, while he remained in complete shock on how the enemy soldiers had met their demise at the hands of their nemesis and sat on the chair with a distant look of shock and disbelief on his face. The others slowly pointed their weapons down, and watched one another in disbelief, wondering what he had just witnessed.

David walked towards snapping his fingers to Daniel's face, while he remained distant, and asked, "Are you okay?"

"You look like you've seen a ghost," Brandon added.

"I just saw one ghost turned more people into a bunch of ghosts," Daniel answered, with a look of total shock on his face.

"Stephanie," Arianna called out softly, looking at Daniel with a distant look on his face, while she kept pressure on Kassandra's wound.

"Yes," Stephanie answered softly, trying to take her focus off Daniel.

"Can you give me some help with this?" Arianna asked.

"What do you need?" Stephanie asked.

"She's bleeding and I need to contain it."

"What can I do?"

"I need to keep pressure on her wound. Can you reach into her pocket and grab the serum?"

"You mean the miracle cure?" Stephanie asked.

"That's a good way to put it," Arianna replied.

"Okay," Stephanie answered, reaching into the pocket of Kassandra's lab coat. "Got it. What do you want me to do?"

"I need you to close the wound before she bleeds to death. So, I need you to inject a tiny dose near the opening."

Stephanie carefully injected a tiny dose of the serum into Kassandra's neck, and watched the wound close within a few seconds, causing Arianna to gently release the pressure.

Arianna slowly walked towards Daniel while he continued to sit in a distant gaze and asked, "What happened out there?"

"It's like he's not human. What he did to those men at the store before was nothing compared to what just happened. It's like committing war crimes over and over. I don't know how Kassandra sleeps at nights seeing the level of brutality this guy continues to commit. And after what I've just witnessed, I don't think that I'll ever be able to sleep again," Daniel said with his face still in a distant gaze, with his eyes completely entranced in deep contemplation after seeing the level of brutality the assassin continued to dispose of his enemies.

The doors of the operating room swung open, startling them as the assassin calmly walked past them, his clothes completely soiled in blood and blade still gripped tightly in his palm. He stopped at seeing Kassandra laying on the bed unconscious from the serum coursing through the body after a delicate procedure.

He glanced at the scalpel and tweezers stained with her blood and saw the tracking device on the metal tray next to them, picked it up, holding it closer to his face, examining it, and laid it back next to the bloody surgical tools, and walked out with the same straight face as he had entered, leaving a sudden chill of fear came over the others, watching the assassin, soaked in the blood of his enemies come and leave without saying a word, as he always did.

"She came here to get the tracking device out, right?" Arianna asked.

"And we did," David answered.

"So, I think it's safe to say that our business is done. And that may be our cue to leave," Arianna replied.

"There's a problem with that. More like 2," Brandon replied.

"What's that?" Stephanie asked.

"Her ass is out cold. And she's the only one that could fly us out of here," Arianna answered, pointing to Kassandra as she lay unconscious on the bed, recovering from the serum's paralyzing effects, as it continued traveling through her body. "The second problem is that the tracking beacon was on long enough to track her last location. So, if she doesn't get up soon, we'll be having more company."

"And that includes more of the horror show. And believe me, it's beginning to get old," Daniel answered.

"So, what do we do?" Stephanie asked.

"The only thing that we can do. Wake her up," Arianna replied.

"How?" Stephanie asked.

Arianna looked all around the room and saw a half used bottle of spirits sitting on the table and said, "There. That's it." She grabbed the bottle off the table, poured some of its contents onto a clean piece of gauze, and held it gently to Kassandra's nose, until she slowly began to regain consciousness. "Looks like some of those nursing classes paid off, after all."

"She's coming around," Brandon said softly.

Kassandra slowly opened her eyes, seeing Brandon's silhouette standing above her and asked, "What happened? How long have I been out?"

"You were out for about an hour. You were out long enough to miss all the fun.

But if it makes you feel any better, the procedure was a success," Brandon concluded.

"But we have good news and bad news. Which one do you want first?" Stephanie asked.

"I'll take the good news first," Kassandra replied.

"The procedure was a success, and the tracking beacon is offline. And that's so much of the good news," Stephanie replied.

"That's comforting. And what's the bad news?" Kassandra asked.

"More enemy soldiers came and more are probably on their way right now. The tracking device was on long enough for them to lock on to our location. So, before more come, we need to fly out of here. And fast," Stephanie replied.

"You see, the thing is, you are the only one who could fly," Arianna added.

"What happened to them? Where are they now?" Kassandra asked, as she struggled to maintain her balance, while she tried to sit upright.

"Let's just say they won't be bothering us anymore. Not those at least. They're splattered all over the walls in the corridors and the others are all over the ground outside. You can't miss them. None of us can, unfortunately," Daniel answered.

Kassandra grabbed the piece of gauze, completely dousing it in spirits, and placed it on her nose, inhaling for a few seconds to revive her senses and replied, "Other than the fact that I'm the only one who can fly, a squad of dead enemy soldiers sounds like good news to me. And if more come, then it's more lambs to the slaughter, and everywhere we go is the slaughterhouse. I can't feel my legs. They feel like jello."

"Either way, we need to leave. And I need to get some sleep," Arianna answered.

"Help me up," Kassandra said, trying to get off the bed using support. "Where's the tracking beacon?"

"It's here. I turned it off," Arianna replied.

"It might come in handy," Kassandra replied.

"Think you're good enough to fly?" Brandon asked.

"Well, we can stay here and watch more horror show if you want," she answered.

"Not an option. We'll settle for plan B," Stephanie answered.

Kassandra slowly wobbled towards the door, leaning on Arianna's shoulder while Daniel reluctantly opened the door and said, "We need to get moving."

She inhaled the cloth for the third time and paused for a brief moment, resting her back against the wall, trying to regain the strength in her legs and said, "Let's get moving."

"The chopper's outside. Unfortunately, the only thing we need to do is get past the horror show," Daniel remarked.

They walked out of the operating room, and slowly stepped into the narrow corridor filled with flickering lights, and witnessed the horror that had unfolded. The walls were riddled with countless bullet holes and heavy blood stains. Spent shell casings from enemy bullets littered the floor, along with the corpses of enemy soldiers sprawled onto the cold, concrete in heavy pools of their own blood, leading towards the entrance.

"If you thought the store was bad," David remarked.

"Well, you're still breathing, aren't you? It's not so bad when you get used to it," Kassandra answered.

They looked at one another in disbelief at Kassandra's fortitude as she remained unfazed from all the unspeakable atrocities that the assassin had left in his wake, while they continued walking through the pile of corpses, and came to a sudden stop, seeing the assassin replenishing their supplies and throwing it at their feet.

He stood up and placed his blade back in its sheath, giving them the usual cold stare, with his straight face, while they stared back with a look of total fright on their faces. He made his departure out of the building, filled with death on the outside.

"I think that it's safe to assume that these supplies are for us to utilize," David remarked.

"Considering the latest turn of events, I don't think that we have much of a choice. We have to do our part at some point. Not that we haven't," Stephanie answered.

They walked out of the doors slowly, when Brandon suddenly stopped, feeling a cold and empty canister of a smoke grenade under his foot.

They slowly walked into the streets towards the convoy of empty enemy transports, completely riddled with bullet holes, and stared at each other in disbelief, seeing more of the carnage the assassin had left in his wake from the bodies that laid sprawled about, impaled and dismembered by the assassin's deadly skill with the use of his trusty blade, turning the pure white snow that blanketed the ground, into a thick dark shade of red with their blood.

The assassin quickly stripped their corpses of their armor and supplies and threw it at their feet, and walked away.

"I think it's safe to say, he wants us to put it on. What the hell? All my clothes were damaged by that piece of glass that tore into my side when we were being chased," Stephanie said.

"Don't take too long, we may have more enemy soldiers heading our way," Daniel replied.

"What else do we do?" Brandon asked.

"It'll have to wait," Arianna replied.

"He only suggested. Don't have to take it if we don't want to," David said.

"But if you don't, you stand a better chance of being ripped apart by enemy bullets," Kassandra replied.

"How are you feeling? Ready to get us out?" Arianna asked.

"I should be able to. Still a little dizzy from the serum. I can still feel it flowing through my system. Take me to the chopper. I should be able to do the rest," Kassandra said.

She sat into the pilot seat and slowly turned on the ignition, while she continued to try and regain her senses.

"Where to?" Arianna asked.

"Somewhere we can regroup and rest before we can continue on mission," she answered.

"And what's the mission, exactly?" Brandon asked.

"Kill the General and secure all my blueprints. That might possibly end this war. I can't afford to allow him to use my father's work as a weapon. I just can't."

"And how exactly are we going to accomplish that?" Stephanie answered.

"We have a mole on the inside, warning us about the General's every move, remember? That way, with him on the inside, we're always one step ahead," Kassandra said.

"You mean if he's still alive?" Arianna asked.

"He'll be fine. And it wouldn't hurt to have a little faith. After all, the odds are against us, and you're all still alive. How's Susan holding up?"

"She's fine. She's still asleep," Arianna replied.

"Okay, hold on," Kassandra said, revving the helicopter engines to warm it up. "And after that, we need to ditch this chopper. But for now, destination somewhere. Anywhere. Nowhere. I really don't care," Kassandra said.

00:07 HOURS. WEAPONS STORE - SOMEWHERE IN CHARLOTTESVILLE, VIRGINIA:

A convoy of enemy soldiers arrived at the store following the tracking beacon from one of the soldiers who had survived the assassin's onslaught.

They disembarked from their transports and cautiously walked through the streets towards the burning wreckage of one of their helicopters, with the charred remains of one of their pilots still inside, and cautiously walked through the front door of the store, their weapons drawn, in anticipation of any form of resistance.

They continued walking through the confines of the store, seeing all the walls and ceiling completely riddled with bullets, along with countless spent cartridges and supplies sprawled all about, until they stumbled across the mutilated remains of one of the high-ranking lieutenants, sitting on the floor, his back firmly pressed against the wall, staring down in a lifeless gaze. His severed wrist was lying on the floor, and his sidearm was still clutched firmly in his palm, with the long wound running from his hip, all the way up to his chest, slicing through his collar bone, which caused him to bleed to death.

They looked at one another with their faces showing collective looks of shock, and continued walking through the stack of corpses sprawled on the floor throughout the entire store in pools of their own blood, tracking a set of bloody footprints, until they came across a sole survivor from the assassin's onslaught.

They walked towards him and pointed their weapons downwards, staring at the pilot, showing the complete signs of trauma all over his face. They waved their hands over his face to try and get his attention, only to receive dead silence from the frightened soldier.

One of the soldiers recognized him and called out softly, "Billy?"

The frightened pilot slowly shifted his green eyes, still with a look of shock on his face, his eyes clouded in tears, staring back at the soldier with dead silence.

"What happened here?"

"It was him," Billy answered.

"It was who? What exactly are you saying? What the hell happened here?"

"It was 0-7," Billy replied, with a distant gaze on his face. "The asset. The General's assassin. It was him."

They looked at each other in a state of disbelief, seeing the state of carnage that the assassin had inflicted upon their forces, making his statement that if they had continued to pursue him, they would meet the same fate.

"Do you know where he is?"

"I wished I did," Billy answered.

The soldier looked at the carnage that filled the store and asked, "Why did he leave you alive?"

"He left me alive to tell you that this is what would happen to you if you continued to come after them."

"Were there any others with him?"

"There was one of General West's men. There was also a child. But mostly civilians."

"Was she with them?"

"She was the one that gave me the warning. He never said a word physically. But those eyes told me everything. They told me everything that would happen if we crossed paths again. I won't get a second chance to tell the tale."

"We must apprehend the Package at all costs, and terminate 0-7. It's the General's orders."

"You can go ahead and get yourselves killed just like them if you want. But I'm not going. General's orders or not. I'm just a pilot," Billy answered.

"If you don't follow orders, it will be considered treason."

"I don't care. You can go on and get yourselves killed. But I'm staying right here with the corpses," Billy answered.

"Grab him," the high-ranking soldier ordered.

Billy quickly pulled the high-ranking soldier's sidearm from its holster, pointing it at them in a frantic attempt to stay free from them, with his hands trembling hysterically, with his eyes filled with tears, and shouted, "I'm not going anywhere! I won't end up like them! Go ahead if you want to! But I'm not going!"

"Take it easy," the high-ranking soldier said, softly trying to calm Billy down, walking towards him with his hands up.

"Stay where you are! Not one more step!" Billy shouted pointing the gun at the soldier, stopping him in his tracks, and pointed the gun to his chin, pulling the trigger, ending his own life.

The high-ranking soldier slowly walked towards Billy's lifeless corpse, blood flowing down his face from the gaping head wound. He grabbed the gun from his lifeless fingers, and nodded to the others to leave.

00:15 HOURS. SOMEWHERE OVER INTERSTATE 64 HEADING TOWARDS ARLINGTON, VIRGINIA, EN-ROUTE TO THE NATION'S CAPITAL:

After hours of falling snow, they were suddenly greeted by the blinding storm, as they continued to their destination towards the nation's capital in pursuit of the General, hovering towards an enemy convoy that pursued them, when the radar suddenly began to beep, detecting enemy presence from a distance, on the dark long and lonely interstate.

"What's that?" Arianna asked. "I can hear this thing ringing."

"That's the sound of enemy activity up ahead. It seems that they've set up roadblocks every few miles," Kassandra answered.

"I'm sure they know that we have control of one of the helicopters right about now."

"So, what are we going to do?" Brandon asked.

"What else?" Kassandra asked. "The same thing they'd do to us. Make sure we have less of them to worry about."

"We're getting close. I'm manning one of the guns," Daniel said, making his way towards one of the gatling guns.

The assassin waited until they were within firing range, and without warning, opened fire on the enemy roadblock, with Daniel quickly following suit, while the others just watched helplessly at the carnage and destruction from the lethal barrage of bullets the guns unleashed upon the enemy position, setting off a chain of explosions.

After the enemy position had been completely obliterated, they watched from the safety of the helicopter the destruction they left in their wake, while they flew past the enemy checkpoint, continuing their destination through the blinding snowstorm.

00:24 HOURS. SOMEWHERE ON INTERSTATE 64 HEADING TOWARDS ARLINGTON, VIRGINIA, A FEW MILES FROM RICHMOND, EN-ROUTE TOWARDS THE NATION'S CAPITAL:

They continued flying when the alarm on their radar suddenly began to sound and grew louder, warning them of the presence of another enemy roadblock up ahead.

"We have another roadblock up ahead," David said, watching the radar seeing countless enemy activity.

"Why don't we find another way?" Arianna asked, grabbing onto Susan tightly, as she slowly began to recover from the paralyzing effects of the serum.

"We have to deal with them eventually. The more we kill, the less we have to worry about coming after us," Kassandra said.

As they approached the enemy roadblock, the enemies' blinding searchlights came on, instantly blinding Kassandra's view. They were suddenly greeted by a barrage of enemy bullets tearing through the hull of the helicopter, causing serious damage to the controls, causing the helicopter to spin out of control. The others clung tightly to safety.

The enemy soldiers watched the flaming helicopter fly out of control, heading towards the city of Richmond and quickly followed in pursuit.

00:32 HOURS. SOMEWHERE IN RICHMOND, VIRGINIA:

After being intercepted by enemy ground troops, they crashed into the city streets, with the deafening impact echoing through the entire area, causing Kassandra to hit her head on the controls, rendering her unconscious from the blow.

Arianna grabbed Susan, while she remained sedated from the serum's paralyzing effects, as the assassin, dazed from the crash for a brief moment, regained his senses, and sprang into action, quickly pulling Kassandra's body from the helicopter's burning wreckage, and resting her on the snow filled streets, while she remained unconscious, and went on to pull the others to safety.

He doused gauze with spirits and gently held it against their noses, causing them to come to their senses.

Kassandra opened her eyes, seeing the assassin standing over her, and rose to her feet, while the others continued to recover from the shock of the crash.

Arianna walked towards Kassandra and asked, "Are you okay?"

"I'll be fine. Are you?" Kassandra answered.

"Your head wound is healing slower. The serum must be wearing off."

"It must be. The numbness is beginning to wear off. Anyone hit?"

"Miraculously, no. Just in shock from the fall," Arianna said.

"How is Susan?"

"She's coming around slowly."

"They'll be here soon. We must find a place to hide," Brandon said nervously.

"But, if we move through the snow, they could also find our footprints," Arianna said in a state of panic.

The assassin walked towards the flaming wreckage of the helicopter and placed a charge on it, to ambush the pursuing enemy soldiers, and patiently waited for their arrival in the frigid, blinding storm.

00:34 HOURS. SECURE LOCATION - SOMEWHERE IN RICHMOND, VIRGINIA:

Celina ran up to Dr. Weaver's room where he slept and knocked on his door with great anxiety and shouted, "Dr. Weaver! We have something! Dr. Weaver, please get up! We've located your daughter, sir!"

Dr. Weaver dragged his exhausted body from bed and walked towards the door in the darkness that filled his room, and cracked it open and said, "What is it, Celina?"

"Sorry to wake you, sir. But, I think that we've located your daughter. We've intercepted a transmission a few miles away from here, from an enemy roadblock that was attacked and had time to send a distress call to another enemy roadblock that engaged them. It caused them to do an emergency landing a few miles from our position, and they are now converging on the crash site as we speak. It appears they didn't have a chance to fight back at the second enemy roadblock. Judging from the position of the enemy roadblock and where they were intercepted, they were heading north."

"Emergency landing?" he asked with a hint of concern on his face. "Is my daughter okay?"

"I can't say for certain. All we have for now is a transmission from the enemy roadblock."

Dr. Weaver quickly revived from the sleepiness upon hearing the news of his daughter's whereabouts, and asked, "Did you get a live feed?"

"After a number of tries of trying to get a signal, we were finally able to get one."

"Is he still with them?"

"Judging from the number of footprints in the snow, she may still be alive. Possibly he's with them. They're being pursued by the enemy soldiers and it's just a matter of time before she gets caught, if she's still alive."

"I need you to keep on the live feed and see the safest routes that we could find around the enemy forces," Dr. Weaver said, putting on his white lab coat. "We leave immediately."

CHAPTER 19: REUNION.

As the snowstorm intensified, blanketing the streets in a sea of white, they saw a convoy of enemy vehicles approaching, and stopped near the crash site where a group of enemy soldiers stepped out into the streets, making their way towards the wreckage, searching for signs of Kassandra, and any signs of the other survivors.

The assassin held the detonator in his grasp, patiently waiting to ignite the charge while he and all the others used the decaying bodies of the vehicles that littered the streets as cover to stay out of sight. He pressed the button, detonating the charge, causing the burning wreckage of the helicopter to scatter in all directions, burning and impaling them, immediately getting them off their trail.

He walked towards the squad of enemy soldiers who laid motionless after being gravely injured from the blast. One of the enemy soldiers took his last breath, and was completely at the assassin's mercy. The soldier bled profusely from his wounds. The assassin looked down at him with a straight face, coupled with his usual cold stare, pointing his side arm to his face, ready to provide him the mercy of a soldier's death to end his suffering, after seeing the extent of the damage. The soldier's entire face and body was torn apart by the shrapnel from the explosion. He stared back at the assassin helplessly and took his last breath, passing on with a lifeless gaze, causing the assassin to place his sidearm back into its holster.

"Where to now?" Stephanie asked, watching the grisly scene that had befallen the snowy streets from the assassin's handiwork.

"Anywhere. Doesn't matter to me," Arianna replied.

Kassandra looked all around the streets until she saw the large metal cover of a manhole that led beneath, and said, "Underground. I'm not being tracked anymore so that means we can move undetected."

"Only one problem with that," Arianna answered.

"What's that?" Kassandra asked.

"They've tracked all the fresh bodies that your bodyguard just piled up in this location. They're bound to send more enemy troops."

They quickly uncovered the heavy metal lid that covered the deep, dark hole that tunneled for miles beneath the city streets, and slowly traversed with their flashlights, giving off their position. They were suddenly greeted by a hail of fire, causing them to run for cover and switching off their lights.

The assassin equipped his night vision hardware that he plundered from one of the enemy troops, and remained still in the darkness, observing the enemy's movements and positions, watching the bright, blinding muzzle flashes of their rifles, while Daniel and a few of the others returned fire, noticing they were the remainder of Dr. Weaver's forces that had survived the General's surgical onslaught. The assassin moved through the darkness, quickly disarming the rebels, until Kassandra finally yelled, "Hold your fire! Hold your fire!" bringing the exchange of gunfire to a sudden halt.

The assassin lit a flare, seeing a visage of Adam's pale face, who looked totally exhausted from the pain of his wound that was inflicted on him. Adam stared back with a look of shock on his face, coming face to face with his would-be nemesis.

Adam looked all around and saw a number of his soldiers laying half-conscious on the floor, after the assassin implemented his deadly skills of hand-to-hand combat. Kassandra said one more time, "Everyone hold your fire."

"Oh my God. It's him," Janet said, lifting herself from the cold concrete floor, after recalling a number of their bouts prior.

"General West? Is that really you?" Daniel called out softly.

"Yes," Adam answered.

"I'm Daniel Jacobs. It's a pleasure to finally meet you, sir," he said, shaking Adam's hand.

"Likewise," Adam answered, suddenly shifting his focus to the young, dark haired woman that stood next to the assassin with glasses, dressed in a once gleaming lab coat, now soiled with blood and dirt from her constant skirmishes of her evading the enemy forces and practicing her healing techniques on the others, trying to place her face. He recognized her and called out softly, with a hint of surprise, "Kassandra? Is that you?"

"Adam?" she called back, looking at his pale face from his heavy loss of blood from his wound, along with the constant stresses that came with war, combined with the physical pain quickly taking its toll.

"My God, Kassandra, I thought I'd never see you again."

"It's good to see you again," she replied, hugging him, causing him to wince in pain from the wound that lay a few inches between his shoulder and heart.

"What's wrong?" she asked.

"Let's just say that your guardian angel missed. But not by much though."

"He's fine now. He's one of us. He doesn't remember everything. But he will eventually. He's the reason why I'm free, and why Susan, and all the others are still alive. Hold on. Let me help," she said, injecting the serum into his veins closing the wound.

"What the fuck are you doing?" Karen asked.

"Just let her do her job. Believe me, I was a skeptic too," Stephanie answered.

"It seems that the heartless assassin has a heart after all," Janet remarked.

"It wasn't his fault. None of this was his doing. He was once a good soldier, until his fall from grace."

"Kassandra?" someone called out softly.

"Yes," Kassandra turned back, staring at a familiar face, and asked in a bit of surprise, after recalling the visage of the woman who called her. "Elaina? Is that you?". Tears ran down her face, feeling the overwhelming joy of seeing her closest friend again after being separated for so long.

"Yes. I thought I'd never see you again," Elaina replied.

"Me too. It's so good to see you again. After so long. Look, I brought you someone," Kassandra said, pointing to the assassin.

"Is that really him?" Elaina asked, watching the assassin, walking away from the pair of bodyguards that flanked her, towards him.

"Yes, it is," Kassandra answered.

The assassin looked at Elaina's face in shock, as he finally came face to face with the very same visage that continued to torment his memories from many years passed.

Elaina slowly walked towards the assassin, despite her bodyguards' silent protest, who were assigned to her by the President ever since the beginning of the civil war, who kept her safe after all these years from the enemies' hands.

"She's beautiful," Brandon said, watching her graceful features. She remained completely unfazed by what she had heard, or what the assassin seemed to be capable of.

"I see why he went through all this trouble to save her. Now it's all beginning to make sense," David said, his eyes fixed on Elaina, while he remained captivated by her alluring presence, causing Stephanie to bump him on his side to stop sharing any more of his thoughts.

"Excuse me?" Kassandra yelled with a hint of jealousy. "We all know that she's beautiful! But the real reason that he was made into what he was, was because he was ordered to kill her and he refused!"

"We're just saying that we see why he didn't follow his orders, that's all," Brandon replied.

"Well, it doesn't sound like that!" Kassandra snapped back.

Elaina walked towards the assassin with a timid and nervous smile on her face, slowly extending her hand to his face and touching it, while they all remained awestruck at her alluring physique.

"Careful now, "Janet said, watching the assassin's cold stare, suddenly becoming warm and welcoming. "For the past few years, I've been bitch-slapped and tossed like a rag doll by this angry assassin. I'd be very careful, if I were you."

"He won't hurt me," Elaina answered softly, looking into his eyes, while the picture of her face continued to play back vividly in his mind, leaving a sudden look of confusion on his face. "If he wanted to kill us, he would've done that by now. He doesn't remember anything of his past."

"He could've had me fooled. Looks like he still remembered how to kill," Janet answered.

"I know you don't remember anything. But it feels so good to finally be reunited with you once again. In time, everything will be revealed to you. I promise," Elaina said softly.

The assassin simply squinted back at Elaina with a confused look on his face, while she rested her head on the armor that protected his body.

Meanwhile, on the surface, another enemy convoy had arrived at the location of the crash site and saw a number of their soldiers lying dead on the snowy road, impaled and burnt by countless shards of broken glass and shrapnel from the crash site.

They continued walking through the snow, and saw a number of footprints that led to the large metal cover of a manhole. They silently descended into the dark recesses of the underground in pursuit of Kassandra and the assassin.

They crept silently in the darkness, and heard the voices of the remaining freedom fighters. Without warning, they opened fire, causing the assassin to quickly shield Elaina, spinning her around, using the armor plating on his back to absorb the shock of the enemy bullets, as he held her tightly.

He placed her in a safe position and looked at the directions the enemy muzzle flashes came from and quickly moved in to intercept, under the complete cover of darkness that cloaked him from the watchful eyes of soldiers, swinging his blade, and quickly eliminating them with deadly precision.

The screams of the dying enemy soldiers began to echo loudly through the dark recesses that tunneled under the city streets, while the assassin continued to engage the enemy soldiers swiftly and silently with his deadly weapon. He suddenly stopped, with his actions telling the tale of what had happened many times before.

Jonathan lit a flare and saw the bodies of all the enemy soldiers laying on the ground in pools of their own blood, completely eviscerated from the prowess of his deadly skills coupled with the use of his trusty blade.

The others lit flares, brightening the dark confines of the underground, and saw the usual scenario of the assassin being the last man standing with his blade gripped tightly in the heated grip of his palm, the blood of the enemy soldiers dripping from his face and tip of his blade.

"What the hell just happened?" Brian said, with a sudden look of shock on his face, watching the gruesome nature of how the assassin punished those that opposed him.

"Now you see what we've had to deal with all day? And that's not even scratching the surface," Daniel answered.

"It's like they were torn limb from limb, completely eviscerated by a savage animal or something. It's like he went from being a man, to a savage beast mode," Janet replied, watching in horror.

Jill walked forward, seeing the carnage the assassin had left in his wake, and suddenly fainted, seeing the gruesome nature of the way the enemy soldiers had met their demise.

They heard the sounds of one of their own writhing in pain after suffering a gunshot wound to his abdomen, the bullet still lodged inside, laying on the floor bleeding.

"It's Anton! He's hit!" Brian yelled, trying to hold him down.

"Let me help!" Kassandra said, running towards him. She slowly and carefully turned him to his side and said softly, "The bullet is deep inside. I can see it. I need to get it out before it goes deeper."

"Here," Brian said, handing over the assassin's knife that he had pulled out of Adam's chest to Kassandra. "Courtesy of your bodyguard, when he left it in General's West's chest during the attack on our base, back in Chesapeake."

Kassandra grabbed the knife from Brian and immediately began creating a larger incision, digging into his wound, searching for the bullet lodged deep within his gut.

After a brief moment of searching, she pulled it from his abdomen, closely analyzing it covered in his blood, throwing it to the floor.

Moments after witnessing the carnage by the assassin's onslaught, Jill had revived after fainting and asked, "What happened?"

"You took a little nap after witnessing "Yours truly," ice those bodies, lying right there on the floor," Janet answered.

"What happened to Anton?"

"He was hit by enemy fire during the assault, It ended badly for the others though," Janet said.

Jill walked towards Brian, who was struggling to hold Anton down from the pain, and saw Kassandra injecting him with the serum, placing him into a deep comatose, as it began to run its course, closing the gaping wound in his abdomen. "What the hell?" she said, still feeling her legs trembling uncontrollably.

"He'll be fine. They both will be," Kassandra answered.

Adam had revived from the paralyzing effects from the serum, and slowly stumbled to get on his feet. He looked at his chest, seeing a tiny scar where there was an open wound from the assassin's knife prior and asked, "What did you do?"

"This serum was one of the things that my father had discovered when he was stationed at the Ivory Coast, 30 years ago."

"That wonder drug saved me weeks of healing. I see now why the General wants you so badly," Adam answered.

"Actually, it's a bit more complicated than that," Kassandra answered.

"The General and my father were once friends, when they were stationed in the Ivory Coast, before they went their separate paths. He knew of my father's work about strengthening the nervous system against diseases by tapping into the human genome strands. Only this time during the war, seeing that you held on for so long, he altered my father's plans and tried to turn my father's research into a weapon."

"What do you mean?" Adam asked, with a puzzled look on his face.

"During the entire war, you were outnumbered and outgunned against the enemy forces, and still are, especially at a time like now, which is the most desperate time for the pockets of freedom fighters who survived his attack, and scattered all about. And of course, being cornered makes you far more dangerous. His plan was to make me tap into the human genome, to accelerate the healing process from fatal or life-threatening injuries."

"What exactly are you saying?" he asked.

"He wanted me to engineer a blueprint so he can create an entire race of super soldiers. But I stalled for as long as I could."

"How far did you go with those plans?"

"I did the blueprints. They were mostly theory, though. I'm not even sure if they could work. I just did something to try and throw them off my scent.

You see, when I did those blueprints, I had to make it look convincing enough that it can look like a practical application, providing that they could decipher it. Or if it can be deciphered at all. Let's just hope that it wasn't too convincing, because if this research was to stay in the wrong hands and analyzed by the wrong scientific minds, then everything that you fought for, and everyone who died fighting this war, would've been in vain."

"Okay. You now have my undivided attention," Adam replied softly.

"Look," she said, pointing at the assassin. "He doesn't have any of those scars healing from a serious injury, and yet still his skills are the best that all of us have ever seen. Then imagine if he could heal from a life-threatening wound, or wounds like these," she said, pointing at the dead enemy soldiers on the cold concrete floors. "Imagine if there are six more like him who could do the same. And we all know if that ever happens, all the skills in the world and no matter how many guns or soldiers we have won't make a difference. Ask them about the trail of bodies that he's been leaving all over the city. All over the state. Look on the floor. Think of the bodies that he alone has left. Now imagine if there were six more like him, which I know for a fact, that there are. Even with his skills, nothing will be enough to stop them."

"And what would you like me to do about it?" Adam asked.

"I need you to help me break into the General's secret base and help me to secure those blueprints."

"Considering that we haven't seen each other in an entire decade, that's a lot to ask, don't you think?"

"I know. It's not safe here. There'll be more coming. We need to leave. I have a plan. I'll fill you in on the details. But we need to leave before more of them close in on our location."

Another squad of enemy soldiers arrived and quietly descended into the dark recesses of the underground passage and followed the trail of footsteps. Without warning, they opened fire.

The assassin once again hid himself within the darker confines of the underground passageway, analyzing the movement of enemy troops, waiting for them to draw nearer. Without warning, he ambushed them in the darkness, causing them to turn on one another, causing a repeat of the agonizing screams of the dying soldiers echoing beneath the city streets, with the enemy bullets scattering in all directions, while the mysterious assassin continued his silent yet deadly crusade in eliminating their presence. It suddenly grew into an eerie silence.

Karen lit a flare and walked towards the grisly scene, suddenly becoming appalled, covering her face and said softly, "Oh my God," watching the assassin standing amidst all the corpses covering her face in horror.

"What is it?" Jacqueline asked.

"Let's just say that we'd prefer to have him fighting for us than against us. This is just another episode of what we just saw earlier. I think you know that by now," Kassandra replied.

"My God. On the field it was bad enough, but this?" Jacqueline answered.

"What now?" Jill asked, boldly walking forward.

"Stay where you are. We know what happened the first time you saw the horror show," Jacqueline answered.

Jill stood next to Jacqueline and saw more of the carnage the assassin had left in his wake for the second time, and fainted once again, falling heavily on the cold concrete floor.

Janet simply watched the mutilated bodies, and fell to the floor for the second time, and remarked, "There we go again."

The assassin sheathed his blade and searched the dead corpses, stripping them of all their weapons and ammunition.

He glanced at Nina and instantly recognized her uniform as one of the enemy pilots. Seeing that she was without a weapon, he unsheathed his blade, walking towards her, as she stared back helplessly, with a look of total fright on her face, with her hands tied firmly in restraints in front of her. He swung his blade, causing her to close her eyes firmly, thinking that she was about to meet her demise, only to feel that her restraints had been severed from her wrists from a single swing of his blade.

She opened her eyes and saw him standing in front of her, staring with his usual cold stare from his cold, chiseled face, and watched her wrists, while she continued to try and catch her breath, seeing how close she came with her brush with death.

He turned back and walked towards one of the corpses and grabbed one of their assault rifles and a handful of clips and slowly extended his arm, handing over the assault rifle with his usual cold intimidating stare.

She hesitated for a brief moment and gently grabbed the weapon from his hand, and said softly, "Thank you."

"She's a traitor! And now she's got a gun?" Janet said loudly, causing the assassin to turn back and face her with his usual cold stare.

She suddenly became shy, seeing the assassin maintaining his cold and intimidating gaze. "On second thought, whatever you say is fine. You know I was only kidding, right?"

"Well, you said you wished he was on our side a few years back in Detroit, Jackson. So, it looks like you just got your wish," Nicole added.

"Like it or not, she's one of us now. And if he says that she stays, then she stays," Adam replied.

"Whatever he says, General West," Janet answered.

"What do we do now, General West?" Nicole asked.

"The same thing we always do. We fight," Adam replied with a renewed sense of vigor, sensing hope with his new-found allegiance with the assassin who almost succeeded in assassinating him to wipe out their resistance.

"Either we remain a small underground unit or hold on long enough until we have stronger numbers. Time will decide. It's good to have you back, old friend."

Kassandra slowly walked towards Nina and said, "I don't know who you are. But since you're dressed in an enemy uniform, there has to be a reason why he saved your life."

"Because I saved him. I suppose that counts for something."

"It doesn't matter now. You're one of us now. But you do know what will happen to you if you compromise us in any way, don't you?" Kassandra asked.

"Yes. You don't have to worry," Nina answered softly.

"I just want you to be on the safe side."

Nicole walked towards her and said, "Thank you."

"For what?" Nina asked.

"For not taking out General West when you had the chance. It's because of that, we live to fight another day. I know now that I can trust you," Nicole said, handing Nina her side arm. "This belongs to you."

"Thank you," Nina replied softly, gently grabbing the sidearm from her hand. "I won't let you down. I promise."

"You haven't. I'm happy that we're allies now."

"Likewise."

"Can someone pick Jill off the damn floor?" Adam asked softly.

"How's your shoulder?" Kassandra asked.

"The wound has completely healed. And I don't feel any more pain. No wonder why they want you so badly," Adam said, exercising his shoulder, seeing if was feeling any more pain from his wound.

"Too bad they won't be seeing me any longer. Especially those idiots. That's what'll happen to the others if they keep coming," Kassandra said, pointing to the corpses that lay in pools of their own blood.

"Are you enjoying this, Kassandra? What happened to you? The Kassandra that I remembered was once a sheltered young girl, with a passion to save lives," Adam asked, with a hint of surprise on his face.

"Does it look like I enjoyed being locked up for an entire decade under someone that my father once loved and trusted like a brother, who willingly became responsible for my abduction? Does it look like I enjoyed standing idly by watching and listening to the very same people who rescued my father from Genesis, and fought for him during the civil war, get murdered by the very same people who were once their brothers in arms, knowing that there was nothing I could do? Does it look like I enjoyed losing my entire family, not seeing my father for 10 long years, not even knowing if he's still alive? Does it look like I enjoy being chased from state to state, hiding from the government because of all my unique abilities? That little girl is still unconscious, almost bleeding to death from a bullet hole in her shoulder, if it weren't for this!" she said, displaying the serum. "She got a bullet just for being in the wrong place at the wrong time. And believe me, they wouldn't lose a single ounce of sleep over it! His grandfather was gunned down just for helping us, and the last I checked, you had a knife sticking in your chest, just a few inches above your heart! Those people standing here before you have lost everyone and everything that they've cared about, because of those people laying on the floor!" she shouted, pointing to the corpses of the enemy soldiers lying on the cold concrete floor. "Today alone, I saw a few people go from having a family to being orphans much faster than overnight! Just like that! And let's not forget after losing my mother in Genesis, You lost one of your own because of him! As a matter of fact, so many lives have been lost because of him, in the past ten years! Or have you forgotten that too?"

"I haven't," Adam said softly.

"Then you of all people should know what must be done since you've been fighting for so long, Adam! How many more do you have to lose in this war? So many young men and women who were mothers, fathers, brothers, sisters, with their whole lives ahead of them just vanished in an instant, fighting this war!"

"I suppose that I never figured your resolve to change," Adam replied softly.

"Well, based on the circumstances, I wasn't given much of a choice," she answered softly.

"Look around you. Bullet holes everywhere. One of your own is still lying on the floor with a hole in his stomach, and a child still healing from this wondrous miracle drug that my father created, and make no mistake, more will come, and they're probably on their way right now as we speak. And whenever they get here, this will serve as a clear warning to them. As I told you, there are six more like him with the same deadly skills, and if he's capable of doing this, imagine what the others can do if they have the special ability to heal after sustaining life-threatening injuries like that in combat, if they can decipher those blueprints I gave them."

"That can't be good," Jonathan answered.

Adam looked at all the corpses that were sprawled on the floor in pools of their own blood and replied, "You're right, Kassandra. If he alone can lay waste to so many, think of what he could've done if he was augmented with these blueprints that you created. This is bad. We really need to come up with a plan."

"We need to come up with one tonight, but first, we need to find a safer place," Kassandra answered. "We need to get moving before more troops come. It'll be better if we moved in any civilian transport that we could find. We stole this tracker off one of the enemy soldiers, to detect enemy activity so we can find a way around them."

Elaina stood in front of the assassin, looking into his eyes with unlost admiration, even after all the atrocities that he'd just committed, gently wiping the blood from his face, hoping that he would soon come to his senses. She looked at Nina, who slowly lowered her gaze, as she still bore a heavy conscience. Eliana walked towards her and said, "Thank you."

"For what?" Nina answered softly.

"Giving me a second chance to love again."

"You're welcome," she answered, with her eyes clouded in tears.

"You could've killed him when you had the chance, but you didn't," Elaina answered, with her eyes filled with tears in return.

"I could only imagine how difficult the choice for you might've been for you to make."

"To General West, we are people. Living, breathing people. But, on the other side, we are expendable. Just assets to be used. And when we've outlived our usefulness, we're tossed aside and discarded like we never meant anything. So, as much as I thought the choice was difficult, I realized that it really wasn't difficult."

"I'm forever in your debt."

"No need. We're on the same side now. My only wish was that I should've made the choice sooner. I'm happy for you finding love in a time like this. I see the way you look at him. I envy the both of you so much. Not all of us are so fortunate."

"He means so much to me. One day, you'll find what you seek."

"There's no hope for someone like me. But, I pray it comes soon, since they don't trust me."

"There's always hope. Just give them a little time. You have gained Nicole's respect, along with General West. That says a lot."

"Okay people, we need to get moving!" Adam called out.

"I agree. This place is beginning to give me the creeps," Jill added.

After they had finished replenishing their supplies, they made their much-needed exodus from the dark void of the underground passage now filled with death of all those that dared to venture between its walls.

Moments after, Dr. Weaver and his small squad of hackers arrived at Kassandra's last location. They walked in the snow-filled streets towards the wreckage and saw a number of dead enemy soldiers burnt and impaled by the shards of shrapnel and glass from the explosion, sprawled lifelessly on the streets. They checked the burning wreckage for any signs of Kassandra's presence.

They followed the collection of footsteps towards the hole and saw it was uncovered and carefully descended into it.

After landing into the dark hole, they lit flares, and were instantly appalled by the grisly site that greeted them.

"My God," Celina said softly, placing her hand over her mouth, watching the terrifying scene in a complete state of shock, and asked, "What could've done this?"

"It was him. He was here. And based on the stripes on their uniform, these were another set of highly trained soldiers, and 0-7 was the only one with the right kind of skills to take them out," he said, walking over the burning flares and mutilated corpses, searching for his daughter. "They must've left not too long ago. The blood is still flowing from these wounds. Still warm. Let's spread out and search," Dr. Weaver said, searching through the dark recesses of the underground, only to come up empty.

Celina walked up to Dr. Weaver and said, "There's no one here. We need to get back before more enemy troops come."

"Okay, Celina. Gather the others and let's return to base. We'll figure out what to do when we get back."

"Yes, Mr. President."

They began making their hasty retreat, when they heard the engines of enemy transports closing in on their position.

"Oh no," Celina said nervously. "They're here."

"Everybody hide. Get ready in case we may have to fight our way out."

"What about the flares?" Celina asked.

"We may not have time to put them out. Just toss them over there, and stay out of sight."

They tossed the flares amidst all the dead corpses, and hid within the darker confines of the underground passage that tunneled deeply beneath the streets, and listened quietly to all the enemy soldiers that quickly descended upon their positions.

After the enemy soldiers had descended into the sewers, their faces transformed into looks of total shock seeing how their fellow soldiers had met their grim fate, knowing that it was the assassin who was responsible for the savage nature of their deaths. They walked through the corpses that laid on the cold, wet, filthy concrete floors, dipping their fingers in their blood, seeing that it was still warm, telling them that their objective had recently vacated the scene, along with the assassin.

Dr. Weaver and the others continued to hide deeper within the confines of the dark tunnels, hoping they wouldn't be spotted by the enemy soldiers while they continued to investigate the corpses of their fallen comrades, listening to their movements fidgeting in the dark, with the lights from the flashlights mounted on their rifles moving all about. They slowly began to make their exit, when a pack of rats attracted by the heavy, metallic scent of blood suddenly scurried past them, trampling over Celina's feet, causing her to scream as she tried to fend them off, suddenly attracting the attention of the enemy soldiers, causing them to ran towards their position.

They quickly opened fire, ambushing the enemy soldiers with a hail of bullets, claiming the lives of a few as they valiantly held their position, resulting in one of Dr. Weaver's staff being gravely wounded during the exchange with a gunshot sustained to his neck.

The enemy soldiers regained their momentum, gaining ground on the young and inexperienced troops, who continued to bravely hold their ground, while Dr. Weaver waited in the dark confines of the underground, waiting for the right opportunity to strike.

As the deadly firefight ensued, the enemy soldiers gained ground, advancing towards Dr. Weaver's position while he waited in the darkness. Dr. Weaver quickly used his disarming techniques to snatch one of the soldier's weapons and use it against him, skillfully eliminating the others.

The gunfire ceased, and they slowly came out of their hiding places, seeing the enemy soldiers lying dead on the cold and blood soaked concrete floor, after the brief but deadly skirmish.

Dr. Weaver dropped the enemy soldier's rifle on the floor, with a look of shock on his face, as his hands suddenly began to tremble uncontrollably, after breaking the code that he'd lived by for so long of not taking a life.

"Dr. Weaver!" Celina shouted, as she came running towards him, nudging him while he stared at the corpses of the dead enemy soldiers.

He stared at Celina with a frightened look on his face and asked, "What have I done?"

"It was them or us! We need to leave before more come!"

"My God," he continued softly, looking at his hand, while Celina continued shouting his name, trying as much as she could to make him come to his senses.

"We have one of ours wounded and he needs medical attention before we lose him!" she yelled, bringing him to his senses. "We need to leave. Please."

"Okay. How many wounded do we have?" he asked.

"Only one. And he's losing a lot of blood, and is in need of medical attention before we lose him."

"Are you sure it's only him?"

"Yes. We barely survived. And if more come, we may not be so lucky to survive another assault."

"Okay, get him on the transport. I don't want any more bloodshed than I've seen tonight."

As they made their hasty retreat, Dr. Weaver looked back at all the corpses of the enemy soldiers among the burning flares, and finally made his retreat from the sewers.

They hurried, loading the wounded soldier on the transport, and began their hasty departure back to their hideout, before more enemy troops could close on their position.

The blood from the soldier's wound gushed profusely from his neck, staining the interior of the transport, as Celina and the others struggled to contain the bleeding.

Celina watched as Dr. Weaver's hands continued to tremble uncontrollably from their recent incursion, while she continued to struggle with the others holding the wounding soldier down, applying pressure on his wound to contain the bleeding, her hands completely soiled with his blood, and asked, "What do we do?"

"There's nothing we can do for him until we get back. For now, just keep applying pressure," Dr. Weaver answered, slowly coming back to his senses.

"He's lost a lot of blood. We can't just let him die."

"I'm not saying we should let him die. I'm just saying that I can't help him until we get back to the hideout. There's nothing I can do for him here." He went over to the wounded soldier, kneeling over him, examining his wound. "All we can do for him in the meantime is keep pressure on his wound. What's E.T.A?"

"About 10 to 15 minutes."

"Hope we make it there in time. Keep pressure on the wound. He'll be fine."

01:14 HOURS. SECURE LOCATION - SOMEWHERE IN RICHMOND, VIRGINIA:

They arrived at the hideout, and charged through the front door, carrying the wounded soldier, clearing one of the desks, resting his wounded body on top of it.

"What now?" Celina asked nervously, watching the Doctor's hands continue to tremble.

"I just need some warm water, and antiseptic to clean the wound before I close it. Hurry. Don't have much time."

Moments later, they brought the warm water and antiseptics, while the others held the wounded soldier down, still trying to control the bleeding.

Dr. Weaver soaked the cloth in warm water and immediately cleaned out the wound, while they continued keeping pressure on his wound.

Celina continued watching his hands as he cleaned the soldier's neck wound while she assisted in keeping pressure on his neck wound, and then took a quick glance at his facial expressions.

The wounded soldier gently grabbed her hand, soiled in his own blood and asked, "What's your name?"

"I'm Celina Bradshaw," she answered.

"I'm Nicolas. Nicholas Swanwick," he answered weakly, his vital signs slowly slipping away from the blood loss. He struggled to remain conscious. "It's strange how we've been working together for so long, and we're only talking now."

"True. I suppose it wasn't meant to be at the time," she said.

"You need to keep him distracted until I apply the antiseptic. Won't be long now, before we're finished," Dr. Weaver said softly, cleaning his neck wound with the antiseptic.

She nodded her head to Nicholas and said, "I suppose the worst things happen for the best reasons."

"Would you've ever talked to me if tonight hadn't happened?"

"When the time was right, I suppose."

"I was hoping that it would've been sooner."

"Better late than never," she said smiling, grabbing his hand tighter, offering her consolation.

She watched as Dr. Weaver finished applying the antiseptic on his wound, and said to Nicholas, "You need to save your strength. You'll have a chance to talk when you're fully recovered."

"Keep applying pressure on the wound," Dr. Weaver said, removing a syringe-shaped vial from his pocket and injecting a tiny dose of its contents into his neck, causing his wound to close instantly.

Nicholas began to feel the immediate effects of the drug coursing through his veins, instantly causing him to feel a sudden sensation of paralysis consuming his entire body, causing tears to track down the side of his face, as he slowly fell into deep comatose.

"You'll be fine, son. Just rest," Dr. Weaver said softly, placing his hand on Nicholas's shoulder.

Their faces went into a sudden state of shock seeing how quickly the serum had begun to work, quickly closing Nicholas's wound, and gazed at each other, mumbling among themselves.

Celina gently released her blood-soaked hands from Nicolas's neck and peered quietly at Dr. Weaver washing the blood from his hands. She stood next to him washing hers in the basin of warm water, wiping her hands on a clean white towel, staining it with the light traces of his blood.

She sat in front of Dr. Weaver, watching his hands as they continued shaking, while he continued thinking about the enemy soldiers he'd just killed and asked softly, "You were once a soldier, weren't you?"

"How did you guess?" Dr. Weaver asked.

"Those disarming skills I saw back there. The way you disarmed that soldier and used his weapon against him and the others could only mean that you were once trained in the arts. Or some kind of military training. Those disarming skills gave you away completely. We may not have the skills like you, but it doesn't take much to see that you were trained in combat. After all this time we've been working with you, you're just a mystery to us. We don't know everything about you, except what happened in Genesis, 10 years ago. Some of it, at least. I suppose this is why they say slow water runs deep."

Dr. Weaver smiled and answered, "That's true. Now is as good a time as any. I suppose. Yes, I was trained in combat. But somewhere down the line, I just gave up on being a soldier."

"Why? It seems like you were doing fine to me."

"There comes a time that your soul gets weary of all the conflict, and all the death that comes with it. So, I just gave up on everything that reminded me of all the things that caused so many to pay the ultimate price."

"I suppose that's true," she answered, watching his hands continue to tremble.

"But I wasn't always a soldier. I only wanted to break the cycle of the chain of what my forefathers were, what they created."

"What did you do before?"

"It's never been a question of what I did before. It's more of a question of what destiny chose me to be. I was just too blind to see it at first."

"What was that?"

"My father was a doctor, like his father, and his father's father. It was my great, great, great, great, grandfather who founded the prominent practice called The Jameson Weaver Medical University in a small town in Minnesota. So, it's safe to say that I come from a life of privilege that stemmed from a respected practice. As for me, personally, my heart was somewhere else, or so I thought. I couldn't see myself living in the shadows of my forefathers, so I tried to be something else other than what I was, so I enlisted in the armed forces."

"What was it like?"

"It had its benefits, I suppose. Then after you come to realize that it's not always what it's cut out to be. And you begin to hear that tiny voice at the back of your mind telling you, ``I should've always listened to what my father said, before I joined."

"What was that? What was that tiny voice at the back of your head, I mean?"

"There's no escaping who you are. No escaping who or what life destined you to be. And he couldn't have been more right. And there I was, trying to outrun my destiny, escaping who I was meant to be. The natural instinct of being a healer and nurturer comes into play whenever the circumstances present themselves. Unfortunately, my adventures took me to many places. Places that I would've preferred to visit under better circumstances. But there was a price to pay in the call of duty."

She watched his hands continue to tremble and asked, "You've never killed anyone before, have you?"

"Before tonight? No. I swore that I would never break my code, until tonight. I never thought the day would come when I would have to. It's so strange that the very same soldiers that we once called our brothers in arms that were once united, now divided, fighting amongst ourselves."

"So, how did you survive when you were in the field?"

"Sometimes, I ask myself the same question," he answered, smiling timidly. "Very often in the heat of battle, I found myself charging the enemy through a thick hail of bullets, and pinning him to the floor, looking into his eyes, with the barrel of my gun pointed right to his face, pondering on whether or not if I should pull the trigger, knowing that he would do the same if the positions were reversed. I suppose that it's something that I should be proud of because it was a million dollar experience that I'd never pay a nickel to live again, because it was too often these wars made orphans. And every time I looked into their eyes, I saw the hopelessness and despair. It made me feel like a piece of my soul being ripped away. While some people resorted to torture to get information from captured enemy soldiers, I used a different approach."

"What did you do?"

"It was simpler and more humane to use the truth drug, because at the time, all I saw was another soldier, like I saw myself. Just someone who was following orders. They try to kill you, and you, them. The only difference is that I just couldn't bring myself to do it."

"How hard did you try?"

"Does it matter? When you're placed in a situation you know from the very beginning whether you're capable of doing something or not. It's just instinctive."

"Like tonight? You did what none of us were capable of doing," Celina said softly.

"Sometimes, the flight response causes you to fight in a way that you never thought possible."

"What do you mean?"

"The most dangerous adversary is the one with his back against the wall. He fights the hardest when he becomes desperate, because it's at that very moment he realizes that his life depends on it even more than other circumstances. We call it self-preservation."

"Like you did."

"Yes, I'm afraid so. And now I must live with it for the rest of my life."

"Don't say that, Dr. Weaver," Celina answered. "These soldiers are professional soldiers loyal only to the General. They would've killed us on sight if it weren't for you. It's because of you, Nicholas is still here with us. You did what you had to do to save us, at the expense of risking your own life, and for that, we're forever in your debt. But you must stop blaming yourself, because all of us sitting in this very room are afraid."

"In the armed forces, they teach you how to kill. But one thing they can never teach you is to block out the post-traumatic stress after you've yet to fight the battle."

"The battle? What do you mean?" she asked.

"Yes, the battle. Being deployed on the field is not the real war. It's just the beginning of a never-ending war that follows."

"Then what is the real war?"

"The real war is the madness that follows after fighting every skirmish you face. It's that never-ending fight that tears away a piece of your very soul every single day and night, seeing all the faces of all the loved ones that you've lost. Even the faces of all the people that you've killed, just before looking into their eyes. Even they come to visit you every night, keeping you awake every time you close your eyes to sleep, after you've finished justifying all your actions, after you keep telling yourself that the atrocities you committed were for the greater good of all mankind. Most call it post-traumatic stress syndrome. But in all actuality, it goes deeper than that. What it really is, is that you're at war with your own soul for taking the lives of all those people who were unfortunate to have met their demise at your hands. On paper, we sign the declaration of unconditional surrender. But in reality, the only way out of any war is death. It consumes you until you leave this world. It's not as easy or glamorous as they make it out to be. It never is."

"Have you ever seen it? The madness I mean."

"I'm afraid so. More than I care to remember," Dr. Weaver answered, looking at the vial -shaped syringe filled with the universal antidote vaccine.

"As a matter of fact, I'm going through it right now. And even before tonight. For over 30 years to be exact."

"I don't understand. If you've never taken a life, how could you live with it?"

"Because of so many deaths that have happened before, in many ways, I feel responsible."

"How come?"

"As I told you before, my time with the armed forces took me many places, until fate grounded me into what I became, or rather what I was destined to be."

"That medicine that you injected Nicholas with. What was it? None of us have seen anything so sophisticated. Not even the military has that, I'm sure of it."

He held the vial to his face and answered, "I was hoping that I'd never have to use it. It's fate. It's a constant reminder of when my father told me that I could never run away from who I was, or who I was destined to be. And when I looked into his eyes, the funny thing is, I knew that he was right. I just didn't want to admit that to myself. What I didn't know was that it would've been the last time that we'd ever see each other again. Every campaign that I fought, I often saw the horror and heartbreak that war left in its wake. So, when I saw all the children orphaned and wives made widowed, it always tore a piece of my soul. So, I set out on a personal crusade, using my families' prominent name and helping to influence a relief effort for all those affected by civil war in war-torn countries. I suppose that it was just my way of showing that not all westerners are warmongers like they often believed, and for that moment, I found peace, seeing the smiling faces of all those orphaned children and widowed women. And it was that one fateful day that changed my life forever. It changed everything."

"What happened?"

"It was a normal day like any other day. Just doing what I always set out to do. We were stationed at a tiny strip providing relief for some of the refugees. Then, out of nowhere, they just appeared, raiding everything, pillaging, and capturing whoever they pleased. The next thing I remember, we were under enemy fire."

"We?" Celina asked.

"It was just my copilot and myself providing relief to the outpost. Was supposed to be just a routine stop. The enemy fire was so great that my plane was severely damaged even before we were airborne. And the next thing I knew, my copilot was seriously wounded, and shortly after, he died from the extent of his wounds after he'd lost too much blood. We were losing fuel and were completely cut off from any kind of help, after we were airborne. And that's when fate made its calling."

"What happened?"

"Didn't know where we were going. The destination was somewhere, anywhere, or nowhere. It didn't matter. We were just flying blind with a broken compass in a dilapidated plane, and all I was thinking about was getting out of that battle zone, and worrying about everything later. All I was thinking about was to survive to see the next hour, or the next day. Just survive for as long as I could, before my fate was to be written in stone. We just had to leave that place before we both became casualties. Our navigation equipment was damaged during the assault, and we ended up flying into Ivorian airspace, and then one of my engines exploded. It was just a matter of time before the entire plane went down. So, I flew for as long as I could, trying to hold on to the plane, and when I couldn't I bailed, I abandoned it to its fate. After I jumped, the entire plane exploded while still in mid-flight, and some of the shrapnel from the blast tore through my parachute. The next thing I remembered was that I was freefalling from the skies. I landed in the jungle with the branches and trees breaking my fall and was dangling from the ropes, severely bruised, and lacerated by them. I can remember the cords from my parachute breaking and falling to the ground. The next thing I remembered, I awoke in the hospital, with a broken leg and a few broken ribs, along with a few scrapes and bruises, after being unconscious for 3 whole days, after being heavily sedated on drugs for the pain I suffered from from my injuries. They said I was lucky to be alive, and it was during my time being bed-ridden, I later found out that they had found the wreckage of the plane and found the body of my copilot. Needless to say that he was burnt beyond recognition. I also found out that I was rescued by a few civilians who lived in a village a few miles away. It was a young woman and her younger brother who spotted me and the wreckage of the plane falling from the skies. Then the civil war between the army and rebels broke out, and from the looks of it, they had more superior numbers than the army. By at least ten to one, as far as I could recall. They were raiding the nearby villages for whatever they could find, killing indiscriminately, so I was transported to an outpost far away to continue recuperating. And in a way, it was a good thing too."

"How's that?" Celina asked with a sudden look of intrigue on her face.

"The civil war had resumed after a brief intermission, and this time, it had waged for months, with a 100,000 people losing their lives, and the national army was on the verge of collapse, then it suddenly stopped again."

"What happened?"

"This time, we would face an enemy worse than war. It was a disease. It was the worst outbreak in the history of the Ivory Coast. Possibly the worst outbreak that Africa would have suffered. If left unchecked, it could've wiped out the entire country for that matter."

"What was it?"

"First, there was the AIDS virus. Then there was Ebola during the civil war. But this time, we were facing the Chimera, and the people were dying like flies. And at the rate that people were dying, there was no doubt that this outbreak had the potential to wipe out the entire country, or most of it for that matter, at the rate it was claiming all those lives. Being that the Ivory Coast was once a French colony, there was a French garrison stationed there at the time, so the local government appealed to them to help take measures to contain the lethal strain."

"What did they do?" she asked softly.

"They implemented The Hellfire Campaign to help contain the threat."

"What's that?"

"They bombed the villages of men, women, and children who were infected with the strain. And to make sure that those villages were contained, they deployed foot soldiers with flamethrowers to burn those who'd survive the bombings. It was a crude method, but necessary at the time, I suppose."

"And what role did our military play?"

"Nothing major at the time. Only providing aid to those who were sick and starving mostly."

"And what role did you play?"

"I couldn't do anything major at the time. Spent most of the time recuperating, with the strange young woman and her brother at my side. So I forced myself to recover quickly. I built a makeshift lab, and began to collect as much data as I could about the deadly strain, but still couldn't intervene directly."

"So what did you do?"

"I helped move as many people from the nearby villages into the outpost, starting with the woman who had saved my life, along with her brother and whatever livestock and anything else we could use for food. Then hundreds showed, and hundreds became thousands."

"And how did it go?"

"Weeks and weeks had passed and the lethal strain continued to wreak havoc on the populace, so I charged myself to find a cure. But nothing was working. And then something unexpected happened."

"What happened?"

"Not only that the virus could be transmitted through bodily fluids, but we later found out that the strain was also airborne, and had reached the outpost and had infected some of the inhabitants, including livestock. We lost hundreds that day, and the livestock, despite having stronger immune systems, eventually succumbed, and we were losing more people, but in all the chaos, a miracle happened."

"What's that?"

"One of the animals had an amazing resistance to the strain."

"Which one?"

"It was a goat. And just as I thought, I figured that if I could experiment with the goat's D.N.A., I could find some type of antibody to create a vaccine and counter the strain. It was just a thought that came randomly."

"Did it work?"

"I used a strain of the virus from the infected blood samples that I'd acquired from the victims, along with the goat's D.N.A., when I realized that I too was infected with the disease, after it had made its way into the outpost."

"What were the symptoms?"

"It starts out with an excruciating headache. It felt like all the blood vessels in your brain exploding all at once, causing the eyes to become flaming red from all the pressure forming on your brain, causing severe bleeding from the mouth, nose, and ears. The pain was the most excruciating that I've ever felt, and in that case, anyone would welcome death."

"Did it work?"

"It was new, but a bit crude. But considering the circumstances, the discovery couldn't have come at a better time. I just found myself regaining consciousness, wiping the blood coming from my nostrils, and it was her again, along with her little brother that found me. With the outbreak running rampant in the outpost, it was a matter of time they too became infected. So, after the vaccine had created antibodies inside me, I had it synthesized as best I could, and had her and her brother inoculated, and continued to repeat the process to have as many antibodies drawn from any and everyone who had been vaccinated."

"So you're saying that the serum is your D.N.A.?"

"Some of it. Along with countless others who developed antibodies with the vaccine. It became compatible with those who were universal recipients especially. Which was an advantage. All that mattered at the time was gathering antibodies to combat the threat, and continued repeating the process, until I was confident that I could turn the table on the disease. The vaccine might've been crude due to our lack of resources, but it was a stepping stone to something greater."

"So what did you do after?"

"Myself and a few others left the sanctity of the outpost, and went to the government to plead on behalf of those who were infected, appealing to them that I had found a solution to combat the strain, and potentially wipe it out."

"Did they believe you?"

"No. And who could blame them after seeing how much havoc this disease had wreaked on the inhabitants? The AIDS virus can live in your system for years without being detected. But the Chimera would take just a few hours. 3 days at most. The strain was 1,000 times worse than Ebola itself. Worse than anything that human history had ever experienced. After I continued to appeal to the government, to tell them to stop the bombing on all the infected villages, they warned me that if I continued to meddle in their affairs, they would throw me out of the country."

"So what did you do after?"

"I had to make them stop. I had to convince them that I was right. The next day, myself and a few other brave souls put on our hazmat suits and bravely ventured into many of the quarantined villages that were next on the list to be bombed, with the help of a tour guide, and inoculated as many people as possible, and had them transported to the outpost. And there I was being who I was destined to be, doing the same thing that I was running away from without even knowing it. It took that one great catastrophe to make me heed my calling. Hundreds from the quarantined villages moved to the outpost. And hundreds became thousands, on their exodus to the outpost, making the long trip with bare feet, with whatever belongings that they were strong enough to carry. In all the despair and hopelessness, they were still looking for that tiny glimmer of hope, seeing how defeated they had become after enduring so much. And naturally, the word of our work got to the government and finally, they gave us the green light to save as many as we could."

"How did the disease come about?"

"If my memory serves me correctly, the first who became infected by the disease was from a mosquito bite. And naturally, many people, not knowing what the problem was at the time, tried to save him and ended up being infected themselves and it just went out of control from that point. Those who were strong enough to travel made it to the outpost, and those who weren't able, we searched for them in as many of the quarantined villages that we could find to get them inoculated. Unfortunately, those who were too far gone from the disease were abandoned to their fate, with the flames that would later come to consume them and take their charred bodies to their final resting place. One of the things that still haunts me is the family we found in one of the quarantined villages."

"What was it?"

"The disease had run almost the entirety of its course. There was a little girl who had survived, but it was just a matter of time before she too would succumb to it. She was too far gone and was all that was left of her entire family. She was sitting there among the dead bodies of her parents, who had met their demise from the disease. She was just there waiting for the disease to run its course. Just waiting to die."

"What happened after?" Celina asked softly, hoping that the sick child didn't meet her premature demise.

"She stretched her hands out to us, asking for help, hoping that we would save her. So young, but somehow, she knew that she was going to die. What could I have done? What could any of us have done for her at that point? I couldn't tell which one was worse. Standing idly by and watching them burn a young defenseless child alive, though she would die eventually, or abandon her to her fate and let the disease run its course, or give her a false sense of hope, trying to administer the vaccine, knowing that she might've been beyond saving."

"What does your heart tell you now?"

"Every day, I tell myself that I should've tried to save her. Maybe I could've. But the vaccine was new, and I didn't know how effective it was. I knew it would work on the primary stages. But I wasn't sure if it would be effective in the latter stage of the virus. I guess I should've tried to see if it would work. I should've. But we were still a work in progress, and that tiny fishing village near the coast became a haven for those looking for a better life, and soon we were numbering tens of thousands, and began to flourish like a real community once again."

When the government heard of my progress in helping to contain the deadly strain, they contacted one of our carrier fleets that was stationed near the Coast of Morocco, and would be coming to our position in the next few weeks. They were given strict orders not to engage any hostile forces, just provide as much relief to help the citizens in the fight against the disease. I continued working on the vaccine and used it on a blood sample of the AIDS virus."

"Did it work?"

"With flying colors. I had done what the rest of the world couldn't do. I discovered the first U.A.V."

"What's that?"

"I called it the Universal Antidote Vaccine. But history only showed that I discovered a vaccine for only that strain. But the reality is with that vaccine, I discovered a cure for any and every contagious disease that has affected mankind. Miraculously, it had a myriad of applications. But this vaccine contained a strain of the Chimera, and in the wrong hands, the strain could be extracted and be used as a biological weapon. Think of this being unleashed killing tens of thousands, hundreds of thousands, even millions. And those who survived the effects of the disease may give birth to generations of children deformed, dooming the other generations to follow. From the civil war alone, during my stay in the Ivory Coast, about 100,000 people had perished."

"And how many perished from the strain?"

"About 350,000 when the outbreak surfaced, before I could find a cure."

"My God," Celina said softly, with a look of sudden awe.

"Just think of the amount of corporations that would try and stop the progress of the vaccine, knowing how effective it was, simply because they go to the world's poorest countries using their citizens like their personal test subjects. So, I did what any sensible individual would do. I kept it to myself. Didn't care too much about the praise because in that moment of despair, that tiny glimmer of hope goes a long way. And it was good from that point," Dr. Weaver said softly, smiling.

"Sounds like there was someone too."

"Yes, there was. Things had quieted down. I was in the final phase of my recovery and I was in love. She was the most beautiful thing I'd ever seen. Just imagine, in an age of war, I found love. From that point everything I did, I did it for her. She gave me the strength to go on. And after months of being with each other in the outpost, we had a son together. After having the first, I found out that she was pregnant with the next, about 11 months after. Everyone in the outpost was thriving and more people continued to come to the outpost in search of hope. My work has done so much to help those people. And it didn't matter to me whether or not the pharmaceutical companies knew. I felt that with the hope that I had given them from certain death was more priceless. The security was light, though we had one of our carrier fleets stationed a few miles off the coast, and the orders to not engage still stood. Just provide relief. Things got quiet and naturally after all that we'd endured, we thought that the war was over. But it just felt like it was a little too good to be true, which it was."

"Did the rebels attack?"

"It started like any other day. The mother of my son and a few other people were doing their chores to and from the outpost like they always did, while my duty was to continue helping fight the disease to completely eradicate it from the face of the earth. Ridding the country of it, once and for all. And that was the day it all went wrong for me. For all of us, for that matter. That day changed the lives of all those who had seen and lived the horror of all the terrifying events that took place. Many of them may be dead by now. But more importantly, it changed the lives of all those who are still alive and dream of those events that took place that fateful day. That day changed our lives forever. It changed mine. That much I know."

"What happened that day?"

"As I said, it started like any other day, and everyone was about their business in the early hours of the morning. Most of us were still asleep in the outpost. Mostly women and children. And an old enemy had returned. Out of nowhere, the rebels attacked. Many of the soldiers in their forces were wiped out from the strain, leaving them desperate and hungry, and in need of medical supplies, after most of the nearby villages were abandoned and destroyed by the bombing campaigns from the French garrison, so they figured that the most likely place they could get all they needed to keep their war effort going was to raid the outpost. They were greater in numbers, but more desperate and disorganized, whereas we were smaller in number and more organized. We had that special training to our advantage. We used our training to inflict as many casualties on their numbers as we could, but they just kept coming. They were consumed by desperation, and that fueled them to survive. She was on her way back to the outpost after doing her usual chores, and was ambushed by the enemy forces, but could only make it so far. She was an arm's length from the outpost. As for me, I ran through the hail of bullets, with no regard for my own life, to save her, when I felt an enemy bullet tearing through my leg. The pain was so sharp that it paralyzed the nerves in my leg. I mustered all the strength that I had left only to feel another in my chest, just a few inches above my heart. And from that point I'd never felt so helpless. Half dead and bleeding, I crawled to try and save her, when an enemy bullet tore through her shoulder, causing her and my son to fall to the ground. It echoed so loudly that I can tell from my experience in the armed forces, that the bullet had come from a sniper rifle. She was seriously wounded and tried to get up and make it into the outpost, but she was just too weak. She'd lost too much blood."

"Did she make it?"

Dr. Weaver closed his eyes, softly, reminiscing on that fateful day and answered softly, "She only smiled back, holding our son tightly in her arms, knowing the time had come for them to die, along with our unborn child. I saw her looking in the skies, and heard the jet engines from afar, and I knew that it could only mean one thing. So, I gathered all the strength that I had left and crawled and crawled, even if it would've killed me. Then our planes flew over and all I saw was a giant wall of flame, consuming everyone and everything in its wake, tossing me off my feet like a sack of dirty clothes. They had called an airstrike to neutralize all enemy activity, even when we were told not to, effectively ending a war that was not ours to fight to begin with. To help bring my soul some solace, sometimes I'd like to think that maybe we didn't have any more alternatives left. I suppose it was a matter of time before we were overrun. I don't know, or maybe I don't want to, after all that happened."

"What happened to her?"

"She was lost during the air strike. She was completely burnt alive. Beyond recognition. I felt like I cheated her."

"What do you mean?"

"It was so unfair. For all the times that she saved me, I couldn't save her. Not even this once."

"But there's no way that you could've saved her."

"I keep telling myself that even to this day. But the problem is that I don't know if I really believe it."

"Sounds like she was really special."

"Agnes."

"What?" Celina asked.

"Her name was Agnes. And her brother's name was Solomon. It was her and her brother who had found me, after I had landed in my parachute in the jungle and took me to the hospital. It was her who had found me in time after

I had contracted the symptoms from the strain. And just this once, I couldn't save her."

"What happened to her brother?"

"Her brother had vanished during the assault, and I didn't see him again until 20 years later."

"Where did you meet?"

"It's a long story, actually."

"We've been listening all night."

"After the incident in the Ivory Coast, I moved back to the United States, trying to adjust to civilian life, but not before I was awarded with the Nobel Peace Prize and the Humanitarian Award for my work for saving all those who were infected. But even that wasn't enough to comfort me after losing her. Nothing was. And if that wasn't enough, I heard that my father had passed after hearing about the incident when the rebels attacked. I was told that he thought that I'd died during the strike. And after being away so long, I never made peace with him. And as the time passed, I tried to put it behind me, and met Jane while I was in the Nation's Capital, during my appointment with the President, and asked her to marry me."

"Did you ever put it behind you?"

"As I said, the military teaches you to destroy your enemies, but the thing that no one can teach you is to cope with all that trauma that you've endured in a war, or the loved ones that you've lost. It doesn't matter how seasoned you are. Eventually it consumes you. Even in my tender moments with Jane, I often remembered Agnes's smiling face. And seeing her face smiling back at me is the war that I fight every night. It's that war that I can never win. That no one can win."

"What did the President want?"

"He heard from someone else stationed in the Ivory Coast that I had often talked about building a haven away from civilization, for people who were displaced from civil war and disease, since the outpost in the Ivory Coast had yielded great results before it was overrun by rebel forces. A place where they can start over and rebuild their lives. A place where they could find hope. So, the government wanted to help pour resources into the project, and soon after, it was in the news and many other countries, including North Korea, plundered many of their resources to help make it happen. After I had gotten back from the Ivory Coast, I just wanted to live a normal life, and forget about life in the service, probably working at my family's practice, continuing their work in the community. But fate just wouldn't let me."

"What happened?"

"They put me in charge of seeing the completion of the Genesis project, and a few years into it, I married Jane and we had our daughter, Kassandra. I was called to go to Haiti after the great earthquake had struck, killing about one third of the population in January of 2010 Seemed a little reminiscent of the Ivory Coast, so we launched Operation Deliverance when the relief couldn't get to the survivors. Only this time, I was not there as a soldier, but as someone who was there to help treat the victims from the earthquake and the Cholera outbreak. After I had done enough, I moved back to oversee the project that took 20 years to build. After it was finished, I vowed to live in Genesis for the rest of my days with Jane and Kassandra, to protect them the way that I couldn't protect Agnes back in the Ivory Coast. Then myself and Jane gave the world our welcome speech to all those searching for a better life."

"I remember that broadcast, though I was very young at the time. It's all coming back to me now. When you broadcasted that message, it felt like the whole world stood still. Never in my life had I seen such unity. You gave the world so much hope."

"It was there I met Solomon. He told me that he was there after his sister was murdered, and managed to hide in the bushes. And after the airstrike, he ran away as fast as he could, until he was picked up by the hospital and later found out that his sister had died during the attack. He was placed into an orphanage, and lived there until he became an adult, and moved to South Africa, trying to put the past behind. He too had a wife and daughter, when we met on Genesis. Turns out that he too was still looking for hope after all these years, like I was looking for myself. My daughter, Kassandra, never understood why I was trying to protect her from the outside world, until the day the uprising happened in Genesis."

"What caused the uprising on Genesis?"

"It was love."

"What? How come?" Celina asked in disbelief.

"It all began with a young orphaned girl who came to Genesis to start her life over. She was one of the enemy soldiers that attacked the Marines who ran through the slums in Brazil, while chasing a war criminal who wanted to live out the rest of his days from the former Soviet Union. She had fallen in love with a soldier from the corp. They were supposed to be enemies, but he saved her anyway. It was shortly after the war that Unified Korea. The troops were on their way to Genesis for some much needed time off. And some of the troops were already stationed there. That day, she was attacked by one of our soldiers, and when she defended herself, she was accused of trying to infiltrate Genesis and cause espionage. It's strange how it made me think of some scandals concerning women that often happened in the military. And this one was no different."

"Was it true?"

"I knew better. I could tell from the beginning that she wasn't the one who actually provoked the fight. But the General didn't care. He wanted her arrested, and some of the troops disagreed. It was from that point on things would never be the same. From one infraction came so much reprisal. So many lives were extinguished that day. The situation was so grave that we had to evacuate that night, by the few who had pledged their allegiance to me. It was 13 against the entire corp, evacuating my wife and myself to the plane, bound to the mainland. It became Unit 13, as they came to be known, and 0-7 was the leader among them. It was him who refused to follow the General's orders on the day that caused the uprising on Genesis. There was a snowstorm, and we were trekking as quickly as we could through it, and it was there I lost my wife, and realized that my daughter was still trapped inside. I boarded the plane and they were still trailing us when we taxied on the runway. And that's when I realized that 0-7 and my daughter were driving, chasing the plane, with the soldiers still giving chase behind them. She was an arm's length away from being rescued. But the storm was raining heavily, and making the visibility almost impossible to see through. There was so much ice on the runway that it caused them to veer out of control, and as the plane flew off the runway, all I could do was watch, as they watched back. During the evacuation, one of the soldiers was fatally wounded, and I left her unattended for just a moment, trying to bring my daughter on board. And when I returned, I lost her. If I weren't distracted, maybe she could've been with us today, fighting with us. But, at the spur of the moment, what choice did I have? The irony is that the same soldier that is now her protector, is the very same one who tried to rescue her from Genesis, during the uprising ten years ago, though at the expense of eliminating the rest of his unit. After the long flight, we were welcomed by some of our allies in South America. From there, we made it to the mainland, and that's when we heard of the atrocities that some of our men had committed, and that Genesis had been deadlocked in the power struggle between the civilians and the armed forces, at the cost of many lives. Both civilian and military."

"What happened in South America? I don't really remember anything about that. Not all the details anyway."

"After the uprising, the entire world went into unrest, in protest against the armed forces, and all our embassies all around the world were being attacked. We were forced to evacuate. The entire world plunged into complete chaos. All orders suddenly became nonexistent. Just complete chaos. The General didn't have enough fuel to make it to the mainland, so he had no choice but to turn to our allies in South America. And when they arrived, they were shocked to receive a rude awakening from the P.L.F."

"Who were they?"

"The Peoples' Liberation Forces. They were a small army but very organized, trained by ex-military soldiers who were loyal to the late president, Jorge Ramos, who was assassinated in 2005, leaving behind his two sons, Alejandro, and Felipe, and a daughter, Isabella. The army was made up mostly of civilians who had joined the fight against the drug cartels and corrupt politicians to restore the country's honor in the fight for democracy, out of retaliation. Even decades after the late president was assassinated, the country was still deadlocked in a bitter power struggle between the two forces, and naturally, they turned to us for help in providing weapons to continue their fight against those who were still loyal to the cartel with connections all the way in Colombia, and many of the other Latin American states. One day, one of our planes were en-route to Genesis and was shot down by guerillas and had crash landed in Peru. A lot of soldiers lost their lives, and the General was less than half strength to repel the attack. No matter how much they fended them off, they just kept coming. Our forces held on long enough to be rescued by the peoples' army. So, they used this opportunity to form an alliance with us. And at the time, being that they had no alternative, our forces accepted. They thought that it was a good way to put a stranglehold on the guerillas' drug financed operations. For rescuing us, we provided them with as much hardware that we could, to help them with their war efforts against the cartel."

"What happened to the alliance?"

"After they heard of the uprising in Genesis, they demanded the release of 0-7 and my daughter, and when that didn't happen, they went to an all-out war. Many of the soldiers of the peoples' army had lost their lives, including the two sons of the late president, Alejandro and Felipe, against the battle-hardened marines, and the rest of the survivors had surrendered."

"And what did the Marines do?"

"They were executed. And they were laid in order as a sign of respect, after they refueled the plane, to get back to the mainland. But the problem is that not all of them stayed dead."

"Who survived?"

"After the General left for the mainland, two of the survivors made their way to the hospital, and gave their account of what happened, and if we thought that things were bad after the Genesis uprising, it was about to get a whole lot worse. And this time, it spread across the world like wildfire. Like a virus. One of the survivors who lived to tell the tale was Isabella Ramos."

"The late president's daughter?" Celina asked in surprise.

"Yes," Dr. Weaver answered. "She's the sole survivor of the president's bloodline. Sadly, she lost her entire family."

"Who was the other?"

"He was another non-ranking soldier in the army. Our government heard everything. The recording of their entire conversation was with some of our very hardware that we had provided them after saving the troops."

"Did the General know they had survived the attack?"

"Not until he arrived at the mainland. He was shocked to see that the authorities were there waiting to arrest him for all the atrocities he'd committed, and received a life sentence in a military prison. And as for those who had participated, they received lesser sentences, for the fact that they were following orders. When he saw the footage of the 2 soldiers who had survived, he knew that it was all over from that point. He realized from that point on, that he'd never get away with it. It was one thing to kill in self-defense, but to murder the soldiers who had surrendered, was something else entirely. After the two survivors gave their testimony, it played a vital role in convincing the tribunal of war crimes, And, at the same time I was reunited with my daughter again."

"Then how did you and your daughter get separated again? And how did he get so powerful?"

"Even after he was arrested and charged for war crimes by the tribunal, he was still highly respected by the people on the inside, as well as the outside. As difficult as it was for the judges to convict him, they had no choice but to do so to save face in the eyes of the public, because the unrest from the uprising and the atrocities had caused too much damage and loss of life, so they were not left with much of a choice. One night, I was out with the President to discuss the possible future of Genesis, and to have all military personnel withdrawn indefinitely. The place where my daughter was supposed to be hiding was infiltrated, resulting in my daughter and 0-7's kidnapping. After our meeting with the President, an attempt was made on our lives, and luckily we escaped. So, in order to keep the President safe, I took an oath to take his place and lead our forces, until things go back to normal, if they ever do, since he told me that I was the only one that could be his successor, for my accomplishments after achieving world peace."

"So, do you know where he is?"

"No. But if I did, for his safety, I wouldn't be able to tell you. All I know is that he's out there somewhere in another secure location like this one, watching and waiting until all this is over. If it ever will be, providing that he's still alive. After the President and myself parted ways when the attempt was made on our lives, you were assigned to me to help keep all forms and communications secured to help keep this place a secret, so it wouldn't be compromised by the enemy. That much has worked so far. And as for the General, even in facing justice of serving a possible life sentence for all his many crimes, his influence grew stronger, gaining supporters in both military and civilian prisons, causing our forces to be outnumbered by more than 20 to 1. And after taking the President's place, the next thing I knew, the entire country went into a state of civil war."

"Do you believe there will be peace someday?"

"As naive as I may sound, yes, I really do believe that. Despite all that has happened, I must bring myself to believe it. Because for all the sacrifices that I made, it seems that nothing good really came out of it. I went from losing Agnes to my wife, and now searching for my daughter, after our brief reunion on the mainland, only to lose her again in all this chaos, wondering where she is, or if I'll ever hold her in my arms again. For me, it never ends. All I've faced is tragedy."

"Wasn't having your daughter a good thing that came out of this? Probably the only good thing?"

"Yes, she is, now that you've mentioned it. And the only good thing, I ever had. I just wish that she didn't have to go through all the things that she went through. And what she's still going through. It just seemed unfair to her. And I can't help but to feel responsible for it."

"None of this is your fault."

"Even so. But when you see so many people die under your watch, you tend to see everything differently, when you think of them leaving their families behind, and making whatever other sacrifices, whether the ones they love, or for their country, or any other cause bigger than themselves."

"I don't understand. After you were reunited with your daughter, why would they take the trouble and not come after you? What made her more valuable? It doesn't make any sense."

"It may not make any sense. But, after I tell you why she was more important to the General's war effort than I was, it just might."

"How come?"

"Would you believe me if I told you that I was the intended target? The night when I was out with the President discussing the future of Genesis, after the attempt was made on our lives, Adam, myself, and the rest of his lieutenants had barely escaped with our lives, after we had thwarted the enemy attack. Possibly, they wanted me alive. But when that failed, they went after my daughter. Where she and 0-7 were hiding was supposed to be a secure location. When I arrived, all I saw was a number of dead bodies. And from that point, I knew we were infiltrated by a double agent."

"Why was she more important if you knew more than she did?"

"The General and I served together in the Ivory Coast during the outbreak. After I discovered the cure, I came with another theory, hoping to put it to practical application. It was strengthening the human genome against diseases, and withstanding hunger for a longer period. The theory basically was to boost the immune system to give the subject a longer lifespan while resisting harsh periods, or life-threatening injuries. He knew of my work, and intended to make good on my promise to see it done, and use it, to try and benefit all of mankind, and possibly save mankind from itself. So naturally, I wanted my work to be my legacy. So, I passed it on to my daughter. And he knew it. So, since he was aware of it, it became obvious that he wanted to use either me or my daughter for a sinister purpose."

"What purpose was that?"

"As I told you before, those loyal to the President are outnumbered by more than 20 to 1. And after all the years in this war, the General thought that our forces would've been crushed sooner. But he was sadly mistaken. So, he ordered my abduction to help with the war effort. And from the looks of it, what I told him that I intended to do. There's no doubt in my mind that this was his plan to create stronger soldiers, and finally place the country under his control. But, he found my daughter instead. And since he had my daughter, I supposed it might've worked out for him or even better."

"What if you were captured? Would you've done it?"

"No, I wouldn't have. I'd rather die first than to take my research and use it as a weapon. I created this to benefit mankind, not destroy it. And he knows it."

"What about your daughter? Do you think she would?"

"Not willingly. If I know my daughter, it's that she's tougher than she looks. Her resolve is as stern as mine. She's very clever, but a bit more delicate. Knowing her, she might've stalled for as long as she could. And judging from what I've seen with 0-7 being made into what he is, I can only surmise that she agreed to participate, to save his life, since he turned his allegiance to us instead of them. 0-7's transformation could've only been the product of constant and painful torture. And it looks like the demon has come back to torment its creator, as we all have seen earlier. If there's one thing that I've learnt in the armed forces is that one would do whatever it took to save a fellow soldier, or the ones they care about, under those circumstances. I may be wrong about this, but it's just my theory. But, I do know this. In the wrong hands, this research can prove very fatal. What became a cure for mankind could end up being its doom in creating a potential biological weapon, or the General's case, creating a race of super soldiers. Things start as one way, and end another, and in this case, that makes her the key to this country having a possible future, if there's any at all. She holds the key that could save us all, or even doom us all to our fates. She's the reason why I wake up every day and fight. After losing so much, she's all I have left."

"Did your wife and daughter ever know about your wife and children in the Ivory Coast?"

"No. I'm afraid not. I couldn't bring myself to tell them, and possibly lose everything that I worked so hard to build."

"What do you think my greatest creation was? Was it the vaccine?"

"That was a major accomplishment, I admit. But, that was only scratching the surface."

"Then what was it?"

"It was my daughter. And still is. Seeing how she blossomed from a sheltered young girl into a strong young woman, knowing that she will be the one passing on my legacy to her children, and their children. And all that brings me solace is that one day before I close my eyes, she'll be back in my arms again. And as for my wife, Jane, every time I saw her smiling face, seeing how happy she was when we were together on Genesis, I couldn't bring myself to tell her, and force the both of us to relive all that pain again. I just couldn't. My only option was to live with it every single day, and let it slowly take away a part of my soul. Possibly until there was nothing more to take, and take my past to my grave. Whatever it took to keep them happy. Not telling them the truth was another demon that still torments me to this day. But, every time when I tried to put the Ivory Coast behind me, it all came back when I saw her smile, only to have the same thing happen to me again, on Genesis. Every night I close my eyes, I have so many demons to fight. I still see all these many souls smile at me from the other side. I still see that little girl that I couldn't save. I can't tell if they're tormenting me, or maybe trying to console me, from all my ordeals, knowing that I did all I could to save them. I don't know what to make of it. But, what I do know is that I've gotten older, and my resistance and resolve has gotten a lot weaker. And I don't know how long I can continue to fight. It's after you fight your battle engaging your enemy, it's from that point your personal war begins when you try to live with yourself, for all the things that you've seen and done. For all the loved ones that you couldn't save. For all the people that you were responsible for, who left whatever little possessions they had, who came to you in search of hope knowing that you let them down, and abandoned them to their deaths, when they needed you most. The sense of feeling that you could've done more. Or you should've tried harder. That is the war that no one can win. Every time I look or feel that scar on my chest a few inches above my heart, is always a grim reminder of that fateful day in the Ivory Coast, when I lost Agnes, my son, and unborn child, forever changing my life, up until the night I lost Jane, during the evacuation from the uprising on Genesis. Sometimes, I feel that God has a wicked sense of humor, letting me linger with all this pain and suffering, giving me something and just snatching it away from my hands.

If it weren't for having my daughter, I often wished that I'd died in the Ivory Coast, or Genesis for that matter, to end all this pain and suffering. And if I was to see them again, I would tell them. Maybe it would help me to ease my conscience. After all, I can't lose more than I already have. Until then, I will keep on fighting, and hope that one day I'll see my daughter again."

"I've never been too much of a religious person, Mr. President, but growing up, I've always heard my parents tell me that God doesn't give us any burden that we can't bear. I can only imagine all the weight on your shoulders, and the tremendous responsibility laid at your feet, and all that's happened to you, you still find a way to and a reason to move on, and never have I seen so much strength in anyone that myself or the rest of us have come across. I've seen people give up for less, but you are a living example to all of us. And I speak for all of us saying so. All of us sitting right before you in this very room, just experienced a small taste of combat, and already felt like giving up. But, you still fight, leading your troops from a place that no one knows about, holding on to hope that we can still turn the fortunes of this war, even in the face of defeat. I suppose that there is a small glimmer of hope seeing that your daughter has escaped and looking for you, with her protector by her side. What I mean to say, Dr. Weaver, is that you're a great man, and for all that has happened you've accomplished so much that many can only dream, and in the thick of it all, keep us safe. And for that, I'm proud to be under your command. And I speak for the rest of us again, when I say that we're proud to be under your command. I couldn't have asked for a better leader. None of us could. We were just children when we began serving with you. Now we've matured into young men and women. Maybe we're the ones that you're destined to lead."

"Thank you, Celina, That means a lot to me," Dr. Weaver said softly.

"The pleasure is all mine, sir."

"It's good to know that even after all that has happened, some people still show a measure of hope. Hope that we can still look forward to times like these," he answered, looking at their faces, filled with intrigue and disbelief, from listening to his tragic experiences that molded him into who he was.

Celina walked over to Nicholas, who was slowly regaining signs of recovery and gently pulled back his blood-soaked collar of his uniform, seeing the tiny scar left behind after his bullet wound had healed, and said, "It's gone. It's completely healed."

The others mumbled among themselves after witnessing how potent the vaccine that Dr. Weaver had created was, making it the greatest medical breakthrough in history.

He walked over to Nicholas, while he continued lying on the table, still feeling the paralyzing effects of the serum and said, "Glad you're awake."

"I can't feel my legs. I can't feel anything," Nicholas said, trying to move, with tears running down his cheeks.

Like all the other soldiers under Dr. Weaver's command, he was young and inexperienced in any kind of warfare, and was recruited by Dr. Weaver's government to help search for Kassandra.

He had dark straight hair and hazel eyes, with a handsome build, and past average height, with his feelings brewing for Celina all these years they worked together.

"It's just a temporary side effect from the drug. You'll be fine. It'll wear off soon enough. Just rest."

"Thank you for saving me."

"Don't mention it. It was my pleasure. Glad to see you're awake. Now just rest."

Nicholas simply nodded his head, resting his head back.

CHAPTER 20: SHANGRI-LA.

02:23 HOURS. BLACK HISTORY MUSEUM AND CULTURAL CENTER - RICHMOND, VIRGINIA:

The Black History Museum and Cultural Center was founded in 1981, and has been striving to commemorate the establishments of Blacks through their visual, oral, and written works. It finally closed down during the civil war that divided the entire nation.

They had arrived at the museum, and quickly established a perimeter, in case the enemy soldiers would attack. The assassin stood guard, unseen from his position, patiently waiting in ambush, while the others walked through the building, admiring the establishment of the oral and written works of the Black minorities that once played a part of their great, yet turbulent history.

Elaina walked towards the assassin, looking at him with a hopeless look of love in her eyes, and said, "I thought you might like some fresh clothing."

He turned back looking into her eyes, squinting in confusion, while the image of her face continued to haunt his memories, causing his eyes to slowly turn from cold, into becoming warm and welcoming, while she stared back looking into them.

He grabbed the clothes gently from her hands, and took a few steps back, slowly removing the blood soaked clothes, dropping them to the floor, while she continued to stare hopelessly at his handsome and muscular physique, lined with the countless scars that he endured from his captivity that showed the horrible truth of the brutal treatment he received at the hands of his enemies. She quickly overlooked them, bringing herself to love him the same, like she had many years before during their previous excursions that made their fates collide.

Unable to contain her restraint from him, she walked towards him, feeling

"

the long, thick scars that ran across the muscles of his brown skin, gently with her finger tips, slowly unbuttoning his clothes, softly kissing him, "I can't forget all that you've done for me. For so long, I prayed that someday, you would return to me. And now that you're here, I never want to lose you again. It's been so difficult not being in your arms, for just another second, let alone another day. Let alone all these years. And even after all this time, I'm still in love with you. I can't lose you again. I just can't."

Though he remained silent and clueless, staring deeply into her eyes, he watched her tears rolling down her cheek, gently wiping them off with his index finger, and resting her head on his chest, holding him closer.

Nina watched from a distance, seeing Elaina holding on to the assassin tightly in a warm and loving embrace with great envy, and a longing to be loved like she once was during her tenure under the General's leadership. After seeing that Elaina had found love in a time of war and peril, her eyes slowly clouded in tears, as she reminisced on her last moments with the man she once loved.

Matthew walked towards her while she continued looking in their direction and asked softly, "Are you okay?"

After being suddenly startled, she quickly wiped the tears from her eyes and answered, smiling "Yes. You startled me."

"I'm sorry. I didn't mean to. I just wanted to take the time off to introduce myself properly. Without the guns pointed to each other's faces, this time. I'm Matthew," he said, slowly extending his hand.

"I'm Nina. Nina Wells," she answered, smiling nervously, gently grabbing his hand, shaking it.

"Don't mean to intrude. If you don't mind, I'd like to talk and get to know you better. Mind if I sit down?"

"You're not intruding. I suppose in a time like this, I could use someone to talk to," she answered, looking into the direction of Elaina and the assassin embracing one another in their tender moment of warm embrace.

"I just wanted to thank you," Matthew said softly.

"For what?" she asked.

"For giving me a second chance to live. For giving all of us a second chance."

"No thanks required."

"When you were sitting in the cockpit of that plane, I could only imagine how difficult the choice was to turn on your own. I really do admire you for that."

"The others don't appear to share your enthusiasm. And who could blame them? All the choices that I made today, and before, I have to live with for the rest of my life."

"To be fair, we were almost wiped out by the enemy forces, and I guess that everyone is still trying to recover from the recent turn of events. It hasn't been easy losing so many of those who we care about who paid the ultimate price in this war. But, me here talking to you man-to-woman, as a sign of forgiveness. I can only speak for myself, at this point. The rest will come around when the time is right for them."

"What made you come around so quickly?"

"After seeing what I saw, today alone, I believe that anything is possible."

"I suppose," she answered.

"You attacked us when we least expected, then turned around to defend us, when we were at the weakest moment of our lives. We're here because of you. You sacrificed everything for people that you never even knew. Well, it's not that you left me with much of a choice, anyway."

Nina smiled and answered, "There's always a choice."

"And I choose to come around. Just like you chose to save us."

"But, so quickly? That's a hard pill to swallow."

"Yes. We were on opposite sides, and we're still alive because of you. You saved all of us. As long as a handful of us are still alive, I suppose there's that small glimmer of hope. And you helped in keeping it alive. I admit, I wasn't too crazy about someone from the other side joining the ranks at first, and I speak for everyone when I say that, but, I'm a fair man, I shouldn't overlook the fact that you saved our lives when you could've taken it. I just wanted to be the one to give you a proper welcome to the resistance. Or what's left of it."

"Thank you. That means a lot to me," she said.

"You're welcome. Then again, it's the first of many."

"Am I supposed to think that you're saying that to make me feel better?" she asked, smiling.

"I don't know. I suppose it's supposed to make you feel some way. I'll let you be the judge."

"Well, I suppose it does," she said, smiling.

"Is that a smile that I see?"

"I suppose it is," she said, chuckling.

"Good. We can use a little laughter at a time like this."

The smile slowly faded off her face, as she glanced in the direction of Elaina and the assassin, still in their tender moments together.

Matthew glanced in the same direction, and asked, "Is something bothering you?"

"Look at them. He doesn't even know who he is or anything about his past, and still she loves him like there's no tomorrow. In a time like this, she found someone to love. Someone to hold on to. It doesn't matter what he did in his past, or all the people he has killed, and still she loves him beyond anything that I've seen. Love is indeed a powerful thing. And that is something that I'll never find," she said, sadly.

"Don't say that. Maybe it wasn't the right time for it to happen."

"Then when is it? I spent so long fighting for someone who treats me like an asset, treating me and the rest of his troops like assets, instead of human beings, expendable instead of irreplaceable. People like me must always have to choose between love and duty. We can never have what the two of them have. I envy her so much. And I envy him even more for finding someone to love, even with all his past transgressions."

"Since when was it ever up to you to determine that you can never find love?" Matthew asked.

"From the moment I began losing everyone that I ever cared about. Every time I got close to someone, the same thing happened over and over again. It never ended for me. It felt like a curse tormenting me all these years. There was that one moment that I was in love with someone, and found out I was a few weeks pregnant, and we had to keep it a secret, for the sake of the war effort. Later, I found out that he was killed in action by General West's forces.

I went into so much grief, and I cried for so long, that I ended up having a miscarriage while I slept alone in my bed. Still, no one knew. After I suffered in silence at nights, I continued performing my duties during the day, like nothing happened. I stayed in my bed all night, until I cried myself to sleep, knowing that I could never bring myself to be close to someone anymore, because I always end up losing all the ones I care about. So, everyday I face the daunting task of trying to rid myself of all the memories, trying to make myself numb from feeling any kind of emotion towards anyone, lying to myself all this time, until the past came knocking on my door, staring right into my face, when I was given the order to kill him. But I couldn't."

"What was going through your mind when you were ordered to kill him?" Matthew asked.

"I know what happened during the Genesis Uprising. I know all the terrible things they did to him before they made him into the monster he is. Where's the honor in killing someone who already has everything taken from him? What more could I have could I have taken from him that hasn't been taken? They already stripped him of everything that made him human. They took everything away from him. Look at him. Even with all his skills, he's alive, but not living. That is a fate worse than death itself. When they asked me to eliminate him, all the memories came rushing back, knowing all that I knew about him. Living with knowing that I'd spend the rest of my days, dying from loneliness, is just another battle that I have to keep fighting," she continued, wiping the tears from her face.

"Not from where I'm standing."

"Why are you being so nice to me?" she asked softly.

"Because we both bear the scars of this long and senseless conflict that has torn all of us apart. And I too carry the burden of losing many of my loved ones."

"What will your friends think?"

"Does it matter what they or anybody else thinks? Everyone is entitled to their own opinion. But to answer your question, I'm tired of fighting as well. Like you, I've lost so many that I cared about, and been asking if I'll ever meet someone and have a normal life, or maybe one day kids of my own, or just someone that I care about, although nothing has been normal since this civil war began. But nevertheless, it would be nice to have someone to care about. So, many lives just vanished in an instant. Bad things happen for good reasons, I suppose."

"Aren't you afraid that I'll use this gun to shoot you?"

"You know you won't. I look into those eyes of yours and I don't see the killer that you were made to be."

"What do you see?"

"Someone who, despite all her transgressions, finally came to the realization that she had a conscience beneath that fierce exterior, searching for redemption, like many others soon to come. Besides, you have enough on your mind to worry about already, and killing me wouldn't ease your conscience. There's nothing to gain by doing it anyway, except an angry mob breathing down your neck. And not to mention that it would be unfair to the both of us, that a fine jewel like yourself would spend the rest of her days being lonely."

Nina wiped the tears from her eyes, and asked, "Is that supposed to make me smile?"

"I don't know. Is it working?" he asked, wiping the tears from her cheek.

"I believe we both know the answer to that. I needed that."

"In times like these, we can all use some laughter, especially after all the pain that has befallen us. I'm beginning to think that all this happened for us to find one another so we can love again. Look at him and Elaina, Frank and Kathy, talking to one another over there, Kassandra and Brandon."

"What about her?" Nina asked.

"Who?"

"The pilot. Nicole."

"Oh her? She's by herself for now. Who knows? She might hook up with General West."

"And her?"

"Janet? Oh, last I recalled when we were getting our asses kicked by 0-7 at Fort Story, she was making out with Anton. Or wanted to."

Nina chuckled and answered, "You're funny. What about you? You think you have a chance with me?"

"I can get used to that idea."

"Fat chance."

"As I said, it was just an idea."

"You've been making me smile just a little too much. Is that your way of trying to sweep me off my feet?"

"Is it working?"

"I'm not saying anything."

"You don't have to. Not since I've been making you blush since we've been talking. And not to mention my charming good looks."

"If you say so. But I do admit that I really needed to laugh. Thank you for that," she chuckled.

"My pleasure."

"Instead of making me laugh all the time, are you even going to tell me anything about yourself?"

"What would you like to know?"

"Everything. Or whatever you'd like me to know. Starting from your childhood would be nice. That is, if you had one."

"I was born here."

"Were your parents from here?"

"My father was from Nigeria. He fled to the United States during his early teens, during the civil war, between the factions and tribes, or whatever you wanna call it. And as for Mother, she was from Sierra Leone. She, too, came to the United States when she was young, fleeing from civil war during the blood diamond conflict, and ended up in the nation's capital, where she worked as many odd jobs as she could to support her family, like most immigrants do. Chance encounter, fate, or however you wish to define it - they met, fell in love, did their business, got married, and had me. That much, I know. But the only thing I don't know is if they went through all the traditional steps in consummating the marriage and all, but then again for the both of us, that's T.M.I. And here I am, nonetheless."

She chuckled and asked, "Are you an only child?"

"As far as I know."

"Are they still alive?"

"Sadly no. I lost my father from natural causes."

"Sorry to hear that."

"As for my mother, from a hit-and-run from a drunk driver when I was just 15. She passed on the way to the hospital. The damage from the collision was too severe for them to save her.

"And a few years later, I graduated from high school with top honors, went to college, and looked for structure in my life, looking for something new. And then, by some strange coincidence, just sitting in the cafeteria on campus, I saw Dr. Weaver's broadcast when he was on Genesis. And from the moment I heard him, for the first time in my life, I realized that was where I wanted to be, and that his guidance would help me be someone who could change the world with his gifts, up until the military came and fucked it up for all the denizens. So, naturally, like millions of citizens, out of support, I took to the streets, and eventually took up arms when the war started, since I always dreamed of joining the armed forces, too. Well, not that anyone of us had much of a choice. Either we collaborate or resist, and I chose to resist. The thing is, I never knew much about weapons, so I had to learn quickly. I'm surprised to see I lasted this long, after losing so many people that I cared about. Frank and Kathy are some of the only few surviving people that I have left. And I pray that I find more of them. Since then, we've been fighting the great war ever since. I suppose I'm very lucky or a natural born soldier, since both my people from both sides of the fence came from that world. And that's pretty much it. And you? I've already seen that you're pretty much one hell of a pilot. What's the story behind that?"

"I come from a line of pilots. Starting from the first World War, when my great-great-great grandfather pioneered it all. He took out a number of Germans, including the Black Baron, before he was finally shot and killed in action. And the second world war, when my great-great grandfather followed his footsteps. He was stationed at Ramitelli Air Force Base in Italy, in the Tuskegee outfit, and later served during the Korean War. My great grandfather served in Vietnam, and was one of the pilots with one of the highest kill ratios, but never got the credit for it, because of the discrimination that Black pilots continued to face during that era. Then there was my grandfather who served during the invasion of Grenada, and later on during the Gulf War. And my father, who served in Somalia during the time of the manhunt of General Mohammad Aidid, which they never found, and Afghanistan, during the hunt for Osama Bin Laden, and Operation Iraqi Freedom for Saddam Hussein.

"He always told me to never forget who I was. Always taught me about the great sacrifices that my forefathers made to earn their place in history. Turns out I did forget who I was when I fought for the General.

"And it was just during the time that the North Koreans had attacked the south, I'd just joined the air force after graduating from college, to continue my families' great legacy. About 50 of us took the exam, and only 3 of us succeeded, with me graduating at the top of the class with the perfect score. And it was from that point on, I was called in to use my skills and have been doing it ever since, until someone told me that the mission was more important than my life. It took me that long to see that I didn't matter being on the other side. I was good enough, until they realized that it was time for me to be discarded like garbage. So, I did what anyone would do. I switched sides. It was the toughest decision that I ever made, but considering the circumstances, it was worth it."

"Are you sure you have no regrets?"

"Can't say that I do, despite the warm reception. But at least I'm treated like a human being instead of being treated like an asset for the government to win a war."

"If it makes you feel any better, those skills were some of the best skills with anyone flying a plane."

"Thank you," Nina said, smiling. "I'd just wish that I'd put it to better use sooner."

"Something tells me you won't have to wait long."

"Thank you."

"For what?" Matthew asked.

"For believing in me. For making me laugh again. I needed to after all that has happened."

"You sound like you won't be needing it, anymore."

"I didn't mean it that way. I can always use it to help me heal. I hope there'll be more of it."

He grabbed her hand gently and said, "Only if you'll let me."

She grabbed his hand in return and answered, "I think you know the answer to that."

"I hope that the both of you are done making out," Jill said, rudely interrupting.

"What's going on?" Matthew asked.

"Now that we've gotten properly reacquainted, General West and the doctor are calling a meeting. And that means everyone's invited, including the lovely turncoat. He's waiting on you, and you know what they say about keeping the General waiting."

"I'll be there right away," Nina said softly, and walked away.

"What's that all about?" Matthew asked. "You're acting like a jealous ex-girlfriend. And I barely even know you."

"She's an enemy of our resistance, and I don't trust her, and I speak for the others when I say this."

"Well, you don't speak for me."

"Apparently not, since you've been having a hard-on for that pretty ass of hers."

"Well, better hers than yours. If it weren't for her, none of us would be here running our mouths, or even our trusted assassin, for that matter. She could've plugged your behind with a load full of lead, but didn't. Me and the rest of us owe her a little gratitude. That means you too."

"The General is waiting. And if this meeting is what I think it is, which I'm sure it is, I hope that her promising you some ass was worth it, because where we're going is a one-way trip. So maybe you should get some before we leave."

"Well, I could say the same for you. And for all the time you've been at war with the rest of us, it sounds like you can use some quality time yourself."

"Not with the likes of you."

"That's fine. I've sent my resume somewhere else. So, I want you to do yourself a favor."

"Which is?" Jill asked.

"Don't knock it till you try it. And don't say I didn't tell you so, either. Now, instead of standing here having a sex talk with you, I have a meeting to attend. Besides, she doesn't take too kindly to sharing, anyways," Matthew concluded, and walked away.

Adam waited for them to gather, and took a deep breath, knowing how difficult the task that he was about to face was, and said, "I want you all to give me your undivided attention. Kassandra has something to say that she thinks that will turn the war in our favor."

"Whatever it is, I'm all ears," Nicole answered.

"That depends," Janet said.

"Say what's on your mind," Anton said.

Kassandra took a deep breath, and replied, "We should kill the General while we're still under the cover of night."

"Yeah, no shit," Janet replied, scoffing, and said, "And how the fuck are we going do that?"

"Just hear her out. I'm sure she has a plan," Adam answered.

"We're still here waiting to hear what suicidal plan you'll come up with," Jonathan answered.

Kassandra felt her cell phone vibrate in her lab coat, and pulled it out. She read the text message, causing her to open her eyes wide, and said, "I have a mole planted inside, and I've just received word that the General is at one of the top-secret facilities. Tonight is our only one chance to take him out and put an end to this war, once and for all. We won't get another chance like this ever again."

"Let me get this straight. You want just a handful of us to storm a fortress filled with thousands, maybe tens of thousands, of enemy personnel, just to kill one man?" Janet asked.

"Yes. He's not just one man. He's the one pulling the strings behind all this, and now may be the only chance that we have to do this."

"I never thought I'd say this to the daughter of a well-known scientist," Janet said calmly, and continued, "But, bitch, are you crazy?"

"How long can we keep running? Eventually, we'll run out of places to hide! We have to make a stand! And it's the only way that we may be able to make a statement to the enemy! The smaller the group, the less likely we draw any kind of attention of being detected, in case you haven't noticed! And the name is Kassandra, thank you," she concluded softly.

"Let's just say we believe you. How could we get close enough to the General to kill him?" Kathy asked.

"The first thing we need to do is blend in. We need fresher uniforms. Those uniforms we took from the enemy soldiers from the White House will stand out. We need to blend in with the lower ranking soldiers to avoid suspicion."

"And exactly how do we do that?" Matthew asked.

"We kill them and disguise ourselves in their clothes, like what we did in the White House before we make our escape," Kassandra replied.

"What about the perimeter? The fences may be electrified. What do we do then?" Brian added.

"I know where it is. It's a few miles away from here. I've taken a few tours around the base, and from what I can tell, there's always a flaw in security during my early days as a rookie pilot. I did a lot of walking around the facility," Nina replied.

"Sounds like you're leading us to our deaths," Jacqueline replied.

"That's enough, Chan. Whether you like it or not, she's one of us now, and I think she's perfectly aware of the consequences, if she betrays us," Adam interjected, pointing to the assassin.

"I hope it's sooner rather than later," Jacqueline replied.

"I apologize for her rudeness. The rest of us are trying to get used to trusting you. Your former allies put us through a lot, if you know what I mean," Adam answered.

"It's okay, General West. I understand," Nina replied softly.

"If she has a point to make, then let her make it. Our lives may be depending on it. We can only be constructive with ideas, not arguments," Kathy added.

"What's your point, Wells?" Adam asked.

"The fences may be electrified. So, to make sure we have a safe passage into the base, we test it."

"And how exactly do we do that? Surely you're not suggesting live subjects, are you?" Jill asked.

"No, we use impact against it. The fence reacts when hit with any solid object," Nina answered.

"And let's just say, if we get in, and I do mean if. The base is filled with tons of enemy guard posts with search lights. How do we avoid them?" Frank asked.

"We use the dark as cover, and make sure we stay out of the light. Though they may not suspect us if we're dressed in enemy uniforms," Nina answered.

"How do we take out the guards in their posts?" Tiara asked.

"If we go long range, we need to get them silent with one shot. And it's important to remain silent."

"The thing is, we don't have any snipers on the team," Adam answered.

Kassandra contemplated for a brief moment and answered, "That's out of the question."

"What is?" Elaina asked.

"Picking them off from long range is out of the question. The best thing to do is to get past the fence under the cover of darkness, and get close to them, and take them out. And after that, it gets a little easier."

"What do you mean?" Adam asked.

"We use him. He's been making quick work of them so far," Kassandra replied, pointing at the assassin.

"There may be another way, but it's far too risky. It's a blind move. In case of emergency, they built underground tunnels that ran for miles, accessible to a number of manholes that ran in a number of directions. If we use them, they may put us right into the enemy hands, especially if they're on patrol. So, the best course of action is to use those tunnels to get us close enough to the enemy base, and when we get in, use the hole within the base as an exit, after we complete our mission," Nina added.

"And how are we going to cover our retreat from the base if we're discovered?" Elaina asked.

"We plant charges on all the fuel depots and hangars filled with planes and ammunition, or just about anywhere that can cause significant damage that can distract and delay them long enough for us to make our escape," Nina answered.

"That's quite an ambitious plan. It's a fortress over there. Do you think we have enough charges to cause that amount of damage?" Adam asked.

Kassandra emptied a large bag filled with charges that she procured during her many excursions on the floor, and answered, "Of course we do. I figured that since we'll be storming the base, we'll need all the help we can get. So, I took as many as I could carry from the trail of all the dead bodies in the city, the store, and the sewers."

"What do you mean, we? The last thing we need is some bookworm scientist getting killed on our watch," Janet asked.

"She's right. It's too dangerous. You're too important to us. To me. I can't afford to lose you," Brandon answered.

"You won't. I'll be fine."

"Give her credit for making it this far in sound mind, at least. For all the things she's seen she should be losing her mind right about now. She's much tougher than she looks."

Janet looked at Kassandra staring back at her with a straight face and answered, "It's your funeral."

"It's my plan. I have to take charge of it, because tonight may be the only opportunity to end this war, or more of you will die. And I'll be a prisoner again, and I'm not going back there," Kassandra replied.

"So, how exactly do we cover so much ground?" Adam asked.

"After we make our way into the base, we split up into different teams. Small but organized, to not attract any kind of unnecessary attention. Then plant charges and wait for the signal to detonate them," Nina said, softly.

"And what's the signal?" Karen asked.

"When the General's quarters gets blown to bits with him in it," Kassandra replied.

"I really don't get it. You came out of nowhere, claimed to be the daughter of a world-renowned scientist, and are now giving orders about killing someone who's impossible to get to. Who the hell do you think you are?" Jacqueline asked.

"It doesn't matter who I am at this point. All that matters is ending this war and the only way to do so is to cut off the head of the snake! Ever since you lost your entire carrier fleet, all you've been doing is running around, scurrying like rats, living in odd places, trying to buy yourselves some time, hoping to strengthen your numbers!" Kassandra replied.

They suddenly grew quiet, knowing there was truth to what she had said, while they contemplated all the close calls of almost being wiped out by the assassin.

"Yes, I know! I heard it all before the sheep returned to the flock!" Kassandra said, pointing to the assassin. "How long can you keep on running? Eventually, they'll find you and kill you, when you run out of places to hide! All of you, even him! He's only one man, and won't always be able to save us all the time! We must act, no matter what you think!"

Karen began to feel nauseous, and began to vomit from the early symptoms of being pregnant.

"Looks like we're about to have a new member of the resistance soon. And it won't be good to us if they're dead!"

"It was the same thing she said, before we placed her ass in handcuffs," Janet said snidely, pointing to Nina. "And why are we even doing this again? That's a little too much information."

A convoy of enemy soldiers had arrived at the museum undetected, and without warning, opened fire, causing them to disperse, assuming defensive positions.

The assassin quickly spun Elaina around, once again shielding her from the barrage of enemy bullets, slamming into the plate of armor that protected his body, while a number of enemy bullets continued racing past his position.

He listened to the enemy soldiers walking closer and gently pulled the pin from a smoke grenade. He signaled the others to run away, as the smoke quickly filled the museum to cover their retreat, causing the enemy soldiers to give chase through the cloud of smoke.

He waited for the enemy soldiers to advance to his position, and quickly lunged his blade, skillfully maneuvering with deadly precision, eliminating them as quickly and swiftly, with a single blow.

After they'd reached a safe distance, they heard the loud roar of the machine gun fire and screams of the enemy soldiers through the thick cloud of smoke, which suddenly stopped.

A gust of cold wind swept through the doors of the museum, blowing away the cloud of crimson smoke, leaving only the assassin standing with his blade firmly gripped in the tight grip of his palm.

Elaina came out of her hiding place, and looked at the carnage the assassin had left in his wake. She remained unfazed, walking towards him while the blood of the dead soldiers continued to drip from his sword, looking into his eyes with unlost admiration.

The others slowly walked through the sea of dead soldiers, inspecting them, when they felt one of the wounded enemy soldiers grab a gun on the floor and stumble to his feet, when a gunshot suddenly echoed through the museum, startling everyone.

Jill turned back with a sudden look of awe on her face, and shifted her focus to Nina, who stood over his corpse.

Nina stared at Jill with a timid look on her face, and said, "He was about to shoot you in the back," and walked away, leaving Jill standing with a look of continuous shock on her face.

"How did they find us? I thought you took out your transmitter, Kassandra," Adam asked with a look of shock on his face.

"She did. I took it out myself," Arianna answered.

"Does it matter?" Kassandra asked. "They won't stop until you're all dead. All of you, and me captured."

They heard an enemy soldier gurgling on his blood, from the grave wounds the assassin had inflicted, and walked towards him. He tried to laugh as he continued to gurgle on his blood and said, "You're all gonna die," and finally drowned in his own blood, while taking his last breath.

"I hate to say this, but he has a point. That's exactly what'll happen if we don't act now," Kassandra said.

"Can't say that I don't agree with you about wanting him dead. But why do you want him dead so badly? There has to be another reason why you want to go inside that fortress," Janet said.

"I can give you a million reasons. And all of them would bring chills down your spines."

"I'm all ears. As the rest of us," Nicole replied.

"Him," Kassandra said, pointing at the assassin.

"What about him?" Adam answered.

"Look around you," she answered.

"Either us or them. They had it coming," Daniel answered.

"I told you before. And I'll tell you again. You're outgunned and outnumbered and putting on a hell of a fight, and that doesn't sit too well with the General. So, he came up with an idea to win the war and that was to create a group of super soldiers, and if that isn't good enough, then think of an entire army."

"You really did say that, alright," Janet remarked, shaking her head.

"Take him, for instance. Look at all the carnage he leaves in his wake. Now, imagine if he was completely impervious to pain, or could instantly heal after sustaining a fatal injury. Imagine that times six more like him, or an entire army with a single purpose, bred to wipe all of you out, and put an end to this resistance permanently, and I don't want to get old spending my entire life being somebody else's puppet in this damn war. And as I said earlier, I'm not going back there."

"How far did you get into those plans, again?" Adam asked.

"I don't know. I told you I'm not even sure if what I engineered is possible. It was just a theory," Kassandra said softly. "But there's a chance it could be made practical application. Just think of what could happen if it was harnessed by the wrong hands. I stalled for as long as I could, and when I finally did something, all this happened. Now, my only chance of stopping anything from happening is to retrieve those blueprints. My father's research was supposed to benefit mankind, not send it to its doom, and right now, we're all that stands between what's left of the human race and total annihilation, because if they turn my father's research into a weapon, then you're all doomed."

"My God, Kassandra. You sure picked a good time to come up with some bad news."

"It's what I've been trying to tell you since we crossed paths," Kassandra answered.

"So you're saying it's a one-way trip?" Anton asked.

"Just as I thought," Jill added.

"Not if we stick to the shadows and blend in. Not if we stick to the plan," Nina answered.

"You're one to talk," Jacqueline replied.

"That's enough, Chan. As I said, she's one of us now. So, now is as good a time as any to prove herself," Adam replied.

"For once, we agree on something," Jacqueline answered.

"I know that none of you trust me, and I don't blame you. I'd feel the same if I were in your shoes. None of this is easy, and everything that I've done until now, I must live with for the rest of my life. I'll be outside," she said, walking away.

"Wait," Adam called out softly. "If there's anything more that you can tell us to help the mission, that would be very helpful."

"What more can I do to help?"

"It would be even more helpful if you can draw a detailed layout of the place."

Kassandra reached into her pocket and handed her a piece of paper and pen, and said, "You must hurry. There may be more on their way right now."

"I will."

After a brief moment, Nina drew a rough sketch of the enemy compound, and said, "This is it. The General's quarters are over here, and you need a key card to enter. And naturally, it's the highest clearance, and the doors are a few inches of reinforced steel. They've made a series of modifications since the late stages of the war. So that means you may have to snatch it from one of the guards guarding his quarters. This is the hangar, and this is the fuel depot, and this is where they store all the artillery shells, so to buy ourselves more time, we need to take out those positions, to create a diversion long enough to escape, and in the process, starve them of precious resources. The only thing we have to do is to remain undetected long enough until Kassandra can procure her father's work from the General's quarters," Nina said.

"If you say this is what you say this is, then we have no choice but to take this mission," Adam said, taking a long, deep breath.

"It is what I say it is. I don't have any other option, but this is the only chance that we may have to do this. We're all that's left between him and total victory, and we don't have much time," Nina said.

"It's settled then," Adam replied.

"I knew you'd say that," Janet answered.

"Susan is coming around," Arianna added.

"Great," Kassandra said, with a big sigh of relief.

"What's the plan?" Daniel asked.

"We split up in teams. Wells, Chan, and Nicoletti, take the hangar."

"Why do I have to be the one to go with her?" Jacqueline asked.

"So you can learn to get along," Adam answered.

"But she's still one of them," Jacqueline answered back angrily.

"She was," Adam answered, pointing to the assassin, and continued, "And so was he. And the last I checked, she saved Nicoletti's ass."

"In order to succeed, we need to be more constructive," Kassandra added.

"Reed, Jackson, and Min, you take the ammo dump."

"Teaming me up with Jackson, huh?" Anton asked, shaking his head.

"I'm not that bad once you get to know me," Janet answered.

"Silverman, Hoshi, and Masaquela, plant charges on the vehicles, while Silva and myself will stay back and cover our retreat just in case. Kassandra and 0-7 will infiltrate the General's quarters, grab the blueprints, and blow him to bits. The rest of you will stay back, and if within half a day we don't return, then you know what to do."

"I pray all this goes well," Nicole answered.

"It will if we stick to the plan," Kassandra answered.

"Before we go to our deaths, can't we at least pray first?" Janet asked.

"We'll do that when we're on the way," Adam replied.

"But how do we travel without being undetected?" Jonathan asked.

"We can use the underground tunnels from the starting point, and they run for miles under the base, all the way to the city. I know where to find one of them from here. We can start from there and inch our way closer to the enemy position. Once we're there, we go through the fence. If that doesn't work, then we try to go through the inside. But as I said, it's a bigger risk of getting caught."

"We need to get moving, before more come," Kassandra said, looking at the front doors of the museum nervously.

"Where do we meet after we complete the mission?" Brian asked.

"The hospital. There's one a few miles from here. We'll wait there until you get back. If you do, that is," Stephanie replied.

Matthew walked past Jill, while she continued to contemplate her close brush with death, and said, "Since we have a game plan, it seems that I'll be getting some ass after we complete the mission after all," and walked away.

Moments after they left, an enemy convoy deploying countless enemy troops had arrived. They slowly walked into the museum, and came to a sudden halt, when they saw a number of their troops laying lifeless, completely mutilated, in dark, heavy pools of their own blood, knowing that it was the handiwork of the assassin. They continued to walk through the corpses that littered the floor, until they found the piece of paper, with the detailed sketch of their position, knowing that it was one of their own who divulged sensitive information, and quickly headed to the door.

03:43 HOURS. TOP SECRET MILITARY BASE, SOMEWHERE IN VIRGINIA:

They slowly and quietly crawled out of the manhole, and carefully walked towards the electrified fence.

"Careful, it may be electrified," Nina said softly.

"Let's test it," Kathy said softly, threw a pebble at its frame, and saw there was no reaction."

"Okay, we're good," Kassandra said.

"How are we gonna get in? It's like a damn fortress there," Janet whispered.

"It's so much ground to cover," Jonathan added.

"We can't come all this way just to turn back," Kassandra answered.

The assassin quickly pulled his blade from its sheath and swung it against the metal fence with one blow, creating a gap large enough for them to walk through right into the enemies' territory.

"Does that answer your question?" Kassandra answered.

"Time for plan C," Frank said, softly.

"What was that again?" Janet asked.

"We need disguises to blend in," Kassandra answered.

"How the hell are we gonna do that without calling any attention?" Jacqueline asked.

"These guard posts are awfully high to move around without being noticed."

Elaina walked towards the assassin and said, "We need to disguise ourselves. Can you help us?"

The assassin quickly moved through the enemy base under the complete cover of darkness, avoiding the searchlights, while the others stayed behind watching, until he arrived at the base of the guard post, and quickly climbed into it, tossing the body of a dead enemy soldier to the ground, while they waited nervously.

"Damn. That was quick," Matthew said.

"I told you not to worry," Kassandra replied.

"We need more," Jill said.

The assassin quickly climbed from the enemy guard post and calmly walked past them, scouting the area for any stragglers.

He snuck up after another unsuspecting enemy soldier, quickly grabbing him from behind, snapping his neck, dropping his body to the ground for the others to strip him from his clothes.

They froze in their tracks, seeing how efficiently the assassin disposed of his enemies, without the giant cloud of smoke that often camouflages his presence to unleash his deadly skills, without any shred of emotion.

Moments after quietly disposing of the enemy soldiers, they dressed in their clothes, and proceeded to begin their mission.

"Okay, we have our disguises. We know what to do. Everyone, split up," Adam whispered.

"Not yet," Kassandra answered.

"What do you mean, not yet? This was your plan in the first place," Adam answered.

"I know. I just need time to get dressed."

"But you had all this time to do it," Adam answered.

"It's cold, and I just needed somewhere more appropriate to do it."

"We'll try the guard tower," Adam answered.

"Too high. I can't climb that high."

"Okay. We all know what to do. Just move out," Adam ordered.

Kassandra waited for the others to move out, remaining with Adam, Elaina, and the assassin, and said, while she covered her chest, "No peeping. If I don't get undressed, we can't complete the mission."

"Stop talking and hurry," Elaina answered.

"Just hurry. You're wasting time," Adam answered, shaking his head.

After a brief moment, she was dressed in the enemy uniform. She picked up her lab coat and asked, "What do I do with this?"

"Why are you asking me?" Adam asked.

"I'll take care of it. The both of you get started. Adam and I will stay here and wait for your signal," Elaina answered, grabbing the clothes from Kassandra.

"Okay," Kassandra replied.

Elaina slowly walked towards the assassin and softly placed a kiss on his lips and said, "Just come back to me."

"He will. I promise," Kassandra replied.

"And I'll be here waiting," Elaina said to the assassin, slowly releasing her grip from his neck.

"We don't have much of a window. It's only a matter of time before we're discovered. Even if all of us are dressed in the enemies' clothing," Kassandra said.

Nina, Jacqueline, and Jill, slowly and nervously made their way through the base, slipping unnoticed by the enemy soldiers who patrolled the vicinity, and quickly slipped into the hangar, where a number of enemy planes were neatly packed in rows, and placed a charge into the section of the nose wheel.

Nina turned to Jill and said, "We need to place as many charges as you can," and said to Jacqueline. "I need you to keep watch outside, in case someone comes."

"Who put you in charge?" Jacqueline asked.

"No time to argue. Just do it," Jill answered.

Jacqueline took one last look at Nina, and slowly walked out with her back facing the door, keeping her eyes fixed on her.

"Thank you," Nina said.

"Don't mention it," Jacqueline answered.

An enemy guard was approaching the hangar and saw Jacqueline and walked past, saying, "Excuse me. Who are you?"

"I'm a new recruit," Jacqueline answered, smiling nervously.

He looked at the name on her uniform and said, "Haven't seen you before. Who are you really? And what's your real name?"

"The name is Chan," Jacqueline answered, watching Nina silently approaching the enemy soldier from behind, and continued, "Jacqueline Chan."

"Then why does the name on your uniform say Jameson? You're an intruder. Put your hands up now!" the enemy soldier said, pointing his rifle towards her.

Jacqueline slowly placed her hands above her head, and saw the enemy soldier pausing, falling flat on his face, from a single shot to his back from Nina's silenced rifle.

Jacqueline breathed a heavy sigh of relief and watched Nina slowly pointing her weapons downwards, with a frantic look on her face, and slowly pointed her hands downwards as she continued looking into Nina's eyes, nodding her head in gratitude.

"We've finished placing all the charges on all the planes and ordinances. And we need to hide the body before we get any unwanted attention. If you so choose, you can shoot me in the back, since you don't trust me," Nina said, lifting the soldier's dead body with Jill, leaving Jacqueline with a frantic look on her face.

Anton, Janet, and Jonathan slowly moved undetected through the enemy base while wearing the enemy uniform, placing charges on whatever transports they could find, when Janet suddenly called out softly, "Wait."

"God dammit. What is it now?" Anton asked.

"I have to pee," Janet answered.

"Seriously? You have to pee now, of all time? Are you serious right now?" Anton asked.

"Yeah, I'm serious. I'm sorry, but I can't hold it," Janet replied.

"Let's go, Min. We need to split up so we can cover more ground," Anton said, leaving Janet to tend to her needs.

"Agreed. I'll go left," Jonathan answered.

A brief moment after they left, an enemy soldier walked by, catching Janet in a compromising position, and said, "The General doesn't like anyone using the premises as their own personal restroom."

"Couldn't wait," Janet smiled nervously. "Nature calls."

"I can see that. What do you think he'd say if he heard of this?" the enemy soldier asked.

"If that's the case, I can't imagine him being too pleased," Janet answered, nervously.

"I was thinking that we could work something out," the enemy soldier answered.

"What do you have in mind?" she asked, knowing what he was thinking.

The enemy soldiers slowly unzipped his trousers and answered, "I'm sure you can use your imagination. We can start off with this and take it from there."

Janet stood up with her pants at her ankles and answered, "Why don't we skip the foreplay and head straight to business?"

"Sounds good to me. I'll worry about that another time," the enemy soldier said, smiling mischievously, when his smile suddenly vanished, as he slowly knelt on the snowy ground, falling face-first, exposing Anton's towering physique standing behind him, with the smoke rising from the barrel of his silenced weapon.

Janet took a sigh of relief and asked, "What took you so long?"

"What do you mean? You're the one holding us up."

"Turn around. No peeping." she said, pulling her pants up.

"Just hurry, before someone else sees you."

"Don't you dare tell anyone about this, you hear me?"

"What we need to do is to hide the body, so it won't attract any unwanted attention."

She gently grabbed Anton by his arm and said, "Promise me you won't tell anyone about this"

Anton glanced at her hand grabbing his arm, pulled it away, and responded, "In case you haven't noticed, we still have a mission to complete. Instead of worrying about yourself, or worrying about someone knowing that you took a piss, is too much information to give about your bush right now.

Besides, I've just seen first-hand how the General's forces treat women. It's a good thing that I'm here to bomb this place to hell, because I want no part of it."

"You have some nerves. I do shave, you know," she answered.

"Jonathan is somewhere out there, risking his life, for the sake of the mission. Let's just hope he's still alive."

"Don't tell anyone about this. Please," she begged, following Anton.

Jonathan continued to traverse through the enemy base, placing charges into the ammunition storage, and was soon joined by Janet and Anton.

Anton grabbed another charge, and said, "I need you to stand watch, while Jackson and myself finish up."

"Ok," Jonathan said, nervously walking out the door.

He stood guard for a brief moment, glancing around nervously, when an enemy soldier came by and asked, "Got a smoke? It's freezing and I can use one right about now."

"Trying to cut down. Too expensive to maintain," Jonathan answered, smiling nervously.

"I'm trying to cut down, myself. I haven't seen you around much," the enemy soldier said.

"I'm new to the war effort," Jonathan answered.

"I'm Kowalski," the enemy soldier said, introducing himself, shaking Jonathan's hand, and slowly fell to the snowy ground.

"And I'm death," Jonathan answered, panting nervously. "And just when I was getting to like him too."

"The both of you owe me for saving both your asses," Anton remarked.

"I thought you'd never get here. You don't know how much I was counting on you to get here and save my ass," Jonathan replied, still trying to catch his breath from almost being discovered.

They carried the lifeless body of the enemy soldier inside, hiding it, and quickly made their way back to Adam's position.

Frank, Kathy, and Matthew made their way towards the transport, placing as many charges as they could, when Frank suddenly said, "Wait. Matthew."

"What is it?" Matthew asked.

"I hear someone coming. Go on. We'll catch up."

"Shit," Kathy said. "What do we do?"

Frank tore her clothes open, showing off a glimpse of her cleavage, and said, "We need a distraction. Use what you got."

"You really picked a good time to take a peek."

"It's as good a time as any to make a fan club, starting with the new guy. Now go on. You need to distract him."

"Only because you asked so nicely," Kathy answered, and slowly walked towards the enemy soldier in a seductive manner, with her cleavage exposed tucked firmly in her bra, and her long, dark, stringy hair dropped to her shoulders.

As the enemy soldier patrolled the vicinity of the compound, he was immediately captivated by Kathy's alluring physique, and slowly walked towards her, with a look of shock on his face.

She slowly walked away into the column of trucks, signaling him to follow her, causing the enemy soldier to follow, as she led him into their carefully laid out trap.

She stopped and watched the enemy soldier coming closer to her, felt him grabbing onto her, and saw him falling onto the ground face-first.

She looked at the dead enemy soldier laying on the snow and said, "Took you long enough. I was praying that he would have the time to shag me before you arrive."

"I was just thinking."

"What?" Kathy said sharply, as she tried to button her clothes.

He opened her clothes and answered, "Maybe we didn't have to show him your rack, after all. We could've just killed him."

"And why are you telling me this now?" she asked.

"Just felt like it was a good idea at the time. Besides, I do have a soft spot for you."

"Well, you'd be pleased to know that it worked."

"I'm hoping after we get back, we can take our friendship to another level."

"I'll think about it," she said.

"Don't think too hard."

"First, we need to complete the mission," Kathy said, walking away.

Kassandra and the assassin slowly made their way to the General's quarters, in hopes of not being discovered by any patrolling enemy soldiers.

Kassandra saw a pair of high-ranking enemy soldiers guarding the door and said, "We can't afford to be detected," as they continued walking.

The assassin quickly drew his weapon and killed both the enemy soldiers with a single shot to their faces.

After they fell to the ground, Kassandra ran towards them, and quickly searched their pockets for the security clearance to open the door, and handed one to him to be activated simultaneously.

After they opened the door to the General's quarters, the assassin dragged their lifeless corpses inside, and cautiously made their way towards his sleeping quarters, with his weapon drawn, while Kassandra trailed closely from behind.

"His room should be over there," she said.

They walked towards the door, slowly opening it and walked in, gently closing the door from behind them.

"I'll search for the blueprints, you plant the charges," she whispered, and quickly began her frantic search for the blueprints.

After her vigorous search through the room, as the assassin continued placing charges all around it, she came up empty-handed, and said, "It's not here. Where could he be hiding it? This is a secure place. It's not here, all of a sudden. Can't just be coincidence. This is where it's supposed to be, unless he knew we were coming. He knows that he can't continue his war efforts without these blueprints. My God. He knew we were coming. We walked into a trap. We need to leave - now."

They were about to walk towards the door, when the assassin paused for a brief moment, seeing the silhouettes standing at the base of the door, realizing that their only way out was blocked by enemy soldiers, and heard the sounds of their weapons cocking, from behind its thick wooden structure that separated them, and quickly pushed Kassandra out of harm's way, when they were greeted with a deadly barrage of enemy bullets that tore through his armor, throwing him to the floor.

Kassandra felt her ears ringing loudly from the barrage of bullets, and after gaining her senses, quickly ran to the assassin's aid, while he laid bleeding from a number of the bullets that tore through his armor, trying to tend to his wounds, when she saw the General calmly strolled through the bullet-ridden door, accompanied by a number of high-ranking officers.

He smiled wickedly, and said in a soft and gentle tone, "Welcome to my Shangri-La. I was beginning to think that I was never going to see the both of you again. Frankly, I was beginning to think that these men were incompetent, which against him, they are, considering the nature of who he is. Today alone, you have caused me a great deal of trouble, leaving a number of my men slaughtered. Then again, I never expect anything less from the corp's most decorated soldier turned assassin along with the world's most brilliant scientists. Next to your father, of course."

"They all deserved it," Kassandra answered.

"They were good men with families that I've had the honor of serving with."

"All the people that you murdered in South America had families too, and so did one of your very own, when you put a bullet in his head, at the Pentagon. And the ones that you murdered the night you had us kidnapped! So many that you've sacrificed, for your senseless ambitions! So tell me, how do you justify trying to murder a seven-year-old girl?"

"This is war, unfortunately, my child," the General answered. "And advertently or inadvertently, many will be sacrificed. Unfortunately, it's the innocent who pay the most, I'm afraid."

"You're going to stand in front of me and say that? The way your troops were trying to kill everyone to get to me? The way you placed a 7 year-old girl in a coma after your soldiers came to murder a number of civilians who were just looking for a place to live? Well, you could've had me fooled! You had my entire family fooled, before your troops gunned my mother down during the uprising on Genesis, even after she welcomed you with open arms, even when my father wouldn't! And if that wasn't enough, you wanted my father to help your murderous war effort, and not to mention, how you robbed me of a whole decade of my life! Then again, that's all you do! Kill, steal, and destroy! You're like the devil in human form!"

The General took a deep breath, and said softly, with a small hint of remorse, "Contrary to what you think, I really do regret what happened to your family in Genesis. There isn't one day I don't think about it. For all of the people who got caught in the wake of the uprising, that inevitably led to the downfall of such a great place. There isn't a moment I don't think of your mother and all the pain that the ordeal I caused your father. But I was bound by my duty to my country at the time, and I couldn't let anything get in the way of that. Not even my love or friendship that I had for your father, unfortunately."

"Even murdering a defenseless young girl looking for a better life? Keep telling yourself that."

The General smiled and answered, "She may have been young. But she was anything but defenseless. She was one of many enemy soldiers who murdered some of our troops, while providing protection to one of the many war criminals who fled to Brazil, after fleeing the many crimes they committed against humanity, after the civil war that broke up of the former Soviet Union. We planned an air-, land-, and sea-born invasion to get him and bring him to justice for his many crimes, but under the command of this war criminal, they were well organized. That day, we lost a number of men. Good men from the hands of the local militia. There were so many of them. But even that couldn't stop us from completing our mission. We lost more of our men running through the slums, until he was apprehended and was finally handed to the

United Nations to face justice for all his many crimes against humanity. And there she was - a prisoner of war, and there he was defending her. Defending one of the many people who helped kill a number of our men. When I saw her in Genesis, I was convinced that she would try to sabotage all your father worked so hard to build."

"What made you any different from all the people that you hunted after committing all those crimes against humanity? Who was the one guilty of destroying what my father worked so hard to build? Who has been a war criminal for the past decade? Who was the one who planned a coup even behind cold prison walls, placing the country in a vicious power struggle, tearing it apart? So, my question to you is what makes you any different? You talk about bringing people to justice, and yet you escaped it, while serving your time. You are such a damn hypocrite."

"I truly never meant for that to happen to your family in Genesis, including all the loss of life. And for that, I'm truly sorry. It's not like I actually got out of bed one day and decided to stage a coup, either. But in life, everything has its course, and this is one of them."

"Well, it won't bring my family back. Or all the people you murdered, now, would it?"

"I know that. But I had a job to do. And there was an enemy soldier running unchecked in Genesis, and not to mention, she had attacked one of my own. And I couldn't let that happen again."

"She was just a young girl, orphaned from war! She didn't know any better! She didn't have the choices that you and I had! All she needed was just someone to give her guidance! She was only trying to change her life when she came to Genesis! And all that changed when one of your soldiers couldn't keep his manhood in his pants, and had nothing better to do but molest her. So yes, she was defenseless, up until his manhood was on the other end of her foot! Or maybe that's how you treat all your women in the armed forces! That they're just there for your amusement, and then you just discard them, after you've had your way! So that makes molesting a young girl out of her mind, right? Simply because he was one of your own? I know what you are! I did my research on you when you were in the Ivory Coast with my father! All the people that you murdered! You talk about bringing justice to everyone, but still you escaped it like the coward you really are, when you were supposed to pay for all the crimes that you committed against humanity! Even from the Ivory Coast, you were supposed to be rotting behind a jail cell."

"There isn't a single day that goes by that I don't think about what happened at the Ivory Coast and Genesis. That was most unfortunate. On that we can both agree. And sadly, it was from that point on that your father and myself went our separate ways. I really wish those things didn't happen to cause our friendship to stray. If I could've gone back to change our time in the Ivory Coast, I would. But I can't. All I can do is move forward, and try and forget the past. The strange thing is, I always knew we would go our separate ways, but never in my wildest dreams, I would've ever thought we would be fighting against one another. Your father had the capacity to be a great soldier. He was a lot tougher than he looked, and passed every grueling test with flying colors, but his only weakness on the field was that he couldn't bring himself to take another man's life, which in my book, based on the circumstances, is very admirable, knowing that the other man wants to take your life in return, and not lose a single night's sleep over it. He never fired a single shot. That's what made him stand out, more than all of us. He wasn't prepared to do what it took to win like the rest of us would do. In any and every given circumstance, he always maintained his sense of humanity. He was only trying to break the long cycle of who he was, of who he was meant to be. And me, on the other hand, am the complete opposite, I suppose."

"You're a murderer, no question about that. No matter what you do, you still find a way to sleep every night. What you called my father's greatest weakness was his greatest strength. You can never be the man he was and still is. He saved an entire country from being wiped out from an epidemic, while you only infect with death wherever you touch. The real cancer to humanity is you."

"That may be so. But I knew all the risks and consequences that often came with making all the hard choices. I suppose that the only thing left to do is to make peace with all that I've done. And no one said it was going to be easy. And believe me, it hasn't been," the General answered.

"You could've had me fooled," Kassandra answered.

"I never wanted any of this. Out of love and respect for your father, I kept you alive."

"So that should make me feel a whole lot better, after you came under the cover of night, as we slept, killed the others and kidnapped us, coercing us to do your bidding. You have a strange way of showing respect for my father."

"As I said, I always knew that your father and myself would go our separate ways. It was just a matter of when. Your father and myself had begun to patch things up after the Ivory Coast incident, up until the moment that your proud warrior and his colleagues had switched their allegiances to your father. And it was then, I knew that time had finally come for that to happen."

"Keep trying to convince yourself of that. We both know that you went your separate ways after you caused the deaths of all those innocent people in the Ivory Coast, and took the credit for all the lives he saved, including trying to murder that young girl in Genesis, causing the entire world to go in a state of unrest, that led us to the civil war."

"That's enough, Kassandra!" he yelled. "You know nothing about the Ivory Coast! You think the research that you did on Genesis tells you the whole truth? I had tremendous respect for your father, and his research!"

"Did I strike a nerve?" she said softly.

"No one would have accomplished what he did in the history of modern medicine!"

"So you took credit for all he did? How could you even sleep at nights knowing that you were responsible for the deaths of all those civilians? Killing a woman and her infant son, and unborn child? Why don't you face the truth about yourself? Everything you touch dies! Everywhere you go, death follows! Everything you touch turns to shit!"

"Stop it! Who are you to judge me? Considering what happened on that fateful day, it served you very well, didn't it?"

"What do you mean?" she asked with a puzzled look on her face.

"Let's just say that if it weren't for that incident that happened when that pregnant woman and her son got killed, during the airstrike, you would've never been conceived. Did you ever stop to think about that?"

A sudden look of shock suddenly grew over Kassandra's face, after hearing the General's cryptic comment, and answered, "What do you mean?"

The General looked back in a state of shock that suddenly came over her face, and answered, "He never told you the truth, did he? After all this time, he kept the truth away from you."

"What truth? What are you talking about?"

He looked into her eyes, and answered, "I've seen that look more times to know that you had suspected something was amiss with your father, when you were on Genesis. I saw that very same look you gave after we made it back to Genesis, after your father removed the remaining shrapnel while tending to my wounds, after being saved by the People's Liberation Forces in South America. You knew something then. I saw it in your eyes, and he saw it too, but your mother missed it, thinking that it was only his anger against me after all these years. I suppose that he wished that I had died in Peru. Maybe if I were in his shoes, I'd have felt the same way. Then again, you're your father's daughter. Not much can get past you, Kassandra. The word smart is not a word that could describe you. It's beyond an understatement. It was from that point I knew that you suspected something, so you went and did your research. Clever girl. Maybe one day, if the both of you were to ever be reunited - and I do mean if - he'll tell you everything you need to know to connect the dots of all the details that you may have missed."

"We will be one day. I promise you," she answered.

"And how would you plan to do that with your bodyguard bleeding on my floor after being pumped with a hundred holes inside him? All that's left to do is to put one more between the eyes to put him out of his misery."

"If he can't find a way, then I will."

"That's why I always liked you, Kassandra. For someone who lived most of her life being sheltered, you always had spunk. You're stronger and smarter than you look. With all that tenacity, you should've been a soldier yourself."

"I am a soldier," she answered.

The General smiled and answered, "It would appear so, since you're all dressed in our soldiers' uniforms, and broke into my quarters. Might I add, I saw my 2 soldiers' bodies lying on the floor on my way in. Good work to both of you. But it wasn't good enough. You left a blood trail. I could only surmise that you were here for only one reason. And that's to procure these," he said, holding the blueprints of Kassandra's work in the air. "If you want it so badly, you can have it."

"You're just giving it to me?" she asked in awe, gently grabbing the blueprints.

"Why not? It's what you went through all the trouble coming here for, isn't it?"

She thought for a brief moment and asked, "What did you do?"

"I put all of what you gave me into practical application. After all, I can't imagine you giving it to me for any other reason. Did you? None of this would've been possible if it weren't for you. You truly are your father's daughter. You did something that your father would have only dreamed about doing to the human genome. Absolutely brilliant. My other scientific minds are doing everything to put it to practical application as we speak."

"My God," Kassandra said. "You don't mean that. You don't know what you're doing. You need to stop, before it's too late."

"On the contrary, I do. Now that I've broken the back of General West's entire carrier fleet, I intend to finish every remaining pocket of enemy resistance, starting with him. The rebels put on a very spirited effort. Outmanned and outgunned. Mere civilians turned soldiers, against battle hardened marines and ex-convicts. Still, they held out for 10 long years. I underestimated him, I admit. I underestimated them. For someone who served under my command, I take my hat off to him. I truly wished it didn't have to be this way, but unfortunately, it ends now, with all my new creations."

"And what about him?" she asked. "Are you just going to toss him to the side, after he took a bullet for you? Just like you slaughtered all these soldiers in Peru after they surrendered?"

A fit of anger grew over the General's face. "I gave him a choice!"

"The truth hurts, doesn't it?"

"He had a promising career ahead of him! And what did he do? He chose the enemy over his brothers! The very same brothers whom he took the oath to fight with and protect our country! Our freedoms!"

"Freedoms? In case reality slipped past you, you're the one who imposed martial law on the entire country! No one here is free! He did the right thing because he saw there was no honor in killing a defenseless young girl! Unless killing defenseless goes in the new norm of God and country. Well, that night, God came first!"

"And look where he placed the both of you. Right back where you started, in the very same clutches of the one that captured you. And starting with him, is the beginning of the end of what's left of your resistance."

"You were a good man once. How do you sleep at nights knowing that you have all this blood on your hands, using the research that my father created to save lives? You turned his research into a weapon."

"Desperate times call for desperate measures unfortunately. Again, I really had to make some hard choices. Time and time, they drove us back, time and time we did the same thing to them. It just seemed like there was no end. Yes, it's true that we spilled the blood of countless of our brothers, but in the end, they were worthy adversaries."

"You talk but you don't hear yourself. Is that how you justify taking away his humanity, and using him to kill all the ones who served under your command? Is that how you justify taking the lives of all those people in South America? They were there for you, like my father was in Africa and Genesis, before you destroyed everything they had, and now you call them adversaries. Why don't you just admit it's just who you are? All you do is destroy. You're the supreme ruler of a broken nation, and more than ever, you're less of a man than you ever were."

"You talk about a good game about humanity. But what makes you different from me?

The last I checked, your proud warrior was your creation. It was your hand that weaponized a great soldier, who laid waste to countless others."

"He always was a good soldier. And he realized that when he and the others switched their allegiances to my father. It was you who turned him into a killer, so don't try to shift the blame on me. You know that you didn't leave me with much of a choice."

"There's always a choice, Kassandra."

"Like what? Turn him into the monster that he is, or let him die?"

"Maybe the next option would have served you better, considering all he did during the last decade."

"I couldn't let him die and you know it. You took that choice from me the moment you put me in that predicament to choose, between saving his life, or turning him."

"What makes you think that you're more inclined to be more loyal to him than the very others who risked their lives evacuating your family from Genesis, just the same? But instead, you chose this one. And because of your hand, he snuffed out the others. The very ones who he saved, running through air strikes, a hail of enemy bullets, whisking them away on his shoulders, dragging them to safety, but in the end, he snuffed them out, all the same. Well, minus General West, of course. You saved a single soldier for the price of 10 others. Well, almost 10. Now tell me, what kind of odds are those, saving one life, only to take the life of so many others, who were a band of brothers?"

"I could ask the same about you. You chose him over the others to carry out your sick, twisted ambitions."

"In this case, the answer to your question is simply because he was the best of all of them. And all I want around me is the best. Who better to have on your side than him? At the time, that is," the General said, softly.

"You knew I couldn't let him die. Not after all he'd done for me and my father. He is the only one who came back and stuck his neck out for me. It was the only choice that you left me with, and you know it."

"Since you keep insisting on me not giving you a choice, it was the very same predicament that those rebels in Peru left me in. After playing this war game for so long, I realized the signs when I arrived at the airfield. The message was clear to all of us, after they'd demanded his release, I realized that the only way was to fight our way out. After all, you were there."

"But after you won, you could've still saved them."

"I think we both know that if I had those soldiers alive, they would shoot me in the back, while I boarded that plane to the mainland. So, for the same reason you couldn't let him die, it was the same reason I couldn't let them live, or have any witnesses."

"I would've testified against you. Would you've killed me too?"

"No I wouldn't. Just find another use for you, like I did during the war."

"You mean robbing me of my youth? Like you robbed him of his mind?"

"Well, the both of you would be of more use to me alive than dead. But, since I am on the verge of modifying the other 6, one of you is obsolete. I'm afraid that he has lost his usefulness. Too bad he couldn't be one of them."

"General, please," Kassandra begged. "Don't do this. If my father's research weaponizes those soldiers, there's no telling what might happen. You can't do this."

"It's already being done, I'm afraid. This great country of ours will be rebuilt in my image, and an entire race of super soldiers will soon be under my control, and I owe it all to you, Kassandra. Now, you have just as much blood on your hands as mine, or soon will. Either way, my victory will be complete, and this great country of ours will be under my complete control, from the Capitol Building, down to the last blade of grass. The night we found you worked out even better for the war effort than anticipated."

"What do you mean?"

"Being the man that your father was, he would've never done what I asked, even at the risk of killing him. And that's one thing that'd be the hardest for me to live with. His character, his selflessness is unmatched. He's truly a great man, but his resolve could be very stubborn. But you, on the other hand, inherited everything from him, and proven to be very clever and resourceful, like him, since you made it this far, but you lack his resolve. I could never make him do what you did. Despite whatever secrets that he may have hidden from you and your mother, his hands are clean. Believe me when I say, I truly couldn't have done it without you. I really mean that," the General said. "Oh, and one more thing before I put a bullet to his head. Thank you so much for bringing the remainder of General West's rebels to their deaths within the walls of my Shangri-La. You saved me a lot of work, bringing the lambs back to their own slaughter."

"How did you know?" she asked, with a hint of surprise on her face.

"I could give you a million answers right now. But for now, I'll do myself some good by savoring this moment of finally capturing the ones giving me so much trouble."

"Who told you?"

"I knew since you drew those plans you would try to stop me at some point. It was just a matter of when."

"What was that?" she asked.

The General reached into his pocket and pulled out a piece of crumpled paper with a rough sketch of the base and answered, "The second convoy of my troops had just missed you by a few seconds after you left. As they combed through your last location, trying to locate you, all they found was a trail of corpses your trusting guardian left in his wake, and this, and naturally they reported it. So we prepared for your arrival, and all your other guests, of course. After all, it's rude to keep our guests waiting."

"My God," Kassandra said softly.

"Didn't it strike you as odd that the electrified fences were deactivated? So the next thing to do was just to let you walk in, and wait for the next indication that you were in my neck of the woods. And when I saw a number of my tracking beacons going offline, almost all at once, I knew my prodigal son had returned, only this time, he will not be going back. And neither will your newfound friends."

"They're all going to die," Kassandra said softly, with a sudden frantic look on her face.

"And one more thing. We also detected the tracking beacon of our traitor pilot, still transmitting. That's how we were able to get a lock on your location, since you had yours and his removed."

"It makes sense now. My God," Kassandra pondered that Nina's transmission wasn't extracted.

"That one tracking that you forgot all about was your very undoing, or as the proverbial saying goes, "The nail in your coffin." More like theirs, to be exact. Just imagine, this place will be their final resting place. No more resistance, and the country is finally under my control after 10 years of all this fighting. And I thought that I might do right by you to tell you that, eventually, the traitor pilot will be captured as well, and I'll make her death as painful as possible, until she begs me to end her life. And on that note, it's been a pleasure chatting with you my dear. The time has come for me to retire."

"They're gonna kill them. I must try and save them," Kassandra said softly to herself, trying to figure a way to escape her captivity.

The General slowly rose to his feet and knelt in front of the wounded assassin, watching the severity of his wounds from all the bullets that penetrated his armor into his body, while he laid helplessly on the floor in a pool of his blood, and said, "I'm truly sorry, old friend. I wished it didn't have to be this way. Please forgive me for doing what I'm about to do."

"You're about to end his life, and now you're saying that you're sorry?"

"In war, sacrifices have to be made. And unfortunately, it has to be some of our own. That's what your father never understood. As I said, he could never make the hard choices."

"My father was and will always be a man of integrity. It's one thing that he will never sacrifice, because he was never a power-hungry egomaniac like you! His integrity and appreciation for human life is worth more than any amount of power than anyone can have, even more than controlling an entire country! He always looked at life as something precious and could never be replaced, unlike someone like you who treats it with contempt and just discards it like it's expendable!"

"We all choose our destinies in life, and he made his, as I made mine. Sometimes, it chooses us to be the villain, even when we never ask to be."

The assassin looked at Kassandra, gave a weak, timid smile, and tried to sit upright, grinning his teeth from the sharp, stabbing pain that continued to persist from the severity of the wounds that tore into his body.

A sudden look of shock quickly enveloped over Kassandra's face, seeing him smiling, after all these years, and vividly recalled the last time he was constantly tortured by the enemy forces, realizing that he was about to play his last desperate act to complete his mission.

She looked at the General and said, "Well played, General. You win."

"What's he doing?" the General asked.

"You said he's been a worthy adversary. Surely, you can give him that. Before you kill him, you can at least show him some respect. The proper respect that he deserves.

You can at least shake his hand. After all, you're the leader of an entire country. A tiny handshake won't kill you."

"Fair enough," the General answered.

The assassin continued to remain upright with Kassandra supporting him, while he continued to bleed heavily from his wounds, with his hand extended to the General. The assassin gripped it tightly with a diabolical smile on his face, and pressed the detonator, causing the confined of the General's quarters to burst into flames, and falling over Kassandra, shielding her from the from the force of the blast, with the giant wall of flames and flaming debris rushing towards them, with much force that the walls throughout his entire quarters quickly crumbled, severely damaging the door of reinforced steel, prying it open.

Adam suddenly came under attack from the enemy soldiers, when he saw the General's quarters suddenly erupted in a giant ball of flame, and quickly gave the order to set off all the other charges to distract them and cover their escape, killing and injuring all those caught up in the vicinity of the explosion, giving them time to escape, as the entire base became consumed in flames from all their resources being destroyed from their carefully laid out trap.

After falling to the ground from the force of all the destruction around them, the surviving enemy soldiers remained distracted, and picked themselves up from the snowy ground filled with shrapnel and debris scattered all around them, and ran over to the general's quarters.

Adam watched the General's quarters burning and said, "My God, they're trapped inside."

"Oh no," Elaina said in shock, looking at the General's quarters burning, knowing Kassandra and the man she loved were still trapped inside, and began to run towards the General's quarters. She was suddenly grabbed by Adam, holding her back.

"We need to leave! There's nothing we can do for them! We need to leave now!" he said, and made their escape amidst all the pandemonium, while the enemy position continued to burn.

The hangars, ammunition depots, and a number of enemy transports suddenly erupted into the enemy compound, causing more panic among the enemy soldiers, giving them more time to escape, while the enemy soldiers remained distracted from more of the chaos that continued to be ensued in the vicinity.

Moments after the blast, Kassandra awoke in the burning building, with the assassin slumping lifelessly over her, as she was completely disoriented with her ears ringing loudly from the roar of the blast, and struggled to shove the dead weight of his body off her. She nudged him continuously to see if he would respond, but to no avail, and carefully began to make her way out of the rubbles of the burning building, and turned back one last time to look at him.

A number of soldiers scurried towards the flaming wreckage of the General's quarters, and saw her fleeing the scene.

She pointed in the direction of the General's burning quarters, and said, "The General's still trapped inside! I'll go and get more help!"

They tried as much as they could to extinguish the flames, until they found the body of the assassin, confusing him with the General.

After moments of remaining unconscious, he slowly regained his senses, after realizing that he was he was being carried from the General's burning quarters. He waited until he was at a safe distance, and mustered as much of his strength as he could, and swung his blade wildly, killing them, and stumbled out of the burning building, while it continued burning.

He continued stumbling through the base undetected, limping as quickly as he could, while the other enemy troops remained distracted, searching for the General amidst all the debris, while using his trusty blade for support, until he came to the manhole, saw the heavy metal lid was slightly shifted to the side, and tried as much as he could to uncover it, while the excruciating pain and the heavy bleeding from his wounds severely drained whatever strength he had left, when he suddenly felt someone grabbed him from behind, causing him to quickly draw his blade in defense.

"It's me, It's me," Jason said, feeling the assassin's blade to his neck. "I'm only trying to help you."

The assassin looked at Jason's bruised face that occurred from their last ruse, and slowly loosened the grip of his blade from Jason's neck and nodded his head. Jason quickly gathered his strength, pulled the thick metal cover of the manhole, and said, "Leave now before we get spotted. I'll keep in touch.

Now go."

The assassin slowly began to descend, and gently grabbed Jason's arm and nodded his head to show his gratitude.

"You're welcome. Now you need to leave. You're no good to the resistance if you're captured and executed. We'll meet again," he said, covering the hole, and ran back to assist the soldiers in continuing the blaze that consumed all the vital positions around the base.

05:49 HOURS. U.V.A. MEDICAL CENTER - CHARLOTTESVILLE, VIRGINIA:

After their long trek through the underground tunnels, Adam and the others had arrived safely in the hospital, where the others waited, greeting them nervously with their weapons to their faces.

"We're back," Adam said, pointing his hands up.

Elaina separated herself from the others, sobbing endlessly after losing the man she loved, while Adam tried consoling her, saying, "Our mission was a success because of them. Their sacrifice was not in vain."

A sudden sadness fell over them as they bowed their heads in silence at the fall of their comrades, when Nina suddenly looked at the palm of her hands, all covered in blood.

Kassandra rushed into the lobby thickly covered in dust from the debris of the blast, with the strong odor of smoke saturated into her clothes, startling them.

Elaina was startled seeing Kassandra completely disheveled in her dusty clothes and strong stench of smoke, and asked, "Did he make it? Is he outside?"

Kassandra took a deep breath and answered softly, placing her hands on Elaina's shoulder, "I'm so sorry."

"I just need to be alone," Elaina answered, while she wept after losing the only man that she ever loved.

"I understand. They'll be here soon. I must warn the others," she said softly.

"Oh my God," Nina said softly, falling on the floor, with the palm of her hands covered in her blood.

"What's wrong?" Matthew asked, in a state of panic.

I'm bleeding. That explains why I've been feeling so strange. I'm feeling so cold all of a sudden."

Matthew took off his shirt, and wrapped it around her to try and keep her warm, while Brian placed pressure on her wound, to help contain the bleeding.

"Turn her over!" Kassandra said, examining her back and said, "There's no exit wound! The bullet is still inside! Fortunately, it didn't puncture anything vital. She's losing a lot of blood! We need to get her into the I.C.U. and have her prepped for surgery!"

"You need to change into clean clothes. I'll handle it," Brian answered.

Matthew quickly lifted Nina off the floor and rushed her into the emergency room, while Brian continued to keep pressure on her wound to help contain the bleeding.

"They attacked us. How did they know we were there?" Adam asked.

"Nina's tracking beacon was still active. We forgot to have it extracted, after she was captured. That means before we came to this place, they may have locked onto it long enough to track us. But with all the interference and the damage that we caused at the base, it'll be a while before they recover," Kassandra replied.

"I hope so," Janet answered.

"He didn't make it, did he?" Jill asked.

Kassandra looked at Elaina sobbing quietly by herself, and simply nodded her head, feeling her friend's sadness.

"No one could've done what the both of you did. Thanks to you, all of us can live to fight another day," Jacqueline said softly.

"Look at her, Adam. It's been so long she's been by herself. She's been through so much and lost the only good thing that she ever had, because of me. I should've listened to you. All I did was get the only man that she loved killed, and at the same time, got Nina hurt. There are no amount of words that I can say to comfort her right now. I've been so unfair to her, just because all I thought about was myself."

"It's because of you we saved more lives. The General can no longer use your father's research as a weapon."

"I wish that were true. We were too late."

"What?" Arianna answered in shock.

"We were too late in stopping him. He already weaponized the others."

"This is not happening," Nicole said. "All this planning was for nothing."

"We're all doomed," Brandon said softly, slumping his back in the chair.

"I need to get clean clothes for Nina's operation," Kassandra said softly, looking at Elena, who continued sobbing quietly, while she sat by herself.

Moments later, Kassandra came out dressed in her usual attire of a gleaming white lab coat over her clothes.

She entered the room where Nina rested, and asked, "How's she doing?"

"She's lost a lot of blood. She's barely here. She's very weak, and in a lot of pain, after I took the bullet out. Fortunately, the plating in her uniform minimized the impact.

And here's the transmitter. This is how they were tracking us," David said, handing it over to Kassandra.

She watched the transmitter covered in Nina's blood, gently deactivating it, and walked over to her bed, and said, "I'm sorry for what happened."

"It wasn't your fault. It was worth the risk," Nina replied, while she laid on the bed, feeling the excruciating pain from her wound.

"You need to save your strength. You need to rest, and let the serum finish its course," Kassandra answered.

"Okay. I'm ready," Nina said, nodding her head.

Kassandra slowly pulled out the vial of serum from her pocket, and injected a tiny dose into Nina's arm. She watched it quickly take its course, placing Nina in a deep sleep and said, "I need all of you to join me in the waiting room. I seriously doubt that you won't like what I have to say."

She walked into the waiting room where Elaina continued crying and walked over to her, gently tapping her on her shoulder, and said, "We're having a meeting in the lobby. Can you come?"

"I just need to be alone right now," she answered sharply.

"I understand. I'll see you later," Kassandra said, and slowly walked away.

She slowly walked to the waiting area where the others waited, and paused for a brief moment, looking for a way to explain the failure of their mission.

"I've seen that look on your face enough to see that something is wrong. We're not gonna make it, are we?" Stephanie asked.

"Did you kill the General, at least?" Brandon asked.

"After we took out his position, there may be a 50-50 chance that he may have survived. It's hard to tell. All I know is that we were too late in trying to procure the blueprints," she answered softly.

"We don't know anything. Is that what you're saying?" Frank asked.

"I'm afraid so. They knew we were coming before we even got there."

"But how?" Jill asked.

"Just after we left the museum, another convoy had arrived. And it appears that they were honing on Nina's tracking beacon all along. They found a piece of paper with the layout that she drew, so they set a trap for us by deactivating the electric fence, and let us get close enough to ambush us. Fortunately for us, we had a well-planned exit strategy. He knew that after my escape, I would try and retrieve my father's work, so he waited until 0-7 and myself were separated, so he could cut us off from you. And it almost worked too," Kassandra answered.

"And not to mention, our best soldier didn't make it," Daniel added.

"Now, do you think it was worth it?" Janet asked.

"You just signed our death warrant. And the sad thing is that we helped you do it. I should've known this shit wouldn't work," Tiara added.

"Either way, they'll be looking for us," Kassandra said softly. "I just had to try and stop them from turning my father's research into a weapon."

"And look where it got us," Kathy answered.

"If only I had gotten there sooner," Kassandra answered softly.

"I told you this shit was a bad idea. We all did," Janet remarked.

"All you did was to give us the best fighting chance of getting killed in your plan," Jill replied.

"Okay, that's enough, all of you! What we need to do is to stop pointing fingers at each other! We're all being hunted, whether we took the fight to the enemy or not! We tried, and didn't work out the way we planned! None of this is her fault! She knew the risks and placed herself in harm's way just like the rest of us, and unfortunately, one of us paid the ultimate price for his sacrifice! But fortunately, we were able to escape, so we can fight another day! We must keep fighting! And what we need is a plan!" Adam yelled.

"You heard what she said, General West. If they used her father's research as a weapon against us, we won't be able to stop them. We don't even know whether we killed the General or not," Tiara answered, in a low defeated tone.

"Yes, Edwards. I heard. We all did, and that's what we tried to stop. But unfortunately, we were all too late," Adam answered softly.

"Up until a year ago, I saw our soldiers bring the fight to the enemy without suffering a single casualty, and we all cheered! Up until yesterday, we lost our entire fleet, and so many good men and women were lost in an instant, and now you're ready to tear each other down! I know you're all afraid, and I'd be a liar to tell you that I wasn't! But the fact remains that we're all that stand in their way, until we can strengthen our numbers! She put herself in harm's way to complete her mission - our mission - no different from us! Her mission was no different from ours! She risked being captured again! What we need to do at this point is to dig in deep and find another way to defeat the enemy! These other 6 soldiers may be genetically modified, by her father's research but it doesn't mean they're invincible! I'm not proud of seeing young men and women go to their deaths, but this is war and sacrifices have to be made, and eventually consumes us! What happened out there could've happened to any of us, at any given time, and mind you, it will if we just sit back and let it happen! Maybe we stirred up a hornet's nest not getting the job done, but with all the havoc that we caused, it showed the enemy how dangerous we can be with our backs against the wall! And if we're fortunate, it will buy us more time until our numbers grow stronger, because our best weapon at this point is our courage, because surrender at this point is no option! I've embraced the fact that I may die in this war someday, but if or when I meet my last moments, I'll do so fighting! We can't stay alive if we fight amongst ourselves! Our only hope for holding out is to put our thoughts together, and come up with a plan! We may not have skills as an assassin, but we're soldiers, and more dangerous as a small platoon than an entire regiment, and like it or not, we're all that's left to salvage what's left of a possible future, so I suggest we act like soldiers!" he concluded, and watched Elaina making her way out of the doors of the hospital into the streets.

Kassandra began to follow her, and felt a gentle touch from Adam touching her on her shoulder, getting her attention, and shook his head, asking her to stay back.

Adam looked at their faces, as they sat among themselves in deep contemplation, uncertain whether he had lifted their morale of the others, as the confines of the lobby of the hospital remained eerily quiet, watching their long, sad faces, filled with doubt.

Matthew slowly arose from his seat and walked towards Nina's room, with his mind still filled with doubt about the success of their mission.

He opened the door and saw she had awakened from her brief slumber, still feeling the effects of the medicine that continued to course through her veins, and asked with a smile, "Awake so soon?"

"Too numb to sleep. I can't feel any part of my body," she said, smiling.

He walked into the room and stood next to her bed and gently kissed her on her lips, and said, "I always wanted to do that."

"Is that the best you can do?" she replied.

"Oh, I can do a lot better than that."

"I'm not getting any younger, you know," she said, smiling.

He bowed his head over to her face, gently kissing her, while she caressed the brown skin of his face, covered in stubbles.

"I'm glad you're okay," he answered.

"It'll take more than that to stop me. But first, I need to get out of this bed."

"You're still too weak," Matthew answered.

"More depressed staying in here than weak," she said, lifting herself off the bed.

"Wrap your arms around my neck," he said, lifting her off the bed.

"Just so you know, you already swept me off my feet."

"Wouldn't hurt to do it again."

"I won't stop you," she said.

He carried Nina to the lobby where all the others waited in silence, with spirits hanging by a thread, and gently placed her on one of the chairs, and sat next to her, holding her closely.

Jacqueline walked towards her and gently grabbed her hand, shaking it, and said softly, "I know how difficult it was for you. I just want you to know how sorry I am for all the things that I said, and to thank you for saving me back there, and for all you've done."

"Don't mention it," Nina answered softly, shaking her hand.

"I never thanked you for saving me either. For saving all of us," Jill said, walking closer. "You could've taken all of us out when you were in that plane, but you didn't. That's more courage than I can give you credit for. And I speak for all of us when I say that. Thank you."

"You returned the favor when you captured me. We're even now. All that matters is that we're on the same side now."

"We're here if you need us," Jill concluded walking away, and patted Matthew on his shoulder.

Kassandra remained consumed by her guilt, knowing that she was totally responsible for Elaina losing the one thing that Elaina loved most, watching her crying hysterically in the narrow, dimly lit corridors of the decrepit walls of the hospital.

She walked towards Elaina and said, placing her hand on her shoulder, "I'm so sorry. I should've listened."

"It's too late for that now. There's nothing that any of us can do to bring him back. He's gone now, and I have to make peace with it. He was a soldier until the end. He died doing his job."

"Is there anything I can do?"

"I don't feel like talking right now. I'd just like to be alone," Elaina said, walking away.

"Okay, I understand. I'll be inside if you need me," Kassandra said, feeling Elaina's pain.

Kassandra walked back into the warmth of the hospital corridors with a complete feeling of helplessness, watching her only friend through the transparent front doors of the hospital, standing by herself in the bitter cold, knowing that Elaina felt bitter resentment towards her for causing the only man that she loved to die on their mission.

Eliana remained standing in front of the door with her eyes closed, completely filled with tears, as the cold bitter winds confront her alluring physique, sighing deeply from the pain of losing the man she loved, when she was suddenly startled from the almost dead and heavy weight of someone falling on top of her, pushing her to the ground.

She pushed him away from on top of her, with a sudden look of shock on her face, trying to come to her senses, and sat upright, looking at her hands and clothes all covered thickly in blood, and stared at the wounded figure in shock, slowly turning him over, noticing it was 0-7. "Oh my God, you made it."

She checked his vital signs, noticing his pulse was very faint and ran inside as quickly as she could, and suddenly came to a stop where all the others remained in deep contemplation about the failure of their mission, catching their attention, gazing back at her face and clothes all drenched in assassin's blood, and shouted, "He's here! He's made it! He's outside!"

"Who?" Arianna asked with a sudden look of shock on her face.

"It's him! He's alive! He's outside, and he's hurt badly! We don't have much time! We need to hurry!"

"Are you sure?" Kassandra asked.

"Yes, it's him! He's lost a lot of blood and needs our help!" Elaina answered, wiping the tears from her eyes.

"You heard what she said! Let's go!" David yelled.

"Thompson and Martinez, have the emergency room prepped and ready for surgery!"

"Okay, General West," Brian replied, running to the emergency room.

"I'll come with you," Arianna said.

They rushed outside to the wounded assassin's aid and saw the armor that protected his body completely riddled with bullets, covered thickly in blood, and quickly picked him off the floor.

"My God," Adam said, looking at the state of the assassin, and asked with a frantic look on his face, "Do you think he can still be saved?"

"There are 6 more like him, Adam! For the sake of my father's work, I must try! He's the only hope for us staying alive, and me not being captured!

And I'm not going back! I have to try!"

"Okay," Adam said, softly.

"We need to get him inside!" Kassandra said, quickly grabbing him by his bloody clothes, causing her hands to slip. She peered at her hands in disbelief, seeing how much they were completely drenched in his blood, causing her hope to diminish.

Barely clinging to life, he opened his eyes with his vision completely blurred from the extent of his injuries, seeing their images of all the others all around him, as they shouted in panic, while rushing to save his life, while they frantically carried him to the emergency room for surgery.

"He's lost a lot of blood, but still showing signs of life! He's barely alive, and we need to hurry if we're going to save him!" Kassandra shouted.

They rushed him into the emergency room where Elaina waited. Eliana gently grabbed Kassandra's arm with a frantic look on her face, and asked, "Is he going to make it?"

Kassandra paused for a brief moment, and answered, "We'll do all we can to save him."

"Save him, please," she said, softly.

"I'll do the best I can. I promise."

"He's the best thing that ever happened to me," she said.

"I know. If I must save him, I need to get going. The sooner we begin to operate, the sooner we can save him. I'll let you know how everything turns out."

"Okay," Elaina answered, softly.

Kassandra rushed into the emergency room when Arianna handed her a scrub before she began operating. She showed Arianna her hands thickly covered in blood and said, "Too late to change into anything else. We can't waste any more time. We need to get started. Now, what do we have?"

"Multiple bullet wounds," Brian answered.

"He's lost a lot of blood. And if he continues losing, he could go into shock," Arianna replied.

"No exit wounds. Fortunately, his armor plate stopped a number of them. But, the ones that got through caused a lot of trauma to a number of vital organs. The man is a living, breathing human sprinkler. Surprised to see he's still alive after all this. He took quite a barrage, and not to mention, he survived an explosion. I don't know anyone who came back from that. Despite all his skills, he's still human, after all," Brian answered.

"Yes, he is. That part of him is still intact. He just doesn't know it. If it weren't for him, none of us would be here," Kassandra replied, pulling one of the enemy bullets from his naked body, dropping it into the metal tray next to his bed.

"I know that, and for that, I'm most thankful. We all are. And I must say that the job you did back there, even if you didn't succeed, was still a hell of a job," Brian answered.

"Unfortunately, the rest of you have a funny way of showing it," Kassandra answered, pulling out another bullet from his body, while medicating his wounds, as Brian and Arianna wiped the blood from his body with a thick patch of gauze.

"Could you blame them for being afraid of him, or the enemy forces, considering the fact that you were too late? After all they've seen, and all you said that the General was planning?" he asked.

"I guess not," she answered.

Arianna watched the tray and saw the amount of bullets coated with the assassin's blood, and watched in awe, wondering how he was still alive, and said, "We've taken all the bullets out. What's next?"

"I need a blood pack. I've analyzed his cells. Thankfully he's another universal donor, like Daniel."

"What if he wasn't?" Daniel asked.

"Then after we supply him with another blood type, the serum would protect him from any symptoms. Either way, he can be cured, but it would work better, and faster, if the blood type was a match," Kassandra said.

"Here's the blood pack," Arianna said, handing Kassandra the blood pack.

"We need to close the wound. He's weak and has lost a lot of blood. What we need to do now is replace it."

She injected his vein with a needle, and watched the blood run through the tube into his veins for a brief moment. She injected a large dosage of the serum into his veins to speed up his recovery.

"What's next?" Arianna asked.

"There's nothing else we can do. All we have to do now is to let the medicine take its course. We need to let him rest. Let's hope we were in time to save him," Kassandra answered.

They walked out of the operating room, and headed into the lobby where the others waited impatiently in complete silence, with their hands and clothes heavily soiled in his blood.

Elaina walked slowly towards Kassandra and asked, "How's he doing?"

"He's still alive, but barely holding on. He's lost a lot of blood, and we've done all we can to stop the bleeding. His vital signs have become stable, but it's still much too soon to tell how his body will react to it. After replacing all the blood that he lost, I used quite a bit of the serum to accelerate the healing process. He took a hell of a beating, not to mention survived an explosion. Him still being alive is nothing short of a miracle. He's still alive after making it this far. He should've bled out after making it through that long passage all the way back. He's resting right now. I'm optimistic he'll pull through."

"Thank you so much," Elaina said, hugging Kassandra tightly, with a renewed sense of hope.

"You're welcome. After all he's done for me, it's the least I could do. I'm just glad that I can help."

Adam walked towards Kassandra and said, "You're just like your father. You've got great courage just like him, and even more than I can give you credit for. And he would've been proud of what you did today, and what you're still willing to do to help the war effort, even if defeat is looming over us, staring us in the face. Even if things don't go the way we planned, that was a hell of a job you did back there."

"Thanks. I appreciate it. And I never had a chance to thank you for what you did for my father on Genesis, and serving under his command after all these years. And it means more to him that you're taking care of me. And that means even more to me."

"Your father is a good man, Kassandra. He accomplished what so many people before him had failed to. He never thought about himself. He always thought about others first. He was the most selfless person that I knew. And still is. It made me look deep into myself that maybe I was fighting on the wrong side all along. And for all the wrong reasons, maybe. I see why he protected you all these years. It's because he saw that same strength in you, since you're his only legacy to continue his work to benefit mankind. The day of the uprising on Genesis, the choice to switch our allegiance to your father came easy for some reason. It just felt like it was the right thing to do. And I just wanted to say that it was a real honor serving with you, like it was with your father, in case I don't make it back."

"Thank you, Adam. That means a lot to me. It would mean a lot to him, to hear you say that too," Kassandra answered.

"I'll hope that one day, I'll get a chance to."

Janet walked towards Kassandra and said, "General West admires you so much, and I really see why now. For someone who isn't a soldier on the field, you show courage like one. I suppose the rest of us should show as much courage as you, especially in times like these."

"We just need to work together," Kassandra replied.

"I'm happy that you're fighting on our side."

"Same here."

Janet watched as Anton got up from his seat, and walked into the corridor, and followed Anton into the corridor, gently placing her hand on his arm and said, "Excuse me. Can we talk?"

Anton looked into her eyes, trying as best as he could to fight his emotions towards her, and quickly came to his senses, glancing at her hand on his arm and answered, "What's on your mind?"

"Did you tell anyone about what happened earlier?"

"I'm a soldier. Not a pervert, Jackson. I went out on a mission to help our cause, not defeat it."

"Thank you, Anton. I really appreciate that. You're a real gentleman," Janet said, chuckling.

Anton looked into her eyes, lost for a brief moment, trying to fight his feeling towards her, as she stared back, and quickly came back to his senses, and said, "Before you thank me, Jackson, I need you to do me a favor."

"What's that?"

"Wash your hands," Anton said, and walked away, leaving Janet to her thoughts.

06:17 HOURS. TOP SECRET MILITARY BASE - SOMEWHERE IN VIRGINIA:

The enemy soldiers continued combing through the rubble, searching for the remains of the General, after they extinguished the blaze that engulfed his quarters from the massive explosion, until a fist suddenly punched through the rubble.

They ran towards his position where they saw his fist sticking out, clearing the rubble from on top of him, pulling him out, supporting him to his feet.

The General stood to his feet with his face torn apart from the impact of the blaze, ignoring the pain from his wound, completely consumed with anger.

The troops looked at one another in disbelief on their faces, seeing that he bore extreme resilience to the pain from the wound that tore deeply into the flesh on his face.

He limped out of the rubble and looked all around the beleaguered base, seeing all the destruction that the small group of freedom fighters had caused, and said, "Their backs are against the wall, and that makes them far more dangerous. And it showed when they infiltrated the base. For someone who once served under my command, General West is truly a worthy opponent, I admit. It just means that I did my job well. As for Kassandra and 0-7, they make a lethal combination together."

"General, you need medical attention before your wound gets infected," Jason said, softly.

"What's the damage?"

"You lost an eye, sir," Jason answered.

"It's just an eye. Small price to pay for what is soon to be a complete victory in crushing the rest of those insects who did this to my fucking face. And if it makes you feel any better, have the doctors on hand, ASAP."

"Yes, sir. Right away," Jason answered.

"Then after, we need to interrogate a few people. Only they knew my whereabouts. Have them detained for now. They'll be executed on my order. But first thing's first."

"Yes, General," Jason said, with a hint of guilt, knowing that he was one of those who collaborated in the attempt on the General's life.

CHAPTER 21: SOUL OF FRAGMENTS.

An eerie calm and silence continued to sweep through the confines of the hospital after moments of waiting for his recovery.

Elaina had finally grown impatient and walked towards the room where the assassin recuperated, peering through a tiny opening in the door.

She slowly walked into the room where he laid on the bed, heavily sedated, with the serum continuing to run its course in the long process of healing, with the constant beeping from the life support system filling the confines of the dimly lit room. She gently grabbed his hand, and laid her head on the bed next to him, closing her eyes.

While he remained helpless in deep slumber, the images of a fortress completely surrounded by a barren, frozen tundra suddenly flashed in his mind, along with the faces of all the lives that he had cut short during the earlier years of the war, including the face of the young woman that continued to haunt his memories, causing his body to convulse violently, as the memory of a man ordering the execution of a number of unarmed soldiers in a remote location of a foreign country, suddenly alarming Elaina.

The sounds of the life support system grew louder in the confines of the room, as his body went deeper into shock, causing a sudden look of frantic to crease face.

She ran out of the room, into the lobby, and yelled, "Come quick! He's in shock!"

"The rest of you, stay here. Brian and Arianna come with me," Kassandra said, rushing into the room.

They rushed into the room, and saw his body still in heavy shock, with the incessant chiming from the life support machine beeping faster, as it continued to fill its confines, and ran over to him trying to hold his body to the bed, while he continued to convulse violently from the past memories that continued to haunt him, when his breathing suddenly slowed.

"What happened?" Elaina asked.

"I pumped quite a bit of the serum into him due to all the injuries that he sustained. Maybe too much at one time caused his body to have a violent reaction to it. I guess. I'm not sure. Though it looks like his wounds have fully healed," Kassandra said, watching the slumbering assassin.

He opened his eyes slowly, his vision completely blurred, staring at the ceiling, seeing the blurred silhouettes of the others that stood at the side of the bed, while he continued to catch his breath from the violent convulsions he'd just suffered, after being heavily sedated from the effects of the serum.

He sat upright on his bed, sweat dripping down his face and chest, soaking into the sheet that was sprawled over him, covering the lower half of his naked physique, and slowly stepped down, with his feet coming in contact with the cold concrete floors, causing a sudden look of newfound admiration on Elaina's face as she glanced at his handsome physique. She regained her concentration, holding onto him, supporting him to his feet, and said softly, "You need more rest. You need to save your strength. You're not well enough to do anything yet."

"Where am I?" he asked.

"My God. Did he just speak?" Elaina asked, with a hint of shock. "You're in a safe place. At least for now. You're in a hospital, somewhere.".

"You were barely conscious when Elaina found you. Or when you found her, for that matter. And not to mention, we saved you in a nick of time. If you had waited a second longer, you wouldn't be here with us right now. Your injuries were very severe. It's a miracle you're still alive," Kassandra answered.

"How long have I been out?" he asked.

"Thanks to the serum, you were out for only a few hours. It saved you weeks, even months of healing. Maybe even permanent damage to your entire body, judging from the extent of the injuries that you received."

He climbed from the bed and wobbled to the door, still feeling the paralyzing effects of the medicine traveling through his entire body, being supported by Elaina and Brian.

They walked into the lobby and saw the others who greeted him with absolute awe and stunned silence as he stared back at Adam's face in surprise, seeing it flashing back and forth in his memory, and said, "You seem familiar. Like I've known you from somewhere, from a long time ago."

"My God, he speaks," Janet said in surprise.

"Yes, you do," Adam said softly, placing his hand on his shoulder. "We've seen each other more times than the both of us care to remember. It's been a very long time. Ten years, to be exact, my friend. I was hoping that it would've been sooner, But better late than never. Things happen when they happen, I suppose. But in any event, any scenario, it's good to have you back. Welcome back, old friend. Welcome back, to the land of the living. I must admit, when I heard when you went rogue on the General's forces, it sounded like a prayer that went unanswered after so long. It felt like the General had finally opened Pandora's box, unleashing that unstoppable force, wreaking havoc on all our enemies. I saw Elaina blossom from a young girl into a beautiful young woman in this war, and when it happened, I figured that it was time that you and Elaina had to be reunited once again, before they finally catch up to her after all these years. And considering the fact that we have one of his pilots fighting with us, I'd say that there's many more to do the same. It becomes inevitable at some point. I suppose that evens things out a bit, considering that there are 6 more super soldiers like yourself hunting us as we speak. I can tell by the look on your face that you have many questions in need of answers. The question is, do you really think that you can handle the truth?"

"Does it matter? I really need to know. I need to know who I am," the confused assassin answered softly.

"As you were told earlier. All would be made clear to you. And now that you're here, what better time to do so?"

"I saw a lot of things. I couldn't tell if they were visions or memories," he said looking at Susan, who stared back, causing his mind to race into the past.

"You were a good soldier once. A good man. A man of great integrity, and honor, before they took it all away from you. Maybe you never meant to be, but, in your past life, you were the youngest, but the best soldier, and most decorated in the entire corps, even better than the General himself. With that tenacity, you could've been a General yourself. You were the best among the entire unit. The best among all of us. The entire corp. Destiny chose you to be who or what you are for some reason. And here you are again, to lead the remnants of what was an entire army. Maybe this time the outcome will be different. At this point, I'm willing to believe that anything is possible. I'm willing to believe that more soldiers will change sides and join our fight. When Dr. Weaver appointed me as his General, most of the senior high-ranking and more seasoned officers switched over to the General. I wasn't sure if I was ready to lead our forces into combat. But somehow, I managed, hoping that the day would come when you'd come back, and take your rightful place among us, and help us win this war, once and for all. And since that time, I often wondered if the war would've turned out differently if you had led our forces instead of me. I'm sure the outcome would've been different. I'd bet my life on it. And now, all I see standing before us is just a soul of fragments. Just a mere shadow of yourself, filled with fragments of past memories you thought were long lost, but that still linger deep within your soul. Or what's left of it, anyway. You're a soldier who's still soldiering on, and now fighting the ghosts of the ghosts long gone."

Karen looked into the eyes of the man that she had once crossed paths with, seeing them now filled with confusion and remorse, instantly reminiscent of the time she stared into them when they were so very cold and calculating, a few years prior during a search and rescue mission over the unforgiving tundra of New Mexico, and now, standing before her with his half naked physique shrouded in the blanket that covered the lower half of his body, with the upper half heavily marked with scars, showing the horrifying tale of all the brutal treatment that he endured at the hands of his enemies before he was turned to carry out the General's orders, claiming the life of Dillon right before her very eyes, along with their brief skirmish in Detroit, including the hunt for Adam's other lieutenants, since the beginning of the civil war, after all his memories of his past came flooding back, finding it difficult to believe that he was the very same man standing in front of her and the others.

Brian peered quietly, like he was savoring the moment, as he was also face-to-face with the infamous assassin who went by the code name, 0-7, who had once crossed paths with Karen, and hunted Adam and the others relentlessly, and continued to stare with a steely gaze in complete silence, finding it difficult to believe that he seemed to be the very the same man who had possessed the deadliest skills as the government's best and most feared assassin, and now seemed defeated by just the constant memories of his past, with his gaze still fixated on his half naked features, that remained completely consumed with mixed emotions of anger and remorse.

"Is that what those visions are?" the confused assassin asked.

"What you see are not visions. They are memories, my friend," Adam said softly.

"Are they just memories of my past? I saw a place like a fortress far away. In a world so cold and barren, lonely, yet beautiful and tranquil. I saw a place where so many innocent men, women, and children were just slaughtered for no reason. Only a child survived. So many other lives lost. Just gone in an instant. I saw another place where so many people who were murdered, by someone who gave the order. High in rank, I believe. So many faces from long ago, who seemed to know who I was. Who were they? What happened to them?"

"Many of those people that you see in your past memories died by your hand, unfortunately. That place where all the innocent men, women, and children were slaughtered, leaving Susan to be the only sole survivor of that unfortunate attack, was a civilian sanctuary."

"Did I really do that?" he said, looking at Susan with a sudden look of shock, confusion, and remorse on his face.

"The high-ranking officer that you see, giving the orders to kill, is the General. That single act placed the entire Latin American nation of Peru in total defiance against us. The fortress that you saw was a place called Genesis. It was a place where people who were displaced and orphaned from war went to start over. After the fall of Genesis, the entire world went into a state of unrest. War between the people and all authority was merely an understatement. It was total anarchy. It became the end of civilization as we know it. Just as Dr. Weaver worked so hard to give the entire planet hope, we destroyed it in just moments. The flashes that you saw during your slumber are the memories of all the people who lost their lives during the uprising. Some of those very same faces that you saw are the ones who were once in our unit. That was the most elite group in the entire marine corp."

"Who were they?"

"The infamous Unit-13, and would soon come to be known as the Unlucky-13. 13 tours together, 13 months, 13 soldiers. The number 13. Those were good days back then. But, I should've known that it was too good to last. I and the others were just too caught up in the moment too much, to see it."

"I don't understand."

"We went to a lot of exotic places together, except they weren't so exotic, if you know what I mean."

"No. I don't. I don't know what you mean."

"Operation Morale. Kiev, the capital of Ukraine, was our first mission together. The morale of the Ukraine forces had plummeted after losing so many casualties fighting against the rebel forces, who had shot down a commercial airliner, killing all 288 passengers on board, making it the worst plane crash since the Pan Am flight over Lockerbie, Scotland, in 1988. It was during that campaign on the battlefield that your legacy was born, and was the beginning of Unit-13, which would inevitably become the beginning of the end for us.

"Operation Nightingale. Bishkek, Kyrgyzstan. There was an uprising that tore the entire country apart, when the citizens demanded the ousting of the president, and at the same time seizing the government, and at the same time driving the Uzbek minorities out of the country. Our embassy was being attacked in the capital, and we were under strict orders to only rescue all of our personnel, and engage if necessary. But, during the rescue mission, we killed a few who were trying to bomb the embassy, so we had no choice but to defend ourselves and our personnel, and the next thing we knew, we found ourselves exchanging bullets with some of the natives, and it snowballed form there in a full-scale war against their forces. By the time our reinforcements had arrived, the uprising had caused the deaths of a number of our personnel, but somehow, we managed to come out on top. I don't need to stress on all the bloodshed that was left in the wake of the attack. It was horrible. Even that was an understatement.

"Operation Foundry. We had received intelligence that a war criminal who ordered the murders of thousands of innocent refugees in Croatia, during the great war that divided the Soviet Union, was tracked all the way in the slums of Brazil, pretending to live a civilian life as a business man, using the militias in the ghettos for protection. And when we received the intel, we pulled another Normandy on the beaches, and worked our way into the slums, fighting and killing a number of the militia during the manhunt, as we pushed forward," he said looking at Elaina, instantly recalling their first encounter.

"Operation Tomahawk. Somewhere over the Magdalena River, in Colombia. We received word from our intelligence that the ones sighted for the deaths of seven of our undercover agents during a major drug deal went wrong. So, naturally, we wanted blood. We hit them so hard, that we literally strangled all their drug supplies to the guerillas all the way in Peru, down to the very last drop. The drugs that we seized and destroyed that day had an estimated street value of trillions of dollars, and was the single largest manhunt since the hunt for Pablo Escobar in 1993. It was bloody. No need to tell you that the Colombians didn't go quietly in the night. They fought to the last man. But, none of that was enough, since their morale quickly crumbled after we destroyed all of their operations.

"Operation Tundra, in the Valley of the Kings, Egypt. After decades of loaning the country's rulers billions of dollars to stimulate the country's fragile economy, they went about starving their citizens unchecked, while these politicians lived prestigious lives. Using all the taxpayers' dollars that we gave them to fatten all their pockets in their offshore bank accounts. And because of it, the country went into total unrest, causing many to lose their lives during many of their protests. So naturally, we were tasked with the mission of ousting the country's leader and all the rest of his cohorts, and bringing them to the tribunal to face justice for their many crimes, and counts of corruption at the Geneva Conventions, or the league of nations. Whichever you wish to call it. And being that it was one of those Islamic states, we were faced with militants who were willing to fight to the death. Like they always have. Needless to say, they were very well equipped and organized, a lot of which was with our weapons that we sold to them under the table many years back. Turns out doing that came back to haunt us. So, you can only imagine how difficult it was engaging their forces.

"Operation Lantern. Took us to the city of lights in France after we got a tip off from our sources that the one who masterminded the attacks, with direct links to Al Qaeda itself, that killed over 200 people, and bombed our embassy killing another 17 people, injuring a lot more, had finally been sighted, after years of hiding. The fight against the insurgents had become so powerful that the French were being so overwhelmed by the rising number of attacks taking place, that the French government requested assistance from us, since we had a long history of being their ally since the second World War. I guess that long-lived alliance that dates back to the second World War finally counted for something for us to recommit our forces to come to their aid.

"Operation Scorching Sands. We did another sea-born invasion, storming the coast of North Africa, establishing a beachhead, and trekking through the Carthage Ruins of Tunisia, and inched our way into the capital, when our intelligence had revealed that some of Al Qaeda's other top lieutenants were masterminding another attack on the mainland, and some of our allies, after the massacre in Paris.

"The saga still continues on this perpetual war on terror. It's like it never ends, and look now - we're in the thick of it, with us fighting amongst ourselves in this civil war, the darkest chapter of our nation's history, doing the very same thing they did before, so I ask now, were we any different at all?

"Operation Rescue. After the President of Peru, Jorge Ramos, was assassinated in his fight for democracy in the year 2005, the entire country went into unrest, resulting in years of fragile truce, between the president's supporters and the guerillas who were backed by the cartels with the bulk of their operations from Colombia, with additional support from Nicaragua and a few of the other neighboring countries in Central America.

Years after, the war reignited, with the government calling on us for support to fight the guerillas, although we did as much as we could to not get involved. And one day, by some strange twist of fate, we were flying over Peruvian airspace, en-route to Genesis, we were shot down. They wanted their revenge on us after we shut down their biggest drug operations in Colombia and the other Latin American counterparts.

"We were shot down, and crash-landed in a location near the Andes Mountains, and lost a number of our men. Good men. And a number of us were injured, and were less than half strength, behind enemy lines. And the next thing we know were swarmed by guerillas. We tried as long as we could to repel the attacks, killing as many as we could, but they just kept on coming, and in a nick of time, we were rescued by the Peoples' Liberation Forces, run by the deceased president's 2 sons, Alejandro and Felipe, and his daughter, Isabella Ramos. It was Isabella who led the charge against the guerillas that day, or we would have surely been wiped out. So, for coming to our aid, our government finally became an ally to the P.L.F., until our forces led by the General wiped their entire resistance, after they demanded your release, and were wiped out in trying to free you. I don't have to mention what happened after the natives found out what happened the General and those who were loyal to him had committed all these atrocities. The entire country went into unrest, protesting against us, attacking all of our embassies, which had to be evacuated. It felt like Kyrgyzstan and Genesis happening all over again.

"The news spread like wildfire, and if you thought it was bad in Peru, it was just as bad here in the mainland, with the people demanding the General and his forces to be brought to justice.

"Operation Stranglehold, Mexico. We pursued the most ruthless members of the cartel who were responsible for the torture and murders of a number of border patrolmen, after completely cutting off their supply line to the United States. So, naturally, the government thought that was going too far. So, they turned to us to rid them, and place a stranglehold on their operations once and for all, like we did in Colombia. After we took Colombia out of the game, Mexico was the next to ramp up their operations. And believe me when I tell you, they were holding their own, even rivaling what we stopped in Colombia. And believe me when I tell you, our success came with a very hefty price, even when they felt the full might of the United States military.

"Operation Chariot, El Salvador. We were ordered to kill or apprehend the suspects responsible for a series of attacks on one of our convoys that was stationed there. Many of them were killed. So, we were called in to make them face retribution, and although we had the last word, that skirmish between us and the guerilla forces who attacked and murdered many of our operatives over there, was not for the faint of heart. The dictator who had direct ties with the militias, gangs, and cartels had the citizens living in total fear under his boots. So, we had to take steps to make sure he could never use that power again, and that had us running through the streets and the jungles. And it felt like another tour of Vietnam all over again. Luckily, we as marines came out on top because of our adaptability. Turns out, we really learned something from fighting the Vietcongs, and that gave us the advantage, and applied it to our campaign in El Salvador.

"Operation Hydra. It was believed that China boasted the world's largest army. And all of a sudden, there was a new faction that threatened to take over and overthrow the government. Some speculated the numbers were bigger than the army itself. Others believed that they were an even match. None of us knew for certain. But what I do know for sure is that they had enough firepower and resources to be a threat to the entire country, since all the major cities were being taken over by that faction. Turns out they were very well equipped and highly organized as our intel revealed. Not to mention they were dedicated to their cause, and would fight to the last man. Which they did. We hadn't seen so much fanaticism since the Pacific theater of the second World War, nor had we seen so much bloodshed since the era of the yellow turban rebellion, during the Han dynasty. And being that we owed billions to China, we were called in to assist. Despite the fact that they had the world's largest army prior to the attack from North Korea, they were not battle-tested like us.

"But the real reason why they called us in was because the word of your skills quickly got around. So, they decided to put us to the test. And in return, they would cancel all our debts if we were successful in thwarting the rebel faction that decided that planned the coup to overthrow the government. Needless to say that they demanded your release when you were captured, after the uprising on Genesis. And from all the events from the past ten years, you can see what it all came down to. Just death and ruin of an entire nation.

"Operation Winback. For decades after the war that separated the Korean Peninsula, that one moment of anticipating the north would attack the south, was a long time coming. That day that everyone was about their business, like any other day. It was just a normal day, like any other. Nobody saw it coming. The bombs just rained from the skies like it was the end of days. So many died. Many more were buried alive under rubble.

The North Koreans swept all across the country practically unopposed. Their attacks were so swift, that nothing stood in their way. China, which was North Korea's ally at the time, asked them to cease all hostile activity and in retaliation, they bombed China, bringing their once mighty army to less than half strength. We were stationed in China that day and suffered a great deal of casualties as well. The loss of life all around was great, and of course, we wanted revenge, but the Chinese wanted it even more. To them, it was the ultimate betrayal. And all forms of diplomacy and history that both countries shared was now out the window. It just dissolved in that single act of betrayal.

"The attack had instilled so much fear on China's other allies that even they didn't want to spare any of their roops for the assault on the North Korean occupation, making our campaign all the more a suicide mission. Our campaign in China was no walk in the park, but my God, North Korea was suicide. We were outnumbered by at least 20 to 1. The odds were staggering against us. Too staggering to secure a victory. So, left with no other alternatives, both our Generals were desperate for answers, and turned to you for the solution, being that you were the best among us. So, we were left with no choice but to attack the enemy with whatever little resources and manpower we had left.

Our resolve was so stubborn, that the morale with the civilians skyrocketed, and even they picked up arms, helping us to push the enemy back across the border all the way back to North Korea. Only this time, it placed the entire peninsula under southern rule, out of vengeance against their North Korean cousins. It was after the war against North Korea, you had finally taken charge of the unit, after the General was begging you to do it for so long. And what better time, too? These were all the medals that you were awarded after all your missions. I've seen you rush into a hail of enemy bullets, or an impending airstrike to save a fellow soldier, and on a few occasions, I've seen you holding out an entire battalion of enemy units and infantry, giving us time to escape, just before the strike came. In the heat of war, I've seen so many seasoned soldiers freeze under heavy enemy resistance, crying like babies, and even screaming for their mothers. But you. You were different from all the others that the General or myself ever met. More than all of us put together. It was like you were a perfect fit through all the chaos and despair that consumed everyone caught in the wake of it all. I couldn't tell if you were just brave, lucky, or incredibly stupid. But whatever it was, it earned my respect, and everyone's else's, including the General's, and even all our allegiances towards you. That much, the old crew can attest to. In the most difficult times, you showed how selfless you really were, that you ended up taking a bullet that was meant for him. I saw that with my own eyes too. We all did. He really did like you, you know. And I supposed that was as good a reason as any. And if you think that was something, our last President prior to Dr. Weaver had the utmost confidence in you. And with good reason too. The outcome of every mission we embarked with you spoke volumes. More than a thousand words."

"That was 12. You said there were 13 missions. But, I only counted 12. What was the 13th mission?" he answered

"Genesis. It was Genesis. Unfortunately, he came to that haven that was supposed to help mankind start anew. And look what happened," Adam answered, softly.

"I don't understand. If Genesis was a place where people came to seek a better life, and start over, why would we attack it?"

"It wasn't supposed to be a mission. We had just ended the war with North Korea and it was on our way to Genesis for some well-deserved time off to celebrate our victory.

And that's when it happened. That's where it all went wrong from that point."

"What happened?"

Adam glanced at Elaina for a brief moment and answered, "Some of our troops were already stationed there awaiting our arrival. And we later learnt that one of our troops had practiced indiscretions towards one of the civilians. Unfortunately, the General didn't see it that way, being that she had a past. So, he used it as an excuse to kill her. He tried to use you as our squad leader to lead the charge and that's when it all went wrong."

"What do you mean?" he asked.

"Dr. Weaver found out and intervened. Seeing that what you were asked to do was wrong, you switched your allegiances to Dr. Weaver. And it was from that point on, that our entire brotherhood began to fall apart. It became 13 of us against an entire army. Hence the namesake, with the Unlucky-13 thing."

"How is that even possible? You said it was 13 of us against the entire army. Who are they?"

"You mean who were they? Are these the faces you saw while you slept?" Adam asked, taking out an old photograph from his pocket.

"Yes. Who were they?" he asked with a puzzled look on his face.

"That look on your face is a look that I've seen more times that I care to remember. They always say that the souls of the past always visit you at nights when you sleep. And from the look on your face, I think you know exactly what happened to them. It was you who saved those men on all our missions together. Just as it was you who ended their lives, after you hunted and snuffed them out during the war. It was you who started Unit-13 all those years ago, just as you ended it during the war. All of Unit-13, with the exception of myself, died by your hand, and I suppose it's safe to say that I am the only one left to tell the tale for now.

"Patrick O'Hara was the best helicopter pilot in the army, and became part of our unit after serving on his tour in Colombia, and was taken from us by your hands after he was shot down by the enemy forces, during his tour back in Arizona, back in 2029.

"Eric Fong was another one of my most trusted lieutenants in the war, who joined the unit after serving his tour back in Brazil, during our international manhunt, searching for a war criminal who fled the former Soviet Union, after it broke into a number of states during the civil war, until you snuffed him out, back in Michigan in 2031.

"Dillon Kim became part of the unit after he was shot down during his tour in Egypt during their uprising to depose the president, in Operation Tundra, and was made captain of our air force by Dr. Weaver, after he took the president's stead, after the president went missing, just before the civil war, when most of the seasoned pilots shifted their allegiances to the General, until you assassinated him back in New Mexico, after he was shot down by enemy fire. It's ironic the same way you found him back in Egypt, was the same way that you found him back in New Mexico. The only difference is that you snuffed him out back in 2030. Santiago witnessed the whole thing when she was trapped in the wreckage of her gunship, and you let her live to tell the tale of what happened, I suppose. Whatever reason you let her live, only you should know the answer to that. To this day, it has remained a mystery.

"Christopher Vaughan, finally joined Unit-13 after he completed his tour in Operation Chariot back in El Salvador, and was promoted to one of my high-ranking lieutenants by Dr. Weaver just before the war, until you assassinated him back in North Carolina, back in 2033. He knew that he was going to die facing you, but gave his life anyway, so that the rest of us could escape that fateful day we crossed paths like we always did for the past ten years in this war. But to be honest, I can't say that myself, or any one of us, were thrilled to have crossed paths with you.

"Paul Alvarez was another great soldier. Young, impressionable, and one of the most courageous men I ever saw on the field. He became a part of the unit after serving on his tour of duty back in Mexico, and was promoted to another one of the other lieutenants during the war, until you murdered him in cold blood, back in the Mojave Desert, in California in 2026. The year after Genesis had fallen. He was the very first one of us to have died by your hand, actually. Right before you snuffed him out, it's like he'd seen a ghost. I could only imagine. It's how we all felt, since you just vanished after being captured only to resurface, as that vengeful ghost, hunting and slaughtering us like cattle.

"Ahmad Evans, from a troubled youth back in the projects in Maryland, grew to be one of the best soldiers that I've ever had the honor of serving with, and another one of my most trusted lieutenants during the war. He joined the unit after serving on his tour in China, and met the same fate as the others. Like Christopher, he made the ultimate sacrifice, giving his life to save the rest of us, before you murdered him back in West Virginia, after we seized the capital, back in 2032. He felt he had to so the fight could go on, but I was running out of lieutenants, and was losing this war. After all, it didn't take much to see. Look where we are right now.

"Henry Collins was another one of my most trusted lieutenants who joined the unit after serving his tour in Tunisia, when we were hunting for insurgents through the ruins of Carthage, all the way to the capital. When you found him, he was seriously wounded in action, after you attacked us, while we were on our way to our secret outpost somewhere in the Mojave Desert back in Nevada. The way I see it, you granted him mercy by taking his life when you did. You granted him a soldier's death. It was either that, or he would bleed to death. Unable to be transported because of the wound he sustained, we left him back, until you found him lying helpless on the desert sands, and snuffed him out, back in 2027.

"Robert Taylor became a part of the unit after serving on his tour of duty in France, and another one of my most trusted lieutenants during the war. He sustained a critical blow to the head from shrapnel that came from an explosion, during one of our missions back in Utah. We left him back, thinking he was dead during the explosion, but he wasn't, and that's when you found him lying in the desert, and robbed him of his life, back in 2028.

"They were all loyal to you. We were all loyal to the cause to the end. They gravitated towards you, because you saved them, even at the expense of you putting your life at risk for us. At least you gave them a chance to say their final goodbyes, before you finally snuffed them out of the war for good. As for Diana Patrick and David Singh, she became a member of the unit during our tour in Kyrgyzstan, and him, during the time we were shot down near the Andes Mountains in Peru. Even to this day, she was the best driver I ever saw. Not too many came close to her skills behind the wheel. They fell in love, fortunately or unfortunately, and stayed back on Genesis to lead the denizens in the uprising against our brothers in arms who became our enemies. Whether they're still alive, I really don't know. None of us did, from the point we lost touch with the outside world. And as for Sarah Jennings, she became a member of the unit, after serving her tour in China after we saved her, when her plane was shot down by the enemy forces. She later led a strike force on the North Koreans, starving them of reinforcements during their occupation of the south, and was once again shot down behind enemy lines in the north, and fought her way out, until we came to her rescue, with our air support. Cold and miserable, she fought tooth and nail to get out of there in one piece. And even after being wounded, cold, hungry, and tired, she still wanted to hop back into the cockpit of a fighter plane to join the fight. She was a lot tougher than she looked. She had some of the most grit that we'd ever seen. But, sadly, she lost her life from enemy fire during the evacuation to escort Dr. Weaver back to the mainland. Maybe if she was still alive, maybe the outcome would've been different. We really could've used these skills in this war to help turn the tide in our favor. Such promise extinguished from all this chaos that became the fall of Genesis. The fall of mankind. After we arrived on the mainland, she was buried with full military honors, with all of us, including Dr. Weaver, Kassandra, and even the General attended her funeral to say our final goodbyes. It truly was gut wrenching to say the least, saying our final goodbyes to her.

"And myself, Adam West, am still here picking the pieces still fighting, even though there is not much to fight for anymore all morale is hanging by a thread, and was the first to be a part of the infamous Unit-13, and, one of the few African-Americans to be promoted as General since the war started, and you were captured and turned by the enemy forces. Hoping that one day, you would return to us and lead us to victory, if there's any hope of having it at all. But, better late than never for whatever forces we have left. I've suffered so many close calls of almost meeting my own demise by your hands, and here

I still am living to tell the tale. I suppose that fate destined me to be the one to tell you what really happened after all these years, before I actually meet my demise at someone else's. Hopefully, it never happens at all."

"But I only counted 12. You said there were 13 soldiers. Who was the 13th?"

"It was you. This photograph of us together was taken after we defeated the North Koreans. And united the entire country under southern rule. And I'm sure they turned against us after what happened in Genesis. We ended up right back to where we started. Out of defiance to us, they shifted their allegiances to the Chinese, only this time, it was the entire Korean Peninsula under the Chinese umbrella. No more 38th parallel. Just another communist regime under our former ally."

"I'm confused. It's like it doesn't add up. None of this does."

"It will. All will be made clear to you, as I once told you. And what better time, since we're all here together at this point? The other irony in all this is we ended up in the same place that we started from. The very same place all of us got separated from. The question is, what do we do now?"

"Did I really do what you said I did?," he asked, with a look of worry and shock on his face, as Adam had laid the truth bare of his past deeds of all the atrocities he committed against all the members of his former unit.

"Unfortunately, you did, Lieutenant," Adam replied softly. "You were and still are the best soldier that I've ever had the privilege of serving with, but unfortunately, your hands are stained with the blood of the innocent and guilty alike. Even more than mine, and all of ours put together in this room, I'm afraid. Since you turned against the General, you alone laid waste to countless of his troops. Not that you were given much of a choice at the time it happened. And now, at this very moment, you're caught up between being the man that you once were, and an assassin they turned you into, and unleashed upon us, like a deadly plague known to mankind. When we arrived at Genesis all hell broke loose. And based on the nature of the orders received, our allegiances quickly shifted to Kassandra's father. So, to keep them safe, we had to evacuate them to the mainland to plead to the president to remove all military personnel indefinitely from Genesis. No need to tell you how that turned out. As you can see, I waited for an entire decade to finally have this conversation with you," Adam said softly.

After the serum had completely run its course through his entire body, the assassin became slowly aware of his tragic past. He gently grabbed the old photograph from Adam's hand, staring at it, his mind filled with questions about his conflicting past.

A sudden look of remorse came over his face, as he looked into Susan's eyes, knowing what had come to pass in the sanctuary, along with her and Arianna being the sole survivors of all the people who were massacred, while she stared back quietly.

"That look on your face is the look of a mind searching for answers. Or knowing deep down what all the answers are, and trying to come to the realization that you really committed all those terrible acts. And rightfully so," Adam said.

"Who am I?"

Adam simply sat on one of the chairs, and took a deep breath, and said, "It's a lot more complicated than it seems, my friend. But what you really are is a soul of fragments. At present, you're the ghost of an assassin's past, in a world doomed with an uncertain future. Conflicted and searching for the truth. Torn between being the man and honor that you once were, to being that lethal weapon that they turned you to be. Forever trapped between good and evil, night and day. Forever trapped between the opposing forces."

EPILOGUE:

07:43 HOURS. TOP SECRET MILITARY BASE – SOMEWHERE IN VIRGINIA:

The General walked into the facility with his face lined with a number of bruises from the explosion where one of the senior scientists waited and said, "Have the test subjects undergone the procedure, Dr. Douglas?"

Like Kassandra, Dr. Andrew Douglas wore glasses, with the contrast of being fiercely loyal to the General, and like all his colleagues, spent most of his life in the armed forces.

He was coming into age, with his hairline completely receding at the top of his head, and showing heavy signs of gray from the years and constant stresses of doing much of the research for the government to assist the General's war effort to crush Dr. Weaver's forces, to place the entire country under the General's control.

He stood alongside the General and answered, "Yes, General. I had them shipped from the capital so you can see for yourself. I hope that you will be impressed with all the specimens, as I am, sir. The blueprints that she gave to create the ultimate soldier were a great success. None of this would've been possible without her. She's truly her father's daughter. I must admit, that none of this would be possible without her. As much as it pains me to say it, she has surpassed me in many ways. All of us, for that matter."

"Indeed, she has surpassed you, and I do appreciate your candidness in admitting the truth about your younger protégé. But to humor you, yes, she truly is her father's daughter. And more so, so much more brilliant than he is. It's in her blood. Thanks to her, this war is about to come to a swift end, despite all her efforts to stall my efforts."

The General slowly walked in front of his remaining super soldiers, analyzing them, smiling and said, "I'm impressed."

"And I would also like to say that what happened to you was most unfortunate. And we will find all those responsible and make them pay."

"Rest assured, Doctor. My subordinates will be dealt with accordingly. Only they knew about my whereabouts, so only they could've relayed position to the rebels. But for now, let me savor the moment watching my new creations."

"0-7 will be sorry for ever going against you, sir," Dr. Douglas said.

The General simply turned back looking at Dr. Douglas with a cold and calculating stare.

To be continued: ZE7RO: GENESIS.

WARNING: All characters depicted in this novel are purely fictional.

9 781950 974108